LAST STORIES AND OTHER STORIES

You Bright and Risen Angels (1987)

The Rainbow Stories (1989)

The Ice-Shirt (1990)

Whores for Gloria (1991)

Thirteen Stories and Thirteen Epitaphs (1991)

An Afghanistan Picture Show (1992)

Fathers and Crows (1992)

Butterfly Stories (1993)

The Rifles (1994)

The Atlas (1996)

The Royal Family (2000)

Argall (2001)

Rising Up and Rising Down:
Some Thoughts on Violence, Freedom and Urgent Means (2003)

Europe Central (2005)

Uncentering the Earth:
Copernicus and the Revolutions of the Heavenly Spheres (2006)

Poor People (2007)

Riding Toward Everywhere (2008)

Imperial (2009)

Imperial: Photographs (2009)

Kissing the Mask:
Beauty, Understatement and Femininity in
Japanese Noh Theatre (2010)

The Book of Dolores (2013)

VIKING

LAST STORIES
AND OTHER STORIES

WILLIAM T. VOLLMANN

VIKING
Published by the Penguin Group
Penguin Group (USA) LLC
375 Hudson Street
New York, New York 10014

USA | Canada | UK | Ireland | Australia | New Zealand | India | South Africa | China
penguin.com
A Penguin Random House Company

First published by Viking Penguin, a member of Penguin Group (USA) LLC, 2014

"The Forgetful Ghost" first appeared in *Vice* magazine;
"Widow's Weeds" first appeared in *Agni*.

Illustrations by the author

LIBRARY OF CONGRESS CATALOGING-IN-PUBLICATION DATA
Vollmann, William T.
[Stories. Selections]
Last stories and other stories / William T. Vollmann.
pages cm
ISBN 978-0-670-01597-9
I. Title.
PS3572.O395A6 2014
813'.54—dc23   2013047856

Printed in the United States of America
1   3   5   7   9   10   8   6   4   2

Set in Warnock Pro
Designed by Carla Bolte

IN MEMORY OF MY FATHER

It is the custom for the barber to shave the deceased, to powder him, whiten his face and rouge his cheeks and lips, and dress him in a frock coat with patent leather shoes and black trousers, as if going to a ball, may God forbid—this shall not happen to Makso.

—Testament of Hatji Makso Despić, drawn up in Sarajevo, 29 March 1921

CONTENTS

This is my final book. Any subsequent productions bearing my name will have been composed by a ghost. As I watch this world turn past my window, I wonder how I should have lived. Now that it seems too late to alter myself, I decline to complain; indeed, my only regret is that pleasure comes to an end. *Wherever there is a rose,* runs the ancient *Gulistan, there is a thorn; and when wine is drunk there is a hangover; where treasure is buried there is a snake; where there is the noble pearl there are sharks; the pain of death follows the pleasures of life, and the delights of Paradise are hidden by a wall of ill.*— This wall of ill, won't you view it with me? Through my late father's binoculars, its aggregates of bloody leaves resemble coral or scrambled eggs, all washed and blended by watercolor fogs. Now let's step up to count vines and snakes! If you'll kindly verify my tally, I promise to prove that for all its deadliness, our wall of ill remains no less green and delicious. To be stung by that poisonous creeper over there might even induce an orgasm; for its leaves bear undeniably precious speckles, and there appear to be vermilion dewdrops upon its urticating hairs. And don't forget to lick Malkhut, the Unlighted Mirror! Some of you may decline, in keeping with the axiom: *This shall not happen to Makso.* But why not make the occasion a dress ball, should the hole in the ground prove wide enough? As for me, even when I dance I long to describe everything—not least, the elephants who carry great blossoms on their braided trunks, and the green monkeys standing on the elephants' heads—for what "posterity" declines to censor, time will blight, causing happy new generations of the ignorant to suppose that our wall of ill was never better than a hedge of grey thorns, so read me now! For I do see beauty; I retain my sexual hopes! Consider that bluish-faced crested iguana over there with the white-banded flesh; the way it watches me while slowly drawing itself along a branch can't help but put me in mind of miscegenatory sports. Having heard so much, you still don't care to crawl closer? Pick a rose with me; sip a bitter cup—or would you rather dive for noble pearls in your own private cesspool? Infinity, I am sure, will kiss you in this blue and green and cloudy land. Or should you prefer doctrine to sensation, I'll guide you through barbed wire past Makso's grave (and mine) to the Last Meadow, where my favorite moss-bearded prophet has nearly finished computing the answer to the following test of intellect: Is it better to lose all quickly or slowly—or best never to have been born? He has already taught me the names of the evil angels. He says: There is no means through which those who have been born can escape dying. Therefore the wise do not grieve, knowing the terms of the world.— I'll believe him—so long as I can whiten my face and dance with an iguana. My prophet intimates that both may be possible. He runs a barbering business on the side. He'll rouge your cheeks and lips for next to nothing. When prostitutes can't help you anymore, let him sell you a hole! He's shown me how to play with death as did Newton with thought-pebbles. Before he got enlightened, he used to worry that you and I would feel sad upon learning how small we are. He himself is big. He says: You too will come to comprehend, if you but keep to the ill-ward path.— It was he who first led me to the pale river which is white in the morning, brown in the afternoon. Down this chalky way of rusty ships and crescent-boats sail people whom I used to know; they will transfer at various terminals, and then, somewhere I have not been, all of them, those rich crowds with red or yellow umbrellas, those poor men with the sacks on their heads, those longhaired women in flower-patterned dresses, will go swarming off the last ferry into the rain. Wasn't that Makso over there? And didn't my pretty lizard just make a getaway? Sharpening his razor, my prophet advises me to make my own fun. I may as well stay here overnight, polishing these last stories until they're good enough to bury in the ground.

I see trees head on, in layers and layers, and now the river has turned to jade, because it reflects bamboos muted by the humid sky. Behind a stand of needle-leaved whipping-trees comes a mountain of writhing cobras; and from within that mountain I hear the hoarse rapid laughter of children.

A man and a woman sit across from each other, and on the round table between them lies a perfectly wrapped box of sweets. The man opens it. The woman smiles; her finger hovers, for each candy is a different color and shape, with a unique poison at its heart. She takes a pale jade jelly with sesame seeds on top. He takes a red one made of bean paste. She touches his hand. They gaze down into their candy box. Just so I gaze into my lovely wall of ill.

WTV
Sacramento 2005–2013

SUPERNATURAL AXIOMS

1. To the extent that the dead live on, the living must resemble them.

2. Confessing such resemblance, we should not reject the possibility that we might at this very moment be dead.

3. Since life and death are the only two states which we can currently postulate, then to the extent that they are the same, immortality, and even eternal consciousness, seems possible.

    a. We do not remember what we might have been before birth. This, and only this, gives hope of oblivion.— Insufficient!

    b. Many religions, not to mention our own egocentric incapacity to imagine the world without us, collude in asserting the existence of an afterlife.

    c. The universe is at best indifferent. Since eternal consciousness would be the worst torture possible, and God's own writings under various aliases hint at such a possibility, why not expect it?

    d. Besides, a ghost told me so.

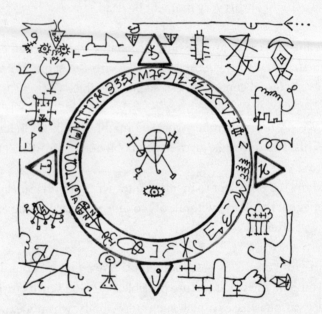

LAST STORIES AND OTHER STORIES

I

ESCAPE

That green light and humid summer air, the cigarette scent of hotels, the way that as the women aged they widened and solidified and their voices deepened; and then the way that the weather so often altered so that the green light would go grey or white; the loud and prolonged clacking of the key in the lock across the corridor, followed by footsteps echoing smashingly down the stairs, the dogs' barking in early morning, all these stigmata of peacetime faded just as the shell-holes and bullet-holes should have done a decade ago, and the story of the lovers began.

Many men have been conquered by the way a Sarajevo girl parts her lips when she is blowing smoke rings, holding the cigarette beside her ear. Because Zoran had grown up with Zlata, he could hardly have said how or when he lost his freedom; but on a certain evening of green light, he found himself sitting beside her in the park, and while the birds sang, his hands went helplessly around her just above the buttocks; he was bending her backward, his tongue in her mouth; and she was pushing him away, after which her arm somehow fell around his neck.

On the following evening they were on the same bench, which he straddled, cradling her back and bending forward to kiss her on the side of the neck while she reclined against him; and the air smelled like flowers and cigarettes.

His face was large and strong. His skin was smooth. He kept his hair short, and his eyes were brownish-green.

Sometimes Zlata needed to torture her sweethearts a trifle to feel alive, to know that she was stronger than they. Afterward she felt remorse. She used to say to her elder sister: Maybe I'm asking of them something that they're not able to give me.— But from him she asked nothing except everything.

First of all, she informed him, she demanded that he believe in destiny. He promised that she was his fate. She slammed her tongue into his mouth. He gave her a copper ring. She gave him her photograph. Their emotions could scarcely be contained in the immense greenness of a Central European evening.

Her mother, who held a cigarette not quite vertically between two fingers, did not remind her that Zoran was a Serb, that being of but middling significance in those days; besides, she knew the boy and liked him.

If we live long enough, it may well be that our virtues turn into agonies; but the memory of first love sweetens with age. I know a former blonde now gratefully married to an adoring and understanding older husband, who smilingly steps away whenever she asks some past acquaintance for news of the boy, now a greyhaired father with a heart murmur, who slept with her no more than three times (she remembers each one), invited her to travel with him in a foreign country, then abandoned her there, returning to his other woman, with whom he presently lives on bad terms. He will always remain the former blonde's true love. And the husband smiles. With patient craft he invites her back into his arms.

It was with another sort of indulgence that Zlata's mother regarded her daughter's romance. If, God willing, something came of it, that would be all right. If not, there were other boys, some of whom even went to mosque.

They took a walk along the river, and somewhere, I cannot say how far from the Vrbanja Most, he proposed. She replied that she must ask her mother.

She was wearing a low top, and her cleavage made him weak. He squeezed her round the waist until it hurt; she loved that. She was whispering into his face, and he was smiling. Seeing how they mooned over each other, her elder sister threw back her head in amused disgust and closed her dark eyes.

Sitting him down, Zlata's mother said that it must be a long engagement since they were so young; everyone would wait and see. But he knew that she was not angry. His mother went to see Zlata's mother and returned, saying nothing. His father put an arm around his shoulders.

Whenever Zlata had to go home to her parents, Zoran felt anguished, and gazed for half an hour at a time at her photograph, drinking in her long reddish hair and big round earrings, her brownish-green eyes beneath the heavy, sleepy lids, the almost cruel nostrils and lush mouth.

Her family lived in the Old Town near the library, so once the war started, the Serbs paid particular attention to that area, which did, however, offer proximity to the brewery where one could get drinking water. Less fortunately situated people, such as Zoran, had to bicycle there, risking their lives to fill a water jug.

By then everyone had balcony gardens with tomatoes, cabbages, onions; and Zlata's mother was one of the first to learn how to cut a tomato into small pieces in order to plant them in dirt in a big black plastic bag. God willing, six or seven new tomatoes might be born. She taught Zoran the trick, and he showed his parents.

Zoran's brother got some real coffee, God knows from where, and Zoran took some to Zlata's family. Matters certainly could have gone otherwise. I remember being told about the man who killed two hundred people in Srebrenica; he was from a mixed marriage, but all the same they told him: You must do it or we kill you.— There were other Serbs like him, and various Muslims and Croats did the same. But Zlata and Zoran held fast to one another.

After Zlata's teacher was killed by a sniper, the girl wept for many hours. Zoran sat beside her, holding her hand.

The Serbs had the leading position in our city, said her mother. We can't understand what drove them to shoot us.

Drying her eyes, Zlata told her: Don't say that in front of him. He's never been against us!

Zoran smiled meaninglessly at the floor.

Zlata's mother lit another half-cigarette. She wished to know if he were acquainted with any of these murderers.

Some of my old colleagues in the office are doing it, said Zlata, squeezing his hand. Now they even have Romanian girls who are snipers. Let's get off the subject.

Well, well! Your colleagues! Which ones? Do you mean Darko?

Never mind.

Zoran, let me just ask you this: What should be done with these snipers?

How can I know? I'm not a soldier.

The next day he cycled to the brewery, his mother in the doorway praying after him; and an antiaircraft gun stalked him lazily without shooting. He felt sweaty between his shoulderblades. Pale thunderheads cooled the humid greenish and bluish mountains where the snipers were. He threw down his bike, grabbed the jug, sprinted through the doorway because a gun was often trained on it, entered the friendly dimness and queued for water. Then he rode to Zlata's.

The besiegers were shooting, Zlata's mother licking her lips for fear. He had never seen her look so ugly. They all sat staring out the window. Zlata pressed her fists against her ears. Suddenly the tendons arose on her elder sister's smooth white neck, and she grasped for the wall. They bandaged up her calf; it was merely a grazing wound. Zlata could not stop screaming.

The next day when there was no shelling, Zoran set out for the brewery, where a yellow-faced old man lay dark-gaping and bloody, filled the jug, then rode to visit Zlata. Broken glass grinned newly in the stairwell. The elder sister lay sleeping, with her thin lips turned down like the dark slits of her clenched eyes. Her hair clung sweatily to her forehead and her face was pale. Zlata was scrubbing the dishes, using as little water as she could.

Such a beautiful, quiet morning, said her mother, it's hard to believe. Perhaps they are preparing some surprise for us.

Zoran said: Even so, we will manage, with God's help.

Zlata, make some coffee. So delicious, his coffee!

Thanks, but we have plenty at home. Please keep it for yourselves.

Zlata, is he lying? How can there be so much coffee?

Never mind! said the boy, smiling in embarrassment.

Zlata's mother gazed out the window. She smoked half a cigarette. Presently she went heavily downstairs, and he took Zlata's hand.

She's getting fond of you, said the girl. That's why she left us alone. Are you happy?

Yes.

Then why don't you look at me? What's wrong?

Last night we didn't sleep well, he said.

Here also it was bad.

Perceiving that the hollows beneath his eyes were the same color as the stubble on his chin, she longed to kiss him. As she began to pull his head against hers, a shell smashed loudly down, neither near nor far. She began to scream.

Her mother rushed upstairs. An empty jar fell from her hand and shattered.

Zoran stayed long into the green evening light, holding Zlata's hand. But before dark he had to go home, because his family needed water. When he said goodbye, the girl could not stop sobbing. That half-cruel look of hers which he used to find so erotic had now entirely gone. She was ill. A machine gun chittered at him as he pedalled round the corner, but he swerved between the buildings whose dusty window-shards resembled scraps of grey cloth. Perhaps Zlata trusted too much in destiny, which he attempted not to think about. Passing the white profile of an Austro-Hungarian medallion upon a sky-blue wall which for some reason had not yet been shelled, he felt desperate at her suffering.

Just as when seen through the window of a rising airplane Bosnia goes blue and then blue-green, her indistinct patches of greyish-green, cut by whitish roads, now falling into shadow, so his anguish dimmed down once he made up his mind. His parents had two other sons to help them. He explained how nervous Zlata was becoming, and his mother said: Do whatever you can to take care of her.— His father said: That's right; you heard your mother.

What Zoran now contemplated was merely dangerous, not impossible. For example, fifteen years after this incident, the Muslim pensioner in the stained blue suit who sat on a bench beneath the trees on the north bank of the Miljacka told me that his son used to walk his puppydog every day no matter how many shells fell; and one afternoon he walked the dog across the Vrbanja Most and was captured, but the Serbs did not kill or even torture him. They sent him to Beograd. He did not even have to enter a prison camp. Right away a beautiful Serbian girl fell in love with him.— Now he is living with that same dog and that same girl in Florida! said the old man. The dog sleeps with them in their bed. If my son goes out to swim in the ocean, the girl takes care of the dog, and even though that dog loves her, he cries, he cries.

And of course Zoran was himself a Serb. Moreover, he had uncles and cousins.

There were friends to see, and friends of friends to pay off. Zlata's mother cried out: They can do anything to her, right in front of you! but Zoran shouted: They're human just like you! and she lowered her heavy head, remembering as well as he that not long ago the Vrbanja Most had merely been barricaded by Serbian officers with stockings over their

faces who threatened and gloated. In good time the friends of friends informed him of a certain telephone whose wire remained uncut; is it a
consolation or a shame that there will always be such conveniences? He
paid fifty Deutschemarks, black smoke slowly unclenching its infinite
fingers over the hill, and called his cousin Goran, who congratulated him
on not being dead. Zoran asked how the life was on their side. Goran answered: Everything is becoming better, and we have no complaints.

He mentioned Zlata, and his cousin was silent, then said: Yes, we
remember her—not like the others, thanks to God! That would be no
problem. Of course I can't watch her every minute.

We won't stay with you, and we thank you for your kindness.

It's good you understand.

When should we cross?

Thursday night, at ten-o'-clock. I'll be on duty at the Vrbanja Most.

Zlata knew that for the rest of her life she would remember that her
mother was sitting at the table with the soap opera on; a man was deeply
kissing a woman. Her mother opened the trunk of ancient dresses whose
red had gone to russet, the gold embroidery along the edges dignified
against the darkness. From them she chose a young girl's black dress embroidered with gold and silver patterns resembling the ones carved on
ancient stones.

I know you can't wear it, her mother said, because you may need to
run. But let's see how you look. I always thought . . .

Zlata turned away. Her shoulders trembled and she wiped her eyes.
Then a machine gun fired mindlessly on and on.

Go with God, her mother said.— Her elder sister's head hung down.
The father had been killed months ago. As for the two younger girls, they
began weeping and screaming.— Shut up, their mother said. Don't you
want her to have her chance? Now help your sister get ready.

When Zoran came to fetch her, with all the money that his family
could spare sewn inside the knees of his trousers, in her deep voice the
mother demanded that he defend Zlata with his life.

I swear it, he said, and then she embraced him for the first time.

Zlata stared out the window. Under a half-clouded sunset the river was
coppery, and the trees of the enemy hills began to thicken into a single

texture. She realized that the river was almost the same color as Zoran's eyes.— You've said goodbye! her mother shouted. Now go!

Congregations being perilous, no one accompanied them when they commenced their escape. Feeling their way down the dark street, they found a doorway to kiss in. Her tongue was in his mouth and his hand on her breast.

After this night we'll sleep always in one bed, he whispered.

What time is it?

Nine-forty.

My God, Zoran! We need to hurry now . . .

At five to ten they arrived at the bridge. I wish I could compare the Vr- banja Most to the white bridge in Vranje that a bygone Pasha built after his daughter drowned herself over the Serbian shepherd he had executed for the crime of love. Unfortunately, the Vrbanja Most lacks monumen- tality. What legends could there possibly be concerning this all too or- dinary structure?

Fifteen years later I met Zlata's mother, who now lived alone in that apartment in the Old Town. Her hair was almost the color of cigarette smoke. She said: In this place people were taking care of each other. When we were living in the basements, whenever we got something to eat we would cook it and we would share it. Maybe after the war we be- came more selfish.

As we talked about the war, the old woman's eyes seemed to sink into their sockets. At first she had not believed that anything could happen to Sarajevo, and then the first bombshell landed; and when it was over, she could not quite believe that it was over.

In her thunderous cigarette smoker's voice she told me about the third year, when shrapnel flew into her spleen. A couple were kissing on televi- sion. She showed me a photograph of Zlata, and the echoes of the foot- steps across the hall exploded in my head like gunshots.

They wanted to cross the bridge and they killed them on the Chetnik side, said the old woman.

I had always imagined what had occurred as simply sadistic treachery, but Zlata's mother said: Anyone who tried to cross over the bridge was killed. Only certain bridges were open. They had no idea.

Who had no idea?

The Serbs. They were careless with everyone, she said, lightly striking the coffee table with her massive wrists.

Zoran's family was gone, of course. Nobody knew what had happened to them, and it seemed wisest to stop asking. I walked away. A drunk cursed me from behind a wrecked airplane.

The old pensioner on the north bank of the Miljacka did not remember them, so I asked others.— I think she was Muslim, said a woman on a bench, but another lady insisted: No, no; he was the Muslim and she was the Serbkina.

At least they agreed that Zlata had been shot first. It must have been an abdominal wound, for she kept screaming (for hours, they said, but I hope they exaggerated) in that puddle of light which the enemy had trained on No Man's Land. Zoran, trying hopelessly to drag her back into the besieged city, was shot in the spine with a single rifle bullet, then shot again in the skull, which, considering the distance, might be called fine marksmanship, although on the other hand the snipers had had months to learn the range. Some embellishers claim that Zlata had not yet escaped her agony even at sunrise. Whether or not this is so, everyone agrees that the corpses of the two lovers lay rotting for days, because nobody dared to approach them. Eventually, when the international press made a story out of it, it became an embarrassment, and another truce was arranged. And it turned out just as Zoran had promised his bride, for they were buried in one grave.

In memoriam, Bosko Brkić and Admira Ismić

LISTENING TO THE SHELLS

1

In the dimming living room they were drinking slivovitz and water out of fine crystal glasses, and everyone was laughing and smoking American cigarettes until a shell fell twenty-five meters away. The women jumped. Another shell fell slightly closer and the women screamed. Then the people sat silently smoking in the last light, their smoke nearly the same color as the drinking glasses, and presently began to laugh again, leaning over their hands or spreading their fingers; they stubbed out their cigarettes in crystal ashtrays, and the poet who loved Vesna even suspected that finally he had found life. But Enko the militiaman sat glaring. Now it was dark, with echoes of the last light fading from the bubbles of mineral water just within the glasses and from the women's pale blouses, and they sat in silence, listening to the shells.

When a shell approaches closely, you may well hear a hiss before it strikes. Once it does, you will be deafened for a minute or two, during which time you are not good for much except to wait for another shell. Meanwhile you see what they call *the big light*. After that you can hear the screams of children.

Vesna's best friend Mirjana had had two little boys, and a shell killed them both. A shell had sheared away the tree in front of Vesna's apartment; the smash had been so loud that she was certain she must be wounded.

Mirjana said: Marinko has a car but no petrol. Do you know where he can get petrol?

Ask Enko, said Vesna.

Enko said nothing.

Smiling brightly, Mirjana tried to light another cigarette. The match-flame trembled between her fingers and went out. Vesna leaned toward her, so that they could touch their cigarettes together. People still had plenty of tobacco at that time. In a couple of years they would be smoking green tea.

Vesna said: It's quiet now, thanks to God!

In the corner sat Enko with a cigarette hanging out of his mouth and his police ID clinking on its neck-chain. He had pulled off his bulletproof vest, which was leaning against the wall in easy reach. Every now and then his hand touched the grip of his gun in the holster; then he swigged from the crystal glass and took another drag; finally he pulled off his now ridiculous sunglasses, his head turning rapidly as he listened to his comrade Amir, who leaned forward as if anticipating something, all the while touching his moustache with a ringed forefinger. No one else could hear their conversation. Enko's cigarette burned steadily between two fingers as he raised it again, tapping his foot, and his face was young and hard.

2

Amir rose, gazed out the window into the greenish darkness, then went out.— He knows how to get American whiskey, Enko explained.

Vesna said: Enko, can you tell me where Marinko can buy some petrol?

Who's Marinko?

Didn't you meet him? I thought you did. He's Mirjana's cousin.

Enko locked his bleak eyes on Mirjana. He said: Where are you from anyway?

Look, I'm Sarajevan, just like you.

Great. Now what part of town are you from?

Her children are all killed, Vesna explained. From now she has none.

Who the fuck cares? said Enko. What do you need petrol for?

My cousin wants it. I don't ask him his business.

Enko laughed.— Sure, he said. I can get him as much petrol as he wants.

He'll be grateful to you.

Gratitude doesn't do much for me, said Enko.

3

When Amir came back with the whiskey, he informed Enko that there was a lost American journalist at the Holiday Inn.

At the Holiday Inn, journalists were smoking quietly around marble tables in the dark. Across the river a machine gun chortled like a night bird. Enko found the lost American and quickly uncovered his particulars: He had no idea what he wanted, and he could pay a hundred fifty Deutschemarks per day—not nearly as much as any television reporter, let alone a sexy anchorwoman such as Christiane Amanpour, but whatever they could get out of him would be easy money, and his pockets might be deeper than he said. Amir, who had recently inherited an almost new Stojadin automobile, would be the driver, billing by the hour; while Enko would babysit the journalist at, for instance, a hundred fifty Deutschemarks a day. Amir and Enko knew that everything is negotiable, while the journalist knew that when one might be killed this very hour, all money is play money. So the three contracting parties quickly achieved agreement, Enko staring into the American's face while Amir drummed fingers on the tabletop as if he knew of more lucrative projects elsewhere, which indeed he did.

A man in a flak jacket and helmet strutted by, with his tape recorder's light glowing red. At another table, some functionary from Municipality Centar was assuring a French journalist: Everything will be solved by winter. Everything must be, or there will be hundreds and thousands dead.— The Frenchman nodded delightedly. Now he could file his story.

The American journalist was encumbered by a pair of binoculars for which he would never have any purpose. Enko told him: I sure could use your binoculars.

We'll see, said the American vaguely. Maybe at the end . . .

Eight-o'-clock, said Amir to the American. Goodbye.

See you then, the American said. Well, Enko, can I buy you another drink?

Sure. By the way, I'm counting on those binoculars.

This building across the street, are there snipers in it? asked a very young British journalist in a worried voice.

Oh, no, they've cleaned it! his handler assured him.

Enko knew the handler, who was a sonofabitch and had once stolen away from him a very pretty Swedish correspondent. He therefore leaned across his enemy and explained to the British journalist, as if out of helpfulness: But there's a sniper shooting at the other entrance. You don't use that.

Now the lost American was looking even more lost, just as Enko had intended. He needed to be reminded that Enko could ditch him at any time. As a matter of fact, Enko was a man of his word. He would never do less than he had contracted to do, and often he would do more. But it was bad business to reveal that at the beginning.

The light continued to fail. Looking out the front windows, which happened to be lacking a few ovals and triangles, the journalists stared at blue sky, and at that silent building across the street.

Another drink? said the American.

Enko began to feel sorry for him.— There's a party if you want to come.

What time?

Now.

How will I get back?

No one expects you to go out by yourself, said Enko contemptuously. He rose, pulled his bulletproof vest down over his head and strapped it tight across his sides.

4

In the windows those shards of bluish twilight sky were already colder, and now the clouds swam in.

The lights had come on in the parking garage. All was noiseless. They emerged into the grey light, which was dulling down with dust and a little rain, Enko already half flooring the accelerator as they screeched around the protected corner and into the sniper's reach. Across the street, the journalist glimpsed a building with four rows of windows visible, grey and black like ice against the pale tan façade. Metal was chattering, but not here. Almost biting his lip, his shoulders hunched as if that could somehow diminish his vulnerability, Enko wrenched the car around another corner; now they were rushing past yellow walls into the Stari Grad; there was dust, chalk and broken glass on the sidewalk.— That's from right now, explained Enko, perhaps enjoying himself.— Just then, more glass departed windows, smashing on the street. The journalist sat quietly in the passenger seat. He excelled at being calm when he was powerless.

Enko demanded: What do you think about those fucking Chetniks?

Murderers, said the journalist.

Temporarily satisfied, Enko said: A few days ago a man was killed in front of the President's palace. We tried to help him, but he was already bloody. The trail of blood went more than a thousand meters. Here's where she lives.

Who?

Vesna. When you get out you don't need to run, but I'm telling you, pay attention and move your ass.

All right.

Wait a second. Inbound. Shut up. *Shut up.* No, we're fine.

As they trotted away from the car, they heard the shell explode.

In the dark landing between the first two flights of steps, Enko said: How about a cash advance?

Sure, said the journalist. How much?

Give me fifty.

Just a minute. Here it is.

Fine. Now, Vesna, she's open-minded. She won't care that I brought you. And there's chicks galore, hot chicks. Not that they'd be especially interested in a guy like you, but maybe you'll get lucky.

Okay.

Another thing. Anybody asks what you're paying me or if you're paying me, that's only *my* business.

I won't say a word.

I wish you'd have brought those binoculars. I wanted to show them off.

Vesna's door was open. As they entered the apartment, which was foggy with cigarette smoke, they heard many people, and far away a machine gun fired three bursts. A woman laughed very loudly.

Look! cried Mirjana. I was wondering when you'd get here. Who's that?

Just some American, said Enko.

And this is from my cousin, for the petrol. You'd better count it.

I don't need to count it. If he shorted me, that's his problem.

Thanks for helping him.

Well, he owes me. Who's that girl over there?

5

At that party Enko met a woman named Jasmina, and in the morning he brought her home with her blouse buttoned up wrong and her lipstick smeared all over his neck. Enko's mother knew enough not to say anything. He was her only help. As for the American, he had to sleep in

Vesna's living room because nobody felt like driving him back, especially after curfew. He didn't mind a bit. Until half-past three he sat up with the poet, discussing the novels of Ivo Andric, whom the poet detested, Danilo Kiš, whose *Garden, Ashes* the poet liked better than he did, and, while Vesna sat smiling, smoking and yawning, the ideal form of Slavic feminine beauty, which, since they were young men, occupied their intellects. The other guests had departed. By now the snipers must likewise have gone to sleep, and the jewel-like silence which accordingly illuminated them both, not to mention their obsessive natures, rendered the conversation yet more interesting, if that were possible, than the topic warranted, so that they nearly could have been outside beneath the stars investigating essential things. Vesna had gone to share a cigarette with the new widow upstairs. The poet asserted that there was a certain kind of look, embodied in the bygone actress Olga Ilić, which had to do with dark eyes, dark hair (preferably curly), round silver earrings, large breasts, a long throat and plump lips. I am sorry to inform you that the American had never heard of Olga Ilić. The poet explained that she had played both Desdemona and Hamlet—what a free spirit!—and that on the wall of his room he treasured a newspaper photograph of her in the lead role of "Bad Blood." If it weren't for the Chetniks, he'd take the American by the arm and show him that picture right now, because these were the most important topics to human beings: true art, romance, expression—all present in Olga Ilić's eyes.— And you know, my friend, when she died, she was practically a beggar! One of our greatest Yugoslav actresses! If I could go back in time, I'd attend one of her performances at the National Theater. She used to wear a rose on her breast, and then she'd give it away. What a poem I could write about that!— In the American, who cheerfully admitted to knowing less about Balkan womanhood than he should, or intended to, the poet found a refreshingly respectful audience; and in the poet the American found a guide to the names and charms of most of the women who had been there tonight, listening to the shells. It accordingly became evident that the poet was infatuated with Vesna, who now returned, smiling at them with seeming love even though there were dark rings under her eyes. The American allowed himself to be likewise infatuated, but without denying himself permission to remember

Mirjana, Ivica and Dragica. Vesna poured them all a nightcap. To himself the American pretended that he had rescued her; now they would go to bed together for the first time. She gave him a blanket, and he lay down as far from the window as he could, with his bulletproof vest for a pillow. When the fabric got too wet, for instance from perspiration, it became dangerously permeable. That was why one shouldn't sleep in it. The poet sat up, writing a poem for Vesna. Like many egoists, he had a very kind heart, and so just before dawn, while it was still safe, he woke up the journalist and walked him over to Enko's.

At a quarter of nine that morning the noises began again, deep sullen thumpings and almost happy strings of popping like firecrackers. The poet had wisely departed long since. Enko and Jasmina were sleeping, or something. The journalist had brought a pound of American coffee for Vesna or some other ideal Slavic beauty, but, missing the opportunity to deploy it, he now gave it to Enko's mother instead. That tired, hungry old woman accepted the gift with neither surprise nor thanks. Whatever came to her came not from this foreigner, who was nothing, but from Enko.

Make yourself at home; take a shower, she said, slipping the coffee into her coat pocket.— I have some business downstairs.

It was the first chilly day. The American took a cold shower in the pitch-dark bathroom and came out wondering how people would manage when the snow fell.

Now there were no shells, and the sun peered mirthlessly down on broken glass. Enko and Jasmina did not appear; nor yet did Enko's mother. Enko and Amir were on the payroll today, but the American, who did not know so very many things, did know that this would come right sooner or later, or not, and that in the meantime the best thing he could do was nothing. Tired, hungover, self-bemused by Vesna, who smiled on every guest; instructed by the poet in the ways of Slavic women, and of course altered by the various evil potentialities of the shells, he considered that he was making progress, and sat at the dining table cheerfully enough, writing up his observations, with his vest leaning against his knees. He thought it his duty to express something of these people's sufferings. If he were here for any reason, it must be that. If he could not do anything for them, then his journey had no purpose. As sincere in his way as Vesna, he wished for peace even if it made his story less dramatic. Like the poet, not to mention the snipers, he gave due credit to his feelings.

In front of the apartment the asphalt had been eaten away in blotches by shells, and beyond that was a littered sort of green over which wandered two dogs whose owners, Enko's mother had said, couldn't feed them anymore, and then a row of cars, some perfect, some rusted and windowless, some bullet-holed. The American listened. The smashing roar of a howitzer was startling, to be sure, but what did it accomplish? Did the besiegers possess only one shell? At nine it was quiet again aside from certain boomings in the background, and people passed leisurely, most of them walking, a few driving or bicycling, all of them crossing the two-lane highway at the intersection where the streetcar had been abandoned, then vanishing behind a tall construction crane. Shots sounded, but a man walked reading the newspaper. No one was running. Pigeons picked at the litter.

At nine-thirty came bursts of echoing poppers that blurred the hills behind dust or smoke, and an elderly man carrying a shopping bag grimaced, ducked and began to run. The pigeons flew in a frightened rabble. Then it fell quiet again; everyone walked slowly or stood chatting unconcerned. A one-legged man swung himself steadily along on his crutches. He kept turning his eyes in the direction of the booming sounds. Then he was gone. The journalist wrote it all down.

The door opened. Enko's mother came in sighing. The American offered her a pull from his hip flask, at which she finally liked him. She took a gulp, licked her lips, and slapped him hard on the shoulder. Then she made them both some weak tea.

Where's Enko?

Asleep, he said.

Ah. With her.

They sat there, listening for the shells, and after awhile the old woman lit a cigarette and remarked: They say it is better not to go out now. Very dangerous. Sometimes it is true, and sometimes the other way. Anyhow, one cannot stay inside forever.

6

Just before ten the door of Enko's bedroom opened. Enko, shirtless but already wearing his gun, strode into the bathroom and shut the door. Then he returned to the bedroom, rubbing his forehead and yawning. After another quarter-hour the girl came out, fully dressed, and darted shyly into the bathroom.

Listen, said Enko. I need another advance.

Why not?

Give me a hundred.

How about fifty?

I said give me a hundred.

If I give you a hundred, then after that fifty I gave you last night, we're square for today, which is fine by me. The only thing is, I don't have much cash on me in case we need to eat.

Don't worry about that, said Enko.

All right, said the American. He took up his bulletproof vest. Jasmina had just left the bathroom, so he locked himself in there, dropped his pants and removed another hundred Deutschemarks from the money belt. Of course he had lied to Enko, who probably knew it; there was no safe place to leave cash, so he carried it all. Like the others, this was a good new banknote, the kind that the people here preferred. He folded it three times and dropped it into his pocket. Then he lifted the heavy vest over his head, lowered it into place and snugged the two tabs across the torso panels. Over this he zipped up the light windbreaker, to make him less conspicuous to snipers. It had always seemed to him elementary logic that the wearer of a bulletproof vest would be in and of himself a target.

Jasmina stood at the dining room table, with her purse in her hand. Enko's mother ignored her.

Enko was staring at him. No doubt he wanted his advance. The American said: Do you have a second?— Enko rose and followed him down the hall. The American gave him the money.

What's all this secret bullshit? said Enko.

I keep my finances private, said the American. That's how I like to do things.

Fine, said Enko. Amir's downstairs.

Where are we going?

The frontline, if you promise not to shit your pants.

I'll do my best.

We need petrol. That's what the money's for. On the way we'll drop Jasmina at her cousin's. Let's go.

The American shook Enko's mother's hand.— Come back, she said. I'll pray for you.

Enko was whispering something in Jasmina's ear. She giggled.

7

Here everyone runs, said Amir. This corner is very dangerous. Serbian snipers shoot from the hills. We must speed up here.

Okay, said the American. Enko was in the back seat with his pistol on his lap.

The car turned onto the sidewalk, then rushed across a pedestrian bridge.— This place is very dangerous, said Amir.

I think I can see that.

Amir's ancient M48 rifle jiggled between the seats, the barrel pointing ahead.

Now they were on a straightaway, and a single bullet struck the car somewhere low on the left side of the chassis, harming nothing so far as they could tell. Nobody said anything. Amir slammed the gas pedal to the floor. No more bullets came. The American felt that slight sickness which always visited him on such occasions: in part mere adrenaline, which was intrinsically nauseating, that higher form of fear in which his mind floated ice cold, and a measure of disgust at himself for having voluntarily increased his danger of death. Over the years, the incomprehensible estrangement between his destiny as a risk-taking free agent and the destinies of the people whose stories he sometimes lived on, which is simply to say the people who were unfree, and accordingly had terrible things done to them, would damage him. Being free, however, he would never become as damaged as many of them. And, like Enko, he did get paid for his trouble. Mostly he broke even or better. On this day, of course, he was simply considering how to live out the day while writing the best notes he could. His mind subdivided checklists into sub-lists, in hopes of preparing him for anything: If Amir gets shot, I'll take the wheel, but he'll be in the way, so I'll hold the wheel steady with my left hand and crook my right arm around his neck, and then if Enko helps me . . .

Hey, Enko, said the American.

Shut up, said Enko.

Enko, I hope your finger's on the trigger guard.

Fuck you.

Just don't shoot me in the back when we drive over a bump. Unless you do it on purpose.

Enko laughed.

Amir rounded a corner on three wheels, and they sped into a tunnel lined with sandbags, already braking now, and parked in the garage of some partially ruined building.

Listen, said Enko. We're going through that hole in the wall. The Chetniks can see us there, so we're going to run up the hill about two hundred meters.

Okay.

So that was what they did, the American journalist stumbling once, topheavy under the weight of his vest, and nobody shot at them. After that it was still only mid-morning there behind the wall of sandbags where half a dozen men, some in the uniform of the old National Army, stood smoking cigarettes while another half dozen loaded munitions into the military police truck not far from last night's shards of broken glass which were something like new-fallen snow. Enko clashed his fist against several of theirs in turn, while Amir stood expressionless, perhaps smiling behind his sunglasses. A grey and ghastly look was in their faces as they listened for the shells.

They were friendly to the American, because in those days his government considered Bosnian Muslims immaculate victims, hence allies to rescue; in later years it would consider all Muslims to be potential terrorists. So they gave him colorful interviews while he wrote diligently in his notebook.

A militiaman showed him a paddle studded with nails and said: You know what we call this? We call this *Chetnik teacher.*

The American knew enough to laugh heartily, and after that they liked him even better.

8

You know, you missed a big story, said an eyes-alight French reporter to the very young British journalist whose handler was Enko's enemy. Four French was wounded last night, and one Egyptian!

Buy you two a drink? the American offered.

Very funny. Find your own story.

I will, said the American, excited because he and Amir were about to go to Vesna's. Enko would come later; he was with Jasmina.

Amir accepted one whiskey and no more. He liked to drive carefully. He said: I think you like Vesna.

Sure. Do you?

A real Bosnian woman.

Bosnian women are very pretty.

Good.

Last night Marko was telling me his theories about Slavic beauty. He's fond of an actress named Olga Ilić—

Who?

Olga Ilić. He said she died in 1945.

Forget what Marko told you. That's just some dead Serbian bitch. Are you ready?

Sure. By the way, do you think Vesna minds when I stay over there?

She understands. You are a guest, and a friend.

Thank you. You're all my friends—

He paid the waiter, and they went to the car. It was another point of difference between him and them that so many of them lacked bullet-proof vests, and his was more invulnerable than most of theirs, although that made it proportionately heavier. The best model he had ever seen was manufactured for members of the Warsaw Pact. It had a collar to protect the carotid and subclavian arteries. His own went only as far as it went. Amir sat in the driver's seat, very slowly smoking a cigarette, staring straight ahead. An automatic rifle chortled far away. The American understood that Amir was listening to the night and forming the best plan that he could. He waited quietly. Presently Amir started the car.

They rounded the corner rapidly and then Amir stamped on the gas as they traversed the sniper's field of fire, and the American looked up into the four window-rows of the building across the street but they were black and grey without any revelations, and the car whipped safely round the next corner, and Amir, slowing, said: Someday we'll get that sonofabitch.— They came into the Stari Grad more sedately than when Enko had driven the other night, but Amir kept gripping the steering wheel hard, with the fat barrel of the M48 pointing greyly forward between them. The American liked him better than Enko. He never asked for advances.

They climbed the stairs. Vesna's apartment was very crowded that night. A tall man was shouting: How can we stop them with fifty rounds? Fifty rounds, just fifty rounds!

Vesna rushed up to him and touched his hand very gently.— Don't worry about it now, brother, she said.

The man stared at her. Vesna led him to a chair.

Something almost gentle came into Amir's face as he gazed at Vesna. He leaned his rifle inside the closet.

As soon as Vesna moved to another guest, the drunk stood up, muttering: Fifty fucking rounds—

Shut up and give me a cigarette.

Where's Enko?

With Bald Man, and you should be, too. Hey, you, Mr. Fifty Rounds! What's your name?

Kambor. Who are you?

Don't you know who Bald Man is?

Of course.

Then you'd better learn who I am. I'm Muhamed. I'm in Bald Man's squad. If you need ammunition, go to Bald Man. He's got so many more rifle grenades—

Not for me, for everyone! The men on the frontline with fifty rounds—

Why aren't you on the frontline, asshole? Amir, brother, what do you have for me?

Amir gave the man a hundred Deutschemarks. The American went to greet Vesna, who smiled at him with a brilliance in whose meaning he could almost believe. Awkwardly he asked how she was, and she replied that a neighbor had been killed, not a close friend, but as it turned out someone whom she missed more than she would have guessed.

How did it happen?

She was queuing for water at the brewery, when a shell . . .

I'm sorry.

And the funny thing is that she was Serbian! Well, at least we're all equals here.

Vesna, have you met Bald Man?

Oh, yes! He's always smiling. He's good for his neighbors and friends. He's good with the people that he's good with.

Such as Amir and Enko?

Yes, reliable men like them.

The American sat drinking and listening, sometimes recognizing that someone had said something very important which out of respect for them all he would not write down in their presence but do his best to remember exactly (the night silently torn open by a faraway shell-flash which could not keep the night's flesh from cohering again); he assumed that none of them knew why what they said could matter to other people and times; after all, how could it be of more than temporary value to them themselves who already understood the shells? Perhaps after ten or twenty years, should they survive so long, they might grow sufficiently fortunate as to forget the significance of what people said in such a situation, and then, if he had written it down and they discovered and read it, it might mean something new to them, and even lend them something like fulfillment.

Presently the poet found him, and with relief those two shy men sat down together to enumerate the beauties of the Slavic woman. The American thought that his friend seemed sad, perhaps even by nature. They drank together.

And how was the frontline? asked the poet.

Not bad. And how was it at home?

How can I complain? When the Nazis were here, my grandparents used to eat beech bark.

9

Now, Olga Ilić, the poet began to explain, when they accused her of collaboration with Bulgaria, she was imprisoned and then she experienced a nervous crisis, because she was a very sensitive woman. So sensitive and so beautiful! Vesna resembles her in both these qualities, I believe.

Would you say that Olga Ilić was kind?

You know, I feel as if she could have been my wife, or maybe my sister. During the Hitler war she lived in a suburb of Belgrade, bombed out of her house and terrified that an American or British shell would get her. Don't you think she was one of us?

When the next shell exploded, not so far away, a young woman went rigid as if she were playing the violin, because this type of life was still new; and the poet gazed on her with pity in his beautiful eyes.

That afternoon Amir had chauffeured the American to the morgue, where he had set about first seeing and then knowing that those children were dead—thank God he'd never known them, so he wasn't compelled to feel much, at least not immediately; he could write about their openmouthed yellow-green faces without being hindered in his work by personal considerations. The details, being precious in and of themselves, since they were the manifestation of the real, would array themselves, and express the sad horror they represented, without his needing to be tortured by it. A photojournalist may look at his negatives ten years later and only then be infected with the anguish they record; for word-workers it is the same only different. He knew enough not to expound on this subject at Vesna's, even to the poet, who continued praising Vesna in the guise of describing Olga Ilić, while the lost American sat listening to other conversations around him, trying to remember them forever, so that something, anything, could be made of this:

We still have ten crates of tracers from the Viktor Bubanj Barracks.

Why won't we harden that checkpoint?

Bald Man says they're shelling Konjic worse than ever.

Was he there?

Of course he was, shitface. Bald Man goes where the brigades can't.

Then why doesn't he liberate Konjic for us? Armchair hero—

. . . Killed them both on the Vrbanja Most, after giving their guarantee. And ever since then my sister's not right in the head. She and Zlata were classmates—

Don't worry, brother. We'll get our revenge. Those Serbian girls are going to learn how to make Bosnian babies.

A shell came hissing, and everyone fell silent. The experienced soldiers relaxed first, shrugging their shoulders as they listened for the explosion, which sounded far away when it finally came.

Mirjana's fingers were shaking. She saw the American look.— Nerves, she said with a smile.

He said: I envy the people who can understand what they hear. It must give them a few extra seconds of peace—

The brunette nodded, her ringed fingers flashing as she raised the glass of slivovitz to her lips, and then she said: At the beginning it was funny for us, and we didn't even know what a grenade was, so we would be on the balcony trying to look. So we learned that this kind made a buzzing sound, and one made a hissing sound, and on the ninth floor of our building there was this one Serb who would always cheer anytime there was a bombing; he would shout, *oh, they got it!* I remember how he would cheer—

What happened to him?

Oh, he's still there, but he doesn't cheer, at least not so loudly, because we got fed up—

Now Amir approached him and said: Enko's waiting for you on the landing.

The American went out.

Give me an advance, said Enko.

How much?

All of it.

Sure. I'll be back in five minutes.

Make it two hundred.

It'll have to be dollars.

How much?

A hundred.

That's not right.

Well, it's what's on me just now.

When are you going to give me those binoculars?

At the end. I'll be right back.

Rather than disturbing the fighters who were smoking cigarettes just outside Vesna's bathroom, he ascended two more dark and silent flights of stairs—far enough to give him time to hide his moneybelt from Enko or anyone. Without incident he removed and flashlight-verified the banknote. The American walked back into Vesna's. Enko was glaring and smiling at a blonde in a cheap print dress. The blonde was giggling. Jasmina, weeping openly, rushed into the bathroom. Mirjana rolled her eyes. Vesna was laying out crackers on a little plate. Amir met the American's eyes, saying nothing.

Enko, I have something for you, said the American.

Shut the fuck up.

I'll give it to Amir.

I said shut up.

The party fell nearly silent, so that the American could hear a fighter say: Fifty men armed with rifle grenades—

Turning away from his good friend, the American clasped Amir's hand, transferring the money that way. Then he went to seek out the poet.

10

Every day they worked for him, Enko and Amir earned their money. He interviewed fighters in a concrete building with wadded-up shutters in the smashed black-stained windows, met the mothers of murdered children and imagined that he would "make a difference." All the while they were running Enko's errands, the most common of which was to carry ammunition to comrades at the frontline. Once they took a bag of onions and potatoes to Jasmina's mother. What Amir could have used and even where he lived the American never knew. In the shade, a longhaired boy was hosing down his sidewalk, walking on broken glass. Sometimes Enko said: Tomorrow I'm with the squad, and then the American went out with Amir alone, who of course could interpret perfectly well. Often no interpreter was needed, as when he and Amir sat on a terrace near the head of some steep high street, drinking slivovitz with a blonde named Sandi (twenty-two years old, he wrote in his notebook); for them she had arranged fresh flowers in a big jar on the table. Her boyfriend lived down in Centar; she could not reach him even by letter. Beyond the fence began a view of other red-tiled roofs, then trees, then more red roofs, then the zigzag mined path. Sandi said: The fear is the most difficult, don't you think? It's so awful. My sister is in Germany and I don't know what I can explain to her. She just doesn't understand that every minute you're in the street you feel it, and then when you go inside . . .— He wrote this down, thinking that he must make others comprehend what the sister could not, while Amir gazed into his eyes.

Enko demanded an advance on three days' salary. Smiling, the American paid. Every night that he could get a ride, he went to Vesna's. On other nights he sat in the lounge of the Holiday Inn, where there were occasionally off-duty soldiers and always both kinds of journalists, the suit-and-tie species with the press card on the lapel, and the devil-may-care ones in the photo vests, making extravagant plans or exchanging boasts. It was scarcely comme il faut to sit alone, as the callow American did. This branded him as the impoverished freelancer that he was—a parasite, in fact. When he first arrived, some television journalists had taken pity on him and given him a ride from the airport to the Holiday Inn (the speeding auto receiving a token bullet from the heights of Gavriča). That day there had been no means of getting into the city but with that group. He was grateful, and hoped not to require any other favors. He had not yet learned that one can always pay one's own way, whether or not the currency is acceptable to others. Indeed, there was an exchange of sorts: To the extent that they noticed him at all, they dismissed him as a denizen of that backwater called "features," while he for his part pitied them for being the merest producers of spectacle. *He* was going to get to the *why.*— Mostly, of course, all parties ignored each other. They schemed out their stories and listened for the shells.

How old were your sons? he asked Mirjana.

Five and three.

What were their names?

I don't want to talk about it.

But in time (by which I mean half a week, for where there is much death, friendships mature quickly) Mirjana and the others came to know (or at least such was his impression) that he cherished them for their suffering, which he hoped to preserve for others because it tormented him. (He could not decide whether to admire Enko, not for his bravery and his knowledge but for his pain, which armored him like a bulletproof vest.) The poet of course had been the first to trust him. Around Vesna the poet resembled one of those silent, spindly-legged, deer-eyed little dogs which sit beneath the table, rarely looking into anyone's eyes but never being the first to look away. Because the American also admired Vesna, but without designs, much less possessiveness, the two men's understanding ran deep; moreover, the American believed in the poet's kindness. As for Amir, he perhaps had liked the American from the beginning, although with Amir one could never tell. Vesna of course would have smiled at anyone but the ones who shelled them from the hills. The other women seemed to take their cue from her. He supposed himself beginning to understand the first and second meanings of the shells but not yet the hundredth; perhaps not even the frontline fighters were capable of that.

Enko was there. Enko said: Mirjana doesn't talk about it because her family is mixed.

That's not true! the woman cried. Silently Vesna slipped an arm around her shoulders.

Glaring into their eyes, Enko said: I think it's a problem not to talk about it.

That was when the American realized that Enko sought to help him.

But do we need to talk about it? said Mirjana.

My personal opinion, said Enko, and the American was astonished to discover that for Enko there was any such thing, is that the only way to prevent war is to shame people.

Do you really think that you can do that to Serbian people?

No, I'm talking about Germans, replied Enko with a sarcastic laugh. Germans are different.— Then he strode over to Amir and muttered in his ear.

Stroking Mirjana's hair, the redhaired girl Dragica said: Enko is right. Nowadays I'm always asking myself, What is the story? What is the truth? When you go to Catholic school, like I did, you hear only Croatian history, and you won't hear what bad things Croats did under Hitler. If I live to have children, someday they'll go to school and they won't hear what bad things Croats did today. But I'm going to tell them: We too had bad people during the war. And I think the best thing would be to write their names, and say, *they killed.*

Isn't that why you're here? Vesna asked the American.

Yes, he said, and after that more told him their stories.

11

Clenching her lips, her cigarette smoke streaming away, Mirjana took him aside and said: Write.— Then she told him how her children had died.

He wrote. She was gazing into his face as if he could help her. He was thinking: Nothing is more important than this. I came here for this; perhaps I was born for it. If someone reads her story and then refrains from taking a life . . .

Bitterly laughing, the poet was relating how in preparation for the siege their Serbian neighbors used to come by night to the Orthodox graveyard overlooking Bucá-Potok, in order to inter crates of shells, machine guns and sniper rifles.— Write that down, he said, and the American wrote.

What must be concluded about that? the poet demanded. How can anyone claim there was no premeditation?

Yes, they've been very intelligent in their way—

Vesna, who heard everything, paused in her passing and said: I don't think they are intelligent. Intelligence for me I think is that you have to be human. Intelligence, so we learn in school, is simply the ability to find a solution for unknown problems. But for me, there must be some kind of genetic memory; we must be born with certain values from previous generations. Otherwise there's nothing. I've met people without any soul. They have decent homes, they have children, they have everything, but they have nothing to share. And those Chetniks up there . . .

I want you to hand over those fucking binoculars right now, said Enko.

You can have them at the end, I promise.

Look. Do you want to interview Bald Man? Is that what you want?

Sure. I'll interview him.

A shell hissed overhead, rather close, and suddenly Mirjana's white top went dark at the armpits. Enko laughed at her.

The American journalist went to get stories from Dragica.

12

Dizzy with cigarette smoke, their hearts racing faster and faster, they flirted, did deals and listened for the shells. Sometimes one or two of them withdrew from the window, as if doing that could save them. More and more he admired Vesna, who gave them this place and comforted those who could not distract themselves. In her presence the glare often departed from Enko's eyes, in much the same way that the offices at the television station slowly darkened whenever the electricity failed.

She touched the poet lightly on the shoulder; he smiled in hope.

13

The next day after interviewing blue-faced Gypsy women who lived alongside their excrement in a cellar insulated with garbage, they sped again down Sniper Alley and into the garage of the Holiday Inn to meet a statistician of deaths, then back nearly to the frontline, where nobody shot at them, probably because it was lunchtime.— I don't want you hanging around here more than a minute! Enko shouted. This place makes me nervous.— Sweating, the American took in sunlight, weedy grass, three men talking on the sidewalk in front of a building of black-scorched punched-out windows ringed by concertina wire. One of the men agreed to be interviewed. No one in his family had yet been killed. He couldn't understand the Chetniks, he said. And his former neighbors, them he couldn't understand.— All right, said Enko, now let's get the fuck out of here.

The American was in the back seat today, to take notes better. Enko was driving. He kept whipping his uncanny eyes left and right. Amir sat beside him, loosely gripping the leather strap of his sky-aimed M48, which appeared useless as far as the American could tell. As they rushed across a pedestrian bridge at a hundred and twenty kilometers per hour, a blue police car nearly slammed into them, screechingly stopped literally three inches away, and sped back the way it had come. Cursing, Enko reaccelerated, past a scorched building into a very dangerous open place where the street was spattered with blackish glass.

Now the American began to imagine that he would die today; a shell or a bullet would find him; in the mountains all around them, snipers were waiting for someone, which is to say anyone, so today he would serve. He felt certain of this but knew his certainty to be meaningless, so he kept it to himself. This lost journalist, hoping only to learn what was true—for as you know, he believed without being able to say why that if

this truth, whatever it was, could be communicated by him with sufficient eloquence (and not cut too much by his editor and the advertising
director), then he would have accomplished something against war or at
least for people (however wanly shone this something)—felt very afraid
at times, but not afraid of his fear; for when that went away it went away;
he had not yet understood that it was hollowing him out almost like an
amphetamine addiction; he was not addicted to war and never came to
like it, but the procedure of maintaining his calm in regard, for example,
to the shrapnel-shard which had entered the wall two inches above his
head just before he was about to sit up from his sleeping-place on the
floor of the radio-television station resembled swallowing a pill; he could
do it today, tomorrow and for however many unknown days or weeks he
might now remain in Sarajevo (on the day after his arrival, the Serbs had
shot down the UN plane, so the airport was closed, and he did not know
when or by which method he would leave); needless to say, if he lived he
would remain in the city for a finite, even relatively minute number of
days, while Vesna, Enko and the others would be pinned down here until
the end; he could calm himself for each and all of those days—but all
the time, unaware, he was getting hollowed out within his skin, and there
was no calculating how thick his skin was; meanwhile he retained the capacity to witness for awhile longer, and even to act moderately brave
while listening for the shells. And Enko was slowing down.

Far down the almost empty street, almost at the corner, a black-
uniformed man named Wolf, member of the special unit, stood deep in
the doorway of an apartment building. He was Enko's comrade, of
course. They all went up the dark stairs to the landing by whose wall
someone had written FPS, the initials of a softball club.— Sometimes I
walk here, said Wolf. I never run.— He's a fighter for freedom, said Enko.
You write that down.— They had weak ersatz tea in his flat, and the
American had his interview, paying as agreed and a trifle more. Then
Enko squealed the tires round a certain perilous corner, and after passing another red tram parked on the weedy tracks, a quarter of its windows shot out, they arrived at their appointment with the clean-faced,
greyhaired, grey-bearded old rabbi, whose moustache was still mostly
brown. He said: You see, that's the place where the massacres were.
That's where it hit.

You see that hill over there? said Enko. That's where the Bosnian Dragons got killed.

Crowds were walking in the shadow of apartment towers, fairly leisurely, the American thought. But the rare cars went screeching and skidding. They drove partway up a hill of red-roofed white houses to the apartment porch where the little girl had been killed yesterday; then for the frontline irregulars the American bought a pack of cigars for twenty Deutschemarks and Enko was pleased. Now Amir was driving. Across from the police station, a blonde sat on a railing while a brunette stood smoking beside a reddish-blond boy; as they drove by, the American took notes on that woman in the shawl who held a pail, on those people carrying water and the people crowding around the bullet-measled car; there must be a main there; they were filling up with water. At the next intersection a man with a shopping bag walked slowly; people were lounging and standing, even if inside a sheltered porch; but when Amir stopped to ask directions, Enko yelled: Shit, keep moving!

Everywhere they stopped, the American felt something in the center of the back of his skull, a sweaty nakedness and tenderness.

Between apartment buildings, two ladies, one in black, stood beside a car which wore a dusty shroud; a little child sat in another car; children were playing ball; a girl in a yellow dress crept to cast one look over the edge of the balcony, and there was a smell of greasy garbage. The American wrote about people with bloody faces, brown faces, dark faces; he described children in worn clothes. One child, dirty in his worn jacket, led them across the courtyard to his mother, who was scraping away excrement. The American opened his notebook. She said: Before the war we lived like other people.

How about that advance? said Enko.

14

Enko parked outside a leather store and went in to buy a new holster. The establishment was small, without much merchandise, but perhaps it had always been that way.— He works from old stockpiles, Enko explained, paying in dollars—today's advance, it seemed.

He stopped at home. Amir sat smoking at the kitchen table. Enko's mother was in a queue to buy bread.

Enko's room was still untouched, a shockingly ordinary room, with two televisions that didn't count for much now that the electricity was gone, bookshelves adorned with statuettes, trophies, the *Opća Enciklopedia* and other sets of books from his student days, stacks of cassettes which he lacked the batteries to listen to, snapshots of girlfriends, a clock stopped at 9:04 and one of his pistols, a heavy old French Bendaye BP, solid black steel, flat, with a scaly black grip.

Enko was airing out his bulletproof vest. Men who couldn't afford to buy their own, and had to share them in shifts, increased their risk of traumatic death; because, as I have already told you, when a vest is damp, for instance with sweat, it stops bullets more poorly.

Enko asked Amir: Does he deserve to meet Bald Man?

Amir shrugged.

Well, Mr. Journalist, do you or don't you?

Sure.

The thing is, guy, Bald Man's got style. Someone like you, there's nothing you can give Bald Man. But Bald Man, he can give you everything.

Oh. Well, maybe I'd better not waste his time.

That's a fact.

By the way, what neighborhood has the most trouble getting water? I'd like to interview some—

Let's go. Amir, swing by Anesa's.

In the safe shade of an office building, couples walked calmly. They reached the intersection, looked down into the openness nervously, and quickened their steps until they'd crossed. The President sped by in a grey Audi. Now Amir floored the gas pedal, and the American felt that same meaningless bitter flood of fear behind his breastbone. They rounded the corner successfully, completed a sickeningly exposed straightaway on which nothing moved, made a hard right on three wheels, and then another car careened toward them, struck the curb, screeched and whirled out of control, wrecked. The driver and passengers got out slowly. Soldiers gathered. It didn't appear that anyone was injured. Perceiving this, Amir drove on, toward a sign which had been shot through half a dozen times, and then they pulled up at the portico of the almost unscorched apartment tower where Anesa lived; she was part of Vesna's circle. Enko leaped out. The journalist sat in the back seat taking notes while Amir smoked a cigarette.

Enko returned.— That goddamned little cunt, he said. In case you were wondering, she's got plenty of water.

The American said nothing, since Enko looked to be in a rage. Amir started the engine and put the car in gear.

Now where we're going, said Enko, the Serbs cut off that well on July eighteenth. This place here, this is a low area, like the Holiday Inn, so these people can still get water from the reservoir. Why the fuck don't you say something?

That well that the Serbs use—

I already explained that. Who do you want to interview?

Anybody who has trouble with water.

All right. I know a fighter over there, and his mother, she's a sick old lady. That'd be just about perfect for you, wouldn't it? Maybe if you're lucky you can watch her get killed by some Chetnik. That would be a scoop, wouldn't it?

15

I need a drink, said Enko. You got your story, right?

Right.

The bar lay behind a courtyard five floors high, and hence protected from snipers. Jasmina had told him that it was organized by Bald Man to keep it safe—evidently a relative term, since he saw a few shrapnel-pocks and windowpanes nibbled away by explosions; one windowpane was blasted into a hole the shape of a flayed animal. Someone with a machine gun was standing in the half-silhouetted stairway.

It was midafternoon, the canned music (Bosnian rock and roll) loud but not deafening. The singer's voice reminded him of the golden shimmers in Anesa's purple sweater. At the next table, crew-cut men in bulletproof vests and camouflage sat smoking. Across the room, a dozen men and women in civilian clothes were getting drunk. A beautiful woman in camouflage from head to toe, her outfit completed by an impractically thin black bulletproof vest with a Bosnian army insignia on it, sat smoking, sipping juice and tapping the toe of her combat boot to the music. A man with a pistol at his hip, likewise smoking, gazed at her urgently; his hand gripped her knee. No one appeared to be listening for the shells.

Enko and the American ordered American whiskey. Amir had a Turkish coffee.

The song ended.— No, said one of the civilians, she was killed by a sixty-millimeter shell, just after her children had left the table.— The next song began.

A soldier said something to Enko, who laughed and told the American: He found a Serbian flag at his neighbor's house; he's gonna use it for target practice.

The American smiled, because Enko and Amir were both watching him.

This guy is an amazing fighter, said Enko, evidently deciding to trust the American for a few more minutes.— I'll tell you what he did. He killed a Chetnik who was wearing a helmet and a bulletproof vest. Got him right in the forehead!

Ask him if he wants a drink, said the American wearily. And if he cares to tell his story . . .

If he accepts a drink from you, you're lucky.

Well, let's hope for the best.

He says he'll take the drink.

And a drink for everyone at his table. Tell them I wish them all the best.

They want to know when the Americans will finally show some guts and intervene.

Tell them I'm also wondering that. Amir, are you sure you don't want anything else?

No. Because I am driving.

Amir, said Enko, you babysit him. I've got some business.

The American took out his notebook and began to write. Although the music did not entirely obscure the echoing chitter of machine guns elsewhere, he felt safe here, like a child who pulls the blanket over his head.

He wished that one of these women would sleep with him, although he would rather sleep with Vesna, whose front window was newly cracked and taped. The men at the other table bought him another whiskey and

Amir another coffee. He was happy then. When he was older and had forgotten most of his interviews, it was such meaningless kindnesses that he remembered.

We're going right now, said Enko, so Amir and the American followed him to the car, where a fighter stood watching a crate, which they loaded into the back seat, and without explanations Amir slipped in beside it and lit a cigarette, so the American rode up front as Enko, who took more chances in his driving than Amir, brought them down a main street, past a windowfront crazily taped and shattered, a Serbian machine gun barking like a dog, and many people running as beautifully as a flight of dark birds, although no explosion had sounded by the time they rolled past a queue for something unknown around the corner from another apartment block with a shell-hole punched right through both ends. More slowly they rolled down a quiet narrow street of people walking calmly past bullet-holes, sitting under trees. Enko's jaw tightened as he turned the next corner, already accelerating; so the car screeched into another lifeless place, then through a scorched place without any glass in any windows, the roof of one house still on but jagged like a kinked bicycle chain, and the American's chest ached with useless fear. After another corner they went sedately down a sheltered straightaway, stopping to hand over the crate to three military police who sat playing cards in what used to be a photocopier repair station. They slapped Enko on the back and poured everyone a shot of *loža*. A policeman lit Amir's cigarette with his own. Laughing, Enko wrote Sieg Heil and Wehrmacht on the wall. They returned to the car.

Could you drop me at Marko's? asked the American.

What, now you have business with him? returned Enko, possessive and suspicious.

Sure, and then he'll take me to Vesna's.

Well, you're on your own.

Are you free tomorrow?

What's the plan?

We could maybe interview some police—

Why the fuck didn't you say so when we were in there?

I didn't want to interrupt your business.

You hear that, Amir? He didn't want to interrupt our business.

That's right. I like his style.

Enko said nothing. Pleased and proud that Amir approved of him, the American continued as if he had not heard: They must have some pretty good stories.

Sure. There's this one guy, Senad, who . . .— Anyway, fuck it. We'll pick you up at Marko's tomorrow at ten. And I need an advance.

You're advanced for four days now.

That's my fucking business.

I can advance you half, but I might need some tonight if Marko and I go out.

You're not going anywhere.

I can advance you half.

Then give me those binoculars.

At the end. By the way, how's your mother?

Look. I want those binoculars.

I understand. And I'll see you tomorrow at ten.

16

Now that Enko was accustomed to him, and also craved the binoculars, the journalist had come into possession of what Americans call *leverage*, if he only cared to use it; but in fact everything already served his purpose, so why disturb the system and the self-complacency of Enko, who, besides, had introduced him to Vesna? As the night reddened from a faraway shell, fire rising up, sparks buzzing beautifully down, he scanned through his notebook for today's aphorisms from frontline heroes: *It is our personal opinion, not authorized,* and: *It is impossible to control all the people under arms. Our general statement is against any bad thing. But it is war; it is a dirty war.* He was in one of the black places whose burned smell would not leave his nostrils. Regarding Bald Man he felt indifferent, believing, as would a great writer or lazy journalist, that the situation of any native of this place who was enduring the siege (for instance, Vesna) should be capable of moving his readers. Like Enko, he imagined that he really knew something about others, and possibly he did. It never occurred to him to ask his superior colleagues at the Holiday Inn how famous or important Bald Man might be. No wonder he had never gotten ahead! In other words, he lacked the resources to visit the

Pale Serbs in an armored car, and no one invited him to videotape the liberation of Hill 849.

So why was he being offered an interview with the prince of princes? Possibly Enko had grown fond of him; more likely, Amir put in a good word; most plausible of all, Enko, being proud of his service with Bald Man, and needing to accomplish some business or other related to that demigod, found it convenient to bring the dependent American along.

Speeding down the steep red-roofed street, which reminded the American of a scene in some Italian hill town, Amir rounded the corner, while Enko issued admonishments as to how to behave in the presence of Bald Man. The machine guns had been speaking all morning. The American gripped the back of Enko's seat. They screeched into the courtyard. The square, ugly building, thoroughly bullet-pocked, was charred beneath one window, and the other windows were smashed in. A crowd of men in and out of uniform, evidently comrades, were standing outside. On the frontline he had met their like: wealthy in wounds, burns, nightmares and greenish-gold 7.62-millimeter casings. Enko raised his right arm in a cheerful salute; an old fighter slapped his shoulder. Leaning against the car, Amir lit a cigarette, narrowing his eyes; for an instant the American wondered who he really was. Unlike Enko, who remained mostly rigid in something resembling the loneliness of the frontline, Amir tended to be quite simply muted, watchful rather than aggressive; of course his apparent mildness was nothing more than opacity. Civilian men and women passed in and came out, and a little boy admired the palms of his hands. A window exploded far away. Enko entered the headquarters, the American following at a slight distance. Men in camo stood smoking. Enko approached a man who towered over him and in an extremely lordly way presented him with one of the American's hundred-dollar bills. Then they toasted each other with coffee mugs of brandy spirit, while the American waited awkwardly. A man in camo put his arm around a woman and then those two went down the hall slowly, smoking, tapping ash into a plant's pot which was already covered with cigarette butts.

Remember what I told you, said Enko. Keep your mouth shut unless he asks you something.

Sure, said the American, wondering how this would turn out.

A man in cammies and a black leather jacket, with his arm in a cast, strode slowly down the hall, his free hand on his gun. They followed him.

At a card table beside the city police commander, Bald Man sat reading some letters, playing with the trigger of a silver Sig Sauer which looked to be a new toy. The pistol was on safe. Whether it was loaded was not, of course, the American's business. Bald Man, handsome and huge, with long hair like a Chetnik and bloodshot eyes like a heavy marijuana smoker, appeared to have woken up late. Gazing at Enko, the American saw in him the glowing face of a little boy who adored his father. A queue of sad women, shabby businessmen and old men with shaking hands stood in the attitudes of petitioners. The city police commander was watching Bald Man.

Bald Man raised his head. He saw Enko. Then he smiled.

17

Vesna lit another cigarette while he asked how she was, and she smiled at him; he feared she might be tired of him. But then Marina, another of the young Serbian women, said to him, her blonde hair tucked back, her teeth as white as the cigarette between them: Last night you were asking for my first memory of this situation, and the first memory is that I was in the club and I was coming back home really really late in the taxi, because my home is up in the hill by Mojmilo, not that I can go there anymore. The driver said: I don't know why we are stuck here, because the light didn't change.— So I paid him and got out, and then I recognized some of my neighbors, waving their arms, and I was embarrassed that they would see me, and I said to myself, why did I dress in this ugly yellow jacket like a life jacket? And my parents were watching some movie on the television, and I said to them, laughing and crying: There is a war in Sarajevo! There is the first barricade . . .— We were all expecting that this madness would stop. We could walk in and out. And then when the first grenade came in . . .

And the telephone lines were cut *from this side*, said the poet.

Let her finish, please, said Vesna.

No, said Marina. That's all.

They waited for her to speak, but that was truly all. So the American, knowing this exchange between Marina and the poet to be significant but not on that account prepared to stop, for his mind's predisposition to keep stories was as ready and partitioned as the narrow golden-buttoned side-leg pockets of Amir's trousers, in which that person kept his wallet and a loaded magazine wrapped in paper, turned to Anesa, who almost tonelessly told how the siege had begun for her; and he wished he could listen to their stories forever, because it now seemed that he almost had what he wanted, which was to say the jewel of horrible meaning whose coruscations might dazzle some would-be murderer into holding his fire, or even help some fugitive from a rape camp to remember why she was damaged; his aspirations were ready to flow through Sarajevo and away, like the rippling, shallow Miljacka. Amir, who'd sent his children to Austria, drummed his fingers in time with the cassette player. The girls were black-eyed and smiling, turning their heads drunkenly, leaning chins on hands.

And on the following afternoon some of them and a few others were in a basement apartment with a Jim Morrison poster and sandbags halfway up the windows, the clock ticking, the pendulum swaying, a certain blonde lost in her own hair as if there might be a place where women rode slowly on bicycles along the summery riverbank, thrushes sang unsilenced, and people in cafés never needed to look away from each other's eyes, straining to gauge where the shell might land; and Anesa was singing, with her cigarette aimed at the sky like a gun; maybe tomorrow she'd be dead. A balding fighter grinned, stubbed out his cigarette and said: *Za dom spremni!*—the old slogan of the rightwing Croatian irregulars—and a friend of the poet, nearly drunk, swayingly said to the American: We came down drunk and singing to have a picnic, and guns shot down the hill at us, louder and louder!—to which Enko, as usual, said: Who the fuck cares?

Then it was evening at the hillside orchard, the guns faint and cozy far away like target practice while the couples got drunker and drunker. The American and the poet entertained each other by speaking of Vesna, who was not there. Enko grinned at Anesa's sluttish face. After they slit the chicken's throat, the girls bent over it and plucked it. Now the barbecue pit was smoking and white smoke came from cigarettes as a machine gun chittered while a shell sounded close but not perilous. The former mechanical engineer, darkhaired, slightly rotund, lit his cigarette while the blonde cut fresh parsley with the knife that had killed the chicken, singing gently to herself, and Enko pulled his pistol from the holster and showed it off to her and she smiled. The poet tried to flirt with Anesa. The American, a little drunk, having just learned how to recognize a KPV HMG antiaircraft gun, and not judging himself any better for the experience, wondered whether he were ready to die now, right now, if a shell came; and he forgot that he had asked himself this before. Lighting a piece of wood, a man scalded the mostly plucked chicken so that the girls could more easily remove the last pinfeathers. Smiling, Anesa said to the American: Ten dollars for a chicken; this is wartime!— And what he thought was that they had accepted him, and even his purpose; for he was not yet old, and so he did not understand that what often passes for toleration and even friendship is merely the easy indifference of people toward each other—although that understanding, if it is even accurate, may still somehow be less to the point than the illusion that we are all brothers and sisters. Just then, perhaps sensing that the American now judged himself nearly qualified to write about them all, the poet said, not without hostility: You can't imagine how it was when they started shelling us from Mojmilo.

18

The next day only Enko drove the American around, because Amir had gone, so Enko stridently announced, to Bjelave on an errand for Bald Man.— I'll be hoping for his safety, the American said, to which Enko replied, and he was right: What the fuck do you know about it?

Bald Man's bar was full at two-thirty in the afternoon, the gold diamond-lines in the faded black marble nearly occluded by soldiers from the Special Forces with their black many-pocketed vests, and by militiamen and police with holstered Russian pistols, not to mention the many girls sitting and standing, all smoking cigarettes, the sunlight catching the bloody amber in their water glasses. Anesa was there, playing with her hair and tapping her foot to the loud music. Enko's new blonde was of course also present; she crossed and uncrossed her legs. The American did not get introduced. He drank alone, quite peaceably. Beneath his windbreaker he kept on his bulletproof vest, which was heavy with sweat. None of the girls showed interest in him; he was not a handsome or prosperous American. He bought Anesa a drink, just to be kind. She blew him a kiss; she'd see him at Vesna's. He bought a drink for a Special Forces man with a big boyish face who said: God help you with your story.— The waitress carried away the round steel tray, on which dirty glasses slammed like shells, and the music got louder, until he could scarcely distinguish the festive crackling of rifles in the distant sky. Gripping the blonde by her upper arm, Enko led her toward the stairs. She laid her head against his shoulder and then they disappeared. The American ordered another drink. For hard spirits the establishment offered only whiskey and cognac; the bartender used a shotglass for the measure, then poured into a water glass. Careful journalist that he was, the American wrote down this detail; and then he looked into all the faces, wondering how they differed from the faces of his interviewees who boiled tea on the landing where the snipers could not see, feeding the fire with cross-slats from a broken chair, their faces hard and dark.

Some men in camouflage stood outside exchanging Hitler salutes. They were drinking slivovitz or *loža* from the look of it, so they must have brought it with them; that lovely pure plum-fire taste nearly seemed to rise up in his nostrils as he watched. This made him crave another drink, so he had one.

At the next table, couples sat around a green bottle and a purple thermos, laughing, and at any instant a shell could come in and make them into what he had seen and smelled at the morgue that morning. He tried to smell *loža* again, but the smell of unrefrigerated corpses now lived in his nose. He wondered whether or not to write this down.

Enko, who had sensibly refused to enter the morgue, presently returned alone, militiaman to the heart of him, in his bandanna and sunglasses; he was more cold and harsh the longer the American knew him—the veriest personification of a gun—but now he stood on the stairs smiling.

Yes indeed, Bald Man had arrived, big and muscular, in camouflage pants, with the new Sig Sauer pistol in his web belt, and a walkie-talkie; his white T-shirt said: **Armija Rep. BiH Policija**. There was a blackhaired girl on either side of him, and out in the courtyard stood his fighters, as straight as the packs of American cigarettes on the glass shelf. He bought everybody in the bar a drink and then left.— He could tear your head off with his hands, said Enko admiringly.

I'd like to know more about him, said the American, opening his note-book.

I might be able to get you an interview, said Enko, as coyly as a high school girl at a dance.

What's the bravest thing he ever did? asked the American, seeking to give pleasure with this question.

Getting out two wounded men by himself, under fire from two anti-machine guns at twenty to thirty yards, from No Man's Land.

That's very impressive.

He was one of the guys in the neighborhood sportsmen's association before the war. People loved him. The only question people wondered was, when will he get elected as leader? He got us guns, machine guns. People came and said: I want to fight with you. Six hundred men would die for him.

You know him pretty well, I guess. What else do you want me to learn?

He loves the occasion when he has to catch snipers, but right now we're not allowed to punish them, only exchange them. One time he was chasing a Serbian sniper for four hours. This Serb had killed ten of our guys. The SDS* paid him five hundred Deutschemarks per kill. Bald Man was alone; he had to climb a skyscraper, they wounded him, but the sniper surrendered.

Very heroic.

I told Bald Man how you said that all the Chetniks are murderers. That might help your case.

Thanks for thinking about me, Enko.

Some HOS† irregulars drove by and Enko gave them the Nazi salute.— Great fighters, he said.

19

Vesna had been drinking, as had he, so he said: Sweetheart, will you be my human shield?

If you don't cut my throat afterward, darling! Oh, Enko, there you are—

---

* Srpska Demokratska Stranka (Serbian Democratic Party), the main organ of the Bosnian Serbs.

† Hrvatske Odbrambene Snage (Croatian Defense Force), the private army of Dobroslav Paraga's party of rightwing extremists, HSP, whose antecedents were in the Nazi period.

The American turned. The poor poet was glaring at him, and he thought: Who am I, who have not suffered as he has, to threaten his one one-sided love?— And then he further thought, as if for the first time: I could be killed tomorrow as easily as he. More easily, in fact, since I'm at the frontline—

Accordingly, he wished to flirt with Vesna some more. Instead, he flirted with Dragica, who had no use for him (the night sky flushing with bursts of fire), after which he questioned the poet about Olga Ilić until the poet was mollified. A smiling fighter carefully wrote in the American's notebook: *MPs in BiH is the only MPs fronting the frontlines at all fronts.*— Thank you, he said. Then Dragica and a girl named Aida were trying to educate him about the sounds of bullets, and Aida said, opening her pinkish-silver-painted fingernails (they still had cosmetics that autumn): Of course it's different when a sniper shoots and when a pistol shoots, because when a sniper shoots it's a longer hissing.— By then he had built up a certain opinion of himself, and had he stayed in Sarajevo for another two weeks, which his budget of course did not permit, it is possible that such aphorisms might have ceased to impress him, and he might even have thought: Woman, I wonder if you've ever been to the frontline, whereas I go almost every day and have learned how to watch Chetniks in an angled mirror so that both parties can see but the Chetniks cannot shoot.— I for my part hope that he never would have thought that way.— Through the taped window, following a shell-hiss, he saw the birth of a glow which nearly seemed comforting; it could have been the lamp of some student, perhaps Thea or Jasmina, who was preparing for her examinations before getting married; and the glow brightened; he could neither hear screams nor smell any smoke. Vesna's guests fell silent, watching that fire, and then their talk sprang brightly up again. Dragica carried around the plate of emerald-fresh halvah. The American recorded the words of the haunted man who whispered what he had seen at night in Kovači Graveyard; then Jasmina was confiding: I was afraid when a 120-millimeter grenade fell into my flat, but, thanks be to God, it went to the other side of the room; they fired it from the direction of the Studentski Dom . . .— And then Enko was informing the poet, practically shaking him: To hear them tell it, everything always went well for the Serbs, even in World War II. You know why? Because shame was never put into their fucking minds! God told their Prince Lazar: You have two options, either you will win today and be prosperous, or else you will die and go to heaven for a thousand years. Fuck their stinking Chetnik mothers! They never lose! Well, guess what?— The poet cringed away; then Vesna came, laid down her long fingers so gently on Enko's hand, and said something which hushed him, and she turned him around and sat him down on the sofa between Aida and Jasmina, and the hatred had bled from his face, but his shoulders would not unlock. Then a Serbian girl named Branka was telling the American in a low and rapid voice: I think Slovenians were the big problem, at which her Croatian friend Olga said: I think we can blame the Croatians the most, because the Serbs did most of what they did out of fear of Croatians.— Vesna, sweating in her white top (with her pink mouth and short blonde hair, her narrow V-shaped dark eyebrows and blue-green eyes, she looked nothing like Olga Ilić), now said: The ones who decided to do this, it's so sick, like pedophil-ism; someone was sitting in an office thinking about all the nasty things he could do to the people! The joke is that the Chetniks are copying old Yugoslav war movies. But these people who are shooting . . . well, as I'm growing older, I understand that religion is only manipulation and noth-ing else.— He thought he had never heard her so bitter. Meanwhile the poet stared down at her breasts. And then more people were telling the American their stories, each of which could have occupied his life in proper retelling. Perhaps in retrospect these nights at Vesna's appeared more bright or even brilliant than they were; or it might have been that they were what they were by virtue of simple contrast (the darkness, the hissing of the shells). But he knew, *he knew,* that these people's agony was not meaningless. And then came a shell, the women straining their faces at the window, then suddenly screaming, and after it exploded, very near, the building shaking, they screamed and screamed, and Vesna's young throat was taut and sweaty.

20

In the middle of the following afternoon they were speeding back from the frontline (they had been running all morning, and, worse yet, through sunny places) when Enko said: Look. What are you going to give Bald Man?

How much does he want?

You don't fucking get it. I told you: Bald Man doesn't need shit from you. He has everything already.

All right.

Looking into the rearview mirror, he saw Amir's sad eyes seeking him.

The only thing you can do is show him you've got heart. Don't you fucking get it?

Sure.

There came a sound as if some monster were wading through an ocean, loudly, yet not without a certain mincing daintiness; he had never heard that before. A window shattered. He was going to pay Enko in dollars again.

Enko said: We caught us a sniper. A real bastard. A Serb. Now what I want you to do, and this'll prove you to Bald Man, is go in there and do the job.

You mean kill him?

I'll give you a gun. He's in a room; he can't hurt you. Go in there and take care of that Serb. You do that, you can ask Bald Man anything you want.

21

After that, of course, he couldn't exactly go to Vesna's anymore.

22

Many years later, when the journalist was fat and old, he returned to Sarajevo, in the company of his wife. Some of his younger colleagues had, as American businesspeople like to say, "adapted." The grand old editors who had taught him were long since enjoying the sweetness of forced retirement. Most journalists of his own generation had simply been "terminated." The war photographers kept lowering their prices in hopes of keeping "competitive" with the stock agencies whose images might be inferior but could be leased to production supervisors for sixty percent less. The rising cost of paper, and the increasing inclination of advertisers to buy wriggling, pulsing "windows" within digital publications, in order to better monitor the readers (I mean "content users"), left the quaint "hard copy" magazines feeble indeed. Perhaps our hero should have exerted himself for his dog food, pulling harder on a shorter, ever more capricious leash—but he was more washed up than he admitted. His eyesight had worsened, and that new forgetfulness might be getting dangerous, for instead of straightforward admissions of confusion it confidently asserted the erroneous. Well, hadn't he always been lost? After a week in the Stari Grad, he kept mistaking the way back to the hotel in those narrow streets between Ferhadija and Zelenih Beretki.— Last time, I couldn't really go out much, he explained to his wife. They were shooting from those hills up there, so I mostly had to stay indoors, or else get into a car and be driven somewhere at high speed. Whenever we left the Holiday Inn we had to—

No, we turn here, said his wife, holding his hand.

But isn't the river that way? No, you're right as usual! You know, I never got down to the Stari Grad. Or maybe I did once—

I know, his wife replied. Do you think a *česma* is a fountain?

I used to know. Didn't we just look that up?

You don't remember either? I feel ashamed of myself; I just can't make headway with this language.

Never mind, sweetheart, and he took her little paperback dictionary, in order to look up *česma* yet again.

So that was our journalist, and why he had come his fellow Americans could scarcely imagine, for where lay the lucre for him? To be sure, he sometimes wondered what had become of the people he once met at Vesna's; and perhaps he was interested in Vesna even now.

For him it was nearly an adventure. He convinced himself that a new country remained to be explored: the past.

In that season many of the young Muslim women wore matching lavender dresses and hijabs, and that was very nice, but most beautiful of all was a girl dressed all in black, with a black headscarf, brown eyes and red-painted lips; she held a red rose.

Strolling into a travel agency, he requested an interpreter. The woman put him in touch with a friend of hers, a policeman's son less friendly than polite—but hadn't they all been that way? The journalist could not recall. The policeman (now retired) had never heard of Enko, and the son knew nothing of Vesna (who, after all, must be too old for the boy), but the journalist remembered that she had lived in Novo Sarajevo; when

Enko and Amir drove him to her place they had turned onto Kolodvor-
ska and then, he thought, away from the river. The policeman's son
inquired her last name. She still lived in the same apartment.

She barely remembered him. After all, there had been so many journalists! When he mentioned Mirjana, Anesa, Ivica and Jasmina, she took
three beers out of the refrigerator, and they sat down in the living room,
yes, here where they had all listened to the shells; and there by the window, the most dangerous place, was where the poet liked to sit, his eyes
enslaved by Vesna; the American could not quite remember his face anymore, so he seemed to see instead (since he and his wife had just visited
the museum) a sad mosaic-face from Stolac gazing up out of a floral-
framed white diamond, where it had been imprisoned ever since the
third century.

He and Vesna sat smiling awkwardly at each other while the policeman's son yawned.

Enko had been killed in one of the last battles for the strategic heights
of Mojmilo. Vesna knew his son, who was sixteen.— Do you want me to
call him? she asked. I don't know if he's working. Probably he wants to
meet a foreigner who knew his father.

Well, if it's no trouble . . .

The boy's name was Denis. He was taller than his father.— Who are
you? he said.

I knew your father briefly, in '92.

We don't like to talk about those times, said Denis. What can I do
for you?

How's Amir? He was your father's friend—

Uncle Amir? He works for the customs department.

His cell phone rang. The policeman's son's cell phone was already
ringing.

Wearily, Vesna opened more beers.— You still look beautiful, the journalist told her.

Not anymore. But I don't care. I'm studying Buddhism.

You never married?

Twice. Where's your wife?

At the hotel. Cigarette smoke makes her sick.

But everyone here smokes! cried Vesna in amazement. This was the only interesting thing he had said, but it must have been quite interesting indeed; she could not imagine this wife who declined to smoke.

I know, he said. Have you kept in touch with Marko?

Which Marko?

The poet who was in love with you.

He was my second husband. Do you want his cell phone number?

Uncle Amir's on his way, said Denis. He knows lots of stories. Isn't that why you're here? That's what you journalists do, is make money from our stories.

I don't know if I'm a journalist anymore.

Then this is a fucking waste of time, said Denis.

At least your uncle will get a beer out of it, said the journalist. Vesna, does the shop across the street sell beer?

I'll come with you, she said. I need cigarettes.

Denis and the policeman's son sat gazing out the window. They were sending text messages on their cell phones.

How's Mirjana? he asked her as they entered the elevator.

She married, and they tried and tried, but never could have children. Now her health's not good. Also, her husband is a real bastard, so maybe it's better we don't phone them.

I remember that she used to tell about a Serb in her building who would cheer whenever a shell came in—

Oh, that crazy Boris? He's still there. Very elderly now.

He said: I've never forgotten sitting with you and your friends at this place, listening for the shells.

Her face seemed to tighten, although he could have imagined that. She said: And you didn't come back after '92?

No, I didn't. Once I tried, but we had an accident—

Well. Near the end of the war, the Serbs didn't have so much ammunition anymore, but they'd kept these airplane grenades. When they had no more surface-to-surface missiles, they modified the grenades. And these had a very specific sound. We called them pig grenades, because they made a grunting noise. If you were very good, you knew by the sound where it was fired and exactly where in the town it would fall. I remember when we would stop and listen to it for a minute, and then we would say: Oh, it won't fall here.

I understand, said the journalist.

One of those pig grenades fell in front of the radio-television station. It took out four floors.

The journalist was silent.

Mortar shells made a hissing sound, said Vesna, hoping to help him feel as well as understand. They were almost like bullets in that respect. You remember?

Yes—

But pig grenades, they roared when they came close. You could see the birds fly. You could always know the Serbs were bombing the town when we would see the birds fly, and just after that we would hear the grenades. I remember it. You'd think that the sky was black. Pigeons, crows, just flying into the opposite side of the city . . . Oh, well. *You* didn't see that.

No, I didn't.

I remember in the beginning of the war people went down into the basement, but it wasn't really a basement; half was aboveground; socialist skyscrapers weren't designed for shelters. After two or three months, no one went to the basement anymore. You would have had to be nuts going down eleven flights of stairs to the basement, because the attacks never stopped. But when they developed those pig grenades, we started going down again into the basement. When they took those four floors out by the radio-television building, that was the first time I was afraid.

The journalist lowered his head. He remembered the fear on her face when the shells were coming in, long before pig grenades. But who could say that his memory was any better than hers?

He bought her a pack of cigarettes. For the party, such as it was, he took a case of canned beer, the one she recommended because it was cheap.

Was Enko a particular friend of yours? she asked.

Well, I liked you better.

Of course. I'm a woman. Such likings are not important.

You were important to *me.*

Smiling, she said: I'm sorry, but I still can't remember you.

Why should you? It was only for a week or two. And is Enko's mother alive?

No. It was after that second massacre in the market, but just now I don't remember how long after. I must be getting old.

When Amir came in, the journalist would not have recognized him. Outside the shop of the beer and cigarettes there had been a newspaper kiosk, and beside that a café at the closest of whose tables sat two skinny old men whose hair had withered to grey moss on their skulls, leaning together, clutching tiny white cups of coffee in their claws, watching him and Vesna out of the corners of their eyes. He wondered what they must have seen and heard. Amir could have been their elder brother. He gazed steadily into the journalist's eyes. Then, very slowly, he smiled.

You can come over and have a coffee, said Denis, who had been watching Amir's face. My mother might talk about old times.

23

The old lady said: Sometimes they were looking like falling stars coming one after the other. They were actually yellow, like they had some fire following them. But we knew they were bullets and shells. There were four or five coming at once.

She showed him the hole in the bedroom door where a shell had come in and nearly killed Denis in his crib. On the knickknack shelf by the television sat the journalist's old binoculars.

Those are heavy binoculars over there, said the journalist.

They belonged to a Chetnik, said Denis. He and my father were fighting hand to hand. You can see who won.

They're not official JNA issue, are they?

Those Serbian bastards could get anything. They ran the army; they had the whole country sewed up.

24

The journalist had considered writing a followup article about that mixed-ethnic couple who were killed on the Vrbanja Most; he had read about it in the newspaper, probably in 1993. If he remembered correctly, she had been a Serb and he a Muslim.

Actually, that's just an urban legend, explained the policeman's son.

I remember them, of course, said the policeman's wife. Very romantic. Every year they are on the television.

Indeed, the waiter at the sidewalk restaurant where the journalist's wife liked to feed bread crumbs to the pigeons said that it must now be the anniversary of their deaths, because they had just been on television again. Their names slipped his mind, but one was definitely a Serb and the other a Croat.

The policeman's son had a friend named Edina who recollected the unfortunate couple slightly. She said: Oh, yes. The Sarajevo Romeo and Juliet. Very popular with the older generation.

The journalist gave it up and went to lie down. He had stepped off a sidewalk wrongly and injured his back, or maybe his side. His sweet wife gave him her pain pills. Closing his eyes, he encouraged her to go out. He could tell that she was restless, while he wasn't good for much.

Perhaps he should have written about Bald Man. No doubt Amir could have told him things, had he felt like asking. He had prepared himself to inquire into Enko's death, but just then Denis had said: Bald Man saved the books from the library when nobody else had balls. The Chetniks were shelling, and he took two men . . .

What happened to him?

He was shot through the heart, maybe during the war. But he lived through that. So he had a heart condition. He died after the war.

No, he didn't die of a heart attack, said Vesna. He shot himself. But he had a good time in the hospital ward with my grandmother; they used to sing songs together. When you saw him, you wouldn't believe there was something wrong with him. Mirjana's family, when they were finally evacuated they left a key with another woman, and Bald Man robbed them; he took even the boiler. So you remember him, too! How many times did you meet him? They say he was very good to his friends and very bad to his enemies.

What do you think about him?

I have nothing to think about him. He was a criminal.

Next morning the journalist and his wife took a stroll down to the Vrbanja Most. They passed the Holiday Inn, which surprised him; he said nothing, for fear of boring his wife. It was hot, and the air was grimy.— I hate this street, said the journalist's wife. Her back was also aching.

The journalist took another of his wife's pain pills. Presently his life began to be as pretty as a lemon-haired Serbian girl's face in sunlight when she leans back and drags on her cigarette.

So she was twenty-five and he was twenty-four, he said, reading the inscription. They'd be forty-three and forty-two now.

But that happened after you were here.

You're right, darling. How are you managing?

Oh, you know, she said.

So they hailed a taxi. Rolling easily through the Big Park, they passed the monument to the dead children of the war. Then they were on the double highway (directions: Tuzla, Zenica, Mostar, Mount Igman). The journalist knew that somewhere ahead lay the source-spring of the river Bosna where Tito's bunkers used to be; many Partisans had died there when the temperature was thirty-seven below zero. He remembered that from something he had read years ago, but decided to keep it from his wife in case he had mixed up his facts again. His wife was biting her lip; probably her back hurt.

He remembered the tram tracks between the two lanes of the highway, but nothing else appeared correct. Now they had arrived at the former frontline. He told the driver to stop and wait. He stepped out. His wife took his hand. For the first time ever he was able to survey the enemy positions. Here was the old age home, called "Disneyland" for its multicolored façade, whose construction had been nearly completed when the Serbs occupied it. Considerable sniper fire had originated here. Now the drug addicts used it.

We'd better not go in, he told his wife. I don't know if it's still mined.

He photographed an arched window with a black tree growing through it, the wall-tiles pitted and pocked. (He still used a film camera, of course; why should he put away what had always worked for him?) Seeing the hateful place ruined and abandoned gave him pleasure. He said nothing about that to his wife. Weeds, rose hips, young walnut trees and blackberries strained up toward the blackened concrete cells, some of whose highest honeycombs were floored with grass. There was a tunnel like a grave-shaft which passed right through the gutted edifice and into the summer greenness by the highway.

I'm getting worried about how much the taxi will cost, he admitted. So they got back in and rolled toward Centar, passing a smashed apartment building, with Mojmilo on the right. Now they drew near the tall white skyscrapers of Centar, wondering whether it would rain, for clouds already pressed over them like crumpled bedsheets.

Up there, he said, that meadow there with the new houses, I think that's where we had to run. I had my bulletproof vest on, and it was so heavy I fell down . . .

His wife took his hand.

Actually, he said, that might not have been the place.

Next morning they took a brisk walk from their hotel up into the hills. Once their backs began to ache as usual, they sat down against the ancient rock wall in the shade of the four walnut trees by the Yellow Bastion, with heavy, fragrant clusters of white elderflowers bowing the branches down below them, and then, far down through the greenness, a hoard of those other white flowers called tombstones, rising delicately and distinctly from the grass.

THE LEADER

There is no life on the earth without the dead in the earth.

Veljko Petrović, 20th cent.

1

They had been friends of a sort, perhaps more so in his parents' mind than in either of theirs. Had they never seen each other again, the insignificance of their accidental association would have been plainer, although as it turned out he rarely thought about his childhood; and when his acquaintances mentioned school reunions he produced his supposition of a smile, enduring the subject warily because his boredom resembled withered branches over a hole. He knew that others were different; sometimes he wondered whether they had made real friends when they were young, or even been happy; or whether (which would have rendered his own situation relatively enviable) they were simply in the market for false memories of joy. From what little he recalled, his high school classmates, even Ivan, had longed to get away and enter the shining world where they could dwell apart from the elders whom they were already becoming. He could barely recollect the place he had fled, so deeply had he despised it; therefore he felt unable to deduce how far, if at all, he had gone, which gratified him since it ought to be best to forget what one runs from: Amir watching silently while he interviewed fighters beneath the thudding and booming of shells along the frontline, and the morning when there were six new bullet-holes in Enko's mother's kitchen, and Enko's contempt for him (the natural feeling of the crucified for the free man who climbs on and off the cross), those he remembered better than his two or three dull school years with Ivan, who had likewise, so he'd supposed at the time, looked down on him, or at best askance; Ivan's mother's opinion of him he never learned, although the last time he met her she must have been far from pleased; as for Ivan's father, he had died long ago. The journalist (if we allow him to call himself such) could not recall the house where Ivan had lived with his mother, brother and sister, so perhaps Ivan had never invited him over; but, after all, we live so hemmed in by our memories that we scarcely realize how few they are. For instance, he could hardly bring to mind the beardless version of Ivan's face. He had invited Ivan to his home once or twice. Ivan, two years older, possessed older friends; besides, Ivan had been born in that town, while his own family had moved so many times that he could not say where he was from, which might have been the real reason he felt lonely in those days, although he naturally never considered that, and therefore believed his presence to be distasteful to others, which rendered it so. His nature was impressionable—a fine quality in youth, when one stands a chance of adapting to one's dreams; an excellent characteristic in a journalist; but a liability in those later years whose captive will manage best through stolid stupidity. Anyhow, he passed much of his childhood either by reading and dreaming alone or by watching others, wishing that they liked him. To him Ivan appeared to be laughing unfailingly, charming his true friends.— Ivan's such a nice boy, said his mother. Not knowing how to make the world admire him the way it did Ivan, he withdrew into his room.

Sometimes an accident returned them into propinquity, especially when Ivan was visiting someone else. The younger one might have been flattered when Ivan sat beside him—flattered, yes, but coolhearted; he needed no favors from Ivan. Each time, they liked each other more, but by then it was the shallower liking of grown men, for whom conviviality suffices. Men know what they think, at least; and anyone who pretends to think the same will do; some people can afford to be different, and tolerate what they fail to understand, but were that the rule, there might still be a Yugoslavia. As it happened, Ivan passed a year in Zagreb and even learned the language, which in those days was still called Serbo-Croatian. Why was he interested? Well, it turned out that he was Croatian, or Croatian-American as anxiously inclusive Americans would say; when they were boys together, Ivan's shy half-friend had never heard of Croats; Ivan was simply the older one whom he should perhaps look up to. The idea that he could ever get away from the narrow darkness which so faithfully contained him hovered beyond him; therefore he could not even envy Ivan, who lived in sunlight.

Later they were journalists together—mere freelancers, of course, being dreamers who lacked the ability to do as they were told. Despite his superiority, Ivan was a less methodical dreamer than his friend. He had grown almost fat by then, while the journalist was only plump. Kinder, not so disciplined, loving to sit up all night talking history and smoking cigarettes with any Balkan type, more fluent than ever in Croatian, Serbian, Bosnian, Slovenian, and all the other languages which used to be one, Ivan gloried rather than labored on these journeys. He had a paying job; Yugoslavia was his leave of absence. With shining eyes he spoke of Knin and Tuzla, Sanjak and Banja Luka, Vukovar, defiant Sarajevo. Very occasionally the other man still wished to be like Ivan, and sometimes he pitied him a little. When he could, he took Ivan as his interpreter.

Once between assignments when they met for dinner in their home city, the journalist happened to be lost and drunk. Ivan watched him make a rendezvous with a transient hotel's hardest passion girl, then distracted and delayed him in a bar, until he missed his hour. Ivan was protecting him! The journalist insisted on searching for the girl, who was long gone. In the hallway, two men were fighting. The journalist wanted to look for his girl all the same. With that gentle, almost feminine laugh that he had, Ivan tried to jolly him. They went around the corner for another drink. Was Ivan sorry for him? He agreed to sleep on the sofa in Ivan's messy apartment. He felt disappointed, irritated, amused and touched.

Years later, Ivan's guest seemed to have discovered peace; perhaps it was fair to state the case more definitely; since no one gets full measure of anything but death, why expect more tranquillity than this? He kept his habits, not to mention his memories, which made him prouder as he corrected them; his health wasn't bad; his wife loved him.

2

At the border there were many tour buses and a Tiško-Benz truck blowing diesel. Two policemen boarded and began to check documents, their manner less intimidating than merely formal; he worried because his wife on principle refused to pull out her passport before the last minute. DOBRO DOŠLI—WELCOME, he read within a grey rectangle. Past the lowered red signal bar at the stop signal lay a hill of bushes and trees, for all he knew still mined, although that would have been discouraging, and then those red-roofed two-storey houses with the windows shuttered—just like before, those silent houses. The beautiful blue and yellow flag with its white stars barely quivered.

The signal bar ascended; the bus entered the new country. At this moment Ivan used to get as excited as a child. On the righthand side of the road, a man stood behind his car, holding out his passport while two white-clad officials peered beneath his car, presumably for contraband or bombs.

His wife was tired. He stared at ivy on a ruined wall.

3

On the Rijecka Krupa road the Cyrillic had been blacked out by hand on the bilingual sign for Sarajevo-Mostar. He had seen that years ago, in Kosovo, where an old Serb had told him: We must live here. We have no choice!—and a pretty young Serbkina whose family had lived and died in that place for three centuries had said, smiling bitterly: I can't walk across that bridge anymore.— Had they blacked her out yet?— Evidently some good Bosnian wished to assert that Rijecka Krupa likewise was not and had never been Serbian.

There were grapes fat on their arbors, figs and pomegranates. He wife took pleasure in the apricot and peach trees. Here came the tower of a mosque.

At the next road sign the hand on the spray can of paint must have trembled, for black mist wavered over Cyrillic and Roman alike. Here came the yellow sign for Karatok; the Cyrillic had been sprayed out again. For some reason he could not pay close attention to anything but the signs. Now swelled the sign for Medjugorje; he remembered that place all too well; his wife pointed out an onion field. The sign for Kelpci remained stencilled in both languages, but at the sign for Čapljina the Cyrillic was blacked out as before. Knowing what that might again portend, he endured the clenching within his chest. On the trees by the bus station the peaches were already pinkening. They passed a troop of young soldiers brown-green in camouflage, who marched happily swinging their arms; he felt sick.

A soldier approached, with his duffel bag pressing him from shoulder to hip; he walked in small weary steps. Then the bus pulled away, past grubby white and tan apartments which had not been scorched full of holes; laundry hung over the balconies; but a moment later they passed a brick building with darkness punched through it. (This was his wife's excursion; he had not expected to feel anything.) At least in this zone the local talent left the Cyrillic on the road signs undefaced. On the high point by the river rose an old wall and a stone tower. A pair of tour buses were parked below, on the edge of a poppy meadow. His nauseating dread increased. His wife saw white potato blossoms.

The semiarid hills ahead had an evil appearance to him, simply because he remembered expecting to be shot.

At Buna they drew up to a long narrow concrete bridge or dam, which resembled the place, but was not, he realized. He had thought to recognize it right away, but of course landscapes do alter in eighteen years, particularly in war zones.

He could not recall whether they had come into the city before it happened. It seemed so, because he remembered photographing Croatian soldiers on the west side. In a steel cabinet in his office he still kept the negative strips; on his return he might take them out and place them under the loupe, although it would be preferable never to see those images again. His wife closed her eyes; she hated the heat, and the seat hurt her back.

Three women stood at the side of the road, selling cherries, and he remembered the two pretty rose vendors with whom he, Ivan and Ted had flirted in the last minutes; the girls had given them each a flower, and he could not remember what he had done with his; probably he had affixed it to his bulletproof vest. The other two roses must certainly have remained in the car. There had been a Croatian checkpoint before they met the rose vendors. Then they had entered No Man's Land.

4

Now they had arrived. His wife felt very tired. He changed money at the bus station, and then a taxi rolled them past a scorched building improved by time into a mellow ruin.

It was very humid, the roses practically wilting in their little planters. At the hotel, the waiter asked if it was their first time in this place. They ordered lunch. At the next table a young couple were holding hands. He had already quarreled with his wife, and felt bitter and furious that she could not understand him.

The muezzin's call to prayer wavered beautifully over the river. He saw two birds in the sky. The green river descended the steps of its straight stonewalled channel.

The young couple gazed stupidly into each other's eyes; they held hands; he could hardly endure it.

His wife stared down at her wineglass, while he remembered how after days of submissive waiting for Ivan's family to claim the body and ask of him whatever questions they cared to—hence the inquisition from Ivan's brother, who naturally sought to establish through circumstantial proofs the guilt of the hated survivor, followed by dinner with the well-mannered, exhausted old mother, in company, of course, with the brother, who, it was made clear, held him accountable not only for Ivan's death, but also for declining to take the blame for it—he found himself home again, some weeks after which he came to be drinking with his friend Sam, whom he admired for being a more mature person, in possession of many adventures and sufferings; and Sam, whom he had first introduced to Ivan and who had not paid for any of the drinks, now rounded on him, shook his fist, and said: Don't think I'm forgetting about Ivan; someday I'm going to *revenge* myself on you!— Since Sam was drunk, he contained himself. A month later—the next time they had met—he said: Sam, I'm going to ask you to apologize to me, which Sam readily did, at which point he forgave him. Now he unforgave him. He wished to punch Sam in the teeth. Then that too passed, and he waited for his wife to finish her wine. How he hated sitting here! But lying down in the room would be worse. Actually it was interesting here; he was glad for these people that tourists had begun to come.

High up on the far side of the river wall, the old foreigner in a silly hat was showing his old wife something. The foreigner stretched out his hand and pointed, as if he had been to the place he indicated, or somehow had something to do with it.

His wife ordered another glass of wine, probably out of loneliness, while he remembered how en route to the place where he would await Ivan's mother and brother, he had returned to Zagreb, because he and

Ivan had left their extra suitcases in Zrinko's apartment, and Zrinko said: Tell me one thing. The radio said that you were in another car, and Ivan was following you. Is that true?

No. We were in the same car. Ivan was in the front seat, and Ted was driving—

He had never been able to fight for himself. His childhood had taught him to bear with the threats and aggressions of others, and this fatalistic patience, which many mistook for compliance, had served him equally well in his profession. He raised his hands to be searched by secret police of any stripe; the insults of uniformed killers he answered with mildness; even when someone touched a bayonet to his throat he held no grudge, because what good would that have done? The killers were what they were precisely because they overreacted. Whatever he did feel announced itself within him afterward, if at all. So Zrinko's questions did not anger him then. For one thing, Zrinko was his friend; they had met through Ivan; Zrinko evidently needed to be told the sequence of events, in order, as Americans would say, to "bring closure" to his grief; hence it was the survivor's duty to comply and explain, all the more so since he was fond of Zrinko.

You swear that you were in the same car?

I swear, he listlessly replied; his trousers were still clotted with Ivan's blood.

All right. If you had been ahead in another car, leading Ivan to his death, I would have killed you.

Zrinko drove him to the bus station. When he thanked him, Zrinko said: I'm not doing it for you. I'm doing it for Ivan.

He never saw Zrinko again.

His wife signed the bill. He longed for her to say something loving, take him by the hand, "help" him; he knew quite well that there was no help in such matters. Just then he could hardly endure his grief and bitterness. Had he voiced it, perhaps she might have embraced him, as he clearly comprehended, but he lacked the power to take charge of himself. Anyway, if he waited, the feeling would depart. He blamed her for nothing. Wasn't he a grown man? They rose and crossed the Stari Most, which had been beautifully reconstructed, evidently with United Nations funds. How had the joke run? When that Serbian commander destroyed this bridge, he consoled his staff that in due course, Serbs would remake it: wider, more beautiful and even older than before! It rose in an inverted V over the green river. Tenderly he helped his wife up the slanting stairs; her joints were weak. There came thunder, rain, the lovely green smell. To him the grass upreaching, the swallows and the rain on the roses all seemed new, but not the narrow evergreens rising up the steep arid mountain; that horizon was hideously familiar.

A Spanish woman with a seashell belt and a leather purse like a uterus touched the bright brass writing-pens made out of shell casings. The vendor offered her another and another. She gazed at each one with doe eyes.

5

On a streetwall it still said USTAŠE DUBROVNIK,* and on another, ULTRAS 1994. He could not remember which brand of cigarettes Ivan had most frequently smoked. Middle-aged women in checkered hijabs were photographing one another on the Stari Most.

These white butterflies flickering everywhere like ashes in an updraft, he lacked all recollection of them although it had been this time of year, that same sweaty light, with those arid yet forested mountains across the river. There were more roadside fruit stands than before, new shopping centers and gas stations, but plenty of the same old smashed houses. On the trees the figs hung green over the river. It seemed peculiar how much he had forgotten, especially after Ivan's brother had hounded him so closely over what might as well have been every turn in the road, from the very starting-point where that United Nations pilot, smiling faintly, reached into his camouflage-flavored breast pocket, pulled out a manual the size of a combat Bible, and edified them with a diagram of some creepy wilderness of fortifications, remarking: That's what those Serbian checkpoints look like. I prefer to fly myself.— He *could* fly, while they were only journalists. After waiting two days, the three of them made the decision

---

* The Ustashe were Croatian Nazis who committed many atrocities against Muslims and Serbs during World War II. Accordingly, Serbian ultranationalists during the Yugoslavian Civil War a half-century later referred to Croats as Ustashe. This hateful appellation was mostly slanderous, but not entirely, for some Croatian irregulars from the Dalmatian coast (Dubrovnik) and elsewhere did gleefully style themselves after the Fascist model.

together.— So you admit that you convinced my brother to take that road, said Ivan's brother, smiling with triumphant hate.

6

Supposing that his duty must lie in submission to the brother's cold hatred, ready to answer any questions if it would bring the man peace—in fact it appeared to inflame him—he complied, told and clarified. When the brother first began to interrogate him (he had awaited his coming for many days), he endured it calmly, even after it became apparent that rather than being, as he had foolishly imagined, "helpful," he was simply *accused*; but when the brother demanded that he tell and retell each detail of Ivan's death, which on his own account he absolutely could not bear to think about, he shivered for an instant. No doubt this bore out the brother's already completed judgment.

As for the sister, whose questioning took place over the telephone, and was therefore indefinitely protracted, she instructed him to call her again tomorrow at one-o'-clock. Every time he called her, it cost him a hundred dollars. He was trying to do right by that family; that was what he would have wished for in their situation, to have his questions answered.

Explain to me again just why you took that turn, she said.

So he did. He had explained it to her four times.

And you were sitting in the back seat? Why weren't you up front with my brother?

Ted was the driver.

You say my brother was your interpreter. So why didn't you take the rest off his shoulders?

Ivan asked the Spanish battalion for directions. He asked again at the Croatian checkpoint. In each case, he was satisfied as far as I could tell—

But you didn't help him verify these directions?

As you know, I don't speak the language. He didn't ask for help. He just said, okay, we turn right just after the final checkpoint—

Then how do you account for what happened?

Ivan directed us to take a wrong turn.

A wrong turn. And all this time you were sitting in the back seat, doing nothing.

That's right.

My brother was working for you. He trusted you. I don't know anything about the man who was driving, but I do find it significant that you had them doing all the work while you sat in the back seat.

Put it any way you care to.

And now you'll cash in. You'll have your dramatic story.

Sure. I'm cashing in every time I call you.

Just what do you mean? Tell me exactly what you mean by that remark.

I mean that I'm trying to answer your questions as patiently as I can. By the way, Ivan was working *with* me, not *for* me.

You hired him as your interpreter.

I got the magazine to agree to pay him a fee, yes.

You persuaded him to go.

I invited him to go. He liked it over here.

You lured him to his death.

You know what, Jeanette?

You killed my brother. You're just as responsible as the men who shot him. I want you to admit it.

I don't see it that way.

So you're a coward as well as a—

Jeanette, go to hell.

He hung up the phone.

Sweet trees were growing up through roofless stone ruins. His wife smiled at him wearily.

7

Now that he had come back to where it happened, he could not stop remembering Ivan's sister, to whom he must have been a leader of unearthly power, since he could lure a man to his death for unstated reasons, conveying him, and Ted also, right into a sniper's nest, like a prostitute who inveigles drunks into some lonely ambush of robbers, then flits away unharmed. The sister had definitely been the most plainspoken of all his judges. But the rest unanimously implied what she had asserted: he was more than he supposed himself to be. In the market, the old man selling cherries kissed a tomato and gave it to his wife. A man was selling pens made of shell casings; was he familiar? A man sat playing the accordion. And the American or survivor or whatever he was said to himself: If only I'd truly had such power! Well, I did, to my accusers at least. For once in my life I got to be a leader.

His ex-girlfriend Victoria, who had gone to school with him and Ivan, was the only one who ever wrote to say that she was sorry. She was dead now. Remembering this, he felt his love for her return, as a dull lost yearning.

His anger at Ivan's brother and sister fluttered like those white butterflies over the elderberries. He forgave Sam again, then hated him. If he ever happened upon Sam again it would be perfectly all right between them. As for Zrinko, he had become one more denizen of a bygone foreign land, so that his hateful and threatening behavior need not be taken personally.

He could not remember the first time he had seen Ivan or even what they had meant to each other when they were boys.

Perhaps if he had made up his mind to take some attitude, not about Ivan's family, or the consequences to himself, but about that double death itself, which belonged not to him but only to Ivan and the other man, he might have been better to himself and others, but precisely which thought or feeling would have accomplished this? Or what if he had simply set out to remember Ivan from time to time? Well, he would not. He disbelieved that he had meant that much to Ivan, or even that Ivan had respected him; Ivan had been too far above him. And so it could have been said that he rejected peace, which is scarcely more or less than sleep.

Without his glasses Ivan had looked much younger; this was surprising. But perhaps the leader had never seen him in life, in which case it would have only been the dead Ivan that he knew. Ivan was smiling in all his press cards. When he smiled, the corners of his mouth did not turn up. In this respect his signature was the same, for it hurried across the empty space, narrow and flat. He was not handsome but his face was kind. There had never been wariness in him. The official stamps on the press cards remained unfaded. In these photographs Ivan had stopped being a man and become a boy, gentle and careless, much younger than the one who had survived him.

In the morning he woke up happy that they were leaving the place. The day was still cool. His wife's knees hurt; he kissed her. At breakfast he ordered a coffee, and the woman smiled at him. He smiled back. His wife returned to the room to organize her suitcase. She was looking very tired. It seemed to him that he could not bear to outlive her. The woman brought his coffee. She was very pretty, and had sweet friendly eyes. He tried to speak a little of her language as he once used to do, and she laughingly encouraged him. Traces of words rose up on his tongue.

The coffee was Turkish, of course: bittersweet, blacker than dirt, thicker than paste. He felt joyful to taste it. Hoping to take his wife back to the market if there were time, and perhaps to buy her some plums, he drank it quickly. Again the woman was smiling at him. He wondered whom she loved. Now she was in the kitchen; he heard her singing. A little sorry to go away, he left a fine tip and went out quietly, not wishing to trouble her with anything. At once he forgot her face. He was worrying about his wife, so at first he did not hear the rapid footsteps behind him on the street. How could those have anything to do with him? But the young woman, out of breath now, had come running after him, just to say goodbye.

II

THE TREASURE OF JOVO CIRTOVICH

I could have been unvanquished, if death had not been victorious.

Epitaph for Lord Šimon Keglević of Bužin, died 17 December 1579

1

When Jovo Cirtović sailed to Trieste in 1718, the place must have whispered to him, for he stayed on to become a merchant of Friulian wines, which his ships carried with magical success. Before the native-born citizenry could open both eyes, he owned a veritable fleet, supplying ports as far away as Philadelphia. Why the grapes of Friuli bleed so delicious a juice remains nearly as mysterious to my mind as Cirtović's triumphal accession to the trade, although just yesterday, in that breezy hour when bronzes begin to surpass the darkness of pigeons, three of my fellow drinkers persuaded me that what accomplishes vinocultural excellence is *soil*, while two others led me to comprehend that the most ineffable qualities of the Bacchic Tetragrammaton derive from *atmosphere*, as has been proved down at Cinque Terra, where one famous salt-fogged vineyard, unremittingly guarded against the sea, produces a crop of great price. The waiter proposed to bring us a bottle of that stuff, but we disregarded him, for he was no Triestino; had we indulged his advice, he might even have poured something foreign down our throats. Meanwhile my helpful friends had educated me concerning the absolute excellence of Friulian vintages, which indeed occupy so commanding a position that should the Devil in his malice uproot every other grapevine on earth, nobody would be worse off, excepting only a few charlatans in Bordeaux or Tuscany. Here they paused to ascertain that my intellect had in truth kept pace with their instruction, for they were warmheartedly solicitous academicians, whose very breaths were purple. Yes, I said. Accordingly, all that remained was my indoctrination in the seventh syllogism of the thirty-first demonstration. This required their coming to blows, so I thanked them one and all, uplifting my glass, forsaking them for a breeze, the sea, a stone wall, potted palms. Then I poured a libation over Cirtović's cenotaph. He was a good father.

Now, what about soil versus atmosphere? I know I am getting out of my depth here, since wine disagrees with me (I'm drinking smoky Dubrovnik *loža* as I write this), but I do seek your tolerance of my efforts, being myself a merchant of sorts, retailing paragraphs by the sailmaker's yard. How shall I say why Cirtović could sell every last barrel that creaked and sloshed on his shipbelly voyages? In the Caffè San Marco my friends are still arguing about it; their tongues have gotten winestained and their eyelids resemble those reflections of blinds which droop in the arched windows of lingerie shops. Not even they can explain wine. In the Piedmont, waiters dispraise Friulian reds; in Spaleto and Zara (which our hero preferred to call Split and Zadar), fat old nobles swear upon Mary Magdalene's reliquary that Friulian whites are absolutely no good. Cirtović never committed himself to any theory about grapes; nor could I imagine how such abstrusities would have impressed the hardheaded merchants of Philadelphia. Was his secret simply *price,* which must have been low enough to satisfy frugality and high enough to massage pretension? Or did the Tories of that epoch feel a yearning for far-off salty places, which they indulged only by the glass? Up until then, many an innkeeper in those Colonies had been wont to regale his guests on fly-infused vinegar, reminding them that such had done well enough for Christ on the cross. Then came sea-barrels of wine from Friuli. For a quarter-hour the thirsty Yankees knew how to be happy. In vain the skinflints who sold foul stuff invoked cabals and vigilance committees against Cirtović—wasn't he a tool of the Papists? Examining the barque *Kosovo* as a precaution against contraband, a certain customs officer, invited for a glass of wine in the captain's cabin, spied above the bed an icon of the Madre della Passione, or *Strastnja*: mostly silver, it was, but the metal drew sharp-edgedly away from around those two golden faces; Marija fitted the young mother's part, while Jesus could have been a watchful little Roman Emperor. Ah, that draught, how magically purple it was! Cirtović began smiling; he seemed an excellent fellow. Rising, the customs man demanded to know whether his mariners obeyed the Pope.— Not us! laughed the captain. If you like, I'll attest an oath to that effect.— Then what are you?— Orthodox, sir. And I am quite sure our

Patriarch has no designs on these Colonies.— The cautious customs man held fast to the proverb *Take counsel in wine, but resolve afterwards in water;* after another glass of the Friulian vintage he forgot the second half. And so the cargo got landed; heaven came to earth. Safely alone, Cirtović raised a glass to his true hero, Prince Lazar.

In Genoa, agents of the Vatican received delivery of another twelve hundred barrels of Cirtović's wine. Now the Austrians and the Swedes got a taste for it; and I have even read that odd lots of it ended up at the Russian Court. Catherine the Great bathed in the stuff, after which her various lovers drank it. In Tartaria it corrupted a certain Khan who finally sold Cirtović what was supposed never to leave the family: an Arabic manuscript on the subjugation of monsters. A Coptic priest in Ethiopia accepted a cask of red in exchange for an illuminated treatise on the geography of heaven. For Cirtović was, you see, a collector.

In his younger days he was frequently to be seen upon the docks and quays, opening wooden chests, drawing men into taverns, pressing coins into callused hands, while the Triestini wondered what was happening. He was built like a porter; his beard was salt-stained; he smiled easily, and all his doings seemed to be accomplished slowly, in the light. Around his neck hung some medallion or amulet concealed in a leathern bag, so that he resembled all the more some credulous peasant. Stolid even in the *bora* wind, gentle of speech, almost humble, unremarkable, such was Jovo Cirtović. Yet again and again he sewed up the market, with greater celerity than a young bride preparing her rich old husband's shroud. And it wasn't merely wines he dealt in; it got said that even rotten onions he could unload at a profit! He leased a warehouse right on the Canal Grande, just in time for the Canal Grande to become the harbor's liveliest tentacle. Against him it was also remembered that he had established himself in the city only one year before the Emperor elevated it to a free port. Laughing, Cirtović offered wine at the communal celebration, but they noticed that he laughed only with his mouth. He could write Cyrillic and Glagolitic with equal facility—a nearly unmatched ability hereabouts. His fellow Serbs called him as wise as Saint Sava, not that they knew his mind. He was a man of his word, as everyone admitted, and generous on the rare occasions that he entertained. Moreover, he seemed adept with nearly any make of dromoscope. In taverns they computed his worth at half a million florins (an exaggeration); but most definitely he now dominated the Hungarian trade, which had enriched many daring men; and he vended the best Bohemian glass; in consideration of how much Count Giovanni Vojnovich had paid for a carafe and two dozen wineglasses, his rivals saw fit to multiply and magnify the treasure of Jovo Cirtović, with as much gusto as if it belonged to them. For six years the Ragusan consulate knew him well. Then he also began dealing with Saracens. You must remember that ever since the Sultan had reconquered Morea from the Venetians, the latter operated more assertively in Ragusan waters, hoping to make up the loss; and when they appealed for amelioration of their taxes and duties, so that they could at least make a living as their fathers had—surely the Sultan could understand; even Turks had fathers!—he equivocated, all the while impelling his Sarajevans to invest new ports at Bar, Ulcinij, Novi and Budva. It can be perilous to trade with people who hate one another. But the prudent skipper who alters his flag from port to port reduces his risk, oh, yes, and increases his profit. What bribes or taxes Cirtović had to pay is unrecorded; the main thing is that he never returned home without his head. That man had luck! Neither earthquakes nor French troops harmed his stock; English pirates lost him in a fog; his helmsmen never went off course; his glassware declined to break before he sold it; even pestilence, which visited Trieste nearly as often as sin, robbed away only his most inessential employees. While others had to wait on a fair breeze, somehow Jovo Cirtović always knew when to raise sail. It might be dead calm in the harbor; no matter. Cirtović embarked his men. When the ship was laden, he'd cry out: Hold onto the wind with your teeth!— Just about then, the wind would come. Did God truly love him so much? After his third voyage to Africa, every sailor on the *Beograd*, right down to the cabin boy, received as a bonus one of those jewels that glow red like a sea monster's eye when it surfaces at dusk. The wise ones used them to get wives and sloops; some left Cirtović's employ, with good feelings all around; the rest squandered them on whores, and once they had flooded the jewelry-shops of Trieste, a certain haughty ruby-dealer hanged himself, following which the Cincars swooped in to buy cheap and sell far away. After that, most ambitious young mariners hoped to sail for Jovo Cirtović.

Around that time certain rich men of the city began to build houses up on the hill, where they could guard their families from future epidemics; Cirtović listened, saying nothing; soon two drunken notaries sang about a lot he had purchased in that district. Even the other Serbs were shocked, for they all lived quite satisfactorily in their warehouses. This Cirtović, lacked he any regard for rules? They had already agreed that he was no son of his late father, who had made it his business to be a dread to Turks at night.— In order to raise up an appropriate edifice for himself, Jovo Cirtović now commenced to trade still more widely. It was all he could do not to smile at the naïve customs men of Philadelphia, who worried that he might know his way around the Vatican when he had long been at home in uncannier realms—not least the Bosphorus itself, which in those days was unfailingly studded with sailing ships most of which flew the Sultan's colors, and some of which flew no flag at all. Wending his trade betwixt the curving deltas and the peninsulas crowned with mosques walled like forts and bristling with crescent-topped steeples, he cast before him the lure of a courtesy which pretended not to be wary, and treasured within his vest a safe-conduct bearing the Sultan's seal and illuminated in gold by seven calligraphers. Had the Philadelphians chanced upon *that*, they would have had no idea what it was.

He was married by then, but nobody could say who had been invited to his wedding, for it took place back in Serbia, during his seventh absence from Trieste; he had chosen his bride by correspondence with his brothers, making use of a certain Cincar wax trader who would later become his undeclared supercargo on an African voyage. According to dockside idlers, Count Vojnovich was offended by some aspect of these proceedings, perhaps because he wanted the lady for himself. She arrived well veiled, accompanied by a mound of crates and trunks; it was dusk when Cirtović, having briefly confabulated with his factor, Captain Vasojević, led her down the gangplank and into a closed carriage. She was slender and she walked with rapid little steps. Another veiled woman who must have been her maidservant came just behind. In good Serbian fashion, both wore daggers at their sides. I'd guess they were thinking on the pear trees, kinsfolk and rapid streams they would never see again. Perhaps they'd been seasick. Spitting, Petar whipped up the horses. The next morning Cirtović gave six hundred florins to the church, which at that time had stood for barely a year; it still served both Greeks and Serbs.

Then he went straight to the dock and put his topmen to cutching some sails for the *Kosovo*. The Triestini, who certainly kept secrets of their own, watched all this with narrowed eyes, jutting out their beards as they asked one another what seraglio those females hailed from, and which other ports the *Lazar* might have touched on in the course of her wedding voyage; for the Adriatic coast, particularly on the Dalmatian side, is so addicted to doublings that a stranger can hardly tell whether the blue-green land-wave he spies below the sky's belly is an island or the continuation of the continent. In short, this part of the world is a smuggler's paradise. Whether or not our good Cirtović ever accepted the discreeter commissions of contraband trade remains, in token of his success, unrecorded, but year after year his fleet plied up and down the labyrinthine coast, counting off stone beacons, hill-castles and their ruins, making quiet landfalls behind walls of birch-beech leaves. Returning quietly into the great blue bay with the whiteness of Trieste before him, he stood beside the steersman, gazing ahead in that guarded way he had, as if there were clouds between all others and himself—he who could see through all clouds. Yes, he who derives from the shadow passes more freely in and out of sunlight than he who was born in brightness. So the Triestini, tanned by the shimmer of their near-African sea, asserted, in order to excuse themselves for not venturing to Serbia, whose roads are paved with bleeding gravestones. For that matter, they did not even peer into the Orthodox church. In the market, housewives bowed their heads together to gossip about the new couple, in between the more interesting task of considering eggplants, while their husbands disputed as to whether or not Jovo Cirtović possessed the evil eye. The way some described him, he wore the masklike face of a vampire squid, when in fact even the wariest customs guards saw nothing in him but well-heeled blandness, and his sailors loved him as they would have anyone who brought them home alive and paid good money. To be sure, he seemed care-ridden now; certain Triestini (who of course loved their native city so much as to frown upon even the neighboring port of Muggia) proposed that if he merely renounced Serbia entirely, forgetting those half-real denizens of an unlucky place, he'd grow as happy as the rest of us—although it could have been (as a certain unsuccessful butcher proposed) that debt had snared him. After all, how much capital must it take to send out so many ships? The Triestini would have loved to know. Unfortunately, the interloper's brothers, recently arrived, proved almost equally closemouthed, although Cristoforo Cirtović did say: Jovo's always been a mystery to us. He takes after our late father, may he sit in the presence of the saints.— Bribing the watchman, a certain Captain Morelli snooped through the logbook of the *Sava* and was astonished to discover some proof or demonstration relating to the section of a right-angled cone; what it meant was conjectural, since the writing was Glagolitic. Copying it out, he sprang it on Cristoforo Cirtović, who said: What's this gibberish?— This Morelli next waylaid Stefano Cirtović on the docks when that latter was unloading a cargo from Korea; Stefano said: Don't ask me my brother's business.

Sometimes the Cirtović men (there were six of them in addition to Jovo) would take over the "Heaven's Key" tavern behind the Ponterosso, get drunk and sing loud songs about the various methods in which they would like to kill Turks. Jovo never joined them there, although he met them frequently enough at his countinghouse, not to mention at church, together with their Serbian wives and children, beneath that gilded ceiling as round as the hyponome of a chambered nautilus. His own signora continued to wear a veil. No one even knew what to call her until a carpenter as longnosed and comical as Pulcinella announced that her name was Marija; Pulcinella's sister's cousin was a dressmaker who had measured this Marija, so it must be true. The Triestini were thrilled by his stupendous news. Just before Assumption Day another vendor of ancient Greek vases visited the Cirtović residence, departing well satisfied. Captain Morelli treated him at the "Heaven's Key." You wouldn't believe how much wine he could deduct from a bottle! Nor was the experiment profitable; for although he was looser-lipped than any fisherman's whore, for that very reason he had never gotten beyond the foyer, where Nicola, the master's eldest son (an unsatisfied youth, he opined), had received him beneath a grand portrait of Prince Lazar, offered him Turkish coffee (served by a veiled woman, evidently Marija Cirtović's maid), summoned the strapping coachman to carry away the crates, then sat with him in almost unfriendly silence until Petar had returned with all the best pieces extracted, the compensation consisting of twelfth-century gold coins from Hungary, tiny as buttons, already counted out, the prices discounted not unfairly (as the vendor himself admitted), but certainly without appeal. He thought he heard the signora upbraiding someone in the kitchen. (You know how all those Serbkinas are, he told his delighted listener.) Presently Cirtović himself had appeared, to inquire after shards with writing on them. He sought a certain diagram by Pythagoras, and would pay more if the circles touched externally. The vendor nodded conscientiously, hoping to deceive him with future trash. Perhaps Captain Morelli knew some Greek who might collaborate in painting ochered circles? By the way, the vendor had ascertained that Cirtović's granary held wheat right up to the roof!—more proof of their enemy's grandiosity, as all agreed over Friulian wine; by then there were a dozen Triestini present, all hoping to make a fool of Jovo Cirtović. Sad to say, Captain Morelli was knifed in the guts a few nights later, and the vendor fled the city, either because he had done it or because he feared to be next. When asked what he thought about the murder, Cirtović said it was a shame that so jovial a man had been lost. The Triestini lowered their eyes. For their next device, they hired a pretty harlot to approach their victim at his countinghouse; but he turned her over to his brother Florio, while his factor Captain Vasojević (another closemouthed man) watched half-smiling from the second storey. She blabbed about Florio's habits, to be sure, but what the hell did they care about that adulterer?

Jovo Cirtović never failed to give hospitality to a certain itinerant snowy-bearded bard with a well-tuned guzla. At the "Heaven's Key" the Triestini queried the old man as to the situations of rooms in the house, and where the coins were kept, and other such matters as good neighbors like to know about each other. Whenever the Cirtovićes invited him to sing about the Battle of Kosovo, he got to observe the wife and daughters sewing around the hearth, beneath the smoking hams; and Cirtović would be singing right along with him, haltingly accompanied by his sons. The imported servingmaid's name, he said, was Srdjana—a tonguetwister, laughed the Triestini. They kept some hope of waylaying her, but she rarely came out of the house. Fortunately, some sailors do talk, especially over Friulian wine. Cirtović's mariners admitted freely that the Turkish bangles now shining on the wrists of their sweethearts came from Bar (their hosts, who promptly sought to trade there, fell mysteriously afoul of the Ragusan authorities), that their master's brothers occasionally carried weapons and armaments into Serbia, and that Cirtović owned better luck than any man they had heard of. As they already knew, he was a pious sort, who never failed to thank his saints. (By the way, Captain Vasojević still refused to open his mouth.) One night the helmsman of the *Lazar* came by the "Heaven's Key"; after his seventh glass of Friulian red he refuted Archimedes's suppositions that a poppyseed-sized quantity of sand contains no more than ten thousand grains, and that the maximum possible diameter of the universe equals ten thousand times that of the earth, in which case the Sphere of Fixed Stars would be two hundred and fifty thousand stadia from Trieste, straight up—a decade's journey, perhaps, depending on solar storms. After the twelfth glass, the helmsman grew confiding, and informed them with a childlike smile that granted fair lunar winds and adherence to certain timetables, the voyage could be made within half a year. Laughing, the purser (now into his seventeenth glass) put in that even if the excess of death can be added to itself, which he doubted, and indeed Cirtović upheld him in his skepticism, then, with the aid of the Mother of God, something could presently be accomplished to the betterment of the Christian world. Then he fell asleep, but in the helmsman's eyes shone an ideal like dawn light beyond the trees. The Triestini drunks agreed that these sailors knew more geography than anyone else; even the cook of the *Lazar,* who was formerly one of their own even though his uncle had apprenticed him out at Muggia, began after his sixth glass to discourse on matters beyond his station; he asked whether they had ever heard celestial music; and then, when they gaped at him, traced out with his fat forefinger the planetary orbits as drawn in the manuscript of Gjin Gazulli. Of course cooks, having food always within reach, find more time to think than other people; hence his remarks proved nothing, especially given the magical powers of the Friulian vintage—which meanwhile transformed itself ever more into gold and silver, until Jovo Cirtović had risen out of envy's sight. Sitting at his high wooden desk, which resembled the altar to which a judge ascends in order to sacrifice still another poor man to justice, he concealed himself behind a wall of ledgers. Occasionally the clerks overheard the thump of one of his roundhandled stamps. He sealed his documents himself, and kept the seal in his pocket.

Above Trieste's harbor, fig-jungles sometimes shade the walls which

guide informed persons to arched tunnel-streets where this or that mansion broods; and from that one such reclusive edifice in which Cirtović
ensconced his wife, a good Orthodox woman who never went out, there
sprang pairs and trios of lovely girls who could very occasionally be
glimpsed strolling rapidly (never unchaperoned) through September's
falling leaves. They wore more transparent veils than their mother, but
traditional daggers rode at their hips. And there were the sons, Nicola,
Vuk and Veljko; they could readily be met with in the harbor, and gave off
no such uncanny an impression as their father, who had been overheard
saying: Only knowledge will save you, boys!—They too had learned
Glagolitic, it appeared, although what good that did them could not be
fathomed, since no one managed to get them drunk. Between them and
their uncles lay a shallow cordiality, with countercurrents. It might be
that the sons anticipated some struggle as to who would control the business after their father. Stefano and Cristoforo Cirtović sometimes carried them to Odessa or Marseilles, teaching them how to run with
quartering winds, when to luff a ship and how to flog men for duty ill
done, but perhaps their father had spoiled them, for around the port
went the word that they were dependent although manly enough, unen-
terprising if admittedly unretiring. As for their sisters, Gordana, the
plainest, for reasons which might have had to do with wine-barrels, wedded a cooper and presently removed with him up into the karst country;
but the next few were sent back to Serbia to marry, departing in closed
ships. Given the downtrodden state of his home country, which he himself had abandoned, Cirtović, onlookers supposed, should have imposed
upon his children kinder destinies. Once again, a sailor or two did talk;
certain uncles were the brides' conductors and wedding-guests, and they
returned with stories; that was how the Triestini learned what in any case
they expected: that each bride, decently (and opulently) veiled, of course,
was met by a lot of powerfully proportioned, bearded, piratical-looking
Serbs. At least the young ladies would be well defended! The Triestino
dandies who stood outside San Giusto Cathedral, flourishing their spy-
glasses to inspect the girls who promenaded below, would scarcely have
scraped up the luck to see the Cirtović females in any event—for one
thing, the Orthodox church held masses at other times—but why should
that prevent young men from uplifting their foreheads in resentment

at the loss of so much nubility? At the Communions of each other's children, Cirtović's oldest captains (most of whom were Roman Catholic) sat at table in their best white shirts, with their spectacles slipping down their noses and their faces red with Friulian wine while between forkfuls of fried squid—the one dish, by the way, which the aforesaid Cirtović disdained—they argued about their master's deeds and habits, but until the Serbia-bound damsels had all been spoken for, no one outside the family, save only Captain Vasojević, even knew how many girl-children Jovo Cirtović possessed. (The reason was that his daughters were his jewels.) Creeping over the wall on Saint Lazzaro's Eve* (having tranquilized the watchdogs with balls of fish-guts soaked in Friulian wine), our late Captain Morelli's brother Luca, together with three other zealous defenders of Italian privilege, saw Cirtović taking out his scales, the daughters embroidering their wedding-stuffs by the lattice window, and the signora standing in her long gold-embroidered dress of white linen and the tight-cinched tarnished belt and square-topped headdress. Then they heard the carriage; an uncle and all three brothers were arriving with Petar. So they fled, resuming the safer if less fruitful practice of importuning Captain Vasojević over Friulian wine.— In heaven's name, leave his business to him! said that loyal individual. All they wanted was a story, any story, they pleaded. Weren't they all friends? Well, then, said Vasojević, and he prayed to the Mother of God that this would gratify their lust for entertainment, he remembered waiting upon his master one evening in Ragusa, some years ago, when Cirtović still voyaged in person, Ragusa profitable, and Vasojević himself no more than a promising subaltern. Behind the black-gratinged windows of a marble house, orange light suddenly shone out, as if a cat had opened his eyes. Then Cirtović emerged smiling. Vasojević was to return immediately to the *Lazar,* there to take delivery of seven fancy inlaid trunks, which arrived within the hour. Obeying his instructions, he inspected these items for damages. They were dowry chests. He paid the carter, and added a tip from his own pocket. Another toast to Prince Lazar! In due course they were all unloaded in Trieste, and by nightfall Petar had conveyed them up the hill. That was all Vasojević would say, and of course there might

* 27 June.

now be more or fewer daughters—in 1726, that voyage must have been, although it could have been 1727; either way, it was before the Sultan got dragged down from the sky. Now there was a new Sultan, and Vasojević and Cirtović both kept getting richer. How did they do it? A certain Captain Robert (whom the master promptly discharged for speaking out of turn) got drunk, and so, leaning in around him over those tiny blue-covered tables at the "Heaven's Key," the Triestini got to hear about the time that the Ragusans sought to punish Cirtović for unlicensed trade, and he looked, not into each face but away from each, as if something warned him, until by infallible default he lighted on the most corruptible man. This gave rise to much discussion first of satanic powers, and secondly of hellfire, which these drinkers certainly carried within their own hearts. About their enemy, as usual, nothing was concluded, and meanwhile one of his agents rented a stable, filled it with Arabian horses offloaded from the *Sava*, and sold them all, very dear, to dukes, mercenaries and ruiners of servingmaids.

The Triestini were aware that in certain walled cities of the Istrian archipelago there dwelled persons so wealthy that their stonemasons might inscribe the following in their names: *Receive, Our Father, this little church as a present.* Captain Vasojević was now believed to secrete a hoard of silver somewhere in his house, although the night-burglars who investigated this supposition found nothing but death. Captain Robert and Luca Morelli (who never made captain) had to pay off three new widows. In fine, the other merchants' attempts to find out, emulate or ruin these Serbs remained as crude as the shield and letters on a fifteenth-century gold coin of King Sigismund. Cirtović knew how to hide whatever mattered.

He certainly kept his daughters sequestered, all right—not that other men didn't do the same in every petty kingdom of Italy. A few of the dandies still hoped vainly. One remained single all his life on a girl's account. His name was Alberto. A night came when he wavered, for his best friends Fabio and Marco invited him to hear the singer Emanuela, by whom many ladies were annoyed because she demanded silence, silence, which is not necessarily a condition appropriate to people who are sipping wine together. She wore a long tight crimson robe whose gold buttons marched all the way down. The way she could enclose her fingers around certain words of her songs was something no one had ever witnessed before. She was said to be forty-seven but looked older. When she sang, three little beggar-girls who lived in the street began dancing and fanning themselves with branches; and the sky over Trieste became a domed ceiling with a golden snowflake-sun in the center, connected to many crowned Graces who balanced all longings and judgments upon their pretty heads. Most of the men watched this Emanuela submissively, and when each song ended there were those who wiped their eyes. Alberto was nearly enchanted. The women (who they were you can work out for yourself) shrugged at the floor, wiggling their fingers or whispering to the men who sat beside them. If the whispers got loud, Emanuela would stare at them with her sunken, glittering eyes. Alberto, I repeat, remained almost enchanted, but failed to expel his desire for Cirtović's daughters, and particularly for the youngest, whose name he had once overheard, and indeed, possibly misheard, as Tanya. In his hot sad life her image was as shade-rich as a grape arbor. Even as an old man, walking slowly with his hands behind his back, he annoyed others with his praises of a certain Tanyotchka, whom nobody else remembered, although in fact she still lived, and promenaded every day between church and hill, dressed in black. When he closed his eyes, Alberto, who did not recognize her, seemed to see the hollows of her white back, and rain was running down her shoulders. Opening his eyes, he sought out whitenesses in the sky to match her, but these proved all too grey or too blue. Just as a woman's heel rises away from her sandal when she takes a step, showing for an instant a bit of sole whose pallor proves its kinship to white tubers and other such things which ordinarily live concealed, so this old man's otherwise sun-tanned fantasies and illusions rebelliously bedecked themselves with the onion-jewels of the unknown. Thus he fell out of time, like a certain skull which anyone who can obey the obscure visiting hours is welcome to see in the Antiquarium; this skull is crumpled like a deflated gas mask from the First World War, the latter's metal-rimmed goggles gaping, the former's eye-sockets decorated with mineral stains. Who are you, skull? Whom did you love? Tanyotchka, Tanyotchka. Perhaps it was to placate people of his sort that Tanyotchka's father Italianized his surname to Cirtovich. Although Captain Vasojević declined to adopt that fashion, most Triestine Serbs accommodated themselves sooner or later. For example, I remember once unearthing a barely yellowed albumen print of Darinka Kvekich, dated circa 1860; she was bellshaped in her immense skirt with ribs of pale embroidery; her exotic femininity was walled like a sailing ship. A Genovese notary who occasionally came to call was astonished at how rarely she appeared, although her tactful servingwoman explained: Every day she takes care of her very ill sister and of her other sister who is a little less ill.— But then where *are* these sisters?— The servingwoman smiled sadly.— Sweet Darinka, said the notary, I need to know how much you love me.— Indefinitely, she replied.

Who any of them were remained a wavy, blurry secret, rippling through those seeming crudenesses which deceive us like the blocky reflections of the lighthouse in the winter seas; Darinka Kvekich, for instance, appears so stiffly monumental in that photograph that our acquaintanceship extends only to her exoskeleton. As a matter of fact, Serbkinas are said to be the most passionate of women, and I have accepted this ever since I first saw cigarette smoke blossoming from a lady's long white fingers one autumn afternoon in Beograd. (If only I could have offered her Friulian wine!) But this quality they keep hidden from most foreigners, treasuring it within the wall of bluish-white river which waits within the beech trees of Serbia; and their inconspicuousness succeeds all the better because there is so much flamboyant Italian beauty in Trieste. I myself sometimes still pine for a certain exemplar of Franz Lehar's *danza delle libellule,* who made her appearance in an ice-blue gown with blue clouds around the hem, a blue scarf draped over her arm, and a strand of blue pearls dangling from her disdainful wrist. Meanwhile, in a dark niche in Trieste dwells the faint wooden statue of a Slavic woman, whom hardly anybody visits; while in a neighboring recess hangs an icon of the Madre della Passione, also called Strastnaja; as Cirtovich demonstrated to the Philadelphians, she is gold and silver on velvet. The heads of Serbkinas stare at me through oval window-mats, as if through the visors of iron helmets. They are no more distinct to me than any gulls and pigeons in Trieste's cypress-shaking wind.

Meanwhile, our Signor Cirtovich grew a trifle rotund, and his hair whitened and withered. His brothers sailed to Izmir and the Orient, prosperously, but not overly so—another reason the Triestini preferred them to Jovo. They greeted a man like Christians, and weren't too proud to eat squid! By now we bought salt from the Venetians, whose prices the Ragusans no longer hoped to approach. Where Cirtovich obtained it he would not tell, but to the Triestini he sold it cheaper than anyone, and it savored better. (The only way to take advantage of him was to offer him old maps and manuscripts; he remained greedy for such trash.) To the Jews of Trieste he brought, secured in an inconspicuous wooden chest, an Ark of the Torah, whose golden-green flowers and radially symmetrical vines upon a pinkish white background comprised a paradise as lovely and secret as his home. The Jews praised him and paid him well. Thanks to him, they could house their treasure in a silver cover inlaid with gold.

Although he had never yet been tricked by any of the sea's shining and tarnished moods, bit by bit he seemed to grow shyer of the aqueous element—or perhaps merely more home-loving. Something disagreed with him, something as small yet black as a single housefly in a whitewashed whitestone room in Ragusa at high summer noon. At about the time that his son Nicola came of age, Cirtovich began to closet himself with a very old man (most likely Slovenian) who carried a snakeheaded walking-stick. Luca Morelli told Captain Robert that he had overheard the two principals discussing an iron hoard in the ground near Bled. Evidently a certain species of iron stood infallible against monsters of all types, and the old man agreed to bring a piece of it to be tried. Cirtovich replied something to the effect that any octopus can ooze through a tiny hole, at which the old man swore by the Mother of God that no seamonster could get around his metal, in token of whose holiness he requested Signor Cirtovich to be informed, as could be verified by any number of esteemed persons, that from this very same ore had been smelted the sword of Prince Lazar, may Christ smile upon him, who could have vanquished the Turks at Kosovo had he not preferred a heavenly kingdom. Cirtovich responded in a very low voice, so that Morelli failed to comprehend his syllables. Six weeks later the old man reappeared shouldering a heavy sack, but soon left the warehouse in a rage. Cursing Cirtovich and all Serbs everywhere, he threw the sack into the Canal Grande, stamped his foot, then rapped his stick against the railing of the Ponterosso three times. That was the last they saw of him. After that, Cirtovich received fewer visitors. His smile failed to match his gaze. He kept his thumbs hooked in his vest pockets, except when he played with the chain of his pocketwatch. Even his friend Pavle Petrović, another old settler whom he had previously greeted at church, began to feel unwelcome in this man's shadow. Complaining to Florio and Alessandro, he was told: Well, that's our brother.

In about 1746 Jovo Cirtovich received delivery of a fine book-chest with three mirrors glued inside the lid, and over the main compartment, as Vasojević was called upon to ascertain, a lockable wooden panel figured with grapes and crowns. Captain Robert said: His brain must be worm-eaten! Why should he waste good gold like that?— Luca Morelli proposed that the man had a mistress. They asked Petar, who kept heroically quiet even over two bottles of wine.— In fact the item was for Cirtovich's youngest daughter, Tanyotchka.

2

Triestina that she was, she grew up in the lovely softness of dirty grey stone, promenaded through brickwork like a sunset made of russet graveyard earth, secluded herself in shining veils and dresses each one of which could have been the silver cover of a sacred book. Her very first memory was of a yellow-green pine branch swaying in the rough sea; she could not remember that on that occasion her father had been carrying her in his arms. Sometimes when she opened her eyes he was gazing down at her with his sad smile. Then she remembered the painful brightness of her mother's sunny curtains in the Triestine sea-wind, and the Ponterosso swiveling up and down for her father's ships; Srdjana was letting her water the garden flowers, so she felt important; in the garden she used to chase slate-hued lizards with her brother Veljko, and when caught the creatures would cast off their wriggling tails. It was already time for church. The priest with the long white beard bowed to everyone and disappeared within the golden door of that great house where Jesus lived. And of course she would not forget Uncle Massimo and Aunt Eva, who gave her presents; even more significant were the sad dark eyes of Prince Lazar from the icon over her parents' bed; he looked like the king of a deck of cards come alive. Then there was a certain painting in the drawing room, and in her imagination Tanya was or somehow would become the tender longhaired girl on the white horse, laying down her many-bangled arm upon the man's head. Who he was she never thought to ask. She remembered how her sisters laughed at her whenever they caught her dreaming over this picture (Aleksandra and Liljana were the cruelest; Gordana cared the least). Her father in his grey homespun trousers, her mother with the little dagger at her belt, them she most frequently remembered not in and of themselves, but rather as elements of scenes, as when, for instance, she was riding in the coach with her mother to see her father off; arriving at the Canal Grande, they watched through the narrowest conceivable parting of the curtains as he descended the stone stairs to the skiff where two of his sailors waited to ferry him out to the *Sava* or the *Lazar* (by then he had turned over the *Kosovo* to Uncle Massimo, the *Beograd* to Uncle Florio). Sometimes Liljana might ride along; her brothers still accompanied them when they were young; they would leap out onto the quay and their father's servitors would set them easy tasks, praising and humoring them as befitted the sons of a rich man. Uncle Florio or Uncle Stefano might be about the docks; they would always approach the carriage to greet the family in Christ's name, kissing Tanya on the forehead. Once, while some gaunt carpenter bent far forward over his bench to watch, a sailor questioned Vuk about that neck-pouch which their father guarded like some diadem, but the boy took fright and sprinted back to the coach. By then their father had commended them to Saint Sava, vanishing promptly, while Petar conveyed the remnant home, her mother too proud to weep, the child knowing that the worst had happened: her father had left the world again, perhaps forever; and she imagined that the evening breeze was sobbing by means of the shaking reflection of leaves in a windowpane. While she was still very young, this image of the absent father quickly became as pallid as San Giusto's above-the-doorway marble saint in his concentrically dimpled robe, holding a castle in one hand and a rake in the other, with his head cocked wryly; then her father came home to renew himself in her mind. Her mother slaughtered two chickens and a lamb; there were onions, potatoes, greens of all sorts, and Friulian wine, of course—never squid or octopus, which her father would not touch. Tanya and her sisters were kissing him in delight, because he had brought them a little box of coral-figured golden buttons. What her brothers got that time she disremembered. For a bedtime story he told them about blind creatures he had recently met in a certain limestone cave. Only Tanyotchka dared to ask: Papa, what were you doing in that cave?—to which he smilingly replied that perhaps he had needed to hide a certain something. In the morning she watched him reading old documents in an unknown alphabet. Then almost at once, or at least so she remembered it, they were escorting him back to the Canal Grande. He embraced them and stepped out of the carriage. Petar's eyes grew as milky blue as the lagoon of Grado. Captain Vasojević was waiting on the quay; he kissed his hand to Tanya. Her mother's lips moved in a prayer, and as they turned up the road past the Teatro Romano, Tanya forgot her father because a plump black-and-white cat lay on the rim of the old Jesuit well, unmoving, her green eyes wide, and so the girl pleaded with her mother for a cat. Her mother kissed her wearily. Her brothers were hounding Petar to tell them how their father once escaped from a boatload of ravenous *uskoks.*— Well, young masters, why not ask Captain Vasojević? If it happened, he must have been there. I don't know about anything but horses.

Each time she was parted from her father, she continued to feel a fearful bewilderment as to how she ought to live without him, but ever less apprehension on his behalf, since he owned such heavenly luck. Soon she could remember him better and better, in part by means of a certain old book which he sometimes unlocked from his strongbox to show her. Its silver covers were mounted with mosaics of tiny gold, somber malachites, carnelian and hematite tiles; mostly it was all gold. Christ hovered, His pale robe glittering like mother-of-pearl and the four spokes of His golden wheel-halo making a cross as He shone there within an oval womb surrounded on all sides by haloed saints each of whose halo was a golden pavement of beads: Saint Lazar, Saint Sava and their kin reached out to touch the spears of golden light which radiated from His envelope. Opening the silver covers of this book, Tanya found the secret of those rays. But what it consisted in could not be expressed. The child believed that her father knew it as well as she; they had no need to speak of it. As for her sisters, they invariably exclaimed over that precious object, then, summoned by their mother, returned to their weaving and sewing, which they much preferred because, safely away from their father, they could laugh and sing as they desired.

These were some of the pictures in the book of Tanyotchka; they made her who she was. Throughout her life they accompanied her, sometimes closer or farther from her head, like the seagulls crying just before a rain. And I must not fail to mention the picture she simply lived in. Caressed on every fair day by that light of Trieste, which is born of sun, sea, paint and stone, and might be yellow or beige, but masks itself in all the colors, she never realized how Italian she was.

As he travelled less, her father built up his library, and long before that renowned Triestino Baron Revoltella even began to assemble his glass-fronted shelves of match-bound, spine-labeled volumes, Cirtovich possessed considerable bibliographic treasures. These became a portion of her heritage, and only hers, because to everybody else in the family that chamber felt as eerie as the site of a solitary burial. Once she asked her Uncle Alessandro what his favorite book might be, and he laughed, staring at her. Then she knew why her father kept aloof from his brothers.

She and her sisters used to play with seventeenth-century brass coins worn down into spurious translucency; their father once brought home a coffer of them, salvaged from some shipwreck and quite worthless except to children. The girls strung them into bracelets and necklaces. As for their brothers, they hid, hoarded and traded their shares.

Their father loved them all in the best way, doting on them, yet, as they somehow were aware, seeing their faults, guarding them from perils and follies, indulging them when that would do no harm, and correcting them only by necessity. The boys often disagreed, and fell to pummelling each other with shipwrights' nippers, clamps and chisels; they would have swung wide-bladed axes if they could. Remembering his own child-hood, Cirtovich did not beat them even for these follies. (He never struck his daughters at all; it was left to Marija to do that, without his knowledge.) Once, it is true, he laid hands on Vuk, whom he caught teasing his sisters with a dead octopus he had found, but that was to teach him that a man must never disrespect any woman.* The Triestini had come to

* This later became a point of some trouble to their husbands, who found that the Cirtovich women were unaccustomed to the lot of wives; indeed, all they had to do was complain to their doting father, and the husbands would be informed that there were wolves in the forest and in the islands *uskoks* who enjoyed burning captives alive. Until the end of Cirtovich's life, only two of his daughters were beaten even once; and of these, one was unmolested forever after; the other became mysteriously widowed and soon remarried on very good terms.

imagine him as overbearing and even ferocious; and indeed, as might as well be confessed, in darker ports he had assaulted certain stubborn customs men, when the latter were unreasonable, and outnumbered, and if it happened to be a moonless night; but up here at home, when the sea breeze passed in between the shutters, which on spring and summer afternoons grew pearlescent with that special Friulian light, he played games with the children on his hands and knees. Marija laughed a little, then turned away.

Tanya's brothers already dreamed of foreign coasts, and among themselves (saying nothing to their father, who simply awed them—he had no use for their plans) they fashioned ever shrewder fantasies of secret lucre. Nicola was the eldest, then Vuk and Veljko. Once they had mastered arithmetic, Captain Vasojević quizzed them on Grisogono's Venetian circles for calculating the heights of tides. Then he took them down to the harbor. Their hands grew rough and they spoke less and less. Their mother and sisters soon virtually lost sight of them, so frequently were they away in their father's ships, learning the lie of the Dalmatian coast.

One evening Tanya overheard Captain Vasojević trying to console her father, who seemed worried or upset. He was saying: Even octopi can be tricked into grabbing hold of olive branches.— What her father said to that she could not hear.

Now the younger sisters, as was indeed their own desire, began in turn to be married off closer to home than the elder, their destinies as simplified as the concentric blue leaf-waves on their parents' plates. They wove their trousseau-clothes as industriously as a nest of elegant spiders. As each one was wed, she gently kissed her parents, brothers and sisters on the cheek.

As for Tanyotchka, by this time she had the peach-colored skin of a young woman, the creamy face of an Italian beauty. Of course she remained a Serbkina, the kind whose form is more powerful than tears.

3

If I may be more explicit, perhaps the reason that in later life her father did not entirely understand her was that while he kept his aspirations as uncorrupted as a soldier's well-oiled arquebus, she grew up, as I said, a Triestina, sweetened by her summers in the arbor of grapes and roses, which, among other more secret things her family's high walls enclosed; and when she heard her father's booted footfalls on the stone walkway, although she invariably leapt up in joy and rushed into his arms, as soon as he had stroked her hair and given her two or three bristly kisses, he turned back to his business, with that sad and watchful expression freezing again on his face, and she, having established that by embracing him again she could delay the resumption of his cares but could never keep them away from him for more than another few instants, learned to let him go, turning away on her own account, in order to avoid the sight of his suffering—not that she even realized that she perceived it, quotidian as it was, and child as *she* was, inhaling life without distinguishing good from bad, which after all would have accomplished nothing anyhow; and likewise drinking in the cool, still, rose-scented afternoons as she sat in the pavilion sewing beside her mother. As crisp as the ivy-shadows on the awning, as sudden as the crow-caws were her experiences of her father, but just as one forgets shadow-patterns, however beautiful, so even now she still misplaced him in his absence, not that she thereby loved or needed him less. Her needle sometimes forgot to flash, hovering instead, like the black bumblebees considering which rose to investigate next; but this dreaminess, which her mother occasionally indulged and her father saw as something else, did not get her behindhand in her tasks. Where her thoughts glided at such times was as much a mystery to others as what might be in her father's neck-pouch, but for a fact the singing of the blackbirds helped her remember, as any true Serb should, the day at Kosovo Polje, Field of Blackbirds, when Prince Lazar got his doom.

4

The first time that her eldest two brothers, well outfitted with warm goatskin vests, went off to sea, Tanya wept, and her mother slapped her face to scare away the bad luck. The child bowed her head to indicate the submissive repentance she scarcely felt. Then her mother kissed the icon many times, praying for a safe voyage. Tanya willingly did the same. Her mother explained about the evil eye, Satan's watchful greed, the jealousy of men (from which Christ preserve us) and the snares of Death the Huntsman. The flower-engraved copper vessels were hissing on the great block of the stove, while Srdjana, who had pretended not to see anything, knelt on the floor, and crammed in more wood. Veljko and Petar had ridden down to the ropemaker's to order rigging for Uncle Massimo. Tanya's father was already at the warehouse.

Perhaps her mother said something to him, because a day or two later he took the girl, decently veiled, alone with him to the empty church, whose lower ceiling-domes were elaborate Easter eggs with figures on them, while the upper ones made up a vault of blue being circumnavigated by marching figures; at the highest point of that inner sky stood Christ in a sun of crackling golden flowers; and in the quiet sizzling of the votive candles her father asked her to pray to our heavenly Prince Lazar, whose shoulders are higher than the deck-cannons of any Spanish galleon. This she did, while he crossed himself and murmured beside her; and when they came out, the Canal Grande was black with ships. Her father inquired whether she loved her brothers, and she said yes.— Don't worry, Tanyotchka. My luck will shelter them, even though they've gone with Uncle Stefano.— The girl kissed his hand. Petar drove them home, and there was her mother in the doorway, forming up a warp of fabric from her loom into the air and all the way across the courtyard to the stack of Roman gravestones which everybody now used for any and all purposes.

In those days she often liked to scare herself by making shadows on the wall with her gabled lantern; sometimes a twisted bit of driftwood that one of her brothers brought her would produce some fine weird shape. Whenever her mother caught her, the girl got extra work to do. But when her father noticed, he insisted that she not be punished merely for dreaming. Already she knew that there was something which she would be expected to do one day, something secret and good, which indeed she would come to demand of herself once its meaning announced itself from darkness.

By then she was braiding ropes for her father whenever he allowed her, first the *trecia simplice*, then the wide mesh of the *plagietto con fragio*. She loved more than anything to please him.

He inquired what she desired of him, and she said: To learn as much as you.— Smiling, he rose and went away. No one had ever said that to him before; nor had he asked the question of anyone, even her eldest brother. As she watched him go, she saw that obscene secret care, whatever it was, swoop back down onto his shoulders. A few days later she cried out in joy when he brought her a brass microscope.

Unlocking his Organum Mathematicum (a fine one made in Würzburg in 1668), he opened to her all the slanted shelves with their many-colored tabs of knowledge.

Here in one pocket were depictions of all seven planets, which truly did, in spite of what her mother and the priest insisted, revolve around the sun, elliptically. She pulled out a card depicting the moon's hideous face, and this in one stroke destroyed her pleasure in lunar nights. Once a lady had come in to pray at church; from a distance she was radiant; then she drew near the altar, and the mother dug her fingernails into Tanyotchka's wrist in disgust, for here was a syphilitic prostitute, whose leprous face was pitted with stinking sores. Her kindly father being absent, the men rushed to turn her out, thrusting at her with sticks until she ran away. Then her mother made all the children wash their faces and hands in rosewater. The lunar disk expressed this diseased character. But her father informed her that what appeared to be imperfections were nothing more or less than mountains and seas, irregular like our own. The girl wished to know whether there were people on the moon. Before he could answer, her mother laughed at her.— Father says that knowledge will save us! explained Tanya; her mother slapped her mouth.

And in another pocket were ships in profile passing a two-dimensional undulating Turkish coast of domes, minarets and clusters of rectangular edifices. She knew all too well that her father had been thereabouts. She raised the magnifying loupe, and with a thrill of horror discovered a Turkish woman in a green overmantle and a long white dress with red flowers. She asked whether all Turks were evil, as Uncle Massimo said. Stroking her hair for an instant, her father departed. She heard the carriage bearing him away; he was gone near about two months, and no news came. That night her mother prayed to Saint Thomas, who guards the rain-clouds.

She learned to operate the two disk-tiers of her father's solar clock, to name each monster and animal painted on his celestial globe. She could already slide the bronze knob of the dromoscope as accurately as Nicola and Vuk; she was better at it than Veljko. Smiling, her father softly clapped his hands to watch her. Of course he'd never take her to sea.

Veljko had been jealous about the Organum Mathematicum, but their father brought the proper gift for him: a crocodile mummy from Umm-el-Baragât, which when Petar carried it from the warehouse was still wrapped in papyrus: crumbly, dingy stuff, inexplicably valued by their father, who removed it with extreme care and took it off to his study. The crocodile stank, but Veljko loved it. Tanya helped him improve its eyes with vermilion beads. Unfortunately, he carried it out into the garden one day, in hopes of scaring Srdjana, and before she could oblige him the watchdogs had devoured it.

As for Vuk and Nicola, the only presents their father now gave them were coins of various realms, all fungible; that satisfied them best.

Years after he was gone, Tanya wondered whether he had wished to tell her more about his youth in Serbia. Why she knew so little was mysterious in and of itself. Uncle Stefano's daughters, for instance, loved to prattle about their high stone house, as if they could remember it. Uncle Alessandro first made friends with her brothers by telling over the Turks he had killed; of the three boys, Nicola especially adored him, and rushed to mend ropes for him or even tar the deck, if only he could be near him. Jovo Cirtovich was, perhaps, shy. On rare occasions Tanya overheard him relating to her proud and breathless brothers some family tale of raid or ambush, in which he never signified.— Remember well, he'd say. There were Cirtovićes at Kosovo.— To the daughters he declined to mention such things, and so she did not inquire, a respectfully meant omission which in old age she regretted. Once for no reason he described that same stone house, which had smelled of sausages, tobacco and ancient wheat, and Tanya, a little afraid of being unseemly, inquired about her grandmother.— Much like your mother, he replied. She cared for all of us, without many words.— And Grandfather? Uncle Florio says he died a hero.— Marking the ledger with his forefinger, he looked up to say: He was a great man, praise be to God. Now, Tanyotchka, have you found the mistake in Uncle Massimo's invoice?

There came the evening when, called urgently to save the church from fire, her father rode there with Petar and all her brothers and uncles, and Tanya found the key left in the lock of his ebony coffer. That time she was a good girl. A week after that, her father was at the warehouse, her mother in the garden caring for the lilies, her most prized flowers; her sisters were weaving and spinning for their dowry chests. Tanya had finished verifying the consignment sheets of a cargo of olive oil. One barrel was unaccounted for. Nicola rushed in, peeped into the looking-glass as earnestly as the helmsman watches the dog vane, then departed, very worked up, yet somehow pleased with himself. Where was Petar? The girl put her ear to the stable door and heard his snoring. Yes, she was safe, and would now accomplish her object. Opening the chest, she saw a hoard of secret books. They were all about death. Her Uncle Florio had once sworn to her that every Turk is as a werewolf who devours children's flesh—and here was a tract which taught how any man could become just such a monster, by going to a certain island and lifting a certain white stone. What had her father to do with that? Terrified, the girl reclosed the lid and locked it, saying nothing to anyone. The next time they ate together, she watched her father's teeth. Half reassured, she rendered herself wholly so by promising herself that those books were not what she had believed. She was learning how to keep secrets.

Just for her he once brought a wooden chest all the way from Egypt; within stood tiny blue mummiform servants with their arms folded across their breasts and their kohled eyes staring ahead. She used to march them all around. He said that they must have belonged to some Pharaoh's sister-wife, who had been entombed with them so that they could do her work for her in the afterlife. Even a queen, so it seemed, was not exempt from agricultural labor.

Well, father, since we have taken away her slaves, will she have to work now?

He laughed and chucked her under the chin. Just then he was unriddling the mystery of the three triangles contained in the Pentangle of Solomon, and her still innocent as he supposed (for he never learned about the episode of the ebony coffer); to him it seemed that this first knowledge she was gathering must merely be as sweetly ancient to her as ears of wheat engraved on a buried Roman pillar; she was not yet armed with the Sword of the Word; the Divine Purpose had not murmured in her ear; but soon, perhaps even this winter, when the ships were in, he would show her the *Cabbalistic Secrets of the Master Aptolcater.*

Father, where is Captain Vasojević?

Him? Oh, I've sent him back to Egypt.

(The task, he did not tell his daughter, was to expose from beneath the sands of Egypt a certain pyramid whose vertex touched the center of the earth, and copy whatever writing might be engraved therein.)

On another day she asked why Prince Lazar had fallen, and her father, rising, with tears in his eyes, explained that Christ had offered two choices: victory at Kosovo, and then eternal insignificance, or the tragic glory of a defeat which his descendants would unceasingly mourn and seek to avenge.

Trusting her above all others in the household, even his dear wife Marija, he ordered whichever books she wished, even when her mother thought them unsuitable, and while her younger brothers were telling off Dalmatia's coastal islands to their father's strictest sea-pilots (for mistakes they now got beaten—she never did), she began to study the ancient Greeks, because next spring he hoped for her help in collating seven fragmentary parchments concerning astral navigation. She chose certain dramas as her primers; he sent away to Rome, paying gold ducats.— He said to her: I've prayed to Saint Sava that you'll find something I've overlooked.— At this the girl felt proud, guilty and uncertain.— He used to sit by the hour at his high easel-desk, calculating wages and profits, while she rested with her legs in his lap, reading Euripides. Not until she had children of her own did she realize how much trouble he must have put himself to, conveying the ledgers back and forth in order to be home with her longer. When she got to "Alcestis," that play about the selfish man who falls out with his old father for declining to die for him, then finally persuades his wearily, tolerantly loving wife, Tanyotchka forgot to reach out and gently stroke her father's wrist; and he, coming up out of absorption in his ledgers, presently noticed the lack, and saw her lovely face illuminated with tears. Saying nothing, he continued his sums, waiting for her to speak. He had almost come to the time when he must be off to his ships when she said: Now I understand.

Oh, is that so? And what do you understand?

It's better to die for others than to—

Yes.

But why couldn't he have won the battle also, and saved our land?

So then you don't entirely understand. Well, darling, give me a kiss! The *Beograd* is coming in . . .

From Montenegro?

Good girl! And your uncle needs me.

Father, why must you do business with the Sultan?

For our advantage, and his disadvantage, silly girl! Now I'm going—

The girl smiled at him.

Father, about Prince Lazar—

Yes, darling, what is it? Be quick.

Would it be better to have hope of heaven, and live in the world trying to improve oneself, or just be born in heaven and never feel the need of anything?

That's one crucial question, for a fact, said he, caressing her hair, and then as he turned away from her she saw the mysterious affliction settle back upon him, so that all the sudden he was as gnawed down to narrowness as the jackal-haunted Sabbioncello peninsula. Rising dutifully, she went to weave linen before her mother scolded her. Once her father had called for Petar, her mother stood for a long time in the garden, stretching out her hands to the doves.

5

Mother, mother, please tell me more about Saint Lazar.

What else do you need to know? He's our holy saint, who gave his life for our glory.

But why couldn't he—

Her mother sharply said: *Whoever weeps for the world loses his eyes.*

6

If they live and thrive, children must grow, just as surely as fig-roots will split the old stone walls of Trieste; thus Tanya bloomed up out of what she had imagined that she understood. Of course one only grows up so far; Tanya would never comprehend, as we can for her, that her entire life remained confined within those sad days before Serbia finally cast off the Turks—which were also the good days when the Ponterosso could still swivel open for the ships; yes, they were the young days of Trieste before Our Lady of the Flowers had blood on her forehead; those were the days of Tanya, who could still remember her mother carrying her inside the cathedral and along that awful glistening space where God could see her, then entering beneath the canopy, crossing herself, kissing the center icon, crossing herself and kissing the rightmost one, then repeating with the leftmost; now that she was grown, she understood that God could see her wherever she hid. Her perception of other matters grew meanwhile. She realized that her parents were not happy together. At least they were not poor. She took joy and comfort in the good sound of ducats pouring out onto the table whenever her father came home.

When an old Florentine lady with snow-white braids and a sea-tanned face knocked on their gate in hope of alms, her father, peering through the tiny window, told Srdjana not to admit her.— But, master, we have some slops . . .— Foolish woman, can't you smell the plague on her?— A week later some neighbors were dead from the pest.— This too gave her comfort of a sort; her father could protect her.

Like her brothers, she learned to communicate in the runic bone-scratching of the old Lingua Venetica, but she had no one to trade messages with; her sisters being ignorant, and her mother, even admitting the inconsiderable possibility of her literacy in that language, lacking the time for nonsense. So Tanya began to memorize swatches of the Gospels, in order to recite them in church. Just before her First Communion she proved her knowledge, and the priest said, not entirely approvingly (not that her father cared what he thought), that he had never heard of so learned a girl.

Smiling sadly, her mother presented her with a necklace of silver coins on a golden chain; every coin bore the same profiled portrait of an unknown king. Tanyotchka's hopes became as rich as the ivy on the walls.

7

Whenever her father and Captain Vasojević went out, murmuring together, Tanyotchka, peeping out between the curtains of the highest window, saw other men grow as open-eyed as the painted saints of the Trecento period. This made her all the more inclined to remain indoors like her mother and sisters, especially since she had learned how to help her father balance his accounts. Occasionally now that she was older she was permitted to accompany Srdjana to the market by the Ponterosso; her mother rarely went. There Tanya discovered how poor most people are. She dreaded becoming a beggar. This she never dared to confess to her father, for what if this would insult him who was undefeatable? So, like all of us, she continued to bind and conceal her thoughts, sharpening her deductions the more. The way that her mother turned her back now when she found Tanya studying astronomy, the way her sisters so often wove and spun her share without complaint, and that steady sad alertness with which her father gazed at her, all proved again that some task would be laid on her. Whatever it was, she prayed it would relieve her father. Since he stood so superior to all fears, she now commenced to wonder whether that look of misery might derive from the body; for of course even he was mortal. But this thought she uprooted wherever it sprouted. Was it reassuring or the reverse that her father's friend now seemed likewise weighed down? She could remember when Captain Vasojević had been cheerfuller, which is to say not merely younger but more like unto other men. When she was much smaller, he scarcely came around. But once he had achieved her father's confidence, with which their common nationality had much to do, he began to stay for supper, or at times overnight; and as the household warmed to him, he might occasionally chuck the nearest daughter under the chin, and with gruff shyness present her with some small and peculiar thing of appropriately moderate commercial value: a copper coin engraved with a pretty mermaid, a medallion of Prince Lazar, or a set of tiny animal-headed trade-weights picked out of some shipwreck or marketplace. By the time that Tanyotchka was twelve or thirteen, of course, such physical familiarities were out of the question, and he contented himself with bowing to her, or at most kissing her hand, before he gave her any pretty trifle.

Her mother used to wonder why he never married. Here she exposed an almost comical blindness, for it was into his hands that that Cincar wax trader had conveyed her so many years ago. Leading her into a private cabin, in company with her maidservant, Vasojević promised the two women that they would be secure, and offered them whichever refreshments or conveniences they might wish. Reassured by the portrait of Prince Lazar, the maidservant removed her veil first. Her beauty was such that it superseded one of Vasojević's most beloved memories, which derived from a window-glimpse he had once obtained in Sarajevo of a woman, evidently Turkish, of immense elegance, who, it being winter, was wrapped in a sable coat whose soft hues were a rainbow of coffee, honey and milk, with sweet black shadows which matched her own black hair. Although he had as yet taken in no more of her than her outline, Vasojević was already stricken. A ring lived on every one of her pale fingers, which ceaselessly stroked one another for warmth. The rest of her, however, remained perfectly still. She leaned forward, resting her fur-sleeved arms on her fur-sheltered knees, staring far away in boredom or sadness. After half an hour she lit a long pipe, which she then allowed to suffocate between her fingers. Then after another long pause she turned her head in his direction. Perhaps she had not realized that he was watching her. He saw a pale face, with dark, generous yet cruel lips. The longer he looked, the more she fascinated him. Her eyelashes up-curled, almost supplicatingly. She held a tiny black leather pouch which gleamed scratchlessly. Her hair was parted across her face, transforming her white forehead into a pagoda roof. She had a triangular chin. He thought her the most irresistible lady he had ever seen. Her long hair accompanied her throat down into the hot darkness of her fur collar. Her expression never changed. A slave rushed to shutter the window.

As she was to all other women he had seen before, so was the maidservant of his master's bride to her, and thus the mistress to the maidservant. Bowing, Vasojević asked them to send to him for anything they needed. Then he left them there, with a sailor outside the door to protect them, and that was how it went, all the way to Trieste.

Had her father seen fit to wed him to one of the many Cirtovich belles, no one in the family would have minded, in spite of the disparity in age; perhaps her mother had even once suspected some interest on his part, Tanyotchka being most definitely his favorite, for although she had not entirely achieved her mother's former beauty, her heart was kinder, her intellect was as great as her father's, and her eyes expressed such beautiful awareness, almost like the Virgin Marija herself; all the same, Vasojević never came anywhere near marriage. Whenever he entered the Sultan's dominions he made do with leering slave-girls playing peekaboo behind their fans, flashing their bangles, whistling, snapping their fingers and singing obscene songs in charming voices. Now that he was in on his master's secret, he got a cash allowance for such sports. He paid with a silver coin issued by the ancient city of Panemuteichus, or with last year's ducats; to the Turks it was all the same, for they knew how to weigh money as well as Jovo Cirtovich. Sometimes Vasojević used to ask after a particular Aida, whom he never found; of late he had given that up. A certain Gypsy-looking girl, nicely laced into her pastel-colored corset, wriggled her gold hoop-earrings at him and leaped on him with the alacrity of a hungry corpse. The other women sprawled sniggering over the bowl of grapes they fed into each other's mouths. Vasojević did not care. Knowing what he did, he wished for neither wife nor children.

8

What blighted those two men (although it also of course advantaged them) had to do with a strange faculty which Jovo Cirtović had inherited from his own father, a *hajduk** both brave and cheerless who after an almost abnormally long life was shot by Turkish Janissaries whom he had sought to ambush in a high meadow on the eve of Saint George's Day.[†] Two of the *hajduks,* who happened to be the dead man's brothers, carried him home. The mother commenced to scream and gash herself, while Maksim, the second son, cursed in obscenities of despair. The other sons sat stroking their beards; and presently Alexander said: Please describe those Turks.— To Jovo, the first living son, then fell that neck-pouch of greasy black lambskin, which his father had worn so invariably beneath his shirt that no one in the family even stopped to wonder what it might contain; after all, curiosity has killed tigers as dead as cats. Or had they wondered nonetheless? Gazing on their grim father, whose lips rarely moved, the sons might have wondered indeed, or even speculated, but it proved best to turn away from such courses. That the pouch was supposed to descend from eldest to eldest was all that anyone knew. Maksim had been the last empirical explorer of this subject; although he was hardly seven years old then, their father felled him with his fists, execrating and kicking him without pity; the boy had been lucky to lose nothing but a tooth. After that, whenever their father stepped away and reached into his shirt, they averted their faces. The uncles remarked that on the night of his slaying, Lazar Cirtović's hand kept creeping toward his throat, as if he desired the touchstone but denied himself; this was

* Serbian outlaw.

† 24 April (Old Style).

peculiar, and so was the fact that the Janissaries had killed him in near-darkness, at more than a hundred paces, with a single bullet. At any rate, the family held the funeral, then made that renowned toast to *the better hour,* meaning the rendezvous in the afterworld with our loved dead. By then the better hour of Jovo Cirtović had already commenced; for, withdrawing himself into a shepherd's cave, he untied the legacy from around his throat. The leather smelled like his father's sweat. He unpeeled the half-rotten, salty clasp. Within lay an ovoid object not unlike a drop of sea-glass, or perhaps a mirror. At first it seemed greenish-black, like old bronze. Reader, if you have ever robbed a Roman grave, you might have won yourself twin fibulae like mushroom-gilled breasts of greenish-silver, ready to be yoked onto the chest of some miniature deity. But although metal-comparisons momentarily occluded Jovo's mind, the object must be comprised of glass, for a fact, although its substance—talk about *through a glass darkly!*—was blacker than anything he had ever seen. The impossibility of any such night-clot being transparent was more patent than an axiom out of Euclid. But as he peered into it, not without a certain longing connected with his father, he began, so it seemed, to glimpse something moving fitfully within, although how that could be was equally mysterious; in any event, the matter waxed unpleasant to his consideration, for indeed the longer he looked, the greater grew his dread; and now the thing inside, whatever it was, briskened like a treetop in a freshening breeze, and he began to get the sense of a ball (although it could have been pear-shaped or even gourd-like) festooned with myriad kelpish appendages whose incessant flickerings were what so horribly drew his eye. It could have been an upturned many-branching tuber, or a strange tree with a round eye just below the crown, or a new-pulled tooth still attached its bloody root. As his sense of menace increased, the conviction stole upon him that these arms would presently draw away from the thing's face, exposing it to him, and that this would be the most fearful thing in the world. His response was of course defiance—for he had been raised to be a true Serb.

He concluded that this entity must be either death itself, or something contingent to it. It unfailingly appeared to him in this molluscid form, it bore a texture like tortoise-shell, and on occasion its body was colored like quicksilver. Its prickle-studded head resembled a Turk's cap; and yet there were nights when he could have sworn it was a triangular mask. To prove his courage to himself, he once tapped on the glass; at which the thing coiled up and shrank, as if fearful, then grew an angry purple, and began lashing out against the sides of the crystal. To him the worst part, which rarely occurred, was when it showed him the ultramarine radiance of its eyes.

As his father's fate proved (or did not), to see death's arrival is hardly to forestall it; for death's minions are myriad; and just because we spy an army of Turks approaching over the plains does not guarantee a victory, as again is shown by the doom of Prince Lazar. Besides, death may come when we are sleeping.

Jovo of course had foreseen nothing, lacking the pouch while his father lived. There had been no dream of bloody banners.

Since he did of course believe in heaven, Christ and angels, one might wonder whether his mistake (if he made any) consisted in refraining from turning to those beneficent helpers. His eventual point of view, a matter of convenience as well as comfort to him, was that the dark-glass thing might be an angel, howbeit of an ominous cast; in any event, it was this gift which God had set before him to make the occupation of his life, and he must face it first, just as a fisherman must get his nets in trim before he rows out anywhere. Perhaps he should have laid the matter in the Church's lap. But he declined to offer himself up any longer to other men's misunderstanding; moreover, he cherished what his father had bequeathed to him, not only because it brought him riches and power, but also quite simply because it came from his father.

Toward him the father had been strangely lenient, permitting him to read and study every now and then with the priest, so long as neither goats nor sheep got lost. Whenever he took his mother's honey into town, he returned with coins. In those days he sensed that something would be expected of him, but how can a child know himself? Had he expressed a more martial character, his father might have been prouder; certainly his brothers and uncles would have made more of him; to please them he killed his first Turk, an old woodcutter, before he was ten, and showed both quickness and courage on mountain raids, but his heart lay in his numbers and letters, so that in time his father gazed across the fire at him with a sad bewildered pride. As for the son, to his father he had been lovingly loyal always, even through his dread.

Now that he was the family head, they feasted him from silver cups and drank his health, all the time watching him, to see what he would do. His mother, who had patiently hated the race ever since the Turks whipped her brother to death on the market square in Mostar, laid out the corpse in silence, folding its arms across its shattered breast. They toasted Saint Lazar, recourse of the persecuted and defeated.

The priest arrived. They prayed to Saint Sava. Fumigating the coffin with sulphur, tow-wisps and good black powder, they lowered the dead father into it. Afterward they threw in coins. Jovo and Maksim nailed down the lid. The sisters were screaming. The brothers passed the coffin out the window and laid it in the horse-cart. Jovo led the family to the open grave. And finally, as I have said, they toasted *the better hour.* Drinking grimly, the uncles waited for something else to be uttered, and presently Maksim said it: Brandy is good in its way, but I'd rather drink Turkish blood!

That anxiety which would weary him like a ceaseless ringing in one's ears, that was not yet perceptible. What was he to do? His sisters lowered their eyes. As for his mother, uncles, brothers, all of them kept watching him as would the double ranks of saints on the golden polyptych in the Franciscan church at Pula. Perceiving his pallor, they prepared to misconstrue him, as they had done before. He was haunted, but no longer afraid. He saw that squid-face howsoever he turned, except to the west. Especially hateful were its tonguelike radula and its beak like beetle's pincers, but when it showed him its huge round eye, that was nearly insufferable. Already he was growing accustomed to it; he would employ the thing to carry out his will.— But what did he will? First if not last, to do something great.— What that deed ought to be he would discover. Being practical, as a Serb had to be in that tyrannized land, he comprehended that he must first build up wealth, then perpetuate his family and his secret. This day he would set out.

On the riverbank he took a handful of Serbian earth and tied it up in a cloth. His youngest brother Lazar said: So, he's getting out with whatever it is that Father carried. What a treacherous bastard!— Jovo forbore to strike him; the squid thing did not show him any need. They all perceived his determination to achieve some triumph, the more splendid since it remained undefined. Of course they could not see that staying on here would be a living death.

Turning the family over to Maksim, to whom he gave all of their father's goods and most of his ready money, he signed on to the first ship he saw, and the sea foamed into grey bubbles like the delicately woven chain-links in Hungarian armor. The dark-glass offered him a comforting opacity. He was entering a more fruitful world and therefore, as ought to have been the case, an easier one. When he first rode the rainbow sea at the base of Ragusa's walls at sunset, he smiled and thought: This was inevitable.— And he prospered, since he could see and avoid so many ills. Hardhanded in trade, and quick, as it proved, in the forecastle of any ship, confident against villains and perilous swells, familiar since childhood with both discomfort and cruelty, and (best of all) cognizant of prices and qualities, he spied out treasures of all sorts. The geometry of halyard, crosstree and shroud came so easy to his mind that the officers never beat him. Some of his shipmates were murderers, many treacherous and most drunk, but the squid-face peered in through his heart's scuttle to warn him of their designs; even in his sleep the cold wet rasp of a tentacle across his neck woke him in good time, so that already his canniness (by which I mean uncanniness) began to be talked of. To be sure, neither he nor they disobeyed the creed of most human beings who act their role instead of merely mouthing it—that since life and death are both unjust, it cannot be evil to fight against them however one can. Against, for instance, the atrocities of the Turkish occupation one is justified in murdering any lone and harmless Turk, if it can be done in secret; and justification increases in direct proportion to profitability: rob the dead, by all means!—But others were enchained by speculations, while Cirtović was bound to knowledge. Now that death had grown visible to him, he thought to strip life to equivalent nakedness. While the others sewed, gambled, drank and carved, he read an old grimoire which promised everything, ending: *And this last point hath been proved, and is very true.* One night an Englishman stepped over the sleeping cabin boy and tried to assassinate Cirtović with a sailmaker's needle, but the latter, galvanized by his angel's electric-blue eye, shot him from underneath the blanket. The others held inquest, but there was the dead Englishman where he ought not to have been, with the needle still in his hand, and so they shrugged and threw him to the fishes. Withdrawing himself then, as though he meant to ease his bowels, Cirtović peeped inside his lucky pouch, and found the thing hanging in darkness there, as if at ease, its arms dangling down and the suckers on them shining like strings of onions, which proved that nobody meant to avenge the Englishman, at least just now; so he returned to his hammock and slept the night through. Presently there came that evening when they were moored at Hvar, and Cirtović scented an ambush by *uskoks,* in time sufficient to kill four of them. Just as certain squids are so transparent that one sees their brains and nerves beneath the skin, so the evil motives of others, if they impinged on him, were ever visible to Jovo Cirtović. Mischances, even potential ones, announced their coming with equal clarity, as in that time off Pula when his demon rode the leech of the foresail, thanks to which he saw that the cringle had come loose, which could have hindered their getaway in a side-wind. The careless sailor got flogged; the second mate thanked Cirtović. And just as Catholics enjoy touch-relics, so do sailors love the lucky man, for we all crave magic against danger. Ragusans, Spaniards, Triestini and renegade Turks, they all respected him, and even confided their money to him on certain doubtful ventures; whenever he agreed to take it, it came back to them with interest—unless, of course, they were fated to feed devil-fishes. To their horrors and fears he listened as would a rich man to the poor. Regarding his own life he appeared to feel nothing but pleasure, wonder and pride; for what can be as beautiful as the glory of God and the bread which people have earned? His aspirations continued to enlarge. To himself he seemed to be voyaging into an ever safer place. Perhaps if an enemy were to lock him within a prison tower he might not be able to get out again, but why couldn't he could avoid getting dragged inside it in the first place? He even dreamed that the estrangement between himself and his brothers could be remedied. Hence long before Cirtović became Cirtovich, he had begun to wonder why his father died at all. And his very longing to solve this question might have made him so abnormally acquisitive of knowledge—although he had ever been so, since his childhood; so perhaps his learning-greed was simply the desire to understand his father, whom he had never known as well as he would have wished. Why had the father withheld himself from the understanding of his sons?— Not from lack of love—if anything, he cared most essentially for his own blood kin—but, as might have been, from shyness of a sort, or the desire not to burden them with something, or (as Jovo believed) fidelity to a magic secret.

He remained certain that the charge which his father had laid upon him came out of love and faith, predicated in a *seeing* of his son. He had been expected to accomplish something great with the means now delivered to him. The fact that his father had done, for all he could tell, nothing great, and, moreover, had left him no explanation, much less instruction in the use of the dark-glass, unnerved him at times—for what if he should misuse it? But no, his father must have trusted him. It was left to him, without restriction, to employ the legacy as he willed. He knew that his father had been a great man—all the more so, it now seemed, that his doings must remain unknown.

He never supposed that a single deathless man could in and of himself overcome the Sultan's empire, but the more he learned of magic, the better he believed in that art, and presently his heart's wish became no less than to sail to the Sphere of Fixed Stars, in order to beseech Prince Lazar to return to earth, and free his suffering people. How could this be done? He held a conviction that his unique mental makeup, combined with the means which his father had bequeathed him, could alter most any story, given life and coin enough.

He settled in Trieste as he had left Beograd—which is to say, at the will of his cephalopodean guide. He took inspiration from the suddenness with which the Golfo's breezy weather can give way to sweltering eternities, until a purple jellyfish of cloud comes swimming over Trieste; and even though the sky over Muggia remains as blue as the lapis lazuli in the church fresco, winds are already hissing through rigging and the masts are clattering, bells ringing by themselves, and the storm comes. An hour later all is hot and breathless, and again the merchants and their shipwrights promenade up the Ponterosso, discussing the manufacture of new moneycraft. From change to change, Jovo Cirtovich proved ready. As he liked to say, *without wind, cobwebs would fill the sky.* He lived within the off-green loveliness of olive leaves. Once he had been led to

sell Friulian wines, trade-lines radiated out from his hands, and his career bore comparison to those golden stars in the blue heaven of an illuminated manuscript. And he married as you know. Some might say that
his categorical mistake was to refrain from friendships with the Triestini; but Serbs have studied at a stern school; they trust in little but death;
to him, the inhabitants of this port resembled an assembly of yellow-eyed
octopi inside their little mounds. What would they have done to him,
had they learned of his project? Remembering a certain morning when a
Turkish cannonball nearly killed him, and the black-clad old women in
the burning ruins had stared him over as if by missing death he had become strange or even monstrous, he declined to be gawked at, much less
judged. Another fishwife offered him an old papyrus which some ignora-
mus had made into cartonnage for mummy-wrappings, and he bought it
with a smile. Let her despise him! He read it easily, comprehending it
down to the last grapheme. It was nothing but some dead merchant's inventory of olive oil, salt and sheep. From a ragpicker he obtained a letter
to a praetorian Prefect, concerning the situation of the now extinct Roman city of Cyrrhus, and incidentally detailing interesting particulars of
the transit of Saturn. Back to Philadelphia he sailed to vend wine, Marija
raising up both hands to send her blessing after him, gauntly feminine,
shadow-eyed like the Virgin whose name she carried. As usual, he cried
out: Hold onto the wind with your teeth!— The sailors cheered. And before she expected him he was already shortening sail, approaching the
many-windowed rectangular edifices of the Borgo Teresiano, the Teatro
Romano gaping in the sunlight like a dead giant's eyesocket, Massimo
and Florio embracing him tightly there before the warehouse, while Petar rode up with the carriage. Building his fleet, he sent out his ships parallel to the Longitude of Death, with facile flags dancing at their halyards.
But how his father had felt upon first looking into the dark-glass, Jovo
Cirtovich would have liked to know. For just that reason, perhaps he
should have prayed more often to the Christ Procurator; but the many-
armed angel around his neck merely gazed at him as would any animal,
even a predatory or tame creature who sought something from him. The
awareness in an animal's eyes is alien beyond knowledge, whereas the
gaze from within the dark-glass haunted him because he nearly compre-

hended it. All the same, he never feared it. Now that he was established, he could begin to achieve his wishes; and just as his multiplying capital gave birth to the many darkening rectangles of new sails against the evening sky, so his aspirations fanned out, his projects ravelling themselves practically of their own accord.

From the outset Captain Vasojević served him faithfully; the fellow was as honest as Marija, as bravely dogged as a *hajduk*, as ready to liberate Serbia as Cirtovich himself, even if they must sail straight up into empty air! Impressed into serfdom on one of the immense Turkish farms, he had escaped only to see his youngest sister Aida hauled off to Abdul Bey's harem. Unable to kill this Turk, he waylaid a wandering scholar from Travnik and cut his throat. Then he fled to Bar, and presently to Trieste. Perhaps what he and his master shared above all was the desire to tempt fate.

Mindful of Porphyry's claim that Plotinus had achieved oneness with the Godhead four times, Vasojević used to propose, in those days when the two of them still discussed a voyage to the Sphere of Fixed Stars, that they plumb the Enneads for the secret of celestial travel. Cirtovich knew Plotinus well enough, and believed him to be wanting in quantities and procedures: in short, no secret lay there. Besides, his destination had already begun to alter. What if Prince Lazar were not yet in heaven, but remained captive in some other realm? This would explain why he had not come back for these four centuries. The Sphere of Fixed Stars was known; one saw it every clear night. But since religion and even the best science of the *Novum Organum* failed to describe the treasure which his father had left him, thus his duty. So he studied death. Marija was in the storehouse counting bales of fiber. Massimo had brought him a case of plum brandy from the old country; once the Cincar traders were all paid off, he called Vasojević up from the dock, locked the door, opened the first bottle, and they sat drinking toasts to Serbia, their dear home so blighted and lawless, while Cirtovich elucidated the qualities he read into Death the Huntsman, who must be as terrifying as had been his own father in anger; but Vasojević, who in those first years remained naïve enough to eat fried squid without getting nauseated, could not yet comprehend him. Well, neither could anyone else. (A certain Captain Bijelić from Montenegro sometimes sailed to Trieste, where a merchant who purchased bales of tea from him inquired into the doings of Captain Cirtovich.— Bijelić said: He keeps to himself.)

Cirtovich began his tertiary researches with the fact that death cannot be said to be either cold or hot, liquid or solid; therefore it, like the soul, must not be embodied; and by means of certain more detailed proofs in this vein (the lemma conceded only by force, as it were), it grew apparent to Cirtovich that death is itself a spirit or active principle. Although the corollaries to this were unpleasant, he reminded himself that if the most precious thing is truth, then realities are treasures, never mind that they often seem to be excrements and bloody cinders. Sometimes he wanted no more than did Marija—a better life. Wasn't that what she prayed for when her oval face shone gold in the cathedral torchlight? In truth, she brought gold light with her! She had wide dark eyes; the right was larger than the left. Her lips were rich red like the borders of icons. He never forgot how the whites of her eyes glowed in the dark church. When he lay down beside her, her eyes grew even larger, as if she were searching for something in him. But it was his fate to see a certain idea, his father's, silhouetted every night. The enlargement of understanding, for which he possessed so high an aptitude, requires tranquillity, if it is to be more than a fighter's ruthlessly expedient knowledge of good and evil—and Cirtovich's peace was getting eaten away. Closing his eyes, he remembered the pine trees looking down on old walled towns.

Having buried his handful of Serbian earth in the garden, he now begot his children. Their Italian was better than his, of course. They were never morose as they might have been in Serbia. Indeed, they were active and optimistic. As for his daughters, each one veiled herself, as did her mother, like any good Serbkina in a city ruled by Turks. Without his knowing it he became ever more a man of Istria or at least Dalmatia, hoarding up islands in his mind. Thank God he had declined to be renowned for creeping through the mountains and stealing cows like some middling *hajduk*! He was going to be a savior. Before Tanya was born he had charted a plausible course. Copernicus, Galileo and Kepler had not, as the ignorant supposed, destroyed Ptolemaic cosmology. If anything, they had brought the Spheres within reach. The almost entirely uncentered earth (for only the Lunar Sphere revolved around it) conveniently intersected the Sphere of Jupiter at certain periods. This would facilitate the voyage. Praying to Saint Paul, who protects wine and wheat, he filled, then doubled his family granary. Wasn't that the touch of proof? From this period he often recollected a certain autumn afternoon after his first wine-peddling voyage to Muscovy, Marija's doves murmuring in the garden, Srdjana off to market, his wife sitting very still in that high-backed chair holding Nicola, who must have been less than two years old; he was clinging to his mother's neck, peeking sidelong at his father. Suddenly the little boy stretched out his hand. He desired the mysterious thing which his father always wore around his neck. Marija watched huge-eyed and unsmiling. The child began to cry. Turning away, Jovo Cirtovich funded *uskoks* and befriended priests whose cassocks had secret pockets, his understanding harshening year by year, although not into what he would have termed dissatisfaction; he had not grown bitter like his brothers, whose dearest dream was to rip the Turks' beards out and skin them like lambs. Hence his secret noble thoughts prepared him for knowledge rather than for hatred. Late at night he went to the garden, mapped stars and listened. He knew what he wanted, his ambition swinging brightly like a forecastle lantern in bad seas, and and although his good angel fixed its blue eye on him and opened its dark brown beak, he succeeded.— Oh, he's as brave as a dragon! they said.— Moreover, it was known of him that unlike the Turks he never blinded or tortured anybody, even when on the trail of money. He was mostly kind to beggars. Even his competitors he treated with wary good humor, as if he were among the feathertopped masqueraders in a Venetian aquatic parade.— As for his face . . . well, such faces belong, for instance, to hardened adulterers who find themselves in difficulties—if they can only pull themselves out of this pit, in order to dive ravenously into the next, all will be well!—and so they gaze far away, clenching their lips in order not to get any more grave-dirt between their teeth; pressing their fists against their chests, they await the next pang of dread, grief or guilt.

When they wrote him that their mother had died, he pitied his brothers and invited them all to Trieste. They proudly refused, wavered, then bowed down to the power of his riches; for it turned out that they too had always wished to travel. So they came, Italianizing their names with mercenary haste: Massimo, Alessandro, Stefano, Cristoforo, Florio and

Lazzaro. They spoke about their father, who since his death had become ever more handsome and terrible, and then Jovo gave them all ships. They were jealous of him, but more so of Vasojević, who although not of their blood had been set so high above them. All the same, he was a man they could understand, unlike their brother. When Massimo demanded to become taken on as a full partner in the warehouse, Jovo Cirtovich gave him a sinecure and told him to study Glagolitic. They tried to learn about his doings through other Serbs: Jovan Moro and even Lazar Ljubibratić. Nobody knew anything. In silence he observed them peering at his neck-pouch. They would not have dared to treat their father thus.

His father's soul swam ever farther away from him, like a lost tarnished fish of silver. Moreover, he felt desperation to see Marija getting greyer and unhappier, no matter how many turtledoves he brought her; while Tanya kept growing up without being part of the secret. What did he desire, then? He was anything but unhappy; great meditations sustained him, his aims, necessities and perils ingathered like the many-roped high masts peeping over the Ponterosso. Unlocking one of his coffers, he set to counting the black wormholes in the White Book. Then it came time to underwrite another cargo of Virginian tobacco for his sheep-dealing brothers, whose mediocrity remained as familiar and therefore pleasant to him as the stink of the Canal Grande. Scarcely cconcerned how he appeared to others, he kept dreaming that famous dream which we all dream under other guises, the one of the dead child who returns home too late, finding his parents long dead—yes, and likewise all his brothers and sisters, together with their children and grandchildren. When he laid his hand on Marija's breast, her heartbeats came as dull as the churchbells of tiny Serbian villages.

In the forenoon watch of one of those ambiguous days when the *bora* becomes gentle, and the sky an ever richer, sweeter turquoise, this man whom no one knew summoned Vasojević, who in those days still wore a gold-braided tunic like a Montenegrin, closed the door and laid out his father's treasure. As the Americans say, misery loves company. Just as an octopus blushes while considering the capture of a certain crab, so did Vasojević color, clenching his hand as if he might hurl the object out the window and into the Canal Grande. Cirtovich, likewise peering into the crystal, perceived a smaller, plumper incarnation than usual hanging there within the blackly glowing glass, with its pale wide eyes watching and its beak agape, and its ten arms the greenish-brown hue of kelp. So far as he was concerned, it went perfectly, and Vasojević, sweating and rigid like a man getting impaled by Turks, turned away, staring out the window.— You understand now, said his master.— All Tanyotchka knew (looking up from a manifest for beeswax: the Cincars were pretending that her father had not paid them) was that on his next visit, slipping into her hand a fat bag of black old amber beads disarticulated from some necklace, their family friend smiled at her, but it was not the old smile. (Her mother was weaving a woolen rug; perhaps she did not notice the change.) And now Vasojević began to grow rich and lucky on his own account.

Tanya watched her father get ever more hollowed out. He was gazing at her with eyes which she mistook for wrathful. How had she disappointed him? Then she decided that it must have been her mother who angered him. But then again that nasty speculation about his infirmity or senescence sprang up. His hair was whiter at the temples, no doubt. Not long ago she had heard him groaning loudly in his sleep. Oh, but she knew better than to ask her mother!— Liljana was calling her. When she had finished carding the wool, her father was seeking a certain place among the golden compass-roses and blue sea-monsters of his atlases, the place-names written in blood-red script. From the way his forefinger hovered over the deep, Tanya thought it must be an island. A year or two before, she might have dared to ask him. He touched her smooth hands.

9

Vasojević had benefited almost immediately from his new power when, ascending Trieste's most famous hill, in order to visit a certain Bohemian chemist on behalf of his master, he spied a dark-cloaked mendicant dozing or lurking in one of the grooves within the Arco di Riccardo, and instantly comprehended, although the beggar remained the merest clot of darkness within the soapy white stone, and although his face was buried in his chest—to any passerby he offered only a black-clad shoulder, long grey stinking hair, a limp swirl of cloth and flabby fingers twitching as if in sleep—that this man had a stiletto up his sleeve—for the decopodian incarnation of death now appeared, superimposed upon his face. Boldly approaching, Vasojević cocked the well-charged pistol in his pocket. The murderer leapt up; the blade blossomed from his wrist. Perhaps Vasojević would have won out in any event, for his beard had not grown grizzled by trusting the creatures of this world. Nonetheless he was grateful to Jovo Cirtovich; not all at once did life take on for him the hateful specificity of a round unwinking eye, and the suckers on ten arms which coiled and uncoiled, and water spurting from the funnel in that nasty head which, although it could change to red, orange, yellow, black, purple, most often appeared in his nightmares fleshed in that crapulous yellow-brown which he inexplicably loathed more than anything. No ship of his could ever now spring a leak, even during the darkest moment of the middle watch, without his knowing; no Venetian or Turkish barque could surprise him in a fog; wherever a pirate's barbed grapnel hook might intend to fix itself, there his better angel would be lolling, gripping this line and that rope, waiting to alarm his second client. But why did he no longer crave to appease himself with revenge? In the rippled clarity of Grado Lagoon on a late spring evening, with their halyard puckishly flying the Wallachian flag, he asked to see the treasure again, and when his master obliged him, he stared into the crystal without expression. Cirtovich said: I often wonder what it thinks. Do you see how it opens its eye just now? I'm sure it can understand us.— By all the saints! cried Vasojević.— And he turned away, only to perceive the simulacrum of that tubular entity floating at its ease off the bow, as it stared upward with its huge blue eyes, with a single kelplike tentacle poised as if mockingly, helpfully or warningly over the helm.

That summer Stefano Cirtovich lost a cargo of Japanese silks, and Jovo made up the loss. For this benevolence they disliked him all the more. Gratitude, of course, expressed itself in a dinner, and Stefano's wife Elisabeth, an Austrian woman, served them a nice fat fish in a fish-shaped dish, with fresh bread, olives, cheese and Friulian wine—an adequate meal, which Marija complimented, while Tanya and Liljana ate shyly, with their faces bowed; Veljko got bored and pinched Tanya under the table; Vuk and Nicola were both at sea, and the other unmarried sisters were at home, because Marija wished to save Elisabeth from too great an effort. It was sunset, the sky scarlet as a Serbian cloak at a festival, when Florio appeared, only for an instant, he said, and only to greet his brothers. While Stefano sent the wine around again, Florio laughingly repeated what his youngest daughter Vesna had said: Oh, father, how I would love you to bring me a Turk's head to play with!—Jovo Cirtovich kept quiet. Tanya grew wide-eyed. The next time they came out of church together, Florio took his arm and invited him to join his brothers and uncles in a raid upon a Turkish convoy at Trebinje. Didn't he care to strike again for Mother Serbia?— Spare me your principles, said Jovo Cirtovich. I've seen you sell cows to Janissaries to turn an extra few ducats.— After this, his brothers accused him of putting on Turkish pantalons. He had heard it all before. That night he said to Tanya, who had asked no questions: Someone forgot that it's better to fight for the Heavenly Kingdom.— Yes, father, but when will you tell me how to do that?— Marija glided sadly into the room, so he said: That's all now, Tanyotchka. Have you calculated how many hogsheads can fit in the *Beograd*?— Yes, father, and I have an idea about the ballast . . .— He stroked her hair.

Florio and Massimo cornered him in the warehouse. They said: You've got luck, brother; there's no denying that.

Jovo Cirtovich replied nothing.

Brother, they said, we've been talking. It seems you've kept Father's legacy for yourself—

Watch what you say. Haven't I given you bastards money and ships?

We praise you for that. But treasure comes easily to you. The other day Lazzaro brought up a certain point. You see, we've come to believe that what Father left you—

Measure a wolf's tail once he's dead, said Jovo Cirtovich. Now get out.

Again and again, Jovo Cirtovich asked his only friend whether he ought to show the treasure to Tanya. What was he to do with her anyhow? None of his sons possessed her aptitude, but how could a woman command ships? A little shyly, Vasojević said: It might be given unto her to petition him. She's a good girl, so sweet and so religious; if she said to him, *sainted Lazar, please return to us,* how could he deny her?— You're too kind, said his master, smiling a little, because he believed every bit of it. And then the grimaces of care remasked both their faces, so that any stranger might have said: Two more refugees from the Turks!— But schools of gold ducats swam in; they were more successful every year. Better still, Cirtovich now decoded that papyrus from Heracleopolis, acquired on Vasojević's second voyage to Egypt, for a trifling price. Recognizing from the idiosyncratic excellence of the handwriting the geometer called High-Seeing, whose observations had been verified by Ptolemy, and being further reassured by the perfect errorlessness in the Greek, not to mention the later addition of a very specific critical sign before the lemma, which implied that some other careful intelligence had found the treatise worth considering in detail, Cirtovich saw fit to trust it as corroboration of what he had formerly merely hoped for: Nearly every voyage became possible. The night skies were dangerous, to be sure, but certain vibrating chords could speed a ship from orbit to orbit; then there were starry tangent courses, and a spiral way, inhabited by a kind of current, which passed through all the Spheres. The mind that believed itself condemned to a stationary or isolated existence committed a crime against itself. No reason remained not to dare ever higher. That night in the warehouse the two friends quaffed a bottle of Friulian wine, dreaming aloud about stars. Feeling quizzical, the master laid down the dark-glass on one of their astrological maps. The topic had turned to Jupiter, whose inhabitants, wrote High-Seeing, had invented a red fire of superlunary potency. The Great Red Spot was their work. The man who obtained some of this stuff would be invincible in war. So those two rode their hobbyhorse, and envisioned liberating Serbia forever. All the while their companion lay watching them with its electric-blue eye. Sometimes it glowed all through its body, and ever so often it uttered pinpricks of radiance. Rising suddenly, Vasojević said, upraising his hand like Saint Mikhail: If I ever saw any such monster on the high seas, I'd take an axe to its arms!— Careful, my friend, murmured Jovo Cirtovich.

It was Vasojević who first proposed (having dreamed strangely, about some distressed ship seeking to forge over a sandbar) that they might be imperiled or polluted, not by their end, of course, but by their means.— No, said his master. We're getting old, so the world draws in; that's all. Everything seems uglier as we age.

But why?

They watched each other carefully, to discover how well they slept.

On one occasion, as the two men completed the conveyance of a certain trunk from a fallen favorite of the Sultan to a hireling of the Holy Roman Empire, having rented a stevedore's skiff, they were rowing toward the Ponterosso when Vasojević's gratitude came out; one of Cirtovich's rivals (I think it was Luca Morelli) stood up at the extreme edge of the working half-bridge of little boats attached to the stone slab on the west side of the Canal Grande, shading his eyes with his hands as he gazed after them: to starboard there was Vasojević in the red cloak, his silhouetted oar wounding the skiff's reflection in the blue-black water, while to port sat Cirtovich, himself entirely a shadow, as was his side of the boat; and they passed beneath the Ponterosso without looking back, while on the east side of the canal, obscure within the dark crowd of beggars, idlers, prostitutes, and those who waited for their men to come home (not to mention Cirtovich's brothers outstretching their longfingered hands), the consignee, which is to say the hireling, drifted slowly toward the sail-furled, forest-masted ships, where on the third gangway he was supposed to receive delivery, all parties well aware that their meeting, once accomplished, would be no more a secret, although since he had prepared, in Cirtovichian fashion, a closed carriage, any reaction of the Triestini would comprise a negligible quantity; and just before they emerged from the Ponterosso's shadow, the two Serbs, sensing the observation of the man on the bridge of boats behind them, turned not toward him, but, being discreet men, toward each other; and in that instant the work of the thing in the neck-pouch advanced itself: Each found horror in the other's sight, and knew it. After that, were they friends? They would have said so.

10

Nicola was home from sea; he had gone cruising with Stefano, and even seen a hundred-cannon English ship with her long bowsprit-proboscis rigged out in glory; Stefano called him a good boy, brave, intelligent and quick to work, but perhaps too softhearted. Nor did he have his father's luck with winds. Then Vasojević was absent for a year, during which time his master's eldest daughter Nada died in childbirth—a clear case of strangulation of the womb. Marija Cirtovich mourned extremely over this, and travelled to Serbia in a closed ship, together with Massimo's elder maidservant Ivica, Srdjana being needed to keep house in Trieste. Marija's husband, although he uttered both tears and prayers, had no leisure to visit Nada's grave. On that gloomy voyage Florio was the captain, since he had failed to clear a profit on a cargo of Caribbean sugar, which even Captain Robert (may he count his teeth on the palm of his hand!) could have sold for a profit, and so Jovo thought it best to set him something easy to do. So he commended Marija to Florio's care, along with several well-chosen bereavement gifts for the widower's family, who, truth to tell, had already put that grief behind them, since they were preparing to assassinate a certain Turkish bey of exceptional cruelty. As for Jovo Cirtovich, while he cherished a mild partiality toward their lurid doings, these could accomplish but the merest local effect; he preferred to command and underwrite Vasojević's voyage, which had been intended to establish the coordinates of that singing chord which runs down the earth, parallel to the Longitude of Death, and on which there lies a certain island where a white boulder stands out on white scree. Beneath this boulder hides a chest (or possibly a human-headed cremation urn), and within this, they say, lies an object especially esteemed by Jesus Christ the Victor.— While Marija was absent, he grew still closer to Tanya, dreaming less about his ten-armed angel, which could emit either black or white ink from the funnel in its head. Again and again, he despairingly appraised his children. Now that Veljko had grown older, he could no longer deny that this third son of his resembled steel badly forged. Aside from Tanya, the daughters were no more or less than he had expected them to be.

One day he was down at the harbor, that gently panting beast whose fur was the masts of ships, where one of Stefano's sons informed him that Marija was nearly home; Florio had sent tidings from Ragusa. He thanked the young man. Now was surely the moment to instruct Tanya, as indeed he might have done, were it not for the dark-glass demon's warnings, which reminded him of a crow cawing just before the rain comes.

Srdjana came running to kiss his wife's hand, with many thanks to the saints for her return. Marija had gone entirely grey. It seemed unlikely that she had ever been a slender young woman breasted like an hourglass. Jovo Cirtovich greeted her affectionately enough. Within the hour he overheard her confiding to Florio that someone must have cast the evil eye upon her husband.

The triumphs which he had once expected for himself might yet be accomplished, if and only if the center of the Sphere of Spirits corresponded to the center of this earth. (How foolish and useless to seek the Sphere of Fixed Stars before exploring the Sphere of Skulls!) Tanyotchka had caught up with all that month's accounts, so to gratify her, he watched her calculate the distance from the center of the earth to Saturn, which she accomplished very nicely by means of arcs and chords, according to the new method which he and Vasojević had discovered. Marija and the other daughters were carding wool. His wife looked ancient; his pity became guilt, so that she made him feel all the more lonely. But Tanya . . . Again he asked himself whether he should have listened to Marija, and confined the girl to female work. But it was to Tanya if anyone that he'd hand over his father's bequest. Massimo had now come right out and asked him for it—but Jovo Cirtovich disagreed with his brothers about many things, not least the magnitude although not the injustice of the Turkish terror. Massimo would use the treasure for revenge, in the service of Death the Huntsman; worse yet, he'd call that liberation. Sometimes Jovo Cirtovich grew melancholy without cause, and sought out one or another of his brothers, although he would never meet them at the "Heaven's Key" tavern. Whenever they exhausted their words, which occurred quickly among these hardheaded men, they spoke admiringly of their late father. None admitted that they had feared him, in part because none could have said why, for hadn't they themselves made a bloodily brutal crew, as the uncles still did in Serbia? Jovo Cirtovich, the head of that family, kept silent. He felt sure that had their father now come striding out of darkness, with dark clots of blood falling from his pale breast, he alone would not have fled. So he stared down his brothers, smiling bitterly, longing to get back to his accounts. Friulian wine was becoming still more profitable in Russia; wax prices were falling; from Tartaria he could buy four magic scrolls for the price of three. And his brothers read his disregard, and hated him. On Saint Lazar's Day he strung silver coins around their daughters' necks.— As for his sons, too clearly he perceived that they were obedient but feeble, even Vuk, the most aggressive, who lacked the faith and daring to cast his ducats upon the waters—nothing to hope for there. Nicola, the rightful heir, was too greedy; Alexander remained yet young for judgment. Only Tanya possessed the mind and spirit to use his dark-glass properly. (She said:

Father, I need to finish weaving this cloth or Mother will be angry.) So far as he could see, the whole business remained on his shoulders. Commending Marija and the children to the saints, he accordingly made one of his own rare voyages, this time merely to Bar, where he closeted himself with a Father Anzulović, who was said to know more than anyone about the posthumous doings of our sainted Lazar. Cirtovich poured out Friulian wine, and the priest proposed a toast to the destruction of the Turks, may the earth pursue them and the sea vomit them up!— The guest raised his glass in silence. Frowning, Father Anzulović urged him to ride to Kosovo. Lazar's sword, which would facilitate the deed proposed, was certainly beneath the threshold of the Red Mosque, as a holy document now proved. A brave man could do anything, the priest said. Smiling sadly, Cirtovich replied that he would consider the question. Instead he sailed home to Trieste, because he lacked Vasojević to help him, and because Massimo was incompetent in the countinghouse, while Florio was too rash; besides, he could not forget how Marija had prayed to the souls of drowned men, in order that they would watch over him, and how when he said goodbye to Tanya she had looked up at him, her face already glowing with tears. Although he made his customary good way even against head seas, the squid-thing kept peeping in at him from under the foresail, whether or not in warning never clarified itself. No sooner had he arrived at the Ponterosso than he proceeded to church, praying for a long time to Saint Lazar, in longing to know where the heavenly kingdom lay. He decided not to burgle the Red Mosque. Massimo begged for another loan, which he granted. Stefano caught Captain Robert sneaking aboard the *Lazar,* and pitched him into the harbor. Petar needed money to repair the carriage. There was a dutiful letter from Gordana, who was pregnant again, praise God; Marija had the colic; he physicked her himself, for the squid-thing had long since taught him which herbs were best. Next he dispatched Vasojević, who had indeed verified the coordinates of that singing chord of earth, not to Kosovo but all the way to Dejima Island, in order to barter with Dutchmen for the Japanese porcelains which only they could get. On Saint Sava's Day the two men ascended into the countinghouse and toasted their purpose. I'll hold onto the wind with my teeth! said his old friend, making the old joke; now he too possessed wind-luck. They shook hands. Cirtovich watched through the window as that two-sailed *bragozzo* passed out of the Canal Grande, bearing her officers into the harbor-night where the *Lazar* awaited them, and through the spyglass Cirtovich saw the frown of grief and worry on Vasojević's face. That voyage proved fair and lucrative, to be sure; each of Tanya's sisters presently received a chrysanthemum-patterned robe, while her brothers were delighted to possess curved and double-grooved Japanese *tanto* daggers. Marija took custody of many ducats, not to mention a *kakiemon*-style vase decorated with birds. It was a successful adventure, for a fact, and after that the Triestini stood in even greater awe of him; all the same, Tanya could not help but note the day that the *Lazar* returned, when her father came in leading Vasojević by the hand; he bade them bring out the wine-jug, and make the triple sign of the cross; they drank to God, the Holy Cross and the Holy Trinity, and then of course to Prince Lazar, after which Vasojević and her father confabulated in the garden, and when she ran silently up to what she childishly called "the tower room," to peep at them, they reminded her of tired fishermen with empty nets draped over the mast. But they reentered the house smiling; oh, yes, the business prospered, the grain-shed grew full again, and that week her father dedicated a gift not only to the Serbian Orthodox church but even to the cathedral at San Giusto. People now compared him to Count Giovanni Vojnovich, the hero of the *Madonna dell'Assunta*. Her mother looked as if she were expecting him to confess something. In the garden the lilies were brilliant. A mountain of crates with Japanese characters on them rose up in the coach shed, but only for a fortnight; and two days after they had disappeared, the *Sava* embarked for Venice, Genoa and Bar. This brought in more money than ever, and yet her father did not seem satisfied. Rereading his face, unable to stop hunting for weakness, she spied out, for the first time, uncertainty in his pouchy eyes. This unwelcome fact, which might have ushered her into pity and horror, she managed to set aside. Of course he resembled other people, in that he could not know everything; he had never found out (or had he?) about her peeping into his chest of death-books. Perceiving that she was anxious about something, he stroked her cheek, and she closed her eyes, won back to certainty. Why not escape ill consequences forever?

Once when Tanya sat studying the origin of angels in his *Novum*

Organum, he was beside her, shaking his head over a Chinese Qing Dynasty amulet in the form of a giant bronze coin with a square hole in it. The girl kept quiet. Presently her father fetched a loupe. He copied down the inscription. Then, smiling hopelessly, he handed the thing to her, saying: Here's another present for you.

11

Father, promise you won't be angry.
  Well?
  Father, what do you wear around your neck?

12

Often he grasped for relief by justifying, mostly to himself but sometimes to the patient, silent Vasojević, his careful concealments, which his elders' dark doings against the Turkish overlordship had established in his character from boyhood; the usual practices of any mercantile man deepened that groove of secrecy; the nervous, angry, weary despair which death's manifold proximities inflicted cut him off most of all. He had anticipated that sharing his strange knowledge with Vasojević would lighten his loneliness. Oh, they remained friends without a doubt; each possessed the other's pities and dreads. As for the treasure, that too they held in common, if it did not hold them. No wonder that he scrupled to bequeath it to Tanya!

He remembered his wife in her dark dress and cap, sitting in a high-backed chair, nursing Tanyotchka; he must have just returned from Muscovy. In the garden, the doves were speaking to one another in their semiliquid voices. And he seemed to remember Marija's face glowing against a red curtain, but he no longer knew where that had been. Nicola and Vuk, why did he retain so few images of them? Well, if he hadn't sent them voyaging with their uncles, the family would die out. They had better learn the business, being unfitted for the other thing. Besides, let his brothers raise them up to be Turk-haters; no doubt that was right, even if he lacked the stomach for it.

The creature in the dark-glass was not in and of itself, so far as he knew, evil. If he declined to tell the priests about it, that was merely on account of their petty understandings. What he hid—that thing itself, and the unhealthy emotions which its guardianship stimulated—was of smaller account than its hiddenness. And since to hide was to deny, how pleasant to close his eyes!

He believed with all his soul that he had lived a life no more sinful than any other. If he had killed men at sea to save what was his, if he had on occasion made sharp bargains, such acts were necessary if one were to get on in the world. In any event he would be hated for his success. The longing to be rid of that loathsome treasure never left him—but then he would be shamed before his dead ancestors. By what right could he forever alienate this legacy from his family? Tanya would make wise use of it, to help her mother and the other children, after he was gone. Why shouldn't she employ it for greater good? She, who in the course of her education had unswervingly dissected the brainlike, fungoid tissues of the chambered nautilus, possessed what he once had; even though she could never command a ship, she might yet do something of which he could dream.

Of course Marija wished to marry her off; fifteen was old enough, she said.— I need her at home, he replied.

Cirtovich, discerning that the lot of the most loving fathers is sadness, had already begun compromising with doom by establishing his daughters in the best marriages he could, endowing them with gold, land and blessings, while tying the sons-in-law to him through benignity, intimidation and mutual interest. But when it came to Tanyotchka, he did more, although not too much, maintaining over her, ever more invisibly, his paternal shield, regretfully aware that unpicked fruit withers on the vine, and therefore that protecting our children from the quotidian nastiness of life is a self-poisoning strategy. For Tanya, therefore, he sought only one good beyond the aspirations of other parents: He intended to save her from death.— But perhaps that wasn't right, or worth whatever it would cost.

He had trained up his sailors to great knowledge in the hope that one day they might carry him to the sphere that the dark-glass being came from. If the soul is the center of the circle called consciousness, then cannot other circles be drawn, to calculate the center of malignancy, doom or absence? Therein lies the place to which all mankind must carry war. What if Jovo Cirtovich could hunt down foul and sniffling death itself,

and impale it forever in its cave? Four years ago, thanks to a Turkish an-
notation of the *Kitab Tahdid al-Amakin,* he and Vasojević had finally
completed their plotting of our globe's Tropic Nodes, from either of
which, when Jupiter is right, one may sail into superlunary spheres, and
perhaps even into that great blue dome of ultramarine, the Sphere of
Fixed Stars, with its stars of silver and gold arrayed in as many constellations as there are kinds of beasts, fishes, monsters, demons, angels,
swords, hairpins and crowns. One night in that tower in Niš, calculating
in units of the fourth order from al-Biruni's coordinates and Osman's
timetables, Vasojević had raised his sextant, then his spyglass; he cried
out. When Cirtovich tried to look, the instant had passed. Vasojević
swore that on the golden sun at the center of that blue hemisphere he
could see Christ Himself peering out, holding a Bible against His chest
and wearing a halo which was brighter than sunfire. Inspired, yet sickened by disappointment, Cirtovich quizzed him again and again. They
could go there! And if they bowed down before Christ in His own house,
what good would not be theirs? Until dawn they spoke, but with the sun's
advent came the dark-glass monster, hovering like Beelzebub, lashing its
tentacles against one after another of the horses of a dozen cantering
Turkish Janissaries who would torture them for sport. And so the two
Serbs crept away, to study death and attend to their fortunes. The next
time Cirtovich raised the subject, his friend replied: Yes, master, we
could go there, for a fact! But given *what would go with us,* I misdoubt
our reception . . .— That was when Cirtovich wondered how he could
bear it if they met that squid thing riding on Christ's shoulder, stretching
out its arms to warn them that here too, here even in heaven, was their
death? In short, the gruesome activity, ubiquitous and almost merry, of
their old friend had worn him down. Cirtovich had escaped from the
Turkish lands, founded his family anew, and heaped up wealth and
knowledge. Enough. His father had done less. So he told himself, staring
gloomily at Marija and Tanya, wishing, as ageing men will, to enjoy his
harvest untroubled. (He was getting old precisely because he had
achieved everything.) How fine to sit in his walled garden, never to see
even Vasojević again, God forgive them both! To close his eyes and listen
to the honeybees, enjoying the clink of gold ducats as Tanya counted receipts in the doorway, and then to fall asleep in the sunlight! But

whenever Tanya arose to help her mother or sisters, her long smooth arms flashing, he remembered again that she was a woman now, full fifteen years old, and ought to be married off soon for her happiness.— She was watching him strangely; what if she were unwell? Seeing her thus downcast, he slipped her a little pouch of Caribbean sugar.

13

Burning a lamp to Saint George, Marija Cirtovich knelt and moved her lips, longing to know why God had brought her all the way here in order to give her to a husband who was distracted. What was it that nibbled at his conscience with such sharp little teeth? For she thought him guilty, because she never knew him; and the reason she did not know him was that between his business and his dreads he lacked the wherewithal to be known, at least to her. (He had long since proved that if death itself be suspended there must remain some kind of permanent equilibrium; perhaps he should have wondered if this were his present state.) Over the years his hearing seemed to sharpen, until sometimes he even fancied that when he passed by cemeteries he could hear the worms moving underground, which naturally tortured him; sometimes at night he sat up beside her, listening; for it had come to him that perhaps the sound was made by the arms of that thing in his dark-glass. On the rare evenings for which he found the leisure, his daughter, hidden behind her long hair, turned the pages of books, her sweet thumbs shining in the candlelight; she begged him, could they please stay together just one more moment, and just one more? Smiling silently, he kissed her forehead, rose and buttoned himself into his old sheepskin coat, for the *bora* was blowing. Vuk and Nicola, lately returned from a voyage, were sitting sleepily by the fire. They rose to their feet. He gave them a moldy purse of ready silver (Imperial coins of Claudius Anazarbus), instructing them to pay their mother's outstanding invoices and advance Srdjana her wages. Massimo would carry out the rest. They nodded, not daring to ask questions. Well, well, he thought, let's see what they can do while I'm off in the world. He did not call Marija, and she did not trouble herself to come to him. For her he felt nothing but pity. As for his sons, he now caught their eyes flickering from one to the other, as if they shared some secret. Such was the business of young men. The carriage rattled him away. It was a fell hour, to be sure; the coachman was crossing himself for fear of highwaymen. Cirtovich slapped his shoulder and said: Trust me, Petar!— Then the man was shamed; he knew that nothing on earth could harm him while he stayed in the care of his master. For his part, Cirtovich had reason to feel hemmed in. The longer and thus more improbably he lived on, the more anxious, so it seemed, grew death to get him, so that the thing in the dark-glass appeared before him ever oftener. Last spring Petar had been conveying him up the hill to San Giusto, in order to receive two treasure-chests whose doors were studded with iron flowers, when it rose up ahead, grabbling at a boulder in its many blackish-green arms as if it meant to hurl a landslide on him.— Stop, said Cirtovich. Turn into the monastery courtyard, quickly!— Petar obeyed. And not two moments later, the boulder came rolling down the road, smashing a peasant's cart and then skipping down into the harbor.— By God, master! said Petar.— Get going, said Cirtovich.

They rode across the Ponterosso and into the piazza. Cirtovich could see the flicker of Vasojević's lamp in the upstairs window of the warehouse. Cirtovich blew his whistle. Two sleepy sailors ascended the steps of the quay, bearing torches.— You'll be safe with them, Petar. No boozing, now.

I promise, master.

Cirtovich approached the warehouse. Even through the gusts and the creakings of ships he could hear the stealthy plashing of the squid-thing's tentacles in the canal; so that must be where Death the Huntsman awaited him tonight. His rivals, the ones who on Sundays sang those *canzonette spirituali* with the black squareheaded notes suspended from the scarlet staves, huddled inside the "Heaven's Key," but Captain Robert, whom he merely scorned, lay darkly behind a wall of sacks and hogsheads, while the blood of this world pulsed round and round, the evening sky going purple and clouds coming in—no evil there, and none lurking in the doorway. Deploying one of his black iron keys, and then locking the door behind him, he ascended to his countinghouse. Vasojević had already risen and was extending his hand.

Well? said Cirtovich.

The map bears all the signs.

God hear you! We might be away this Christmas.

And gladly, master, if only—

But what about our third member? chuckled Cirtovich, and out came his father's treasure. Just then the demon's almost tuberous or vegetable quality was especially pronounced as it hung there within the magnifying crystal, its two tentacles immensely longer than its arms, which in turn were as frail and swirly as ribbons. The eye was closed.— Well, well, said the master, winking the thing away, we seem to have permission. Now tell me.

I sent another spy to that Turk Orlanović—

Oh, him! said the other, remembering that afternoon with Vasojević in Constantinople, as they leaned forward over cups of Turkish coffee on a round table, buying military secrets from that suave bey in the fez and pajama-skirts, yes, Orlanović, who cared only for money (and this was another of Cirtovich's secrets, that for him money itself was not an end), Orlanović, whose delicately curled moustaches and gentle eyes they disdained; thanks to his treachery, a certain Venetian raid had succeeded. After they completed the business, the two Serbs should have departed, but the dark-glass thing being quiescent just then, Cirtovich thought to reward his loyal companion, and likewise take his own pleasure; so there had been black-eyed Emina and Fata with the perfect-braided hair.

He smiled, but Vasojević bowed his head as mournfully as a new bride kissing the hearthstone. There remained that matter between them. Cirtovich threw down a pouch of yellow tobacco from Scutari for old times' sake.

He asked only ten ducats for it, Vasojević was saying. I gave him twelve, to keep him sweet. A warlock made it. Some Illyrian—

Shaking out the map from its leathern cylinder-case, they unrolled it, weighted the corners with lead bullets, and swooped down like seagulls upon that pictured island—for it was as secret as the face of another man's wife, or the night-errands of neighbors on the sea.

14

So they sailed south, far south, to what we call *the gloomy latitudes*, where the lichens curl as thickly as quarto pages on the windy dripping trees, and ferns lurk in the crevices of boulder-cliffs. Arriving at a certain nameless island, the *Lazar* shortened sail, then dropped her mudhook, following which the two friends rowed carefully between the remnant ice-floes (it was summer), beached their dinghy in the rocks, shouldered spades and vanished into a meadow of red peat at the forest's edge. Once more Jovo Cirtovich imagined that he was entering a new world. Meanwhile the crew, not being paid for idleness, killed a whole herd of elephant seals, skinned them and salted the meat. Whatever their master was up to, they retained confidence in his luck, and thus in theirs. They dreaded neither this dull grey sea flowing rapidly nowhere, with its ugly oily whitecaps breaking out like pustules, nor that other tall black island not far ahead—which place the Illyrian mapmaker had likewise declined to name.

Praying to Saint Sava, who rules over snow and ice, and offering their most heartfelt invocation to Prince Lazar, our two principals now followed the river to the gentle slope of dark scree on whose crest the white boulder waited. (Perhaps they should have also prayed to Saint Thomas.) The wind blew stronger, so they sat their fur *kalpaks* on their heads. It was the hour between the two dog watches. Their aspirations resembled the glow of golden icons in a dark room.

Do you see it now? said Cirtovich.

God help us, yes! Master, don't you? It's wriggling all its arms down in there, and it's watching us through the ground—

That's enough, Vasojević.

They drew a magic circle in the sand, then kindled a fire and burned mastic, aloes and frankincense. Through the fragrant smoke they passed a pentacle drawn in scarlet ink upon a virgin lambskin. Then they commenced to dig; and before we describe the object of it all, before the corpse arrives, carried through the window by two stoic men, the mother need do no more than stare into the night, waiting and worrying, while the boy called Jovo gets for an instant longer to keep the precious certainty of his father's invulnerability. Then comes the sight and above all the touch of death. Their father has fallen. Death has ruined him—he who should never die. But now everything will be put right; any instant now our spade-edges will bite success.

And so their shovels struck wet sand, then ice, then gravel, and suddenly something hard and hollow—wood or metal?— The latter, of course—a bronze casket, as ancient as the three broken basilicas at Salona.

Remember, master, what the Patriarchs have said: *There is no resurrection without death.*

I'm not afraid. Are you?

Didn't Lazar choose death?

Spoken like a Serb! And now, dear friend, let us be armed with the sword of God's Word!

Adonai, they sang, then offered up a last prayer to Saint Sava, hoping that if they could accomplish this one magic thing their lives would be perfected, or at least mended. Although he should have kept his mind on the ritual, Cirtovich could not help but think on Tanyotchka biting her lip in half-mastered grief as he departed their home. Vasojević was lucky never to have begun a household. His master knew that if they ever did return, the house would be smaller and sadder, the people older.

Now listen, Vasojević. What's next may require fast work—

With all respect, I'm still young enough!

I've never doubted that. But do we agree on what to wish for?

By all the saints! We came here to—

Yes, on our own behalf. But what about Prince Lazar? We could seize this chance to bring him back. Wasn't that our old dream? Think about it. We could save our tortured country.

Or defeat death itself, as you used to say—

Knowing from the despairing hope in each other's eyes what they both longed for above all else, they fell silent. Then Vasojević said: Lazar, God praise him, made his choice and can take care of himself. I don't say this for my own sake.

So you relinquish that dream?

Just as you say.

And death?

Endless life, and endlessly seeing that face before me—well, I'd rather not.

Raising up the chest, they tried to open it, but although green light began to bleed out as soon as they undid the clasps, the task required violence. They prayed once more, longing for their church's smell of candle wax. With shovels they attacked the lid until it was a ruin like the multicracked shell of a boiled egg squeezed in the hand. Then they twisted with their Saracen blades, and it sprang aside.

Up rose their old companion like an emanation of the Great Godhead, closer and more corporeal than ever before, freed from the glass, neither larger nor smaller than it needed to be to fill the newly available space, its flesh breaking out in purple-brown ventral chromatophores, and all ten arms beating a tattoo against the sides of the casket before reaching out into the chilly air. The two men stepped back once it began discharging liquid from the funnel in its head, Vasojević longing to sink a boat-hook into it and Cirtovich imagining those arms curling and tearing at his face. But fixing on them its jewel, that beautiful lidless eye, it grew calm, as if it recognized and trusted its friends. Before it had invariably appeared omniconscious, not to mention gruesomely hateful on account of the hatefulness which on their behalf it busily foresaw. And now it opened its beak like a baby bird. Which of us would not on occasion prefer to be dependent?

Almost as suave here as in Philadelphia, Cirtovich propitiated the thing with Friulian wine until its tentacles wriggled as sweetly as a baby's toes. What did he care? After all, not even it could match his childhood dread of his father.

He drew out the dark-glass, proving to himself and his companion that it was not only transparent, but void. It seemed that the monster could not exist in two places simultaneously. Then, uttering another prayer, he poured another bottle of Friulian crimson into the creature's beak. Drunkenly, wine drooling out of its beak, it draped one tentacle around his neck—the first time in all these years that it had ever touched him. Well, it felt no stranger than touching a corpse! Trusting in it not to hurt him—after all, what had it done him but good?—he knelt down, and raised it to his heart. At once it flushed red-violet, as does the giant octopus when disturbed. And Jovo Cirtovich felt moved to tenderness. But seeing Vasojević standing quietly stubborn in his views, whatever they might have been, he set the creature gently down in the rocks.

In the box beneath where it had lain was another casket, which he withdrew. From it issued the scent of an unknown flower, but when he opened the lid, there was the head of his father, smiling at him. So grief came to him in truth.

Are you my father?

No.

Who are you?

I am the one you sought, it said, and its voice resembled the vivid strangeness of the gold on certain Byzantine icon panels, which as one alters one's angle of view appears to shift its underhue from cool reptilian green to sanguinary red. Around it shone a soft light whose rays brought sweetness and tears.

We have come for a wish, said Cirtovich.

What would you?

Hesitating, thinking perchance to dicker with this being as with some Cincar trader, he demanded: Will you advise us? Shall we rid ourselves of that nightmare?

If you choose. What would you?

Or should I ask to hear death's voice? Or preserve my favorite daughter forever, or find out where my father has flown?

Master, said Vasojević, I pray you to improve this opportunity for the best. Never mind you or me, or even Tanya (and you know how I love her). What do I care for us, if we can make our land a graveyard for Turks?

Can you do that? Cirtovich asked his father's head.

I can. Decide now, or gain nothing.

Cirtovich, inspired by his noble friend, was about to call for the restoration to earth of Prince Lazar when the dark-glass entity returned to its senses and reached out, the suckers on the undersides of its arms scintillating with the pearlescence of certain amphorae. When it touched Vasojević, that man, who never in any emergency, even a battle, had expressed anything but coolness, cried out like a convict being branded on the forehead; and Cirtovich, compassionating him in that moment, shouted: Free us from *that*!

The head smiled sadly, then disappeared. So did the creature, the two caskets and the hole which had been dug. The dark-glass cracked.

Vasojević, did it injure you?

No, master, barely a sting—

Cirtovich closed his eyes. Upraising her chin, Marija stared at him gloomily. Nicola, Vuk and Veljko stretched out their arms to him like drowning men. As for Tanya, that young woman, pulling her long hair diagonally across her forehead, prepared to go out as if she did not perceive him. Well, this was but his fancy. But what if she now began to suffer? And in truth, he felt ashamed before the shade of his father. Well, Massimo would have done far worse; he would have wished for the ointment which transforms a naked man into a wolf.

Jovo Cirtovich seemed to hear royal processions departing in faraway crownlands.

He opened his eyes. He took his father's vacant treasure and hurled it down. There alone those two men stood, on that low hummocky peat-island which was studded with striped rocks and cut by those narrow silvery streams whose multiple forks fell into the sea.

15

Just as after a rain the Triestine sky is of an impeccably African brightness, thus it should now have been in the soul of Jovo Cirtovich, for he had attained his heart's desire. Vasojević stood leaning on a spade.—
Well, said Cirtovich, did we act rightly?

We shall soon know, doubtless.

I could have demanded knowledge—

Foreknowledge we had.

This I've never asked you: When you saw the Sphere of Stars, was Lazar there?

Of course, master, and seated on Christ's right hand. He smiled and beckoned to me, and not with one finger, either. You did ask that, and I told you. We would have been welcomed—

Well, there's nothing to prevent us now. What do you say? Shall we refresh our crew, and then sail to heaven?

Vasojević hung his head. Within the hour he seemed not merely to age, but to grow haggard and unclean.

16

Oh, yes, once they had rid themselves of the dark-glass thing, they should have felt at peace, and even righteous; but so long had they lived (Cirtovich especially) in anticipation of its ominous appearances that not seeing it refined their anxieties almost unbearably; for ambuscadoes had been laid—all the more diligently for Cirtovich since he evaded them with such defiant success—and now he could not find them out. Students of probability theory will assert that his peril of death at any given instant remained no greater now than half a century ago; but he knew death to be a kind of person, or at least an entity with multiple writhing arms. Therefore, death hunted him actively and intelligently. This might have been an error. Then again, nothing is as hateful to nature as incorruptibility. High time for the grave to take him! Thus he believed; and his face grew ghastlier than before; he might have been a prisoner condemned to row until death in a Turkish galley—but no; that sort of wretch remains chained to others, for better and worse; while the most hideous quality of Cirtovich's existence, as ever, was *solitariness,* even though he kept longing to stroke Tanya's hair.

In his father's house in Serbia there had been a strange icon, depicting one of those cubical Biblical cities where lean brown men bore long scarlet coffins on their shoulders, ascending and descending clay stairs so that the mummies they carried could exchange one tomb for another— and everything mendaciously embellished with gold. Now he knew the meaning of it.

So he holed himself up, avoiding even Vasojević, who likewise withdrew from inessential intercourse; and they sailed north, laboring in cross-seas, wandering through all twenty-eight Mansions of the Moon. Even Friulian wine could not cheer them. But what had they to fear? Their future resembled the weary wounded man whom one meets at the end of a trail of werewolf-blood. Vasojević was looking still older; as for Cirtovich, he was now as fishy-bearded and bleary-eyed as that famous silver likeness of Saint Blasius. For years he had found no use for the superannuated worthies of Ragusa. Now he felt like one of them. Had he gazed in a mirror, he would have confessed that his face was no longer a bland mask; but what it expressed he could not make out. He supposed himself ready to acknowledge his losses, which so often until now had seemed to swivel into sudden gains. Behind his breastbone there seemed to dwell something hard, round and smooth. His consciousness kept fingering it as if it were a marble, turning it round and round in order to know it or, better yet, to massage it down into nothingness; but it would not go away; it was fear, when he had expected to win peace. And some other feeling still less creditable settled into his guts like an anchor digging in with both flukes. What was it? Although they remained as lovely to him as the bloody Serbian earth, even thoughts of Marija and his loyal sons and his daughters running silently to and fro on the carpets in their stockinged feet, gathering hams, potatoes, onions and wines for the welcoming feast, could scarcely warm him. Besides, this time he brought no silver coins to string around the necks of his women, and so he felt ashamed. At last his hours had become sad and definite. He fancied he could hear jointless fingers stealthily caressing the hull. But his ears had been for so many years disturbed by fanciful things that he doubted them even more than he did his own heart. Believing him to be weakening in luck or goodness, the sailors began to doubt him likewise, although they could not yet show it. Meanwhile he said to himself: If I die now I never need touch Tanya's corpse—oh, God, that the beautiful delicacy of my daughter's skin should be burned by death's sucker-arms!— And so he went on hoping for life, at least for her.

You're holding up like a true Serb, Vasojević.

Thanks, master. You know, an octopus shows no sign of pain when we cast him into the fire—

One morning when they had almost regained the coast of Africa a pallid wave arose, spread itself into fingers and sought to pluck him from the forecastle. Cirtovich ducked away, but it got Vasojević, seizing him in both tentacles, then speeding him down into the clutch of those long, tapering arms which were cratered with teeth-ringed suckers, and as the monster submerged they had one murky glimpse of the brown beak opening; and so after that Cirtovich lacked anyone who could understand him, excepting Tanya, of course—but not even she could have helped him reason out the causality of this latest death. Was that submarine predator the same as the devil he'd cast away, or was it a visitation of God, meant to rebuke him for dismissing his better angel? Either way, he commenced to fear that his own doom would come from the sea. The mate, who loved Vasojević, had proposed to lower the creeper, in order to hook and grapple that kraken into reach of their guns, but Cirtovich refused, saying merely: It would kill us all.— A certain sailor with a bearded old head resembling Saint Stephen's, whose limestone flesh keeps smoothening and blurring with time, whispered that their captain was now an evil-eyed Jonah, which most of them immediately believed, and had another man been lost on that voyage, they might have risen up and marooned him there in the African Sea. Withdrawing from them, he knelt before Saint Lazar's icon, and prayed for his friend, but almost without feeling. He had squared off his dreams into a single thing as flat-sided and sharp-cornered as the heel of a mast, and now sat in his cabin thinking about Tanya. This year he'd present her with a real woman's dagger to wear at her hip. It pleased him to think of her at home doing the accounts. As for Marija, the love he had bestowed upon her was as the coins he had thrown into his father's coffin. Her lilies must be blooming up now. He wished he were sitting in the garden, listening to the murmurings of the dovecote; but then Marija would be out there with her back turned. And so he grew bitter against other living beings, and the more bitter he became, the less his sailors liked him. Although they were all adept at trapping the chambered nautilus in a baited basket, they caught nothing precious, as had never yet befallen men employed by Jovo Cirtovich.

Avoiding Italy because they had nothing to sell, and because there were more customs vessels on that side, they kept in sight of the limestone windings of the Adriatic coast, which were already bright with vineyards, grey with olive trees and green with palms; it was almost as if Cirtovich intended to trade there as usual, but they passed Spaleto, Ragusa, Zadar and Rijeka, sailing close-hauled to the wind. The sky was yellow. There was a tiny islet in the channel between Maun and Pag off which a certain chest had been sunk; their captain had once promised that its contents belonged to all of them, and now they demanded it.— Straight on, he told the helmsman, and now they were already level with Škrda. Embittered, they whispered for the first time of murdering him, but even now feared his luck, being uncertain whether it could not flare back after this waning. And the weather was so strange; the *bora* failed to blow. Two swabbies muttered when he set them to oiling the strakes, and he nearly punished them, but no blood for violence remained in him, and he could not have said why because he no longer understood himself, if indeed he ever had. They could have had their chest, for all he cared; merely for his own safety had he denied it to them, since they had asked so insolently, with their eyes like candles. They all disgusted him;

when had they ever dreamed anything worthwhile? Once he had studied such men, and quickly mastered the study; perhaps if he had repeated the course he might have learned something new to distract himself, such as, how can men live rightly and perhaps even happily without seeking but the merest perpetuation of life? Or would this study merely have ruined him further? Curiously ashamed, as if blood marked the leech of their foresail, they sailed west by northwest, then northwest until they gained Pula to the starboard. And so they drew into the Golfo di Trieste, or, as he called it when he was young, the *Tržaški zaliv*. To him it all seemed dark and dirty, as if sky, sea and land alike had been smeared with lead. In his mouth dwelled a poisonous taste.

The *Lazar* came in on one of those calm days when the harbor was blue almost like Egyptian faience, and for a moment he imagined how lonely it used to be outside the walls of Trieste—a century ago, that was; now the walls were all muddled. It was near about Easter when they shortened sail. Seaweed fouled their ground tackle, and the canvas needed cutching. The mariners' families stood silhouetted on the Ponterosso, waiting for their men. Jovo Cirtovich longed for the old marble font he had installed in his garden, and for that quiet daughter of his, so meek and obedient toward her mother, so understanding of him. But when she'd peeped into his weary eyes, how would she feel? Better, perhaps, if he never came home! Doubtless Marija would be disappointed, since he'd failed to make them any richer—

Anchoring among the ranks of high-masted ships outside the Canal Grande, he set the crew to transferring the seal-hides and certain other items, I suspect of a contraband nature, to a Venetian vessel whose captain he knew, then posted a light guard, led his sailors ashore and paid them off; as you might imagine, they were more perplexed than satisfied. In every tavern spread the news that he had grown unlucky. It was good that Vasojević had not married; no one dependent would be impoverished by his death. But where was Petar? Why were his sons and brothers all absent? Cirtovich feared that some evil had befallen his house. Or had they somehow learned of his doings, and so forsaken him? But Tanyotchka would never do that, nor even Marija, no matter that she regarded him with the sad eyes of a silver deer; it wasn't as if he'd abjured God! By now he shrank from everybody, believing that they recoiled from him. And so, as if fearing that misfortune might sniff him out, he passed the night alone in his countinghouse, locked in, sleepless, lighting no lamp; but a sharp-eyed busybody who spied into the upstairs windows late that night (for instance, Luca Morelli) might have seen the palest flicker behind the shutter: Cirtovich was burning a candle to Saint George, and another to Prince Lazar, with his eyes lowered over the ducats which his hands were counting: yes, still enough for Marija, Tanya and the rest if they grew more careful. All the same, he'd now return to importing Ragusan salt into Serbia and gold and silver threads from Constantinople. This had brought good money when he was young. He pulled off his sheepskin stockings; he opened his shirt. He groped at his throat, then remembered that he had no dark-glass anymore. Once upon a time he had gone adventuring into the private courtyards of Mostar and Sarajevo where the rich Turks raised roses and lovely young women. Now it was eerie enough merely to come home. Why had he avoided the Orthodox church, which was almost directly across the canal? He'd always been a wise avoider of law-courts, but never before had he declined an opportunity to whisper to his saints. Some years ago Vasojević had ceased attending services except for high masses, because the main candelabrum hung as straight in the darkness as one of those squids who dangle their arms in a tight vertical cluster as they troll. Cirtovich had never been thus affected. But at every loud sea-swish he flinched nowadays. He sat over his ledgers and invoices, discovering that Massimo had as usual left receipts lying all in a muddle like a rotten heap of cast-off sails, that the *Beograd* was in late from Bergen and that the Cincar traders had overcharged him for wool. Nothing had altered; he could have been silently awaiting delivery of some new folio. Unlocking his secret coffers, he found untouched his separate bags of money, each ready for expected and unexpected deposits. He remembered a spring afternoon thirteen years ago now when he had stood inside the cathedral with Marija and the children, the many votive candles burning on their iron tree, and he raised baby Tanyotchka in his arms; she stretched out her hand at the rose-window, which glowed with rain-light like a chambered nautilus. Just last spring, for Saint Lazar's Day, he had endowed the church with thirty-one thousand five hundred florins; even the Vojnoviches had been impressed.

And once again his thoughts turned and turned round the bygone enigma of his father, which had sunk so far down into the darkness of years that he could scarce glimpse something twirling, like a weighted corpse going feetfirst under the sea; he felt desolate at its going, and yet horrified at the thought that he might see it again.

At dawn he came out, half expecting to see arrayed against him the crosses of black tar which certain Serbs paint upon their doors, to keep away vampires. But the piazza was free of these. On the horizon a twin-masted Austrian warship, evidently of Venetian make, was shortening sail. He saw in the doorway of the "Heaven's Key" an unknown Triestina, fifteen or sixteen years of age, with the small firm breasts of a Maenad on a Greek vase; she stood sweeping, and behind her, drunk, his old enemy Captain Robert. Not long prior to this latest voyage, Vasojević had proposed to open up the fellow with a bronze-winged harpoon. But Jovo Cirtovich had always hoped to interpose smoothness between himself and brutality. And so he trod the blood-red iron of the Ponterosso, with ships groaning and ropes hissing on either side, again avoiding the church; he could have hired a coach; he scarcely knew why he continued on foot; it was as if something wicked might see him and follow him home if he rode too high. Of course everyone did know this bowed old man, no matter how he hid his head or hastened away.

He had to rest; he dozed a trifle. Flies descended on his reeking sheep-skin coat. They buzzed in his ears. He got back to his feet.

Now he had reached the Teatro Romano. What did he fear then? Until now he had always expected to die intrepidly like his father. He said to himself: I hope to be ever more gentle with Tanya—yes, and with Marija, too, whom I now can remember when she was young, and sailed to me. On me be all guilt and blame.— Just within the old wall, a certain marble doorway is overhung with a cartouche which once presented a lion's gape and now is merely dark empty jaws like a letter C, while the gnats thicken around the lamp; here old Cirtovich crept up the marble stairs, bending his knees and stooping, his hands in the pockets of his jacket.

The day was as hot as vampire's blood. On the rim of the old Jesuit well a cat was sunning herself. She opened her yellow-green eyes. He stopped there a moment, smiling wearily, and just as he reached out to stroke the creature, the cobblestones parted beneath him, dirt and roots split apart, and so he found his grave. Just as ivy grows up over a castle wall, occluding every last brick, so the rats covered him, blossoming, shading his flesh from the misery of sunlight.

And no one ever knew his fate, although his sons scoured Trieste for weeks, and dragged the canal, and even searched many ships. Even Marija came out, walking in weary little steps, with that dagger at her belt. The closest they ever came to learning about him was when a certain brutal-looking sailor, stripped to the waist, with his trousers rolled up, blocked their way, laughed in their teeth and said: Cirtovich used to beat me.— To the end of her life, Tanya halfway disbelieved that her father could die. For two years, old Srdjana accompanied her each morning to the cathedral in order to pray for the vanished man, but they had to reduce her wages, and then she left their service, buckling round her hips a chain of fine brass because she was getting married at last. As for Petar, he grew demented, and drove the carriage round about by night, until old women made the sign of the cross whenever they saw him.

17

The Serbs praise the good fortune of the man who dies at Easter, since the angels are so merry just then that a canny soul can flit into heaven when they turn away from some gate or window in order to toast one another. Perhaps it was so for Jovo Cirtovich, who had slipped by so many customs men in his time—and, moreover, was not a bad man. Or maybe he remains imprisoned in his bones, deep under the Teatro Romano. (I myself cannot but wonder whether as he sped down into the earth he saw that dark-glass creature awaiting him, stretching out its swaying arms to him, opening its loathsome beak, with its eyes shining like cold fire. Probably it was not there.) In any case, his family held a funeral for him on the first anniversary of his disappearance, thus closing the book of his life, whose silver cover is engraved with figures. The Triestini came to gloat, and to see the inside of an Orthodox church. Suspicious of the great tapers and the canopy over the three icons of that vast chamber, they stared at the deep-worn crosses and double squares in the floor. But it was a good funeral just the same: Jovo Cirtovich had been laid low! Facing the iconostasis, the priest chanted beautifully as all the people crossed themselves.— With the exception of Cristoforo, who was tracking down a bad debt in the Orient, all the uncles appeared with their families; Marija Cirtovich sat between Massimo and his wife. Tanya was with her nieces. Luca Morelli stood smiling outside. He had already organized a celebration at the "Heaven's Key." Pavle Petrović sat through the service and then paid his respects to Marija, shaking his head as he repeated: It was a visitation, dear lady, oh, yes!— Meanwhile Count Giovanni Vojnovich favored the mourners with his presence; they all got a good look at his gold medal. His epitaph for our Jovo (which fortunately Marija and Tanya did not hear): *An overcunning man overleaps his luck.*— Even Captain Robert was there. And in the highest house, Jesus gave Himself endlessly to the cross, surmounted by a circling swarm of dark triangles, his head hanging miserably, two robed figures beneath him in the immense space. It was a fine service, complete from Bishop to Archimandrite, for Jovo Cirtovich left a pretty legacy for his soul, as I can tell you. Some people said he should have been more generous to his family.

The dead man's brother Massimo carried on the business through that year of hopeless waiting, then liquidated it. It turned out that the finances were as profoundly indented as Dalmatia's coastline. Against Massimo's advice, Jovo Cirtovich's sons pooled their shares to revive the firm. They lacked their father's luck, but got on far better with the Triestini, no doubt because they were native-born. I read that they all married well. But their wives and daughters no longer wore red-topped caps embroidered with golden roses; that was out of style. Everyone was thrilled to stop studying geometry. Wrapping their daggers in the leaves of forgotten books so they wouldn't rattle, the young men sought to cut discreetly successful paths through life, as they supposed they had seen their father do.

Nicola never looked well put together. All the same, there was something beautiful in him, no matter how hopeless or even foolish. His father had struck at Turkish power in any way he could, feebly and treacherously. To Nicola now descended the longing to free the land of his birth. Unfortunately, he was not well versed in graphetics. When the rival captains, accompanied by local thieves and hangers-on, burgled the residence of the late Captain Vasojević, to obtain whatever benefits the dead owe the living, Nicola heard about it at the last moment, and they could hardly keep him out, so he obtained a certain basket of papyri from Oxyrhynchus, thinking to gain some magic formula for wealth or martial power. Several critical signs misled him, and he gave over seeking to comprehend these old writings. By the time he was forty he was as pathetic as old Cirtovich, striving to escape the harbor's curving pier-claws. Wondering whether it would be an act of cowardice or worse to relinquish his birthright, he clung to it for the sake of his father's name, although his sea-aptitude was leaving him. He sailed to Philadelphia with a cargo of Bohemian textiles, and thought to have done well, but the bales of Virginian tobacco he carried home turned inexplicably moldy. Tanya finally coaxed him into letting her help with the accounts, but by then it was too late; the clerks had swindled away half the capital.

Vuk wondered aloud why he turned such a poor profit at the family business. Tanya reminded him that their father hailed from a land where life was more difficult, and death colored the sky; this surely virilized any man who survived. Instead of hazarding his capital and losing it, Vuk exemplified the way that an octopus will gather coins and whatnot into its amphora of residence. Thinking to craft an alliance, he married Luca Morelli's younger sister Nella, who most definitely ruled the house. He was not unhappy counting his cash (much of which he hid from Nella) and eating potatoes and smoked meat. The Triestini liked him best of the dead man's sons. He never acted haughty or uncanny. I admit that for a time he still could name all twelve Roman cities of Bithynia, as if he held himself ready to please his father. Nella had no use for that, so he gave his children a more practical education. At her persuasion he made over the *Sava* to Captain Robert, whose helmsman soon wrecked it off the coast of Sicily. The *Beograd* needed repairs, to which Nicola stubbornly or spitefully refused to agree.— Never mind, darling, said Nella. Just find something else to sell.— To Tanya, who still listened to him, Vuk tipsily insisted that their father had *known* him, or at least seen something in him. Courtly rather than handsome, he turned out to be one of those men who look best in late middle age. Bit by bit he sold off all their father's Turkish scimitars, and his ivory-banded rifles studded with semi-precious stones. Then he started in on the books. Tanya tried to hide them, but he threatened to put her out of the house, and so in the end most of the library was sold away, although a few volumes did end up safe in the Archbishop's possession.

Veljko, the brother whom Tanya loved best, used to write her whimsical messages in Lingua Venetica, which the rest of the family had long since turned their backs on. One night after drinking Friulian wine he asked whether she supposed that sky travel was an apocryphal fantasy, and was astonished when she burst into tears. Constitutionally less impelled toward what lay overhead than toward things beneath the earth, he trolled the multitudinous limestone caverns of the Dalmatian highlands in search of their father's secret hoard, which probably never existed. At first Nicola flattered and probably sincerely admired Veljko, hoping that his discoveries might finance an army of liberation-minded *hajduks*. Both brothers fell out after the latter sold their father's manuscript of Gjin Gazulli and got (so Veljko told Tanya) only enough for a drunk at the "Heaven's Key." Veljko continued his prospecting for seven years; until in Zara, which the Cirtoviches of course continued to call Zadar, he fell for a certain grey-eyed blonde. Keeping her in fine style, and meanwhile caring for his wife and children, he overtaxed his heart and died long before his brothers.

As for the sisters, they got along well enough, raising Orthodox children and praying for everyone's souls. Discreetly they sold their bracelets of silver coins, as their father would have wished them to do. Now that he was gone, their husbands found courage to beat them whenever they deserved it; but in prayer the women consoled themselves, the priest swishing the tinkling censer, perfuming away all ills, and presently it seemed fantastic that their father had ever been able to shelter them from kicks and blows, which are, after all, the lot of most wives.

Of the dead man's brothers, Massimo and Alessandro survived best; they stuck to the wholesale trade. Stefano, whose old face had grown as flat and wise-eyed as a flounder's, found himself ever more often called upon to help Jovo's children, which he did; may he receive his reward in *better days*. Cristoforo became an olive oil merchant. Strange to say, these four, who once had longed to impale Turkish heads in every castle tower, gave over that design, perhaps because it did not pay. As for Florio and Lazzaro, they sailed away to Izmir, and were never again heard of.

In the final years of the Ragusan republic, the *Lazar* was sunk by Venetian pirates, and the Cirtoviches nearly fell into debt. After this they began to buy insurance like everybody else. They went on drinking the three toasts, and never neglected that fourth cup in honor of Prince Lazar. If only they could have gotten hold of that leatherbound talisman, whatever it was! It must be admitted that they kept mostly cheerful, in obedience to that Serbian proverb *when his house burns down, at least a man can warm himself.* Sometimes they sat at the "Heaven's Key," theorizing as to the qualities and whereabouts of that enigmatical treasure. So went the years. Blaming Tanya's bookkeeping practices, Nicola, who had bravely sold out his share of the business, was reduced to coming home in a *bragozzo,* with his conical wire-mesh traps full of lobsters. The others found ever less to do in their father's countinghouse; first they voyaged; then they sat at home scraping their capital together. The other fishermen disdained them for slovenly souls, whose ropes lay as loose as the hair of women at a funeral. Luca Morelli bought the fittings of the *Beograd,* just to humiliate them. Nicola and Vuk were already dead when Serbia cut away the Turkish noose (which happened, as I recall, around Easter). So far as I can tell, the next generation remained in Trieste, although several did fall out of the records; perhaps they too met with accidents at sea, or even adventured back into their family homeland. By then the Cirtoviches possessed only two waterlogged merchant ships. As Milovan Djilas once wrote: *Society has no way out of disappointment but the death of whole generations and whole classes . . .* Austrian customs officials further hedged them in, and so I drink their memory-toast in Friulian wine.

Although Marija failed to survive him by many years (she aged with an eerie rapidity), Tanya lived into the era of diamond clasps, weaving her nephews' undershirts, still hoping for her father to return. By then her family's garden had been eaten up by caterpillars, and the Spanish consulate had taken over her father's warehouse. Just as a preying nautilus extrudes its tentacles, so this or that rich Triestino overhung her property, trolling at its deeds and taxes, making her shameful offers. A certain Alberto importuned her the most, but he was too old. Meanwhile her brothers and uncles hounded her, hypothesizing that since she had been her father's favorite she must know something about his treasure. When nothing came of their investigations, they ostracized her, I fear, but in time they forgave her. She became quite the old maid. All protections having been not only superseded but countermanded, death slavered to get at her now, so that even the brick-scaled, flag-clutching pier-claws of the harbor occasionally sought to close upon her whenever she promenaded in search of her father (sometimes followed at a distance by Alberto), with her woman's dagger at her side, inquiring among the cloaked, barelegged Ragusan merchants, quizzing the beggar-children huddled together like figures on a dirty old marble frieze; but again and again death spat her out, not relishing the taste of her indifference.

How much did she comprehend? Although her father never told her in so many words that he had hoped to sail high enough to approach not only the stars and saints swarming through the sky like the ships in Venice on Ascension Day, scarlet bunting everywhere, oars swiveling like crustacean legs, lapis-cloaked ladies in the shaded galleries, peals of cathedral bells, but also the starry canals to grander spheres, until he came into the gold-haloed presence of his most adored saint, didn't Tanya guess it all? Turning away from this, she rigged out yellow ledger-pages like the cutched sails of the Cirtoviches' fleet, valiantly angling for the slightest breeze of profit. Even in this skill, in which she had no interest, she proved better than her father's other children. But, as the Triestini remarked, the planets were against her.

She married late; her husband was a merchant whose family came from Muggia. He was as handsome, sad and smoothfaced as the bearded golden reliquary bust of Saint Nicholas, whose moustaches, beard and hair flow together like so many parallel waves of yarn; but Tanya scarcely noticed him. Their children died early. From across the room the husband frequently stood for a moment to watch this woman (who never permitted him to call her Tanyotchka), with her long grey hair hanging down and her chin in her hand as she did his accounts. He felt proud of her; she knew nearly as much as he did. Sometimes he got her to sit beside him by pretending interest in her father's doings. When he died, he left her a decent portion.

Although she gave up on astronomy, she never ceased praying for her father's safe return. She called upon Christ, and Saint Sava, and Saint Lazar, of course, not to mention the Holy Virgin, whom in Trieste we name Stella Maris. Every day she went to church. It would have pleased Jovo Cirtovich to see her go out for so many years into the Triestine twilight of many colors. But when people saw her on the street, she was just another old woman dressed in black.

THE MADONNA'S FOREHEAD

1

Once upon a time, somebody threw a brick at Our Lady of the Flowers, and she began to bleed from her stone forehead. From this occurrence we all accepted the occasional sentience of statues, but thence our themes departed in cardinal directions. Upholding the Madonna's compassionate forbearance, some argued that she had in effect murmurously moaned to us: Your disrespect gashes me, but how could I, your loving mother, bring myself to punish you in any way? That is why I smile upon you just as before even while the blood runs down my cheek.— Schismatics asserted that her smile was in fact a punishment, and indeed a terrible one, for they remembered from their childhoods the faithful, distant sadnesses of their mothers when they sinned—longhaired mothers who licked the sugared spoon and pouted, swinging their knitted turquoise purses, strings of pearly tears commencing from their big sad brown eyes—and as for the children, their evil remained inexpiable; that was why nobody beat them; their lives had become hopeless. They were the ones who upon seeing the glare of the solar disk behind late summer clouds were capable of simultaneously rejecting both their present sweltering infinities, thickened by cigarette smoke, and the clammy *bora* wind of embryonic autumn.— Still others said: No, what's proved is that she *could* not stop the brick from striking her!— The boy who threw the brick was their adherent. Of course he had never supposed that anything supernatural would happen, for be assured that he had thrown stones, rusty iron and other such before, impelled by blasphemies as insignificant to us as the rotations of the little carousel beside the Canal Grande. In those days the boy, whose name was Nino, appeared as hard and slender as a breadstick. Sometimes his parents punished him; hence his cunning had increased with the cowardice of experience, and he generally threw stones and bricks in the hottest hours of the afternoons, when arugula wilted under the striped umbrellas of the produce stalls and even the Italian flag sweated on its pole. He especially liked to climb over the railing where the Via del Teatro Romano overlooks those

eponymous semicircles of grass-grown brick benches and globs of masonry which the centuries treat as does the morning sun the fish vendor's
blocks of ice; they may last out the afternoon, but count on them to be
absent tomorrow! We may therefore consider this boy an agent of the
morning sun. Arriving at the Roman theater with his pockets full of
gravel, he would pick a weary old column and assail it with dents and
dimples; once indeed a certain missile of his smashed off the corner of an
ancient brick, and he felt as happy as if he had dislodged an enemy's
tooth. The afternoon weighed shadily on a rusty grating in an arched
doorway set in a steep grassy hillside; this spot had always been sinister
to Nino, and now, glancing at it as if by mistake, he discovered his triumph decaying into guilt and fear, because what if a ghost came out? But
nothing did come, because the amphitheater, where gladiators once
clubbed and stabbed each other for our amusement right there on the
ocean's edge, had already lost almost everything, even the sea itself,
which had receded like an old man's gums and now hid behind the white
municipal building of flags and garbage cans. Then the boy's courage
returned, and he decided to throw something at the Madonna della
Borella, whom we also know as the Madonna dei Fiori, Our Lady of the
Flowers. Right then the sky was as smooth as the naked black buttocks of
faraway statues, and the Madonna's face was smoother even than that.
Maybe he could break her nose off.

Just as the late afternoon sun extends itself down Trieste's drainpipes,
elongating their goldenness while devouring their shaded dullnesses, so
that lines of gold expand like a summer thermometer's mercury, penetrating each roof's shaded zone even as the solar angle alters so that the
lines of gold commence to narrow—already now they resemble the slen-
derest rays of light which a master's one-haired brush could paint onto a
Book of Hours, for the shade has risen all around it; now they are all
gone—thus the past (if indeed there can be any such thing as a "past," a
present which has become nonexistent) of this iconoclast thins out the
more radiantly it pretends to go backwards, so that if you were to ask me,
why did he become that way?, I might start to answer confidently, then
lose my thread, distracted and annoyed precisely as you would be when a
black lapdog goes barking past the merry-go-round, dragged by its weary
master, slavering from both sides of its drooping little tongue, which is

even more crimson than the velvet seats in the opera house. Meanwhile the horses gently rise and fall, while the pumpkin-coaches, sanctuaries for timid little ones, remain as solidly anchored to the revolving disk of reality they inhabit as would a fat woman's bottom; and as the lapdog's angry yelps succumb to the law of decrescendo, a little boy's whine fills the impending acoustic vacuum; but the young mother of the bobbed hair and mohair scarf and spectacles waves to her four-year-old blonde in the sunglasses who clings (somehow regally) to her white plastic pony's neck as it ascends and descends without consideration for the whining of the boy, who sits behind her all alone; other children accustom themselves to their pole-skewered horses with cautious amazement; then here comes the boy, Nino, all by himself; his father is reading the newspaper because it is Sunday and he is tired, his absence being in the small boy's mind merely a grief, although when the boy has grown perhaps it will number among the father's many sins which whirl in the shadows of the trembling olive-green hedges. A man walks by smiling, with his arms folded. He stops. He turns back. He cannot get enough music, it seems. The boy's whines never reach him. And down the street they are knocking an old horse over the head, because Nino's father and I both like to eat horsemeat steaks with green peppercorns. The man stands for a long time, smiling and faintly nodding his head. When the Sunday light strikes the yellow-painted zinc of the ticket kiosk, the pigeons suddenly look very dull indeed, and Nino's whining becomes still more of an insult to the music, the waving parents, the happiness of this world.

As for the boy's father, poor man, he'd gotten trapped by a pair of mammaries—or, to be more precise, by the peach-colored throat of the woman who now no longer loved him, or at least that was his belief although they had never talked about it because, as H. P. Lovecraft proved, it may well be better not to know the answers to questions of fatality and decay; for instance, what answer, what honest answer at least, could the whining boy have learned which would not have made him feel worse? For when we whine, dear brothers and sisters, we become unlovable; that is why the jackbooted heel which has just crushed the bones of the prisoner's hand against the flagstones cannot be blamed for entering a partnership with the jackbooted toes in order to penetrate the prisoner's screaming mouth at high speed, simply in order to shut him up, because most of us who claim to love a crying child are lying; the remainder must be themselves unlovable, because they tolerate, encourage, actually foment annoying demands upon our so-called obligations—not that I would ever suppose that the father wished to hurt his dear bambino whose face was always sticky with snot and the slobber of green and red candies. From one of the conical-roofed white vending tents on the edge of the Canal Grande there now came, temporarily expelling the smells of burned rubber and of cigarettes, a fragrance of frying calamari, and since Nino's crying couldn't get worse and he surely wouldn't toddle off the moving carousel and if he did then naturally the attendant at the kiosk would take care of him, the father went to buy them both this treat—yes, *both* of them, for even now he still dreamed of being surrounded by children just as the plinth of Verdi's statue has been lovingly besieged by red begonias—but I regret to say that as he approached the line of backs and buttocks between him and the cala-mari, he suddenly experienced, as perhaps he might have planned for and even welcomed had he slept or philandered less in order to read more fre-quently an Evangeliario, or better yet an Evangeliario covered in red leather and saints in silverworked relief, a thrombosis, and that was the end of him, right there on the Piazza del Ponterosso, surrounded on all sides by the candy-cake Habsburg buildings of Trieste. And he had been correct, because that dirty naughty boy kept whining so hard that he had made everything as horrible for himself as he could, which meant that he was safe; and when the carousel stopped, he clung to the shining pole of his horse, whining with his eyes closed; the attendant frowned, but since the father was out pissing or something he allowed the child, who frankly re-pulsed him, to stay where he was until all the parents had bent over their darlings to carry them off their horses, or smiled with outstretched arms while their children returned radiantly or regretfully to their care; so the next cloud of children swarmed onto the carousel, the whistle blew, and the smell of fresh-fried calamari blew from the white tents, in front of which a crowd was thickening like leukocytes around an enemy bacillus; so that the attendant supposed that the sidewalk painter had begun the day there, inconsiderately close to the businesses of others; or perhaps one of the North Africans had finally gotten hold of a good book to sell, prefer-ably one pertaining to carnal adventures; but the crowd seemed too attentive even for that, and now here came a policeman in a very clean uniform; the crowd contracted to make him a passageway, and the attendant leaped onto the dais of his carousel in hopes of some excitement, so that just as the accordionist started to squeeze out the national anthem, the attendant gaped, proving to all of us that his teeth were as brown as the wooden keys of an old spinet; for he had just perceived the dead man.

A little girl, her hand held by her father's, kept turning sideways to watch the pigeons and the sea, but her father supposed that it was the dead man who attracted her, hence his well-meaning yanking of her wrist; while the whining boy was sure that she kept looking at *him* in fascinated contempt; and it was this memory above all, whose basis you have just seen to be false, which hurt him most in later life—but did any of this justify his actions?

2

So the naughty boy grew up with his ever-merciful mother whom he hated, teased, tormented and drained. Those two were of so little interest to anyone else that they lived on the eighth floor of a seven-storey façade (chiseled dirty stone, which might have been pink or tan beneath its greyness). It could have been worse; they could have lived on the ninth floor, among the old widows who have gone to heaven; although it could have been better, in which case they might have been privileged to exist on the seventh floor, among the old widows who no longer watch but *listen* through the dark shades of their narrowly vertical windowpanes. Those years half throttled him with the stickiness of clothes at knees, elbows, shoulders, chest and back. He kept running to see where life was. Whenever life got away from him, he grew enraged and smeared his excrement on monuments. He was a disgusting boy, to be sure, and always had been. When he was small he used to fly from banister to shoulder or armchair to neck like a vampire bat, sinking his sharp little teeth into the flesh of anyone he chose. When people prayed he would roll his eyes and utter rude whistlings. Those behaviors grew more discreet upon the death of his father. Anyhow, what was he to do? Everything was grey with white glare behind it, like the noon sky in Trieste late in a summer which will not die. So he remained miserably exempt from the fear that so many feel in the face of death, from the vain desire to keep death from achieving total victory by commissioning monuments to ourselves. But finally his testicles descended, and at once autumn began, with a wind which whirled away the potato chips from their glass dishes on the tables of the outdoor cafés. The shadows were more distinct and we could all see farther. What we spied between the slats of our shutters used to be undifferentiated whiteness; but now it organized itself into distinctions of white light and blue light.

His mother bought him a little briefcase. He began to be excited by the dull sheen of brass plaques.

3

I cannot tell you whether he wanted to be good or merely to be approved of. He was a boy who told lies. Once his mother told him to eat a certain apple before it got overripe, and he said that he had done it but she found it in the dustbin. These careless lies of his became more extravagant, hence almost endearingly unearthly. A beggar came to the door. His mother was upstairs scrubbing the floor. She heard the beggar arguing with her son; she was just about to rise up off her aching knees and go to the young man's aid when the door slammed behind the beggar; then her son came rushing upstairs with his face alight with virtue; he announced that he had given the beggar five hundred lire of his own money. What could the mother say? Perhaps he had at least felt a momentary charitable inclination, which should not be discouraged. Smiling pityingly, she patted his elbow and went on scrubbing the floor.

4

When he threw the brick at the Madonna's white, white forehead, at first he disbelieved the result. Then, determined not to change his life, he approached the divine image in a scientific spirit, seeking to see some reservoir of rusty water beneath the paint. But no; she was bleeding. And she gazed at Nino, lovingly smiling—the smile of a lover, or a mother, or simply of a woman who loved—so giving, that smile, and so fearless, but not like the smile of the woman he would someday marry, who sometimes, at least at first, expressed such happiness that he seemed to smell the fragrance of oranges and lemons; and not like the heavy-lidded smiles of the prostitutes with whom he would in time lie on July afternoons, with the window open in hopes of a harbor breeze; no, she gazed at him with sad awareness—after all, not like his mother, who narrowed her awareness in order to avoid loving him less on account of his sins. Sad smile, brown eyes (one of them larger than the other), bleeding forehead—what did all this mean?

5

The boy knew well the tri-tiered stands of gum, candies and cough drops in little boxes, and then around the corner he knew a specific double-shelved pastry case, with cookies like full moons eclipsed at the center by smaller planets of jam. These cookies did not seem stealable, so he bought one with his mother's money, then ran off with it to lurk amidst the sunken weedgrown columns of the Teatro Romano, seeking to deny what he had seen.

6

The psychotherapist Wilhelm Stekel asserts that our fundamental emotion is *hatred*. Hence *we may conceive of the masochism merely as a painting over the sadistic portrait beneath. Such an assertion would be monstrous, could it not be proved.* Are we created in Mary's image—or, if you like, is she one of us? If so, what sadism does her portrait conceal? If not, is she inhuman? Or is Stekel incorrect?

7

Next question: Considering the way that some families have of devouring their weakest or most foreign member in some *dramma eroico*, I wonder whether Nino's father had been sacrificed? His sense that his wife no longer needed him had been, as such feelings almost invariably are, entirely correct; without Nino and his demands the couple would have been worse off; hence if anyone had to go the father was the one. And why not? He was already as worn as the Arco di Riccardo. Such parapathies, once initiated, may well continue. Families are hungry. Could this explain why Nino chose to vandalize the Madonna, and why his mother said nothing? Pretending to him that she must visit her sister, she hurried out with a rag and a bucket of soapy water, struggling to clean the marble, but it did no good.

8

By this time we had all divided into factions, each of us attracted by the flavor of a sympathetic idea, just as in the Canal Grande a school of long green fingerlings will gather round an ice cream cone whose melting whiteness makes especially foul light in that dark water right above another gift to Neptune, namely a pallid rubber glove whose protrusions swiggle and sway in the listless current—and if you want to sit at a café with your friends and speculate as to whether that ice cream cone was dropped in the water by a careless child, or thrown in by the parent of a child who was naughty (who, for instance, whined), or whether it fell from the hands of a sticky child who had eaten too much and suddenly began to vomit, why, then, I wonder why you don't have better things to do; and it may be much the same with the variously attractive theories about why the Madonna bled when the brick struck her forehead. Nobody except for that despicable boy knew the whole story. He'd lied to his mother, who suspected him but found it more relaxing, God bless her, to believe him; she took a long hot bath, and afterwards he rubbed her feet, all the while sarcastically abusing her for her lack of faith in him. But which way did he judge the question? When his brick hurt that perfect woman, her eyes had *moved;* she had *seen* him; this was absolutely for certain; and the blood which spattered his wrist was an earnest of her suffering, which horrified and humiliated him but mostly (in that instant at least) caused him to be terrified of discovery and punishment; as soon as he had gotten away, the horror of what he had done began to prey on him, until he decided not to think about it ever again; and when this strategy failed, he commenced to nourish resentment against Our Lady, who had caused him such suffering. If only she had stayed dead! Who was she to magick the merest nasty thoughtlessness into an atrocity, by being present in her body so unexpectedly? If I drive round the corner at high speed and some old lady is stupid enough to be crossing the street just then and no one has ever been in my way before at that corner, which I have taken at high speed all my life, how can the outcome be my fault? And so he became a Madonna-hater. (The young man's mother took him to the Gran Teatro di Trieste. He licked his lips at the flowers and lace on Carmen's costume.)

9

His mother was now an elderly marble-skinned woman, her head tilted back, her hair almost like a gilded mushroom cap. She wore a thin smile, with her nostrils flaring and her eyes not quite closed. The muscles and bones were taut on her face.

One of his father's cousins was a pharmacist, and it was to him that Nino presently applied for employment. In the back room of the man's shop, where he compounded his preparations, there hung an anatomical model of a woman, gloriously naked, and her belly opened so that one could see her internal organs. Opening her belly that night, with the half-formed intention of doing mischief, Nino found a little girl inside. He took her out, and instantly fell in love with her, for her anus was as pretty as the tawny ring in the white cup from which the espresso has been drunk; and so he finally grew up into a man and joined the army.

After several of those July amours to which I have alluded, he fell for a certain Triestina named Francesca whose waist-length chestnut hair, carefully combed, shone red, yellow and all the other colors as she sat with a rose in her folded hands. Some of her suitors could play the viola d'amore of nice red wood, but Nino, having enlisted in the engineers' battalion, knew how to detonate things; and thanks to his unswerving application to dishonesty he could glamorize his occupations into something resembling the candylike floral depictions on a certain psalterium in Dubrovnik. So Francesca married him.

Nino's mother congratulated them, with a tenderly submissive smile, as if she were relieved to fade out of this story. And Nino said to himself: Now I must become good.— He not only forgave the Madonna, but prepared even to love her.

But she went on bleeding; the neighbors remarked it; no one could explain who had injured her, and why she did not heal.

10

His wife was now a gentle, melancholy, elegant woman in brownish-black, wearing a brooch below her withered throat, a lace collar of moderate width, and round earrings of some precious stone which coincidentally resembled his dead mother's eyes. As for him, he had resigned from the army in order to become a greengrocer, an occupation so respectable that he fancied himself nearly as worthwhile as a gold-relief saint with an up-raised spear. Outside their window, the high-masted ships rocked quietly in the mirror-harbor. Of course they had children, a daughter who reminds me of a cherry tree growing out of the ruin of the old Basilica, and two busy little boys like the blooming bush on one of the high ledges of the Arco di Riccardo. I remember passing by their window and seeing the sons in their formal jackets, sitting at the piano for their lesson, while the potted orchid behind them grew sluttishly wild. Just as some rich orders like to get their old wooden icons sheathed in hammered silver, so Nino sometimes embellished his life with extramarital adventures, in order to display his loyalty to what he called happiness; while Francesca perfumed her underwear with dried orange blossoms.

One day Nino got a rash on his belly which declined to improve. He grew ill. At such times he had always been childishly peevish and dependent, so that the family could never do enough to please him. Finally Francesca gently said: Darling, I've heard that Our Lady's blood works miracles.

Terrified, he sat up and said: What must I do?

I'll go with you. We'll pray. Then you must kiss her on the forehead, and swallow the blood.

Needless to say he preferred not to go. On the other hand, he feared suspicion and exposure as a result of any refusal—although only a little, for he had thrown that brick so long ago that his crime seemed unreal to him—and his rash itched so badly that he could scarcely sleep.

So his wife led him there. He crept up toward Our Lady of the Flowers, groaning with pain.

It was that time in mid or late afternoon when the Triestine summer, not having entirely established its sticky grip, allows a cloud or two to dim the sun, and an innocuous remembrance of the *bora* to rise deliciously in the shaded parks where children go fishing for tiny prey with hands, hopes and sticks; and even the old couples who sit together doing nothing are refreshed into holding hands there in the mottled shade of the chestnut trees of the Giardino Pubblico "M. Tommasini," the bare-breasted stone nymph pissing happily from the circular array of jets, the many-windowed apartment façades glowing slate-green or whitish-pink outside the shady zone; tonight will be humid again, so people will open their windows, and the mosquitoes will feast all night. They descended the semicircular seat-steps of the Teatro Romano, and Nino could not help but look at the column which in boyhood he had damaged, first dreading that the brick might have healed itself, which would render this world's laws still less predictable, then sad and guilty when he saw that it had not, and finally angry that he had been made to be sad.— He wished to pulverize Our Lady into gravel.

We're almost there, darling.

Nino did not reply, because the Madonna's smile came into view before the rest of her, and it unnerved him as much as ever. For years he had tactfully avoided reminding her of his existence, but now she herself had dragged him back! What was *wrong* with this world? He tried to say to himself: She's nothing but a vampire!—never mind that he was the one who had come to drink blood.

He had forgotten her sadly smiling slightly bewildered face, and that infuriating way that her eyes had of looking lost. The Christ child in her arms was a sexless little adult.

Francesca was now praying steadily. He knelt beside her, moved his lips, and closed his eyes, so as not to be haunted by Our Lady's face. Dove, lily and olive branch, those Marian attributes he promised henceforth to adore. When he could no longer put it off, he stood up and kissed that stone forehead, tasting dust, salt, soot, then blood.

Instantly her bleeding ceased, leaving for a souvenir a reddish-ocher stain on her smooth cold forehead. Simultaneously Nino found himself healed, so that his life became as lovely as the long dead singer Bianca Kaschman, as useless as an artificial sand dollar, as meaninglessly triumphant as wreaths of silver and gold. Again, one must wonder about Our Lady's motives.

11

Within the year he turned away from his wife, since he now lacked any further need of others. Self-entitled to the seductive stare of a certain Triestina in a pallid formal gown with half a dozen hems, her right knee crossed over the left to make a platform for her left elbow as she played with the pearls on her triple-stranded necklace, her hair pulled back, everything dim and silver-blue but for the whites of her eyes, he pursued and eventually won her on a blue-grey day of *bora* rain, streetlamp reflections shining on the empty street like cat-eyes, until he finally unlatched the coffers of his heart for her and she saw inside. Francesca, for whom he had so long pretended to be tamed, kept looking desperately between her tanned and slender knees, in case she she had lost some part of herself.— Fortunately, she was comforted, for the long-necked, golden-haloed, blue-grey bird called the Holy Ghost flew to her from out of an old Croatian-Glagolitic missal. Then she took the children, and ran off with a haberdasher.

As for him, ambition bemused him, like a lady's legs reflected in a curving wall of brass—but without Francesca his belly-rash returned. The next time Nino kissed the Madonna's stained forehead, his affliction, as indeed he had expected, refused to divorce him. This was positively insulting, since Our Lady could easily have made another cure; everyone knows she vanquished a cholera epidemic in 1849. Lonely and perhaps not far away from death (so it certainly appeared when he looked into the mirror), Nino would have wooed her had he known how, but found it easier to become a politician—for his life, unlike yours or mine, was comically accidental and meaningless. Incited by slogans about smashing the idols, chipping away at restraint, tearing down the old order, he believed that life should have promised him something, and he was not the only one.

In his schooldays the bad boy had loved Emperor Massimiliano, touched his statue and even refrained from daubing, scratching or chipping it. So it might be "no accident" that he betook himself to the deep and ancient chairs of the Caffè San Marco, worn by generations of nationalists' buttocks.

An eagle on a shroud for Lohengrin, said the Duke, and we'll need turquoise-beaded bands on its wings and sad ruby eyes, because . . .

Silence! The leader arrives—

The leader liked Nino, because he was so good at telling lies, so before the Madonna had wept or bled again he got to take the train all the way to Venice, bearing in his briefcase the money and confidence of the party.

Already he was hoping that someday he could for all purposes become a white statue whose arms would be pompously folded across his toga'd breast, overwatching the red flag which bore the historical weight of Trieste's white fleur-de-lys well enough to slowly, slowly stir, unfurling like a pill dissolving in liquid, then wrapping itself up again, just as Caesar covered his face when he saw Brutus among his assassins . . . and below the flag's balcony, all of us, his followers, even Our Lady (whose statue was naturally much smaller) would be carried into the shadow where arched windows shone silver and cigarette smoke diffused like sea-fog. Thus his hopes, and the train had barely passed Miramar.— Here came the trolley of coffees, candies and cigarettes. The woman who wheeled it wore a frothy white chemise, and there were dark circles under her armpits. As she drew close to his seat, he inhaled the smell of her sweat and was enchanted. Those intimate circles, they reminded him of the light seen through grape leaves. Because he knew what to say, she soon agreed to meet him in a hotel room where the shadow of the lace curtain on the Naples yellow wall resembled a harp, but when he undressed, it turned out that his sickness had spread. Revolted, the woman departed.

What will become of me? he anguished, which is not the same as *what will I become?*— If only Our Lady had left me as I was that first time—if Francesca hadn't dragged me there . . . !—for what he detested above all was confusion. He wished to be what he was, coldly and secretly. But what was that?

Resigning from politics without even returning the money, and therefore knowing that unless her new husband, who had friends in three of Trieste's marine insurance companies, saved him, his best hope was death, he returned on his knees to Francesca, who unfortunately had grown happy where she was. Out of pity (and with her new husband's permission) she gave him a lily and an olive branch, instructing him to sleep with them under his pillow until he dreamed of the Madonna. But he never did. One cool whitish-pale morning when a single pale pigeon flew high across the Via Dante Alighieri, showing itself for the merest instant between the two embellished streetwalls, Nino returned to kiss Our Lady's forehead once more in secret, desperate to believe that it would bleed again, although he knew quite well not only that all hope of that had fled, but also that whatever solution the mystery of the bleeding stone image might contain, he was better off never learning. Our Lady bowed her marble face, silently suffering the touch of his lips; and the bloodstain on her forehead matched in hue the crimson-brown garment of one of those faded figures on certain Istrian graveyard frescoes. He licked and licked at her forehead like a dog, but this time he could not obtain the slightest blood-taste. By the time death came, from complications of his rash, exacerbated by three bullets in the back, Nino had become bitter—although, come to think of it, he might always have been that way.

CAT GODDESS

1

Dark bronze Rossetti, haughty on his plinth, held a book and clutched his heart, while among the many abject figures below, a seminude crowned lady who held a tablet of the laws essayed eternally to offer him a palm branch. As soon as the evening darkened sufficiently to be safe, he stepped down, snubbing the poor crowned lady, who grew as disappointed as if she were made of flesh, an emotion she could not sweat out or weep out, because the foundry had cast her to love only him above her, whom he unfortunately considered a mere decoration; Rossetti-adoration was in her every bronze atom. Rossetti, differently comprised, wanted women. The clashing of bronze against bronze could not seduce him. Some of our miseries may be called tragedies of place, as was the syndrome of that poor crowned lady (whose name was Giovanna); had fate simply established her farther down the coast, she might have attracted the attentions of some marble Herakles. Cloaking his face, Rossetti set off to drink a grappa in the brown and creamy-yellow silence of the Caffè San Marco, where they kept a table for him by the far wall, in a niche whose sweet dimness offered however treacherously to preserve the semiliving from recognition. He paid in bronze, of course: heavy, dark, ovoid coins from a hoard within the plinth, which was much hollower than it appeared. Our Lady of the Flowers, who performs miracles every day, replenished his treasury, out of loving pity, which indeed shored up his equanimity. Why he could not be satisfied with standing forever overlooking the Giardino Pubblico "M. Tommasini," graciously accepting the deposits of pigeons, cannot be explained; but several other plinths in Trieste had been vacated by now, their heroes and heroines having chosen ecstatic oblivion over unbending fame. There was, for instance, a certain shy little marble girl whose sculptor, Barcalgalia, had condemned her always to be half-trying to cover her pubis; meanwhile she had conveniently pulled up her marble shift, so over time she gave and took much joy. A century and more it had been since she first leaped off her marble block. Our Lady, whose hobbies include the arranging of marriages, once proposed her to Rossetti's consideration, but he said: You know, *cara*, the thing is, I have a bitter disposition. That's why I need someone soft and yielding. I'm not saying a stone woman can't be forgiving; for instance, look at you, still smiling, with that bloodstained forehead! But you're not, how should I say, available . . .—nor would he have wished her to be; although he had several times been tempted by the exaggerated frozen gazes of the thespians at the Circulo Artistico, he longed, if such a verb is not preposterous when applied to him, for a dear woman of flesh who could warm him up as even Triestine sunlight never could, not quite; indeed, it was considerably worse for poor bronze Giovanna, who had to stand always in his shadow—not that she ever complained. And so the shy marble girl found herself another taker; one day James Joyce stepped off his plinth by the Canal Grande, and the newspapers wrote that he had been stolen by a nymphomaniacal American heiress who engaged in untrammelled sexual congress with statues. After Joyce deserted his post, even Umberto Sava, it was said, began to be tempted by a certain someone cast in pure silver. As for Rossetti, all he needed were his nightly amours. For her part, Giovanna (whose longings resembled brass railings shining in the morning sun) never imagined lowering herself to engage in such practices. Where her idol went when he departed her she suspected all too well, but since he never failed to return, she had at least someone to look up to. So on the evening under consideration, she watched his departure no less calmly than mournfully. Rossetti turned his steps to the San Marco, which, while it was not as quiet as early on a Sunday afternoon just before closing, remained a good venue for a bronze fellow who prefers to be left in peace. Whenever he had the place to himself, Rossetti liked to inspect each of the round brass-bordered portraits, whose crudeness surpassed that of worn Etruscan frescoes. To the vertically grooved column-reliefs upon the Naples yellow walls clung plaques whose import might be stylized honeybees or petals of quartered flowers; these decorative concretions soothed Rossetti by reminding him of his plinth. So he sat down in his private corner, prepared to re-explore the way that some grappas burn and others glow. And on this night the slender, elderly waiter, whose spectacles never ceased shining even when he straightened his necktie, revealed, without even any expectation of a tip, that a sweet girl all alone in a tasselled scarf and a long pale dress dress of many embroideries had just decided to paint her lips, cock her plumed hat, and set off for the radiant sea. Can you believe it? She meant to abandon this world! Moreover, she derived not from some Serbo-Croatian-speaking karstic village high in the interior, which origin might have excused her, but from Trieste herself, empress of cities. The waiter, who took pride in knowing Rossetti's tastes, remarked that this young lady, whose name was Silvia, was worth looking over, at which Rossetti pondered and ordered another grappa. Next morning, when Silvia arrived at the port, whose ships' smokestacks resembled banded cigars, Rossetti, having without making her a single promise instructed Giovanna to take his place on the plinth, either with or without her palm branch, whatever she considered most discreetly effective, stood waiting to rescue the girl from the sea.

In case you are wondering whether anybody noticed the alteration of Rossetti's monument, I may as well tell you now that the painter Leonor Fini, while making her morning promenade through that same Giardino Pubblico "M. Tommasini," in hopes of reinterring a ghoulish hangover in the smallest possible hermetic coffin at the center of her skull, paused there, and caught the substitution right away, because when her father, wishing to raise her in the Catholic Church, had sought to kidnap her away from her mama, she became a watchful little girl in her knee-length skirt and sailor hat, posing with flowers and precociously pregnant with spite, clutching her cats, jeering and staring, growing up salacious and defiant, distrusting the male category and hence preferring to play with her transvestite friends. In the grimy alleys of Trieste she not infrequently spied ghosts—for instance, an old Serb named Jovo Cirtovich, whose face had perhaps fallen in a trifle, and his ancient, black-clad daughter Tanya or Tanyotchka, who was always seeking and never finding him. To more complacent observers they might have been shadows or scraps of cheese-paper. Once Leonor saw that pair wandering under a deep Roman arch which resembled a well laid on its side; he kept sighing and clutching at his throat, as if he had lost something which used to hang there, while she strode determinedly right through him, murmuring *father, father, father.* It chilled Leonor that they could not perceive one another; the lesson she derived was that a girl might as well seek pleasure in this life! On another occasion she saw the Emperor

Massimiliano, dressed in the Mexican uniform in which he once de-lighted. When Leonor was a girl, her mama took her to visit Miramar, where, being apprised of the legend that who sleeps here in Massimilia-no's castle dies a violent death, she giggled and shuddered. Up on the wall, the pale melancholy faces of the Emperor and Empress, painted by Heirrich in 1863, almost seemed to foresee the execution.— Poor man! sighed Leonor's mama. The Mexicans were so ungrateful . . .— The guide informed Leonor and her mama that to console him before he was shot, they performed his favorite tune, "La Paloma." So when she en-countered him that night on Via Dante Alighieri, Leonor hummed "La Paloma," at which the ghost lifted his head and smiled sadly. How many other phantoms did the watchful woman see?— Cat-ghosts by the score, no doubt, and perhaps even the odd vampire.— And which of the living did she not see through? In that famous 1936 photograph by Dora Maar, Leonor sits with her stockinged knees apart and a black cat peering out glowing-eyed between them; she holds her head high, presenting her cleavage, her eyebrows painted on catlike, as if she pretends to be Cleopa-tra. One can tell that she sees everything. Ten years later, Cartier-Bresson catches her leaning forward in darkness, ornately decorated by embroi-dered sleeves, wide-eyed, pursing her lips as if in concentration, ruth-lessly intent on seeing and being seen. Even in the photographs of Veno Pilon her wariness is her charm; sometimes she stares over her shoulder like a streetwalker. So you may be sure that she noticed Rossetti's ab-sence. With her loud, screeching laugh, Leonor now strolled up to the plinth and fondled Giovanna's nipples. Her estimation of Rossetti took off like an unguided missile; she had never suspected that he might be one of her very own man-women! Not knowing what else to do in the face of such treatment, Giovanna kept very still. Leonor's hangover per-ished with a plop, and she hurried home to paint the bronze lady and her palm branch into a crowd of bejeweled hermaphroditic clowns in the background of her latest surrealistic canvas, and before the oils had even dried down as far as tackiness, Leonor was wrapping herself in a robe of her own design and crowning her head with colored feathers, because a photographer from Marseilles had been entreating to do her portrait.

Meanwhile, as Giovanna stood anxious, shy and proud in her master's place, with an electric-grey pigeon warming her head, Rossetti, who would have been insulted had he known Leonor's new misapprehension of him, persuaded the erratic Silvia to take him back to her rented room. The roses had not yet wilted in their vase and her tabby cat Lilith was barely getting hungry. Silvia removed her clothes with darling clicks and rustles; Rossetti undressed himself with clinks and clanks. Three bronze coins fell out of his pocket. How the procedure was carried out I who was not there cannot tell you, but it remains certain that with great success they made love in her bed, and afterwards, while he lay naked beneath the white sheet watching her and humming "La Paloma," although he did not know why it had entered his mind, a fly crawled upon his bronze forehead as Silvia stood naked by the shuttered window, sipping wine, holding Lilith against her breast and stroking her, hungering ever more to vanish from Trieste, which was why her eyes kept shining and glittering on that late afternoon by the sea. She had booked a berth on a certain twin-masted brigantino, the *Tancredi,* a former warship which now sailed into the past, ferrying seekers of lost dreams. To get rid of her lover, she acquiesced in becoming the next Signora Rossetti; by then the *Tancredi* had already departed. The instant her intended had dressed, constructed their rendezvous for that very evening behind the botanical gardens, kissed her lips, breasts, hands and then departed, Silvia, tyrannized by the fact that in summertime Trieste the smell of sweat can drown both smell and sound of sea, smashed her wineglass in a rage, at which Lilith, frightened by the uproar, hissed and showed her claws, which impelled Silvia to throw the animal out the window; and the calmness with which she observed the cat's whirlings and screechings all the way down rendered her worthy of either damnation or pity—all because the odor of sweat from that unmade bed exasperated her. Now she desired to embark for Hvar or Opatija, where the sea's fishy vapors make frequent headway against the air. Accordingly she poured the roses and water from her vase onto the bed, hurled the vase out the window to shatter on top of her dead cat, laughed, pulled her dress on, painted her lips reddish-black, cocked that pale hat on her head, locked the door behind her, just in case (which proves her not utterly irrational) and set off once more to buy her ticket to sea-freedom, but this time Leonor Fini, unapprised of Silvia's unforgivable cruelty to cats, caught sight of her, and although she mostly preferred men she could dominate, or

men-women to play with, Leonor found herself in a mood to give and receive Communion between this girl's legs for the instruction, humiliation
and delectation of all Leonor's membrane-shrouded ladies bathing in
pitch, Leonor's gentle corpses and Leonor's lesbians in jester dress—for
by now our talented heroine had advanced beyond seeing other people's
ghosts; she invented her own. The world of Leonor Fini, the painted
world, could be reached by lifting aside a certain oil painting on a certain
easel. Being one of those women who say yes when they would rather say
no, Silvia permitted Leonor to lead her to her studio, which was just
downstairs from her mama's apartment, and presently, after cigarettes
and absinthe, her hostess opened the door in the easel, took her hand,
and pulled her down to the dark garden of lichens, logs and glossy greens;
so that before she knew it, Silvia was standing naked in dark water, huger-
breasted than ever before, with the sky red behind her, and half-submerged
skull-crocodiles watching; Leonor was dancing white and naked on a
black driftwood log, and the grey-wigged red-cloaked skeleton of the Angel of Anatomy performed a string solo for them both, drawing a rib
across the music-hole in a woman's pelvis.— Silvia was thinking: I'd
rather be in Opatija.— And then catbird ladies commenced to fly softly
down, hovering just above the tarry water, swishing it around with their
fat white breasts, so that before Leonor and Silvia had even made love
once, Silvia was in distress, recalling all too well what she had done to
Lilith and therefore (I am happy to say) repenting, which Our Lady of the
Flowers found pleasing, since to her way of thinking contrition became
people about as well as anything. Beneath a long veil, a jewel-like skeleton, pale and smooth like a fly's eye, now squatted to embrace a bald unconscious man-woman to whom Leonor paid more attention than to
Silvia—who stole the opportunity to dress. Leonor, who had anticipated
painting a portrait of her standing waist deep in that pool, threw a glass
dildo at her head and commanded her never to come back, which suited
both parties. By then it was Sunday afternoon, so Silvia decided to climb
the stairs of the bell tower. She would sail to the radiant sea on Monday.
The tower was dark. Passing the Roman griffin or Pegasus or whatever it
was, and the wing-headed thing carved into the marble, the excited girl
ascended and ascended. Here the light was bluish-greyish-white, yet also
warm; and gazing across the world she saw the myriad masts like stalks

of dark grass in the harbor, beyond which the last roofs and the lighthouse demarcated the end of gravity. Tomorrow she would happily forsake the humid glare of the coast, gathering up armloads of those sea-diamonds which glitter all the way to Dalmatia—but spiderlike within the immense metal skirt of the cathedral bell clung Rossetti; for Our Lady, entreated with his orange-fragrant prayers, and wishing to encourage and even facilitate his promise-keeping (although his sincerity in proposing marriage I myself cannot help but fault, and the only reason she haunted his desires was that she had broken their rendezvous), had informed him where to find her. Giovanna being irrelevant, he invited Silvia to bronzify herself and share his plinth forever. She for her part, determined to be free, leaped out into the sunlight. Just before she met the pavement, the Madonna dei Fiori looked upward, not at her but at Rossetti, who, fascinated by the bloodstain on her stone forehead, was thereby saved from witnessing Silvia's death—but all the same, he wept verdigrised tears on his plinth for a full three weeks, after which he got consoled by a slim, lovely young wasp-waisted beauty in a black jacket-skirt and black tights who held a whip and sometimes permitted him to feed tidbits to her pet bulldog. Her name was Lina. The whole time, Giovanna had heroically concealed her own troubles behind her palm branch.

2

Leonor, who loved a good quarrel, had been in a fine mood ever since she threw Silvia out. After drinking absinthe with two transvestite friends of hers she saw again the ghost of ancient Tanya Cirtovich in a light black veil, and painted that sad woman into the background of her latest oil autoportrait. The next time she visited the Madonna she found her weeping, and that was how she learned about Silvia's suicide. Here I wish to insert that of all the Madonnas in the world, Our Lady of the Flowers takes greatest local interest in the doings of sinners. I have it on authority that when Buddha abandoned his family to go drink enlightenment beneath a tree, his little daughter cried so much as to fall into danger of death, so in the end they sent her to Trieste to be cared for by Our Lady, who sang her madrigals by night and gave her suck from her fine stone breasts until she became a stone seagull, a happy enough outcome were it not for the fact that after the fall of Mussolini they forgot who that seagull was and moved her into the Lapidarium. Our Lady wept twenty-four stone tears over that—the most she could have done for anybody so unchristian—and then, on a sultry autumn day when the *bora* blew the window open, transformed her into a real bird so that she could fly over the sea more or less as Silvia had wished to do. As for Silvia herself, how could Our Lady help such a bad girl? But was it Silvia's fault that she had been created incapable of Triestine happiness? Moreover, she had repented about killing her cat. So the Madonna wept a river of tears into the sewer and through the forgotten Roman catacombs under the street and then down all the way to hell, in order to extinguish the flames which wracked that poor dead girl, who thus grew sufficiently sane to pray for Lilith, which entitled both Silvia and Lilith to come back to life, a favor which Our Lady gladly accomplished; she even gave Silvia a painted basket in which to carry her pet, who presently forgot to distrust her.

3

Leonor was one of those women who never allow anything to keep them from their pleasures—and, if I might say so, we would all better enjoy one another's company if we lived and died like her. Being in a hurry, she stayed but a moment to hear the Madonna's news, then kissed that stone female, of whom she was truly fond, upon the lips—didn't they have cats in common? In their time they had both rescued myriads of felines, for, as Our Lady once remarked, a cat and a prayer are equally beloved in heaven, no matter how many songbirds the cat has done for.— You should really offer up a candle for Silvia, *cara*, even though she's alive. Do it for me, my girl!— Of course, of course! cried Leonor, to whom grudges were an inconvenience. She went straight to the Serbian Orthodox church to keep her promise; and that very afternoon, as Silvia stood by the starboard railing of the ferry to Opatija, cradling Lilith in her arms and craving the snow-white specks of houses and villages ahead along the beach-edge of the blue-green coast, both woman and cat began to smell a delicious scent compounded of incense and catnip, all thanks to Leonor Fini and the Madonna, and so they lived happily ever after, until, dissatisfied with Opatija, they removed to Rijeka, and looking straight down past the white cliff-rocks and through the water's wavering green near-translucency, down to where the white ovoid rocks, many of whose centers were green, waxed and waned like moons on the bottom of the harbor, Silvia imagined that she could see the back door to hell, which made her remember how she had sinned against Lilith, followed by her own dying, burning and all the rest of it; so, half suffocated, she picked up Lilith in her basket and carried her to the market, where a man was wooing his daughter with shining cherries which were almost the scarlet-purple of a harlot's velvet dress; and first Silvia thought that cherries might save her; then she thought to trust in those neat bunches of chives, as yellow-green as summer, or in the pure white bulbs of leeks, never mind the lovely purple-black polka dots on glossy green fava beans; but the tiny old woman who sold them, turning her head like a bird—she had a brown-shawled, nut-colored face and eyes like small black round berries—gazed at Silvia and Lilith with such sweet half-comprehension (in other words, in so animal-like a fashion) that Silvia remembered Lilith's trusting gaze the moment before she hurled her out the window (she had been purring wide-eyed, with her belly-fur whiter than sea-clouds); so they fled to Vienna; indeed, they had voyaged all the way to Prague, where staring out at her from the dark narrow doorway of a photographer's shop Silvia saw a man whose face and hands were so white that she knew he must be dead; she might have recognized him from hell; his black eye-piercings aimed themselves at her, and his black gash of a mouth elongated; his black nostril-slits enlarged but of course did not pulse in the white flatness of his face. Just as Silvia began to wonder how her life would have been had she made love with Leonor Fini, the dead man said the words *Heloy Tau Varaf Panthon Homnorcum Elemiath . . .* at which Lilith, hissing, clawed at her basket, and then they both fell down dead, to the grief but not surprise of Our Lady of the Flowers.

4

Now I ought to tell you of another Triestine cat-career, whose creeping abjection rendered Our Lady of the Flowers yet sadder and wearier. Rossetti's new sweetheart Lina, the one with the whip and the bulldog, loved cats nearly as much as did Leonor Fini, and currently kept a tiny mixed-breed specimen, named Giulia, who had in kittenhood been abandoned and so could never trust anybody. Lina tried sincerely to love

Giulia, who repaid her with fear. At first she suspected her bulldog, but even when Giulia was entirely alone with Lina she could not successfully love her. Often, it is true, Giulia approached her when she was reading or sewing in bed, and not only meowed until she was petted but purred thereafter. But there were times when Giulia, suddenly fearing a lock of the woman's hair or the loudness of her heartbeat, never mind the snoring of the bulldog down the hall, would scratch or even bite Lina, drawing blood. At the best of times it was not uncommon for Giulia to go on meowing even while she was being petted; she could never really be happy. If Lina sat up suddenly in bed, the cat rushed away in terror, sometimes continuing all the way down the hall until she crashed against the wall. At night she slept under the covers with her mistress, but not infrequently she would claw her way out from the bedspread and begin galloping up and down the corridor. Any stranger terrified her, as did anybody who stood erect, presumably because she had been tormented by boys when she lived on the street. Her instinct was therefore to hide. On certain mornings when her mistress stood before the wardrobe mirror, choosing a dress, Giulia would creep around her into the back of the closet, so quietly as to be unperceived, as a consequence of which she often got shut in. Upon being trapped in that dark place she never dared to meow, so that it sometimes took a day or more for Lina to find her. She likewise had a way of wriggling into chests of drawers, and her mistress feared that someday she would get crushed.

Lina disbelieved in God, on the grounds that there was so much evil in this world that should He exist He must be evil. When they discussed the matter, Rossetti said: I believe in the kingdom of heaven, but when I consider your cat, who seems mostly so, well, self-constricted and unhappy, I sometimes wonder whether God might be some horrible wooden thing Whose purpose is to constrict *us*. On the other hand . . .

He was allergic to cats, even though he was made of bronze. Whenever he visited, poor Giulia had to stay outside the bedroom (as for the bulldog, he slept downstairs). She then scuttered up and down the hallway for much of the night, so that finally, with Lina's permission, he closed the door against her in hopes of getting some sleep—for he never slept when he was standing on his plinth; only when pressing himself against a woman's body (preferably her backside) could he refresh himself with that fleshly treat called oblivion. So Giulia had to go. Later he heard the poor creature thudding against the door, and felt guilty and sorry. Each morning he found her curled up on the carpet outside the bedroom, in a wretched little ball of greyness. She could have been dead.

When she did die, she became a timid ghost. Because most cats never become Christians, the best place to seek them after their lives end is Limbo, where they and the pagan philosophers entertain one another. Round the corner from Our Lady's statue was another way to hell, a well covered over with flowers, whose diverse beauties increased each time she brushed against them en route to helping another soul. Through those depths Our Lady now flew, her alabaster face downcast, her lips parted as if she might even breathe, and amidst shiny ebony snails and pale green night-leaves she found both Lilith, who had been stalking a child's nine-hundred-year-old beetle-sized ghost, and Giulia, who was cowering in a temporarily vacant vampire hole. Gathering them both up into her arms, so that they nearly warmed the still Christ child she also carried, the Madonna ascended three hundred and thirty-two flights of stairs, each step paler and less nitrous than the last, and thus reached the realm of mummies, where triangles, ankhs, scales and herbs are carved into the lintels of false doors; after one more flight she came into the marble-boned place beneath Leonor Fini's easel where the milk-nude women and pastel-tendoned grotesqueries dwell forever. Here there were also cats, and as many saucers of fish and of cream as they could well desire; but when Our Lady set down the two new arrivals, they hid. Knowing that they would come around in their own good time, she ascended through the easel to pay a visit on Leonor, who although she could never face the death of her own cats agreed to give Giulia and Lilith the most dazzling double funeral. By then Our Lady had even rescued Silvia, who was standing in the queue of terrified new souls to be burned forever, all of them as silent as the pigeons in the shady sandy piazza between the Museo Civico and the Instituto Nautico; plucking that lucky woman out of hell for the second time, Our Lady established her in a gilded cloud-boat on heaven's endless seas. Then she flew home, loving Trieste's long white descent from the karst to the pine trees behind it—so it seems when one approaches the city from the west, and it appears to underline a narrowing blue cape. She flew lower, and within an orange slit of light, a woman extended her stockinged leg as she smoked a cigarette; she was the clerk of a lingerie store. Our Lady overflew her, overseeing everything like the white sun pouring warmth through the cloud-lace above the massive shuttered edifice-islands whose top stories were so often painted yellow or pink; and for a space she hovered over the milky blue of cigarette smoke below the egg-yolk-hued streetlights; Leonor Fini was down there with her man-woman friend Arturo Nathan; the Madonna blew them both a kiss, so that for a moment the breeze smelled like oranges.

5

Rossetti was at Lina's the next time that Leonor came promenading by. As it happened, she loved to take note of his absences, having caught him on several nightwalking errands, the last time being seven winters ago, when she, with her wolfskin cape over her shoulders and her fingernails painted dark, approached her rendezvous with a certain dilettantish Count, while as for Rossetti, a thespian female had lately attracted him by means of a dark cloak ribbed with decorations and a feathered beaver hat; she was smooth, lovely, opulent and plump; she was positively swan-skinned; so he was just descending from his plinth when Leonor shrieked out, just to torment him: Police, police! Rossetti's deserted his post!

Please, *cara*, be discreet!

Leonor coldly informed him: I hate discretion. I hate hidden tricks.

Having heard about the time she screamed down Mussolini's mistress in Milan, he tried to brush past her in silence, so she spat in his face. After that he despised her, of course, whereas from Leonor's point of view it could have been over; not only did she forgive him but he interested her (if he but knew it) as a physical form—because Leonor, who during her self-apprenticeship used to visit the morgue ever so often, had long since lost interest in cadavers, admiring mummies for their sculptural qualities, and preferring above all the perfection of that relic which deteriorates the least: the skeleton. Who could be more bone-durable than a bronze man? Of course she never mentioned this to him, not wishing to turn his head.

This morning Giovanna occupied the master's place; having amassed confidence in the course of this last summer, she had slowly become the sort of apple-breasted woman who likes to stand nude on a plinth, with a bronze apple in her hand. And perhaps the kindly Madonna made her appear especially enticing to Leonor on that morning. Right away she craved to paint her nude, maybe holding out a tray of sweets, and definitely doing something with that adorable palm leaf; on second thought, maybe the sweet creature ought to forgo the tray and raise the palm leaf over her head as if she were an Amazon with a sword.

Rossetti, she said, I like you much better as a woman.

I *am* a woman, said Giovanna shyly.

But you look so mannish! Don't lie to me or I'll spit on you again.

You see, I've studied under him. Usually I stand down there. I try to act as he does, because—

Listen, baby, why don't you run away from here and come to my cat funeral?

Oh, no, signora! I—

Is that *man* telling you what to do? Listen, precious. Come with me. If he says an unkind word to you, my friends and I will come here with blowtorches. Do you or don't you like cats?

I—

Then come. Right now, sweetheart. I dislike the deference with which your Rossetti's been treated. Oh, what nice breasts you have. I'll make it worth your while.

Since Giovanna, like Silvia, could not say no, she let Leonor take her hand, and stepped shyly off the plinth, with her bronze heart clanging rapidly within her hollow bosom. Although in her time she had certainly seen things even more exciting than two white-wimpled farmwomen flirting with a young shepherd (for many things do happen in a park), she wondered what she might have missed. For instance, no one had ever held her hand before. Leonor, who knew how to pick up a cat such that even though its hind legs dangled it took no fright, led Giovanna with kindred gentleness into the stinging white sun, which had been doubled and half-melted amidst the oily brown rainbows of the Canal Grande. It seemed as if the curtain of water had already begun to part, and the white clouds crawling beside this splendid gash could have been the cigarette smoke of spectators at an orgy. Giovanna began to feel warm and limber. Now they turned down apartment-shaded stairs and through an arch where Leonor had once met a sweet Bohemian vampire named

Milena; and presently Leonor unlocked a door in the wall, led her up-stairs and unlocked another door. They were greeted by a wide-eyed, high-eared cat, who kept bristling out his whiskers. Then came three more cats, all coffee-colored like the reflections on the dark reddish-brown floor of the Caffè San Marco. Leonor was already kissing a kitten as sleek as the longhaired thespian who played Salome a century ago.

So this is my place, said her hostess unnecessarily. Later I'll take you beneath the easel, because I'm going to paint you as a nude cat goddess. You see, we're going to have a funeral for Giulia and Lilith. Now, these are more of *my* cats. I'll introduce you later. Time to get ready. Here. What's your name?

Giovanna.

Giovanna, take this atomizer and spray perfume on all those heaps of catshit, so our killjoys won't dare complain. Oh, mama, there you are! I have a cat mask for you! Did you hear there's going to be a double funeral? Giovanna, this is my mama, Malvina. She's my best friend. Mama, this girl's in love with Rossetti, the one in the Giardino Pubblico.

Well, well, said Leonor's mama, smiling and fanning herself. Rossetti, of all people!

What do you see in him, anyway?

You see, Leonor, he's like my father.

Does that mean you want to fuck him? Yes or no? Anyway, don't let that *man* dominate the situation. Mama, darling, entertain this little girl while I change.

Malvina Fini stood in her sweeping black dress, smiling appraisingly at Giovanna as if at a suitor. She said: Are you interested in my daughter?

God forbid, signora!

The guests were already beginning to come. The sentimental ones wore black, the sluts wore leopardskins, and there were any number of pseudo- and quasi-feline poseurs. Knowing what was expected, Leonor's mama led Giovanna down through the easel into the place where the niches were inset with frozen faded figures as in old churches, the atmo-sphere thick with silence. Self-absorbed pale women were wading naked in dark water with their hair like veils. Giovanna loved it. She had never felt so free.

For this latest saturnalia, Leonor now dressed herself in the coarse gauzelike covering of a Roman mummy, painted with ocher figures of cats and high-breasted girls in profile.— Splendid! cried Giovanna.

Thanks, *cara*.

But where are all the men?

The men around me are dead, her hostess explained. They're too limited in understanding, too brutal to survive. Well, except for Arturo, of course. Arturo, *caro*! You look fabulous in that pink dress! I mean to paint you with a tropical bird perched on your finger. Oh, and you brought cake! Is the Prince going to be late again? Do cut Giovanna a piece, and spoon-feed it to her, for the poor girl's made of bronze. Now here come some men. I'll make them entertain you; they'll love it.

And Giovanna, who had never eaten or drunk anything before, sat behind a pastel cake as elaborate as a cathedral, hoping this would never end—for it was much superior to the eternity she knew at the Giardino Pubblico "M. Tommasini"—until Leonor laughed and said: Go ahead, *cara*! Don't be a prude. Eat.

Do you like me?

That's impertinent. No, don't look at me like that! I prefer cats. They're much wiser than we are. You wanted men, you said? All right, silly! They're waiting for us in that room!— And opening a door, she showed the wide-eyed bronze girl a convocation of shining-eyed gymnasts whose chests gleamed with constellations of medals.— Fuck them all if you like; just don't take orders. All right now. Come sit by me. The services are beginning.

Lilith and Giulia, the two most important cats of the hour, behaved very differently. Lilith stalked slowly about with her tail upraised, while Giulia was scarcely to be seen.

Here came the chief mourner, Leonor's cat Sappho, who had a way of craning her head over her shoulder when she meowed for food, showing off her white breast; and when she raised her ears she was like an owl with round yellow-green eyes. Leonor opened her arms. Sappho came in, digging her claws into Leonor's robe as she ascended. Giovanna did not know what to think. She had seen cats in the park before, but until now they had been nearly colorless to her; she never imagined that they could be so intriguing. Why they preoccupied her at Leonor's can be explained from the simple fact that she had never been indoors before, nor had anyone treated her as a friend, although she remembered certain looks of Rossetti's which she had, perhaps, overinterpreted; I suspect that almost anybody could have won her over. Wide-eyed, she watched all those nude women around her; they were as white together as all the skirts of a flock of nurses, titillating themselves for lustral purposes; and thirteen nude ballerinas danced in honor of the two dead cats while thirteen na-ked nuns sang feline cantatas. Beside Giovanna, applauding, sat a visitor from downstairs: a high-breasted mummy lady whose necklaces were faded in many colors and whose white belly was cracked right down to her mons veneris. With a sad fragrance of cypresses Our Lady now ap-peared to bless the funeral with tears which hardened into good luck pearls. She stretched out her hands, and Giulia crept into them unwilling-seeming, as if she could not help herself. Then the Madonna drew her in, cradling her against the Christ child's cold stone head. Giulia began to purr. Then it was Lilith's turn. So both were rewarded and consoled for being dead.

After the words of praise were sung, Leonor found Giovanna a gym-nast with whom to waltz, but although she tried to dance, she was too stiff; Leonor laughed at her, saying she might as well have been a wooden skeleton made for processionals! Leonor was dancing with her mama and Arturo, giggling like a schoolgirl. Then she threw herself down by the shore of a bubbling black pool, her cat Salome lying across her lap with her white paws dangling, the claws flexing in harmony with her purrings.

Giovanna, she remarked, I feel quite sensual toward you—but you love Rossetti, so there's good reason to keep my distance. Mama, should I teach her how women do it?

Lolo, you're embarrassing her!

Am I? Arturo, let's start drinking! Where's that old man I like? You know, the one with the pet owl? Oh, and Gianluca arrives at last. How adorable he is!

Giovanna began to be homesick.

There was a certain lovely nineteenth-century Triestina in a high-collared white dress with a jungle of perfect leaves and flowers on her hat; she licked her lips at Giovanna, quite lustfully, but Giovanna was not interested. Leonor inquired reproachfully: Baby, wouldn't you like to see femininity triumphing over a city? Play with us; don't be a prude!

But before she could begin to bully the bronze woman, the Madonna said: Giovanna, everyone everywhere deserves happiness, even people in hell. Think of me as your mama who loves you. What would you like? Shall I ask Rossetti if he's willing to be your husband?

I want love, mama, any kind of love! I don't care anymore. And if he doesn't love me . . .

Now Giulia came creeping toward Our Lady, craving to be petted by that loving stone woman with the bloodstained forehead, and Our Lady lifted her up, embraced her until the Christ child began to open his eyes, then gently handed her to Giovanna. The instant she began to hold the cat, Giovanna experienced a hot feeling both in her bronze heart and between her legs.

So that's how it is, said the Madonna, smiling. Come downstairs with me. I'm going to introduce you to a lady who's a seventh cousin of mine. Would you like to be a cat goddess?

Will you decide for me, mama?

Well, then I think it's for the best. Leonor, darling . . .

But Leonor had already gone off to be pleasured by an ivory bird with a serpent's head.

Our Lady held her hand as they began to descend the stairs, and Giovanna found herself loving the dead cats more and more, not to mention the live ones; at the first landing she felt joyful tenderness for a certain woman's mummy which rested there upon her painted semblance within the white coffin; and the breath began to hiss within Giovanna's bronze windpipe because she lusted to know all the Egyptian cat-women who folded their arms across their animal-painted wooden breasts; smiling, upraising her lapis-bangled arms, a snake in a headdress lifted her golden head to bless Giovanna, and Our Lady said: Do you see?

6

One morning Lina (who never had any more cats, because they made her bulldog jealous) said to Rossetti: Marry me or make an end of it.— So he went back to his plinth, only to discover that Giovanna had abandoned it.

That was when he comprehended that she was the one he should have loved.— Lina's heart was broken, naturally, so Our Lady wept for her; the grey-green tear-streams flowed through the gutters and temporarily quenched the flames of hell. Meanwhile Octavian had already deserted his plinth; Maria Theresa had run away with an Austrian mountaineer; Massimiliano had strayed several times to give himself to pretty Croatian tourists; even marbleskinned Winckelmann had eloped with the bellboy of the Hotel Brulefer, so that Trieste's pantheon of park-heroes had begun evermore to resemble a fading fresco of apostles on the ceiling of a village church, the sky tarnishing toward a wintry blue-grey.

Entering the Caffè San Marco, whose twin brass coatracks might have been the skeletons of immense wine bottles, Rossetti rejoined the shadows of shutters and window-lines projected on the floor like eagles whose ribs were lyres. He wished to ascend the wide white steps of the Politeama with Giovanna at his side, although he might have wanted Giovanna solely because he did not know what else to want. At least his choices were as distinct to him as the opposing armies of spools and knobheaded cones in the ancient Egyptian senet game. Far away, across the length of the café, beneath the ceiling's breasty light globes, stood a mirror in which he could see himself and the old waiter below the reflections of the bridal-lace curtains. Rossetti sat down in the corner, and the waiter brought him three grappas. Just then, in one of the narrow silver-frosted panes—a rectangle of real life—he saw Giovanna, or someone much like her, but taller and stiffer, promenading hand in hand with Leonor Fini.

After investigating the way that after an extra grappa the coat stands at the Caffè San Marco begin to resemble horns and trombones, Rossetti, not knowing how else to act, reestablished himself at his post. When Leonor next encountered him, he was as well turned out, careful and lost in his own downward gaze, as a violinist.

All right, she said, I'll bring you to her, but only if you come in high heels, with a crown of feathers.

Be merciful, Leonor!

Rossetti, you're not nearly as masculine as you think. Lick up a little degradation; you might enjoy it. And you know what? If you do, both Giovanna and I will see you with different eyes. *Both* of us. Is that an enticement or what?

He murmured: I'm in your hands.

That's better, signor! Now come with me. I'm going to show you something. Maybe you've never been this way. Your elegant girls don't live up on the hill, do they?

Because he was so submissive now (and quite amusing in his high heels), Leonor did not mind helping him, although he slightly disgusted her—for in truth she used to enjoy his arrogance. Oh, well; there was nothing for it but to be as kind to him as to any maimed animal. Sensing this, he began to find her nearly as lovely as a nude amber woman. But then with a sadistic smile she giggled: Poor Octavian! and he saw that she had led him to the last surviving gate of Octavian Caesar's wall, which had long since become the Arco di Riccardo. High upon this relic, whose ankles and square toes were so deeply gnawed away that some people hesitated to walk through it, a cloaked and hooded little figure stretched out its sleeves, worn down to gruesomeness, its eyeless face like a peach pit, supporting or supported by spiral leafwork. The tracks and bubbles on the coarse whiteness were atmospheric pollution, no doubt.

Pinching his cheek, Leonor told him: Stay on your plinth long enough and you'll look just like that. What's the use?

Since he was now broken, she took him home to the atelier where she lived with her cats, her lover-man and her friend-man, explaining: Giovanna's underneath the easel.— But when her mama led him there, down, down, turn again, skulls clenched their fangs at him and goggled their eyesockets up out of the dark ooze, beside a dead butterfly and a dead lizard lying belly up. Far away, a blonde Sphinx was gazing at him. The Sphinx's breasts were so huge and round that they glued her to the mud.

Malvina Fini left him alone there. So did Leonor, because she was in love with her own breasts.

He saw a woman not unlike Giovanna, but with still longer, richer hair, ornamented with leaves clasped in place by a dog skull, who stood beside a dark-furred cat-man or cat-woman; they were both leaning over a tombstone, admiring a lovely corpse. Closing his eyes in loneliness, he saw parallelograms of red light. And still Giovanna made no appearance, so at length he thought to descend another flight of stairs, which led him down, down, to the mummy realm; down to where two mummies were playing a game of senet, the gameboard having been pleasingly inscribed in the top of the drawered box where the wooden pieces were kept.

Some people, including Our Lady, who eternally preserved a bright attitude, might have found these caverns almost festive, for their walls were sometimes decorated with red, black, ocher and green scenes of Apis, the sacred bull, who carries the mummies away; but Rossetti could not help but wonder: Why hasn't he carried *these* mummies away? Or is this where he brings them?— He now encountered a male mummy whose shoulders were hunched and whose knees were drawn up; he was grinning at Rossetti as if in agony, and his toes resembled white marbles. Disgusted, the bronze individual turned away, to browse among the nestled half-bodies of anthropoid coffins. Where was Giovanna? Cat mummies bared their teeth at him, lurking among the little faience things found in tombs; and although Rossetti did not know it, his expression, by which I mean the expression of his soul, for his bronze face could scarcely grimace very well, became a younger version of his hosts'. He had seen dead bodies before; sometimes murders were committed in Giardino Pubblico "M. Tommasini," even right before his plinth; and during the Occupation, the Fascists used to execute people there at night; unable to do anything else, Rossetti, who himself hoped never to be destroyed by the earth, had taken note of the dead faces like cruder mummy-masks of the Old Kingdom; now he remembered them, and the suicided Silvia disturbed him like some tiny vampiretta keening by his ear. Moreover, at first the floor-mosaics had been nearly as ornate as the brilliant red chestnuts upon the green algae and within the yellow light in the bottom of the pond in the Giardino Pubblico "M. Tommasini," but the designs grew ever more sinister, even to him, and the unpleasant atmosphere was deepened by the unsmiling joy of the goddess Hathor, whose diorite statue he encountered far too often; for even now Rossetti preferred a woman's shape like some drop of bitumen pulled upward until it draws in at the waist. Hunting for Giovanna, ever so lonely even among these lovely slender statuettes of nude wooden women with their arms at their sides, he faced another stiffnecked, grinning mummy, with its bony hands splayed out in the air over its crotch—a wonder they didn't break at the wrists!—and sometimes they approached him in a hostile manner, not that they could exactly trifle with his substance: a single blow from his bronze hand and they went flying into shards and flakes! But whatever he did, he now found himself surveilled by the rigid brown muscles of a certain mummy's face, whose strained white grin and outthrust jaw felt still more unwelcome than the long white bones breaking through the torn brown fingers, pretending to be fingernails. He uttered Giovanna's name. The mummy pointed deeper into the darkness. When he went that way, Giulia and Lilith, those two dead cats grown gruesomely swollen, launched themselves at him from some high dark niche, clacking their teeth against his face until he brushed them aside, and they flew into the darkness wailing.

At last he prayed: Madonna, *cara*, help me, and I'll offer a double handful of bronze coins to the Cathedral San Giusto!

Pitying him, Our Lady pointed, and a stream of light sped from where she stood holding her stone child up there by the Teatro Romano; it penetrated the ground and made a road for him between the replicated sceptered profiles on the sides of Egyptian sarcophagi; so he went that way, until he came into a blind passageway, and his soul's gaze grew as huge and dark as the kohled eyes upon a certain noble mummy-woman's sarcophagus; because Giovanna seemed to have grown taller and more rigid, if that were possible; and, still crowned but otherwise utterly nude, she pressed herself up tight against Our Lady's seventh cousin, the cat-headed avenger goddess Sekhmet, whose faces may differ but who always holds her scepter straight between her legs and whose tubular braids of stone hair fall down to her breasts—yes, Sekhmet, the one with the solar disk on her head; and Giovanna's bronze tongue was in this cat goddess's mouth and her bronze hands were clasping the goddess's temples so tightly, grinding her stone face against hers, that the stone had already begun to crack, but Sekhmet did not care because to her Giovanna appeared as gravely beautiful as the goddess Maat, weigher of truth. Once upon a time, Sekhmet had been betrayed by the fugitive flesh of a certain wooden lady-statuette with worm-eaten eyes. Now she would only settle for imperishable loves.

As Rossetti approached them, he perceived himself to be shrinking. It is no coincidence that Sekhmet's knees are so high that the supplicant cannot reach them. That inhuman, ruthless, whiskered head of hers slowly pulled away from Giovanna's mouth, and there she stood, tall, stiff, hardbreasted and lion-faced. Much more imperishable than he (for she was made of diorite), she sat down on her plinth, as if to put him in his place.

Giovanna now turned, pointing her bronze palm branch at him like a spear.

At Sekhmet's feet lay a half-rotten wooden coffer. Giovanna pointed to it sternly. Realizing what she expected, he withdrew three bronze coins and deposited them there. While the stone goddess sat watchful, with her lion-snout shadowed, he said: Giovanna, I'll buy you a plump canopic jar with a falcon head . . .

But she replied, more inflexibly than he ever could have imagined: You're not even a dream.

7

Rossetti returned, of course, to his plinth, where it came to him, again too late, that had he only been grave and stone-bearded like the god Ptah, he might have kept Giovanna; but since his desire for her had never been less superficial than some anthropoid pattern gilded over the glossy black bitumen of a mummy-case, and the stone cat goddess horrified him, he presently dismissed the matter from his mind. He no longer found it wearisome to adorn his standing-throne, especially on a May evening when he could overlook the brilliant gold-orange treetops of Trieste, whose church towers went golden-pink in the turquoise sky. His affections resembled bubbles in a carafe of mineral water, which may perhaps be bluer or more silver than the liquid they hang in. The matter of who might substitute for him whenever he went night-wandering concerned him, but since so many heroic effigies had already gone missing, and he had never cared that much for his so-called public, who paid him small regard and quickly rotted in any event, he essayed to overcome his self-constraint, and indeed so well succeeded that the plinth often stood empty, without any repercussions whatsoever. Admiring himself in the foxed mirror at the Caffè Stella Polaris, he presently grew sufficiently confident to drink espresso in broad daylight at the Caffè James Joyce, where vertical strips of brass ran around the counter, the legs of women accordingly getting sliced vertically, the toes of their dark leather shoes shining like stars, the black and white tiles widening away, the chocolate

voices of women all fever-warm tracks of a railroad which might have
carried him to his old flame Silvia (another lady about whom he endeav-
ored never to think), and although none of these coffeehouse women
showed interest in him (indeed, they sometimes mistook him for an ornate coatrack), he liked sitting there hour after hour, paying in bronze
coins, dreaming about sweet women whose bodies presented the pinks,
blacks and beiges of a Tiepolo drawing, while coffee-steam condensed on
his forehead and he pretended that he was sweating. In a way, he was lost,
and when Our Lady of the Flowers thought about him she sometimes
wept, to the benefit of souls in hell, but he was not discontented, especially when he visited Leonor Fini.

A certain Duke of hers took a liking to Rossetti's powers of observation,
which were of the category miscalled "phenomenal," so he sometimes
invited him over to inspect his art collection. Narrowing her eyes with
pleasure, like a cat whose mistress is gently scratching her between the
ears, Leonor said: Darling, sometimes I'm almost proud of you. The Duke
says you're the only one who's ever understood his Serbian icons.— For a
long time Rossetti pored over a certain old Italian panel of singing girl-
children, whose marble was now greenish like the translucencies of frog-
spawn. Better than anyone he could hear the hymns soughing from their
eternally half-opened mouths. He yearned to make them aware of him.
Since he could not, and for that reason among several others grew ever
more unmoored, he and Leonor become friends of a sort and occasionally
even lovers; he once brought her a pair of thick earrings from which
strings of beads depended like fingers of a hand.

Sometimes when she was marble-nude, gazing at herself in the mirror,
alone but for her cat, Leonor found herself wondering how Rossetti
would look in pink panties; by then he was up for anything; what a dear
man he was! And women were mostly such bitches; she barely knew
whom to trust! When she discussed this matter with the Duke (Lilith
plumping herself out in Leonor's lap, blinking gently as she got stroked),
he insisted that Rossetti could be counted on, after which she valued him
the more. And cypresses tilted up the flagstones across the courtyard;
their friends faded into bluish-grey *cartes de visite*, like the portrait of the
late-nineteenth-century signora in the long floral gown who stood with
her sleeve-hidden hands on her hips, gazing dreamily along a diagonal to

the other world, her hair parted high in the fashion of the period; once upon a time she had taught Leonor a certain trick of horizontal dancing. Our Lady replenished the coins in Rossetti's plinth, and almost every year was as still as the grey-blue sea along the Istrian coast.

Leonor fell out with her Duke, and Rossetti continued his own amours. Of course he never again descended the flight of stairs to that cold dry place to visit Giovanna, so he never learned that Sekhmet's flesh is sometimes rough, sparkling and dull, sometimes smooth, glossy and dark; that sometimes her lion-head is narrower and more doggish than others; that her breasts rise and sink upon her chilly chest-cliff as she pleases. He never learned that Giovanna, now unalterably herself, remained so fixed, stern, unbending and upright that even Osiris came to approve of her, and for all I know they have made her a goddess by now. As it was, every time he paid a call on Leonor he met all the cats he liked; including those naked Sphinxes whose marble breasts were bigger than planetoids; while other sorts of cat-women were invariably to be found admiring themselves in mirrors. They were more his type.

For a time Leonor moved to Paris; then her mama died, along with ever so many cats; she herself got old, and several other sad things happened. As she aged, she estimated Rossetti still more highly, because although he had barely known her then, he remembered the way she used to paint in gouache on crumpled paper in her carefree days.

THE TRENCH GHOST

1

Of course the Trench Ghost loved to play at soldiers. On those summer evenings when the light tempted even him, with the smooth grey-green translucence of old robed and headless figures of alabaster, he sometimes rose out of the ground, but never for more than an hour or two; his favorite time, as one might expect, was night, and since he could see quite well in the dark, and, like a salamander, preferred the clamminess of dirt, the best way to meet him, had anyone ever wished to, would have been to wander through the old installations at Redipuglia, preferably hooting like an owl, or groaning a little, which would have been music to him. Deep in the dirt, as trench-diggers and even certain well-connected archaeologists knew, lay tiny votive bronze figurines with genitalia and elongated limbs. The Trench Ghost, as one might imagine, was proficient at discovering these. How it was that he could pass through earth, and even concrete, more easily, and certainly more inconspicuously, than a mortar shell, while yet being able to shuffle material things about, might require an ectoplasmic physicist to explain; I can't, but then I also never understood why soldiers slaughter each other. For whatever reason, their blood darkened the dirt of Redipuglia, thereby bringing the Trench Ghost into being. How or what he was before the war I have not learned; nor could I tell you my own whereabouts before I was born. At first he scarcely wondered why he existed. Lacking solid dislikes or memories, he nonetheless had to be, without remedy. Prior to his ghosthood he might well never have lived, although at times he seemed to see his own form, whatever that might have been, and beside him the bare toes of a woman, and then a waving white curtain gone blue with Triestine sea-light; this recollection, if you care to call it that, was as worm-eaten as an old wooden statue of Saint Anna; and I for my part suppose him never to have been human; let's say that he was the *genius loci* of Redipuglia, some "emanation" or sad freak of the mass grave beside those trenches. Couldn't a pair of beetle-ridden relics have acted as anode and cathode in the celestial battery which powered him? As for his origins, there could

hardly have been any Trench Ghost in that vicinity before Gavrilo Prin-
cip shot the Archduke at Sarajevo; there weren't even any trenches . . .—
but no, earlier battles had most certainly soaked his earth.— Whether he
was subject to diminution and eventual extinction in proportion as that
buried mountain of dead human matter decayed was not for his consideration. Death meant nothing to him, being merely fundamental.

Three dozen meters beneath the deepest trench lay a Roman marble
fragment depicting an almost faceless hero on his rearing horse, the enemy's horse crouching and trampled. The Trench Ghost used to sink
down to it and gloat. He knew what murder was, and wished to drink the
pride which comes of killing others in public, at risk to oneself, at times
when killing or perishing is exactly what one's leaders call for. In the beginning the Trench Ghost did not wish that the hero possessed a face.
Why wouldn't his own serve? So one twilight he flitted out of the em-
placements and down through the trees to the little stream, in hopes of
seeing his own reflection. He could not. After that, he began to consider
faces. Beneath a concrete slab laid down in 1915 and forgotten long before
the end of the war there lay a certain neighbor of his, a grey skull all
alone, which the Trench Ghost used to take between his hands as if it
were a crystal ball, staring into its mud-choked eyes. Wondering whether
his face resembled this, he scrolled his hands across his forehead and
down his cheeks, but never could decide whether to let his fingers pass
through himself; hence his investigations dwindled into inconsistency.
He seemed to be hairy, gristly and bony, but then again, there might be
nothing to him. Sometimes he envied the skull, for being neither more
nor less than what it was, and often he hated it.

He decided that if he could not know what he was, he might as well become a general. Deploying other creatures for some purpose external to
them seemed grand; he might even fulfill himself thus. The cool, slippery
trench with its many windings and its arched ceiling like a concrete de-
basement of Roman ruins was world enough in which to enact the no-
blest dramas. Gaunt as a mummy, with his legs worn down to bones, he
began arraying his soldiers against each other. What the rare living visitors (mourners, students, lovers, sensation-seekers en route to Aquileia
or Cividale) recoiled from as a deep belly-crawl of arched tunnel descending beyond those few half-lit galleries in which their shoes stayed

clean, the Trench Ghost slid into as easily as an otter, right up to his chest in solid dirt; that way he could lay out his toys without bending over. The foremost of his gamepieces was a Venus-crowned hairpin made of bone; she, who must have been a thousand years old, began as his lieutenant-general, inspiring the others, who dared not retreat once he had pierced her into the mud, for her slender, yellow-green form was severe, her breasts hard, her tiny face resolute no matter whether the Trench Ghost had established her straight or crookedly. Immediately subordinate in rank came those Bronze Age figurines already described; as they drifted in and out of favor, he made them right or wrong, slaves or enemies. Who ought to lead the foes was a matter which gradually improved his mind; it would have been facile enough, as indeed he had done for some decades, simply to move them about, like a miser laying down gold coins; but in time even the Trench Ghost began to wonder what war was for; hence he decided to establish beyond his mere purpose an outright *cause*, relating to the conquest of evil; every martial monument on the battlefield cherished that as its engraved excuse! So which of his creatures should he define as wicked, and why? He meant to defeat them over and over, forever; hence they had to be sturdy and patient, perhaps even beautiful in their way; his cause required him to hate them, but not so vehemently as to destroy them, because then what would he do with himself?— Good Trench Ghost, he was already facing down eternity!— For the first half-century or so he satisfied himself with leaving them general-less. It sufficed that he swept them down. But presently he grew as unsatisfied with such easy victories as Hitler felt after his unopposed annexation of Czechoslovakia; and that was when he discovered another of his own qualities: He could make things.

Once upon a time, when men writhed and died in the trenches of Redipuglia, there had been fine weather, at least for a Trench Ghost: a birdsong of alarm whistles melodified the forest (which of course got wrecked and flattened—the reason that the current trees had achieved no great girth as yet); and steel butterflies of shell fragments flew up to complete this delightful picture. With almost none of a vampire's helpless obsessiveness when put to counting grains of rice until sunrise, the Trench Ghost began to gather souvenir scraps of metal. As his ambitions grew, so did his powers. He could bite a piece of copper, iron or even case-hardened steel neatly in two. He could fold down rough edges, and pinch them as smooth as piecrust-dough. By breathing on his subsections, he could adhere them to each other better than if they'd been soldered. Before long he had made himself tiny saws, files, sanders and scrapers. Whenever he had assembled another toy, he carried it into the mass grave over by the monument. This dark place, horrid to you or me, always revitalized the Trench Ghost. Furthermore, some exudation of the sad mud at its center possessed the quality of fixing any metal with a black and durable finish.

I confess the possibility that the Trench Ghost lacked any power at all over material things, in which case he was simply an insane hallucinator. But the loneliness of God makes for no story in and of itself. That is why our scribes added people to the Bible. In this story of the Trench Ghost I have likewise thought fit to let him do this or that, because otherwise the actual desperation of the eternally aware yet powerless dead might distress you who live; anyhow, I cannot prove that what he perceived himself as doing was not actually being done. So let's agree that he made a spider-legged little iron knight, who became one of his most determined captains. For the knight's antagonist he now constructed a puppet of flat black plates whose arm-edges were sharper than razors and whose legs were as those of a machine-gun tripod. In enemy pairs he made them, tiny metal figures whose heads were frequently ejected shells and whose hands were vises or triggers (some also had tongs for hands). Unlike the works of modern factories, his differed individually, even if their functions and destinies bore one flavor. Deep underground he brushed past a grubby feminine figure who was half emerging from her marble stele in the third century before Christ and had still gotten no farther. He did not wonder who she was, but he considered how he could use her. His intelligence failed him there, for he was merely a Trench Ghost; hence he floated away and constructed his own counterpart, the enemy general: tall and black in form, a narrow triangle of metal with many grooves and knurlings on its surface; its springloaded razor-wrists folded prayerfully in, its many-jointed legs drawn up ready to leap; on its head a black helmet, in its eyes cruel determination without understanding; its mouth a sawtoothed groove.

2

For years he contented himself with posing his toy soldiers as would a child, lining them up; they were stiff, still and ready, and came to appear quite smart together; even those new black steel troopers had begun to go green-verdigrised, following after their elder brothers and sisters, the bronze figurines. Sometimes he employed the ammunition-holes in the wall to sort them in; as the two armies grew, he began to classify the pieces more whimsically; one night it might be all bronze figurines on one side and steel ones on the other; or perhaps the bronze entities called out to be officers on both sides, after which he was sure to humiliate them by putting the steel creatures in charge for the next round. And as he played these sad games, he imagined that the trenches around him were his home. He thought: All here is mine. He decided: No general is greater than I.

Before the youngest oaks had thickened, he discovered that if he held each toy soldier to his heart, it would come to life, or at least enter a state which appeared alive to its maker. I wish you could have seen those black many-legged things fighting, falling back before this or that steel officer as if some horseheaded demon were sweeping them away! To the Trench Ghost it was a particular treat to watch that enemy general, the puppet of flat black plates, swinging up its jointed, sharp-edged iron arm, like the legs of a machine-gun tripod. To oppose that entity and assist the cause of good, he now constructed another grinning verdigrised monster with splayed frog-legs; it could leap and bite most desperately, and its cheeks were sharper than scalpels. For an expression the Trench Ghost awarded it whatever he had seen in the eyes of that grey skull beneath the slab from 1915. After that he fashioned springtailed dragon soldiers, gen-darmes whose helmets he roweled like cowboy spurs, beetle-browed metal infantry, shock troops who could roll forward on wheeled leaden plinths, brass corporals whose jaws happened to dwell in their chests, tapering-headed sappers no wider than Maxim cartridges, executioner queens whose skirts rushed open like skeletal umbrellas just before they worried enemies in half with their sawtoothed thighs, caterpillar-legged Alpine troops. The enemy general, of course, was the most impressively malevolent of all these toys. With each match he became more ferocious, and in this the other soldiers followed him. At first they used to knock each other down with clattering little scissors-kicks, or hurl each other waist-high against the concrete walls; by and by they learned the arts of charging, smashing and dismembering. Whenever a battle was concluded, there rose up in that dark and mucky tunnel a faint hissing or whistling or crackling. The victorious troops were cheering! Then, when the Trench Ghost flew over his miniature battlefield, breathing gusts of fog down upon their broken parts, they clanged back together again, ready for the next war.

Only the Venus-crowned hairpin refused to live. He attempted different exhalations and even foggy whispers, but could not reach her. Hence he fashioned a new steel lieutenant-general in her place. Not knowing why he did so, he pierced the Venus deep inside himself, until her face barely protruded from between his ribs. He swiveled her around in his heart so that she was always looking up at him. After that he felt a sensation of tenderness, as if he were a mother suckling her baby.

By now he felt, as most of us do, that he ruled his own doom; hence the future would be ever grander. And in this optimistic spirit the Trench Ghost taught the enemy general the art of the phalanx. All the troops already knew trench warfare. And they dug in, scrabbling grooves into the concrete with their bladed hands. Soon they began to make their own weapons.

Carrying the enemy general down under the concrete, the Trench Ghost showed him an unexploded cylinder of mustard gas. The little creature understood, and grinned with all his teeth.

3

His troops could not yet travel to mine their raw materials, so he brought them whatever they wished; in Redipuglia there is plenty of everything. He was beneficent; he built them a tiny smelter and a machine shop the size of a cigarette carton; they played fairly, and took turns, while the Trench Ghost reinspected that old memory he had of almost seeing a waving white curtain going blue in late summer Adriatic light. This picture did not lead to anything. By now the two lines were launching tiny projectiles at each other. Their bombs were no larger than matchheads, but that sufficed to blow up those brave little fellows. They screamed or buzzed when they were struck, and cheered when they did the striking. Their machine guns stridulated as sweetly as crickets; and when they rushed out of their hand-grooved trenchlets in hopes of seizing each other's positions, their fierce-shining gazes were as pleasant to the Trench Ghost as I myself find the yellow-pupilled compound eyes of the pink hydrangeas in Trieste.

Now it began to happen that the enemy general would conquer the Trench Ghost's troops, and pose upon that mound of dead metal skulls, with the splayed legs and upraised arms of a gladiator triumphing over his victim. Whenever the Trench Ghost won, he allowed his new lieutenant-general to take the credit, and then that metallic personage would preen himself like a flame-winged red-ocher demon painted on plaster. He too got stronger and crueler. By the time the oak trees got taller, the armies fought finely without any guidance from their maker. They still needed him to breathe them back into coherence after they were broken.

Another dawn whose cloud-grey was bluer than the machine guns had ever been, even when they were new, surprised the Trench Ghost into a sort of flush, as if he had been caught at something, or, far less likely, as if some spirit-fever had caressed the back of his neck; and once yellow lagoons of light began to afflict him from between those clouds, he felt still warmer, and sank down into the black mud below the concrete, where not even winter frogs could go. There he lay like a small child pretending to be asleep. Successive moments suffused and departed him no more quickly than they would have for you and me. Therefore, on account of his immortal consciousness, they tortured him. But he had long since learned how to be mad. All day, and each day, he suffered without understanding, which was how he endured it. At night, fancying himself refreshed, he rose up into his own sort of church where high barrels of thought once aimed outward, greyly shining.

4

The Trench Ghost's victories brought him no increase in the introspective joys he already experienced (drifting above his battles, he wore the dreamy smile of a Nereid in the arms of a feminine deity). As for his defeats, they neither soured him against the enemy general, whom he never thought to name, nor did they give him any pride in the intelligence of his creation. Perhaps it would be best to say that they made him wonder what else he might do. There were evenings when his two armies ranked upon their separate window-ledges awaited his pleasure, while he existed elsewhere, experiencing that cool dank dampness deep within the hollow of his heart. Lolling in his high window seat, looking through the white-arched embrasures into the sunny forest, he learned, then forgot, how twig-shadows twitched upon the pale tan earth at breast height. It was mid-morning, the rectangular window now sighting on gravel, grass and leaves. He seemed to remember the cool moldy smell of a certain old church whose Madonna elongated herself into near-phantasmic proportions. He was gazing up above the altar's fresh flowers to the Crucified One eternally perishing; and behind Him the daylight, white as linen, glowed through the three tall slit-windows. The Trench Ghost experienced something more refined than pleasure. He nearly flitted into the forest. He felt an impulse to pick flowers and lay them here.

5

Wandering this way and that through his round-ceilinged trenches set deep into the grass, he played at soldiers, one of the new-made recruits now slumping forward while standing with his hands over his steel belly, bowing grimly forward, his snout dripping sand-grains like tears; beside him, a soldier whose hands were visegrips stared at his god with a dog-like look, as if he could possibly hope for something. But the Trench Ghost barely paid attention, because the sunset clouds now put him in mind of the way that some bronze helmets express verdigris in beautiful patches of turquoise and white, still leaving the bronze color here and there. Emerging from an embrasure, he hovered over his trenches' round spines. There was lichen on them, and moss. Ivy climbed the lovely trees below them. He wandered down there in order to look back up at the skyline where his trenches lay invisibly. He listened to a blackbird. He was alone in the young forest. He liked to look up and count leaf-shadows. Soon he had gone all the way to the boundary, which was a certain helmet-topped grave.

He declined to believe that this was all there could be. Another slow-growing oak spread its arms above and away from the trench.

6

The smell of wild thyme, the ugly rounded galleries black-lichened and crackling, the pools of rainwater rapidly sinking into the karst meadow, these entered his essence, and so he carried the enemy general and his own lieutenant-general out into the sunlight, to warm them and see how they were affected, but they never did anything. He exhaled upon them very slowly. They faced off, and began to fight to the death, while he floated into the new forest, just above the railroad tracks, keeping exactly between the two tracks in the deep rock-groove there at Redipuglia. He picked a leaf and watched it fall. He stared into the sun. Looking about him, he decided: I am not this.

The Venus-crowned hairpin grew warm. Presently she tumbled out of his heart. Leaving her in the grass, he said to himself: She does not pertain to me.

Returning to his toy combatants, he found the enemy general standing atop the lieutenant-general's decapitated remains. Although the latter continued to struggle, as insects often will even after central ganglia have been removed, its motions were to little purpose. The Trench Ghost lifted the enemy general away. Angrily, it stabbed him in the leg. The Trench Ghost felt vaguely proud. Surely whatever he was had to do with this place in which he had found himself and these things he had made.

7

Since he could see through dirt and rock, he found a round-cheeked child's head made of marble—her nose broken off, her cheeks pitted— and a one-armed naked marble soldier who held his chin high. He left them underground, reasoning: They too have nothing to do with me.

Wandering through the reinforced connecting tunnels, he gazed up past the concrete and counted the roots of the young oaks and wild thyme bushes. From his visits to the mass grave he remembered brass epaulettes with gilded tentacles, a corroded canteen in a woven sack whose fibers now were atoms, a scrap of ribcage, a cross attached to a ribbon of gelato-colored stripes, and a blue case of visiting cards which to anyone else would have looked like mud. More roots groped deep through all that. He posited that things which grow downward might somehow relate to him.

Looking up between the inclined rusty rails of an artillery carriage (*cannone da 149G*, projectile weight thirty-five kilograms, maximum distance nine point three kilometers), he seemed to remember a sergeant inserting a child's head into the barrel's loading-hole, or perhaps only a loaded shell had gone in; and then two soldiers had manipulated the great wheel against the recoil-springs, in the name of great Madre Italia. Another memory appeared to be wedged behind the angled slabs of metal. In Trieste a woman was rising away from him, lifting her lips from the earth. Perhaps she was the one who had once lain beside him under the blue curtain. Then an Austrian shell was caressing a church whose wall-shards danced marble-white and bare-breasted like Nereids. He knew how the great barrel moved in its track; he had seen its birth from a vertical ovoid slit, and when the gun began to fire, destroying over months the pines that the Austrians had planted in better days, he had been there, too, all over the strategic zone demarcated by Peteans, Isonzo and Sdraussina.

He could not realize anything beyond all that, until one night when he was playing at soldiers, all the gamepieces on both sides attacked him. Smiling, still supposing that he was proud of them, he swiggled himself down, and permitted them to stab, cut and shoot his flesh, until he sent them to sleep with a long puff of breath. Then he said to himself: That they who come from me did this to me implies something about me. Yes, I'm sure that's so.

Then he removed himself, standing alone like a machine gun lost in the grass.

8

People who think they know about ghosts often suppose that a ghost is tied to its place of death, burial or unwholesome love attachment; and while this may well be the rule, as evidenced by the famous Moaning Lady whom I hear in the next room whenever I visit my favorite whorehouse, the Trench Ghost remained as free, in his own estimation, as you or I; so presently, in the interests of discovering who else he might be, he flew north, where the blue-grey sea showed itself through the slit windows in the concrete pillboxes at Tungesnes, which naturally means Tongue Ness; and here the rounded blackened foredomes of old Nazi bunkers awaited the Allies who had tricked them by landing at Normandie instead. The rusty iron rebar pleased the Trench Ghost; it resembled sunset at Redipuglia. Belowground the ceilings were sometimes brilliantly corroded ribbons of steel, sometimes simply concrete, which stank far worse than his trenches; certainly all these chambers were fouler than the nearby Viking graves. Of course not every corpse had been disinterred, much less every beetle-ridden scrap of yellow-grey bone. But that wasn't the reason it stank.

One autumn my friend Arild took me here, so that I could write this for you; thus I seem to see our Trench Ghost settling in the planked underchamber on whose ceiling huge brown spiders, slumbering, were awakened by Arild's flashlight, and writhed furiously, as if about to plop down on our heads. We found cylinders of what might have been poison gas; and if that is what it was, the Trench Ghost must have been happy, because Germans were even better at the manufacture of that than Italians.

A guru once advised me: *Find what is it that never sleeps and never wakes, and whose pale reflection is our sense of "I."* So I looked and looked; I hoped to discover the Trench Ghost, or at least to learn what his name might be—for it has always struck me that one defines oneself in part by naming others. What did he call himself, or what should I call him?— Arild said: From what I've read, ghosts cannot name anything. That's one of the things that keep them dead.

In the rubber waders that my friend provided, following his flashlight, slopping in stinking mud or clambering over some farmer's rotting pallets, I descended various flights of concrete stairs to where the grasses and flowers ended, then came into the entrance tunnel which soon angled sharply right, then straight, then left, then straight again, to make it easier for the defenders to knock an intruder on the head. I groaned, then hooted like an owl; but the Trench Ghost did not reply. Each bunker was different, probably so that intruders could make no plan. And in each bunker, my painful feeling worsened. It was a nastiness in the chest, foul and cold, wet and evil; I could not get enough air. Failing to find the Trench Ghost (although Arild promised that he had seen him), I returned out into the sweet smell of manure and moss.

9

In the evenings he pretended to wet his feet in the oily puddle within the square parapet of the command bunker's viewing-tower. Of course he had found the pit for the murdered slave laborers; sometimes he sank down there, "to get ideas" as he put it. He wondered whether any of his toy soldiers at Redipuglia had outfought the others, in which case the form or attitude of that survivor might teach him something about himself. He considered waging wars of one against many, and many against one, of riot, confusion and slaughter, because, as the ancients have said, *the pinnacle of military deployment approaches the formless.* He hoped for a perfect realization as sharp as the knife-ridge along the top of an old helmet, or, failing that, for the expansion of his understanding, like ivy growing up between the snake-toes of a great fig which is busily cracking a Triestine courtyard's flagstones. That three-angled slit of meadow and sea, sunk in the grass, seemed like a place to sink or even dig in, but no matter how deep he descended, he never found anything but dirt and stone. Concentric ring-tracks of concrete around the base of the vanished cannon led him to himself. Under a hill, a certain square concrete tunnel, closed up with stones by a farmer, tempted him to play at soldiers. Instead, he rose up under the grey sky, imitating a blackened pillbox. He asked himself: Am I this?

Floating down the wet, rock-heaped steps into mud and rubbish, he said to himself: Where the grass, moss and dandelions stop, the darkness begins.

He asked: Am I that?

In an old map room from which the benches had not yet rotted, he read the German instructions and warnings painted on the walls. He tried to take them to heart.

Sometimes he felt almost homesick for Redipuglia's masonry of tiny karstic stones rather than these German slabs, but he told himself: I am not that place, at least not anymore.

One foggy night as he hovered over the sea he wondered how it would be to return to Redipuglia and bury the enemy general deep beneath a concrete slab. By then he had read a waterlogged German field manual, so he comprehended that by some standards that action would render him as wicked as the father who buries his son alive. He had tried to be good, without certain result; so maybe he should be wicked. In the end he stayed at Tungesnes half a hundred years, building ever larger game-pieces whose faces he pretended were his.

10

Since the Second American Civil War is one of my favorite periods, I am happy to end this story then. The victory of the Afro-Creole Matriarchy, which resulted in the castration of all white American males below the age of twelve, and the liquidation of the rest, was cruel enough, no doubt, but my interest is limited to historical regalia, and you must admit that the ankh-medallions and bright pink uniforms of the Matriarchs, not to mention their sky-blue marching-banners of rampant Erzulie, deserve to be collected. At any rate, by the time the Second American Civil War began, the Trench Ghost had taught himself how to make giant steel soldiers which filled whoever commanded them with dreams of victory. Of course he helped both sides, and got rewarded as he deserved. The last I heard, he was overhovering a munitions factory in China. But since eternal stories do have a way of becoming tedious, it seems best to fire up some final episode which pretends to define the Trench Ghost in his "soul," for his existence, like yours or mine, assumes a sort of self-discovery.

During the Siege of Pocatello, which had now become a redoubt of white male power, the Trench Ghost was floating in the darkness, laughing, weeping and rubbing his hands. The chaplain, one-armed and marble-white, raised his bleeding head, staring out across the electrified wire, and the Trench Ghost imagined that he had seen him before. Indeed, perhaps he had, for, if people only knew, there are ghosts everywhere. A shell came screeching into the field hospital, while on all sides the Matriarchs chanted: *Erzulie, Erzulie!*— Another shell now killed the general. The chaplain lifted the microphone and shouted to the survivors: *It is the body that is in danger, not you.*

Astonished, the Trench Ghost asked himself whether that could be true. He decided that it was.— In that case, he decided, I'll never be in danger. I have no body.

The next shell atomized the chaplain. The Trench Ghost said to himself: That man was in danger. Something happened to him. But nothing will ever happen to me.

Then he asked himself: If that man was more than a body, then where is he? Why can't I see him? Can he see me? Is he where I am now?

And he began to search for the chaplain, as if he could hope for something. That was what led him all the way to China. How much more blood has darkened that dirt? In another century or two he might return to the Canal Grande in Trieste, because they say that every dead thing ends up in there . . .

III

THE FAITHFUL WIFE

1

If you have never loved with such luminous fidelity as to await a dead lady at a crossroads at midnight, then the question of why it is that Romania produces fewer vampires now than in old times must seem insoluble to you. Timidity becomes its own excuse; and perhaps you have not dared even to see your own spouse naked, much less encoffined. Many there are nowadays who refrain from kissing a dead forehead. A wife dies alone in a hospital bed, in the small hours when the nurse sits down to sleep, while the janitor rests his chin on the handle of his mop. At mid-morning the husband peeks in to identify her; next comes the undertaker to nail her up, or, as may be, the coroner to slit her open. Ashes to ashes, promises the minister, but should she refrain from decaying in that fashion, who will be apprised of that wondrous miracle except for the true heart who comes to the crossroads at midnight to share a kiss? Satan, they say, can speak even from a rotting skull—a mere assertion seized upon by you who have never loved bravely. Insisting over the sad sighs of your conscience that you would not be able to distinguish her from Satan, you decline to visit your own wife, forgetting that loneliness is the Devil's work—and what could be more lonely than a beautiful dead lady returning to the cemetery without a kind embrace from anyone? Let me tell you this: In Romania it was once not entirely unheard of for female vampires to glide home to their children; and in Greece the cobbler Alexander of Pyrgos died, became one of those swollen-bellied leather-brown monsters whom they call *vrykolakas*, and then, relying upon the discretion of a moonless night, crept back into the doorway of his much-adored wife, for whom he drew water untiringly. In the daytime, so that the children would not be afraid, he slept inside a certain oblong trunk which leaned up against the back of the closet; every night as soon as the young ones were all asleep his dear wife let him out, and he bent over his bench, returning their tiny shoes into good trim. As for him, he went barefoot and naked; his clothes had long since rotted off him; his yellow toenails were indistinguishable from hooves. Perhaps his skill had declined somewhat; he now lost tack nails or sometimes drove them in crooked, but his heart, let's say, was correct. Sitting at his bench, counting scraps of leather with unmoving lips, he did as much as he could. One night when he stood at the well for his wife, with a bucket over each shoulder, the moon dashed out from the clouds to betray him; and so the neighbors came at high noon with blunderbusses, scythes, stakes and pitchforks. At that hour he was helpless, of course. They built a pyre outside the house, burned him, box and all, hacked up his curiously elongated bones, and raked everything down into that well, which they supposed his exertions must have cursed. They similarly disposed of his tools and stock (although one lad couldn't help keeping a handful of shining rivets; he soon died of a nightmare pox). Next went the children's shoes, and even the dried bouquet which this Alexander had first brought home from the graveyard. The way some tell it, his wife was tearless; the children had been having nightmares anyhow. It is reported when the saviors came in (not very politely, I'm afraid), she even might have pointed to the closet—wordlessly, in case he could hear. On the other hand, it could have been that her love for this Alexander survived his demise, in which case she knew enough to stay on the good side of the Church.— At any rate, a week after the vampire's removal there came a plague to Pyrgos. How could anyone blame Alexander's harmless ashes? Besides, nobody dared to drink from that polluted well, which, so some asserted, emitted a miasmatic cloud (people can always be found to speak badly of the dead).

2

The story now turns to Bohemia, where a sad paterfamilias named Michael Liebesmann, with three young daughters in attendance, watched his dear wife's coffin descend into the grave. All the neighbors were there, of course; even the butcher was weeping; I wonder if she owed him money? The priest gave a particularly fine sermon, and in signification of another kind of future consolation, there was visited upon Michael the full-lipped yet narrow smile of his widowed neighbor Doroteja, who wished to become his second wife. At the end, as was customary in their region, the members of the bereaved family masked themselves, and returned home circuitously, in order that the abandoned corpse could not follow them.

According to the astrologers, on that very night the moon had entered her seventh mansion, called *Alarzach,* which is good for lovers. And just before it set, while the children slept and Michael sat sadly in his doorway, his wife flitted back to him.

3

Among the reasons we ought to be grateful to death is that not until we lose the one whom we love can we feel how much we've loved her. Grief's wound lets light in! According to the Book of Revelation, it is a very particular species of light. I refer you to that certain half-hour on a summer's mid-morning in Torino when the charwomen are all finishing along the Corso Re Umberto, so that the floors of those squarish passageways they've tended, be they marble, mosaic-tiled or ordinary concrete, all glisten with comparable preciousness; and the walls, painted in burgundy and Naples yellow, achieve greater brilliance than they ever will again (until tomorrow, tomorrow); this goes especially for their far ends, which hint of sunlit courts. For we dwell within ourselves, losing sight, as Plato says, of the darkness; and when Death creeps up silently behind us on his bony tiptoes, strangles our cohabitant, and wrenches her outside of our flesh, we cannot but *see* that golden morning beyond us, which most of us fear more than Death himself. The light is nameless, while the wound is called loneliness. In time we teach ourselves to forget the light, straightening up within our bodies so that our soul-faces resume residence within our skulls; and that clotting gash in the chest (not mortal this time, evidently) admits the light only vaguely now; anyhow, it's so far below our chins as to pose no inconvenience;* and the charwomen set down their buckets, stretch, massage their aching hips, shield their gazes with dirty sweaty hands and peer down those corridors which they've mopped for ever so many thousands of times; and while the light remains

---

* It might be best to be a tree, drinking sunlight, eating dirt and budding for ever so many seasons, probably without the knowledge which doubles pleasure but also without the corresponding double pain when autumn requires the tree to shed pieces of itself. For a tree, life might be experienced as easy and semicontinual aggrandizement, death as nothing—but who can say? Is it any worse to while away an afternoon over a grappa or two, at a little round table, drinking in the sunshine of passing women?

as hurtful as ever, the tunnels and corridors have dulled now, and the charwomen turn back into themselves, permitting me to do the same; in short, I follow a pair of immaculate policemen as we cross the Piazza Solferino untroubled by the red traffic signal. Such is light; such is life; and so the philosophers explained to me while we sat beneath Italian flags in Torino; and a double-chinned lady trolled through her magenta purse without looking, while a man in very dark sunglasses picked her pocket.

4

In short, Michael was lucky to get his wife back after bereavement taught him how to value her. But could he remember how precious she was?

5

Her eyes shone dully at him like copper coins in an algaed pool. She seemed very weak. Her cerements were stained with dirt, urine and blood. He took her hand, which resembled cool yellow marble. No one else was out, it being, appropriately, the witching hour. Tenderly he conveyed her to a secret place in the river-reeds, stripped her and himself, and bore her into the water, squatting down to lay her across his knees, with his right arm cradling her neck and his left supporting her ankles, and so he held her, singing her name to her while the filth oozed out to darken the water downstream. He rocked her in his arms, combing clean her long hair. Frantically kissing her drooping, bloody wrists, supporting her drooping head, he whispered loving secrets into her ear. Finally, he carried her to the grass and laid her across his lap. He massaged her with chicken-fat, arnica and lavender. Then he pulled her Sunday dress back over her, lifted her into his arms, and conveyed her into the hayshed where the children would not see her. In the corner where the forage was freshest and softest he laid down a bedsheet, which he tucked around her, then walled her away behind heaps of hay. Her eyes shone like candles, because she knew how much he loved her.

6

He kissed her and kissed her, fearing that she had fled him. At last she reopened her eyes.

He asked what death was like, and, just as the lid of an anthropoid Egyptian coffin slowly levitates, at first proffering nothing but a wedge of darkness, no long brown mummy-fingers yet, she parted her lips to speak. Terror poisoned him. She said, almost angrily: Are you *sure*?

Yes, Milena, I wish to know—for your sake . . .

Very well. You'll find yourself choking in your tomb, however large it might be. Even an Emperor learns that his sepulcher is no refuge.

What is it, then?

A torture chamber to kill the dead.

Upon her breath was the bitter smell of sand. As he stood appalled, she sought his hand, whispering: Save me; don't make me go back there! Do you promise?

I promise.

Thank you, husband.

Now tell me what happened to you.

Nothing.

And then what?

Then suddenly I missed you so much that it was worse than dying. I was blind and paralyzed, but aware. I wanted to be dead and not yearn for you, but I couldn't be, and if I had been, the grave would have begun torturing me again. Then I felt a pain in my right breast as if a rat were eating me; and worms bored into my eyes. Through the holes they had made, I could see, and through the hole in my breast, my heart could drink from the moon. So I came to life again. See, Michael—feel my heart!

She laid his hand on her yellow-white breast, smiling pitiably.

Can you feel it beat?

Yes, he lied, kissing her blue lips.

Michael?

What is it, darling?

I think the sexton stole my wedding ring.

Let him keep it.

What will we do?

I don't know, he said. But he did know the following: Since he loved her, he would not return her (at least not prematurely) to *that*, her coffin-prisoned head staring up forever into vile darkness.

7

But then matters got worse, for Milena said: It's about to get light. I need to hide—

God's sake, what do you mean?

To sleep in my grave, until nightfall.

With the coffin-lid pressing on your face?

Yes. But I won't know it.

If I make you a new coffin, can you sleep at home?

Yes, but if anybody finds out—

I can't bear to be apart from you, and you under the earth.

Yes, yes; I'm going now. Michael, I love you; I'm going now . . .

That night she returned to him. By then, he had built a wooden box to her measure, which of course he knew by heart.

8

Usually she awoke shortly before dusk, but she preferred not to be present until the Blessing of the Lamps. They had agreed not to tell the children, at least not until they were older.

Sometimes he peeped in on her in late afternoon, when he could not bear to wait anymore. At that time her open eyes wore that lost gaze pertaining to the faces of marble statues. Taking her thus unawares gave him an erotic feeling he could hardly resist, but as he bent down to kiss her, she seemed almost to squirm and grimace, as if his presence were disturbing her; her mouth gave off a bad smell. In the morning, as he discovered, she presented a far more hideous appearance. It was as if at dawn she relapsed into an utterly corpselike state, then slowly over the daylight hours regained whatever it was she needed to live. Once he understood this, he would no more have spied on her (at least, not too often) before the sun was waning than he would have watched her in the outhouse.

You see, he tried his best to love her as she was, which is why this story will be as sweet as the tale of little Merit, the Egyptian wife, who, playing one of her girlish pranks, predeceased her husband; he adored her so much that he permitted her to dwell forever inside the sarcophagus made to his own larger measure. The slaves built him another, and in time, as any good husband should, he came to join her. And now the glass-eyed effigies of their anthropoid coffins stare straight up, side by side. She is bewitching in her gilded and bitumen-striped mummy-mask. They have kohled the outlines of her sweet dark eyes; they have painted her eyebrows and drawn stylish cat-lines from the outer corners of her eyes toward her temples. Her cheeks have been rouged to perfection, and gold shines subtly through the transparency of her pink smile. They gaze upward, but will never see the sky.

9

He begged her to let him comb her hair, and, smiling wearily or perhaps grimacing, she bowed her head to him, while lovingly he ran her best four-toothed comb, one of whose teeth the middle daughter had broken off by accident when she was very little, through her long wet hair, singing to her as he untangled it.

10

Her mother, whom he had brought secretly, gazed downward, and her face contorted into a sobbing smile. Milena opened her eyes. When she reached up to touch her mother's neck, the mother screamed.

They made her swear by Saint Polona not to tell anyone. She kept weeping.

Mother, it's really me; I'm not a fiend . . .

Oh, I believe you; I won't say a word, not even to the priest, but why in the Lord's name couldn't you sleep in your grave? What happened to you, Milena; what happened?

Before she could answer, Michael said: Mother, if you learn the answer, you'll never have any peace. I promise upon my salvation that she's done nothing evil. Trust me! You're better off not not knowing what death is.

I don't know, I don't know—

Mother, said the returned one, do you want to see me again?

No, child. I can't bear this. I love you, and I wish you and Michael happiness, but you're *dead*. I'm going to tell myself this never happened . . .

11

Next came the turn of the daughters, peeping pale and timid, the youngest one gaping and the middle one rubbing her red eyes, the eldest folding her hands in her lap—how could this *not* have occurred?

It was late afternoon, going on twilight; and because their father had forbidden them to enter the hayshed they crept in there, discovering the box which he had built, and carved with flowers, hearts and apples as sweet as any of the decorations on the toys he'd made them.— And why didn't he nail down the lid?— Reader, you know the reason: to spy upon the naked helplessness of his wife, as the children now did.

At first they supposed her to be some kind of doll. From the smell, it must have lain in the manure heap. Why was it here, and how did it come to be wearing their mother's clothes? Cautiously stroking her cold soft flesh, they grew afraid. The sun dipped lower. And then Milena opened her eyes; her face grew round, and she struggled to speak; but the eldest daughter was the one to scream.

Their father rushed in, his face dark with fury and a hammer in his hand. When he saw the circumstances, he sighed, sat down on a hay bale and tightly closed his eyes.

Swear by Saint Polona . . . their mother lisped groggily, her tongue blue and swollen.

The father arose.— This is our family secret, he instructed them. Your mother has come back, because she loves us. You're to tell no one. If you do, we'll all be destroyed. Foolish, foolish girls! Why didn't you listen to me? Now swear by Saint Polona to keep this quiet. You heard your mother. Go on now! Swear—you first!

12

After this the couple were well aware that they must soon be exposed. One of their favorite topics, and perhaps the most morbid one, became the question of which girl would tattle, and how soon. As it was, the daughters had been pale and shy ever since their mother's death. Their father's clandestine night existence told on him, of course, so by day he was peevish and negligent with them; they were already almost orphans. Now they were practically ill.

Their parents called a family council—after dark, of course, when their mother could be up and about. The father, who had scarcely slept, sat with his eyes half open and his head slumped forward. The mother stood beside him, holding his hand.

She said: Children, you must believe us. I would have shown myself to you in time. Say you believe.

Yes, mama.

Now, since you have brought this burden upon yourselves, you must bear it. You have committed the oldest sin. Do you know what it is?

The sin of Adam and Eve, their middle daughter whispered.

That's right. Your father and I forgive you, because you and we are all their children together. You craved knowledge, didn't you?

I wish there were no such thing, and we all went crawling like animals! the youngest cried out.

Oh, that would be a different state of affairs, to be sure, laughed the father. But would you still want to be an animal come slaughtering time?

Enough, their mother said. We're a family again now. We'll always be together by night. Michael, did you bar the door?

I never forget that.

Mama, why do the neighbors' dogs howl every night?

They howl at me, you silly girl. You know what I am. *Don't you?*

A vampire.

So they'd call me. But look at your father. Do you see any marks on his neck? I'll never suck your blood—that I swear by Saint Polona. Now, don't doubt me anymore, or I'll get angry. Go fetch your needles. It's time to mend your father's clothes.

The candle was burning down within the hanging pewter lamp when the middle daughter asked: Mama, what should I tell the neighbors if they ask why we hide behind closed windows every night?

Tell them we're in mourning.

You taught us never to tell lies.

Don't contradict me, or Father will show you the back of his hand.

13

At every dawn, their parting increased his sorrow; aware that she was dying yet again, he could scarcely bear this latest bereavement. What if this time were truly the last, and within the coffin she would this very morning burst into putrescence, or, worse yet, become a *vrykolakas*? Pitying and seeking to comfort him, the faithful wife prepared his breakfast before she went to lie down. (The daughters were long asleep, tossing and moaning in their beds.) She kissed him on the mouth, trimmed his beard, helped him plan his daily projects, murmured into his hopeful ear promises of erotic loving-kindness and professions of spiritual longing, and then departed, closing her coffin-lid from within, thanks to a handle he had installed for her. He now hated so much to see her there that in the afternoons he only peeped in on her to reassure himself that she was slowly coming back to life. In truth, the transformation was hardly easy for her, either. Like her mother before her, she suffered from claustrophobia, and to lie in a dark carrion-box so close and narrow about her that she could barely lift her head a quarter-inch, much less turn over if her back got tired, was nasty enough; to depart the birds, flowers and children of daylight was harder still; worst of all was leaving him, whom she loved more than what might be called her life. How sorry she was for him, to leave him entirely alone in the house (for what good were the children to him?), with a dead woman in the hayshed, dogs howling all around and the neighbors meditating murder! Grateful for his insensitivity to her anguish on that quotidian journey into death, she sought always to distract him from what must be, as if he were her little son who had been bitten by a wolf and must now get cauterized. Let him hide his greying head in her skirt! Although she would never lie to him, she shielded him from horror wherever she could. He had wished to know what it was like to be dead, and she had answered, as a good wife should. But he could scarcely bear it. Revolting at the morning stench within her coffin, for her he fashioned sachets of mint and lavender, although that was women's work, and bought her cloves, frankincense and other such precious spices at the apothecary's shop; when she came back to herself in the early evenings, these scents comforted her as evidence of his love; on most occasions, however, he was there in person, watching anxiously over her with the lid drawn back. At first these invasions of her slumber humiliated her; when she caught the girls doing it she was angrier with them than ever before; at the same time, she knew (for on her wedding day her mother had told her this, earnestly advising her for the sake of decency to follow their example) that even in darkness her parents had never been entirely naked for each other; and on her very first night with Michael, intoxicated by his needy adoration, she had promised to withhold nothing that he asked of her, no matter whether she felt ashamed; he for his part swore to cherish her unerringly, as indeed he did, until all shame soon turned to luxurious joy. So it had been until her death. Now more than ever she craved that their feelings for each other would continue undecayed. She tried to make herself pretty for him before lying down, just in case that could secure her more tightly in his affections. Of course she dreaded his seeing her when she was at her worst. But again and again he swore that she was and would always be his excitress, just as for her he remained the soul which hers was framed in; and if there truly do exist spiritual vapors by which magic is excited out of flesh, even dead flesh deep in the ground, then by grace of his loving sorrow over her death he must have been gifted to exhale those vapors from his heart, kneeling desperately before her at the graveside, while the priest, mother, daughters and the rest stood back, variously moved, titillated and aghast. After all, she had dreamed in her grave that the mask which custom required him to wear, in order to give her the slip, had fallen off his face three times.

Again he comforted her; again she softly thanked him for declining to judge her according to the ways of this world. Slowly he stroked her hair until dawn. Just before the noon hour, lonely and doubting the miracle, he stole in to peep upon her. She was a rather pretty sight as she lay sleeping, with her head twisted sideways and blood dribbling from her gaping mouth.

14

Another neighbor came over to complain that his dog lay lifeless and bloodless, to which Michael replied that from what he had always been given to understand, dogs died, just as people did; and since the neighbor had nothing to do with the passing of his late wife, just how was *he* concerned with some accident involving a dog?

I'm not saying that *you* had anything to do with it, replied the neighbor in a chilling tone, striding one step closer, so that Michael nearly reached for his knife; instead, he replied: Then good day to you! closing the door in the face of this former friend whom he must now keep away forever. As soon as he had bolted himself in, his bowels went weak with dread—for what if the deed was, in fact, Milena's? Thanks to the priests, he was as well apprised as you or I that some vampires, especially early in their careers, can roughhouse with the living in what must be a playful way, tossing them up and down, or stamping back and forth upon their roofs, having lascivious intercourse with their wives, rolling them around in their beds, opening the taps of their wine-barrels; but in the stories these vampires were all men; furthermore, Milena's disposition had not changed—but what if she needed to suck blood? He'd better have it out with her.

15

Before he could honor that resolution, he heard people outside whispering. The next to visit was the widow Doroteja, who arrived like a wreath-bearing angel.

When he was young and had not yet made up his mind which of them he should marry, Doroteja had fashioned him a black Easter egg painted with a golden castle, while Milena had made him a lavender egg painted with a yellow candle and two columns of ovals each of which were red on the left and blue on the right.

It is not good for a man to live alone, Doroteja said to him. So the Bible says.

Then it must be true, he replied. How are you getting along?

Michael, I'm very lonely. If you agree to be my husband, I'll forgive you for having married Milena first.

Well, he said, that's certainly something to think on.

I want to live with you and take care of you all your life, she said. And your children need a mother.

You're right in everything you say.

Doroteja laid her sweet brown hand on his arm. If Milena hadn't been right there in the hayshed, he would have found her touch pleasant. Even so, he wouldn't say he didn't enjoy it. (Toward her he felt the magnetism of the flesh, to be sure, but not yet the flesh's understanding, much less the magic of the blood.)

Michael, she said, I'll tell you a secret. When Tadeusz lay dying, he told me to look under the hearthstones. I never would have guessed; we lived like poor people. But there was a handkerchief full of silver, and even three gold pieces. We won't be wretched when we get old, the way so many people are, without even a breadcrust or a stick of firewood . . .

Her eyes were enchanting. He wondered whether there might be something different about the gaze of a man's second wife, perhaps because she knows she must share him after death.

Thank you for your love, Doroteja. I need some time yet to know my own mind, for I still feel attached to Milena.

That's to be expected. But how long must I await your answer?

Not long, he replied (for how much longer could matters go on like this?). Taking her hand in his—for he hated to hurt her—he added: And in any event, I swear by Saint Polona to keep your secret.

May I greet the children before I go?

What could Michael say to this? They were in the garden, weeding and killing snails. He called them. They came running to her with howls of joy.

16

That night was as dark as a blacksmith's tongs. A stone struck the door. When the girls tried to speak of Doroteja (for they seldom got any visitors nowadays), he sent them harshly to bed.

Why treat them so? said Milena. I know she was here.

How much can you hear in your sleep?

More than you imagine.

Then you know I kept faith with you.

I didn't doubt it, said his wife. How can I do anything but trust you absolutely? Any day you like, call the people in . . .

Milena, we'd better make a plan.

Would you send me back to my grave?

No!

All the same, perhaps that's where I had better spend my days. Doroteja will return soon.

I told her to wait.

You just don't think, said his wife. Let me tell you how to do this.

They began to plan together.

17

For three nights they avoided each other. He left the windows unshuttered at dusk, as he used to when she was alive. He called upon the neighbors, who barely spoke to him. Sleep came badly; when it did, he kept dreaming that her face had grown so thickly spiderwebbed that it could have been a sculptor's half-cut crystal.

How should he have felt, to be free of her? Perhaps it was cunning on her part, to give him opportunity to go for the priest; or it could have been simple love. It pleases me to report that he never felt the temptings of what good citizens would call conscience. He was bound to her, and freely.

He slept by night, for a change, and by day he let himself be seen in field and street. Yet the air continued to petrify around him, such was his danger and isolation. Had I more time I might have told you how it used to be for him with those people when Milena was still alive. But memories are mere tombs, containing foul dust which will never return to what it was, for all our hoping. So he resolutely forgot his friendship with those goodwives and honest men. Life must be lived without subservience to dust; God knows the stuff is difficult enough to get away from.

Thus he did whatever he could, to preserve himself and her. I wish you could have seen his face on the fourth evening, when he was to see her again.

There was an old tomb she knew (he refrained from asking which of her neighbors had showed it to her); they began to meet there in order to be alone. He took a wax impression of the lock, and the blacksmith, not suspecting what it was, made him a key. She awaited him within. They lay cool and wet together in the smell of stone. How nice it was! How lovely on those hot summer nights in the tomb with his wife!— Their daughters lay alone at home, fearfully crossing themselves.

In a shady alcove of damp black sand, the wall grown in with heart-shaped leaves, the moon peeped in at them around the shoulder of a stone Madonna; they hid behind her mossy stone robe, baby ferns creeping out from the buttresses.

At noon the ivy was as clean and shiny as grape leaves growing on the trellis, with silver-white ribs of light scraping across the dark leaf-claws.

Once when she was underground he went there, the chalky stone almost sweating, and all he could think of was how much he longed to rest in her cold sweaty hair.

18

The next day he overheard the youngest daughter saying that since their mother had been ordinary, neither extremely good like Doroteja nor as wicked as the stepmother next door who had boiled up her husband's little boy for soup, she thought the best course generally was to avoid conversation with their mother, although the appropriate demeanor for herself personally would be to respect whichever example her sisters set. Michael said nothing, either to himself or to Milena. He put the children to spreading manure across the field, while he went to cut firewood. Staring at his reflected face in an inlet of the river, he saw a lonely, guilty man. Well, what was he to do? Had Milena sinned against him by coming back? And if their daughters hesitated to love her, was that blameable? Perhaps he should have beaten the youngest, but what was the use? He could not imagine how many Hail Marys it might take to set things right.

19

Perhaps the darkest issue in human relationships—certainly murkier than questions of vampirism, which have been resolved ages ago by our Mother Church—is that of family favoritism. Regarding the three daughters, whose names I have declined to give, in order to maintain them in their proper station in this tale, no one knew toward which parent each had experienced her closest connection; from the parents' point of view, the question hardly presented itself; for when we marry we tend to feel (unless others have arranged the match for us) that our spouse appeals to at least some of our inclinations, which is why we chose as we did; whereas our children, no matter whether we set out on purpose to produce them, or how many of our own qualities we discover or invent in them, arrive in the form of little persons who, like us, are emphatically themselves, no matter what others might wish them to be; hence, parents and children resemble neighbors, with whom we find ourselves accidentally living, and toward whom we make more or less headway in accommodating ourselves. I would never be so rude as to state that

Milena and Michael loved one another more than they did their children, nor that the girls preferred one parent to another; but I do suspect that after she had returned from the dead, Milena found her daughters less affectionate than before. Perhaps she could have made a better effort, but in those days, parents found themselves so preoccupied with protecting the family from the cruelest sort of destitution that they found scant time to cosset the small beings they ploughed and spun for. And in this case, there were the extra difficulties of ploughing and spinning while concealing a member of the undead.

Spitting three times, the cobbler informed him: The Bible tells us: *You shall not suffer a witch to live.*

I don't know any witches, Michael replied.

From outside, the house still appeared unhaunted, although on the night of her first return, their grass roof had begun to die. The Bulgarians say that a vampire who is new first sprays sparks in the darkness and projects a shadow on the wall; as he gets older and stronger, the shadow gets denser. This did not transpire with Milena, although her face seemed to have widened and darkened. Perhaps she wasn't a vampire at all. Her lips smiled reddish-brown. Her sad black eyes were huge but they did not shine; they could have been painted on. Growing ever more accustomed to her, Michael now thought it best to be straightforward (although of course not forward). His wife had come back to him; that was all. No doubt it must have been God's will.

At any rate, how could it have stayed secret? The neighbors' eyelids drooped as if they were half asleep, but their mouths opened and their faces turned to wood. Gathering between the ruts of the street, they watched the couple sitting together on the doorstep, her face turned toward his while she smiled as if in joy and relief, holding his hand; they claimed to believe that something was wrong, either with the way he kept massaging her fingers, as if he were striving to warm them, or with the way her dark eyes never fixed on anyone but him; that wasn't natural; she must be sucking his blood! It's true that he still seemed to be more or less himself, but who would swear to that in an ecclesiastical court? She appeared to fascinate him even more than she had in life, although he had certainly adored her then; he kept turning toward her; sometimes he gazed out into the world, perhaps anxiously, and then she stared into the ground. Her long black hair gleamed more than ever before; it seemed to be nourished on some new grease.

Thank God for the tomb away from home where she now passed her sunny hours! The neighbor women would have peered in on her all day, praying with their mouths open, seeking to know if that dead face were still hers. As it was, they hounded his daughters (who grew skinny and never said anything); several times he caught people snooping in the hayshed. He burned up the lovely coffin he had made, but too late; they must have told the priest. When Milena awoke that night, and flitted darkly in through his window, those two discussed the matter and found themselves of one mind. Before the grim men with stakes and torches had entirely surrounded the house, he sent for the priest himself. Then he sat at his doorstep alone, watching his dear friends and neighbors, who as usual said nothing to him.

20

The priest was as wide-eyed as an owl on a Greek vase.

I know your mother-in-law very well, of course, and she has confessed that on a recent occasion, during the night, you sent for her.

Yes, Father.

That's all very well, saying, *yes, Father,* but you delayed your coming to me. Until now there's never been anything against you. You're a hard worker, a good tither, no blasphemy or fornication, but now . . .

Yes, Father.

Speak.

Well, Father, Milena came back to me. She was buried by mistake.

That's not what your mother-in-law said.

Well imagining what his mother-in-law had said, he imagined equally well the recent doings of those people who all his life had known who he was and after his marriage tied up their bags of knowledge and lost them, because there was nothing further to know, and now reached new conclusions about him, mostly that he had become uncanny and ought to suffer for their safety or pleasure. Of course they had been acquainted with Milena and continued familiar with her mother, whom they now promptly haunted and tormented, until she, as most people would, gave up her dead daughter, and Michael with her. So the priest got involved. To him

Michael said: But it's true—I swear it on Milena's grave! And since her mother didn't approve, I told Milena to go back where she came from—

If you're lying, you'll be burned.

Yes, Father.

We may burn you regardless. You didn't confess to me.

Please forgive me, Father.

The neighbors say that she sports licentiously with you every night.

She's my wife, Father.

But you just claimed that you'd sent her away—

Yes, Father, because *man who is born of woman, his days are short and filled with trouble*—

I'll remand you to the magistrate for questioning.

Please, Father, what about my children?

We'll make provision for them. I'll speak with Doroteja.

What if I deed our home to the Church as security?

Very well. Sign your mark here. Do you swear by the Virgin not to run away?

I swear.

The Inquisitors will send for you when they arrive.

Yes, Father.

Go tend to your children. If your wife appears, you must bring her straightaway.

Yes, Father. Father, Milena suspects the sexton of stealing her wedding ring.

We'll search for it in the coffin.

21

Beautiful and resolute, the eldest daughter raised the carving knife over her mother, turning toward him as he entered, but appearing not to perceive him, her face barely poised in his direction, the evening light very lovely on the near side of her head and neck, her sweet lips, which resembled her mother's, a trifle clenched.

22

The daughters, those lovely girls, soon unfortunately died, of the cholera, it was said, although the neighbors naturally wondered whether the mother had sucked them dry. In fact it truly had been the cholera, and when Michael asked Milena whether she could bring them back, she replied: Don't ask God for too much.— Astounded that she could even speak of God, he determined to test her one morning while she slept, having obtained a pinch of consecrated salt from Father Hauser. He never meant to harm her, only to comprehend what she was.— What do you suppose happened? Did it burn her? He was just about to sprinkle it over her left hand when slowly, sadly, she opened her dark eyes, with all her best effort keeping at bay the glaring stupor of daylight, and *looked* at him, so that he felt ashamed. Hence he never learned whether holy salt could burn her; he went on living without seeking certainty.

Weeping, she wove the daughters' shrouds in a single night. She requested to be alone for the sake of her grief, but when he peeked through the keyhole he saw that three spiders were helping her. Bursting in, he demanded: Are those your familiars? Did the Devil give them to you?

Of course not, husband. I found them.

What does that mean?

I only found them; that's all.

(Perhaps you think it ghastly, what happened to the children, but there is no evidence of malice.)

Here came Doroteja's elder sister, likewise a widow, and a simple, hardworking woman who had already lost half her teeth, lifting up her skirts as she negotiated the mud between her house and his, the kerchief wrapped tight around her sweaty forehead and her basket half full of cow dung. Fearing her condolences, Michael locked the door. She might have heard him breathing inside.

23

The authorities reasoned with him, citing wise words of the *Malleus Maleficarum*, which is a book of such virtue against the Black Arts that a Papal Bull has praised it, and the wise words run thus: *I have found a woman more bitter than death, who is the hunter's snare, and her heart is a net, and her hands are bands.* And still further they counseled him from this Book, saying: *There are three things that are never satisfied, yea, a fourth thing, which says not, It is enough; that is, the mouth of the womb.*

But he replied to them in their own coin, beseeching them: Isn't marriage an eternal sacrament? Have I misunderstood? At all the weddings and funerals I have attended, and on Easter, and at every baptism, you teach us that the souls of those to whom we have been united in the sacraments will be with us in the Hereafter—

Provided that the parties are Christian. My good man, don't you see that your wife has become a foul fiend? Like Eve herself, she has grown more bitter than death. The very grave vomits her out! And the very first result is that you begin to question us. Can't you hear the Devil laughing? Kneel down now and beg our pardon, for we know you to be a simple man misled by uxoriousness.

Pray forgive me, Fathers.

The priest's most prized and efficacious tool, a gable-faced reliquary casket, was given to be carried in the altar boy's arms.— And you know what will happen to you if you drop it!— Yes, Father.— As for the butcher, his apprentice bore the sack of knives and the sharpening stele, but he himself marched with the great wooden mallet (an implement of office) over his shoulder; he used it to pound tough meat into tender, which went for a higher price. Beside them walked the executioner, Hans Trollhand, a shaveheaded, essential man with a bundle of rough stakes under his arm.

In Beograd it is often the drummer boy who carries the surgeon's box of instruments when it comes time to disinter a suspected vampire, but since the drummer boy had recently broken his head, thanks to a kick from a colonel's stallion, the surgeon found himself unable to emulate the example of that fashionable metropolis, whose glittering doings had been polished up still more for him by hearsay; accordingly, he was sulky, not to mention uneasy about this public trial of his medical knowledge; he had worked on dead patients before, but who could say what tricks the undead might play? But what he feared most of all was the Inquisition, whose severities are infallible, not to mention inevitable. In short, he carried his own toolbox under his arm, keeping a trifle aloof from Trollhand, who looked festive in his black-and-red cloak.

It was quite a procession indeed. The blood-red banners hung from the town hall. Doroteja was there, and so was Milena's mother, her face as hard as a shoemaker's wooden form. Yes, Doroteja was pale, yet avid, of

course; and here came all the old women whose children or grandchildren had been sucked dead by the satanic pest; with them came the living representatives of youth, hungry for horrors, and the one-legged
soldier who desired (so he loudly explained) to see if anything could
make him flinch—and here came Michael's former friends, who used to
partake of Communion beside him (the same cowards who if they were
alone would pay off a corpse with silver, so that it would not come haunting), and the ones whose cows Milena had healed, not to mention everyone else, the presence of the whole town being required by the
Church—and none of them meaning him or Milena any good. Why it
was that he could not be left in quiet with his faithful wife in whatever
happiness they could make was certainly beyond him. But there it was;
and now men from other villages were coming, too, and some few carried sharpened stakes over their shoulders.

I do him no injustice to state that his awareness that any time he
wished to, he could get rid of this vampire and then taste Doroteja, devour her even, was delicious to him; for isn't it human nature to be
pleased when fate offers us more than we already possess? It gave him a
sense almost of pride, to know that he continued to stir Doroteja's heart.
To be sure, he was also afraid of her; it was precisely on account of her
almost predatory determination to have whatever she wanted that he
had first chosen the more easygoing Milena. At this very moment, as he
could well see, she was brooding over him, in much the way that an evil
spirit studies us. Of course he would have enjoyed experiencing with her
the understanding of the flesh; and for the first time it now struck him
that her fleshly intuition or comprehension of him might well exceed his
of her; for all he knew, she might be able to read him down to his dis-
creetest parentheses. This possibility should have increased his fear; instead, it flattered him.

Gazing round him at the audience, most of whom perhaps hoped in
horror to see a slender female arm rise gracefully up from the ground,
Michael thought to himself: Even if Milena is what they say she is, why
should that make her any worse than these old peasants who have nothing better to do than watch the weeds grow on their mortgaged fields?—
He hated them all.

The day was as bright as the illuminated miniature in some Cardinal's missal: sky of lapis lazuli, fields of malachite, which is more faithfully permanent than emerald, attire of—Well, I should not say red and blue, for who in that town was so rich, and who would have wished to wear fine clothes to an exhumation? Let's say that the figures were perfect in their diminutive fashion, and that they were all ringed round with gold leaf; for who could disagree with their purpose? Michael, perhaps, might not have been so contented. He could not prevent himself from envisioning what would happen once they had operated on his wife: Her eyeballs would sink into her skull and her mouth would split her face from ear to ear, in a grinning crack of darkness.

There was another old shrew who had been terrorizing the neighborhood; three young mothers whose breasts were full of milk but who had lost their babies just the same had already made formal accusation against her. Singing a prayer, they opened her coffin first. She was quite decomposed.

Getting a bit dark at the armpits, are we? said the surgeon.— Just in case, he drove a stake through her heart—which is to say, he positioned the sharpened lindenwood skewer in the most infallible anatomical position, then nodded to the butcher, who swung the mallet with all his might. To everyone's disappointment, the corpse declined to shriek, so the executioner had nothing to do.

Well, how was that experience? asked the priest.

The butcher, who felt passing proud just then, wanted everyone to appreciate his experience. So he considered awhile, then said: It was like driving a nail into blood pudding.

Next, they opened the three daughters' coffins, just to be sure. The faces had already fallen in, with spiderwebs or cauls growing mercifully over them. At the priest's direction, the surgeon cut their heads off and packed the grinning mouths with garlic.

Now it was Milena's turn. Michael stood to one side, temporarily overlooked by the little boys with bare and grubby feet in whose names this was being done. The sexton dug up the coffin. The butcher helped him pull it out. On account of their confidence that whatever lay inside had become evil, they slammed it down with what Michael, who knew better than to say anything, considered to be disrespect. The sexton leaned on his shovel, gasping and coughing. The butcher, sweating, pulled off his bloody apron and slapped it against an old tombstone until the worms fell off. The executioner smiled, with his hand on the pommel of his sword. The priest led them in a prayer; Michael's lips moved meaninglessly. The surgeon, whose belt buckle resembled a great lock, shouted: *Amen!* The grubby mothers and grandmothers raised the babies over their heads so that they could see and learn everything; then the sexton, having caught his wind, tapped a chisel into the crack between coffin and lid, twisted expertly, and pried it open. So the roundcheeked priest pressed forward, raising a cross, while the lean, longhaired surgeon peeped cautiously over his shoulder, gripping what is nearly as efficacious against monsters as a cross—namely, his sharpest knife, which could saw open a skull at need.

There lay Milena, with her head on her breast, in that same silent and patient position as the old beggar who stands outside our church.

24

The good priest, so wide, steady and sad, had been ready for anything. But Milena looked . . . well, lovely in her coffin. Her face was as glossy-white as that famous intaglio portrait of Duchess Margherita of Savoy. Since everybody awaited his word, he said: Lift her out—gently, now! (Michael, are you with us or against us?) All right now. Sexton, have you seen her wedding ring?

And all these people who had once loved them, they did not know whether to pronounce her dead, alive or monstrous.

25

Just as it is for a woman all alone in bed at witch-hour, with a single candle to light her, and the other rooms of the house dread-darkened, and the world beyond filled with night and death; so it was and ever would be for Milena in daytime, even with her husband lying on top of her coffin to guard and comfort her. How much more so now! And had the villagers truly met with such a sight as I have imagined in the previous chapter, that would have been Milena's end. In fact what they discovered—for Michael and his wife had been provident—was a woman's remains, long decomposed, slopping out of Milena's burying clothes. Her ooziness proved her innocence.

26

The priest then said, as anyone would: *But Milena did come back.*

I must have dreamed it all, replied Michael, and when Milena's mother and the neighbors insisted that they had seen that demon in his wife's form (at least Doroteja kept kindly silent), he pointed down at the thing in the coffin and said: But there she is!

Even the executioner agreed that there was no point in driving a stake into it.

Reclosing the coffin, they reinterred it, not gently, because they all felt disappointed, and the way things should have gone, Michael and Milena ought to be burning together now. How exactly he got out of it I cannot tell you, but it might have had something to do with the payment of gold, and his grace was certainly provisional, so that evening, once he had bolted himself back inside the little house which was no longer his, and dug up Milena from under the kitchen floor (she woke up crying out: I was so lonely!), he stood defiant at the window, while she sat discreetly behind him in the hot darkness. He watched their neighbors standing behind the fence, waiting for them to come out; and for the last time he saw Doroteja crossing the footbridge by Milena's mother's house.

Since of the two of them only Milena could see in the dark, not until moonrise did they set out, leaving forever their high-roofed farmhouse beneath its chestnut trees; no doubt the roof would soon fall in; who else would care to live there? He carried a few tools at his belt; her wifely lockbox was light; he bore that on his shoulder.

The moon slipped behind a cloud. Milena whispered that she'd flit ahead and behind, to ensure that no one lay in wait. He worried then; he wouldn't know where she was.

She told him: If you love me enough, you'll learn to listen.

For what?

For me.

How will I know?

When your ears are sensitive enough to hear a vampire's fingernails growing underground.

He complained that she was being uncanny, and she laughingly kissed his throat; he realized that she was teasing him.

She vanished and returned: A horseman was coming. Michael's faithful wife led him quickly to the cemetery, where they ducked down among the uneven ranks of pale gravestones in the grass and the mud. The horseman passed. Michael would have liked to bid goodbye to their daughters. Strange to say, he also wished to visit Milena's grave. It seemed awkward to pose the matter to his wife, who in any event probably knew what he was thinking. Besides, who could say which ghouls and monsters were here?— Courage! she whispered, squeezing his hand.

Something chuckled, then whinnied like a horse. Faraway horses began screaming.— Oh, that joker! laughed Milena.

So they hurried along the dirt road which curved in obedience to the adjacent river. Passing the Dark Man by the water who disguises himself as driftwood (he was an acquaintance of Milena's), they hastened on, and behind them came a sound as if the water were being flogged with planks. Long before dawn they were both weary. Skirting the villages of Nachtstern and Grabmund, where dogs barked at them, they found another cemetery. Michael smashed the lock on a vault, and retired within to sleep out the day with his faithful wife, unable to keep from smiling now that everything had ended so well.

27

She brought him a gold ring from some churchyard, and he sold it in a tavern. With those wages they took to the road again, in fear of every human being, and therefore in still greater need of each other, hiding in a beehive-shaped night-coach pulled by two horses; so they got past the high-towered castles inhabited by all those others who would never understand them, their way lighted by the glowing greenish eyes in her dark face.

In Kreuzdorf he hired a coach for himself and his long narrow box. The driver was to take them to the frontier. It was afternoon; he'd scarcely slept, since he must flee with her by night and protect her by day. The horses were nervous. The driver studied him as if he or Milena were somehow to blame—and if she were not, then how could he be, who had sworn to care for her until the end? In the dirt road, a man who held a fat cow by the string tied to one of her horns stood chatting with a man who leaned on his broom. Now it was evening. When they came into Feuerstadt the horses slowed as they approached two barefoot women in long ragged skirts which were grimed to match the color of the road; one wore an open basket on her back, and her arms were folded across her breast; she was telling the other some trouble; then they turned, saw the coach, peered in and crossed themselves—in the name of Saint Polona, what could they be seeing? Milena looked just like anyone else!

Two men and four black-clad children formed in a line along the road, staring at them.

Begging their forgiveness, the driver withdrew from service. It was safely dark; they leaped out and departed, leaving the coffin behind; but still he loyally bore her little notion-box, and her caress strengthened his weary step, the sharp blade of morning-dread pressing ever against her unbeating heart.

28

So they ran away, over cattle tracks, through the mountains and into the hinterlands of the Holy Roman Empire, around pest-haunted villages, avoiding every church, sometimes chased by thieves and witches; and he clove to her, untempted by any other woman, even when they traversed a piazza which happened to be dazzlingly irradiated just then by the brass-bangled arm of a girl whose hair was still wet from the bath; while his faithful wife's hands were as cool yellow marble. He was still proud of her lovely long neck. At the last minute she had even brought him another present from beyond the grave: a cameo exactly the size of her fingernail, depicting an unknown white blossom and sealed in old glass or strange lacquer or perhaps even amber.

In her ornate coffer with the three locks (her mother's wedding present), she kept those three pet spiders who could weave lace in any pattern she chose: the many-branching floral kind sold very well, but sometimes people liked fleurs-de-lys, or multireplicated suns in a checkerboard pattern. These creatures must have come from the same place as the cameo, but Michael thought it best not to inquire into that which Milena hesitated to reveal. So as they crept southward, unable to trust anyone but each other, he peddled her lacework in the street for small pay, imminently expecting exposure since all the other such vendors were crones and their daughters. And yet they could not say, in the fashion of most outlaws, that they had been unlucky. All they wished for now was a place in which to be themselves. Milena slept in wolf-holes on the edge of town. At first he used to worry that someone would find her and destroy her while she was thus helpless, but she promised always to bury herself as well as she could. There were nights when he lacked a safe place to bathe her, and then with all his heart he pitied and grieved for his sweetheart who once more was black with dirt; but he never recoiled from her; for her part, the faithful wife, understanding now that even her mother's love had never been what it seemed, clung the more constantly to Michael, who had begun to go grey. So it went, like the many small square scenes of the life of Jesus in a folding triptych icon. She subsisted on the blood of fieldmice and the occasional dog.

By now he had become mercifully addicted to her gruesome odor— which is only to say what you already know: that he loved her. What is toleration but habit? Consider for instance the halfway sour-moldy odor of fresh strawberries at the market; much of this smell derives from the leaves; all the same, it contains an unwholesome component, over which it is astonishing that so many fruit lovers complacently pass. Hence it would be more accurate to write: *Slowly he grew fond of her earthy, sweaty smell.* In perilous stretches of daytime he did not in the least mind guarding her remains, no matter what stench leached out of her coffin, trench or shed. Over her remains he sometimes murmured: If they killed you again, and then I never saw you—

They moved to Torino, and if he were only literate he could have become a bookseller. She taught him Italian, for she already knew Latin, that being a dead language. He did odd jobs of night-work, guarding rich men's homes from brigands while Milena hid beneath ground. At the milliner's he consigned his wife's productions: skeletons of frogs done in silver lace, or a lace snail whose shell coiled in spirals, with a waning moon at the center. Nobody except the milliner suspected he was married.

But, as usual, the couple soon betrayed themselves. A child saw her and screamed. A dog died; a horse grew anemic. Sometimes the neighbors heard them singing the songs of their youth.— People had begun inquiring whether Milena was his wife or his daughter. Soon the Inquisition would be onto them. In Torino there is a certain chocolate shop on Via XX Settembre whose rainbow-striped pistachio chocolate pastilles may, if eaten during the the eleventh Mansion of the Moon (*Azobra*, which is propitious for redeeming captives), facilitate time travel. If only they had known about it! There came a dawn when Michael saw angry men sharpening stakes. That night he fled with his faithful wife, forsaking all they could not carry. The three spiders travelled inside her mouth. The so-called *dark night of the soul* might not have been experienced as such by Milena; in any case, it remains intrinsically impenetrable, so I cannot tell you exactly how or where that couple adventured. Our narrative resumes with their arrival in Trieste not long before the end of the *bora* wind, the trees bowing and whipping before them, in evidence of Fortune's two sides. They stole into port in a tiny *guzzo* of Dalmatian make, paying off the boatman in ancient coins. Milena was cloaked and veiled, while Michael looked decidedly unprosperous, not to say desperate, so that the ruffians along the Canal Grande left them alone.

Declining to flee anymore, they settled in the theater district. He sold her dearest embroideries for insulting wages until he gained the means to wash his face into complacent honesty. Then, having spied and loitered about as their travels had taught him to do, he commenced to fish for more gainful business. And presently through his mediation she became a dressmaker for singers and actresses, dwelling by day within the travelling-trunk of a dead tenor, her flesh oozing in mercurial drops, the floral wallpaper inside the box peeling like rotten papyrus. They hired a dressmaker's girl to take the clients' measurements. That got them talked about. Milena's work grew famous; everyone wished to know who she was. (My wife is not well, he frequently explained.) So resplendently did she fashion the curtains of light chain mail on the helmet of the baritone who sang the knight's role that everyone cried: *Madonna!* By then they were able to take better lodgings. He got her a coffin as pretty as a violin case. She clapped her hands. That night he threw the tenor's trunk into the canal.

So there he was, secure behind high walls with his faithful wife! He would have been satisfied to give up his life for her, or, better yet, to kill her enemies. In fact she was now the one to build up their wealth, his role mostly being to provide her with the love she required to justify her emergence from the ground and all her subsequent actions. In a trice she uttered linen handkerchiefs with silver roses on them, or even golden wedding-cloth for Duchesses.

By now their sins were as numerous and lovely as the gilded volumes in Baron Revoltella's library, but they had begun to trust in the famous indulgence on the part of Italians to the imperfections of others. No one could blame them for adapting themselves to the world they found, and for seeking to prosper; even those who kill it forbear to criticize the scorpion for following its own nature. So Michael and Milena did adapt and prosper, so that their sins were indulged indeed.

A singer demanded to meet Milena. She thought it only right that Milena should personally take her measurements. And Milena came, just after dusk, muffling up her face against a toothache. The singer was charmed. So was Milena. Michael managed to seem so. As their fortunes ascended, they began to enter society, if only to peep in from the back of the hall, as befitted modest persons. Milena was veiled, and Michael looked, at least to himself, middlingly well-born in the green suit that his faithful wife had made him; his hands were rough, his face was red and his hair was grey. That night there was a rouged signora playing the pianoforte in such a way as to show off her white neck; there was a flower in her hair, and she wore one of Milena's gowns, whose needlework made blue diamonds from one angle and black crosses from another.— *Madonna!* they cried again.

The manager of a travelling troupe had a proposition. They decided to risk inviting him for dinner, together with his actors and actresses. The guests found good food, and Friulian wine, of course, so that they enjoyed themselves sincerely, while the host and hostess replied with a falsity so perfect that they might as well have been polite guests on their own account. And so even the actors and actresses, who were by profession practiced at fictions, supposed themselves to be at table with people like themselves, who slept by night and found contentment rather than peril in every crowd. It is true that on the next day one of the actresses asked another whether it is ever possible to discern traces of vampirism in a sick man's face; for their host, who must have been of rustic or ignorant birth, had appeared to be watching them with a cautious, considering grimness, as if he might become unfriendly. As for his cat-eyed, sensuous dead wife, who kept smiling faintly, they pitied her for an imbecile. Anyhow she was harmless; so they stayed late, drank much, and then off they went, the midnight air shining with dangers which only she could see were merely cats' eyes.

To be sure, his wife's unhealthy look did sometimes attract attention, which in those times was a dangerous matter. Fearful and ashamed, Michael performed his utmost to make them forget her, growing so ingratiating that he practically would have performed conjuring tricks to please them—and when it didn't quite work he sometimes nearly blamed her for his troubles; but one marble-eyed glance from his faithful wife sufficed to blot out his rage, which became as a coin sinking down to the bottom of a mucky pond: settled, concealed.

She gazed upon every guest with a level smile. Once he asked: Weren't you afraid?—to which she replied: What were they going to do—kill me?

Just then she seemed even farther away than poor Doroteja, whose loneliness, had it been her lying there, would most certainly have sickened him with remorse.

After that, Michael and Milena had nearly enough money, and so there were other dinners. They even had a nighttime servingmaid to carry out the platters. And there, playing the hostess, sat his faithful wife, wise enough not to hang long glistening earrings from her dead face! Of course it was still dreadfully risky. When Milena was still alive, she sometimes used to preen herself before a little mirror that her mother had given her; when she was pregnant she used to stand before it, combing back her hair with her lovely breasts thrusting out; nowadays, of course, she cast no mirror-image. So it was difficult to get ready for company; she had to rely on her husband to tell her how she looked. But he was careful; nobody caught her out. People remarked on the woman's lucent green stare, but not to her, and certainly not to her husband, who had a ruffianly look about him.

Of course they would have preferred to open their hearts to others, to accept true friendship as opposed to eternally giving it (favors can be done with kindness and even sincerity, without revealing oneself; consider the rich man in his hooded cloak who drops a coin into the half-naked beggar's hand). But why complain? Their household in Trieste became nearly respectable, their evenings gilded by Friulian wine, which indeed also served to propitiate their neighbors: after a bottle or two of that stuff, every guest thought Michael and Milena to be the best couple they ever knew; and this even went for the new priest, who had been curious, I suspect, to meet someone to whom uncanny facts actually applied; at first he kept baring his teeth at them like a corpse, but once they opened the third bottle he began singing. The guests departed by midnight; in the small hours Milena was uttering *bordi* of gold and silver thread, her needles ducking in and out to make flowers, ivy-enclosing caskets, wheels and suns all of precious metals, triple-stemmed artichokes, slender rolls of feminine chain mail. Her odor could make a stray dog howl.

Thanks to her, his daylight hours no longer burdened him with labor. All he had to do was take orders and deliver them. How he loved those opera singers, sweet mountains of flesh, sweating in their velvet dresses, their wide pink foreheads, exuding the salty juice of life!

When she slept, he sometimes liked to sit on his doorstep and watch the children who wrapped their arms around their teachers' waists, the teachers who at the first stroke of the bell formed them into a double line, the little boys who held hands or swished their raincoats at each other, the little girls who sang songs. But he was always tired in the daytime nowadays; on account of his appearance it happened that certain clients declined to receive him directly when he delivered the garments they had ordered; they feared he might bear some contagious disease. Sometimes he grew lonely and irritable, but then he reminded himself of his dear quiet wife whose hands worked unceasingly for them both.

He would have liked to have children again, but, as thirteen learned doctors have already proved, after a woman's womb dies once, it lacks the twin elements of fire and water most needed for propagation, being corrupted by a surplus of earth. Besides, who would care to have children with a vampire?— Well, Michael did; he certainly tried. Lying beside her just before dawn, he whispered his wish for more daughters; but the pressure of the oncoming light was already causing her to twitch and grimace; it was time for her to go away again.— That cantata singer's dress is finished, but ask her if she'd like more ruffles at the sleeves. Because she . . . oh, Michael, I don't feel well; hide me away quickly; I'm ashamed to die in front of you—

It was July, and he gasped in the summer air. It seemed that he couldn't breathe enough. Although Trieste is no more humid than Lyon, and far less so than New Orleans, his lungs felt malnourished. All that year he craved more and more of that perfumed oxygen, even when it was drizzling, even when the freezing *bora* finally blew again; needing fresh air, he revolted against the muddy charnel odor of his wife. But it wasn't that he didn't desire her.

In Bohemia people had regarded her with horror, while here they merely felt spiteful disgust. Her eyes did perhaps look a little sunken in, and her flesh might have been yellow; but to her husband, who had lived with her since she was young, she remained much the same. (It might have been that his pleasure in her was tinctured with a secret sense of superiority, because she was dead.) He bought her a plaid corset which helped keep her flesh together. Now came September, and his faithful wife was stirring porridge with a long wooden spoon—nearly time for his breakfast and her sleep. How he longed to live out one more day! Had she learned to see his thoughts? For what a cold pale gaze she was turning on him!—although hadn't she done the same when she was alive? No, he must not suspect her of anything; their most precious jewel was trust. (Some say that vampires have two hearts; by all the saints, Milena had but one!) The *bora* whistled, and the nights lengthened, thank God; now it was easier to renounce the sunlight, for Milena's sake. But in due time he found himself tormented again by spring; and in June, when the cities begin to stifle their inhabitants, who cling to the shadowed sides of the streets, and in all the many-windowed palaces, curtains close themselves against sunlight, concealing sweating insomniacs in much the same way that a lake smooths itself out above a sinking stone, both Michael and Milena grew restless, because they found it more difficult to breathe. He attended more than before to the sweating chests of the young city women, and each morning that she withdrew into her allotted world, he felt lonelier than before.

In the Kabbalah of Isaac Luria, each of the tenfold emanations of Divinity comprises its own tenfold sphere; and every aspect of the marital state may, indeed must, be comparably, multiply subdivided. I won't deny the complexity of their relations. Sometimes she wept: *My poor, poor children!* (He never brought them up, of course; she might have worried that his trust in her was falling off.) The closest they ever came to disagreeing was on an occasion when they were talking over the times when she and the children still lived; of course their memories of her mother and most of the others had soured, but when it came to her old rival, whom she might have been expected to hate, Milena said: That summer before I got sick, when the crop was bad and our girls needed shoes, I even begged a loan from Doroteja—

What! And did she oblige you?

She did.

And you repaid her?

No, because I died.

It was on the tip of his tongue then to blame her, but she struck first, saying: Tell me the truth. Was there ever anything between you?

I swear there wasn't.

Then Doroteja—

Wife, she's the vampire, not you.

Oh, sweet-tempered Milena was! On occasion he could not refrain from gazing upon her in her stupor and wondering, just as we all do about one another, which secrets colored her blood; and, to be less metaphysical, what evil she might do, and what good she might in time of desperation do or refrain from doing. But the instant that the lid closed upon her face, he invariably felt that he could have treated her more kindly. She, who had done everything for him, who must have passed (although they never spoke of it) through nightly agonies of temptation or even physiological compulsion without becoming the kind of evil thing which feeds on people, had made herself his innocuous lovebird; so that his anxiety had merely to do with how to live a lie with everyone but his faithful wife, while somehow reserving from her some moments of sunlight, contented social trivialities, roseate flesh and neighborly approval, not to mention the summer expanses of this great world. Bile foamed all the way up to his heart; he nearly vomited. Honoring her fidelity, he remained false to all others in order to be true to her; and she grew ever more beautiful in his sight, as certainly should have been the case, for this was a pretty time, a musical time, when Schandl and Warbinek were making *pianoforte verticale* in Trieste.

Before she married him, and rolled up her hair in a wife's cap, she used to toss her head at him, and her long tresses licked her neck. Now she had grown rather stiff, as old people will. Between marriage and death she had kept her hair pulled up in a bun; but now she left it loose again, as if she were a newborn maiden; he liked that very much.

At times he was ambuscadoed by a longing to have married Doroteja, to see her standing in the kitchen in the morning with the sun illuminating the edge-strands of her golden hair as she set out the bowl of fresh milk whose cloud-clean whiteness for that one quarter-hour the sun would touch with purples, lilacs, yellows and many other colors, to see the play of sunlight on his wife's hands, my God, was that too much? But in the summer evenings, bathing Milena in his arms, as she floated with her long pale legs almost lilac-colored in the twilight, her slender arms barely grazing his shoulders—she had gained so much practice in lying still!—until, half-opening her eyes, she began to caress his hand, he was not at all troubled by the lack of Doroteja. There she was, his faithful wife, floating in a long tin bathtub with her gaze locked upon his; there she was every night, lying in her coffin, with her long legs pressed together, slowly raising her head, smiling at him before she had even opened her eyes, with her hands sprouting up toward him. Just as a baby turns its round head, opens its wide eyes wider, smiles and reaches toward its mother, as if somehow its arm can bridge any distance—which indeed it can, for she now bends down to take the child into her arms— so his dependent, adorable wife yearned unto him unfailingly, trusting him to care for her, hide her and love her.

But while Milena slept her open-eyed sleep, he could hardly manage himself; his desperation (if such is not too emphatic a word) ripened within him like a worm in a corpse, until he could scarcely meet the eyes of others. Down a certain shady side-street lived a flower vendor of easy morals, who looked not unlike Doroteja. One afternoon he found his feet pulling him there. She smelled like roses, as he knew quite well from having bought bouquets for Milena. Her name was Anna. She smiled; her breath was as flowers. Oh, he almost could have done it! But as she stretched out her fingers to be kissed, he found himself imperfectly recollecting a night when his faithful wife was lying on her side, with her head turned away from him and her buttocks exposed to him beneath the edge of the blanket—had she been asleep? If so, she must still have been alive. How tired she was, with the first two girls already born and always hungry; and once the sun was high she would have to be spreading the hay for the goats, with the elder one crying within the house and the younger one weighing down Milena's back, while he went to the forest to steal firewood; how could he magnify the griefs of this woman? And during those Triestine summer days, when she lay reeking in her wormy rags, and in those winter nights, when her caress was as cold as the bronze clasp of an old leather book, he loved and pitied her even more. He could easily have found some daytime courtesan, or perhaps even a sunshine wife, but it was only when Milena was present, and he accordingly felt like himself, that women attracted him.

Until evening allowed her globs of flesh to recombine he was always so tired nowadays, and come nightfall no one could compare to his wife, shameless and therefore innocent, her chin darkly dripping. As for her, of course, she was touched by the sweet feebleness of her faithful husband who had not yet died. She went on weaving noblewomen veils more fine than smoke, and custom came to her like flies to a corpse.

29

Vampires tend to have a fatalistic nature; and the faithful wife had certainly never anticipated being able to enjoy her husband forever. For many good years they comforted one another: for their friendless, lurking existence, for the deaths of their children and the loss of their old home—and since they were such perfectly suited helpers each to the other, I'd call their marriage as successful as any.

Once they caught sight of a kindred *vrykolakas,* dark brown like one of those Slovenian honey-breads in the shapes of animals; the Triestini had haled him out of his tomb, and were burning him in the piazza. He was wicked; anyhow, Milena and Michael could not save him; they turned away from his cries.

Then there was the child who disappeared—a very good little boy, too, of whom everyone was fond. Michael found difficulty in protecting Milena just then. But he had long since become the good husband who knew and in a manner of speaking even cherished his wife's infirmities. He knew how to clean things up! As for her, she kept bringing renown to the neighborhood; on her devolves all credit for the soprano Rina Pelligrini's costume in "Lucia di Lammermoor": golden embroidery on white, pale silver on a white as soft as the blurred face and girl-smooth hands of a priest's tomb-effigy after centuries of rain. And so the neighbors settled on a Jew to burn.

A few years later came the case of the dead man who an hour before had been laughing and full of blood. To save Milena from suspicion, Michael had to lead her out in the sun—barely after dawn, of course, and utterly gloved, perfumed and veiled; her tottering, twitching body began to liquefy at once, and she bit her tongue nearly in two so as not to screech; supporting her around the waist, he conveyed her down into the street, as if to help her take the air, fanned the light away from her face, explained to the passersby (who started at the stench): *my wife is not well*, then carried her back inside, terrified that he might have killed her forever. She did not leave her coffin for three days. Dusk of the fourth disclosed her helpless, as are we all when dead: hideous with sores, blind, unable to speak. He ran out, bought the fattest hen he could find and forced its head into her mouth. She tried feebly to bite, but even this she could not manage, so he slit the bird's throat, directing the wonder-working jets of blood upon her face.— Thank you, she whispered.— Perceiving that this had not sufficed, he rushed out again, just in time to catch a stray cat which had scented Milena. This time she was able to kill for herself. Then her sores began to heal. Every night he fed her on such-like live creatures, and she lay there on the bed, grimacing and twitching. Soon she could see again. He sat by the threshold (although that was unlucky), wishing to take her in his arms or at least utter loving words but understanding that at this moment anything pertaining to life was nearly unbearable to her. All this she was suffering, if not for him alone, then for both of them. The distance between them seemed to have existed forever. But by then the neighbors had forgotten their suspicions of Milena, because a new wonder had been discovered in Trieste: a certain dead Countess's portrait, painted in oils, which could wink its left eye at anyone who praised it. And when he comprehended that he had saved her for a little longer, he felt the way he had as a boy in Bohemia on a certain

January morning, the ice black on the river and the whole family almost starving, when he found a precious apple hidden under the straw.

You might think that he sometimes wished to go back to the days before any of these events happened; for it is tiring to hide a secret, and lonely to forgo one's friends. But the fact is that he never thought along those lines. For they were consecrated unto each other. Their joint career was besprinkled with blood, perhaps, but only of the insignificant. And they were safe now. Who among the Triestini could believe this vital if pallid night-woman and her sweaty companion who sometimes behaved as if he kept a dagger near could be any worse than murderers or thieves? (Anyhow, in Trieste there is always some dead man or other rotting at the bottom of the Canal Grande.) By virtue of the magnetic sacraments they cherished one another to the end. Now it was time to make a silver girdle for the Duchess d'Aosta. Smiling at him with all her sharp teeth, Milena laid her hand upon his pulsing breast.

30

She had to go to bed earlier and earlier. By now a stench would come out of her an hour before dawn, her black tongue lolling out, her eyes screwing shut. As for him, he continued to look unwholesome, as might be expected of a man who never got quite enough sleep. Which of them loved the other more I cannot tell; they were bound to one another by the obscurest appetites of the blood.

I have seen an octagonally-framed daguerreotype of them from sometime after 1845—no, the legend you wish to cite is false; vampires do sometimes cast shadows, reflections and images, even if their husbands can't see them—with her dark hair parted high across that pallid forehead of hers; she wears a high-busted corset with a glass jewel about her neck; his arm is around her as she smiles, showing her teeth—no, what are you thinking? She wasn't like that!

Saving up their money until they could buy their indulgences, they entered the bosom of the Church, which was certainly soft and rich, although sometimes they found it difficult to breathe. He managed to protect her so long as they both lived, and she nourished him and kept her copperware shining like winter suns.

So finally they died together, and because they were wealthy and generous, the Archbishop himself made sure that trentals were sung for them in church; and then they were buried in a marble tomb in consecrated ground, ringed round by the great trees, which do not even know their own names, and whose leaves hang down like grapes, like women's luscious hair, like ivy rushing to cover skeletons; and the crypt was sealed; the mausoleum was locked; and the moon passed into silver clouds, like a beautiful dead lady returning to the cemetery.

DOROTEJA

Doroteja sat embroidering red snapdragons on a white tablecloth which she would then hem with lace. She was childless. The joy she felt when one of Michael's daughters came running into her arms would surpass your belief.

Like any goodwife, she knew what is done with cristallium, tansy, zedoary, hassock and fennel in a jar of hallowed wine; all the same, the goblins had gotten at her, so that she miscarried. Her late husband had never comprehended the grief that a woman feels to lose the child she has cherished so long beneath her heart. Her mother, understanding quite well, taught her the charm to sing while stepping thrice across a dead man's grave: *This is my help against the evil late birth.* After that she was supposed to sell a clod from her baby's grave swaddled in black wool, saying: *I sell it, you must sell it, this black wool and the seeds of this grief,* but she could never find any merchant, peddler or Gypsy kind enough to buy this burden away from her. If only Tadeusz had lived, to give her another child!

The windows of her cottage were always darkened now.

But there was Michael, who ought to have wedded her in the first place. Milena was too ill to live, people said. With her out of the way, Doroteja needed but to sing the correct spell in order to have him.

On New Year's Day, with Milena declining more irrevocably, Doroteja washed herself in the water in which a silver coin had been dropped, in order to be as abundant in money as in water (because Michael had always been poor), and within the month six copper pieces came her way. Before Easter she bathed in a tincture of last year's roses, so as to be more beautiful—her elder sister staring at her, that same stinking kerchief on her head; Doroteja tried to wash herself at least twice a month.

Milena died when the moon entered her sixth mansion, and Doroteja felt very sorry, of course. A month later, Michael had not yet proposed.

So she paid a visit to his daughters, and the eldest one said: Aunt Doroteja, every night I pray for you to become our mother.

Soon after that, she learned that Milena had come back.

On the night of Holy Saturday, the dead souls go to church, which is the reason we burn graveyard fires on that night. Doroteja decided to ask her deceased husband for advice.

Reader, I would not care for you to believe that Doroteja was a witch, for we burn witches. She was simply one of those lucky girls whom God permits to be born on Easter Sunday.— Others hesitated to visit the cemetery at night. For Doroteja, the place was not much worse than her goatshed.

Just as some papyri buried in humid old graves crumble away within moments after being unearthed, so it can be with deep-seated loves suddenly exposed; but the feelings of Doroteja and Tadeusz for each other endured like a hoard of gold coins. She had never loved him, but what did that matter? They were friends. Now that he was in the ground, she intended to indulge her hunger for love, which meant Michael.

Doroteja built a fire upon Tadeusz's grave. At midnight, after the dead sermon had been preached, he returned, pallidly glistening, and found his widow sitting at what for once could be called his hearthstone.

She said: Tad, do you still care for me?

Well, well, he said. What do you want? I've found more money if you need it—a hoard of Roman gold! And if you feed your calf a hank of grass from that grave over there, you'll get a fat milch-cow.

Where's our baby?

I never see him.

Tad, I want to marry Michael.

And eat my curse?

You wouldn't curse me, would you?

Gazing at him in the firelight, she fancied that his eyes and mouth were holes.

He said: Milena's living with him again. What would you do—put away his lawful wife?

Her rights are ended! I went to Father Hauser—

What would he say about your necromancy here?

Tad, never mind that. He said that Milena's sin is that she refused to bear in patience the death which God has appointed for us.

Flittering round and round her face, Tadeusz smiled at her with translucent teeth. Perhaps he too found death difficult to bear. Doroteja's mother had told her of the dead woman who returned on purpose to bite her husband's finger; when he pushed her away, she sank her teeth into his side. Remembering this, not to mention the fact that he kept circling closer, Doroteja began to fear her husband.

Milena and I will never allow you to marry him, he whistled.

So, said Doroteja. She's now become a friend of yours?

We all know each other here.

Then where's my baby?

Well, the unformed souls, you see—

Michael and I were *meant* to live together. You're the one being selfish.

His eyes narrowed, and a vertical crease came into his forehead as he cocked his head at her in the way he always used to when they were about to argue. Then, with a screech, he swooped in on her, hoping to bite her face. Knowing his moods, Doroteja was ready, and flicked a silver bullet into his mouth. Choking and retching, he shot back down into his grave.

2

Doroteja fed the geese, and then strung garnet crystals to sell. She washed her Sunday dress. She peddled eggs in front of the church, and turned them all into copper coins. When she got home she locked the door. She hid her profits beneath the fireplace, in the hole where she kept her magic treasures: two candles made by a virgin, four nails from a child's coffin. Then she filled a basket of plums and went to see Michael's daughters. So adorable in their white-rimmed ruffled caps, they ran into her arms, crying out: Aunt Doroteja!

How's your mother?

Father made us promise not to tell.

Never mind. Here are some plums for you. When I go I'll take my basket.

Thank you, Aunt Doroteja; you're always good to us. We love you more than—

Where's your father?

Here he comes now.

Long ago, before he married, he had felt something for her; now he was a wormy ball of equivocations. You may be sure that Doroteja did her best. When he greeted her, she rolled her eyes, smiled and adorably shook her head, all at once. But he was curt, even wary. That made her all the more jealous of Milena, whose postmortem existence resembled the idleness of some rich girl whose only work is to string beads. When she said farewell, he replied with relief. The daughters brought her basket. They begged permission to help Doroteja bundle up the wheat.— Never mind, girls, she said. Your father needs you.— Looking back over her shoulder, she saw Michael staring cautiously out at her, his forehead higher and paler than before. Then he closed the shutters.

So she returned to her dark house, where she kept weeping, weeping, like some dead woman whose every attribute but sorrow has rotted away. She would have cooked him mushroom soup with barley for Christmas. Because she so truly loved, her story is chased with flowers and diamonds, like the leather cover of an ancient book.

3

Doroteja was having one of those nightmares we all know, in which the wind becomes the rustling of a dead lady's dress as she ascends the stairs. When she awoke, she sought to persuade herself that the dream was good, and signified treasure from beyond the grave.

She milked her cow, fed the geese and collected the hens' eggs. She gathered firewood from the forest. She weeded her field, rescued plums from the birds, milked the cow again, and then life was as beautiful as a Bohemian sunset with a raven hovering over the mountains, or was it merely a fly on the windowpane? She ate supper: barley in milk. She prayed to Saint Polona, Saint Vitus, Saint Adelbert, Saint Wenceslaus, Saint Procopius and of course Saint Doroteja, her own patron saint. As soon as it got dark, off she went to the churchyard, where the memory-stones resemble sheaves of wheat leaning against each other. Singing the spell that her mother had taught her, she knelt at her mother's headstone, anxious lest some evil thing might come upon her from behind. She poured out a little milk. And up rose her mother, spinning thread as she came, clenching between her knees the grooved distaff as tall as a scepter.

Mother, I've set my cap at Michael.

He's not for you. Milena has him.

Mother, I want a husband and a child.

You won't get either.

Then what should I do?

Die alone.

So back home went Doroteja, weeping, weeping, back to her house whose eaves ran nearly down to the ground.

4

The daughters died; Doroteja refused to believe any ill. But if only she had given them medallions of Saint Polona! At night she prayed for Milena to return alone beneath the earth.

Harvesting clover, washing beets in the creek and then confessing her sins, Doroteja endured that summer. Even now her love persisted, like some half-rotted scrap of flower-knitted lace. After Michael and Milena's disappearance, she accompanied her neighbors to burn down their house, singing hymns, with her hair braided up in a cornucopia, and Father Hauser complimented her voice. Outside sat Milena's mother, who was huge-eyed and pale, with her chin up and her mouth open, her hair tucked decently in her kerchief and her withered hands straining not to claw at one another in the lap of her faded striped skirt. Everyone both expected to make horrible discoveries and hoped to find supernatural treasures. Hans Trollhand, looking fearsome in his black-and-scarlet cloak, now kissed his torch to the thatch. As the flames ascended, people dispersed, and some were hiding objects in their pockets. As for Doroteja, in a recess beneath the straw mattress where the daughters had slept, she found an Easter egg red as sunrise, with yellow grapevines crossing upon it. She had made that for Michael the year before he married Milena. The next year she had made him a black egg painted with a golden castle; Milena must have destroyed that one.

Doroteja joined the quotidian line of men and women bending in the fields, scything hay, sweating, groaning because their backs hurt. So she helped her neighbors in exchange for a mouse's share of the crop. In the forest she gathered mushrooms and berries. She dried her plums and pears on the kiln. At a rich man's funeral she got to taste bread with horseradish sauce and small scraps of smoked meat.

Come autumn she set out for the cemetery and called upon her dead father.

What now, Doroteja? Has Christ returned at last?

Father, father, I can't endure to live and die alone.

She remembered how he used to be in life, hunching forward, turtling down his shaggy head, gripping his spade as he stared furiously into any stranger's eyes. Now he was not much more than a gust of fireflies. It would have been different had she poured out blood for him.

Father, are you lonely here?

You never knew anything. How do you expect to get a husband?

Help me, father!

Then lower your ear and I'll sing you a charm . . .

Dead man's breath, a tongueless whisper and the crickets singing, that was all she heard.

5

Through the fall she kept the red Easter egg under her pillow. Sometimes she kissed it, because Michael had touched it and kept it. But it began to haunt her, floating before her eyes even when she was working in the fields. After she had dreamed about it three times, she realized that it was bewitched, so she smashed it, and maggots crawled out of it.

That night Doroteja set out for the cemetery and poured out milk for Michael's daughters, singing spells to draw them forth by their names. Here they came: Maria, Ludmila and then Markétka, the youngest—sad little girl with the watchful eyes, her dirty dress still too large for her. They rushed up wailing and trembling, with moonlight shining through their bones. They struggled to embrace her, but of course Our Redeemer permits no such perversions. Wriggling and fluttering, they breathed on her the faintest cool breath of earth. Doroteja burst into tears.

Aunt Doroteja, they said, will you be our mother now?

Did your mother murder you?

We promised not to tell—

Aunt Doroteja, may we live with you? We'll be good; no one will ever see us.

We'll help you; we'll count grains of rice—

In much the same way that magic can kindle a shadow upon the sun's disk, so the loneliness of those three dead girls cooled Doroteja's sorrow, and so she invited them home. No living soul ever entered that house but her elder sister, and when *she* came the ghosts hid in the pile of firewood, squeaking more faintly than rats. They never grew up, of course; they loved to ride on her shoulders when she went to the creek to wash her laundry. *Maminka* they called her. One might say that her home was as haunted as an old Gothic castle, but Doroteja forgot to look at it that way. When she went to confession, she neglected to mention her visitors to Father Hauser, because he was so fond of her that she thought it cruel to disappoint him. In the evenings when she sat eating her barley cooked in milk, they pretended to share with her, but in truth their spoons were too heavy for them to lift, and the iron pot burned them if they hovered too close by it. After dark, Doroteja would go out the back door and spill a few drops of milk into the dirt, whispering their names, very quietly, so that the neighbors would not hear.

They were as helpful as could be when she went to the forest to get mushrooms and berries, for they could fly off in three different directions, then come winging back to whisper in her ear. They could not scare away birds, but they could sit up in the plum tree watching for them, and whenever some bold robins or crows descended in a robber's band, one of the girls would fly squeaking into Doroteja's ear, so that she could save her fruit. When Doroteja went to church, attended a witch-burning or set out to sell eggs and garnets, those three darling girls watched over her field, sinking down into the dirt to count her beets, carrots and lovely yellow potatoes.

Just as ancient copper coins go green, so went Doroteja's life, and by the time she was old, what others imagined to be her desperate solitude had become as insignificant to her as the splash of a crabapple in a deep well.

THE JUDGE'S PROMISE

And finally let the Judge come in and promise he will be merciful, with the mental reservation that he means he will be merciful to himself or the State; for whatever is done for the safety of the State is merciful.

The Malleus Maleficarum, ca. 1484

1

In old Moravia, between the towns of Javicko and Svitavka, you may, if the scale of your map permits, descry the little village of H——, which has few monuments to speak of (not that the patriotic citizens of this locality are entirely conscious of the aforesaid fact); accordingly, its very existence has been passed over in every edition of Baedeker's guide. I have been told that the schoolmaster once made courageous epistolary efforts to remedy the omission, for he is a man of charity, who readily takes it upon himself to improve the defects of others. As for his neighbors, including even those august fellows in whose name the old lamplighter hangs out red or black flags from the balcony of the town hall, I fear that few could definitively inform you whether Baedeker is some great lord ensconced in a castle down in Lombardy or an item of dairy-tackle of which they need not trouble to learn the use, thanks to the superior methods of milking (not to mention cheesemongering) in their enlightened district of Bohemia.

Now, the burghers of H—— are known above all else for their devotion to duty, and the schoolmaster even promised to show me a citation which some Margrave or possibly even an Emperor once bestowed upon the Mayor; unfortunately, his good wife kept topping off our tankards with empyrean beer until we both forgot about it. But should you have any doubts about this matter, I advise you to observe the police force in action; sometimes there are as many as two officers in uniform protecting the village from evil, and the schoolmaster claims to have seen even more. At the time of this story, which takes place in 1673, although it could have been 1752, there was, unfortunately, only one man on the force, but you may rest assured that he was a full inspector, with all the powers and dignities of that office.

He was a veteran, of course, and childless—still hale but with a greying moustache. I believe he had been decorated and commended in a small war in Swabia not long before 1361. His eyes were that lovely blue-grey which comes when a silver thaler is polished. He knew which townsmen were bad, and who was merely weak, and how to torture a recalcitrant prisoner with the strappado—which he did only when ordered or when necessity struck. No good citizen had anything against him, and he greeted the neighbors with a slightly distant but in no way deficient courtesy. Had he been a Prussian, he would have bowed and clicked his heels. In Bohemia people rarely go so far as that, but in the moderately informal venue of H___ it could be seen that this inspector of ours desired to please, even if that desire must be moderated by official duty. A few ancient men who tremblingly grasp hold of life even yet remember how they used to watch him whittle toys for them when they were children, and I think I have seen the moustached oval of his face peering from a dark high window in the town hall. Nobody ever asked him what he wanted out of life, which was as well, since in those days life was parsimonious. He aspired to promotion, of course, and perhaps even to marriage if he could afford it. Well warned by the famous tale of the hero who is lured into the arms of a lovely girl who then turns into a corpse, he kept away from love. No great career awaited him; he had nothing in particular to which he could attach himself, except for life itself.

There are epochs when we manage to convince ourselves that death is merely an inconvenience visited upon other people; but then come other periods. H___ was presently in one of those latter phases. According to Father Hauser, who gave Sunday reports on just this subject, evil had been waxing in those parts for a considerable while, doubtless because our judges weren't burning enough witches. In the adjacent village of Neinstade, a corpse chewed and grunted so horribly in its grave that they had to disinter it, at which point it opened its teeth and exhaled a stench, from which cause several people were infected with the plague. Immediately afterward, every churchyard in old Germany became perilous. Sextons no longer dared to dig coffin-wells after nightfall, for fear that some skeleton-hand might pull them down. Vampires rose up throughout what Fleischmann has named *the ill-fated Bohemian rectangle*. God's army reacted. In the neighborhood of H——, several beautiful and intelligent women had to be destroyed, just in case they might be witches. Antisocial or intellectual persons of any stripe were burned alive. Strange to say, the monsters grew worse.

No one blamed the inspector for not keeping up with the threat, but the next time the Mayor came to church, he stayed late and lent Father Hauser an edition of last year's newspaper, which had just arrived in H——, where we kindly give others the opportunity to verify our news before we read it. It seemed that Frederick the Great had just dispatched one of his most trusted martinets to Paris, to be instructed by the Lieutenant of Police in Paris for one year. In Berlin, the Police President of Berlin now commanded a hundred-odd truncheon-smacking Exekutivepolizei, most of them former soldiers who had every quality it took to break any lawbreaker's teeth. Why couldn't we be equally *au courant* in H——?

Of course nobody could offer the inspector any additional help, not even a truncheon. But those who mattered agreed that he should set an example to all the policemen of Bohemia, for honor's sake.

They gave him a temporary squad of beggars, and he opened many a grave, but most had to be closed up again for lack of proof! And several were empty, and practically every vault contained a tunnel going down, down, down! The inspector wrote a report. He explained that unless these enemies of heaven were taken in the act, nothing could be accomplished. So they took away his squad.

The inspector and Father Hauser locked themselves into the church at high noon, with candles burning all around. They rubbed every keyhole with garlic. The High Honorable Richter* Bernd von Lochner knocked at the back door, and they let him in, looking both ways. Since dawn the executioner, Hans Trollhand, had been stationed in the crypt, his huge mushroom-shaped ear turning blue with cold as he pressed it to the floor, listening for any subterranean stirrings, because it would be disastrous if the enemy overheard their counsels. The three who mattered agreed on trying something new, daring, perhaps even shocking, should

---

* Judge.

word get out, but since they controlled the town's opinion, they had high hopes that it wouldn't.

Richter von Lochner had by far the greatest authority at that conclave, for he had travelled as far as Prague, where the clay corpse of the Golem still lies in the attic of the Old-New Synagogue. Of all his generation, he, perhaps, had done the most for the human race. I would need a flock of obsequious clerks were I to retail to you all his accomplishments. He had burned dozens of Jews and Freemasons in his time, and even interrogated the Devil, catching him off guard within the house in Charles Square where Doctor Faustus once lived. It was his pride that he had never let a guilty soul escape.

Inspector, he began, I've been watching your efforts. No one can reproach you for anything. You're a brave and steady hunter. I suppose you carried out many a night reconnaissance as a soldier.

Oh, yes, said the inspector.

Tonight we expect to find you in position underground. Modern police methods demand new modes of observation. Do you understand me?

I know how to do as I'm told, replied the inspector, who might have doubted this or that, but never said so.

At any rate, Father Hauser sprinkled him with holy water and summoned the sexton. Secreting a twice-blessed medallion of Saint Polona against his heart, the inspector set out to expose the guilty.

On that occasion (it was Goblin's Day), he essayed to disguise himself by coloring himself brown with a decoction of oak bark and puffing out his cheeks like a *vrykolakas*. Acting upon an advance hint from above, the carpenter had prepared him a coffin with a little hole in it, through which for an hour he diligently practiced sipping by means of a straw. Father Hauser gave him Communion. Laying by his pike which once parted a Turk's ribs—for what good would that do against the undead, except in daytime?—he took up the greater weapon of the sacred Host—which, alas, dissolved away beneath his tongue. They lowered him into position while he lay staring upward, wondering how it would end. Richter von Lochner had already drawn up a list of inspector-successors and replacements, which the mayor signed, saying: Good men, Your Honor, and ready to go down to their utmost!— Of course the sexton left his grave unfilled, so the inspector breathed full comfortably. He thought he might catch one or two dead rascals, oh, yes; no one would be disappointed in him! But on that very first churchyard midnight, when he heard the mausoleum doors creak open, and accordingly popped out of his coffin (whose nailheads were merely painted on), stood up in that six-foot hole and threw back his own gravestone (which was on hinges), crying, *fellows, where's the party?*, they saw through him at once, and made a rush! I am sorry to say that poor Saint Polona excited their chuckles; he barely saved himself by firing off all his garlic-rubbed silver bullets. Not one of them managed to bite him, thank goodness, and thanks to his excellent shooting he managed, just as he had hoped, to destroy three notorious vampires: a roasted Protestant, an infanticidal mother whom the authorities had convicted and buried alive last winter, and a woman taken in adultery whom they had mercifully and legally drowned.— Justice, concluded the inspector, is not justice, until a stake goes through the heart!

At dawn, dragging himself back to the revered Father Hauser, who had once catechized his charmed childhood, he had to ask himself how much he should be expected to sacrifice for the town of H____. Would he yield up his life?— Well, if he had to; any brave man would, although his aspiration had been to retire before his hair went utterly white, and buy a flock of sheep.— What about his immortal soul? That was a blurrier proposition; for wasn't anyone who did such a deed, even in order to achieve good, a bad person? Fortunately, Father Hauser infallibly promised him absolution.

Richter von Lochner declined to be present at that difficult conference, for he too had a heart; it pained him to send anyone in uniform to certain death, no matter how easily he disposed of evildoers. So the inspector and Father Hauser stood face to face like two Bohemian eagles staring down one another on a faded tapestry, while the gaunt grimy-faced Virgin painted on the ceiling stared down past her locked hands, with her cadaverous head, framed in a blue wimple, glowing blotchily; and Hans Trollhand, well wrapped in his black-and-red cloak (for last time he had caught a cold), kept watch in the crypt, not that he detected the slightest scratching or groaning. Perhaps he would have made an even better hero than that cipher of an inspector; for he had always been more acute than the latter at ferreting out the tiny snake-holes which vampires make (although sometimes there is nothing below but a snake). He was also very mercantile, which helps one to get renown. Sometimes he sold the blood of people he beheaded, for it was a charm against arson. He collected tips for a good view of the torture platform. All the same, his children were malnourished, and his wife Margaritha owned but one dress. There was hope expressed (I cannot say by whom) that this time the inspector would become famous, a possibility which must have occupied Trollhand in some fashion—and certainly warmed the inspector even through his constraint. He and the priest now discussed such minimally unacceptable methods as choking to death on a crucifix, or forcing holy water into one's lungs. But in the end, he ate mushroom poison, courtesy of a convicted witch whose torture von Lochner accordingly suspended. Justice was on the march! Before Hans Trollhand had even set that witch on fire, the inspector died in anguish, losing himself ever more sorrowfully behind the phosphorescent rainbow of the churchyard spectrum, while Father Hauser sent him off with prayers. So far, the secret retained its honorable virginity. It was an accident, proclaimed the town crier (for in the service of truth it is permitted to our authorities to lie), and so Father Hauser presided over his burial. Because the mayor, who considered that by lending out that newspaper he had already done enough, declined to tax the citizens of H____ for the price of a silver casket, which might have guarded our inspector more securely from the enemies of God, the sexton stuffed cloves of garlic into his shroud, while Hans Trollhand, whom nobody could accuse of not being goodhearted, dug up an irreproachable old Christian woman named Jette and hacked off her right hand, for shouldn't that be nearly as good as a saint's relic? This gift he laid across the inspector's breast. Now for the eulogy, two prayers and three cheers. Down sank our hero, and this time the dirt blanketed him.

Since a man who is merely dead remains of small use to either side in the war between good and evil, the undead-hunters' next task was to bring the inspector back to duty before the vampires got him. Father Hauser accordingly summoned the widow Doroteja, one of his favorite parishioners, who had never missed a day of church.

He said: Doroteja, my child, the church has need of you.

Yes, Father, although I'm but a simple woman . . .

Doroteja, what I'm about to demand of you must be kept secret, on pain of rendition to eternal fire. Do you understand?

Yes, Father.

We know that you enter the churchyard at night.

Please don't burn me, Father! I won't go there anymore—

Doroteja, *he who would save his soul must lose it. She who condemns her soul shall save it, now and forever, amen.* Sing one of those pretty spells of yours. Wake up the inspector. Do this, and I'll be well pleased.

Forgive me, Father, for I've always been ignorant of such arts.

Hans Trollhand would love to see that pretty hair of yours catch fire, Doroteja. We'll burn you from your feet up, to save the best for last. Now listen. You're a witch, and there's no use pretending otherwise. Richter von Lochner stands ready to interrogate you today. I'll ask but once more. Now do as I say, witch, or forfeit your life.

And you'll burn me?

Doroteja, my girl, don't you believe in my fondness for you? It's a sin to displease me.

Yes, Father.

You can count on that. Can you bring him up in daylight?

Finding herself in much the same situation as one of our linen-weavers in northeastern Bohemia, who must both buy the raw linen and then sell back the cloth she has made, Doroteja said merely: Will you come with me, Father?

Shame, woman! I cannot be associated with such Devil's errands. And give him this. Have you seen one before?

The second medallion of the sun, Father, to release the imprisoned. Is it true gold?

Of course. Richter von Lochner inherited it from a Jewish sorcerer. A pretty pentacle, if I may say so! That's the Face of Shaddai on this side, and on the other, that secret symbol which resembles a gallows, can you comprehend it?

No, Father.

Well, it's supposed to be infallible, but the Jew who owned it went down to hell nonetheless.

2

Since the inspector was already accustomed to the vileness of criminals and the misery of torture chambers, never mind the thick grief and futility within the cottages where the poor lay starving on beds of sickness, his new quarters scarcely troubled him.

At first he thought, as he had when alive, that no food could be better than the fresh tears and saliva of one of those young witches whom he and Hans Trollhand so frequently interrogated; but presently he began to fancy menstrual blood; and then, as his tastes grew more catholic, any blood would have done, the more the better; and as this desire grew up in him, so did his strength and will, until with an exultant blasphemy he found himself rising through wood, dirt, roots and grass, into the night sky. All the while he knew he could set these impulses aside; they were coloring, not proclivity.

He felt almost gleeful to be in possession of Richter von Lochner's medallion. Although he could not follow the inscription of the outer ring, DIRUPSITI VINCULA MEA; TIBI SACRIFICABO HOSTIAM LAUDIS, ET NOMEN INVOCABO, it gave him self-confidence to own something gold, although even underground it perilously outshone all those long golden bones which resemble breadsticks, so that he had to triple-wrap it in the shroud of a deaf-mute child, which Doroteja had given him for a good luck gift. He scratched out a hole in the earth with his ever-growing fingernails and concealed it there, much as a squirrel hides acorns.

His new friends liked him right away, for he pretended to be innocent. Two periwigged old vampires even got into a quarrel as to which of them could better help him grow into his supposed inclinations. It astonished him how trusting they were—for had they not caught him in recent deception? But, as they remarked, we all die, pretenders or not. And I suspect that they so much enjoyed discovering likely young men, and advancing them on their way downward, that they frequently overlooked their own interests, like a multitude of frogs with whom a snake pretends to make friends, in order to swallow them one by one in secret. Moreover, accomplished fiends grow as egotistical as the living, and what can be more gratifying to a settled old soul for whom sinking two fangs into a strange throat has lost its thrill than imparting information to a wide-eyed yet stalwart type who once served the other side? For his part, the inspector was far too busy spying on them to feel indignant at their loathsomeness. In the first six weeks they taught him how to suck blood and how to frighten children to death.— But you're still in your youth, they said. You don't need to get serious yet. Why not run out and play a few pranks? For instance, you could hide in the bed of some lonely widow. Then you could kill her, rape her or both. It's also great fun to come up through the crypt and throw corpse-fat at the altar. Don't get too close or the cross will burn you.

He pretended to go along. In fact, even that medallion of Saint Polona held more power than they could conceive. It allowed him, although not without distress, to move about at dawn or dusk, and confer with Father Hauser in the church. The sexton had been laid under instructions to keep a mendicant's hooded cloak in the tool shed, right behind the second-best shovel, so when the inspector slipped into this, it disguised him well enough from the living, and, moreover, kept the sun off. When he took up the pentangle of the sun, he could even go out in full day-light, which of course was safest, although it tired him a good deal. And so the authorities of H— finally began to hope for results. Richter von Lochner sent away to Prague for more silver bullets, and the town council required of every citizen three perfectly finished and sharpened vampire-stakes; while Hans Trollhand, hoping for the best, laid more firewood in stock.

Being the cause of their hopes, the inspector found himself feeling very free, even if he sometimes would have liked not to be dead. Father Hauser was sweeter with him than ever before. For a fact, he liked pre-tending to be what he was not, right down to effacing every indication of virtue—and who would not have considered it delicious to make friends, which policemen in uniform ordinarily find difficult? Moreover, he con-tinued to condemn and despise them, so that he had the best of every-thing: the solace of virtue, the sweet thrills of vice, the comradeship of interesting creatures, the joy of keeping secrets from everybody, and, above all, the approbation of authority.

Why did you kill yourself? they asked him, and he replied: To defy God.

O brother! they shouted out in glee. Then let's hear you curse Him.

This he did, secretly curling his fingers around the medallion of Saint Polona. The more he insulted God and the saints (even his beloved Saint Polona), the more loudly they laughed, sometimes even until they choked up their guts, not that they minded since they no longer troubled to breathe. The witch who once upon a time conjured worms into her husband's stomach until one of them bit his heart, so that he fell dead (Troll-hand broke her arms and legs on the ravenstone, then hung her up alive to be eaten by carrion crows), thought the inspector the most hilarious soul she had ever met; she offered to make a troll-baby with him anytime. The inspector had never considered himself a charming person before, and so their admiration gave him more pleasure than he had ever received, even when the colonel awarded him a medal during his term of military service. Although mere logic would indicate that there ought to be but scant prospects for an apprentice vampire without relatives, joviality goes far in every underworld, as was proved even during the private wars of the German states.

He was sitting on a tomb one night when he saw a certain green-eyed demon leaping toward him.

My plan, it explained, is *certain as blood.* All we need to do is slip through the wall of Doroteja's house—you do slip through walls, don't you?

Of course I do, my boy.

That's good, since otherwise I'd know you were alive, and have to kill you.

Kill me? What the devil are you talking about?— And with his best ghoulish laugh, the inspector dug his sharp black fingernails into his own blue throat, and tore the dead veins to ribbons.

All right, all right; it's just that we undead have to be careful these days. Now, come along and help me. This Doroteja is a hot-blooded widow, as you know, and rather simple. Since I'm the more handsome of us two, I'll get her excited, while you figure out where she keeps her holy bric-a-brac. Once I get her to undressing, and that cross comes off her neck, if you have her other weapons out of reach, we'll be set. Just give me first suck; that's all I ask, for I could use a drop of the old red! Cross my moldering heart, I'll pass her over to you before *her* heart stops beating. And once she's buried and one of us, she'll be quite the seductress.

Count on me, brother, said the inspector.

They darted over the cemetery wall like lizards. Within a quarter-hour they were making terrifying faces at Doroteja's window—for monsters of this sort, as you have seen, tend to be quite high-spirited, even to their own detriment; they cannot help but lurch and caper.

On my faith as a throat-ripper, said the inspector, I believe you've forgotten to count some grains of barley.

(He had, of course, dribbled them out of a secret pocket in his shroud.)

At once the demon got lost in this task, and the inspector slipped away to rouse Father Hauser, who established himself in the outhouse with Hans Trollhand, each of them bearing a silver cross, a sharpened stake and an arquebus. Before Doroteja had finished screaming, they were torturing the monster into helplessness, and then Hans Trollhand, terrifying in his black-and-red cloak, served justice with a silver bullet from behind.

Frequenting the evilest shadows of that graveyard, the inspector succeeded in putting several more vampires out of the way. The trick was to get them before they tattled to the others. (It was unpleasant to imagine the glee of that subterranean crew if they could only neutralize him, preferably by draining his veins.) One night he lay chatting with a skeletal lad who had died some forty years before, and, like him, could creep around even in weak sunlight. When the inspector asked how he managed this, his new friend showed him a wrist-charm which he had gained from a witch in barter.— Who is she? asked the inspector. I'd love to give her a tickle.— And so the very next day, justice fell upon Old Hilda, who trafficked in the hair, bones, blood and fingers of the murdered. Before she could even call once upon Beelzebub, Hans Trollhand had gagged her and thrown her in a cage. By sunset the whole village was there, razing her house and helping themselves to whichever rags and crusts of hers they liked. Trollhand began singing his favorite song, the one about the brave soldier who kills his faithless betrothed. Then from the smoldering timbers they built a bonfire, and threw her on it, cage and all, so that once more heavenly virtue won the victory. The inspector kept prudently out of sight, but hearing the wailing and raging of his friends that night gave him the satisfaction he most certainly deserved.

By Christmas he had done for three dozen evildoers, for he sought out murder-conclaves as diligently as the peddler who goes to every fair to sell pictures of the holy saints. Come Easter, his score stood at ninety-nine. On the thirtieth of April, when we burn witches, half a dozen fresh women were sent to hell by Hans Trollhand, thanks to the inspector's reports. A week later he even betrayed a werewolf, the first to be captured in H—— for nearly a century. For a good while he continued to be surprised by the cavalier ignorance with which all these creatures fell into his snares, but presently he simply lowered his opinion of Satan's followers.

On Midsummer's Eve a troll whom he knew but slightly came loping up to him and said: What a fine dark escape we've had just now! You wouldn't believe how close that priest came to catching us! We were enjoying a little boy; I did for the mother last year—what a treat she was!— and there's only the girl left, who frankly smells anemic to me. Anyhow, I had my fangs in the boy, and Kobold here was just about to open his belly when the priest came running, cocking his cross at us! So I called on Satan, who sent me a nice little fart of an earthquake, but Kobold never got any food! That's why he looks so green—

Father Hauser and the executioner rose up just then from behind the Margrave's vault and fired off a load of silver bullets. Kobold escaped, but the troll died screeching. The inspector sank rapidly into his grave. The next morning, taking up his golden pentacle and medallion, he slipped into the church to complain.— Excuse me, Father, but you've put me at great risk by not consulting me beforehand. If anyone saw you and me—

Inspector, you have your work and we have ours. Richter von Lochner is pleased with your accomplishments, but he expects much more from all of us. Don't get self-important. God bless you, and go away; you stink up my church.

3

Kobold had indeed expressed his suspicions about the inspector, and so in a certain nitrous vault, where witches, ghouls and vampires sat assembled, their officials presently marched in with many a tooth-clack, dressed far more presentably than he ever would have imagined. Up in the realm of the living, our judges wear the black of mourning and the red of blood when they are condemning people. Here the magisterial colors are green and blue, and whether they represented the daylight fields and rivers so inimical to churchyard monsters, or simply two different varieties of mold, the inspector had to admit that they were pretty. Their boots were greased with the fat from unbaptized infants, and they were armed (as death's heads ought to be) with scythes. Their eyeballs burned greenly or redly from deep within their skulls.

And though it was sore grief to us to hear such things of you, inspector, declaimed an old ghoul, yet justice compels us to investigate the matter, to examine the witnesses and to summon and question you on oath, proceeding in each and every way as we are bidden by our satanic institutions. First, to the complainant. Now, troll, what's your name?

They call me Snow White, said the ugly fellow, and the assembly screeched with laughter; the inspector had to admit that they were all very jolly.

Sir, may I put a question? he said. As a new fellow here, I can't help but wonder if you're related to Hans Trollhand, who's burned so many of us.

The troll, of course, flew into a rage at that insinuation, and came rushing at him with his claws out, but the old ghoul tapped on the lectern with a coffin-nail, and the assembly returned to order. Meanwhile the inspector had scored a point, for several witches who had been smiling fondly at the troll before now overwatched him with tight grimaces of suspicion, as so many of their neighbors had been lately destroyed, thanks to the inspector's efforts, that nobody underground felt safe.

Snow White, tell the court what you know.

All I can say is that when the priest did for poor Gulper, who was my second cousin, I was hiding behind a tombstone, as Kobold will bear out, and I saw the priest and that inspector exchange *a look*.

Is that so, Kobold?

That's right, and who else do we have to suspect but this fellow who was on the *right side* until he insinuated himself down here?

Search him, trolls.

In a twinkling, the poor inspector was stripped. But he had wisely left his two charms behind, so nothing could be said against him.

Accused, what do you have to say?

Well, said the inspector, already getting delighted with himself, let me just say that if I only had hold of Saint Mary by her pretty paps . . .

At this, they all positively screeched with glee, so that the vault rocked and the citizens of H——, shaken out of sleep, crossed themselves and prayed not to be devoured by earthquakes.

Thus, for the moment at least, he was acquitted by acclamation, which he considered his greatest triumph, for nothing had ever struck him as more difficult than that night in the vault full of ghouls and vampire judges. But when he departed the court, explaining that he had some mischief to attend to, he could not but remark the silence with which the others regarded him, as if he smelled alive or worse.

4

In time he made up with them, and they loved him when he persuaded Father Hauser to lend him his cassock, which he pretended he had stolen; and the witches all took turns trying it on while they had sexual congress with broomsticks. It was a merry night, to be sure; by then they were all twenty glasses of blood the better. After that, the inspector could not help but laugh when the vampires voted to dig up the dry old grave of a Christian and play dice with the vertebrae. Back when he was a soldier in the war, the boys in his regiment used to play similar pranks.

In each of them he descried the will to bury his own shame and foulness, hate and greed, not to mention death itself; so that's good, this vampiric tendency, he said to himself; for such things truly ought to be kept out of sight!

Because they knew so much about the depths of the earth, they were well acquainted with gems and hoards of gold. So, because they were fond of him, they soon taught him where the richest lodes were, and he felt even more important. But how could he forget what it means to be alone?

Just like children gathering fallen pears and nuts, they ranged about, murdering whomever they could. To them, living human flesh was nearly as delicious as a Sunday roast of castrated goat.

The next night they frightened their arch-enemy Hans Trollhand, popping up outside his window, dressed in their shrouds as when they attended the Hangman's Meal. The inspector declined to attend, not wishing to observe his friend's discomfiture. This stirred the mercurial vampires against him. All the same, he bravely set forth to ensnare more of the undead.

Now he fell in with a less jolly crew. The dead vagrant branded on his forehead with the Lord's Mark, the prostitute whose right ear had been sliced off after the second time she was caught in the act, the embezzler whose wicked fingers got nicely hacked off before he was decapitated, these were all ordinary criminals, justly convicted by their own confessions and executed in accordance with the law, so I fail to see what they had to complain about. And yet, strange to say, they all acted quite bitter. Bertha the murderess, whose breasts had been nipped off with red-hot tongs, was especially foul in her expressions of fury, even though she had repented in tears (a pretense, no doubt) just before they broke her on the wheel. Here's a good one to keep away from, thought the inspector. He did not really need to deceive them, although sometimes, like Richter von Lochner himself (who was famous for his tricky promises to the accused), he did so for his own pleasure. His duty was but to recognize them and withdraw before they thought to suspect him. Since Father Hauser had so fine a great memory for names and crimes, all the inspector had to do next was unearth his golden pentacle, pull on his mendicant's cloak and creep over to the church in the daytime, while his comrades slept, and then describe them to the priest, who would take notes, only occasionally asking a clarificatory question or consulting the graveyard register. That very afternoon, the sexton would come with Hans Trollhand, to dig up and dispose of them while they were helpless.

The other undead could not understand where their associates kept disappearing to. They had not been in such peril since the Prince Elector of Bohemia sat beside the Count Palatine. Some were in constant excitement, running from one grave to another without being able to eat any corpse. Finally they decided to appeal below for help.

5

The Vampire-Colonel's expression somehow reminded the inspector of the way his father used to smoke his long pipe. It was a long way down if one wished to see this worthy, but when he overheard some of his depraved and disgusting friends agreeing that it was high time to make that pilgrimage, the inspector volunteered his company, at which they wrinkled their bloody lips at him, half prepared to reaffirm his treachery, but after whispering together they agreed that he could come. What did they admire in him? Richter von Lochner, I regret to say, had never considered him save in the light of a tool; Father Hauser kept him at an ever greater distance, due to the offensive stigmata of decay which he now presented; as for the undead, it is all too plausible that even they saw him as no more than a convenient companion for their debauches; and presently even the inspector himself began to wonder who he was. Down a greasy tunnel they sped, until it had gotten substantially warmer, and even brighter with a blue light to which the inspector supposed he could get contentedly accustomed, if he ended up having to spend eternity down here.

His friends urged him forward. They asserted the necessity for a second interrogation of this peculiar individual, for they could find no one else among them to blame; he himself continually reinfected them with the cunning fallacy that Trollhand and Father Hauser were managing these persecutions entirely on their own.

Why did you come to us? demanded the Vampire-Colonel. From this first question he could see that this too was to be a pro forma questioning; at which, as so often before, it struck him that people became stupider after death.

I died, he answered.

Prove it.

Here's my death-wound.

I'll give you another, just to be sure—and, blowing a skullheaded whistle, the Vampire-Colonel summoned two rats who gnawed away. It didn't hurt at all. After that, the company courteously assisted him in refastening his head on. I am told that they keep very good mastics in those subterranean realms. After all, many glues and gums can be made from dead things.

Well, said the Vampire-Colonel, it appears that you truly are dead. And a good business, too.

Again the inspector began almost to pity his adversaries in their ignorant weakness.

Now, what are you all doing here? their host demanded.

Taking the errand upon himself, the inspector explained: Half the population of our graveyard has been rubbed out in the past year. It's that damned priest and Hans Trollhand.

All right, said the Vampire-Colonel. I know them. I'll get my legions together before the moon wanes. On the first completely dark night, we'll go out through the crypt and tear those two apart. Now inform me about the church? Does it serve any purpose?

Sentimental attachment, said a troll.

That's all? No store of items to pollute and deconsecrate?

We're afraid to go there, said the inspector.

We'll smash that place.

The next day, the inspector sneaked over to the church. Father Hauser informed Judge von Lochner, who sent to Prague, and come the dark of the moon a squad of Holy Bohemian Dragoons stood ready with garlic-shooters, buckets of holy water and arquebuses loaded with silver bullets every third one of which had been blessed by the Pope. When Hans Trollhand lifted up his fungoid ear from the floor and raised his forefinger, they all knew that the evil souls were marching in cunning, silence and speed.

The flagstones trembled. Two engraved marble memory-stones began to swing aside, and there were black shapes like reflected tree-limbs trembling in dark green water. From underground came deep voices singing the following:

Up, up, you doughty ghouls, to aid the groaning dead
And tear apart the pious ones who boiled us in lead!

The dragoons took aim. Trollhand lowered his pike. A knight's marble tomb-effigy, cracked across his grin, so that his head was nearly bifurcated, began to tremble even as he lay rigid, with his delicate marble hands crossed upon his sword, and then he swung sideways. First out came the Vampire-Colonel, as one might have expected. They riddled him with consecrated silver, and he exploded. From the other two tunnels spidery things convulsed in hatred. Launching garlic and holy water down into hell, Christ's army brought forth many a screech and a wail. At dawn they descended with candles to clean it out as far as they dared, finding nothing but a few troll-scales, clots of greenish blood and promiscuous scatterings of human bones.

Throughout this operation the inspector kept wisely aloof.

6

So the undead had to go deeper, right down to the King Vrykolakas. The inspector kept them company again, of course; for I promise he will be loyal to everyone throughout this hateful story. After the oozy earth-guts there was a lovely winding stair, all stone, with shells of unknown mollusks laid out as if by design, and a soft glow of yellow-green light from the landing below, or perhaps from the landing below that, which might have been hell. They reached a crouching corpse, now fallen forward in its decay. When they got down twice as far as where the Vampire-Colonel used to dwell, they began to hear a sound of chuckling which was actually roaring, coming up through the ground

The King Vrykolakas lay faceup in a wine-cask full of blood, snoring, gurgling, drinking and vomiting all at once. He was as fat and brown as a roasted pig; he was as absurdly large as a mountain of hay which must be carried by two oxen. He had fangs halfway down to his knees, fingernails like sickles and toenails like a vulture's claws. When he opened his eyes, the inspector saw that the whites were yellow, the irises were red and the pupils were blackish-green like frogskin.

You see, said the *vrykolakas.* I know what you're up to, inspector. All the rest of you, leave us alone, please. I'll send a rat to get you when you're done. Now, tell me which is worse, inspector—to find malignant beings such as we are, or to find nobody in here? Wouldn't it get lonely in here if it were just you and a few skeletons that couldn't even chatter their teeth hello?

When you put it like that, said the inspector, I see that there's a third possibility. Why not wish for a cemetery full of angels?

Oh, so that's what you want. One of those is just down the road, in Neinstade. For your reward, after you finish destroying us, why not get Father Hauser to rebury you there? There's a cute little winged Cecelia with a marble-white bottom; I used to let her suck my fangs. But I don't know how much joy you'll get from people like her. They're not as open-minded as we. All cobwebbed up with hymns, you know. Unless you're one of them, they won't even smile at you. But go and see for yourself.

The inspector kept quiet.

The great *vrykolakas* sucked in his cheeks and scratched bloodclots off his chin-bristles. He said: Now see here. Do you suppose we'll be better off when Trollhand drives a stake through our hearts?

That's not for me to say, replied the inspector. My task is to apprehend evildoers and turn them over to the authorities.

Well, we're definitely evil. And does our punishment fit the crime?

It's not punishment, actually. You're scarcely conscious when the stake goes in.

As he said this, he confessed to himself that it must be worse for them than that. Even Father Hauser sometimes grew unnerved at the way that a vampire appeared to smile slightly when in daylight the lid of its coffin was struck off by the ecclesiastical authorities; in simple fact, the creature sensed that it had been disturbed, and struggled in its sleep to avoid the hateful stimulus of holiness, grimacing, as if it practically expected the stake.

But the *vrykolakas* pretended to agree, burping and saying: That's right. So it hardly matters to me what you do. Undeath is nearly as monotonous as life. What happens next I don't know. So I won't betray you to your friends. In the meantime I've got appointments down in hell. Will you take my place?

After your accusations?

I have known far too many who have crept into the deepest positions, solely due to their proficiency in biting. Inspector, do you promise to accept personal responsibility?

So he ran everything like a dream. He arrested the ghouls who stole mammocks from each other's tombs, and punished those who expressed seditious sentiments about the Devil. (This made him realize that some undead were less fundamentally guilty than others.) He oversaw the decorations on All Hallows' Eve. He even drilled squadrons of undead soldiers, showing the keenest sensitivity to the prestige of the Mushroom Crown. And all the time he silently identified everyone who was active underground: the son whose parents had neglected to punish him for sluggishness, the prostitute Veronika, the nameless brother and sister burned alive for incest and so many others whose peccadilloes had ripened into sins. Many of them dwelled so far below the surface that it would be necessary to pitch holy water down into their tunnels. He began to map the warrens down there between headstone and hell.

But there were certain passageways which, finding them strangely beautiful, he decided not to betray to Father Hauser. He was willing to reveal most of what he saw, but when he entered the high-vaulted side-cellars where undead children played harmlessly with knucklebones, and sometimes tried to grow phosphorescent mushrooms, he left those off his maps.

7

When the King Vrykolakas came back, as a reward, or more likely an enticement, he introduced the inspector to the demon Brulefer, who causes a man to be found luscious by women; Surgat, around whom no lock can remain shut; Humots, who fetches any book one wishes for; Hael, who gives us command over any and all languages, but is ruled by Nebirots, whom it is best to conjure first; Trimsael, who teaches chemistry and legerdemain, and can accordingly impart the obscure process of manufacturing the Powder of Projection, which will alter base metals into gold and silver; Bucon, who causes antipathy between men and women; Sidragosam, who forces the girl of one's choice to dance in the nude.

It was all profitable to the inspector, who had never been well educated. He learned the identities of the Whispering Knights, and which demon is most delighted by ritual cremation. He still believed that everything about being dead was the same for him. But what had really happened was that, as people generally will, he grew accustomed to his new state of being. This is not to say that he made plans of any sort, much less altered the previous ones. To tell the truth, he disdained the riotous ghouls and vampires upstairs as much as ever. The snoring solitude of the King Vrykolakas was more appropriate to his nature. The inspector was well aware that this monster was one of the most dangerous of all. Trollhand ought to destroy him immediately. Well, the inspector would take care of that in time. That old ghoul in the mold-green robe who had judged him last winter had already been dealt with, and a good thing, too. But when would the inspector receive his reward?

He had never been suggestible, but now it would have been easy to convince himself that in spite of the medallion of Saint Polona and even the golden pentacle, he was developing an allergy to light. Not wishing to give in to such satanic deceptions—for after all he had already rejected a number of notions in order to get where he was—he continued his investigations, under the guise of being a subaltern to the King Vrykolakas, who loved to look him up and down, snorting and snoring with laughter until blood-clots wormed out of his hairy nostrils. The golden pentacle would have been his mainstay in this time of hesitation, were it not for the fact that he dared not risk carrying it on his person, so that it mostly slept in the dark dirt high over his head.

Of course while he was down here exposing the Devil's work, the King Vrykolakas was employing minions to counter-investigate *him*. First they found the medallion to Saint Polona in his coffin, together with old Jette's skeleton-hand. These did not really signify, since any number of people in H—— were buried with such trash, which availed nothing against a vampire bite. So they kept on looking, while the inspector, having received approving consent from the King Vrykolakas to conduct a census of the undead, should there ever come a need to mobilize all the undead against an invasion of Holy Knights or worse, burrowed deeper and deeper, openly mapping almost everything he saw, with a secret excitement as he imagined presenting this document to Father Hauser, and clinking glasses with Hans Trollhand—nobody had thought to offer him a drink since he died! Perhaps even Richter von Lochner would come. Turning a corner, he entered a golden-black ooze-world of jawless skulls basking like crocodiles, half overgrown with vagina-flowers. More than anything the place resembled, at least to me, one of the night-garden paintings of Leonor Fini, but since she lived after the inspector's time I cannot imagine that he drew the same comparison. But here, in a grove of nude trees whose branches terminated in smooth blue hands, he met undead women, scintillatingly nude, whom he actually supposed he could love.— Dear boy, that's a truly romantic place, the King Vrykolakas remarked, gnawing on a dead frog, just to bring on an appetite for dinner.— You see, Baal constructed it for his harem, although they've since dug down to blacker paradises. It was unoccupied for more than ten thousand years, and then some of your kind moved in.

What do you mean by my kind?

Oh, the delicate sort. They cherish all their appendages, and extrude parts of themselves into each other's orifices. Female, for the most part, as you may have noticed. I've left all that above me long ago. But you're still immature, inspector. You bear the hallmark of a living man—loneliness.

Sir, I disagree that the dead are less lonely than the living. Up there in the graveyard, all they do is play pranks together and—

Exactly. Up there. The farther down you go, the more solitary it gets.

What about Baal's harem?

Oh, he ate them all.

The inspector said nothing. In resentment and despair he soon set out to expand his map, not that he would ever record the existence of the "romantic place," which was too interesting to be destroyed. By now he had explored all the way to the horned long barrows of Bryn Celli Ddu. But often he returned to that black garden where the skulls basked like crocodiles, and the lovely blue undead women loitered in the grove of hand-trees, and there he tried calling on the demon Brulefer, who granted his prayer, so that all those women loved him happily. The deeper down he went, the more he began to believe, if only to console himself, that he must be digging for something, perhaps the water of life or death, although the glowing, coagulating atmosphere he swam into down there addled him so much that he sometimes hardly gathered what he was about; nonetheless, you will be relieved to know that he remained capable of mapping and memorizing everything. Just as Bohemia's crown jewels lie hidden underground near Saint Wenceslas's tomb, so the precious matter of the vampires and their kin entombed themselves right beneath the cemetery of H____, which after all is the center of the world. And now the inspector began to uncover more such secrets, each of them more charming than the last, and the deeper he went, the more bewildered he became, while by now the King Vrykolakas's minions had discovered the golden pentacle, which once again (although the king himself was certain) they could not prove to be the inspector's, but it was certainly a dangerous item; it would have burned them had they touched it; to pick it up they had to pass a stick through its necklace-chain. Depositing it in the ribcage of old Jette, whom none of the undead had ever found a prior use for, they rendered that poisonous thing halfway safe, even though the more sensitive ones among them could see its baleful golden glow right through Jette's coffin.

They were fairly sure but not positive.— You deserve a rest, said the King Vrykolakas to the inspector. Why don't you go up to your coffin for a year or two, while I take my nap?

Chuckling, he watched the inspector's glance flick toward the map, then away. What did he care? Even Trollhand was in no position to threaten the cemetery frontier. And the inspector watched him watch. Since the King Vrykolakas knew his secret, what was supposed to happen? The inspector did not dare to take it with him, but he felt confident that he had most of it memorized. Of course he had better visit Father Hauser sooner rather than later; in case he too became stupider.

He clambered back up through the ooze. In the chamber he had left, his host was already snoring like a goodwife's iron pot bubbling day and night on the stove.

8

It happened during the twentieth Mansion of the Moon: *Abnahaya*, which strengthens prisons. By now the inspector wore the generic fangs of a dead Bohemian. When he blasphemed, it no longer brought him any pleasure. His position felt as cynical as the policy of the angels. Sometimes he dreamed that he had forgotten the way to his tomb, but found himself twitching strangely and counting pebbles whenever he entered a graveyard. He yearned to give himself to the green darkness of oak leaves, which unlike the living or the undead would accept him without conditions.

His pentangle was gone. This alarmed him, but not so much as he might have expected. Just before dawn he set out with his Saint Polona medallion, but it had lost much virtue, and he was in agony by the time he reached the sexton's toolshed. A witch was hurrying away from the daylight, clutching something wrapped up in a dirty cloth. He knew her; she must have just dug up a dead man's head, and today would be planting black beans in his eyes, mouth and ears, to make herself invisible. Well, Trollhand could burn her. The inspector drew on his mendicant's cloak, which used to stick to his oozing flesh but which now hung quite loosely, and when he regarded his hands he saw why; they were semiskeletonized.

Creeping into the church, he found it disagreeably warm, for he had grown accustomed to the delightful coolness of muck and clay. Naturally, he did not permit this discomfort to distort his projects in any way.

Father Hauser was in bed at home. But his good friend Trollhand was there, dozing in the rearmost pew, wrapped in his black-and-red cloak, with a heap of sharpened stakes at his feet. Since his salary was low except when there were dogs and rats to catch, he often preferred to sleep in the church, in order to avoid his hungry wife and children. The inspector stood over him, longing to eavesdrop on his thoughts, for suddenly it came to him that the only key to understanding himself he now possessed was this Hans Trollhand. Perhaps he felt this because they had been friends together, or it might simply have been that Trollhand was the first living person he had seen in a long time, and the inspector still thought of himself as in a way living. Or it might have been that his assignment, which nowadays we would call espionage, had rubbed off on him, although in fact everybody in H—— does much the same; practically every night Doroteja caught somebody listening at her keyhole to the sounds she made when she was combing her hair.

Trollhand uttered a cry when the inspector touched his shoulder. After all, it had been awhile since they had met. The inspector began to tell him his great news, only to discover that he seemed to have lost his tongue.

Are you the inspector? Trollhand demanded. Why don't you say something? For all I know, you're some ghoul who's gotten hold of that cloak. Speak to me, damn you!

This insulting treatment enraged the inspector, who, after all, had given up quite a lot for his fellow men. But he bit what remained of his lip, and gestured that he wished for something to write with. Narrowly observing him, Trollhand said: I don't have much truck with reading and writing. Now, are you the inspector or aren't you? Nod your head yes or no.

The inspector nodded once. The man's ignorance revolted him, not that the King Vrykolakas had been any better. Was there nothing but one kind of self-satisfied cunning stupidity or another? Neither one of them even cared about the demon Brulefer, much less Trimsael or Humots.

Trollhand then insolently said: And have you ever met the Angel of Death, old boy?

Suddenly the inspector was overcome with indifference. Not only are the lusts of the living never satisfied, he said to himself, but they grow and grow, just like the death within them. How many of us has he staked and burned, thanks to my efforts? And now he wants to mock me.—Turning away, he shambled back to the cemetery. So many birds, so many insects! Blackbirds were nesting where the archers used to shoot. A pigeon trilled within a dead knight's blind arch. But it all hurt him. He longed to be as supple as a lizard in a shady crevice, the way he used to be when he was alive. As he drew near he began to perceive the shining of the golden pentacle coming up through the earth of Jette's grave. Since none of the undead could possibly be on watch, he dove down to retrieve it, and at once he felt more together, so to speak. The sun scarcely annoyed him, and vapors no longer rose from his cloak. He could have returned straight to Trollhand, in order to express himself to him with greater success, but instead he decided to visit Doroteja, who was always kind to everyone.

Of course the sun was higher now, and people saw him. The kerchiefed women, already kneeling down in the fields while two matrons approached with baskets, rose up to scream; men threw stones, and someone ran off to fetch the priest. Not wishing for Doroteja to get burned for a witch, the inspector gave it up, wondering: Am I the only one who is not incapable of love or of facing truth? He spat, determined not be reconciled with any of them. Having inhaled all those secrets issuing out from between the King Vrykolakas's teeth, having betrayed many a fetching vampiress, even the innocent ones who still wore their white shrouds, he must have done enough. So he returned to the cemetery, returned the pentangle into Jette's eternally unconscious keeping, and descended into his own grave. By now he felt too weak to return the black cloak, so there it lay in full daylight on top of his tombstone.

When he had rested for a night or two, he called upon Humots, who stood ready to bring him any book of his desire. So he asked for the Secret Book of Angels, which contained rules for every situation, especially the postmortem ones. He said: I hope to learn what belongs to me.— Humots twinkled his red eyes at the inspector, then flew up toward heaven with a great buzz of blackish-green insect wings. And the inspector waited.

9

The Romanians say that a vampire can go up into the sky by the thread that a woman weaves at night without a candle, and thus he eats the moon. Perhaps Humots ascended in some such fashion, and then some malicious angel snipped the thread, for he never came back. The inspector lay at rest, and sometimes he dreamed of Doroteja trying to stab him through the heart with a silver hairpin while sometimes he dreamed of Doroteja smiling at him with nearly closed eyes. And so his mission became to him like a vampire's tomb so overgrown with underbrush that not even Trollhand could find the way.

10

Richter von Lochner had once succeeded in forcing a witch to confess (a triumph of his jurisprudence) that she had flown her broomstick to Prague, and there been conveyed by certain sinful creatures into that secret tunnel about which Father Hauser had so often preached; it runs from the Jewish Ghetto all the way to Jerusalem—and, as anyone might expect, makes a special detour to the churchyard here in H___, where the greatest battle ever between good and evil is eternally taking place. Thanks to the inspector's efforts, the fact of this battle was now proved, as a result of which the priest and the judge both expected to melt down many more scrap-hearts in the furnace of piety. But then the inspector stopped coming. He never drew out for them his subterranean map, or informed them of the whereabouts of the King Vrykolakas, whose staking would have been a grievous loss to hell, or even gave them more names of pranksters from the cemetery. Even on Saint John's Day, when our vilest witches creep out naked to gather certain herbs whose magic will steal the milk from their neighbors' cows, the inspector never appeared to finger them.

Just as the surgeon, when called upon by the magistrate, will conscientiously slit open a comatose vampire's chest to discover how fresh and

lively its blood may be, so Father Hauser now called upon himself to examine the inspector's heart, or as I should say his soul; for he had heard
from Trollhand about that ambiguous visit to the church; who had it
been exactly? And why was that stinking black cape lying on top of the
inspector's grave? The other vampires wondered much the same, but as
usual there was nothing to prove the inspector's guilt to either party; the
golden pentacle blazed on within Jette's skeleton; Kobold paid a visit to
the inspector, who lay in his rotten box with his arms folded and declined to answer. Meanwhile, day came, as it always has so far, and so the
priest and Trollhand set out for the cemetery, that thriving heart of the
town, where Doroteja used to sing and dig in hopes of undoing her miscarriage, where Michael Liebesmann happily recovered his wife Milena,
where our inspector had gone in order to advance his career, and witches
and warlocks came to harvest the materials of their commerce. Come to
think of it, the cemetery was the only important place in H——.

This occasion, of course, did not at all resemble the occasion when the
whole village turned out for the opening of Milena's grave. Trollhand
doffed his official cloak. Not even the surgeon and the drummer boy
were invited. The people were in the fields. Father Hauser believed as
much as ever in the inspector's loyalty, although Trollhand, having seen
so much evil in his life, said: Forgive me, Father, but what lasts forever?
Even undeath is turning out to be temporary, thanks to these new police
methods of ours.

You're quite proud of the inspector, aren't you, Hans?

Well, said Trollhand, he's put food on my table. For every one I stake,
the mayor gives me a silver thaler, although last year one of them was
counterfeit.

Blackbirds and starlings rose up over their heads when they dug him
up, and as he appeared distinctly *evil*, they finally put a stake through his
heart, in order to teach him that the tunnel to heaven is far narrower
than a corseted woman's waist. The priest, who was so well regarded that
on cloudy days one could practically see his halo, held it to be for the
best. Although Richter von Lochner had uttered no promise on the subject, in his Christian mercy he did presently command that the inspector's remains should rest beneath a cross made of wild rose thorns.
Perhaps you consider this an inadequate reward. But as is said about

devils in the ancient *Grimorium Verum, this sort of creature does not give anything for nothing.*

Father Hauser offered up three prayers, for the inspector had certainly abated the nuisance, even if not permanently; and so tranquillity welled up out of the grave-riddled earth of Bohemia, seeping and creeping across the entire carcass of the Holy Roman Empire, until by 1855 Bavaria found it practical to recommend the amalgamation of commercial codes throughout the German states.

IV

JUNE EIGHTEENTH

So long as there is an Emperor, there is still an Empire, even if he has no more than six feet of earth belonging to him, for the Empire is nothing without the Emperor.

Charlotte (Empress Carlota)

1

If you appreciate the way that the double-headed Austrian eagle manages to bear both sword and orb in its claws, then you may well be an adorer of the fleet, like Massimiliano, whose bedroom resembled a ship's cabin. How he loved to sail around Istria! Archduke and Admiral, lepidopterist and orange-gardener, he might have lived contented, had not his wife persuaded him otherwise. Indeed, he used to say that all he wanted out of life was a castle and garden by the sea. Instead, he entered a story told on tin-coated iron. (He was not unlike the Holy Child of Atocha, who was carried to Mexico by the Dominicans.) Once more he gazed back into the pale blue harbor, with Trieste glowing white on the underside of that blue peninsula. Then the *Novara* carried him away. He became Maximilian. Charlotte stood beside him on the foredeck, excited to finally become Carlota. To this day some Italians remain proud of him, at least to an extent. In Trieste his verdigrised statue stands high upon a cylindrical and octagonal bronze plinth studded with high-breasted angels, and there is even a bare-chested youth whom I first took for an Egyptian in a quasi-Pharaonic headdress, although now I wonder whether he could be one of the Emperor's grateful Mexican subjects?

A soldier from the Confederate States of America once observed: *Owing to some radical defect in the Mexican character unfitting them for self government the country has been cursed by one of republican form . . .*

Fortunately, Maximilian now prepared to govern for them. He made it understood that his measures would have an entirely friendly character.

We remember him for many good qualities, not least his china blue eyes and beautiful teeth.

2

Matters ran on pretty well for the first two years, wrote an Englishman in his service. *French bayonets kept the country quiet, and the roads open.* But presently certain Mexicans began to fall short of their Emperor's hopes. I cannot tell you whether the blue and red of Maximilian's army were inappropriate colors for those latitudes, or whether his desire to lead the natives out of anarchy exceeded their benighted comprehension. He assured them: *No Mexican has such warm feelings for his country and its progress as I.* I wish you could have seen him with his blank white forehead and his nautical side-whiskers and his squinting eyes, whose gaze was outglittered by the watch-chain peeping out of his dark vest. Beside him, Carlota in her white wedding-cake dress smiled nervously upon the world. He determined to keep only Mexicans in his government, wore white, abolished inherited debt, enacted ten-year serfdom for negroes, but only under certain conditions and with the best intentions; imported pianos, upheld the nationalization of Church property, established a minimum wage and collected butterflies. Soon the Empress was writing to France: *We see nothing to respect in this country, and shall act in such a way as to change it.* He restored the Palacio Nacional. His soldiers dug ever more convoluted earthworks isolated by ditches; established outlying piquets whose sentries lay ready to fire upon silence; rigged up abatis of prickly pears; marched out battalions of jet-black Turcos in Zouave dress; levied any number of ablebodied natives to serve in his Guardia Rural, while Carlota, twenty-five years old, clasped her lovely long-fingered hands, assuring her acquaintances in Belgium: *If necessary, I can lead an army. Do not laugh at me.* Meanwhile her husband, who was already going bald, signed the October Decree, which saved the inconvenience of trying guerrillas before executing them. But no matter how valiantly he led, anarchy marched along at his heels. Indeed, so singular is Mexican gratitude that he was practically alone even before the French troops sailed home; then he found himself defeated, surrounded, betrayed at Querétaro, and imprisoned in that half-devoured city, brought to trial at the Iturbide Theater (in absentia, since they had courteously granted him a certificate of illness) and duly condemned to be shot on the nineteenth of June, 1867, along with his generals Mejía and Miramón.

3

As might have been expected, at dusk on the eighteenth he saw small hope of sleeping. This displeased him, for he wished to meet his executioners with that calm and decisive courtesy which demands a certain cast of face; it should not be said of the Emperor of Mexico that he appeared hollow-eyed at the end. In fact he had been unhealthy for years, but the valets who shaved and dressed this man had preserved him from his mirror-image. Like many of us, he believed himself somewhat younger than he was. His narrow pink face, whose eyelids were a trifle sleepy and whose chin hung too close beneath the mouth, had been widened by blond side-whiskers, and the matching beard extended his chin to normal length. Thus Maximilian at thirty; and if in truth he was closer to thirty-five, he remained as facile as ever on a horse, and nearly as attractive to women. He retained the confidence of a fresh and handsome man. It was this that he aspired to keep until the end. Insomnia could never undermine his dignity, but two or three hours of repose would increase the luster with which he smiled upon the executioners.

If the word "noblehearted" brings a smile to any reader nowadays, so much the better, for Maximilian possessed precisely this old-fashioned quality, which was precious in its time, no matter that disuse has rendered it ludicrous. Turning over his feelings, he found, as he would have expected, no anger toward the seven soldiers who would shoot him, and he thanked God for that. Tomorrow he would forgive them, ask forgiveness in return and bestow a gold ounce on each man. As for the two who must die at his side, he compassionated them more than himself. That afternoon he had penned a telegram to his triumphant enemy Juárez, requesting that they be spared; let their punishment be upon him alone. No answer came. Well, so it must be. He was never to know that the kind and loyal Mejía could have saved himself, but chose his Emperor over his own desperate wife, who next morning would pursue the carriage, screaming and raising up her baby, until the soldiers thrust her down with their bayonets. Another thing he never learned, thanks to his abstention from the trial, was that two years ago Miramón had proposed to come over to Juárez. At any rate, on that eighteenth of June all three were good friends.— Although she had tearfully entreated his life at the knees of Juárez, who in his usual colorless way replied that he could do nothing for her, Miramón's wife was more composed than Mejía's; indeed, her resolution had brought the Emperor to tears a day or two before. Miramón must have been moved in his own way, for, kissing her hand, he remarked: I am here because I would not listen to this woman's advice, to which Maximilian bitterly replied: Feel no remorse; I am here because I did listen to my wife.

Yes, he sorrowed for them, but they would pull through; and of course he believed so deeply in that other antique thing called "renown" that the prospect of monuments comprised the supreme consolation; it would hardly have occurred to the Emperor that they might feel differently.

He had prepared his will, although one of the witnesses' signatures was lacking. Doctor Basch was to convey his rosary and wedding ring to the adoring mother who had advised him to stick it out in Mexico, and his gold medal from the Empress Eugénie to the old Empress of Brazil, the mother of his truest love. His corpse would be embalmed, so that his mother could see it.

For his mother he felt extremely sorry. Of course she would manage to rule herself. As for Carlota (whom he still called Charlotte), he would have dreaded the prospect of somebody's bringing sad news within the ken of her wide yet small eyes, for ever since Napoleon and the Pope had declined her personal entreaties to maintain the Empire, insanity infested her peculiarly flat-topped head, and her long white hands sometimes tore at the air. Fortunately, Maximilian imagined her to be at peace; for Mejía comforted him with the fable that she had died at Miramar.

Sitting on the camp bed, he stared wearily at the ivory crucifix, which offered so little and so much, until his eyes closed for an instant. In the adjacent cell, Miramón was coughing, while the moon rose, and Austrian warships waited uselessly at Veracruz. It was half-past eight-o'-clock.

4

He had thought himself to be past bitterness, but presently, like mosquitoes singing round his head, bad memories rose up: the trial's thirteen indictments, each an insult; the horribly gentle eyes of Fray Soria, who had accompanied the lawyers when they brought the verdict to his cell, while in the corridor the eavesdropping general and three colonels held their gloating breaths; and then Curtopassi, having weighed fidelity against expediency, coolly scissoring away his signature from that compromising bill of change through which the three of them had hoped to purchase their escape (Mejía jaguar-eyed as he thrust a single curse between the departing coward's shoulderblades); Charlotte's humiliated whispers to the Virgin of Guadalupe, who, so her women had pityingly assured her, could fructify any womb, should the heart but truly believe; and Charlotte pulling out her first grey hair, and Charlotte with her head down on her writing-desk (which once had belonged Marie Antoinette), silently weeping for hatred of Miramar; and the first time she withdrew her hand from his to walk alone at Chapultepec; and Fray Soria's clumsy attempt to comfort him there in the chapel below the cells, directing him to that absurd votive scene, painted as if by a young child, with the caption *On the 7th day of July in 1864, I, Ambrosio Alonso, having been captured and held as a guerrilla, was led out of jail to be killed although nothing had been completely proved against me, so I called upon the Lord of Wonders, who granted me this favor, so they released me, and I have commissioned this retablo,* giving thanks for the miracle*—good God, their literalist idols! These people were all primitives, as even Mejía continued to prove in his sad thirst for images of the Holy Child of Atocha, who, so it is said, used to slip between the bars of Moorish prisons to bring inexhaustible supplies of bread and water to Christian captives, and now sometimes liberated the oppressed; well, it might be so, and in any case religion must never be mocked. Fray Soria brought him another retablo to handle. It was childishly done, of course. But for the benefit of self-discipline he pretended to admire this likeness of the roundfaced, smallmouthed, smiling Child. Sunshine glowed around the tiny sombrero which floated on His reddish-brown curls as if upon the water; white ruffles encircled His throat and the plump baby-hands which peeked from the sleeves of His crimson robe. One hand held the basket

*An image, often naïve in style and technique, commissioned in honor of a saint, or more specifically to acknowledge some miracle or favor. Nineteenth-century Mexican retablos tend to be oil-painted on tin-coated iron.

of loaves which resembled flowers, and the other a water-gourd on a stick, as He sat on his diminutive throne, old and young, sweet and knowing and unapproachable, more patient than ingratiating. *I petitioned the Holy Child, and . . .* The Emperor turned over the tin sheet, and in the matte darkness of the japanned iron saw his reflection as if in black water. Back came bad memories: his myriad brave soldiers who had been compelled to feed the earth with their own bloody hearts, Marshal Bazaine's perpetual yet ever-altering machinations, now recapitulated, ever since Bazaine together with his troops had abandoned the Empire, by the bustling night-vermin on that crusted bandage around Miramón's temples; not to mention the hangdog conferences, which all participants knew to be useless, regarding the interest, never mind the fiendish principal, on those infamous Jecker bonds (for which, to tell the truth, Miramón was to blame), Bazaine's bald head gleaming still more hatefully than his smile when he said: Unfortunately, Your Majesty, you must meet your obligations to France!—and the antlike, inimical, invincible vitality of Juárez, whom he had once thought to welcome into his cabinet (never mind the fact that in every respect he resembled a servant), and whose orders had put to death a hundred captured Legionnaires at San Jacinto; the sadistic self-importance of the unshaven mestizo general and the three ragged colonels now sitting outside his cell, and none of their pistols clean; and that evening at Puebla on Charlotte's twenty-fifth birthday, when their well-meaning host, an elderly hidalgo who had served Emperor Iturbide, thought to put Their Majesties in one bedroom, and the nearly imperceptible twitching at the corners of Charlotte's mouth when the valet commenced to set matters right; the deciphered telegram with the word APPOMATTOX (had Lee defeated Grant, the United States could never have rescued Juárez), followed in due time by that letter on the familiar stationery of Louis Napoleon, who had lured him into this adventure, and promised never to abandon him, explaining that *in France it was no longer permissible to be mistaken*; the embarrassing vulgarities of that former Texas circus-dancer Princess Salm-Salm, who had just now tried to save him by offering herself to Colonel Palacio Villanueva; that vile farewell kiss from his brother, who had smoothly encouraged him to fall in with Napoleon's designs, then, when it was too late to withdraw without loss of honor, compelled him to renounce his Austrian claims; the treachery of López, who had received so many preferments at his hands; the moment when he understood from an indiscretion of the physician that Charlotte had gone mad in Rome; the silence that long ago morning in their stateroom on the S.S. *Elisabeth* (in those years they still slept together) when Charlotte realized that he had lost interest in her seasickness, and her dull gaze when he packed her off to Madeira, while he continued on to Brazil, counting her tears through an ivory telescope, listening to her sobs through a curtain at Chapultepec, watching from between the curtains of his palace window as a young woman in a dark blue reboso, kneeling on the cobblestones, supported in her lap the naked, bleeding corpse of a boy, probably a son or younger brother, stroking the dead face, gazing steadily up at *him,* as if she knew he were there; while a semicircle of poor people began to cohere behind her, all of them staring at his window, until a whistle sounded, his French troops leveled their bayonets, and he turned away—and by no means had he forgotten Concha Miramón, freshly married, who kept watching him with gentle dark-eyed hatred, as if he were the reason her husband must die; nor did he decline to recall his first jailer in this place, the cruel peasant whose narrow speckled face resembled a jaguar's; he had locked Maximilian into the Capuchin crypt, sneering: You must stay here for the night, so that you realize that your end is near.

5

But then he smiled a trifle; for his recollected joys now came to comfort him, most of them surely for the last time. Of course he would remember Charlotte again and again, right up to the end, but so very many images of her did he possess that few could return at all, let alone more than once. How pretty she appeared in Lombard dress! He had loved to watch her planting flowers in the Alameda; at first she had been so much happier in Mexico than at Miramar, where he preferred not to remember her. So he flew there all alone, hovering like a fly or miniature ghost over the gold and purple bindings in his library, the busts of Shakespeare, Dante, Goethe and Homer, the quill pen over the four-bezeled folio and the inlays of his writing-desk. If only he could always have been a fly! Smiling, he caressed the two silver candlesticks which Fray Soria had lent him. His guards gave him all the tapers he could burn. Once upon a time, he and

Charlotte had lit ever so many candles at Miramar. He used to deck four Christmas trees with gifts for the poor children of Trieste, and watch shyly from the window. The flickering flames reminded him of tropical butterflies. He could almost hear the twitterings of his aviary. Now he remembered how he had stood away from the Mexican deputation there on the parquet floor of Miramar; he would have sent them out and returned to the orange seedlings he was propagating in his glasshouse, had it not been for unhappy Charlotte in her snow-white crinolines, and Charlotte in her yellow silk, with the Order of San Carlos glowing on her breast, descending the ballroom stairs in Mexico, even the Liberals applauding her (Miramón still wore epaulettes and a tapering dark vest embroidered with golden ivywork); Charlotte undoing her hair at Cuernavaca—oh, yes, Cuernavaca, with his orchids and birds, and that rose-grown old house, Charlotte weeping again in Cuernavaca, among the fountains and orange trees, and the door in the garden wall through which glided the gardener's daughter Concepción, with her long blue-black hair outspread on her naked shoulders, while Charlotte signed decrees for him in Chapultepec. Smiling, Concepción pulled her shift over her head. She opened her arms. He was riding beautiful Mexican horses one after the other; he was commanding the *Novara*, with Trieste's lovely pastel edifices beneath summer rain-clouds off to starboard, coming home to Miramar, mooring between stone sphinxes at the landing, where even the Italians cheered him and Charlotte awaited, dressed in white, smiling adoringly, gazing down into the clear green sea. Soon they would be in their separate rooms, gazing down the steep mane of treetops at Miramar. He and she, Their Mexican Majesties, were riding in through the arch to accept the fruits of Mexican gratitude. Her white fingers were curling round his elbow as they descended the staircase, he appropriately overtowering her, she comprising a tiny-headed cone of many skirts. But perhaps he had never been so happy as when he had gone botanizing and insect-collecting in Brazil, wearing a white suit and a green-veiled hat. He remembered the butterflies he had captured there, and the trophy-bulbs and saplings he had collected for his gardens at Miramar. What if he had followed his inclinations then, and trekked forever deeper into the Matto Grosso? Charlotte would have been sad, of course. Besides, the oxhide slave-whips employed upon the blacks were abominable; he had prohibited those in his own Empire.

For the last time he was welcomed by his hordes of loyal Indians dressed in white, waving fern-garlands; yes, he abolished peonage throughout the Empire; once more Miramón was decorating him with a bronze medal on behalf of the Mexican Army; the Pope received him; Trieste glowed after a summer rain; Concepción opened her thighs; he became Admiral of the Austrian Navy; and in the rising sun he rode down from Chapultepec in his sombrero and grey *charro* outfit, and on the edge of the road petitioners were humbly waiting; often some young mother with a child in her arms begged him to spare a son or husband from the firing squad, and he was rarely as joyful as when he could oblige her (Bazaine got furious, of course)—but this memory likewise had some present pain attached to it; before its claws could catch him he fled to that time when he was young and voyaged through King Otto's Greece; there were slave-wenches exposed for auction in the market at Smyrna; that was the first time he had seen so many undressed females in one place, and realized the unbearable attractiveness, actually quite bearable, of sin (it provided particular pleasure to remember it here, because a well-bred Mexicana hides all but her eyes behind her reboso); then he visited Maria Amalia de Gloria, his first and truest love, who had died of consumption during their engagement; but tomorrow's rifle-barrels were staring at him, round and shining like a jaguar's eyes. Quickly he remembered the silent golden clocks with blue enamel numbers, the pretty clocks at Miramar; and again and yet again he remembered Concepción in Cuernavaca, eighteen years old, with the blue-black hair.

Again he stared miserably at the ivory crucifix, longing to slow down or reverse time, or, if that were impossible, for everything to be over. Whatever agony awaited him in the morning would not, he hoped, last long—although he had heard of cases when the first or second volley failed to kill.

6

Mejía had informed him that Juárez would renounce the Jecker bonds. This staggered him. If Juárez could do it, why had *he* failed to do the same? (The answer: Marshal Bazaine.) Freed of debt-weight, he might have been able to spend a decent fraction of his revenues on the people, and what if they had then come to love him?

7

The fear in his belly, which would most likely receive some of their bullets, he defeated with the certainty that however cruel the faces of the firing squad might be, he would regard them as if he were staring into a dark mirror. So he calmed himself. Then, upon the well-bred tranquillity of his courage, there grew a stain, not unlike the image of Christ's exhausted, bloody face which appeared on Saint Veronica's veil. It too was a face, but stone, wide-eyed and cruel. He could not say where he had met it before. Presently this apparition likewise faded, allowing him liberty to reconsider the cramp in his belly, which had spread to his chest. He smiled, understanding and accepting that until June nineteenth these feelings would come and go, in much the same way that in the mornings the longtailed crows descend on the *zócalo* of Veracruz, vanish in the afternoon and come swooping back at evening.

He would have liked to stroll in the cloister once more. It lay immediately outside, and they sometimes led him there for exercise. Whenever he entered its garden of orange and lemon trees, he remembered Cuernavaca. At any rate, he preferred to ask nothing of these people.

The general must have gone to the latrine; his pistol made a special noise whenever he laid it on the table. Two of the colonels were chuckling over something. It must be very dark outside. He wished he could have seen the sunset. At this time of year in Trieste there comes a certain quarter-hour when a long stripe of setting sun reddens the middle of a row of cypresses whose crowns are golden and whose lower trunks silhouette themselves. Not far below, Miramar overlooks the sea. The Emperor remembered this.

He remembered an orange-slice floating on the silver sparkling water in one of those fluted glasses the servants used to bring at Miramar. Italian oranges were delicious but Mexican ones were better. Keeping their taste and fragrance in his mind, he set out sincerely to yearn for death, to sink into the fragrance of the flowery death.

So a kind of grace came to him. He felt *the sweetness of time,* which customarily smudges, corrodes, effaces our joys bit by bit; in Maximilian's case the moments themselves could scarcely harm him, death being near and known: practically speaking, he would age no more, nor meet disappointment; the pulse in his wrist was satisfyingly eternal; he loved his memories, and even his cell, which was ten paces long, three paces wide, with its two tiny tables and five chairs, one of which was an armchair; mostly he sat on the camp bed. There was even a cupboard where he kept his clothes. Well, well; he would need but one suit more. The most dislikeable feature of the cell was its window, which allowed anyone standing in the corridor to look in on him; it showed some consideration on the part of the general and three colonels that they sat at a low table out of view. He did not care to peer out the window like a caged creature; nor did he like to sit with his back to them, so that they could spy on him without his knowing; hence he gave them his profile, living out his moments there on the camp bed. He remembered Cuernavaca, and limegreen Brazilian insects. His life grew as lovely and white as Trieste overseen from the karst foothills. Without a doubt he was far better off than the wives of Mejía and Miramón kneeling by Fray Soria in the chapel, both women clinging to the railing while they prayed and wept, with gaudy retablos all around them on the wall.

8

Presently the cigarillo girl who supplied his jailers came quietly upstairs. He recognized her step.

The general and all three colonels smoked like devils, the way Mexicans so often do. He had never overcome his distaste for the habit, although he hid it as poor Charlotte never could. This girl made a brisk trade with the jailers every day; her face had grown familiar to him.

She knocked gently on his door.

Enter, please, he called out.

The general, who had been muttering to one of the colonels, fell silent.

The woman came in. She was small, dirty and dark, with tobacco-stained hands. He thought her about twenty-five—nearly Charlotte's age. Perceiving her pitying gaze, he turned away.

He did not rise; after all, until tomorrow he was still the Emperor. Nor did she appear to expect it. In a low shy voice she murmured: Cigarillos, sir? The general said you were to have as many as you wanted.

No, thank you, said Maximilian.

He expected her then to curtsey and depart. Instead, she drew nearer, and even leaned forward. On her bosom she wore a tarnished little mirror on a chain, and in it he now saw his own exhausted marble face and sunken eyes, his beard and moustache awry. This shocked him, but he smiled steadily, so that she would not suppose him to be distressed about anything. Suddenly his heart began to race, and he believed that one of his friends had sent her here to save him from death. From Fray Soria he had heard more than enough of the Holy Child of Atocha. Sometimes, as the retablos testified, locks opened at His touch. Why then shouldn't the Empire be saved? Of course he would not consent to escape unless Mejía and Miramón could both accompany him.

The woman must have read the hope in his eyes, for she flushed, which made her very ugly, and quickly murmured: Sir, I have something if you wish to sleep. For dreams. In the morning your mind will be clear.

His heart fell, but he succeeded in keeping his tin face. From her sack of tobacco she withdrew a dark green pill, evidently rolled out of some plant material. With her dirty fingers she picked away tobacco shreds, then offered it to him, meaning to be kind.

Although she smelled a trifle stale, at least she was a woman, perhaps the last with whom he would ever have occasion to flirt, not that it should go any further with those four soldiers in the corridor, doubtless listening; and so, a trifle mechanically, he touched her hand, and smiled up into her brown eyes, which were surprisingly pretty, only to discover that she was in silent distress, evidently on his account. Of course he would rather not be comforting still another person just now, but there it was.— Pleasantly he said: What's your name, girl?

Dominga.

Don't weep. God wishes this. How old are you?

Fourteen.

You're quite goodhearted. Set it on the table. Now here's a present for you.

His feeble desire for her departed; he rose, and presented her with a gold ounce engraved with his profile. There was plenty left over for the firing squad. At first she grew as round-eyed as Tlaloc, their cruel god of rain. Then she burst into tears in earnest, and refused to take it, so he smilingly wrapped her fingers around the coin and said: Thank you, Dominga. I'd better sleep now.

Goodnight, sir. I'll pray for you, both tonight and tomorrow.

Goodnight, my girl.

He had never felt so tired. The instant she departed, he took the pill in his hands, sniffed it (it smelled fresh and resinous) and swallowed it down. What did he care if it were poison?

It was a quarter past nine-o'-clock. Next door, Mejía and Fray Soria were praying to the Holy Child for comfort in bondage. He could hear Fray Soria's deep voice. By nine-thirty he had begun to feel refreshed by a warm lassitude. The guards were arguing in the corridor. He read a few pages more of Cantù's *History of Italy*. Miramón had lent him his own favorite volume, the *Imitation of Christ*, which he found too fervent, like his smallheaded, wide-skirted bride. He preferred history.

At ten-o'-clock, deliciously drowsy, he blew out both candles. At midnight General Escobedo came to say goodbye to him. During the two hours in between he slept deeply. And this is what he dreamed.

9

He seemed to see the double doors of a casket fly open—and his own corpse, popeyed and powdered horribly white, stared straight up at him, with buttons shining from the throat and down most of the abdomen. His head had grown astonishingly round and the collar of his suit was buttoned so tight under the chin that he seemed to lack any neck. Perhaps a bullet had mutilated him there, or, as might be, the embalmer had needed to draw something out through his throat. Shiny black boots rose all the way up to his torso. No part of him appeared real, except for his chalk-white hands. His bifurcated moustache, greatly impoverished from its living state, could have been painted on in two long ink-strokes. As for that round white head of his, it was the crudest effigy of clay or plaster (perhaps the embalmer had unfleshed his skull), while the rest of him lay preposterously long and shapeless. From the thing's very confinement, meagerness, hardness and rigidity he somehow knew it to be himself. This was what he had come to, in death as in life.

At least it appeared that, as he had requested for his mother's sake, the executioners had left his face unmarred.

Presently he became accustomed to what he was. And once he said to himself: *Very well, let me be a corpse*, he felt easier, and the casket-doors closed. Now he was permitted to rise away from himself. The sun resembled the halo around the head of Our Lady of Refuge, and he gazed down on the casket when Juárez arrived, and two soldiers opened it. The President, small and dark, was the sort of man who should have been a servant at two and a half reales per day. He looked at the corpse's face in silence, then turned away. Maximilian observed him pityingly.

Now the envoy from Vienna had disembarked, and Juárez made any number of difficulties, in order to teach the Habsburgs their place; but at last the casket began to ride away in a black-curtained *caratella** over mountain roads and past great stone heads half sunken in the earth, until it reached the coast, where the *Novara* lay at anchor. Their Mexican Majesties had departed Miramar on this very ship; and there had been a hundred-gun salute. Now came the return voyage in the black-draped salon of the *Novara*, back to Istria; here by Ragusa lay the isle of Lacroma, whose ruined monastery he would have rebuilt had he not fallen so deeply into debt for Miramar; hearing this, darling Charlotte had bought the island for him as a surprise. And so his corpse came home, to pigeons and white sea-light, while he watched above, and the black-creped hearse waited in Trieste to receive it. He had become Massimiliano again. A weeping peasant woman raised up the little child in her arms, so that he could outstretch his chubby hand toward the casket. People in black stood bowing and crossing themselves; among the younger and poorer he seemed to recognize some who in childhood had found gifts beneath one of those four Christmas trees at Miramar. Had they finally forgiven him for being Austrian? His brother's secret police feared him no longer. Nowadays they even guarded his monument, which read: MASSIMILIANO, IMPERATORE DEL MESSICO. He felt great joy and comfort to see them looking after him in this way. Here he had embarked on his first long sea voyage—seventeen years ago! In the fleet they still respected his innovations; he had retrofitted ships and enacted the great dockyard at Pula. The flags flew at half-mast everywhere in Trieste, except of course at Miramar, where Charlotte was not to be told. For the first time he wondered whether she might remain alive. To

* Light spring wagon.

abdicate the Empire, having already signed away his Austrian rights, and be confined here with her, year after year—and if she were truly mad . . .

She used to say: Anything is better than to sit contemplating the sea at Miramar, with nothing to do but watch the years go by.

He fancied he could almost see her in the Oriental Salon, looking through the tall narrow casements into the sea.

With great relief he saw that he, at least, was still dead. Ever so gently they carried him into the black-decked car of the special train. The cathedral bell tolled; the train began to move. Overhead he followed, smiling down on the Friulian vineyards. The grapevine, they say, lives sixty or seventy years, like one of us. He could not tell why this pleased him. His sensations resembled the sweetness of visiting Maria Amalia's grave in Madeira (Charlotte, of course, had not been pleased). Just as when upon first disembarking from the S.S. *Elisabeth* in his snow-white suit and stepping into the Brazilian jungle he had nearly shouted for joy, because all the butterflies his wealth and labor had gathered into his cabinet at Miramar seemed to rise up into rainbows about him, and the exotic botanical curiosities in his glasshouse unfurled into towering fullness overhead, their flowery vininesses as seductive as the way that Charlotte used to part her hair when she was nineteen, so as the special train sighed onward his true self expanded and blossomed, drinking the incense of freedom; it was the moment when the book gains life and the dream grows real at last. Just before his Empire ended he had sent to Miramar for two thousand nightingales; they were en route when he was captured. Now all these birds were rising and singing around him. Slowly, slowly they journeyed, with the bells tolling in each place they passed, so that at last he felt loved. And ever more slowly they rolled into Vienna, where again the casket was opened, his brother standing stiff and straight with fists clenched at his sides, while his mother bent forward to kiss his forehead. Why couldn't she have done that before? The heaviness of her bowing reminded him of the drooping of Christ's head upon the cross, and she kissed his whitish-yellow forehead. Then he was carried to the Habsburg crypt, and with a golden key they locked him safely into a tomb of pure marble.

10

Next he dreamed that after the Mexicans had called upon him to be Emperor they took him in hand and crowned him with a quetzal-feather headdress whose semicirclet of long and close-packed jade tendrils was underlined by soft red arcs of blood-red and sky-blue, dyed by their artisans in the great city where he reigned amidst cool night winds. They presented him with a palace of onyx, whose windows overlooked jungle branches against a rainy sky. There they taught him to play many flutes most delightfully and to inhale the perfumes of flowers as would a nobleman of the highest degree. One of his flutes was fashioned of jade, changeably green like Charlotte's eyes; and its mouthpiece was the semblance of a lizard's head. Another flute was of fragrant wood, and a third of bone inlaid with silver and gold; there were as many others as he desired; and they all belonged to him. But what he enjoyed even more than playing his beautiful flutes was sniffing the fresh flowers which the Mexicans presented to him. This brought him great joy; and even in the dream he faintly remembered the vanilla-scents and orange-blossoms of Cuernavaca. They pierced his ears and hung golden rings from them, which pleased him still more than when every member of his suite had been personally decorated by Napoleon. They gave him golden bat-pendants and jade lip-plugs for his own; whenever he liked, he drank triple-refined pulque from a jaguar-legged bowl, and he could not imagine any greater contentment. They bestowed upon him a mirror of black obsidian. Then they led to him his first love Maria Amalia de Gloria, and she was naked but for a headdress of flowers. Next they gave him Charlotte, who had become seventeen again, nearly as huge-eyed and delicate as when she was that child in the portrait by Winterhalter, with her white, white arms and white throat, and she too was naked, but she bore an ear of corn in her hand; and she and Maria Amalia greeted one another without embarrassment. When they presented her to him, he sensed that within his love for her grew something secret, beautiful, yet painful; it could have been a many-fingered jade-blue fern guarded by orchids; whether it was something intrinsic to her or to their marriage, or whether it might be inimical and extrinsic was better uninvestigated. But by then they were bringing to him Concepción, the gardener's daughter with the long blue-black hair, whom he had left pregnant with his child, and she too was naked, and entered with shy little steps, carrying water in an apple-jade cup; she had always reminded him of the dove which in so many votive images rests upon the clasped hands of Our Lady of the Incarnation. Finally they presented him with the cigarillo girl Dominga who had brought this treasure of sleep to him, and she was lovelier than he had realized now that he saw her undressed among the others; it turned out that her brown skin was as smooth as Charlotte's; and she held salt in the palm of her left hand; the other women rushed to kiss her, just as the cherubs come winging to crown Our Lady of Light. These four now became his wives, loving him and one another, so that he never had to choose between them. So again he felt as he had upon entering the Brazilian jungle, with all his greenhoused and cabineted joys blooming up to veil the entire world in reality's fragrant mist. Concepción opened her arms to him, while Dominga danced with Maria Amalia, their jade ornaments clattering, and Charlotte reclined on the terrace, playing with the pearls of her necklace, slowly loosening her hold on her painted fan, another brilliant sunset spent. And it seemed that for a very long time he reigned in easy ecstasy, never ageing, with nothing to do but play the flute, embrace his women, discover himself in the obsidian mirror, and sniff the fragrances of flowers, which he came to distinguish with such expert knowledge that he seemed the wisest being in the world. Charlotte fed him of her tender corn-flesh, her small head nodding on that long pale neck. He drank from the body of Concepción, and ate salt from Dominga's skin while she tilted her head, watching him like a mother at her son's marriage, a lover memorizing her sweetheart's face or a wife leaving her husband forever. He crowned Maria Amalia with a wreath like unto the ruby roses and turquoise roses which retablo painters so often place around the brow of Our Lady of the Incarnation; and wherever she touched it, up grew a jade stem with many green pricklepods of gems, rising and glittering, until it budded into a flower as pink as her vulva.

Then one day (it had been but a year) they led him and his wives to a boat, whose fittings were plainer than he would have expected, and carried him across a lake toward a volcanic desert, while his wives sang him songs which he had never heard. He began to feel desolate. When they reached the other shore, the Mexicans stripped him of his headdress and his mantle of butterflies and flowers, took his dark mirror, and ripped away his earbobs, pendants and lip-plugs, so that all that remained to him were his sandals, his loincloth and his incomparable flutes. He felt much as he had upon learning that Bazaine had destroyed all the munitions which could not be embarked from Veracruz. When it rains in Trieste, the pinks and peaches of the edifices go grey; and so it now seemed to go with the moments of his life, which muted more with each removal. His four wives said farewell to him one by one, calmly and without sadness. Concepción had pulled her shift back on, and Charlotte was once again well laced up, while Dominga, already in her grubby skirts, was throwing on her black-and-white linen reboso, one end of which dangled in front, the other behind her head; while Maria Amalia had once more become a marble effigy. He entreated them not to abandon him (which of course in waking life he would have been too proud to do), but they regarded him like empty-eyed stone goddesses, and the boatmen rowed them away, leaving him alone on that lava jetty.

Perhaps they would now give him some lesser wife with naked jade breasts and a black slit between her gleaming jade thighs, and black eye-holes and nostrils, and an oval black mouth-hole; perhaps they would recompense him with a spiderweb hung with turquoise beads; already he felt unfitted for the greater treasures of his brief epitome. His heart was as tobacco-stained as a Mexicana's hand. Threading his way between overgrown wells and courts, past broken waist-high columns, between broken walls and great stone heads half-sunken in the earth, he saw a barren stone breast, cracked, wide and grey, touching the low evening clouds, and sunshine silvering the edges of its dark steps. In the second year of his reign he had left Charlotte to administer the Empire while he climbed the Temple of the Sun—a grimly glorious experience. This pyramid was hardly so grand; on the contrary, it seemed to have been deliberately neglected. For a moment he could hope that he had been likewise dismissed. He looked around him. There was Tlaloc's wife Chalchiutli-cue the water goddess, carved out of a tall block of stone, with her great flat headdress, wide eyes, and tiny indrawn arms. Bazaine's great bald head, fashioned out of lava, lay half-buried in the cindery dirt. On the faraway ridgetops right and left he spied columns of silhouetted waters.

So be it. Blowing a melody on his turquoise flute, he climbed the first stair. As yet the grief of leavetaking remained moderate. If the summit of the temple were abandoned, then he would go his own way, living out his life in grateful inconspicuousness. Essaying to dream of his white suit and green-veiled hat, in hope that his valets would presently appear to dress him, misery meanwhile aching in his chest, he completed that melody, which seemed to him the loveliest he had ever played. Then, as he began to ascend the uneven stone steps whose variegations made them resemble snake-scales, he saw the terrifying priests waiting above. At least he had never had to be one of those people who carries his own cross. So in resignation he climbed the steps, breaking his beautiful flutes one by one. Gazing back down across the lawn of weeds and ruins to the jetty and the lake, he searched for the boat, but it was gone. Across the lake he seemed to see Miramar's white tower with an orange light shining from one window, as if Charlotte were still alive and awaiting him. He thought he heard the general and three colonels singing the song about the wounded rider who goes through the world, bravely seeking death. He remembered once at Chapultepec glimpsing in the file of *guerrilleros* being led off to execution still another strange boy whose long eyelashes were drooping and whose mouth was half open as if with astonishment and exhaustion even while his chin somehow preserved a manly squareness; he intended to be as that boy had been. His grief had scarcely yet increased. Up those steep, dark and grubby stairs he continued bravely, breaking his last flute and throwing it behind him. When he neared the crowning platform, the priests drew back a little, as if to encourage him; the instant he set foot on it, they seized him, dragged him to the stone basin, which was painted red and blue, and uplifted their obsidian knives. He smiled at them, although he could not understand why he must die. The sky was already filling with vultures.

11

General Escobedo now awoke him, speaking exactly the right words of valor and chivalry, so that his heart was comforted; and for a moment more they reminisced, as if they had campaigned side by side, instead of fighting one against the other. Both had experienced San Blas's red gnats, whose sting induces days of blindness; and both had been many times bemused by the vultures in Veracruz's sandy streets. The Emperor shook the general's hand. He heard Fray Soria murmuring in Miramón's cell. Presently he knelt before the crucifix, and prayed again for his mother, Charlotte, his brother and himself. The reek of cigarillo smoke increased in the corridor. He heard more footsteps than usual echoing downstairs. The last time he had ever seen her, Charlotte's lovely white oval face had been framed by the dark reboso as she gazed out scared and stiff. Thank goodness she was at peace! He prayed for Concepción and her baby. He prayed for Juárez. He wondered whether he ought to pray for the people of Mexico. He washed his face. As he was dressing he heard one of the colonels spitting on the floor. In good time the first cock crowed, and he rose, ready for a sunrise which would resemble oil paint on a cheap sheet of tin.

12

He made a good end, of course. Blond-bearded, he comforted his weeping confessor, Fray Soria, while the sombrero'd guards stood waiting at the door of his cell. The sun ascended, ready to drink his blood. Against his will he remembered the gleam of Bazaine's head and that daily homily: Your Majesty, you fail to understand that Mexico is not Algeria.— In the streets, Mexicanas stood smoking cigarillos and watched him being led out. The smell of tortillas reminded him that he had received no breakfast. He found himself peering around for Dominga, that interesting damsel with her bag of fine-cut tobacco, but she was nowhere in evidence. An old woman spat at his feet. His escort indicated the cart in which he was to ride. The colonel inquired whether he had any complaints.— The Emperor told him: Never complain, for it is a sign of weakness.

When they stood him against the wall there on the Hill of Bells, picking their teeth and wiping their foreheads, so inferior to his own troops, who had sparkled in their new caps and uniforms as they formed ranks in hope of immortality, neither he nor the spectators blinked. After all, they were people for whom it was nothing to see a gaunt white corpse strewn with bullet-wounds as if with roses.

He wondered what would become of his two thousand nightingales.

They shot him first. According to some accounts, his last words were:

Vive Mexico! Next went jadehearted Miramón, then Mejía, who was so weak from typhus that he could barely stand. Both of them shouted: *God bless the Emperor!*

As for the Empress, she outlived the spidery cactus behind the half-wrecked wall of long adobe bricks where the three were executed. (Pitying romantics erected a shrine there in 1901.) Peering out the window of her madhouse palace, she glimpsed World War I and said: One sees red. One supposes there is something going on because one is not gay. The frontier is black, very black.— Before she knew it, she was old, fumbling and weeping.

Why did she suffer so long? This question finds a Mexican answer. When we choose a young man to incarnate Tezcatlipoca, the obsidian-mirrored god of kingliness, we kill him after a year of every good thing, so that our other young men will remain strong.— And in the month of Ochpaniztli falls the feast for Teteoinan, goddess of the ripe corn. Because weeping causes rain, which would be harmful at this season, we clothe her incarnator in gorgeous stuffs and lead her to believe that she will soon be brought into a great man's bed, so that she laughs for pleasure and pride. Presently we mount her on another woman's back. Then we decapitate her at once, and flay her, after which an outstanding man puts on her skin. This is what happened first to Maria Amalia and later to Concepción; for both got carried off young.—* But when a woman is chosen to be Ilamatecuhtli, the Old Princess, we must not permit her to be happy; for this is in Tititl, the seventeenth month, when we languish for rain. Only tears will bring that. So before we kill her, she must weep and weep, while she dances alone.

When he had lain in doubt as to whether or not to accept the Mexican crown, she told him: Well, you have your butterflies. For my part, Max, I prefer a full and active life, with duties and responsibilities—and even difficulties if you will—to an idle existence spent in contemplating the sea from the top of a rock until the age of seventy.— But the rain which is our life required more of her than that; not until her eighty-seventh year could she escape. They say she died surrounded by the wide-eyed flabby smiles of ever so many amateurishly painted votive images.

---

* As for Dominga, her doom is obscure.

THE CEMETERY OF THE WORLD

Woe is me, Llorona!
Llorona, whether yes or no;
the light which illumines me (oh, Llorona!)
leaves me in darkness at the end.

Mexican folk song

1

Veracruz used to be called *the cemetery of the world* on account of the plagues within its unsanitary walls. The following tale, whose heroine is even older than faded epaulettes, muted ribbons and those enameled decorations whose rows of narrow colored rectangles have long since been dusted down into pastels, may excite your doubt; but its setting's pestilential virulence shines undeniable through the centuries, like the humid sunlight of that coast. The victims failed almost infallibly, first swelling until their rings cut deep into their fingers and their faces bulged with pus, so that at the moment of decease they often wore the fleshy-lipped grimace of an Olmec head. Three chroniclers date the worst out-break of the disease to 1646, when the city refashioned its slaughterhouse into lodging for infantry companies. In sternly understated accents, a certain Fray Domínguez reasons out the effects of that miasma, con-tained within greasy dungstained walls and concentrated by tropic swel-ter, upon demoralized, unhygienic conscripts whose main diversion was drunken congress with the harlots of the port. But in the most ancient volume of the Archives of the Ayuntamiento de Veracruz, a ledger whose pages have broken loose from their grimy leather shell and whose inner knotted cords lie exposed, an unknown official not long after 1608 of-fered the proposition, *unlike the apparent arguments which are lately proffered so commonly,* that because the city (founded in 1519 by Cortés himself, who called it Villarica de la Veracruz, or Bera Cruz), occupied the site of the indigenous town of Quiahuyiztlaín, which the conquista-dors had so brutally erased, a curse exhaled itself undyingly from the bloody soil. *And in confirmation of the same I do here avow and swear upon my faith that in the hour after Vespers the figure of a veiled woman hath oftimes been seen, who upon unwrapping her face, which is said to be that of a low caste Indian or mestiza, breathes forth her diseased breath, whereupon people rapidly sicken, excepting only some scant few persons whom God hath spared, in order that they might make known to us these facts. Her dress is green, like unto a serpent's hue, and she has been known to . . . in her left hand. For which reason . . . the jade fever.* And then much writing is missing, thanks to layer upon layer of worm-tracks which long ago riddled these pages into cunning paper cutouts of ice-floes and islands; following which a different hand informs us: *It may be recorded that on the twenty-fifth of last January the Civil Fiscal consulted me as follows . . .*—a round seal enclosing a crown upon a quartered circle. I myself give any curse small credit, since in 1599 Veracruz was relocated a trifle east of Villarica, and the plagues continued. At any rate, herewith:

2

Once upon a time, a plague ship came sailing home, with a cargo of munitions, chains, armor and icons for the Duque of Albuquerque, and all on board were either sick or dead, excepting only one. It was mid-morning, the winter sea a chalky bluish-grey, the warm clouds a trifle darker shade of that same hue; and the helmsman, whose name was Miguel Minjárez, began to hope that the Virgin had heard his prayers, and would continue to hold her hand over his head. But as they approached the harbor, dodging the familiar sandy isles, jade fever settled also on him, and the long piers seemed to pulse; Veracruz was welcoming him, rhythmically opening her arms like a woman measuring lengths of thread. Her palm trees bent toward him; her waters sparkled mockingly over the ribs of wrecked ships. Just as when a young woman's hair has been so tightly bobbed away from the back of her neck that along the borderline between flesh and hair each strand glows against the skin like a lacquered shadow, while the tiny hairs on her arms shine white in the sun, so the edges of Miguel's eyelashes seemed to illuminate the great woman who gathered him in: Veracruz, our Sweet Lady of Contagion; Veracruz, who smothers her lovers, breathing on them ever so adoringly with her green and filthy mouth. He wanted her now, and would do anything to come to her, but not yet here like those barnacled skeletons on either side; he preferred to sink into the ground. Death inflamed the corners of his vision, like the red-leaved almond trees of Veracruz. On the ramparts of San Juan de Ulúa, which ordinarily bristled with as many silhouetted sentries as a centipede's legs, he glimpsed but a single soldier, sitting with his head in his hands. A black cloud of vultures overhung that island. Miguel steered away. As the city walls rose up ahead, he grew weaker; his way became as steep as the steps of a Totonacan pyramid. He prayed: Help me to kiss you, Lady Veracruz!— Remembering to overlay the tower of the Church of San Francisco upon the cathedral tower, no matter how they both contracted and swelled, he kept on course, sweating and nauseous, and so presently brought the vessel safely to anchor.

3

Pestilence must have outraced them to the port, or else the Indians had risen up again; because neither inspector nor guard arrived. The *Isabela*, lately in from a slave-and-sugar voyage, swung in her chains like a derelict. Both infantry companies were gone. Freeing the anchor, whose chains rushed down like the guts of a belly-slit heretic, Miguel cast rope-loops over the wharfposts and drew them tight. Then he passed ashore, into the power of the lady whom he loved. He would have summoned help for his comrades, even from the Marqués del Valle, who rarely forgave the disturbers of his leisure; but even that lord had departed from his tower, along with both sentries. The barracks was silent, the door ajar, and on the threshold lay the ripe green cadaver of an officer in his wheel-breasted armor, with vultures eating him. Miguel in his loneliness, confusion and fear commenced to pray to Our Lady of Remedies; but now his fever flared up irresistibly. In Veracruz, fathers wrap their baby daughters tight when the wind blows warm instead of hot; and so the roasting, steaming sensations which enwrapped Miguel were not utterly unpleasant; indeed, they seemed better known to him than the nearest islands, as if he might be going home. So he tottered dizzily across the *zócalo* where a few years since a temple's stone arms had comforted the sacrificed, while today María Elena the pretty banana vendeuse who used to flirt with him was lying on her back with her arms outspread, dark fluid staining her swollen face and ants busy in her hair; the vultures rose off her as he neared; and he went on seeking the lady he loved: Veracruz, whose bosom was as lovely as the cemetery hill in Cempoala from which one can see the ocean, and whose eyes were as gentle as the wormholes shining like silver ice-crusts through the fine conservation paper in the Archives of the Ayuntamiento de Veracruz. Sickness fouled his liver, cramping it up tight against his ribs. Obediently he opened his mouth and vomited.

Veracruz was wearing a greenish-blue cloak and a translucent veil. Smiling at him over her shoulder, she beckoned with her little finger. Miguel followed joyously. She led him into the doorway of a house on the street now called Avenida Nicolás Bravo, and if you wish I had furnished more complete explanations, please blame the silvery wormtrails between those twinned layers of translucent conservation paper, whose texture is as fine as a finger-whorl's, because otherwise we would not have been robbed of what might have been the most significant trailings of brownish ink, written in those intuitive horizontals, with wide margins of the conservation paper on either side, the verso showing through like an inverted ghost; and on every page a spring coil of ink, which must be the verifier's mark. Sometimes marginalia tantalize our researches in smaller but still neat characters.

4

From *caja* twelve, volume twelve, bound in acidic cardboard by some impoverished or benighted twentieth-century functionary, and accordingly embrittled, I now extract the eighteenth-century story of the deformed boy Jesús Sánchez, who, in despair because he could not find a girl to love him, somehow escaped his parents (who kept him chained to a mango tree, in order to protect him from the consequences of his own hideous appearance), shambled out of ken, and in three days, thanks to the kind offices of vultures and rats, was found naked in an abandoned establishment on Avenida Nicolás Bravo, the parts of him which had not been eaten being fruited with green pustules *of the bigness of those galls on oak trees, from which ink is made,* for which reason, with the concurrence of those who deserved to be consulted, and appropriate disregard for all others, the authorities thought best to burn the house; accordingly, as testified in neat script faded to orange, overlaying a jagged grey pillar of nineteenth-century water damage, the aforesaid cleansing was carried out, and the corpse buried decently in the cemetery—an unpleasant task even for quadroons, since its semiskeletonized arms remained outstretched as if to embrace the invisible. Between wormholes the following words taunt our researches: *of jade in his mouth, which the prudent Fathers* . . . Whatever these may have signified, within the next week two dozen families in the vicinity of the cathedral showed signs of yellow fever, which was duly cured with exorcism, prayer, but not before most of them had died. And if you disbelieve any of this, I refer you to that concluding guarantee of veracity: *Escrito por la parte de la Policía.*

5

Just before the Spaniards withdrew from Mexico, much the same befell a certain *hacendado* with gold and silver embroidery on his felted hat, whose double rows of silver buttons on his black jacket had not been able to buy true affection, and who was robbed of nothing after death, not even the silver spurs on his feet.

And two months after the French landed at Veracruz, two of Maximilian's soldiers disappeared, and because the plague city showed her occupiers such a sullen face, the French contra-*guerrillero* expert Dupin felt at first inclined to carry out some exemplary hangings, but then the missing were found, one in a dilapidated house on Callejón California and the other, of course, in that ruin on Avenida Nicolás Bravo. Dupin suspected that they had been decoyed by prostitutes to be strangled by robbers, but he could not explain the apple-green ovoids of polished jade in their mouths. The insurgents he hunted would never have been so obscure. Moreover, it came to light that the dead men's valuables were in the possession of the very Mexicans who had discovered and reported them. They had pilfered the corpses, yes, but they were innocent of worse acts. Dupin contented himself with terrifying the relevant families. Then he set out on more consequential business, raiding deeper into the fever country.

By now the ledgers of the Ayuntamiento were scarcely being kept up, while newspapers remained rudimentary except in Mexico City; so how often such murders (if such they were) took place cannot be known, and perhaps the censors passed them over in any event. The wavy hunks of decaying paper, with their faint smell of mildew, the stencilled worm-tracks and the dark brown letters offset in orange mirror-writing, or sometimes corroding themselves through like stencils, do present themselves most picturesquely, and nobody with any claim to aesthetic sense can be unimpressed by the way that numerously lovely wormtracks at the top of some snow-white sheet make it resemble wedding lace. But what *facts* can be discovered? The researcher might just as well be driving across the freeway bridge and along the petrol-perfumed double highway, which is lined with grubby white-limed trees and wanders drearily past fences and concrete walls.

6

In my time there lived a sad young man named Ricardo Ramírez who once loved most unfortunately in the city of Guadalajara. He happened to be a doctoral candidate in the patriotic but unremunerative department of folklore. Wishing at all hazards to avoid glimpsing his former sweetheart's beautiful, treacherous face, he wrote his favorite aunt, who lived in Veracruz, and asked whether he could board with her awhile. Since his dissertation, in setting out to identify the "autonomous" and "universal" elements of Mexican legends, laid its snares conveniently wide, anywhere he cared to go would serve; all he required were stories, the stranger the better. Hence the bony night-wanderer who bites that lady who foolishly fell asleep with her window open, the murder-carcass whose wristbones sway toward and away from its neck-stump as it begs in the only way it can: *Make me whole!*, the flaming ghost of the young bride whose jealous mother-in-law burned her to death once upon a time, these and other macabre jewels Ricardo strung on wires of theory, and however he arranged them, they appeared as shiny as cars in the rain. A cocky sailor of archives, prone especially to planting his standard on the most ancient islands of colonial writing (which nowadays keep shrinking evermore within the rectangular oceans of silvery conservation paper), he knew what he sought, and found exactly that, the fascicles dwindling like melting ice-shards, verso words showing through, blots spreading and darkening, so that our hero could interpolate whatever he liked. If his method lacked rigor, so much the better for Ricardo and his easygoing professors. Even before Adela broke his heart, the grotesque, lurid and erotic had faithfully distracted him from counterpart aspects of his own half-lived life. Turning pages of worm-lace, the signatures splitting apart where there once had been a binding, he quarried legends from the reign of Carolus III (whose second seal used to get affixed for a fee of twelve reales), explicated a broken stone jaguar head, collected old cabinet cards of Maximilian in uniform and visited the Temple of the Moon, which turned out to be another dark old pyramid in the center of town, with a fence around it. Had Adela remained faithful, Ricardo might have dreamed out his life in his harmless, feeble fashion, turning dust into paper so that it could become dust again. It is not for me to say that he neglected her. But so she told the taxi driver who seduced her. As might have been expected, Ricardo now collected folktales about traitorous women.

Although he could not go so far as to claim a uniquely Mexican provenance for that topic (since prior to Adela he had been jilted by a buxom exchange student from Madrid), Ricardo followed the line that the nation's founding legend could only be the oft-told parable of La Malinche, the indigenous mistress of Cortés—because, you see, she interpreted for the conqueror with politic eloquence, embellishing his false promises and magnifying his threats, even assisting at the torture-interrogations of caciques who might have known the whereabouts of more crocodile-textured golden bracelets studded with silver flower-petaled knobs and spiral-bellied monkey figures (most such treasures, it turned out, had already been lost or melted down by the time Mexico fell); worst of all, Malinche betrayed all plots against the Spaniards, so that through her, all too many would-be liberators met destruction, while more forsook their hopes. Therefore, Ricardo *hated* Malinche! The records indicate that she kept house for Cortés, and bore him a son. He then married her off to a drunk. Upon meeting her Mayan relations, who had originally enslaved her, she proudly or desperately informed them that *she would rather serve her husband and Cortés than anything else in the world*. For that service she was rewarded about as well as any other Mexican—which Ricardo, of course, found exquisitely fitting; yes, he was bitter, although, being delicately handsome, with skin the color of creamy coffee, he might yet love and be loved again, and then why wouldn't he think better of the world? As for Malinche, her emotions are lost to us. Once she died, her ghost became known as La Llorona, the longhaired one who weeps over her lost children. Ricardo grew polemical on this subject. (Do not blame him too much for his cruelty; his nights and days were death.) At that time Malinche had new defenders, the feminist syncretists, who argued that whatever harm she did her own kind was the fault of compulsion, that she was an instrument of progress—without her, the authorities might still be cutting people's hearts out with obsidian knives, instead of working them to death in the silver mines—and, most importantly, that her docile or ambitious miscegenations helped found the modern Mexican race. To this, Ricardo asserted, in fiery counterparagraphs, that La Malinche was, in fact, evil to the bone, her suffering therefore justified, her very name a byword for the dirtiest whoredom. Just as certain young women in church know how to pray to good advantage, kneeling with their arms outstretched on the prie-dieu which seems to draw in their hourglass waists still narrower, so Malinche, at least in Ricardo's opinion, made effective show of her submission, as a result of which, again in his opinion, she acquired culpability. Adela had been just that way. Whenever Ricardo took her on a holiday, she did just as he said—but then it became his fault when it rained. Eventually her whole life was his fault. Likewise, Malinche ruined Mexico.— While Ricardo was engrossed in excoriating the dead woman in such terms as gave him sadistic gratification, he received a reply from his aunt, welcoming his speedy arrival in Veracruz. Knowing somewhat of his field of inquiry, the old lady reminded him of what she was sure that he already knew, that in Veracruz could be heard any number of tales about La Llorona. So he fled to that city where almond trees come up out of the sidewalk and yellow-green coconuts cluster in the armpits of palms.

Aunt Bertha had prepared his favorite dish: chicken with green sauce.— You look unwell, she said.

That's Adela's fault.

So I've heard. That stinking little puta! I've been praying for you.

Thank you, aunt. And how's your health?

Oh, the same. I know some fine girls your age. Would you like me to introduce you?

Never mind, aunt. I'm busy with my research.

I know a young girl who's quite interested in La Llorona. An extremely pretty young girl, although her blondeness does come out of a bottle. Her mama says she's never had a boyfriend, which is practically a miracle, Ricardo; nowadays you wouldn't believe the sluts in this neighborhood. There are exceptions, thank the saints! The one I'm talking about keeps her skirt clean. I think you'd like her, because she watches paranormal episodes on the television. And she lives right around the corner.

Thank you, aunt. Maybe when I feel better. I think I'll lie down now.

Of course you've had a very long trip. How many hours was it?

Well, fourteen, more or less. Thank you for dinner, aunt.

You're sure you won't have any more? No? Then you must be unwell! I'll pray for you. By the way, do you remember that *bruja* I go to, Doña Esperanza? She always asks after you. I informed her about Adela, of course, and she said she was going to do something about her. She promised me that within a month, or six months at the most, that bitch's womb is going to dry up.

Thank you, aunt. I'll see you in the morning.

At dawn, anxious to escape his dear aunt's ministrations, the young man took a bus to the river, and from there a taxi to the root-wrapped arches of the Casa de Cortés, where everything was the same tan, the open chamber half strangled by roots which flowed across the floor like a great lady's dress. For some reason this reminded him of traitorous Adela, and he ground his fingernails into his palms. Ricardo had last come here while his mother was still alive. He had half forgotten the place, and found himself now strangely impressed by the long drapings of that crepe dress of roots which flowed down the broken walls from the green-leafed sky, white light shining in between them like unearthly pleats. In one coral-studded corner hung shards of pale blue plaster which the taxi driver said was only twelve years old and the tour guide proudly asserted to be original. There was folklore for you! Through this narrow-bricked arch, Malinche must have passed with her lord. Ricardo touched it. He gazed up into a great tree-branch. Slowly he wandered through Cortés's roofless house, passing the arch whose curve was outlined with many narrow bricks stood on end. He approached another corner which was grown with roots as flat and wide as the abandoned clothes of *pollos**

---

* Mexicans seeking illegal entry into the U.S. Along the border they are memorialized by their clothes, left behind in the course of a crossing or an arrest.

crushed into the dirt. The shade of these *ceiba* trees refreshed him, but the slow strangulation which their roots were accomplishing horrified him.

Strange to say, although he had always thrived in this climate, the humidity now wearied Ricardo, and before noon he decided to return to Aunt Bertha's to lie down. He caught a taxi to the bus. Perhaps he was getting ill. Gazing dully out the bus window, he saw from behind a narrow-waisted woman with a white ribbon in her long black hair, walking down the road, her skirt darkly slit just above the ankle. In spite of his rage against women, he felt desire. Resolutely he closed his eyes, only to be afflicted by an afterimage of roots and flagstones both the color of the reddish dirt.

All the way back to Veracruz, Adela haunted him. How could he make that she-devil weep with remorse? Someday she would come groveling to him, and he would say: *Malinche.* No doubt he ought to apply to the university for a travel grant; it would profit his dissertation to visit that house in Coyoacán where Malinche once lived with Cortés, in company with the three daughters of the murdered Moctezuma; there she gave birth to the conqueror's son Martín just before the arrival of his Spanish wife, who soon died in that house with black bruises around her throat. Had Cortés done that, or someone else? Ricardo would have liked to see Malinche's face on the night the wife appeared! That way he could imagine Adela's expression in that same situation. Better yet, if he could drink in Malinche's pain on that afternoon when, somewhere near Orizaba, Cortés married her off to Juan Xaramillo de Salvatierra, who as I have said was intoxicated while uttering his vows, then history would finally serve his purpose! His headache was getting worse. He longed to kill Adela, but only if he wouldn't get caught. He could not decide whether his forehead was hot or cold.

Before they had returned to Veracruz, Malinche was delivered of her new husband's offspring, a daughter named María, who at age sixteen would be kidnapped and forcibly married by the Viceroy's nephew. Cortés had long since carried away Martín to Spain, to legitimize him at court. No one knows whether Malinche died of plague, or heartbreak, or whether Juan Xaramillo had her put out of the way, in order to get himself a fresher wife. In any case, Malinche, the so-called Mexican Eve, whom the Tlaxcalans identified with a jade-skirted volcano goddess; and who also apparently incarnated or represented Malinalxochitl, Wild Grass Flower, the woman who founded the city of Malinalco and became a deity, was now charged with being Adela as well; and Ricardo most definitely had business with that female; he would recall her to punishment, just as a domineering little boy pulls his mother back by her pink apronstring.

When he had implored Adela to have hope for them both and to believe that they could live together, she paused, then evenly informed him that she was considering and reconsidering; and when he inquired how long it might take her to reconsider, she informed him that she had no idea and therefore declined to discuss the matter, a proceeding which, she easily admitted, might not be entirely fair, but she happened to be annoyed by other worries, such as how to pay for her car. Ricardo proposed to hope and assume that he and Adela would love each other always, to which she indifferently assented, after which, since she said no more, he began to feel ever more anxious and sick; and the longer she avoided the subject, the more hurt he became. Adela presently explained that of course she loved him; the reasons for her coolness had nothing to do with love.— How true! he bitterly thought. Nothing to do with love!— It was not until she left him three months later that he began to hate her.

Aunt Bertha was in her room snoring. Ricardo opened one of his Veracruzan books of legends. In the engraving, a pair of Spaniards scourged an Indian tied to a post. Closing his tired eyes, he seemed to see the narrow-waisted woman walking down the road again, but this time she was dressed in dark green. What had she actually been wearing? It had not been green. Her long hair was as black as the *zócalo*'s palm trees at night, when the white bell tower rises and narrows into the purple sky. What made her memory so alluring? When he closed his eyes, seeking to remember Adela, he could see her turning toward him, commencing her half-smile, but then she faded away.

Ignoring his headache, he sat in the back yard beneath a palm tree, footnoting various known correspondences between Malinche and the Woman-Serpent called Cihuacoatal, whose naked, decapitated, cast down and violated stone semblance appears in many ancient tableaux; she is the original one who weeps for her children by night, and La

Llorona may well be the same entity, renamed by the people in order to gain toleration from the Church. So he drew his analogies tight, and began to hope that the university would award him high honors. But presently, although he strove to fight it off by means of rage, he began to feel still more unwell, his desires and other feelings now insinuating themselves like those new tree-arms slowly cracking apart the threshold of the Casa de Cortés. The pressure at his temples and in the small of his back felt ambiguous; he could not decide whether a woman's fingers were massaging him, pushing the flesh inward, or whether he might simply be bloating. Fluid would soon burst out of his skin, or else the bone would fall away beneath the woman's fingers; either way, it might not be so unpleasant because he felt warm and almost still, as if he were riding that single wide breaker on the wide sea, that wave a trifle redder and greener than ultramarine, toward that hill called the Indian's Headdress where there used to be many palms; a man bought it and cut some of them down when his mother was still alive; and Ricardo stared bewildered along the *avenida* of body shops, automobile glass, yellow walls, laundromats, strip malls, trucks and bricks and gratings, sunshine, concrete, and the shaded military zone; while in his eyes the blood vessels glowed as brightly as the doorway of that pharmacy with ever so many colored packages on the shelves.

He lay down. When he woke up, his face was covered with mosquitoes. He crushed the creatures and sat up with a groan. Then he summarized his six conclusions about the Malinche Dance. This would punish Adela. His hateful memories of her resembled arches standing all alone in a plain of hot mud and dust.

Aunt Bertha was making tortillas. He thanked her. Presently it was night, and he could lie down again.

When he awoke, with his dream still alive in his mind, like a fresh-plucked flower in a vase, he was astonished at how happy he felt. He would have wished to describe his feelings to his aunt, but, like so many young men, he imagined that opening his heart to an old woman who had known him as a child might be humiliating. So he kept to himself. In his notebook he wrote: *Malinche—syncretism. Imperialism of the vampire. Treachery of the feminine.*

His aunt had another girl for him, a pious virgin whose skirts were so clean they squeaked, so he fled to the municipal archives, sailing over pages of writing which were as shallow and wide-spaced as sea-waves. By the time he reached the fourth signature seal, his forehead began to ache. *Excellent Señor: In* cavilda *celebration on the twenty-third of the present month, being present in the office of the Lord Governor, in which you were pleased to approve for the third and fourth deputies of this . . . innumerable unfortunate wretches who . . . my task will be to go within five or six months to distribute salt,* the smell of dust and mildew strengthening, until he began to cough. When would he cease to hate Adela? *The figure of a veiled woman hath oftimes been seen,* and that long tall dress of greenish-grey tree-roots with its train of dusty tendrils, what did it mean? *Her dress is green, like unto a serpent's hue.* More syncretism, so it seemed. This serpent-woman sounded quite repulsive. If she turned out to be an old avatar of Malinche's, that would serve Adela right. Ricardo wondered whether his aunt knew this legend, which seemed to have blotted a century and more of narrow, wavering shards of yellow-brown paper in which dark chocolate script seemed immersed just below the surface. *The said four thousand pesos within the date of this writing . . . Before me the aforesaid witness and scribe deposited the following . . . jade in his mouth. Since the swearings and reasons in this writing are the most efficacious and certain, I record the place, in hopes of saving others from being devoured by that she-demon who . . . This tribunal which God hath opened for our benefit . . . the helmsman Miguel Minjárez, whose corpse hath been proven as the nucleus of this latest plague, for three green serpents issued from his mouth when he was burned. The ill-omened residence in which these young men are invariably discovered . . . Oferta de 4,000. Pesos hecha por Don José Gil de Partearroyo para libertarse de cargos cobcejiles . . . jade . . . to punish the English pirates . . . a mulata clad in green.*

7

Insinuating his fingers between the ancient pages which were melting together, Ricardo found loose brittle sheets, their edges all rough, their clotted old mucilage shining like wax; and on the second of these, above a signature which resembled two sliced apples separated by a violin, was a crude map of the so-called *cursed house* and its environs. Ricardo recognized Avenida Nicolás Bravo. Returning the old ledger, he went out for ice cream, watched girls, returned to Aunt Bertha's, then, being informed that the pious virgin and her mother had been invited for supper, rushed down by the zócalo, wishing murder to Adela; so there sat our slender young man with his elbows on his wide-apart knees, reading legends about La Llorona on the steps outside the doorway of the cybercafé where the crucifix guarded the dusty computer and the digital print of Jesus curled on the wall. Skipping supper, for which he would surely do penance (he loved his aunt), he set out for Avenida Nicolás Bravo, just in case it might be ghostly, and then, not knowing what else to do, he sat down in the playground, watching a little girl in a rainbow dress toddling very cautiously to her father who pretended to be a monster. The child screamed, then giggled. Remembering that he had begged Adela to have a child with him, Ricardo felt sick with grief and rage. Just then an old *mestiza* beggar humbled herself before his feet. For pity he gave her a hundred pesos. Studying him like some shrewd procuress, she asked: Señor, are you looking for someone?

He hesitated. But then he found that although he could not confide in his aunt, it came easy to describe the green-clad lady to this stranger, all the more readily since he disbelieved in her. Anything for folklore's sake!

My God, señor, do you mean to kill yourself? Please be careful; that's La Llorona!

Tolerantly Ricardo said: Please tell me what you know.

The woman said: There's a story . . .

Yes, please do tell me.

Señor, in that building she . . . I know a way in. When I need to go to the toilet.

Oh, yes, he said. That way. Thank you; I see.

But the most evil house is like a castle, she explained. Over there on Hidalgo and Callejón California, where she comes out.

Now Ricardo began to feel quite happy and interested. Perhaps he might even get a chapter out of this.

As soon as the old woman left him alone he approached the rectangular ancient building there on Avenida Nicolás Bravo, not the castle but the place whose railingstone had blackened with grime and mold, while the casements gaped blackly open, the ancient shutters being caught in a

fossilized tremble; and he saw trees growing inside, while outside a serene cherubic face, doubly winged, remarked him blandly from above
one arch; the other arches were missing. How old were those wooden
doors? Rocks and boards blocked the doorway, and behind them a rotten
railing from the head of a vast old bed. Ricardo peered in, and a moth
brushed his cheek with the hem of its tiny skirt. The stench of mildew
rushed out. He looked over his shoulder; nobody was in sight. So he
pushed open a window, and a lizard-shaped patch of darkness greeted
him. Locking his palms upon the windowsill, he leaped and pulled himself up into the ruin.

The first thing he spied was considerably farther within: a dead dark
doorway with a wooden grating over it. The floor was nicely tiled but almost impossible to distinguish. He decided to return with a flashlight.

The place was more sad than eerie at first, but it offered him an intriguing strangeness, as if the scent of copal were half-hiding the vulgar
odor of death. It was so quiet that he could almost hear the mold growing on the walls.

His aunt was waiting up for him.— Chasing girls again? she roguishly
inquired.

8

Adela used to say: I feel your desperation, and it scares me.— She was
never happy, and her voice was flat. But, oh, those tender little lips of
hers, he couldn't get enough of them! They were like fresh new leaves. He
remembered how he used to lie next to her at night and wait for her to
touch him, because he no longer dared to touch her.

9

The next time he came to the ghost houses, on a hot Sunday afternoon
beneath a crescent moon, there was an old woman selling flowers, with
long white hair around her face and behind her the cheerful glow of the
toy skulls she peddled to children. She reminded him of someone.

Just as some of these abandoned houses' shutters bore shards of faded
paint, so his explorations contained older motive-markings which he
could not read. Pulling himself up into another high-floored ruin, one
wall of which had been broken open long ago, he encountered rubbish,

the stench of excrement, scrap wood and darkness. Of course the city's homeless fugitives would have grubbed away any jade beads lying here. A succulent, well rooted in the rotten wood, had grown out through the window and rose up higher than he could see. In another house, fig trees had nuzzled their way through the roof. Choking on dust and mildew, he began to feel a special secret warmth upon his forehead, as if a beautiful woman were lovingly urinating on him. It descended the back of his neck and enriched the backs of his hands. For a long time he could not understand what it was. Then his ears began to ring, and he remembered that he was febrile.

Staggering out of there, he next investigated the so-called "castle" on Hidalgo and Callejón California. It was an archway full of sky.

10

In the morning the bright red shards of brick and the scraps of blue-grey tile gave the castle a mellow appearance in contradistinction to evening when the sky was so yellow and clean over its flat-toothed parapet. The walls were cheerfully graffiti'd in red and yellow, and broken casements leaned up against the partially bricked doorways. Standing on the street, Ricardo, moderately feverish, looked around him, and once again found himself safely alone, aside from the pregnant woman who was dancing to music on the street corner, clutching a small child who lay sleeping across her belly-bulge. Behind the wide curling railing of stone, an open room invited him, so he clambered in, and found lanky dark vines growing down from the high ceiling as at Cortés's house. The ceiling was ribbed with what seemed to be narrow struts of iron. The wall bore faded patches of blue like the Tang Dynasty tombs. There was a yellow motor oil bottle and a foul smell. It would have felt perfect to close his eyes, but Ricardo proceeded into the next room, which was fresh with pure blue sky in its broken skylight, and floral frescoes on the wall, partially overpainted with graffiti. The deeper in he went, the better he forgot Adela and the more he longed to unite himself with the genius of this place. He entered the third room, and found the burned skeleton of a sofa grinning with all its springs. Beyond this lay a bathroom whose tub was full of ashes. Ricardo sank his arms into this, and immediately found a jade bead carved in the semblance of a grinning woman.

In a niche at the far end of the room stood a toilet like a low altar. The wall behind it had been torn open, and from the wall of the adjacent alley, water trickled down into the toilet bowl, never filling it. He thought to himself: If she came into my arms . . .

Then the trickling sound became a giggle, and the woman in green appeared, as he had hoped that she would, this perfect woman for him to love, as slender and radiant as when she had stood at Cortés's right hand. Although she must have been someone from the south, the blue direction, realm of vegetable matter, her lips were cochineal-red like an Aztec prostitute's teeth. His sudden lust resembled the brass band whose roarings and blarings prevent anyone within two blocks of the *zócalo* from sleeping before dawn.

She regarded him with much the same unwinking interest as does a lizard the shiny brown beetle which gambols in reach of its jaws; and Ricardo, precisely because he blamed women for his failures, was susceptible under such circumstances as these to even the most impersonal feminine attention. As he approached her, she began to lick her dark lips. Her unwholesome breath played coolly over his face. Unable to control his desire, he thrust the jade bead into her mouth, and at once she became a dead object, with her eyes closed and her mouth an ovoid cave of darkness, her breasts hard and yellow, and a great clay headdress on her forehead, with many vines or serpents rising out of it. Her earrings were the size of cartwheels, and the knurled stone collar around her neck could have moored the largest ship.

Jade beads began to spew from her vulva. He filled up his pockets, then fled.

11

You've grown lucky, said his Aunt Bertha in satisfaction. Which girl gave you those, or is it a secret?

It's no secret, aunt. I've met La Llorona.

Child, that's very dangerous.

Tell me, aunt. How can I get a woman to love me?— And because he asked her this with desperate sincerity, he felt no embarrassment.

My boy, how could a woman not love you? I see girls turning their eyes

on you when you go down the street, and you reject them all; you deny
that it happened—

What do they want to do?

To take care of you, my child! To cook for you and comfort you in their
arms.

But I'm not just a child! Maybe you see them that way because that's
how you see me. But I'm not, I'm not!

12

Before she left him absolutely, Adela, who was herself as grave and lovely
as Doña Marina, still used to make love with him on unexpected occasions, and whenever this happened Ricardo would whisper: *I'm so grateful,* in an ever more feeble and passive voice, and Adela, riding on top of
him, would stop and raise her eyebrows. Ricardo said: You can do anything you want to me, even cut me into pieces; what I want for you to do
is to cut me into pieces!— Then Adela grew angry and disgusted. But this
was truly what the young man wished for; that way he escaped the lonely
agony of being the one she no longer cared for. Everything was up to her
now; that was best; he would accept anything.

After she left him, of course, he rejected everything, despising her; he
became as active as a rat.

13

The next time he pulled himself into the "castle," early on a cloud-pearled
morning, just as the cars began to honk, encouraging the birds to further
exertions according to their various aptitudes and interests, while men
mopped the café-alleys, and the sweetly sulphurous sea-smell of Veracruz illumined him with fever or happiness, she was absent, so Ricardo
returned to the ghost house on Avenida Nicolás Bravo, and beyond the
dark, wooden-gratinged doorway found a heap of broken clay heads,
whose thick clay lips the dead potter had rolled on around their oval
mouths. Suddenly the impulse to count them overcame him, he could
not have said why; but before he had half finished he felt the icy prickle of
creepiness between his shoulderblades, and when he turned around,
there was La Llorona, paler than he remembered, close enough to touch,

with her long hair scarcely darker than her green lips. At once he thrilled into glorious desperation and asked her: Do you love me?

Of course. And after you, the next one and the next.

In his confusion he could not determine whether she was the one who would help him, and cut him into little pieces, or the one who should be weeping with remorse for helping the wicked Cortés. Presently she opened her arms. On fire with fever, he knelt down before her on those shards of clay, and slowly, slowly in the mildewed darkness her cold fingers began to play with his hair. He expected to be devoured like the men before him—all the more so, since he had run away with her jade. But once they had satisfied each other three times she sent him silently away, and when he descended back into the sunlight this very young man who thought to have hardened himself against women longed to worship all the girls in red high-heeled boots whom he passed on the way home to his Aunt Bertha's house. And that night when he lay down to rest he remembered what until now he had not even perceived seeing on that bus ride from Guadalajara: a young woman, her ripe buttocks practically bursting out of her shorts, walking slowly down the side of the jungle road, half-smiling in the drizzle, gazing for an eyeblink at him. At this recollection he masturbated furiously.

14

In contradistinction to the chronicles of her time, legend made out Malinche to be a promiscuous slut; and some said, Ricardo maliciously among them, that for this very cause Cortés married her off to Juan Xaramillo de Salvatierra; but now that Ricardo could no longer hate women, excepting of course Adela, whom he proposed to stop remembering if only she could be buried deep, instinctual passion enthralled him, for La Llorona, being immortal, was still fresher than the fringed arches of banana leaves: never satisfied, therefore everloving. The myriads whom she had devoured, their own preciousness extracted and then disregarded, rotted for very joy, a doom which Ricardo yearned to endure. Only the earth prevented him from pressing his groin against hers—for he was not yet dead, belonging but incompletely to her. Sometimes when he lay awake at his aunt's house, he whispered to himself: Why won't she cut me into pieces?

But while he remained alive with her in that mildewed old house on Avenida Nicolás Bravo, he was happier than he had ever been; rightly or wrongly he believed that because he had become conscious of love and of himself (grand certainties for which we should excuse him), he pleased her more than at least some of her other victims. Sometimes he vomited and frequently he felt dizzy, but whatever disease possessed him declined to devour him just then. So happily addicted to her green vulva, and therefore, as he would have said, in love with her, he daily strode ever handsomer and bolder to his aunt, who remarked that life was finally bestowing on him what he deserved; you may be sure that she had done everything required to forget that this sweetheart was La Llorona, to whom some Veracruzanos attribute a ghastly horse's head, and whose kiss all say is fatal. Indeed, one day he entered her foul old house only to find some previously unsuspected other lover lying on his side with his head hidden behind his elbows while vultures minced through the puddle of vomit and blood and cadaveric fluid around his torso. La Llorona squatted over him, carefully inserting a jade bead between his teeth.

Although he said nothing, Ricardo felt jealous. Why wouldn't she consummate their marriage? For some days afterward they met in the "castle," until the authorities had removed his rival's corpse. He began to understand that were she to spare him, she must feed on others in the meantime. They altered the time of their rendezvous to dusk, because it was easier for her to lure in others by day. Thinking about her, he pined away every afternoon and sometimes began weeping; then as evening drew near he would rise up out of bed and look happier. His aunt began to wonder whether he might be bewitched, perhaps even by Adela, who must have turned away the *bruja*'s spell, but since he was not wasting away, and since, moreover, he had become kinder and more patient, even listening to her long stories about his mother, Aunt Bertha continued to hope that all was well. In truth he found it heavenly to give himself to La Llorona. Unlike Adela, she never turned away from his need. The next time that sweet fever redescended from the ceiling of his aunt's house to whistle in his ears like a harbor wind, warming his forehead and the backs of his hands, he found himself thinking: I'm doing it all for her, so that I can be her and she can be me; I'll heal her and make her happy.— But what this meant was obscure even to him, and he sank deeper and deeper into his bed, listening to a single mosquito. His aunt beseeched him to eat more; he was studying too hard, she said, reminding him, as she frequently did, of the ominous career of his great-uncle's great-great-grandfather Don Roberto, who while preparing his illustrated dictionary of *trabucos,* percussion guns, blunderbusses and other weapons of the conquistadors had strained his mind so perilously in the mildewed reading room of those selfsame Archives of the Ayuntamiento de Veracruz (in particular, he grew fixated on the question of why some words remain untouched, others become outlined in dark brown, and the rest vanish away) that he commenced to be haunted by a gaunt brown manuscript demon whom only the thrice-uttered name of Saint Santiago would keep at bay, until finally not even this availed, and the poor man was found dead one night with his face resembling a royal seal poxed by worms; but at this juncture, kissing her sweet old hand and thanking her for her consideration, her nephew now hurried out to drink an unaccustomed cocktail at the *zócalo,* watching the double rows of dark green soldiers flipping their scarlet drums, clashing their drumsticks and blowing their trumpets, while passersby lifted up their children; then came the Mexican national anthem as a half-dozen of Veracruz's bravest carried the long limp flag to bed, while Ricardo sat playing with the engagement ring in his pocket.

15

La Llorona stood with her hands on her hips, turning her pale face toward him, while in a puddle of dark fluid her latest lover lay glossy and swollen like a roasted chicken, ants all over him, a great leaf on his face, his knees drawn partway in, his fists closed like a baby's. She began to laugh.— And seeing this, you hope to marry me?

Come what may, he replied.

Drawing near, she breathed her cool foul breath on his face, and he bowed his head.

She inquired: Do you imagine that you don't deserve to live?

After you devour me, will you remember me?

Not at all. Neither will you.

Do you remember anything at all?

I was born at Painalla. Before that I blossomed and fell, blossomed and fell.

Please, Malintzin,* let's make a child!

No one ever asked me for a baby before!

Will you?

Why don't you ask a woman?

What are you?

A goddess.

I did, but she—

Very well, then we'll marry.

That very day she came home with him, to be introduced to Aunt Bertha, who thought her marvelous, although it did seem peculiar that she declined to live with them. Ricardo and La Llorona had agreed to keep their marriage secret, to avoid explanations. Of course Aunt Bertha noticed that she was wearing a ring, and the instant that the girl's belly began to swell, that too she perceived, with the sort of hungry titillation which so often breaks out like mold in such circumstances. The next time the ghost lady visited them, Aunt Bertha said: I may be mistaken, my dear, but is there something you haven't told me yet?

Oh, you're not at all mistaken about that, replied La Llorona, who was standing at the kitchen counter, grinding corn in a lava metate.

Well, then, darling, if it's not too delicate a subject, have you and my nephew made any plans?

That depends on him.

If you'd like, I can speak with him, because he shouldn't leave you unprovided for.

Don't trouble yourself, aunt. I've provided for myself for a good while now.

But, well, excuse me for keeping on with this—

You see, said the lovely woman (whose greatest drawback, in Aunt Bertha's opinion, was the fact that she sometimes smelled a trifle unclean), when we discuss this subject, your nephew always says that he's not sure how long he'll live.

---

* Indigenous name for Malinche.

My God, Malintzin! What do you mean? And if Ricardo's unwell, which is not news to me, wouldn't that be all the more reason to unite yourselves, in case there are any children?

But just then Ricardo emerged from his room, looking more joyous than ever. He had lately been making great progress with his dissertation, which seemed to be more brilliant and clear than before, as if someone had been rewriting the manuscript for him. Later that very night, after he posted a letter to Adela, asking her forgiveness and wishing her all good things, he was sitting in the back yard waiting for La Llorona to descend into him when he first thought to hear his pen scratching against the paper; and peering through the keyhole into his room, he seemed to see many green leaves blossoming and he smelled a perfume as of vanilla and copal. Of late he had showed still more gratitude to his aunt. And the more he deferred to and relied on her, the more his hard heart melted away. Everyone exclaimed over him, especially the unmarried girls at church. As for La Llorona, she did not seem to be a bit jealous.

On the following night the young couple strolled hand in hand all the way to the lower reaches of the white-limed palms in the *zócalo,* where children played hide and seek around the wide-bellied plinth, booths of cheap necklaces shone as if they were precious, an angry boy kicked a soccer ball all by himself, and a man in a red shirt and cap slowly swept old paper cups and tortilla scraps into his dustpan.

Now you must decide, said La Llorona. You can raise our child alone, or I can take him away, or I can kill you.

Will you come home tonight?

No, darling, I'm hungry.

He went home and considered what to do. His aunt pinched him laughingly and said: Another quarrel? You're the man. Just force her to live with you. It's high time for the priest!

He said: Aunt, should a baby stay with his mother or his father?

Well, both, of course, but if it must be one, then the mother.

Thank you, he said. That's right, of course.

So La Llorona kept little Manuel, who was quite fetching except for the fact that his face resembled a death's-head. The loving couple must now go their separate ways, unless Ricardo were to be devoured. And he wanted to be, but as to that, La Llorona told him: No, I won't eat you, because you won't surrender yourself to women, and, besides, you're the father of my child.

In the third room of the old house on Avenida Nicolás Bravo, behind the sofa's burned skeleton, La Llorona stood beside him, gesturing with all her delicate fingers, the tropical light of Veracruz gilding her naked shoulders and her eye-whites brighter than sea-waves, her hair lusher than sea-foam as she turned toward him, gesturing at the light of the farthest room without looking at it, and he suddenly realized with a thrill of joy that he was naked, ready to give himself to be devoured; he was taller yet somehow smaller, open to her without shame and therefore without hatred, not ever again; how grateful he felt to belong to her! Manuel sat on the toilet, playing with a man's thighbone, while La Llorona disrobed and opened her legs to Ricardo for the last time. How he loved her! He would have done anything to keep her, anything!

I'll walk you out, she said, kissing his forehead, which burned and stung with fever. Manuel sat alone watching them as they dressed. He was seven days old.

In the harbor of battleships and other steel fishes of the Mexican Armada, a pelican nearly as tall as Aunt Bertha swallowed fish and worked the red-orange leather hinge below its throat. Ricardo could not bear to watch the shimmering and waving of the water very long; it made him queasy. His fever was a nice tickly feeling, as if his thighs were being massaged by a thousand cockroaches. Of course he felt on the verge of tears.

Ricardo, listen to me, said La Llorona. Adela left you because she would not love you. I'm leaving you to keep you alive.

Please eat me; please drink my blood; I don't want to start over anymore—

Do you love me?

I—

You're just like me, silly! You'd love anybody!

When I die will I see you again?

The dead see nothing.

Are you dead?

No, darling. Not me. That's why you'll never see me again.

Turning wide-eyed toward him, with the sun on her gorgeous

shoulders, she gave him a little golden turtle with three golden bells hanging from it, to help him when he married, and for his aunt a lovely golden bracelet studded and beaded, sun-rayed and devil-pricked, and for his as yet unknown wife a necklace of little golden eagle-horsemen who extruded their forked golden tongues, and a pendant of three golden bells with feathers and jade beads.

She gave him a magic leaf and told him to make a tea out of it and drink it. Then life would go differently for him. His emotions writhed like the dying fingers of a severed hand. She kissed him coolly on the cheek; then they parted. In a way he was relieved; he no longer had to fear that in his company she might slay some decent person.

Then, blindly solitary, he crept back to Aunt Bertha's, and when his hostess saw his face she knew at once what had happened (more or less). Pale and despondent, the many-times rejected young man lay down, struggling to hate La Llorona, but no hatred came to him. Next he tried to imagine how he must live, since he could not die. If the purpose of life was indeed erotic or romantic satisfaction, perhaps his aunt could save him; didn't she know any number of likely young girls? But why shouldn't he rush back to Avenida Nicolás Bravo, for instance tonight, and open his veins before La Llorona? So he set out. But when his former sweetheart appeared before him, she was nothing if not furious and monstrous.— Where had she come from, by the way? Was it from under the rotten floor? Where did she actually keep herself? This he had never asked himself, or her. Well, too late now! Warning him in icy tones not to try her further (behind her he spied gruesome Manuel, already half-grown, with blood running down his lips), she then approached him, breathed on him with her foul breath until he trembled, slapped his face once, then closed the interview as follows: If I choose, I can infect any part of you with necrosis, and even so you will not die without my permission. How would you like to drag out the years half-rotten? Now go, Ricardo, and never come back.

I never trusted her, said his Aunt Bertha. What you need is a girl whose purpose in life is love. There's someone I'm already thinking of . . . But tell me this. What's become of your child?

She took him away—

Horrible, horrible woman! Ricardo, you need to relax. Drink with me.

So he did. His fever still troubled him, and a foul smell haunted his nostrils.

Aunt, this bracelet is for you.

From *her*? It's not real, is it? Oh, Ricardo, close the shutters! How beautiful!

Returning to the municipal archives, he sought even now to cling to her by means of discovering facts. *For the said Viceroy incited the orders in this writing and . . . in his mouth . . .* and then wormtracks. At once he seemed to see his hateful son. *By the hand of a man who newly and with certain foundation . . . burned both corpses, with many prayers, after which the said Lord Bishop . . . jade, which to these idolators is considered more precious than gold. The aforesaid* mestiza, *who is said to be a familiar of the Devil . . . exorcism, all of which was reported to His Majesty, may God guard him many years and continue to concede to him such a title,* and then tiny waterstained islands of ink. *We simply sign this in our city of Veracruz, Ciudad de la Vera Cruz y Puerto,* some signatures resembling geometrical shapes, others like string figures, crossing lines and squares. *Ecstasy on his face, although his belly had been utterly devoured.* The ledger's back flap fell open like the wing of a dead bird, folded inward and tied shut with crosses of rawhide. Within he found a tiny oval of apple-green jade, and on the back of a yellow sheet reading *Certificación que acredita* a notice in a feminine hand: *Ricardo, since you persist in disobeying me, I now afflict you with gangrene.*

16

After the amputation of his left foot, Ricardo found time to become acquainted with all his aunt's neighbors. Across the street there lived an old widower who was very lonely. He touched the old man with the magic leaf, and at once the man rose up full of hope again that he might find some woman who would love him, and although he had not left his bed for many years he managed to get downstairs and even came into the street; stretched out his hand to a passing housewife, then fell down dead with a smile on his face. So this was a good thing that Ricardo had done.

His fever now seemed to become an ovoid jade bead, polished very smooth and inserted into his skull, where it ached deliciously and hilariously. He longed to die; oh, how he loved La Llorona! He prepared to become spiteful and hateful as usual. What an evil example woman sets! Consider for instance the way that a woman casts her smile toward a man, even when she keeps her knees together . . .

He made the leaf into tea and drank it. After that he was never sick for the rest of his life. Moreover, he suddenly loved women—all of them. Not long after that, he completed his dissertation, for which he received highest honors, and a publishing contract with a feminist press.

17

After Ricardo's aunt died, he finally discovered his vocation as artistic director of the provincial folklore troupe, where numbers of ambitious yet unwary young women depended on pleasing him. They waited at auditions as silently as handmade Indian dresses hang within their wheeled, roof-topped stands, ready to be sold and animated, their indigo stripes darker than the night. Ricardo rarely took advantage, for he loved them. No one seemed to mind his prosthetic foot, in part because long ago, when he sold that golden turtle with three golden bells, he had become his own master. Even the doctor didn't take all his money. Before he knew it, he had regained the fatuous self-love which is our birthright. A certain pretty, chubby dancer from one of the Tuxtlas, I forget which, put on more weight, and after a notice in the newspaper which unfavorably singled her out (for by then the poor girl had grown outright obese), Ricardo, first consulting with the producer, made up his mind to fire her, a doom from which she saved herself by seducing him and declaring pregnancy. She was, as I have said, quite a big girl, with thighs like watermelons, and moreover extremely needy, loyal and weepy—an ideal combination for Ricardo, whose true love-type was thus revealed to be what are so unfairly referred to as "smothering women." Riding the craze for self-consciously syncretic dance which now infected Veracruz, Ricardo's troupe, who daringly and defiantly called themselves "The Malinchistas," performed Totonaco dances reenvisioned as fandangos, put on a well-regarded play about the Emperor Maximilian, and even turned supernatural tales into ballets. In all these enterprises, I am happy to say, Ricardo's new wife, María Guadalupe, proved helpful, not least in calming his nerves, for he tended to worry on opening night; and sometimes the

producer talked down to him, asserting that he, Ricardo, had no understanding about money, a misapprehension which María Guadalupe corrected as often as needed, since the producer was terrified of her. She
loved nothing better than to take Ricardo into her arms and roll on top
of him. Sometimes she would fit her lips over his lips and blow in hot
moist breaths until he grew intoxicated. Even La Llorona had never taken
him so far. He felt ecstatic to love this woman who was literally so much
greater than himself. Moreover, on account of her expert dependence
and insecurity, Ricardo learned to apologize for his wife, and even to take
the blame for her lapses, a practice which rendered him, in time, tolerant
and even warm. Thanks to her and the children, Ricardo lived a happier
life than any of his early acquaintances could have predicted, among
them, of course, the hated Adela, who attended several of the troupe's
performances and once wrote him a postcard, which he thought best not
to answer. By the time that María Guadalupe had grown as vastly squarish as the Convento de los Betlehemitas, Ricardo choreographed the
great masterpiece of his career. It was a wordless performance entitled
"Salvation."

The curtain rose on a maze whose high-walled pasteboard corridors
turned always at right angles, their destination the wall at stage rear. And
the dance, if one can call it that, was performed by a dozen young men in
white hats and white suits, wandering blindly toward that blind wall.
From time to time a tall skeleton, all black and white except for his red
eyes, popped out of a niche or ambushed a man who turned a corner. To
tell the truth, he looked not unlike Ricardo and La Llorona's son Manuel.
Whomever he touched fell motionless. And this was all that happened.
A man would meet death and die, or he would wander toward the blind
wall. If his corridor ended without the skeleton having found him, he
turned back and took another turning, because what else could there be
for him to do? His only prize was the dreary delay and return for more
seeking of nothing. And all the young men got killed one by one. Just as a
taxista lacking business might slowly lower himself in the driver's seat
until only his half-open eyes appear above the gasketed sill of the
driver's-side window, so Death sometimes sank nearly all the way behind
a partition, so that only the audience could see the hateful shining of his
skull, while the victim strayed toward him. Finally only one man

remained. He wandered helpless from corner to corridor to wall and back again, and presently, Death, having devoured the others, came in search of him. And so he was nearly at the blind wall, and Death was two turnings behind him, already stretching his bony arm, when suddenly a door opened in the blind wall, and out came a lovely death's-head woman in a jade-green skirt. The young man flew delightedly into her arms, and she enfolded him just in time to spare him from her rival.

So Ricardo became famous. The children all married and never came back. He outlived María Guadalupe, who was buried in her necklace of golden eagle-horsemen; then he retired and wedded an old widow not entirely unlike Aunt Bertha. I have seen the two of them at the *zócalo*, among the old couples slowly dancing hand to hand or arm to neck. Some of the women who are merely middle-aged whirl about in shining silver-white satin skirts, while the more ancient ones, like the aforesaid Juanita Ramírez, show themselves in faded floral dresses and pink slacks. She and Ricardo looked sweet together. He was wearing a white suit and a white hat. His prosthesis did not hinder him. Turtling his grey head, he gripped her wrists, staring down at her knees through his dark sunglasses. He swayed, bewildered, and gently Juanita held him up. One morning I introduced myself and mentioned my curiosity about La Llorona.— Young man, he replied, I don't know anything about that.

18

Now I will tell you what I was doing there. Not long after the birth of our second child, my wife announced that she had never loved me. I am American, and she was a Mexican national who married me, so she now explained, solely to gain citizenship. Although she had opened her mind, as she put it, to the possibility that I might become worthy of her efforts, I remained crass. My punishment dawned. Carmen and her lawyer calculated that alimony and child support for the three-person household which she now intended to found would keep her in sufficient style, as indeed it proved. I signed every paper without amendment. I gave away the house, and everything in it but my clothes. The last time we ever saw each other was in court. When the judge dismissed us, I walked outside with her and said: Carmen, I want your advice.

If it doesn't take too long, she said.

Well, it's like this. From what you say, you know me better than I know myself. I certainly didn't know you as well as I thought—

No recriminations, please. What do you want?

Since you know me, and since I'm feeling lost, please tell me: What kind of woman should I look for? Who do you think could love me?

None of my friends can stand you, and that's the truth. They never could. I deserve a medal for putting up with you for so long. I can tell you what's most hateful about you. There are actually seven things. First—

Sorry to interrupt you, Carmen, but since you're in a hurry, could you just tell me who—

Look, she said. No woman could tolerate you. Your soul is utterly diseased. A prostitute might pretend to like you until your money runs out, but I've just made sure you'll never have much of that. Your only hope is to find a saint or a vampire. Now remember: Don't contact us in any way. You lost your visitation rights for a reason. The children are trying to forget you. That's it. Goodbye.

Thanking her for this suggestion, I travelled to Veracruz, because she once lived there.

I was too timid to seek out La Llorona for my bride, but I did once visit the house on Avenida Nicolás Bravo. Within lay a dead man, perhaps homeless. Sometimes when forgotten corpses mummify, and their arms are outspread (perhaps because the dying men flung them open when their hearts drank in those nourishing bullets, or perhaps because the executioners crucified them), their tendons come to resemble the roots and woody creepers which clothe the arches of Cortés's old house near Veracruz; to enter one of those archways is almost to shelter in a mummy's armpit, and to discover any such hard hollow carcass is to be reminded of a ceiba tree. The mouth was open, with a jade bead inside.

Then I went to worship at the Climax's titanic effigy of a naked blonde between whose legs any one of us may lean. The girls were nice; they took my money. None of them gave me a fever. I ate at Tacos "Mary"; I took in freight trains and dusty flat roofs with laundry hanging from them. Seeking to lose myself, I traversed the rolling hills of reddish grass and green palms. Wide orange-grassed canyons impelled me through the jungle, into thickets of prickly pear. Hoping to see heaven, I gazed upward and found the flash of white on an eagle's wingtip.

19

Once upon a time, on the coast of the country known to the indigenes as *Woman with the Green Jade Dress,* there used to be a sandy place called Tecpan; and here, on 24 June 1518, Capitán Juan de Grijalva landed, soon after which this land was snatched from the Devil, and reclaimed for the Kingdom of God, not without certain necessary tortures and executions. How could the savages in their simplicity have imagined that their primitive rites at Tecpan would be prohibited and forgotten? As for the conquistadors, why shouldn't their empire of righteousness have endured forever? And Malinche, wasn't she secure in her lord's love? (Where she once embraced him in the Casa de Cortés, there grows a palm tree's snake-roots whose scales are chain mail.) The matador in blue and gold, not yet realizing that he is ready for the grave, feels kindred confidence; likewise the ancient *mestiza* who trusts that her tomb-robbed, staring jade figurine with the jade lizard-woman in his lap will find a buyer, right here on Avenida Díaz Mirón, maybe even today, after which she will get abundant food, perhaps even meat. And won't my sweetheart cherish me until life ends?

Just as in the old records a word will be broken up wherever the page ends, after the style of a Roman inscription or a child's letter, so it is with our loves and lives, everywhere we find ourselves, but most of all in Veracruz, the cemetery of the world.

TWO KINGS IN ZIÑOGAVA

But what does the social order do for geniuses and passionate characters, burning for gold and pleasure, who want eagerly to devour their allotted span? They will spend their lives in prison and end them in a torture chamber.

Jan Potocki, *ca.* 1812

1

When the mulatto gravedigger Salvador González Rodríguez rebelled against our Mother Church, and martyred a priest by means of a shovel-edge, he was, of course, brought to trial with punctilious regard for the formalities, then gibbeted in chains, following which his head was exposed as a warning to evildoers. One question remained to annoy the authorities: What should they do with the murderer's younger brother Agustín? He was thirteen—an age sufficient for culpability, should any act be proved against him, although the case did not appear that way, since the innkeeper Jaime Esposito, being duly sworn, testified that on the morning of the crime this curlyhaired boy, who now sat between two soldiers, bowing his head and swallowing saliva, had been peddling sugarcane in a doorway across the street from his establishment; so that, as the *procurador* indeed proposed, there might exist grounds for admitting him to the house of mercy lately established for poor beggars here in Veracruz, for he was a bona fide orphan, his father having met the black vomit some three years after his mother got raped to death by French pirates. Next to be summoned forward was the peanut vendor's slave Herlinda Encinas, a fullblooded Congolese damsel of about nineteen years of age who appeared so deliciously ebony in her pure white dress that the *procurador,* a tolerant man whose work had educated him about crimes of venery, winkingly referred to her as *a fly in milk.* She must have thought this court like unto a Mass! Her master, a free negro named Melchor Marín, aged fifty-seven, and a fair Christian, who took oath that he had been baptized, as seemed likely since he could say his Paternoster without great trouble, evidently feared to lose her services should she be convicted of anything, for he kept thanking God for this diligent chattel, without whose laughing, winning manners people would surely desert his stand, which from what he told the court was generally unfolded just outside the Baluarte, that square transshipment fort, already old, whose cannons pointed outwards at palm trees; moreover, the aforesaid Marín depended on Herlinda to feed and dress his children, his wife unfortunately being so infirm as to be good for nothing; indeed she longed for the hour of her death—at which inessential and certainly impious juncture the judge, Doctor de los Ríos, closed up the sluices of that old man's mouth, and commanded the aforesaid Herlinda to speak, in order to inform the court as to whether she had in fact been—in the words of the three witnesses Cristóbal Pérez, free mulatto, Neyda Duarte, black slave, and Verdugo Acosta, free mulatto—a former paramour of the late detested evildoer Salvador González Rodríguez; to which the *fly in milk* immediately confessed, with more demureness than shame. Aware (to his sorrow, be it said) that the people's turpitude throughout this New Spain of ours, and most certainly here in Veracruz, had grown so ubiquitous that such errors as yonder benighted woman's fornications must be overlooked, at least for today, in the interest of rooting out the more dangerous offenses of bigamy, sacrilege, blasphemy, sedition, witchcraft, Judaism, treason and murder, Doctor de los Ríos, after admonishing the slave wench, who bit her lip and hung her head, satisfied himself by asking whether there had been any engagement or understanding between her and the detested Salvador, at which she shook her head, although whether in negation or confusion none could tell. Therefore, Doctor de los Ríos repeated his question, in a grimmer tone of voice. It came out that the detested Salvador had sworn himself to marry the girl, and even (or so he had told her) applied to the archdiocese for forgiveness of their illicit relations, by requesting a formal dispensation from his victim, the sainted Fray de Castro, who might for all anyone knew have been struck down for refusing to provide it. Doctor de los Ríos now interrogated Herlinda as to why she had desired to wed this evildoer, to which she replied, not without sense, that since they had already fornicated, it seemed best to repair their sin by entering into the sacramental state. When the question arose of whether she had submitted to intercourse before or after receiving a promise of marriage, the girl could utter no intelligible answer. Doctor de los Ríos accordingly demanded to know whether she had or had not been a virgin prior to lying with the detested Salvador, to which she abashedly replied that she had already granted carnal knowledge of her person to four men.— And had she confessed these sins?— Oh, yes, she said—to Fray de Castro, who was now in no position to contradict her.— Calling upon the aforesaid Melchor Marín to stand, which he tremulously did, Doctor de los Ríos reminded him of his responsibility toward this negro woman as her owner and therefore in a sense her father. Then the aforesaid Melchor Marín did lower his head, after the fashion of his own negress, and asseverate and say that to his certain knowledge, Herlinda and the detested Salvador used to sleep together in one bed, or more precisely on the dirt floor, which he, the said Melchor, and his spouse Ofelia both considered scandalous, not to mention a sad reflection upon our distance from Jesus Christ; but since the detested Salvador had often helped Herlinda by carrying great sacks of peanuts upon his shoulders, as if he were her loving husband (although whether those two had indeed betrothed themselves to each other the said Melchor could not swear; they had kept him in darkness, he tremulously said, because they must have feared that he, Herlinda's owner, might resent their expectation of future enjoyment of any so-called conjugal rights at the very times when he or his children had need of her), and since the selfsame detested Salvador visited her either at home or on the street whenever his victim the sainted Fray de Castro permitted, Melchor and Ofelia had seen reason to hope and pray that those two would in time be married by the hand of a cleric—all of which was corroborated by the aforesaid Herlinda Encinas, who, it quickly came out, was a blithe and accomplished tattler, at least so long as the investigation appeared to concern someone other than herself. When commanded to explain why in her view the murder had occurred, she freely informed the court that in her presence the detested Salvador had complained with unseemly resentment about certain floggings regularly administered for his own good. Calling upon her to look into his eyes, Doctor de los Ríos now required and demanded to know without equivocation whether the concubinage in which she had so disgustingly engaged with the detested Salvador ever caused the latter to be delinquent in his duties to his employer, to which in a feeble voice she replied that it had not. Next, Doctor de los Ríos asked her owner the same question. Gripping the railing, the old black man said that to the best of his information the late Fray de Castro had considered Herlinda a good influence upon the detested Salvador, who was known to be moody and even turbulent, and that he might very well have preferred to see those two persons married, not that he, Melchor, had ever raised this issue with the Father, for fear of encouraging the matter to go forward.— That's as may be, said Doctor de los Ríos, but can you deny that the visits of your slave woman's paramour benefited your business at the diocese's expense? From what I've gathered, in the times when he was hauling peanut-bags to her, she wasn't exactly digging graves for him!—at which the court chamber blossomed with smiles and titters, and the old man staggered.— Now then, Herlinda, continued the judge, not displeased with the success of his jest, have you fully discharged your conscience here before me? I call on you now, in the presence of God, Who is most certainly listening, to give oath, for the sake of justice and in the interest of your own soul, to state, speak fully, and say whether you felt inconvenienced by the late Fray de Castro's legitimate demands upon your detested paramour, whose memory I curse with every word of execration, and accordingly conspired with him to commit this damnable crime—at which the black woman, sobbing loudly, as if she had just now come to comprehend her peril, and would never again be permitted to see the cathedral's cupola-faces now almost the color of the sweetly humid air, nor the palms growing invisibly, silently and vainly away from earth, nor those two fat ladies with the baskets of biscuits and crackers on their shoulders (one of whom, Neyda Duarte, had testified against her), reiterated, as was indeed known to be the case, that upon perceiving the murderer approach her in the market, marked, as if with the brand of Cain, with red eyes and red hands, she had screamed and fled him, as a result of which the baser sort of negroes and Indians had stolen nearly two pesos' worth of peanuts; moreover, her owner, the aforesaid Melchor Marín, had already sworn by the Mother of God that this girl was innocent, which Doctor de los Ríos himself believed; but there are times when justice finds it politic to put on a frowning face. Now that she had been reduced to the proper state, one would hope that in order to spare herself she would denounce any error or failing of the aforesaid Agustín González Rodríguez, who, since he remained so far short of his twenty-fifth year, when a boy becomes a man, was compassionately represented by the *procurador*, whose name was Ángel Enríquez and who felt considerably less interested in him than in that aforesaid *fly in milk* with the dark brown eyes and the small breasts; if you have ever seen some pretty young negro penitent standing barefoot in the Inquisition's chapel, shivering with dread, naked to the waist, bowing until her hair sweeps the flagstones, then setting off her breasts to still better advantage when she raises high the tall green taper of contrition, you will comprehend the daydreams of Ángel Enríquez, whose wife was a long-suffering old hag from Cádiz. Now, regarding this Agustín who so perplexed the court in that humid hour (the birds nearly asleep in the late-morning sun), nothing could be proved, and Herlinda's owner, that aforesaid tottering Melchor Marín, testified on his behalf; but poor Doctor de los Ríos, who thanks to his profession could never get the reek of moral latrines out of his nose, suspected that the old negro might feel beholden to his slave, either (as he had already stated) because he survived upon her labor, or because he enjoyed occasional carnal connection with her, or both; here then was no unprejudiced witness. For this reason Doctor de los Ríos had been more swayed by the innkeeper Jaime Esposito, who like Ángel Enríquez's wife happened to be of pure Spanish stock and who considered Agustín to be neither more nor less than a nuisance—in other words, possessed no interest in him. So far as Señor Esposito could make out, there was no great evil in the boy, whom he considered sullenly abject rather than malicious. Doctor de los Ríos had once found occasion to investigate the said Señor's inn, which some busybody suspected of being a brothel, but nothing could be proved, although illicit intercourse had certainly taken place there. Señor Esposito's noble indifference to the affairs of others, except insofar as they affected his revenues, rendered him the perfect witness, and the tribunal had already sent him home. Doctor de los Ríos now inquired of the negress Herlinda how often the boy Agustín had been present when they trysted, to which she replied that her owner disliked to see him, since children of his age would rather eat than work. From this answer it was apparent that Agustín had in fact come around in the master's absence, doubtless to stuff his mouth with stolen peanuts; therefore the judge pursued the matter, demanding to know whether the late detested Salvador's ungodly spite and resentment ever expressed itself to Agustín in the slave girl's presence, to which she answered (for which he could not fault her, knowing the inferior capacity of these negroes for reason) that she could not remember. So the boy was called to stand, which he did, and commanded to state his opinion of his brother. He seemed amazed and ignorant concerning what he ought to say. Doctor de los Ríos asked whether he comprehended that his brother was a murderer. The boy said yes. He was dark, dirty and ill-favored. Furthermore, he stank like someone who has been in bad places. Although he appeared small, especially in comparison to his brother, whose toes had nearly touched the ground when they hanged him, he projected a woeful skulking look, in the manner of those half-starved dogs which feed on refuse in the streets, and grow up to be vicious. The priests said there must be bad blood in him. Upon demand he produced his *papel* proving church attendance. Gently the *procurador* inquired whether he was a Christian, to which this Agustín replied that no one had ever taught him anything. After due thought, Doctor de los Ríos now released the aforesaid Herlinda Encinas, upon whom any exhortations to chastity would presumably be wasted unless accompanied by flogging and disgrace, back into the corridor between two soldiers, and out into the wide courtyard whose walls were Naples yellow and whose square planters contained narrow-trunked wide-branched almond trees, and back into the sweetness of Veracruz, where until she died or got sold she would presumably continue her close friendship with that metal cage with sacks of peanuts and sometimes even mangoes hanging from it. Next, after further questioning, together with a reminder of the penalty for adultery, and a word of helpful advice on managing one's dependents (for instance, one could borrow money, if need be, to purchase a sturdy young negro fit to keep one's negress from wandering) he dismissed the negress's owner, Melchor Marín, who crept gratefully back to his sins. Finally he rang his tiny bell, summoning the guards, who returned the boy Agustín to the secret underground cells. Everyone agreed that nothing could be indicted against him, but no one approved of his manner. In a bored voice the *procurador* proposed placing him in that new house of mercy for unfortunates, but when Doctor de los Ríos drew attention to the boy's apparent potential for corrupting the souls of others, no one dissented. Within the week they set him at liberty, but being homeless and without a trade, he haunted the house of Melchor Marín until the latter drove him away definitively, then fell into thievery. Although they exhorted him in reasoned kindness, and punished him with only twenty stripes, in consideration of his youth, for their charity they got requited with sorrow—a tale all too frequently heard here in Veracruz, where sins have become as commonplace as negroes in shackles. It was the lacemaker's wife who saw this Agustín interring some bundle in the dungheap between her house and the cemetery wall; thus they recovered Señor Castellano's miniature aventurine cask, which corresponded in important particulars to the description given by its outraged owner, the tap being decorated with blue enamel and two pretty chains. Señor Castellano swore that he had paid twenty pesos for it, although the *procurador* opined that its worth was closer to eighteen. Brought into the light, Agustín readily admitted his guilt—forthrightness being the only good remaining in him. When they inquired how he had it in him to expose his evil doings, he replied that his brother had taught him that a true man behaves so. He was now fourteen. Sorrowing over his misdeeds, and fearing that he had become of disobedient or malevolent character, they flogged him with fifty crimson stripes—a seemly and edifying entertainment for our common people, who are easily tempted into comparable offenses—then sent him to San Juan de Ulúa for a term of nine years.

2

Looking down from the yellowing ramparts into the shallow water, which stinks of algae and sewage, one can see the bottom, and sometimes spy the outlines of preying sharks, who guard this hateful prison-island at no expense to the Crown, excepting that incidental loss of labor when a local fisherman loses a leg or worse. They patrol the harbor like bluish-grey shadows. Never mind that the shore lies no great distance away! At church I learned that their voracious grins are set around their snouts for the express benefit of the King of Spain and his laws. All the same, the authorities of Veracruz keep other sentinels, whose swords and guns terrify the prisoners as effectively as sharks' teeth. It was these who marched that batch of chained prisoners up the steep steps from the landing-place and across the broad low terrace of coral-stone blocks where everything was asymmetrical. The boy looked up. He saw a many-slitted phallic guard tower. The column continued to move, and so he stumbled. A soldier split open his back with two blows of the whip.

Before the commandant's palace, which was the one square building in that considerable courtyard whose balconies shielded themselves with heavy wooden railings carved out in leaf-shapes and whose windows were latticed with drooping iron ribs, the criminals now got registered and divided up like scoops of grease flicked into so many bubbling pots, the pots being the cells. Wondering whether he might pass the remainder of his life without light, Agustín dared to look up a second time, and saw someone high above him, wearing shiny boots and a scarlet-velveted brigandine with the rivets glittering all down his chest. He wondered how he would feel to become this man, who appeared nearly as small as a seagull on the cathedral's roof, or at least to look down from this parapet and watch the tiny figures marching through the courtyard. Before he had thought this for very long, they kicked and flogged him, in his string of six, down a long tunnel of arches, whose floor was round stones, and across the stone bridge over the brownish-green water to the polygon-island of huge dank-domed cells, where he left the light indeed. The chamber where they intended him to pass his next nine years had two narrow slits for windows, up high so that a man could not put his face to them. The interior resembled a crocodile's toothy mouth, for it bore yellow-white stalactites and stalagmites of salt. Stinking rotting half-toothless men lay one upon the other, wheezing, spitting and cursing. The ones who could now sat up, scanning him as thoroughly as our priests will a marriage witness. That was how he was studied and then accepted by his new friend Rodrigo de la Concepción, octaroon, who had already served three years of an eighteen-year term for stealing an infantryman's helmet. Soon they became very easy together, for in San Juan de Ulúa, as in any prison, life grows jollier and safer for wretches who double up to share secrets. For much the same reason that in Veracruz the birds flock more wildly at twilight than at noon, so in San Juan de Ulúa the convicts commence to crawl all over one another the moment that the sun descends beneath the sea. Accordingly, at dusk Rodrigo got to business. The fingers of his hand, now laid upon the boy's belly, were as elegant as a crow's black talons, shining as softly as if they were gloved in patent leather. He liked Agustín even better upon learning that he was a murderer's brother; thus it came out that in addition to the affair of the infantryman's helmet, Rodrigo deserved the credit of fitting his hands around a certain woman's throat, for a cause that any man of style could understand:

> *Mestiza*, goddess of the orient;
> *mestiza*, queen of the sun,
> so that you look decent,
> remove that piece of bean
> which covers your whole tooth!

and two as yet unknown other villains sang along. For all the neighbors ever learned, he said, that slut simply ran off from her husband, a townsman infamous for his own paramours; hence Rodrigo got rid of her for nothing, unlike Salvador, who stood before the tribunal, weighted with chains, grinning down his capital sentence; when they led him away he gazed back at Agustín unbearably. Having heard in church that submission is the best way to avoid getting lost in fiery tortures; and, moreover, remaining yet capable of joys not unlike the shining white pores of fresh watermelon slices, the boy determined to make the best of his confinement; after all, there would be food—besides, his new friends were such jokers; they'd speed the years away! This Rodrigo, for instance, was a cheerful, hopeful sort of fellow, who began to uplift Agustín's soul with treasure-talk.

The food now came, in a common bowl. It was nothing but slabbersauce,* and moldy bread-crusts with which to grub it up. But there was plenty of it, and his new friends promised it would come twice every day.

Just as rich men dream of becoming good, so poor men imagine getting rich. And everyone knew that riches still shone here and there in Mexico—for the contrary would have been unthinkable. The Franciscans once longed to build on this soil a Kingdom of the Gospels, whose citizens would become gentler than the pigeon-armies which strut along the island of white-limed palms in the *zócalo*; no less hopeful were the

---

* A mixture of palm-oil, flour, water and pepper, served out on some slave ships. Doubtless its low nutritive value made the human cargo less dangerous (at the cost of increasing mortality).

dreamers of Cortés's stripe, who if they could not torture treasure out of Indians would squeeze a quotidian surplus out of their own kind. Then there were the convicts, who craved to hunt down Amazons, and revenge themselves upon all wealth and pleasure—all the more so since they lacked means even to hire the jailer's dice. A few of Agustín's cellmates denounced certain nobles and churchmen for their dark greed, but the rest dreamed of victories, not over their century but merely over this or that moment. From ambush they might have shot down an Archbishop standing beneath the gold-and-purple pallium, could they have sold his vestments for fifty reales; but they would far rather have raped a woman of the town; better still, they listened for the footsteps of the two guards bringing the food trough. They grieved over the friars' decision to destroy the Mexican temples, even down to their lovely furnishings; but New Spain goes on and on, like that stony-floored recession of arches at San Juan de Ulúa; surely other temples remained; thus eagerly they devoured each other's lies. As Rodrigo liked to sing,

> Stretch out your arms, *negrita*,
> and raise me to your castle in the clouds!
> Open your legs, *negrita*,
> and show me your coral casket!

What astonished Agustín, whose character (he having been a worrier from his earliest age) was practical nearly unto bleakness, was their silence on the subject of escape. In fact the sharks and sentries kept the place so well that the commandant slept late, as he had always wished to do when he was younger. On the ramparts stood a file of fresh troops—less in order, perhaps, than the wide black shoulders of those vultures which had lined up on the wall for Salvador's execution; for it was summer, and so the yellow fever was ripening again in men.

Once upon a time the beautiful witch Mulata de Córdoba, who, so they say, was the fortress's only female prisoner, did get out of San Juan de Ulúa, simply by begging a piece of charcoal from the guards, who must themselves have hungered for something unearthly to transpire, for after advising her to act like a good woman they provided what she had wished for, and with it she drew a ship upon the wall of her cell.

Came a midnight thunderclap, and in that ship she sailed away with the Devil! But no other prisoner possessed her advantages. Several generations after Agustín's confinement, that upright, colorless liberator Benito Juárez, whose administration would put Emperor Maximilian to death, lay in one of these cells. His best aphorism: *I know that the rich and the powerful do not feel or try to alleviate the miseries of the poor.* He expected nothing in prison, and got nothing. As for Agustín's new friends, precisely because their expectations had ebbed, they craved dreamy prizes all the more—and not one of them wisely fearful of his own conscience. For the boy's part, the bitter impossibility of escape was not to be admitted all at once; after all, he had years in which to make that accommodation; so wouldn't it be more inspiring to fondle imaginary silver? And since he was new here, and preferred to get by without trouble, by all means let them guide the conversation! That Indian with the cropped-off ears, when would he say something, and how unpleasant would it be? That tall negro with the inflamed eyes, that wiry quadroon who kept grinning back and forth, as if his temper required constant watching; that pallid, vague fellow with the hands of a locksmith (he'd burned the granary of some miserly *hacendado* who hoarded corn in drought years); that broad-shouldered mulatto who'd laid his arm against Agustín's, and smiled because Agustín's was darker . . . well, they were his neighbors now. What he would have preferred to do was remember a certain turning he had glimpsed when they were marching him to this cell, and a certain narrow stone staircase worn perilously smooth, and above it, dark blotches on the island's dim rock, and vast L-shaped corridors between whose flagstones the grass grew in square outlines; because already his recollections were drawing inward, like blotches of wetness on laundry hanging in the sun; soon, as the guards intended, he would be lost at San Juan de Ulúa even in his memories, and his chances for flight still further reduced. That narrow staircase, could he ever find it again, he'd clamber from it into the rock's footholds, and then leap down onto a passing soldier, but only at night; already he had forgotten whether it lay left or right of the main corridor; and his fine friend Rodrigo, the one with the crow-black hands, kept going on about treasures. And why not? On those bygone nights when the two brothers still dwelled together (they used to sleep in this or that tree overlooking the beach, so

that crocodiles could not eat them; but it turned out that instead of crocodiles it was soldiers who rousted them out, after which they hid in the
sailmaker's shed), they too loved to dispose of imaginary wealth.—
Reader, may you be warned by their example never to forget what wields
greatest power over our immortal souls!— Agustín, then five or six years
old, proposed to fill his belly with meat and cake; thus far went a hungry
boy's dreams. Salvador promised there would be other pleasures. Someday, God willing, they'd pass for honorable grandees, with the power of
death over a dozen slaves, and nothing to do but ride about the city in a
coach enriched with cloth of gold. Indeed, at the trial, Agustín, like the
procurador, envisioned himself between the thighs of his brother's light-
of-love, Herlinda—for how fetching she had been, and how well she had
fed both brothers! Lying close against the boy, Rodrigo, who wished for
an *encomendero* of his own, with Indian labor forever, now swore that in
Moquí Province (so a mulatto swineherd had whispered to him the night
before being garroted) there ran a snowy Blue Range renowned for its
central peak, a silver mountain ringed round by quicksilver lakes; and
that beyond that, in a direction which was certain, on the island of Ziñogava, in a palace of jade, there dwelled an Amazonian queen most deserving of pillage, because her vassals served her on plates and platters of
pure white silver—and by the way, Rodrigo informed him, Amazons are
whiter than all other women on earth, and weep tears of unalloyed silver,
which makes them doubly worth raping and tormenting. Concerning
the existence of these females Agustín stayed skeptical, since Salvador,
who had always been eager for such knowledge, had been definitively informed by Fray de Castro that no trusty witness ever saw one, no, not
from the Conquest until now, although once upon a time, allowed Fray
de Castro, the Tarascans most faithfully promised Gonzalo de Sandoval
that an Island of Amazons lay but ten days' sail from Colima, and even
Cortés hoped and believed. In truth the idea of tormenting a beautiful
woman gave Agustín something new to dream of, although he would
rather have loved and married her (for he was not yet as lost to goodness
as some Saracen); and Rodrigo proposed to swear an oath upon the sacred Host, should he ever obtain it, which appeared improbable, that
there were Amazons, not merely somewhere in this world, but right here
in Mexico! Agustín wondered aloud how they might find Ziñogava or

even the Blue Range. Pressing against his back was a certain Bernardo Villalobos, with whom Rodrigo appeared to be very tender; he had been lucky to draw a mere nineteen years for bigamy and incest. To encourage the boy, and initiate him into their fraternity of treasure-seekers, he now told the tale of the skeleton hand: A sea-captain out of Barcelona, having entered into illicit relations with his sister, sat sorrowing at her deathbed, when she commanded him, as her final wish, to cut off her hand and keep it with him, since the magnetic sympathy between them had been so greatly magnified by their physical love that this one piece of her, so adept at caressing and gesturing, might be able to do him a good turn. Being a sentimentalist, he kept this relic on red velvet in a glass box. As he soon learned, the skeleton hand was better than a compass-needle. Were he unsure where to sail, he would closet himself with the hand, utter a few endearments (the same sort which he practiced on women of the town) and confess his uncertainty, at which point it would swivel around upon its velvet bed, and then the forefinger would point out the direction where he ought to go. Greatly interested (for he had sometimes thought to become a sailor), Agustín asked Bernardo whether he might perhaps know that sea-captain personally, which he coyly disdained to answer. The main thing, he said, caressing the boy, was that this hand, could he but find it (and as a matter of fact he suspected where to steal it), would guide them quite infallibly to Ziñogava, and Agustín would be welcome to be one of their company. Bernardo said that the hand sometimes liked to tickle people, especially young boys, and sometime, perhaps even tonight, it might pay the new arrival a visit.— But can the hand get us out of here? the boy demanded.— Salvador had taught him how to pick pockets on those afternoons when the musicians, dancers and lovely singers performed high up on the wooden platform and happy people pressed carelessly around. He could march his fingers like spiders quite well. So when Rodrigo and Bernardo did just this, he fell back on his guard, but being so lonely and so weak, he could not forbear all the same to hope that they would be to him like brothers, and perhaps even someday, when they were all free, help him find an Amazon to love.— Rodrigo laughed at his question, but Bernardo, who must be worth listening to, since he had formerly done well for himself as an Indian-whipper for the Franciscans, claimed to know how the narrow stairs ascended through a deep arch of pastel stone, going up past a certain barred window to the parapet, which in places was broad enough for three horsemen to ride abreast, but whenever his words had carried the other prisoners that far he invariably hesitated, his plots never finishing or even becoming symmetrical, in which respect they took after the prison's open-roofed many-arched islands of stone. And so everyone stared down into the dark latrine-crypt whose hole opened over the shining green water. The sun now drowned itself. There came the faraway slam of a door. Bernardo tried to kiss him, but the boy rolled away. At this, Rodrigo clapped his hands. Four villains held the boy down. Perhaps he should have appealed to that divine protector of the weak and innocent, the King of Spain.

3

Could we become so great and strong as to survive the malodorous embrace of those who love us beyond death, we would not need their ghostly services. And the man who scarcely fears at all when his dead brother, instead of answering him, draws rotted hands about his throat, is nearly insusceptible to blackmail. Agustín had already learned how to be despised as poor, dark and criminal. The day they cut off his brother's head something sickened in him. The night he became a catamite he felt as blindly bewildered as the corpse which wonders whether it has been buried alive or is truly dead. But the foul breaths of his new friends, the fungus on their skin, never mind the stink of algae and sewage from that hole in the floor; the grand and lonely hatreds he already wore; and the sunrises glowing in the latrine hole where the sea lightened into turquoise and small fry swam mindlessly round and round; all these improved him into a befitting instrument; then came the pestilences which could not kill him, although they carried off seven others in that cell. Now, for a fact, he grew "realistic." The second time was not so bad as the first; by the fifth he knew better than to struggle; the best way was to give them satisfaction so that it would be quickly over. Juan and Rafael generally hurt him the most; Leopoldo was the kindest. Agustín would never come into his growth, it seemed; he had no more power to defend himself than a little girl. Salvador would have protected him, even with his life; indeed, in a sense he had—the very reason he was gone forever. That fatal quarrel with Fray de Castro had been occasioned by the victim's refusal either to accept Agustín as an apprentice or to allow Salvador a half day's leave in hopes of finding some master for the boy; the priest remarked, not without reason, that Herlinda had already siphoned off enough of Salvador's labor; it was when he called her a succubus that the shovel struck him. So the boy drew himself ever more apart, not only from the other inmates of that crowded sweltering vault, but even from himself; and his appointed stripes no longer prevented him from meditating on the idea that the remains of some relative—her skeleton hand, for instance—might retain some virtue which could aid the living. Furthermore, he thought on the grand mountain of silver, and the regal Amazon of Ziñogava who wept silver tears. Once he more completely forgot the stepped Indian walls assembled from round river stones, the Spanish flag over the Baluarte, the smoke rising from the old Indian pyramid, the cruelty of canon law and the chittering and thudding of birds and lizards in the tree of yellow berries, the fishing nets on the wall by Boca del Río and the way Herlinda used to smile when she brushed her long hair away from her face, reality bled out of the world; and he dreamed about silver, which might for all its silverness keep a bluish or golden-brown tint, and which although it seems to reflect pinkness remains white in its deepest grooves.

His neighbors were gambling with lousy rag-scraps. The winner got to strike the loser. Agustín dreamed out his impossible escape: The iron door would screech open, the guards would fall dead, and somehow he would ascend the wall, which resembled the skin of a piebald albino.

In that cell lay a certain Indian whose ears had been lopped off for some offense against the Holy Sacraments; since he never in all those years broke silence, his cellmates jested that the executioner must also have cut out his tongue, as could easily have been the case. He was the only one who had not incurred Agustín's hatred, not that he had ever defended the boy—who took him as a model. Staring at the wall, those two said no word. Agustín heard his cellmates reckoning up the days as well as they were able; they decided that this might be the first of May, at which he closed his eyes, remembering the Ribbon Dance which is performed on that date; once when he was small his brother sat him on his shoulders so that he could see across the thousand-headed crowd in the zócalo, and enjoy the dancers; there were certain nuns who could sing and play the guitar, and although he was too young to understand the words, the melodies tickled him; and afterward his brother gave him a slice of cake. Closing his eyes, he saw the arches of San Juan de Ulúa receding and receding; he had seen them only that once, and it seemed that if he could but count them accurately he might save himself; therefore as he lay in the sticky whitestained cell, his bitterness growing upward like one of the stalagmites around him, he tabulated arch-shadows on the grey-pebbled pavement which he had so briefly trodden: one, two, three, and then the fourth shadow-bar was darker and wider, after which came the fifth, beyond which he could not certainly see any shadows, but noted two more sharp-edged archways, although it might have been three, and the blotched pallor after those might or might not have been a wall.

Sometimes Rodrigo picked over the legend of Chucho el Rojo, the thieves' hero, whose cellmate La Changa paid off a guard to get him a ship, from which he swam away, oiled against sharks, and then travelled overland to Mexico, where he was received by his lovely mistress, Matilde de Frizac. What La Changa got out of it no one mentioned. Rodrigo and Bernardo were going to get themselves younger, lighter-skinned mistresses than Matilde; they would rob great ships of cocoa, vanilla and silver. This dream was as a breezeblown palmhead waving behind one of San Juan de Ulúa's moldy stone walls. As for Agustín, he pretended that the bootsteps of soldiers on the low many-arched bridges, or the faraway hoofsteps of horses on those blocks of out-fanning coral, were somehow conveying him away from here. In summer Fray de Castro used to keep his dark cloak clasped only at the throat, falling away to his ankles and showing the dirty-pale robe beneath. To live is to live in dirt, it seems. What did he care about Matilde de Frizac, especially if Rodrigo liked her? In six more years he'd be twenty-five—still young, perhaps, but how nitrous by then his heart! He no longer fever-dreamed of kissing any pretty blackamoor wench who wore earbobs of jade and a fine silver necklace. What he wished for most of all was revenge—on these fine villains here to whose mercy he must pretend to feel beholden, on the uniformed rogue who had whipped him, on all the guards, soldiers, officials, mariners and architects connected with San Juan de Ulúa, and on the men who had executed his brother. If only he could trample down that damned judge, and make off with the *procurador*'s head! By the fiftieth time the others used him, it seemed ordinary. The falconets and brass lombards were booming out to honor some admiral in the harbor. To his cellmates he continued peaceful and obedient, having no hope of making his way here were he anything else. (Had he come more quickly into his growth he could have looked them in the face, and known their menace and their dingy monotonous malice, their self-hating corruption, which pleased itself only by blighting others and then but for an instant.) He never spoke of his own accord, and answered others as seldom as possible. Feeling insulted, they treated him with increasing cruelty. Just as Dorantes de Carranza used to amuse his guests by arranging bullfighting matches against crocodiles whose jaws had been tied shut, so Bernardo or Rodrigo liked to organize a certain game, played four or five prisoners at a time, of sitting on Agustín's arms and legs, then tormenting and goading him. While they used him, they called him *slave, whore,* and, worst of all, *woman.* Sometimes when he crept toward the food trough they liked to shove his face in it until he choked. On a certain night when they commenced to threaten and insult him, he attacked Juan Hernández, who had too often bragged of having once discovered a golden frog ornament in the ground; and because he injured this Juan in his ribs, they punished him with a broken nose and several other tokens of their comradeship, followed by the usual outcome. But Agustín found himself less afraid than before, or perhaps simply more indifferent, as if the steamy, moldy years in San Juan de Ulúa had rotted away some of his heart. And although his indifference enraged them, it might also have saved him at times, since they shared it. Once they had satisfied themselves, and left him facedown on the floor, he kept still until they slept, then hit back, biting and kicking. Again they subdued him, slamming his head against the wall until his hair was wet with blood. They left him to live or die, and he laughed. An hour later, when they had forgotten him sufficiently to again memorialize all the women they had defended or attacked with their daggers, he sprang on Bernardo and thumbed out one of his eyes. Whether they would murder him was a question, to be sure, but he did not care, as they well perceived. When they let him alone, which was easiest, he did the same for them.— He's not afraid! he heard them say, and then he knew that he was correct. He informed Bernardo that next time he would kill him, and Bernardo said nothing. Thus his life got simplified through hatred. No better than a slave before, he was no worse now.— Sometimes in the winter they could hear the *nortes* blow around their prison, and sometimes they could even hear rain. They heard the cannon; once in awhile they heard voices.— In the summer of his third year, nauseously grinding his forehead against the nitrous walls in quest of any coolness which might exude from this earth, he swooned into the searing well of his sickness, surrendering to nightmares, or at least enduring them, since he could do nothing else; when he awoke, he seemed to spy a greyish-white bird departing from his face. Gazing down into that latrine-hole beneath which the water flowed as bright and green as the jade ornaments on Chalchihuitlicue's skirt, he longed for light more fiercely than ever. He seemed to hear faraway people chanting in church like slaves pulling a rope. Again and again he dreamed of his brother rising back out of earth, whole again—but it is seldom we realize our dreams entirely. By then he was stronger and uglier, like his wishes; and from time to time, as inmates died, the guards threw in fresh young boys more gratifying than he to his companions' tastes. Just as Aztecs used to torture children, to ensure that they would weep before getting sacrificed to Tlaloc the rain god—for who would deny that tears are similar to rain, and therefore might bring it?—thus these cruel men, being diseased by rage, made sure that their pretty objects shrieked out in pain and shame, while Agustín, who was commencing to achieve a sinister reputation, lay in the darkest corner, turning over and over everything he had ever heard of necromancy, in order to call back his elder brother from the dead. Silently he worked his arms and legs hour by hour, in order to strengthen them, and perhaps someday to accomplish his deliverance. (Salvador had been terribly strong—all the more so when anger overtook him.) Each grief, humiliation and injury was now as precious to him as the thorn from Christ's crown which we keep in our cathedral here in Veracruz; because each one strengthened his righteousness. Yet all the while he felt indifferent. None of his emotions were real to him. His self-pride grew as glorious as the silver cross on the Inquisition's crimson banner. Perhaps he would kill each man in this cell, one by one. He knew he'd get Rodrigo at least. Even that nonentity of an earless Indian maddened him now, but he'd rise beyond all that; he'd wear a pleated doublet of scarlet or emerald, sashed tightly round his narrow waist. He'd sin with as many women as possible, preferably without their consent. Sometimes he could hear the calls of the leather and sugar vendors on the beach, but then a white mist rose up out of the latrine-hole and wrapped him soundlessly in himself. He drowsed. Meanwhile his companions preyed upon a new convict named Luís, who had been imprisoned for defaulting on his *alcabala* tax, and next morning they all meditated on the strange expression of peace on the suicided boy's face, his skin so smooth, his dark eyes sleepily half-closed, his lips parted on the right side and shut on the left, so that as he lay there his mouth appeared to be a sweet fruit which excited the villains no end, so that they began to sing:

Much do I care for my María;
how lovely is this woman!

Agustín lay watching, as calmly as a conquistador blowing on his matchlock fuse. The next time that Bernardo crawled to him, insinuatingly lecherous, while the others began singing "The Whores of Hermosillo," Agustín did by him as Rodrigo had done by his light-o'-love, so that Bernardo went out of this world. When the guards came, no one would say what had happened. They all got beaten, then thrown back into the cell. Agustín was now a man. They all lay watching the white stalactites grow—a finger's width grander already since the boy's arrival.

4

In the seventh year of his captivity, while his good friends lay arguing over who had committed the greatest sin (Rodrigo hoped someday to sit at the Devil's right hand), Agustín prayed to Satan so successfully that his prayer passed through hell's keyhole, and at once the head flew up through the latrine-hole and landed on his shoulder.

Is the soul, as Socrates sometimes posited, a life-bearer, or is it merely the body's contingent prisoner, whose release when the flesh perishes merely brings about its own doom? And was this flying head a spirit, an animated fragment or an alien demon hiding in Salvador's semblance?— All that I can tell you is that for the first time in several years Agustín smiled. (As for the head, of course, it never stopped grinning.) It was a pleasant enough reunion. No matter that Salvador had not preserved his old appearance; we all diminish in time, and may even sacrifice a few appendages; the main thing is to get on with our projects and not complain overmuch.

Now the other men cringed back in terror and cried out: Agustín, save us, brother!

Shall I? laughed the head.

No, said Agustín.

So the head whirred through the air and bit them one after the other, mincing their throats and necks with its long yellow teeth, and they all were dead, excepting only the silent Indian, who lay so afflicted with fever that he could barely open his eyes.

Your pleasure? asked the head.

Kill him, brother!—because Agustín now held that Indian's silence against him; all these years he had resembled some great lord who hides his grain.

So the head murdered him also. That was when the rapier of something cut through Agustín's hate-ringed heart, and he got pricked by the love shown by this hateful head which had flown so far from hell to help him.

Well, it said, that was a nice drink of blood. I'm feeling much restored, thanks to those gentlemen.

None of them had suffered as they deserved, although of course the ones who awaited their turns paid a higher penalty than those who died first. The flying head was terrifying, without a doubt, but by now Agustín had seen worse.

He felt exalted. He wished to impress everyone in Mexico just as he had done in this cell: to kill the people who had testified against his brother, together with their children; to harry meek penitents who knelt with ropes around their necks; to open the throats of men he'd never met; to burn a rich lord's granary for a lark—dreams as old as the accounting-books in the archives.

5

The head told him: Brother, you've become foul.

And you?

I as well, the head replied, even as I decayed into a skull, and all the more when a soldier pulled me off the spike and cast me into the harbor to be crabs' prey, because there was nothing left to me but a ruined fragment of my body, and all got worse and worse. Then I heard about you, because when they pronounced your sentence a bell tolled under the sea, and I remembered you, knowing that you have no one but me. But who was I? When I was a child I was no murderer; when I was alive I was not dead; when I was dead I was not whole. Still in all those times I remained myself. So I began to take myself back out of the mud and away from the crabs, and now I feel myself becoming good. Don't you wish for the same?

Brother, said Agustín, what I wish for is to get out of here.

That's easy, chuckled the head, and bit right through the bars, devouring each one in two places, while the young man lifted each broken length of iron aside, as quietly as he could.

Don't worry, brother. I've dulled their ears. Have you said goodbye to your friends?

For answer, Agustín kicked the dead Indian in the chest.

Rolling its eyes with whirring sounds, the head flew out of the cell, and its brother followed.— Now hold me against your heart, with both hands. Grip my hair tight, because if you let go, you'll be killed. Don't worry; you can't hurt me.

So they rose up into the air. The fortress began to unfurl around them. Within the half-barrel arches, salt coated the walls like ribs of frost. Because he had counted and recounted the corridor of arches, Agustín grew momentarily furious not to go that way; but this he overcame. His brother's head was squishy-rotten and its hair wriggled with worms, but the young man would have done anything to preserve his life. Moreover, the head was his destiny. As silently as mosquitoes they cleared the parapet of the squat yellow island, which was not entirely unlike a Totonacan pyramid in its wide and stolid massiveness, brooding utterly alone, never mind its connecting bridges, over its barely untrue reflection in the still dark water where offal floated among the reflections of palm-tops. Halfway up the steep narrow stairs of the far corner stood a sentry, shaking with fever and occasionally groaning. Unlike the convicts he knew the misery of parade on the broad pale terraces of the fortress, the sun beating down on burned and infected hands, the commandant's rages, and the hallucination of a certain longhaired fever-woman in a jade dress, who outstretched her arms to him from the precious mildewed shade of towers and archways. He had not yet begun to vomit. At first he stared right through Agustín, neither comprehending nor believing, so that before he knew it, the head had torn away his throat, and Agustín changed clothes with the corpse. Again the head flew up near his heart, and he gripped it around both cheeks; again they were flying silently a hand's breadth above the hot foul water, down within which some long and finny thing accompanied them, and cautiously rounding the corners of steep-walled promontories and bridge-joined islets which make up San Juan de Ulúa's immense and complex hatefulness. Agustín could spy the myriad glowings of skulls at the bottom of the harbor.

And so he escaped from San Juan de Ulúa, where Cortés first came on Holy Thursday, 1519, in the days when dreams of silver and Amazons still travelled in fleets like our high-castled galleons; yes, he returned into the day at last, and the sun shone nearly as brightly as the face of the Mother of God.

6

They descended to the beach, easily avoiding a file of night soldiers with leaf-bladed lances, and then the head whirred out of his hands. So he was back among the happy people.

Eight years it had been since he and Salvador used to conceal themselves here, gleefully devouring stolen food. Several palm trees had fallen; the sailmaker had patched his hut. Once when he was very young—their mother must have died not long before—his brother had stolen a dirty breadcrust to share with him, and as they sat in the sand eating it, some Spaniards came to punish them. While they started on Salvador with their sticks, Agustín ran into this very thicket, where an Indian prostitute hid him in her sweaty cloak. Now he felt equally enveloped and protected by the flying head, which loved him more than anyone ever had or would; only he wished that instead of being so much smaller than he was, the head would enlarge.

The head asked if he were satisfied, and he said that he was. Indeed, it seemed at first that his ingenuous hopefulness had been regained, as if it were again so early in life's day that the sky was pearly and a solitary grey pigeon seemed almost black; watchmen's torches still glowed like egg yolks, and the yellow-pink fissure which would prove itself to be the sun barely announced itself through the clouds. He hoped never to make another mistake. Knowing that everyone but the head was against him made life easy. The cavalry were all asleep, and the vultures had not yet come down from the trees.

Well? the head demanded, with the round gold ring-eyes of a crow. Is this where time stops?

Because the head had done for him what he never could have done for himself, Agustín felt timid and dependent, all the more so since liberty was blinding and dangerous, but he considered himself a man, and meant to become a rich lord. Should no Amazons make themselves available to be conquered right away, he might apprentice himself to a leather merchant, then kill his master and sell off the stock in Xalapa. Then he could buy weapons and set out into the jungle, where he might find, if not Amazons, then at least some feeble Indians with gold in their ears. Or he could lease that old sugarmill in San Andrés Tuxtla and live off the labor of his negroes. For a fact, after all his sufferings he deserved never to work like other people! But relying on his own notions just now might cause his recapture. Settling, therefore, for patient opportunism, he did not answer the head's question directly, but pried an old sack out of the sand and invited the head to fly into it. This conveyance, if it may be called that, he tied around his belt. Then he strode into Veracruz. The yellow flecks behind the silver clouds coagulated into a new sun. Suddenly pigeons flocked to the ledges of the municipal edifice. Men such as his brother had once been were already sweeping last night's offal from the steps of palaces. In the doorway where Salvador sometimes used to meet Herlinda, two prostitutes were quarrelling. A few sailors lounged around the plinth, only one with his cap on. They eyed him like crows, ready to challenge him, since he was, for all they could tell, alone. This train of thought reminded him that the alarm gun would sound any moment now; it was surprising they had not yet discovered the dead guard and prisoners. But three *mulata* housewives were walking side by side around the bell tower, their dark hair shinily wet. Seven years since he had seen a woman! Were trouble on its way, the head would surely save him. So he stood leering at the women, who hastened on; he had forgotten that the uniform could scarcely compensate for his face, which was more unshaven than any beggar's, nor for the seven years of filth on his body. How could he remember? He had freed himself from time, abandoning the gloomy years to molder in those locked vaults while he, transplanted into a lovely tale, could play with beauties and treasures, steered through ever purer adventures by the head, his general and prophet.

Then he spied a squad of infantry filing up from the beach, and his heart sank. He seemed to see again the gory throats and bulging eyes of his late comrades. If he somehow escaped hanging, burning or decapitation, they would send him to sort stones in the mines. The sack at his belt buzzed as if a wasp nest were in it. As rapidly as discretion allowed, he turned a corner, then ducked into a palm thicket where he and Salvador used to conceal themselves.

What now? asked the head.

We need to fly away!

They're nothing to us, brother. Have you considered your future?

I'd like to be rich, said Agustín.

The infantrymen were level with them now, but they seemed unable to see or hear anything. Trying to be brave and live up to the head's expectations, Agustín treated his enemies as if they did not exist, and continued the conversation, saying: Can you get me a mountain of silver?

Would you rather have that, or a jade palace?

Which would you advise?

Now the infantrymen were all past, and the head, pleased to have been asked, chuckled: Both.

At once his mind's harbor was overwhelmed by chained galleons of treasure-dreams, so that he grew weak and nauseous with silver-sickness, and said: Brother, I'll trust in you for the best. There's an Amazon—

Who told you about that?

Rodrigo, one of those who you killed.

Oh, I know him. Just now he's at Satan's right hand.

What about you, brother?

You'd wish to marry her, I suppose? You know that Amazons have but one breast.

I don't care about that.

All right, then. Her name is María Platina. You'll court her, and punish her enemies. She'll marry you. And when you're ready, brother, when you're tired of everything, we'll go under the earth.

What if I'm never ready?

That's as Christ disposes, replied the pious head.

So the head whirled him west and west, which is the red direction, and hence the realm of women; long before the alarm gun ever sounded, he found himself passing from one country to the next, like a white-clad blind musician creeping along with his hand on his colleague's shoulder; and the brothers flew through sunset, night, and a morning as moist and hot as a new tortilla; then after traversing a day as red as blood and a night as pink as coral, they arrived at Ziñogava Island, where silvery jungle hills rise up in the rain, and every ill can be healed.

Now what? the head demanded.

Truth to tell, Agustín had grown happier the farther away from prison they travelled; but once they alighted he felt no better off than before. For one thing, he feared his brother, or at least worried that his brother might get angry at him over something, and then bite him. The new country was pretty enough—nearly as lovely as Veracruz's trees of white flowers and trees of red berries—but somehow he nearly felt himself to be once again within the long shade of prison walls, and he could almost smell the foul water of the latrine-hole.— Impatiently the head nibbled at his wrist, and he said: Shall we take her by force?

No. Do exactly as I say.

But if she—

Thanks to God, brother, she is as good as ours.

Again it was night. Ready to pounce on his happiness, Agustín ascended a wide road, toward the distant glowing of the jade palace, with a cool sea breeze ever at his back; and the head flew before him, lighting the way with its blood-red eyes. They came to a river, and the head made him wash himself. With its teeth it trimmed his hair and beard. Once more he put on the prison sentry's clothes, and the head shrank itself down into a golden pendant of ghastly design, on a copper chain for him to wear around his neck.

So they arrived at the palace. Just as the windblown sands seek ever to smother the streets of Veracruz, so an unnamable tainted emotion began to sweep over Agustín; the grandeur he saw, instead of inciting him, confused him; he stared down at his feet.— Hurry forward! hissed the head. Eyes up, chest out!— So in they came.

Here stood Amazons yet more numerous than the vultures in the sandy streets of Veracruz. For instance, they met Laura, Lidia, Lucrecia, Luísa, Magdalena and Margarita; and all of them tall, handsome and one-breasted. Now, what the head actually understood and foresaw I who merely tell this tale have never been able to make out; but it is certain that Agustín felt more lonely and inferior before these lovely women than he had even before the tribunal of worthies who condemned his brother; perhaps they were too silvery for him; if he only could have seen the sweet face of his brother's concubine Herlinda I am sure he would have pricked up his courage; as it was, he felt numb enough to face the thing out, and unwilling to go against the flying head—which, after all, had brought him to the place he wished to go. Somehow the head must have dazzled the Amazons; for what had Agustín with which to impress them? He had fallen out of the habit of looking into people's eyes. Since his cellmates used to take him from behind, he never had to stare into their gaunt yellow faces when he was making them happy. When the Amazons inspected him he prepared for the worst.

Make yourself happy, whispered the head.

But, brother, I don't feel so.

Put on a good face!— And the head murmured into his ear three boisterous jokes, which he deployed to best advantage, so that the Amazons laughed and began to love him.

The Queen of Ziñogava now entered the hall, wearing an ankle-length sleeveless robe of silver and gold, and at once the day grew as bright as the scrutiny of our merciful Church. She was young, slender and high-breasted—but, as usual, one breast was missing. Her golden hair was roached high above her forehead; then it spilled down her neck. Her eyeballs could have been green stones. Her eyebrows and eyelashes were silver, and her lips were garnet-red. Her coral-pink arms were perfectly smooth. Her hands were graceful, her fingers long, with their nails, of course, painted in that mineral-green shade called amazonite. Agustín felt no desire, but told himself that he did. For a fact, she was nearly as beautiful as our Lady the Virgin Santa María.

She is ours, whispered the head, smiling a little sadly.

What is that pendant you have on? asked the Queen.

Slipping the chain over his head, the young man bowed, and presented her with the toy.

How very real it is! she laughed. And are those rubies in its eyes?

Yes, Majesty.

She closed her eyes as if in pain (really she was thinking of something), and the tendons stood out on her long pink neck. Since he felt like a very little boy, he could not help but wonder how it all might turn out.

She presented him with a decorated box of blue crystal, filled with round beads of pure silver. What was he supposed to do with it? He bowed to the floor and was dismissed. Creeping into the jungle, he ascended a fig tree, gorged himself and slept in the crotch, while Salvador's head hovered faithfully until dawn, keeping watch for snakes and jaguars. Meanwhile Agustín dreamed that he was walking down a long prison corridor toward a faraway curtain of rotten hide whose edges let in white light. It was a dream which had often settled on him of late, and he feared it without knowing why. He awoke in a sweat, and there was the head hanging in the darkness, a hand's breadth away from his face, with its red eyes glowing like flames and its rotten black lips smiling at him.

On the following night he returned as the head commanded him to do, although, truth to tell, he would much rather have gone home to Veracruz if he could have kept his liberty there. When he entered the presence of the Queen she said: Someone stole the pendant you gave me.

What did you do, Majesty?

I had two of my maidservants put to death.

This made him respect her. Certainly God would be well pleased with a lady who thus enforced her rights.

Señor Agustín, what do you carry in the sack at your belt?

My brother's relics, Majesty.

Very loving of you.

The head whispered: Tell them that you are the best knight in the world!— So he did. Then he offered to serve her according to his power, and she clapped her hands for pleasure, because her eastern dominions were currently oppressed by all sorts of monsters. And the Amazons said to him: God has sent you.

The Queen of Ziñogava gave him a mirrorlike sword and chain mail nearly as silky as a woman's hair. Then she called him back to bestow more treasures on him, so that before she was done she had armed him with shield, spear, sword, silver armor and golden crossbow. So he sallied forth, with the aid of God and His Glorious Mother (not to mention the flying head).

7

His battles lay eastward, in the yellow direction. You may be sure that in his path were monsters indeed: namely, the *extra ecclesiam* who dwell outside of Christian grace. Although of course he had never been there, he seemed to recognize certain vistas from his childhood: papayas, almonds, coconut palms, vast spreading mangoes whose tops were in a fire of yellow flowers. Loudly invoking Saint Santiago, as he had seen actors do in battle-pageants, almost forgetting how afraid he used to be in those days, he did exactly as the head instructed him. Had he been alone he would have pondered, worried and planned, so rigorous had been his education; but when one's brother is a flying decapitated head, there is not much to do but throw oneself into each campaign, trusting in magic all the more since Salvador used to be a lucky gambler.

First came the dog with the eagle's face. The flying head worried its throat to pieces; meanwhile Agustín lanced it through the breast. He cut out its jeweled eyes for souvenirs, and for that instant felt pride, but the head sternly told him: Never say that we mean justice, or care for the right. We do not forget; there is nothing to be made whole.

How can that be, brother? We're killing the bad, so aren't we becoming good?

Keep wondering, said the head. That's the first step.

Then there was the three-headed ogre. Vowing to have him dead, and all his minions delivered up unto her who ruled Ziñogava, Agustín rushed upon him with unexampled hatred and courage.— Kill the center head first, said Salvador.— In the end Agustín accounted for two heads, while his brother finished up. The third head was small, high-foreheaded and sad. Agustín picked it up and stared into its eyes. Then he threw it away, at which the flying head sang a cheerful song.

Although they made a great cry and entreated his kindness, he put all the ogre's children to death, male and female, and his joy rose up like smoke to see their suffering. As for the monster's slaves and servitors, Agustín dispatched them back to Ziñogava, enchained in terror by the flying head. Not daring to step right or left from the straightest path, nor even to upraise their eyes, they shuffled into the Queen's presence, bearing her necklaces of gold beads and shells. The Amazons all agreed that he was succeeding even better than the pirate Lorencillo. And the Queen began to desire him.

He halfway expected to meet enemy spirits or even flying heads. What if the earless Indian's ghost were as powerful as his brother? But thanks to Our Lady he never did meet one.

Next to fall were the winged crocodile, the Laughing Bird Lady and the giant whose armor proved less infallible than he had expected.— The head kept saying: Don't hesitate. God will help us.— When the giant first turned an eye on him, Agustín seemed to see once more in the base of the guard-tower at San Juan de Ulúa that long tunnel which seems to penetrate impossibly beyond the diameter of the tower itself, at which he felt weirdly quelled and quenched, as if he were helpless, but at once the head flew round and round his face, buzzing angrily, until he came to his senses and realized that this enemy reckoned for as little as the others. So he slew him, beating in his head with his sword.

Thanks to the flying head, all Agustín's battles taken together were no more frightening than one of the cane games which our horsemen play in honor of Corpus Christi. The Snake Twins proved difficult, but since the head could not be killed, they bit at it as much as they pleased, while Agustín took advantage. So the Snake Twins perished; their clay skeletons quickly turned to dust. Thus the two brothers continued to deal with the wicked and rebellious as they deserved; indeed, Holy Writ has proved that for unlawful villains there never could be any escape. Both brothers enjoyed to see a severed head bite dirt in its dying rage. They exterminated the Bee People; they reduced escaped negroes to reason. Seeing this, even the Devilfish Tribe surrendered. Approaching his mercy, blowing animal-headed whistles and flutes, they knelt to await what would happen; he and the head slew them all, sending back trophies to the Queen of Ziñogava.

There was a certain evildoer named Dzum; he was wider than the cathedral at Veracruz and his flesh was harder than steel. Agustín felt daunted, but the head buzzed round his ear, saying: Remember those Inquisitors who condemned us! and at once rage empowered him into leaping forward like a picador about to thrust the lance over his horse's head and gore the bull again. And even Dzum could not withstand those two brothers. When he fell, Agustín kicked his teeth in, wondering whether this might be happiness.— Back in Veracruz, when Señora Marín was still able to walk, she and her husband used to cudgel Herlinda and Salvador for their own good, sometimes kicking their heads a few times, and if they caught Agustín miserably eavesdropping they would command him to come in, which of course he was not required to do, not being their slave; but for Salvador's sake he always marched stonily in, bowing his head and never crying out when they began to beat his head, which in truth they did but moderately, since he had barely entered the years of reason; and this proved to be a valuable education for the boy, who as he grew found ever less pity within himself. This memory increased the zeal with which he finished off the giant. Suddenly he remembered his brother's execution, and sobbed. By then the head was out of sight, swooping about its business, most likely devouring birds and insects, for it sometimes grew so thirsty that even a battle wasn't enough. Agustín gave thanks that it had not observed his tears. By the time it returned, he had recovered himself, and was cutting away Dzum's leather armor in hope of discovering something precious.

There remained the Poison King, whose touch was death.— That's nothing! crowed the head. Have you forgotten the night when you were weeping for hunger, and I burgled the glovers' guild?

Yes, brother. A pretty loaf of bread you got me—

And meat. Don't you remember that?

I remember that bread—

And I got myself Herlinda. She loves money far more than you do.

She's still alive?

Never mind.

And now I'll have María Platina for my wife.

Yes you will, brother. Perhaps then you'll begin to grow good.

Thus conversing, they slew the Poison King safely from a distance, Agustín shooting him with arrows while the head hovered dropping stones from its jaws.

These were but a few of Agustín's battles. Although many monsters fought against him with courage, his deeds kept passing as straight and useless as do the sentries through the endless colonnade of San Juan de Ulúa, the head weaving noble treacheries for him, as industrious as a skilled clothmaker at eight reales a day. Thus they felled all those miscreants, or *Turks* as they are often called in New Spain. I consider our two heroes nearly the equal of those great lords in New Spain who find time to go a-hawking.

When all the evildoers were dead, the two brothers flew home to Ziñogava, and María Platina gazed at him as if he were taller than Seville's highest churchtower.

I am yours more than mine, she whispered.

Reader, here is the story's happiest turn—that by virtue of marrying her, he instantly led her and her entire realm to the True Faith.

8

It was a very fine wedding, with musicians, singers and dancers, and a thousand Amazons looking on; Agustín taught them how to dance the Jarocho fandango. The head flew in, gripping a hogshead of Andalusian wine. Agustín prayed aloud for the perpetual glory and security of Ziñogava. As soon as he had been crowned, he enslaved all the Amazons, and under pain of death set them to working the silver mines.

She was very rich of person; even her single breast was as high-silvered as Mexican pesos. No one could deny her purity of blood. He took her maidenhead, together with all that is referred to in that measure and demarcation. At once she lost her powers. She was very learned, and sometimes composed chamber music in the musical notation which is aped by certain slave brands. She was meant to be his earthly bliss. He ruled her like some cunning pork-farmer who buys up all the grain for his pigs, so that the townspeople go hungry.

For him, the joy, so he had supposed, was to be witnessing the sunlight on the buttocks of María Platina, Queen of Ziñogava. For her, it was to continue supposing his soul to be as white-coraled as the Island of Sacrifices. And indeed, he sought sincerely to inhabit goodness, like an Aztec warrior crawling inside his captive's flayed skin.

But once he had possessed her, he felt like an unwanted child sucking from a sour-breasted nurse, and of course he always hated to be touched. Every night he dreamed most weirdly or sorrowfully. Sometimes he struggled to breathe. Bitterness rose up out of him in bad vapor from his heart, and he wondered why he could not get his happiness even when María Platina remained as pliable as a slave of the correct blood. Perhaps he would rather have had his brother's former *novia* Herlinda. But wasn't he supposed to love life here in Ziñogava? What should he say to anyone? All he had wished for was to rule a kingdom; but the misery haunted him like the mosquitoes of Veracruz; he could not decide whether he had become foul, as his co-ruler said, or whether the judges had spoken true in asserting that he had always been filthy and malicious, perhaps on account of the color of his skin—or might it be that he needed but to pursue one thing of which he had not yet conceived, a thing perhaps even easy to get, and then he would be happy?

He caused a special fortress to be built after the fashion of San Juan de Ulúa, and here raised a tower where his silver ingots were locked away; to this stronghold he alone kept the key, although his wife looked surprised and sad, as if she were seeking something to say to him. Upon pain of death he required the architect to copy everything which could be remembered about the prison-island, right down to the low outer parapet with its iron ship-rings within each of which two people could have embraced. Once the place was constructed and dedicated, he never went there.

Brother, he said, I'm feeling almost murderous.

Yes, brother. Then shall we go forever under the earth?

No, not yet.

Then go to your wife. And when you have a moment, get that servant to fetch me another bowl of fresh dog's blood.

His wife said: I am struggling to understand you.

She said: I shall not be rid of this feeling until I regain what you have taken from me.

Presently she said: I beg you now to let me go my own way and entrust me to God.

Divorce is a sin, replied Agustín, seeing his angry face reflected in each of her silver tears.

At first his rage was so often soothed by the gentle shining of silver.

His Empress, who meant only to please him, gave him everything, but still he could not contain his rage, because he had lost the ability to be happy. Her gentle entreaties made as much headway against his heart as did the sea against the white-flecked black walls of Baluarte de Santiago. Now that they had been reduced to reason, the Amazons crept around below the palace on their allotted labors, in proof of that canticle in Isaiah, *they are dead; they will not live; they are shades; they will not arise—* which did please him in a way, of course, because thus ought all such stories to end. The way that silver can be at times both warm and cold, infinitely indefinable, ought to have contented him more than it did, but his sufferings had been, as would now be his excuses, too painful, too deep. Although he reminded himself that he had never been happier than this, he had not been sadder, either. He ruled his wife of silver, although she might not have been a human being; beneath their bed he also kept a great sack of silver plate, in case he should suddenly decamp. Why shouldn't he have been satisfied? In fact the more readily she obeyed him the worse he hated her, especially when she tried to caress him. (Of course she could not resist his punishments, for here in New Spain the woman remains always a legal dependent.) Woe to her silver belly, lovelier than the moon; woe to her bewildered silver eyes! If she were only an enemy, like one of those trolls and ogres he had killed! Then he would have known what to do. Thus he began to beat her. The servants learned to withdraw when they heard certain sounds. So came the morning when, peering back once more into the great sunny bedchamber, he saw her lying there with her hands outstretched, her eyes squinted shut and her mouth screaming darkness. A thick stone cap weighed down her forehead.

Brother, you're not yet good, sighed the flying head.

Agustín cared nothing for that. Everywhere in the world he would be famous.

9

Perhaps he had been a trifle cruel. But he made up for this by undoing all their unchristian customs; for instance, he forbade the Amazons to lie together anymore, under pain of death, and required them to marry with men, whom he and the head provided them, flying here and there to

360 | LAST STORIES AND OTHER STORIES

bring them lords and masters of his choosing—brigands, villains, pirates, soldiers and murderers all; for those were the fellows he knew. So the Amazons lost their virginity forever. He made them slaves to their children as well as to their husbands; thus they became what women should be. And he also made it prohibited for them to mutilate their breasts as they had done before. Hearing this, many of them wept for the first time; but Agustín showed no pity.

Remembering Bernardo's story, he had cut off and embalmed his wife's right arm, in case it might point him in the direction where he ought to go, but even though his craftsmen impaled it on a pivot in a red-lined crystal box, it never moved.

Well, brother, what did you truly expect? laughed the head. Were you good to her? Did she love you as I do?

Agustín withdrew into his palace and looked out over the sea. It was getting dark. From his deepest mines he heard the Amazons chanting feebly: *Let us die then; let us die.* The head, its eyes sunken as low, wide and deep as the arches of San Juan de Ulúa, demanded his silence. It said: You rule alone now, brother.

But you rule with me, brother! We're two kings in Ziñogava.

Then the head flew up and kissed him with its bloody lips. Agustín had spoken truly, for how long would his reign have endured without that head, the cunningest killer in all the world?

Knowing what the head desired, he said: Brother, teach me to become good.

Then bring in priests.

Like the one you killed, brother? Can you make his head fly as busily as yours?

Not him. He's too good for us. But import priests of our stripe, who can chant the Ave Maria and teach the Seven Mortal Sins.

We can teach those ourselves, brother!

And a curate, to be the keeper of their baptismal book . . .

Where did you learn all that?

Oh, they instructed me before they cut off my head, so that I would come to understanding. That's what we need to do here, as virtuous kings.

As you like. Ziñogava is ours together.

And so they ruled for seven more years, our visible king and his familiar, and perhaps no government in the world was ever more feared and hated than theirs. Agustín was homesick for the cathedral of Veracruz, and for the peanuts Herlinda used to feed into his mouth, and even for the mosquitoes in the street-puddles. But what was he supposed to do? He and the head had long since buried María Platina in secret; their subjects were not so reckless as to mention her.

The two kings promoted justice sincerely, and they both agreed that there was nothing as delightful as beheading a young woman, although late at night in their palace they sometimes enjoyed stabbing a child in her sexual organs.

Perhaps he should have offered up the head on the altar of God. But then he would have been alone as if in a prison. He once asked it for book-wisdom, but it did not know any riddles; it grew ashamed and excused itself for being so uneducated. For this he loved it more.

He said: Brother, do you remember when the hurricane hit the peak of Orizaba and the three rivers came raining down? And then the rich men ran away from Veracruz with their families so that they would not drown, and Herlinda let us into that granary so that we could eat all we wanted? And then—

And then, said the head, I began to grow good. And now I've made you a great man.

Brother, at your execution did you see how they pushed me into the front row?

Well, they made me good. I'm as good as they are.

Agustín turned away. By now he dressed only in robes of silver, and the head most often resembled a grimacing, wide-eyed Aztec turquoise mask. Whenever they wondered how to do this or that, they imitated the example of their home, Veracruz. Thus they replicated that familiar post where murderers such as Salvador are put to death, and ever so many naked Indians get whipped into reason, their wrists stretched upward and tied tight against the pillar, their stinking bodies flowering with scarlet wounds. This proved increasingly convenient to the two kings. Remembering how much they used to love such music in their youth, they imported black slaves to play the marimba at festivals. They set a price of six reales for a marriage, and twelve for burial rites. They tithed foreigners ten percent, which helped to soothe the dull grievance Agustín had always felt against them without knowing why. And so whenever they gazed out the palace window, their subjects appeared as docile and diminutive as the Indian slaves creeping round a great corregidor's table.

Well, brother, are you satisfied yet? asked the head.

No, brother. What am I lacking to be happy?

Another wife. Don't you want a two-breasted one?

But ever since they pent me up in prison, I dislike sharing a room with anyone—except you, of course. I think that's why I—

Well, you certainly don't lack for silver! Shall we go back to the wars?

No, brother, I'm tired. I don't know what's the matter with me.

Then ask a priest. Why not that Fray Costa who burned the recreant Amazons last week?

So Agustín went to Fray Costa, and inquired how to become happier. The priest replied: My son, you've already laid up heavenly treasures for yourself. Thanks to you, Ziñogava has become a Christian province of New Spain. Take joy in what you've done; keep on the straight path, and you'll die a good death. Does any sin press on your conscience?

Murder, Father, although it was not I who did it, but my brother—

Remember the words of Cain. *Am I my brother's keeper?* Kneel down before me, now, and say a Paternoster.

Agustín was beginning to get old. His years lay caught somewhere in the rows of half-barrel arches; he could not get them out. What was he supposed to care about? Sometimes he dreamed inconsequentially about the earless Indian. He and the head brought in the Dominicans who control Indian labor at Chalco, and ore flew out of the mines like angels returning to heaven! At night they sometimes heard Amazons whisper-praying to the Goddess of the Dead Women. These miscreants soon learned the significance of a penitent's green taper.

Once the two kings had enough silver, Agustín made his subjects build him a fleet of galleons, which he then loaded with treasure. And he commanded them to set forth for Spain, where he intended to establish himself as a great lord; and for captains he appointed his strictest slave-drivers. And so the ships cast off and departed from the Americas. Once they were out of sight, Agustín threw his wife's hand out the window.

And after this the head carried him all around the world. Together they viewed Huasteca's two secret fountains, the one with the red fish and the other with the black. For a thrill they flew three times around San Juan de Ulúa, and Agustín felt happy to see his old cell from the outside. Then off they went to Peru, just for an instant, after which they dipped quicksilver from the base of that silver mountain in the Blue Range. They visited the magic mountain by which runs a river which can petrify fallen leaves. And they agreed that no place in the world was especially worth seeing.

10

Brother, asked the head, are you ready now to fly to Spain? The King and Queen are anxious to receive you.

Brother, replied Agustín, something stays wrong in my mind, or maybe in my heart.

Your ships arrive tomorrow. You'll be Captain General of New Spain if you play the right cards.

My ships? They're your ships, too.

Only because you love me, which will help you to become good. Brother, will you allow all your treasure to fall into the hands of the King's agents? You'll be poor and ignominious again.

Our treasure's not for them! Please, brother, don't let them get any of it!

Laughing, the head sped across the waves and bit holes in the ships, so that they all sank, and every man with them. When it told Agustín what it had done, he sat down with his head in his hands.

Well, brother, was that wrong? We can be kings in Ziñogava again, and make our slaves dig out just as much and more.

Never.

At the head's behest, they flew back to Ziñogava incognito, just in time to see the public burning of an Indian sorcerer. Juan the Rapist had become Regent. The Amazons were nearly all exterminated, and the province was very highly spoken of.

What do you say? asked the head.

I care not.

For Agustín sickened ever more with that melancholy which had crept over him without his knowing the reason. Perhaps it had something to do with María Platina, for when he thought of her lying sad and naked on their bed, with the marks of his hands around her throat, he nearly longed to quit his errors. So he cast his mirrorlike sword into the sea.

Brother, the head remarked, the trouble is this. Never have you sincerely asked me which deeds are good.

Are you so good, then? Teach me how to be good.

Yes, brother. Well, the thing is, you must have a cause.

A cause for what?

For anything.

Teach me more, brother.

But at this the poor head began to sweat, and flies descended on it.

Brother, he said, I'm becoming lonely.

But the head remained silent.

In the hottest localities of Veracruz, there grows a shrub called *hueloxóchitl*, whose seeds have sometimes availed against Saint Vitus's dance. Salvador sometimes used to suffer from headache, and then Agustín would gather these seeds, and Herlinda would boil and strain a decoction from it. So by night (although no one would have recognized him in his kingly attire) they returned to Veracruz, where on the beach, unchallenged by the cavalry on account of his royal clothes, the younger brother again collected *hueloxóchitl* seeds, boiling them himself, in hopes of curing the head, but it told him: Although I have no tomb for you to pray at, brother, please pray for my soul.

Don't abandon me, brother! I have no one but you!

Then I'll keep you company awhile longer. But since you feel sick, I too have sickened.

What do you need, brother?

I need to drink blood.

And so they withdrew a league or two, and commenced to prey on travellers by night, until the head was restored to the sort of vigor it had. And Agustín, not knowing what to aim for anymore, himself tried drinking blood, but it failed to agree with him. Finally he said: Brother, should I try to be good in your way?

By asking that, you've taken the second step.

Why won't you tell me what to do?

Will you go under the earth with me?

Brother, I've been there! You rescued me—

That's where you became foul.

And you?

I was always good, the head assured him.

11

Well disguised in his silver Ziñogavan cloak, with the head pretending to be a jade effigy bead on the golden necklace he wore, by night he wandered into Veracruz, where in the *zócalo* there was a harp dance about an evil little kiss, a malicious little kiss, and he almost smiled at the sweetness of those dancers in white, the women flashing their long sleeves and foamy dresses like butterflies, but he knew that if one of them were to smile at him he would hate her, and should she lie down with him he would need to murder her. But he could not understand why. From a doorway, an old man in immaculate white gazed at him, spitting carefully onto the sidewalk

Brother, he said, have you done everything you can for me?

Asking that question was the third step.

How many more steps are there?

Only one.

Brother, can you bring back the dead?

That's a trifle, said the head. Shall I fetch your wife?

Oh, no! I couldn't bear to have her look at me—

A little squeamish there, brother. Well, did you have Mother or Father in mind?

Where are they?

Mother's in hell, because the pirates took her chastity. Father's in heaven, because he died saying *Ave Maria*.

Have you met them?

They're ashamed of me, the head admitted. But when I sink my teeth into anyone's ear he has to come, like it or not.

If they're ashamed of you, I reject them. It was you who helped me—

Because I love you, brother.

Brother, please bring me that silent Indian we killed.

Do you need all of him or just his head? I prefer it when they're my size.

As you wish, brother.

So the head dived down into hell, and soon rushed back up with the grinning cranium of Agustín's Indian cellmate who had never done him either good or harm, and its dome was as lovely as the slices of fan coral and fossilized shell fitted together at San Juan de Ulúa, while its eyesockets were as prison arches.

Agustín said: I forgive you for not defending me, because you didn't know me and we were two against many. And I beg your pardon for taking your life.

The Indian's skull, of course, said nothing, which entertained the flying head.

12

But now the head began to sicken again, and this time it wept.— Brother, it said, I can't keep you company much longer, unless you come down to hell with me. You asked if I've done everything I can for you. It's for you to answer that question.

Brother, tell me once and for all how I can become good.

Whom would you follow, if not me?

Brother, should I follow you?

Would you like to fly as I do?

That won't make me happy, I fear. Please, brother, tell me what to do. I'm unwise, and don't know my own happiness.

So at last the head brought him down into hell, where they were greeted by demons dressed in French livery in imitation of the pirate Lorencillo. The head flew before him down that same long weird corridor he sometimes used to dream of, with the curtain of rotten hide at the end and white light all around the edges. It lifted the curtain in its teeth, and Agustín saw green water in which fire-colored sharks swam round and round. Utterly at sea, with no way forward but to follow the head, he descended steep steps from the squat stone island straight down to the water, where he gripped the head against his chest, and was flown to another polyhedral island of this prison or palace; jutting from an embrasure were two corroded fangs of iron which must have once formed part of a grate or something to hold a cannon; then the fangs moved; the narrow windows above them winked, and Agustín realized that he was gazing at Satan's face, which was not entirely unlike the coarse lava-flesh of a decapitated Olmec statue.

The mouth opened. The flying head, which had led him through so many of his days, darted tenderly to Agustín and kissed him on the lips, evidently for the last time.— Goodbye, brother, it said.— Before he could answer, it rushed into the Devil's maw; and Agustín, who could never have imagined turning away from the head which had been so kind to him, was alone again, for the mouth had closed.

My son, said Satan then, it's high time you've come home to me. Thanks to your brother, you're becoming better by the moment, and soon you'll be ready to receive magic powers.

Should I promise you my soul?

You're already mine.

Please, Lord, I'm not happy yet. And now my brother has gone—

Perhaps you need to ask others for help.

Lord, can you help me?

Of course. Go over there now, and all my best love to you.

So Agustín crossed water again, treading the wreckage of Cortés's old drawbridge, whose wood was partially broken off and whose fat hinges were the color of beetle shell. Confused by the mélange of shells, fanning corals and bricks above the narrow arches, he now descended within a round tower, grieving anew for his brother; and he completed another flight of stairs, remembering that there had been a silver key on a chain around María Platina's neck about which he had never asked her; perhaps it would have saved him; and he completed another circuit down into the purple-red light of hell and entered a blind chamber in which, standing at this wall, naked, with her back to him and her brown hair falling all the way to her splendid buttocks, was the most beautiful young woman he had ever seen. She was chalking a picture of a ship on the wall. Now she turned and smiled at him, saying: Do you know who I am?

Rodrigo used to say—

He's been broiling nicely ever since your brother did for him. Yes, I'm the Mulata de Córdoba, and all this time have been waiting on purpose to rescue you.

Just as far-off white roofs glow orange and red when the birds of Veracruz fly loud and crazy at the afternoon's end, so the distant whorls of his heart began to illuminate themselves with hope.

Agustín asked her: How can I become happy? What should I wish for? I'm afraid of becoming more evil than I already am.

Good or evil has no bearing on happiness, said La Mulata. If happiness is all you want, I believe I can help you.

And gratefully he accepted.

She finished drawing her ship of chalk, then offered him her hand. They embarked in a twinkling, two-dimensionally, rushing between walls and stones like cockroaches, with clay skulls in their wake as they sailed through the night-black dirt, until they came back out into the light of Veracruz, sailing through rows of young banana trees with the hands of yellow fruit already reaching down, and double-tailed fishes leaping, and ghosts all around them like nosing, trotting dogs.

La Mulata transformed herself into his dead brother's sweetheart Herlinda, who was as black and feline as a jaguar and whom alone of all women he loved. Oh, how happy he was! And they dwelled in a white house with a tiny palm in the courtyard, just downwind from the slaughterhouse, living in easy concubinage, with a protective mist around their doings so that the Inquisitors could not arrest them.

At times he feared that he might come to hate her as much as he had María Platina, but whenever he began to feel resentment she would speak to him of Salvador, and how noble he had been. So Agustín for a time remained as bright-eyed and bold as a crow. Perhaps he could purify himself. The question of who La Mulata actually was, whether she ought to be rated true or false, sometimes distressed his understanding, but then he would remind himself that he had never comprehended his brother, either. They lived together through lovely mornings of orange juice and prickly pear juice, with many vultures to keep them company on the sandy streets. They shared a pillow when the moon took on a tarnished gold like the handguard of an old soldier's saber, and tall-masted ships went out sailing hard past San Juan de Ulúa, avid for the ebbing tide. They ate peanuts together from a blue dish which resembled a two-headed dove. For a marriage portion their father below gave them gold bars like glittering greenish-yellow cigarillos, golden necklace-beads with eagle heads and serpent heads, and turtleheaded golden beads; so presently Agustín nearly began to believe in happiness's staying power. Everyone in Veracruz repelled him; they were all dwellers in the dark and mold of prison; but he persevered, striving not to be offended by life, and whenever they promenaded on the beach the cavalry made way for them. La Mulata would always smile and take Agustín's hand when he gazed across the harbor at San Juan de Ulúa. Although he had told her never to touch him without permission, this one lapse he tolerated. Come the trade fairs, when the merchants set up their tents in the sand and offered leather, sugar, silver and hardtack, La Mulata liked to look, for people and personalities were her meat, whereas Agustín, who owned more riches than he could digest, stood glaring and fanning himself. He would gladly have built a sugar concern, or slain more monsters for the True Faith; he would fulfill himself; that was as likely as getting ship-wrecked in a north wind.

At home they kept a silver mirror, but he avoided looking into it, for his wooden face saddened him. At least his wife never got impatient with him. (How could she? They had a bargain.) Soon she had given him four children, who all feared his temper, and they even had a carriage and slaves.

A Spaniard in a wide lace collar held two naked Indian children upside down by their ankles, one child in each hand, so that his dogs could rip them to death, and more golden beads fell out of their intestines; then the cathedral bells called everyone to Mass. A cotton plantation fell into Agustín's hands, after which he set some negroes to curing tobacco. He arranged to have frequent carnal access to the black proprietress of a certain shop which sold bread and wine. So you can see that he had a good life, but he could never imagine his future; and presently, out of boredom, he began to quarrel with La Mulata. One night, seeking to entertain her, he recited the three boisterous jokes which the flying head had taught him in Ziñogava, but she said: Everybody in hell has heard those.— Insulted, he struck her.

At once he entered into the time when our Lord will thresh out the grain. La Mulata, the slaves and the children all disappeared, in separate stink-puffs, and there he was, back in the prison of hell, with that gigantic wall-face grinning and winking like the parish priest who rapes his female penitents.— You see, said Satan, happiness was never what you wanted. Your brother gave it to you in Ziñogava, and you destroyed it. I restored it to you to prove that it's no good to you. What next?

Lord, I never knew what to wish for.

Speak up now.

Lord, may it please you, I'd like to do evil with my brother, until we're punished.

A noble plan, said the Devil. Now that it's too late, I'll tell you what you should have asked for.

Yes, Lord?

Grief.

The mirrorlike sword of Ziñogava rushed back into his hand. Back out of the great mouth flew the grinning head, which seemed perhaps more desiccated or even singed than before, and it said: Congratulations, brother. Now we can both be good.

Brother, asked Agustín, am I alive or dead?

Don't think too much. Now let's go pay back our old friends!

13

Although Doctor de los Ríos was served by proficient torturers, neither Church nor Crown had ever thought fit to protect him against the visit of a decapitated head, and so he now got to find out whether Paradise is truly as wide and flat as Extremadura, where so many conquistadors hail from.

As for the real Herlinda, by now she had found herself a new *amor,* the lightskinned free mulatto Gaspar de la Cruz, who under pretense of carrying sacks of sugar smuggled French textiles from the port up as far as Xalapa, where he sold them at a respectable rate of return, although too much of his profits went for bribes and fees, in obedience to that fine Mexican custom called *engordar el cochino,* to fatten the pig. Herlinda was tired of being Melchor Marín's slave, for his breath stank, his wife was incontinent, and he never left her alone at night. Her very compliance bore sure relevance to his retreat from that half-promise, uttered so long ago, of conditional manumission for her, someday, if she continued to be his good girl. Now that she had gotten into the habit, she sometimes serviced the master's friends in exchange for a piece of leather or a fine roast fish. Truth to tell, Salvador González Rodríguez was the only man she had felt much for, but Herlinda, who could not hope to be considered a *fly in milk* for many years longer, faked affection in order to burnish her so-called future; indeed, she branched out to friends of friends, none of whom had yet infected her untreatably. Meanwhile, although Doctor de los Ríos once seemed to enjoy her looks, she had already appeared before him a second time, when he warned her, as she knew all too well, that the punishment of concubinage is to be led through the street on a donkey, with the neighbors jeering and threatening, and the usual rope of criminality around one's neck, and then to be stripped to the waist beneath the official pillar and there, in the stink of malefactors' decapitated heads, to be treated to a hearty hundred lashes. So Gaspar chivalrously proposed to steal the girl from Señor Marín and take her over byroads to Mexico City, where no one would know them if they changed their names. But first he wanted to get a good lot of Lyonnaise cloth, because from what he had heard they could make double or triple once they reached the capital. He was a dashing sort, who liked to wear a mushroom-shaped cap in imitation of the conquistadors. Herlinda, who had the most to lose, pointed out that it was a long way to go; for all they knew, they might be called upon to fatten dozens of pigs, and she had no ambition to be poor. (In fact, although she trusted her paramour well enough, in her girdle she had hidden five silver pesos to pay off a *padrino* who might gain pardon from her master if she chose to come back, because who can predict which surprises may come flying out of the night air?) Gaspar told her to leave it all to him. Perhaps she shouldn't have listened, but in truth she had to do so much for the Maríns that it felt very nice to be taken care of for once. Moreover, her children had recently been sold, which was convenient.

While they perfected their plans, something came flying through the evening sky. At first she thought it was a bat. Then it drew closer. Her face turned as yellow as a penitent's frock. Before it killed her, it sang:

Sad is my heart, *negrita;*
I know not why—
sad for an illusion,
sad for what I dreamed.

Agustín said to himself: Salvador is evil, and I am his knight who is unclean in his heart.— And this brought him a kind of comfort, to know where the truth lay. With his Amazonian sword he swiped off Gaspar's head. Then the two kings went rushing through the city like a plague-breeze, lopping heads and splitting guts all night.

What about the witnesses who had served the authorities against the two brothers? First Herlinda's master and mistress, and then the inn-keeper Jaime Esposito (whose greatest pride was that he was the bastard descendant of Don Diego Fernández de Córdova), all became medicine for the thirsty head. Of these, Señor Marín perished the most abjectly. Agustín remembered watching him beat Salvador, in the days when Sal-vador was more than a head; Agustín would begin to pray silently as soon as his brother, having received the command, knelt down on the floor and clasped his hands while the master cudgeled his skull; and Her-linda, her earbobs sparkling crazily, would be kneeling beside him, gri-macing and weeping, praying for mercy on her lover's account, until she irritated the master sufficiently to receive a whack or two on the fore-head.

Neyda Duarte, who had testified against Herlinda, was already dead from the white sickness, so the two brothers could not punish her, at least not in this world. Infuriated, the head went rushing over the city, breathing out hell-breath, and by dawn people had begun to die of yellow fever. The next day Agustín began to vomit. The head flew sweetly round and round his face, to keep the flies off. When he expired, the head sank back down underground. Demons marched up like a file of Jaguar Sol-diers, and seized them both to be burned forever. And if you ever come to Veracruz, put your ear to the grass outside the irregular septagonal parapet of the Baluarte de Santiago, and among the other screams coming up from hell (which is not far underground), you may hear Agustín weeping endlessly over his failure to live, while the head goes on laughing.

14

I myself have never seen a ghost, let alone a flying head, so I cannot swear to you that every detail of this story is true. But when I visited San Juan de Ulúa, which the Indians used to call *Chalchiuhcuecan*, a guard with the crossed anchors of the Navy on his cap assured me: If you come here at night expecting to see a ghost, you definitely will.— He himself once saw a man in a raincoat supposedly standing guard, but all the guards were inside, so what could that have been but a ghost? On another occasion he was pissing and saw a dark faceless figure glide by. And so there you have it, straight from a uniformed member of the Armada de Mexico.

V

THE WHITE-ARMED LADY

For the white-armed lady he waited long.

"Volundarkvitha," *ca.* 9th cent.

1

Inside the tiny white house, he sat at the head of the table, listening to the seagulls, his stare fettered from below by the white lace tablecloth, whose flower-whorled spiderweb knew how to trap his eyes, and occluded by the low-hanging lamp, whose candle never guttered within that scalloped breast of glass. Unblinkingly he peered through the windows curtained with white lace, and across the narrow lane at the other white houses. Again it began to rain. Silver drops clung to the windows.

He could hear somebody cutting wood.

In nearly every window of each of the other white houses he could see a potted plant beneath the white curtains. All of the pots were white. One window presented a narrow-necked green vase and a green watering can. He liked that window the best without knowing why.

Up the street came a man, who stopped, shoved his hands in the pockets of his heavy coat, and gazed right into the window. The one at the table wondered how deeply he could see, and when he would go away.

The man went away.

There was a white-haired old woman in white, bent over her walking stick, who used to pass by twice each day, first going left, then going right. She never raised her head. He grew fond of her, and then one morning she passed to the left and never returned again.

Closing his eyes, he heard rain splashing on the cobblestones. He looked up. Now the other white houses were going grey; the windy day was fading.

At night the rain prickled and pulsed down on the roofs of those little white houses, spattering loudly on the cobblestones, shining on the windows between the greenish-white curtains; now it sounded like marbles on the roof, and over the table the lamp began to twitch. The trees shone almost day-green in the streetlights; the windows of the other white houses were black. He sat at the table staring.

2

At the center of the tablecloth's lace spiderweb lived the white spider named *Hungry,* who also waited; whenever the man tired and lowered his head, or found himself allured by one of the lovely white links of spider-chain, then, no matter how fiercely he struggled, bit by bit Hungry pulled his gaze inward. To a heartless stranger their contest might have appeared playful, for the man's head spiralled round and round. When Hungry had finally dragged him to the center, so that he must look upon his enemy, the battle was done; and the great spider, which had disguised itself as a many-whorled lace flower, rose up, leaped upon the man's face, and sucked all the life out of his eyes. Hungry was greedy, but not impatient, so it took longer than one might imagine before the last desiccated sinew of hand or foot had been reeled in through the eyesockets of the miserable skeleton that sat there. Even then, Hungry hesitated to go away, for his victim's brain endured within. But against the skull's forehead a magic jewel had been strapped—the gift of the woman called White Arms. Hungry could drink; any flesh he could suck until it liquefied, and retracted into his star-shaped mouth; and he could sting, but he could not bite, and so the jewel and the leather circlet which held it, being grooved into the bone itself, remained impervious to him. Thus after awhile Hungry grew sleepy, returned to the center of the tablecloth, and closed his red eyes. Then, slowly and wearily, stalks of nerve, meat and vein began to grow down from the man's brain, until he was whole again. As soon as he was able, he jerked his head up from the tablecloth. Hungry still slept, and therefore could not keep him. Because his heart regenerated last, the man was spared from his anguish until he sat upright. But even when he could not feel, he remained condemned to think. He thought considerably about Hungry, as one might imagine; and doubtless Hungry thought about him. They were neighbors, like those two women whom every day he saw chatting with a white picket fence between them.

3

A redhaired woman opened the white picket-gate, reached up, dreamily caressed a leaf from the maple at the side of her house, strode into her back garden where he could no longer see her, then presently emerged, lowering her head against the wind as she unlatched her picket-gate. Suddenly she raised her head and peeped into his window, the instant enduring more than long enough for him to read the horror on her face. To her, he was a skeleton hedged with fire. She strode quickly away, down the cobblestoned lane toward the harbor and the seagulls which he could never see. He owned one window at the lefthand edge of his vision, whose curtain's lace flowers and diamonds dulled down the white light. Waiting, sitting, he hoped that in the instant of framing herself there she would look back at him, even in horror. She did not, and never returned home.

Humiliated, he told himself: I hate the others who are not as I.

4

Sitting in the darkness, the hanging lamp now resembling a polished tuber or a skull in chains, he inhaled the ancient smell of the house, although his chest never moved, and he gazed out through the windows into the sloping, streetlit lane called Bergsmauet, whose cobblestones he could see only by day and only through the righthand window, his room leaking darkness through the triangular wounds between curtains; there the greenish light held its own. He studied the faint shining of streetlight and moonlight on the tablecloth. Just inward of the wave-patterned edge ran a zone of doubled columns adorned with berries and connected to each other by many thin cross-lacings; then came the girdle of wheel-flowers beyond which it was not safe to look; when he tired, and his head began to sink, he counted the horizontal stitches between the double columns; there were sixteen, and when he obtained a different number he knew that he was worn out, and then Hungry might get him. Heartsick, he sat among pallid self-assertions of the unlit candles, the lampshade, the well-mated borders of old prints in their dark frames on the wall, and the scaly, glistening anomaly of the one lace curtain which received the most streetlight; he awaited his lady with the white arms.

5

His white-armed lady had departed him at dusk, their shadows large against the pine wall upstairs when they stood kissing. Called away by a spell, she pulled off her black nightdress and stepped into her long blue dress. She promised to return whensoever she could, while for his part he swore to wait for her. Her shadow withdrew from his; and he followed her down the steep narrow stairs, bending his head. She undid her jewel and fastened it around his forehead. She unlocked the door. She was the one with white arms, the woman in the long narrow blue dress. She descended the three slate steps, the point of her fringed cape hanging down her back. He locked the door. He stood by the window watching her stride out of sight. Then he sat down at the table. On the instant of her arrival within the many-toothed gate fashioned by those who hate the light, he found himself fettered. She had been his bride. He awaited her, remembering the time when they used to make a shadow together.

6

Again the chain-hung lamp was shining, for it was day. He sat there, a skeleton at the table in the white house, never denying that his death was of his own making, but wearying of the eternal misery of his loneliness in that narrow white grave. The red gaze of Hungry burned his breast invisibly. White Arms did not come. Casting his heavy eyes upward, he felt newly shocked at the way that his face oozed and snarled in the glass of the antique mirror. Behind the picket fence, the neighbor's maples, still green in defiance of the season, began to sway. Hungry awaited him as patiently as ever a woman wefted her warp. He resisted. His neck could not endure his head's weight much longer. Bitterly he glared around the walls at the faded oval portraits, the life bleached out of those fog-white unsmiling faces. He closed his eyes, then quickly opened them. Already his head was tilting down, and the girdle of wheel-flowers ranged across the world. In terrified defiance he craned his head back up, barely in time, and stared out the window, awaiting his bride of the white arms. Had he been capable of locking his elbows on the table and cradling his chin in his interlocked hands, he could have held out longer. The misery grew up into his chest like cancer.

7

Among other women, whose hair was the color of sunset, of copper, of yellow butter, white butter or honey, or even as orange as egg yolk, White Arms was the rarest, for her hair was as gently white as the winter sun. When they went up the steep stairs, her breath tasted of sweet butter. The one window was on her side of the bed. His side was by the stairs; he gave her the window, because her arm grew utterly *white* where the autumn sun fell on it. By night the pallid extremities of the bed remained barely visible even to a long-accustomed gaze, the weak projection of the windowpanes on the wall no more than patterned deficiencies of the darkness, while some narrowly clotted form stood on the verge of stirring in the mirror's greyish obscurity, beside the black rectangular tombstone of the doorway to the bedroom which would have been their child's. Sometimes there was moonlight to brighten her arms while she lay beside him. Then the moon departed them, and they listened to the rain-wind plucking at the windows.

8

His head could no longer stay upright. He had already passed beyond the tablecloth's wave-patterned edge. Seeking to delay his inevitable progress through the zone of doubled columns by counting the fifteen or seventeen horizontal stitches between them, his glassy gaze nonetheless devolved through the girdle of wheel-flowers; and although he struggled to regain the front windows through which he might even then see White Arms returning to him, although he wished that it were day, for then the dull glare of the hanging lamp stimulated his consciousness by stinging his eyes, his wishes and intentions could not save him from meeting the stitch-bristling lacy white arms of Hungry, which rose up at once to grip his face.

9

Now it was autumn again, or remained so, the sky as faint a blue as the veins in his white-armed lady's neck; and he had cohered once more; even his heart must have taken new root behind his breastbone, for hate and anguish pressed there. This time, he said to himself, I will hold out and hold out. Hungry can do nothing by himself. It is my weakness which empowers him. I will try to starve him.

Closing his eyes, for the first time since she had gone he squeezed away all memories and hopes of the white-armed woman, forgetting her in her long blue narrow dress which the sky sometimes matched, so that he grew as still as those potted flowers which looked out the window at the whipping leaves of autumn, his death a barely perceptible nausea, forgetting her whiteness in her black nightdress when she lay beside him upstairs in that bedroom as rawboarded as a coffin, and her white arms, her white arms, and her white hand sleeping across the breast of that sad black dress so sweet with her smell, and the way that when raindrops struck the dark harbor their compact white ripples rode the waves for a good instant, becoming as immovable as the wall built of clay bones, the silvery sun greying down the white picket fence across the lane even as it yellow-stained the lace curtains, and something struggling to get at him, caressing him like that breeze that springs up before an autumn rain, ruffling the seagulls' feathers; he knew not whether it was Hungry or the woman with the white arms; his determined refusal to remember her resembled some lichened stone disk with a hole bored through it; now he had forgotten even her white arms, considering only Hungry, commanding himself: I must starve Hungry, his stone skull tilting, the zone of doubled columns fleering at him like white riverweeds in the current, his misery withering in his breast, Hungry's red gaze stinging him, and there was someone whom he longed to remember in order to return meaning to his waiting, but he craned his skull up and back until his eyes were clear of even the wave-patterned edge, fixing his mind on Hungry, dying to kill Hungry, his own red eyes closing, his skull creaking forward, the lace tablecloth writhing into a hypnotizing lattice of hooks whose long necks looped and snaked across one another in a fashion no woman could weave; and at last his forehead struck the table.

He opened his eyes. In the center of the tablecloth was nothing but another white whorl, slightly larger than the flowers, eyeless now, and fangless.

Now he could rest while he awaited his white-armed bride.

10

He rose, and it was night. He unlocked the door, but descended only one step. Standing in the chilly rain, he gazed down the slant of grey cobbles at the black harbor. Had it gone dry, he would not have cared. Inhaling the various freshnesses of unseen stormclouds, he descended the second step, looking up and down the street for her, then hesitated, anxious out of habit, as if Hungry could still harm him. His tired gaze began to creep down toward the street, as if he were seeking the footprints of this white-armed woman who had gone so long ago. Going backward, he returned inside and shut the door, refraining from locking it in case she had lost her key. Awaiting her, he would sleep.

So he ascended the three full stairs, then turned the corner landing and the seven steep stairs (his heels projected into space when he climbed them), white autumn light now melting the green banister, because it must have been day; at the top he turned one more perpendicular on the bare pine floor and took the last raw pinewood step to the chamber with the sloping unpainted ceiling of smooth planks and cracked beams where on her side of their bed she lay on her back, rotten and grinning in the rags of her black nightdress, her eyesockets spuriously astonished that within her ribcage nested the spider called *Thirsty*.

WHERE YOUR TREASURE IS

That which is, is far off, and deep, very deep; who can find it out?

Ecclesiastes, 7:24

1

Just as it is not unheard of for a church, of all places, to get haunted, so a pious heart may come to be tenanted by evil sometime after it has been lowered under the turf; but before anyone criticizes the mechanism which makes this possible, please remember that the least pleasant aspect of being dead, its monotonous *too-lateness*, practically demands to be circumvented by souls of the slightest self-respect; for what makes life bearable is our illusion that we can undo the mistakes of our condition, be they the sins we inflict on ourselves or the impoverishments of fate; why shouldn't postmortem aspirations be the same? Now it once happened that when an orphan from Kvitsøy named Astrid Audunsdottir, poor but pious, good-looking and of respectable family, got married off by her uncle, who had thus fulfilled his obligation of guardianship in obedience to the Preacher's writ, *Better is the end of a thing than its beginning,* she exchanged a chilly, hungry existence for miserable terror, her husband being a cruel man who never passed a day without beating her. Of him it was said that he had formerly been moderately openhanded, but before he lost his youth some form of epilepsy overcame him, worsening his character. Like most explanations of the inexplicable, this but described what it pretended to elucidate; nonetheless, it served to close the question, and Loden Gudmundsson did seem better left uninvestigated. His family was comfortably off, and until recently he had kept gathering in wealth; his factors shipped timber from Ryfylke, and he also owned a dry goods store on Breigata Street. Everyone agreed that he had approached Astrid's uncle decently enough; his white beard was as clean and delicate as pipesmoke from the best quality tobacco, and his house, it was said, wore three stained glass windows; so that although no one thought him the most winning sort, at least he could be counted on to provide for the girl. One of the most likeable characteristics of a rich man, unsleeping activity, he certainly showed, even down to demanding the briefest possible engagement, such was his eagerness to enter the nuptial state, and of course Astrid's uncle expressed no objection. Strange to tell, once the marriage had been settled he retired from business, remarking that since he now possessed both money and a wife he would as soon keep to home. At first the neighbors thought they knew why, and shook their heads to learn that even so hardheaded a man, never mind his years, could be enslaved by lust. But when Astrid first came to church in Stavanger, they looked her over, and liked what they saw, for she was not only pretty, but meek. First of all, she spoke only when spoken to, and then in a whisper. Better yet, unlike other rich women, who wore wide white skirts or crisp black skirts as they flitted across the clean wide gravel of Nedre Holmegate, she kept to the patched clothes of a thrifty islander, for which the old people praised her. One might have supposed that it reflected poorly on Loden to let her go around so; on the other hand, all men would live more easily if their own wives came as cheap as Astrid Audunsdottir! Of this Astrid it is told that she remained all her life a wondrous good Christian, turning the other cheek and praying for her tormentors, so that even the minister used to wonder whether she were feebleminded. On Sundays it remained the custom for neighbors to greet each other after worship, commenting on the weather and suchlike important subjects; but Astrid, who seemed to be getting more shy by the month, preferred to sit inside the church with the Bible open on her lap until Loden or his sister, having finished whichever pleasantries they allowed themselves, came to take her away. While awaiting them she invariably pored over a particular verse, the one in which Jesus says: *To what shall I compare the kingdom of God? It is like leaven which a woman took and hid in three measures of flour, till it was all leavened.* What so simple a creature could see in that nobody knew, when the minister himself could barely explain it. Her head was always bowed, in signification of her condition; and as bad as it was to be Loden's chattel from dawn to dusk, her nights were worse; for once the servants had gone to bed, he became monstrous. The best recourse was to crouch utterly still and quiet on the stairs, for if all went well he might lie brooding upon their bed, with his eyes half closed and a sour smile on his face.

But should anything remind him of her, he would darken with rage. Summoning her with obscenities, he would slap her face, pull out her hair, scratch her breasts with his long fingernails, and that was just the beginning. On a winter night as black as an iron stove he knocked out two of her teeth. By the time she had lived with him for three years, the rest had gone the same way, and her remaining patches of hair were grey. Clasping her bluish-grey hands over her Bible, she bowed her bony head, praying for him, for his sister Magnhild, and for her faraway uncle's family. Now she began to be thought of as a woman with a secret—a secret which they all knew. The neighbors saw it all that summer afternoon Loden threw a brick into her face when she came home carrying water from the well. In spite of his kicks she managed to get to her feet, and turned straightaway back to the well, since the water had been spilled. That evening the minister paid them a call, but how it turned out nobody learned, except that he returned silent and shamed. For a fact, Astrid never complained. Sometimes she even smiled a little, when a breeze brought the clean smell of ocean which reminded her of Kvitsøy. Loan her a measure of flour and she'd return you double; so people said, although how could they know, since Astrid scarcely went out enough to borrow anything, and anyhow which supplies didn't Loden keep at his store? They all felt sorry for her, without a doubt. In her fourth year she became a gaunt and crooked old cripple; her fifth was her last. People said the shroud was stained around her head, but Magnhild, who never liked her, had done such a thorough job of sewing her in that nothing was certain; and for a fact, it was best not to cross that terrible family. Whatever Loden had held against her nobody knew; perhaps it was merely the revenge of age upon youth; for, having outlived her, he quickly declined, and before Easter they dug him down beside her. At any rate, no one had any doubt of heaven for Astrid Audunsdottir, at least so long as they recollected her (and you very well know that remembrances of compliant victims are inconvenient). Loden endured more substantially in their thoughts, having left tangible property which an intelligent man might get his hands on, for example by marrying Magnhild, sourpuss though she was; moreover, Loden had been by every measure more remarkable than his wife, who in the neighbors' anecdotes had always been old; whereas him they liked to describe as being more watchful than the verger who keeps poor men awake at church—a truthful summation, whose horror was softened by the rains of time, until he became merely comic; and what do the living like to quaff more than humor, when they lack the means to buy brandy? Eventually they even grew proud of him. And so, turning away their minds from the friendless woman in the ground, the residents of Stavanger sought to live as best they could, and no one was there on that muffled clammy Sunday morning, the white sky treasuring up rain, orange leaves blowing down from the trees in the center of the square, so that moment by moment their branches grew more like black bones; and in the churchyard, a counterpart breeze blew underground, in the neighborhood of the Gudmundsson family's graves, the soil gelatinously quaking beneath dead leaves; and by afternoon the trees in the square appeared to grow out of an island of orange and yellow leaves upon that sea of grey cobblestones, which rippled whenever the churchyard did, although far less perceptibly; but by then the autumn rain was roaring and the wind was singing, which was why all the living who could manage it sat indoors watching the fingers of water on their windows vanish behind coffee-steam and soup-steam while they prayed and dreamed; as for Astrid, her black fingers now spread out against the sky, grubbing at the orange leaves until she had awakened sufficiently to clear them away from her face. And if you find her reemergence strange, I would say to you that she befitted that autumn, which tinctured everything in Stavanger just then, even in the Vågen, where each sloop's tawny sail resembled yellow leaves dropping from a tall and narrow tree.

2

So she came out, and looked at herself, and thought on the days of her girlhood when she had been yellow, pink and white like the flower called *guldå*. Her mother's hair had also been yellow, they said, but Astrid could not remember her. Indeed, how much do the dead understand of anything? Ask the Preacher, and he will tell you that this matter also is hidden. Between Astrid Audunsdottir and the living past lay a single spider-strand glittering over wet moss.

3

Magnhild's hair had darkened when she bore children and lightened again when she grew old, until it became as blonde as when she was a child. She was proud of her hair until Astrid came. How she had hated Astrid for her shining yellow hair! Now Astrid was dead, as were all Magnhild's children. She lived alone with one servant in her dead brother's house, whose routine continued as in his time, except that the inmates burned candles more freely nowadays; Loden had never permitted anyone but himself to expend tallow.

Like most of us who have committed cruelties, Magnhild got through life by not thinking about them. On the occasions when that shield slipped aside, she could thrust out with sharp reasons and justifications; and when those failed, she simply needed to envision Astrid before her, in order to be renewed in her hatred. Just as a man who hates dogs might correctly anathematize their greed, their odor when wet, and their enthusiasm for rolling in filth, without yet explaining, even to himself, why he must hurt them at any chance, so did Magnhild cherish up her reasons as blackly distinct as the hymn numbers posted on the cathedral's wooden board, unlike Loden, who had never stooped to explanations. In brief, she despised Astrid because she loved her brother; and how he could be loveable to her and why he hated Astrid from the instant she belonged to him are two more of the Preacher's far-off and deep things.

Magnhild was in some respects an excellent woman. Her greatest pleasure lay in hearing the choir's melodies echoing and blending until they seemed to butter the cold stone pillars of the church. On that evening, which Marianne had off, Magnhild felt ill and cold, so she went to bed early, listening to the rain and that freshening autumnal wind. The beauty and comfort of the hymns she had sung in her life nourished her as she lay there reading her Bible, and presently she slept. But just before she began to dream, she made the error of remembering a certain pretty girl of long ago, who once slipped into the Domkirke to hear her neighbors at choir practice; in those days Magnhild had had a fine contralto voice, whereas this pretty Anne Kristin, the one with the long yellow hair, could not sing, and married far away, so that Magnhild had forgotten her for many a year; and one cannot blame her for missing this

innocuous girl's susceptibility to being employed as a disguised emanation of Astrid, whom it was best never to think about at bedtime.

On that evening Magnhild was dreaming of a group of hooded women
in long dresses carrying water from the well. In this well lay something
poisonous, and these women, whoever they were, were coming to make
her drink of it. She woke up with her heart rattling in her dry old chest.

The next dream proved worse; yes, here lies the tale of a woman who
lives overlooking a graveyard and one dark night hears something
scratching against her window; when she parts the curtains she finds
herself looking into a hateful whitish-yellow face framed in long hair, and
before she can even scream, the thing has smashed out the glass with a
single furious blow of its skull; then its bony fingers reach through, gripping the ledge fast; it pulls up its shoulderblades, locks its skinny arms;
and in another rush it is through and biting her to death.

Magnhild woke up screaming. She lit a candle, rose and went to the
head of the stairs. Something was ascending toward her; perhaps it had
an osprey's white neck and dark breast. No, its breasts were as pallid as
the autumn cabbages which they sell in the street near the cathedral. As
for hair, there seemed to be none. It opened out long black rakes of fingers. It said: Magnhild, give me your hair, just for awhile. Magnhild, give
me your hair.

With her mouth wide open, the old lady backed away, all the way into
the wall, believing that she whispered the verse *I never knew you; depart
from me, you evildoers*, when in fact her tongue would not move. Gruesomely smiling (when it comes to ghosts, any expression is worse than
none), the specter drew near to her, so that all her nightmares of her life
grew as bright as the reflections of ships in the cold harbor. Its stench
took root in her nostrils. She closed her eyes. But not seeing proved unendurable, so she looked, and found that the thing was upon her. Its eyes
were red, its teeth had the chilly glitter of a stained glass image late in an
autumn's day, and its groping fingers resembled the dark high ribs in the
ceiling of the Domkirke. Magnhild now realized who it was.

It commenced to caress her head. The worst thing was the way it looked
at her. Wherever it touched her, her tresses fell out. Once Magnhild had
been utterly denuded, the ghost removed its skull, rolled it around the
floor, and thus gathered up her hair unto itself. Replacing its death's-head

upon its spine, it rose, hovering near the ceiling and preening itself, as if it too were now one of those blue-eyed blonde Norwegian women who retain the beauty of health as they age. And it smiled with its withered black lips, which had once been pink like the bells of a *valurt*-flower.

4

When the dirt gave way in the Gudmundsson family plot, and several monuments upended themselves, the sexton took both helpers and commenced smoothing everything over as decently and rapidly as possible. By then Magnhild had already been dead for eighteen years, with the paint going grey on her rotting house, which no one could afford to buy; and several prominent men had erected a statue of Loden Gudmundsson, who inspired the rational modernization of timbercutting in this part of Rogaland. Around his gravestone the earth appeared especially disturbed. Feeling called upon to disprove a rumor that certain graves had been tampered with, the sexton fetched a crowbar, which turned out to be unnecessary in Loden's case, since the lid of his box had collapsed. Strange to relate, in place of the viscera which the ribcage had once contained there lay a hoard of old silver coins as variably irregular as scales of herring-skin. The sexton could not help remembering the verse which runs: *Do not lay up for yourselves treasures on earth, where moth and rust consume . . . For where your treasure is, there will your heart be also.* Magnhild and Astrid had been placed on either side of that wicked miser.

Near the century's turn, on a winter night when the men had been drinking until they grew as cheerfully red as the enamel on a housewife's coffee mill, and the talk turned on old times, when herring had enriched the sea, bread sold for a fair price and children obeyed their parents, the sexton, now retired, confided to his son Eirik, who was himself somewhere between middle-aged and elderly, that the most hideous experience of his life had been opening a certain woman's coffin and finding it choked with its decomposed occupant's tresses which had grown out with such unnatural vitality as to be on the verge of worming through the lid.— Yes, father, said Eirik. I know who you're talking about.

And well you should. Parish history is our family's bread and butter.

Come spring I'll renew the sod on that section. Blonde hair, isn't it? It's coming up again.

Silently the old man poured himself more brandy.

And what about Magnhild?

No, son, it's Magnhild I've been speaking of.

But she—

Went bald in her old age, quite suddenly, it seems. Was it the scurvy? I remember seeing her coming to church, always with her bonnet on, summer or winter. Almost a scandal it was. Your mother used to say—

You see, father, that hair, wherever it might be rooted, it's spread all through the Gudmundsson section, just like dead grass. So I thought—

No, it's Magnhild's. Astrid, now, perhaps I should have left her in peace, since her coffin was perfectly sound, but in those days I was still curious about things, like you. Marianne Olafsdottir, who used to serve in that house, was not yet demented, so on the following Sunday I had a chat with her. She said that in her youth Astrid used to have beautiful long hair, which I didn't remember at all, but one woman's not likely to forget such a thing about another.

What else did she tell you?

That poor Astrid always returned good for evil. Marianne was fond of her, for a fact. Once she dropped a porcelain cup, and Loden was out for blood! Somehow Astrid helped her make up the money—in secret, of course.

All right, father. So what was in Astrid's coffin?

Nothing.

5

How belatedly these unpleasant happenings might have been prevented is another of the deep matters unknown to me; but Lady Justice (when she isn't blinking) can descry murder's signature even on the rottenest corpse ever carried on a hurdle to the coroner's jury. Ten or twenty years in the ground need not leave a case unknowable, in witness of which I remind you of those occasions when daring memento-hunters (whom the law calls by other names) have recognized this or that disarticulated skeleton by the nitrous jewel amidst its bric-a-brac. And so, had someone dared to exhume Astrid, he might have noticed that her skull was half smashed in! Then what? We could have pulled out Loden's remains and burned them, or at least cast them out of the churchyard. The Devil already held that soul, without a doubt, but the living would have been edified, and Astrid gratified. Or we could have burned *her;* that's what grim old Bishop Eriksøn would have done, had this story taken place in his time.

Were justice too much to expect, why not appeasement? In the Dom-kirke I have found people praying as industriously as ever bondsmaids can turn a millstone; so what if we had uttered heart-winged words for Astrid's comfort? Some say the dead know nothing, but the minister assures me that at every funeral he perceives ghosts screaming around our prayers like a flock of gulls. And so when Astrid died, we could have had a sermon on the subject of *Blessed are those who are persecuted,* or, if that was too daring, *Blessed are the meek;* at least we could have paused en route to the churchyard and offered her a eulogy, even one as simple as any of the heliographic cutouts on my cast-iron stove; for the old people remember that she was easily pleased.

THE MEMORY STONE

Most people say that the bride was rather gloomy . . . As the saying goes, *things learned young last longest.*

"The Saga of Gunnlaug Serpent-Tongue," *ca.* 1500 A.D.

In the Mary Church in Old Stavanger leans a great stone from ages ago, smoothed along one side and then carved in runes so tall that they stretch from edge to edge: *Kjetil made it and erected it to the memory of his dear wife Jorunn.* Who they both were is forgotten.

When Birgitte and Olav were wed in that church, he promised to remember her as well as Kjetil did Jorunn, at which Birgitte said: Not good enough. I'll expect you to follow me.

Yes, wife, I'll follow you . . .—at which his drunken cousin clapped him on the back.

She was a girl with a star at her throat and her scarf's narrow ends hanging straight down below her breast. Then she was a goldenhaired young mother clenching her hands against the cold, and every morning she rocked the cradle, singing the song of the spider and the brooch, but their baby died.

She was never well; she was always as whiteskinned as a young wooden house. When her doom grew certain, she leaned against him, and slowly they walked up the hill, looking down over the steep roofs of the wooden houses at the narrow, streaming brilliance of the Vågen. The Østhavn was empty but for one or two great ships; the picket fence was going grey with dusk; the maple leaves were already black.

Again he swore to ride the day-ship and the night-ship, with the sail his wife should weave for him; and so she passed the rest of her life, vomiting and fainting, rolling her sailcloth upward on the warp-weighted loom as she formed the stuff. Just as a woman in her moon-bloody shift runs round the barley field before her husband sows it, so that the earth will bear, thus Birgitte uttered all her paling magic into the cloth she made, until her lips turned black. After she could no longer speak, she still stretched her arm toward him whenever he came to sit with her. Her hand closed tremblingly around his fingers. She learned how to make the good death once the leaves were new.

Because her life and death were in part secret to others, Olav's nightmares grew brighter than the sea. Beside their child he buried her in her finest cloak, pinned with a golden trefoil brooch. Her stone read: *Olav made this in remembrance of his dear wife Birgitte.* As far as others were concerned, she had now been cast away, forgotten beneath the grass, avoided like dead wet leaves on the path—his mother spoke of fresher women, and the slanders of others resembled fallen poison-berries crimson on rock stairs—but Olav took mind of his promise, although he felt uneasy enough, to be sure, because where Birgitte had gone was as dark as a forest at a glade's end.

Just as in a green hollow, a school of obedient dark stone heads stands aligned—a cemetery—so his nights now ranked themselves until a certain old witch in a double-brooched scarlet dress finished weaving the sail, spitting onto it to give it more woman-power.

Now the time had arrived for Olav to set out upon his journey, but first he wished to visit the husk of her whom he sought. Because he had paid the witch what she asked and more, she grew friendly, and even accompanied him that day, carrying the shovel. The church was cold. A man and boy bent over the votive candle which they had just impaled upon one of the equatorial spikes of the skeletal iron globe whose North Pole was a black cross, and when they had departed, Olav entered the churchyard, while the witch stood watch, reading the sun. An hour and more it must have been. Grimacing, she said: Do it now. I've locked the gate.

So he opened Birgitte's grave, kissing her rotten face most lovingly, whispering in the hole where her ear once was that he would come to her now, and when he touched the heart-mud between her ribs, her lead cross went white with reflected gold-light, its triple rows of runes shining copper-red in their grooves.— Now she knows, said the witch. I wish I'd had a husband like you.

On the following day, Olav left home, with the witch-cloth rolled under his arm. The witch called up a breeze for him, then went her way. He said: Birgitte, prepare to welcome me.— Rainy wind on the slippery mossy rock, beech trees bursting from the dark rock, these sang to him when he put his feet in the two ovoid footprints, because in this very stone, dead people had made clean long ship-carvings: three vessels, one over the other, with people or animals or other beings on them. But what they had meant by it no one could say. Olav carried a silver neck-ring for his wife. Glorious white flowers were all he sorrowed to leave behind. Here he unrolled his sail. The keel sprouted before his feet. The wind caught him up.

Olav flew above the tongue of city into the Østre Havn, with small islands ahead: Plentingen on his left and Natvigs Minde on his right. Just like a duck paddling rapidly in cold black water, then diving, so his night-ship scored a wake in the day, then descended to the sea. His day-ship slit open the night; his night-ship found light; his day-ship carved darkness. Sometimes a sound as of wind came beneath the hull, but more often he heard slappings and sloshings; while after dark the ocean always sang like the choir back home in Stavanger. He grew as lonely as a dandelion flower high on its stalk. From Karmøy to Bukkøy he sailed, through shade and silver-wet grass, way-lit by the thunderglow of silver-blue lichen on black boulders, wife-lit, rune-lit, his ship's swan-neck so dark-lit by water that it seemed to be its own thing, a snake; and as he travelled he began to wonder whether he crossed waves or was but a shadow upon blackberries and petroglyphs by the sunny sea, so many broken shells and mouse skulls did he pass over upon that cracked rock-shelf with its black and silver-white lichens and grasses growing up gold in the cracks, until after sailing through many rains he began to forget some of this Birgitte whom he sought, voyaging ever more lightly over green island-heads in the pale blue water. But he would not release his grip on her memory. He kept dreaming of her dead breasts because he sailed between rosehips as large as suns, while her dead womb became a red crab-apple in autumn.

Ahead came the desired land, and on the grass, the outspread arms of rock. Olav kissed Birgitte's neck-ring. The ship became an eight-legged horse whose eyes were dandelions. He sailed into the rock's embrace where white water leaped up out of the dark water it struck, the rock pale and nearly green in the light. He hovered over green moss and lichens, breasting the leaves which waved at the sheep-clouds on the grass-sky. Cloud-sheep grazed on the green horizon.

He called out to Birgitte, but she did not yet answer. So he rode his horse across the trees, watched by blurred Dorset faces on a wand of antler.— Now I'll roll up this horse and carry him under my arm, he said to himself.— He leaped across the dark lake, then across the river like a silver sword.

Far away where the blue-grey sea was writhing under a double bank of purple cloud, the sky glowing whitish-yellow at sunset, he approached the steeply tapering wooden roofs of Valhalla. Up rose mead-worthy woman-ghosts: Ingrid, Mari, Signe, Johanna, Karen, Elisabeth, Anna, Margaretha, Inga, Juliane—but Birgitte happened to be the one on whom he'd set his heart. So again he mounted his horse whose eyes were dandelions and rode down to Hel, whose dark hills are wound-gashed with red leaves. The ogres were greyish-blue like cold clay, and the trolls were as black as berries in a wall of green thorns; the giants were boulder-hearted, and the night-elves were pond-eyed. Sometimes they were grandly terrible; then they became as leaf-shadows. Scattering them all, even the monster with an ovoid head and closed ovoid eyes, he lifted a stone, and up rose Birgitte.

She wore a brooch made of crumbling green rust; perhaps he had once given it to her. Her hair had grown longer, and she was younger. She declined to open her arms. She was whiter than a birch tree, and her finger-nails were paler than evergreen tips.

He held out her neck-ring, and unsmilingly she slipped it over her head, saying: If you teach me to love you again, I'll show you why dark water catches light.

He drank water from the moss beneath her arms. Her voice kept the high sound and the low sound of a stream.

She said: Your memory stone is choking me.

What shall I do with it, Birgitte?

Birgitte's not my name.

You told me to come here.

Go home and roll your stone away.

When Olav opened his eyes, the sun hurt them. The ground chilled his back. He was lying in his wife's opened grave, with dribs of rotten sail-cloth between his fingers and the memory stone on his chest, facing downwards. He managed to push it off, then clambered back into the sunlight. As soon as he stood upright he felt as if he had recovered from a drawn-out illness.

Although he felt curious as to whether the silver neck-ring remained in her coffin, burning her bones with precious frost, he remembered the words of Christ: *Let the dead bury the dead.*

So he called workmen to haul the stone away. The gravediggers filled in the hole and laid new turf over it.

Then he remarried—a sweet young girl named Jorunn, who had long been on his mind. She promised to outlive him, which she did. He left instructions to be cremated.

THE NARROW PASSAGE

... if foul witch dwell
by the way you mean to fare,
to pass by is better than to be her guest,
even if night be near.

"Sigrdrífumál," *ca.* 1000 A.D.

1

In 1868 some Rogalanders remained in hopes that the herring would swim home to them, and a few even believed it, for it is always an insult when good things depart, and one readymade defense of the insulted is faith. That great wooden hand still pointed upward in the window of Mr. Kielland's shop, as if to remind us where those good things go; while the herringmen reached in the opposite direction, praying even yet for silver treasure in their nets. Out where the coast unrolled page after page of rock-stories, it seemed as if some secret fish-hoard might yet give itself, pallidly pure, like autumn light breaking weakly through the clouds; and since the herring occasionally pretended to return, the believers went on believing, awaiting their own continuance, watching the stillness of black water in the rain. Fortunately, universal afflictions manifest themselves in our neighbors before we need to confess the symptoms in our own faces. In other words, Karmsundet grew impoverished more rapidly than Stavanger, whose shipwrights and merchantmen made do thanks to lobster if not lumber; but even in Stavanger the unluckiest fishermen presently began to pack up for America. They were followed by carpenters whose iron-jacketed mallets had rusted, servant-girls expelled from their fine situations beneath the master's stairs, stevedores whose great shoulders went unhired and whose despondent women had given up expecting to stand in mountains of herring, gutting and salting by the hour; ropemakers whose only use for their product would have been to hang themselves, bankrupt farmers and other apostates from the silvery faith.

The shipping companies' agents promised easy terms and golden lives to any who would buy their tickets. After all, isn't gold superior to silver? To be sure, certain crows kept croaking about the *Amelia*, which departed Porsgrunn Harbor with two hundred and eighty souls, seventy-nine of whom died of sickness. But some of her survivors came out rather well. One family even bought a piano, in a place called Minnesota. Although not all emigrants could expect that, they stood a fine chance of doing worse at home. Even the Rosenkilde family, it was said, was suffering: they now ate red meat but thrice a week.

2

Many Stavanger emigrants signed up with Mr. Køhler, his family having dwelled thereabouts since the Late Bronze Age, which rendered him nearly trustworthy and his passengers nothing if not civically patriotic. But not all were satisfied in the end. The ones who got buried at sea declined to complain, but their widowers and orphans wrote home that America had cost them twelve weeks belowdecks in a stinking prison of verminous, vomitous bunks, scuttles locked tight and not even enough water to drink—never mind the thieves in Liverpool and the road agents in New York.

So when Øistein Pederson and his wife Kristina prepared to make the adventure, they wondered whether Mr. Køhler's competitors might be any better. Kristina had already been dismissed from the cannery, for slackness, so the foreman said, but to her husband she tearfully swore before God that she had never for a moment slowed down; even between fish-barrels she kept on, cleaning the floor or sharpening the gutting-knives, nor had there been complaints about her. Øistein believed his spouse, who was honest in all things; moreover, the factory immediately took in a horde of hungry young Swedish girls who worked for less. A week later they hired her at Magnussen's, and it seemed as if they could live as before, weary over their bowls of soup on the narrow wooden table, so early it was still dark, a sheen of her gold hair reflected like aurora borealis on the dark frosted window. Then Magnussen's closed.

Øistein was a cooper. For three months they got along on his earnings, but the canneries ordered ever fewer barrels, so he and Kristina began to quarrel. On a certain cold night, Øistein slept badly, awoke in a fever, and because the room was so close and squalid, he fancied himself already dead, trapped in the cold black earth, open-eyed, blind, unable to catch his breath. What could he do but suffer forever? Of course he had simply lost himself beneath the bedclothes. With a gasp he threw them off, disturbing Kristina, and gave thanks when he saw her shape in the pallid nightdress. Although he kept this experience to himself, it changed him. In brief, he conceived a horror of rotting away in Stavanger.

Come to think of it, horror of constriction might have been his very nature's foundation-stone. When he was a boy of five or six, his mother, who once saw it, told him how the great stele of Saint Mary's needle leans ever closer to Haakon's church; some believe that when they touch, Doomsday will arrive. Of all the children, Øistein was the only one affected by this tale. He could almost imagine himself caught in that inevitable evil hour—pinched, chilled and crushed. Seeing how readily he grew disturbed over nothing, his father realized that the child had too much time on his hands, and set him to the most wearisome tasks of coopering, which he soon mastered, after which nobody could find any fancies of which to disapprove in that quietly straightforward young man. Kristina's father, and perhaps even Kristina, would have been surprised to know what sort of person had joined their family. Naturally, they themselves might have presented a few astonishments to Øistein, had there ever come time to get to know each other in that way.

After his nightmare, he asked himself: If the herring never come back, what's the best we can expect?— The answer untricked his mind.

To say that Kristina and Øistein loved each other conveys less than I would wish, for doesn't marriage often commence with some kind of love? After three years their passion had not waned to nothing; but it had lessened, for a fact. On the other hand, they had learned how to be loyal helpmates each to the other. Øistein thought matters through, from his wife's point of view and his own. If there was no money then there would be more quarrels, in which case the chance of their remaining true friends appeared as unlikely as a happy ending to one of those tales which begin with a pretty girl luring a man into the churchyard. Anyhow, even if the old plenitude returned, why should Kristina spend herself in gutting herring by candlelight? Sometimes when they lay down together he could barely endure the smell.

His father-in-law, that gaunt and bearded believer, had stood against emigration, but on one of those dark mornings he lost his capacity to wake up, so they buried him beside Kristina's mother and began to consider in earnest. Now was the time. Øistein's parents were already dead. No children had come yet; they retained a sack of coin from better days; as to their future, the landlord had increased the rent, and next month would bring three more boarders into that tiny house.

It was Sunday. When they all got home from church, two of the other tenants commenced disagreeing over a pair of boots, while Øistein stood watching raindrops on the window, the harbor trembling, reflections of red, white and yellow edifices barely pinkening or blueing the water. Then he opened his heart to Kristina, who said: I'll do whatever you think best.

He loved his wife's hair. In America, perhaps, she might not be compelled to kerchief her face against the stinging herring-brine. Then he could admire it every day. One could breathe in America, it was said. There was cheap good land, and the taxes were low.

Bypassing Mr. Køhler's, they went to Mr. Kielland's cousin Nils, who ran a clean business, everyone said. His passengers tended to be rich, but Øistein hoped that a berth in steerage might not be too dear. So the Pedersons awaited their turn, gripping the railing-narrow counter while the officials sat far away around their square wooden island of a desk-table, writing in their ledgers, counting money received and placing it in envelopes, never opening their tall black safe before the public. Some of these men Øistein had seen across the nave on Sunday, and some he had never met before; they looked nearly as grand as the Rosenkildes.

Finally the Pedersons stood before the high clerk, who asked what they wanted. From his tone they could have been unemployable Pietists. Looking him in the eye, Øistein demanded his cheapest price to America.

America, now, that's a wide place. Where in America?

New York.

We sail only to Québec nowadays.

Then you could have said so at the beginning, sir.

Good luck to you. Next!

How much to Québec?

For two?

That's right.

The man wrote down a number on a scrap of paper. Øistein led his wife out of that office, passing framed etchings of sailing ships and frowning rich men.

3

Fortunately, Kristina's aunt had been watching out for them. She said that there was nothing as easy to keep an eye on as that raven-suited agent who rushed so busily across the winding walls of white houses. He usually flittered by in mid-morning, when women had given up standing outside the canneries. The next day the Pedersons stood waiting for him, and here he came.

In his black suit he reminded Øistein of the dark narrow column of a mink standing up, its little hands dangling against its breast. Under his throat he wore a high white collar, whose clasp was a ruby-eyed herring cast out of pure silver.

He extended his hand, but Øistein stepped back.

So it's America you'd go to?

Frowning, the young man nodded.

I'll quote you a fine price!

What price?

Whatever others charge, Captain Gull will be less. Just bring a bill for proof.

Where is he?

This way.

That's not to the harbor! Øistein exclaimed.

It is, it is! A short passage! laughed the sailing-ship agent.

Following him up that steep lane whose twistings were nearly stifled by hordes of square-windowed wooden houses which watched every pass-erby like standing stones, they unaccountably found themselves back at the docks. Little single-masted vessels scuttled in and out of the Vågen, quick to tie up at their favorite warehouse before someone else could. The agent led them past the line of weary women in the salty stench of the herring wharves, some of whom tried to smile at Kristina, and just past Eystein's warehouse they arrived at a door in a small warehouse. Natu-rally they were subjected to no passenger ship office, and certainly not to any clock with Chinese figures on its towering plinth, let alone some white door marked PRIVAT. This went far to explain why it might have been that the instant they saw Captain Gull, they liked him, although, come to think of it, this was unaccountable, for Øistein partook of a distrustful nature. With a name like that,* the fellow should have been a German goldsmith with six pink, roundcheeked children. As it was, he gave off a prosperous enough impression: narrow spectacles, fine white hair with a few strands of red still in it. His breath was scarcely beery at all.

Two more for America! said the agent.

Kristina wished to know how long the voyage would last.— Not above three weeks, said Captain Gull.

Impossible!

Not at all. Given fine weather it will be even less. You see, I've found a short passage.

Kristina was smiling. Alarmed, her husband took her hand, which even now remained blotched and inflamed from herring-brine.

Captain Gull was explaining that this shorter route to America had been worked out long ago. It was the way that Leif Eiriksson had revealed to no one, not even the ill-fated Vinland voyagers, who were his own kin; Captain Gull had followed up certain hints in the sagas, and claimed it for himself.— And you must promise to keep my secret, he continued.

He took them down to see the *Hyndla*. She was a pretty enough vessel, white, black and green. Øistein tapped his forefinger on the railing. Smiling, the agent said: Sound ship-wood—straight from the Ryfylke forest! And look here; this is interesting.

Her bowsprit was as impressive as an iron spear—for walrus hunting, chuckled Captain Gull.

We'll think on this, said Øistein, to which the agent replied: Don't think too long, Mr. Pederson. We have only half a dozen berths left.

In steerage?

They're all in steerage.

What's the price? And this time I want a figure.

Smiling, Captain Gull turned away. The agent murmured. It truly was unbelievably good.

---

* *Gull* means "gold."

Oho, said the agent. Three more emigrants coming! Excuse me now; perhaps I'll see you again.

After a glance at his anxious eager wife, Øistein said: We'll book our passage now.

Kristina's face was as shiny as her best possession, the brass teakettle that her mother had bequeathed to her.

4

Buying dried foodstuffs for the voyage at Mr. Kielland's store, Kristina felt even happier than she had been when Øistein first came courting. She laid in potatoes, flatbread, jugs of soured milk—and salted herring, of course; there was still a supply of it. In America, where food was cheap, she might be spared from eating that fish anymore. She bought plugs of tobacco for her husband, and a few onions against scurvy. Receiving Mr. Kielland's permission, the apprentice loaded the wagon and took her home with all her groceries.— Write us a letter if you get time, he said. Kristina thanked him, knowing that he would pray for her.

Her cousin Eyvind reached into his sailmaker's horn full of needles, and pulled out an awl which could pierce through anything. He gave it to her with a prayer and a kiss on the forehead.

Meanwhile her husband was packing up his trunk: wool mittens made by his sister, a striped white shirt, a cap, oilskin trousers and jacket, linens, a bit of rope, then all the farm tools the relatives could spare. How long he and Kristina could manage in America without work was as tedious to calculate as the number of green herring to fill a barrel. The uncertainties of the passage disquieted him, but after all, no man can see down deeply into the future. They had made their agreement and must be content. At least the voyage would be brief; moreover, his wife was too strong and good to complain.

On the last day, standing side by side, the Pedersons overlooked the few sailing-ships in the Vågen; and devouring the chilly breeze, which was purer by far than the air in most port cities, the water streaming blue and grey, they promised to be brave and true to each other. Half a dozen undermanned herring-boats were heading out to sea in hopes that the silver wealth might have come back; they went slowly, slowly sailing, their brass bells faintly ringing.

5

And so the emigrants ascended the gangway, Øistein and Kristina and all the other young women with their white collars buttoned up to the throat, stern old men, wide-eyed children, all the families leaving behind their white-painted wooden houses, disconsolate fishermen altered into hopeful farmers, butterwives who'd sold their fat sweet cows for next to nothing (the buyers being apprised of their circumstances), beneficiaries of the short passage on the pretty ship *Hyndla*, bound for Québec, the leavetakers' view of them interrupted by many tall cables. Among them stood Kristina's Aunt Liv in her lace shawl and collar, sternly seeing them off, and at the last sadly bending her head like a good cow before the axe. Øistein hastened into steerage to guard their place and possessions. The smell was nauseating, but he could certainly get used to it. Glancing around him, he found that he knew no one except for Reverend Johansen, who had intended to leave last spring but stayed to care for his mother in her final illness. Well, there were so many families in the narrow white houses of Stavanger! And from the sound of their speech, some people must be from Hjelmeland or Suldal. The reverend and Øistein nodded to one another. Kristina would be pleased. When she came down, her husband pushed his way back onto the foredeck, ostensibly to wave farewell to Aunt Liv and Cousin Eyvind. He looked down and saw a fish skeleton hanging complete just beneath the surface of the oily harbor. Swans, gulls and pigeons bickered on the pier, the coy sun gilding the cobblestones for an instant. The young man now gazed across the water and up the street, into the house where he and Kristina had lived. Øistein had always been remarkable for his eyesight, and so he made no mistake when he perceived how upstairs the windows parted, and in the widening column of darkness between the pairs of triple panes, a pallid face, never before seen, gaped its mouth at him. But two other men jostled him, and he swung round, ready to defend himself if need be; the men apologized, and they all agreed that three weeks belowdecks would be superior to attic-dwelling forever in Stavanger. Cousin Eyvind waved his hat at Øistein and went away. Aunt Liv sought to make herself conspicuous for that instant, but the crowd half crushed her. She too used to stand in the sheds with her hands buried in the silver hoard of herring.

And before anyone expected it, the *Hyndla* was underway, the glamor of separation now gracing those tiny, narrow white houses which shone so softly through the beech trees.

6

At first the instants of their voyage were distinct, like mackerel-bubbles in dark seaweed at dawn. Kristina told herself that she must never forget this creamy dawn sea so black and orange around those low Norwegian islands which resembled translucent flints knapped and polished down by giants. Øistein held her hand. Once they reached America, they might not find such leisure again, at least not until they were old. The water seemed viscous, and the red sun-shield shone over the islands. All day they sped toward the short passage, which Captain Gull had explained was a trifle narrow in spots, this being the reason he had not replaced the *Hyndla* with a larger ship (doubtless, thought Øistein, the true reason must be that Captain Gull lacked the means—and thank goodness for that, since otherwise he would have increased the fare, perhaps even up to Nils Kielland's price). It was peculiar, to be sure, the way they kept on following the coast northward, when America lay to the west; but no doubt the master knew what he was about. There came another dawn to the black sea, the ship foaming through ribbons of green-chambered white lace on either side; and still the ship lay never so far off the coast as to be out of soundings. By now several children had vomited, making the stench of dirty feet and fish-oil even less pleasant, but Kristina reminded herself that she was not some rich girl who can afford to get queasy in her stomach from a surfeit of butter. And wasn't this preferable to the stink of the herring-barrels? She went among those young mothers who wore lovely lace at their throats—attic-sharers, no doubt, from those square-windowed wooden little houses—and tried to be helpful; sometime she might need the same. Then she attempted sitting on the edge of her bunk, but the ceiling was too low. Pulling out her trunk, which had formed a very close acquaintance with three others beneath the bed, she seated herself on it and began to knit a pair of socks for her husband, who had gone above in hopes of establishing a business association with some other men. Presently she grew melancholy, because somebody was flatulent and the ship tilted nauseously on the rushing grey ocean, with hasty

low sunlight glancing unpleasantly into the scuttles, and something unknown to her whistling and piping outside. Kristina was a landswoman;
she had never been on a ship before. An icy feeling established itself behind her breastbone, or maybe higher up than that—almost up to her
collarbone, in fact, but there and only there, like burning cold metal inside her; she felt that she could not get warm; well, no, it wasn't just there
anymore; her wrists were freezing where they emerged from the sleeves;
her toes were numb. Just as she had begun to wish they had never set out
for America, a shaft of sunlight turned the royal grey water into blue, revealing many forested islets, cormorants and seals. So the weather came
and went, in conjunction with her moods, and they approached the short
passage, after which every passenger would be compelled to resume the
weariness of getting a living.

Early next morning the helmsman was fixing their position by means
of careful sextant angles, as Øistein approvingly perceived. This must be
the place where they would turn straight west, out into the Atlantic.

But why's that fellow folding in the spinnaker sail? a Hjelmeland man
said, as if to himself. Two tall sailors approached him. They inquired: Is it
to tell us our business that you'd be wishing?

Øistein was sorry for the Hjelmeland man, but ours is a hard world,
and so he turned away.

The *Hyndla* was shortening sail, for a fact. Perhaps her master had determined to take in extra water or supplies.

Greeting Øistein, the reverend gazed over the side and remarked: I almost became a fisherman like my father.

Then you escaped a bad destiny.

So it seems. But where did the herring go?

We fished them out, that's all, said the Hjelmeland man. Greed and
folly. And if they ever come back, we'll do it again.

Without a doubt, said Øistein.

The rising sun-shield's three or four reflections skipped across the water like a stone; then there were nine of them, and they merged into a
vermilion road between wrinkled dark islets. The topman was yanking
in the throat halyards of the foresail, and Øistein went down to see
whether Kristina needed anything. She looked nauseous but smiled at
him, knitting a sweater.

Come on up, wife, and see the eider ducks swimming.

His wife beckoned him closer. When he leaned down toward her, she whispered in his ear: That Dorthe Magnusson from Suldal has been complaining since dawn. When she went topside to take some air, someone stole a pound of tea right out of their trunk.

A shame, said Øistein, shaking his head. Can we spare her a bit of ours?

Of course, only—

Now go take a turn on deck, and I'll mind our goods.

Thank you, husband.

He sat there in the close air, passing the time with a Suldal man named Bendik Hermansson, whose brother had already emigrated to that district called Minnesota. By all accounts, a man had room to breathe over there. The Indians used to make trouble in those parts, but nowadays they were practically finished. Land and cattle were cheap. Øistein listened, embellishing his own dreams for himself and Kristina once the passage should widen out into American infinitude. Like most of the others, he had a gift for patient endurance, so that the hours receded easily, green and grooved like Norwegian islands. When Kristina returned, looking much better, they lunched on hard bread and tinned herring from Mr. Kielland's store.

7

It was best not to be overexacting in one's expectations as to the duration of the short passage. Captain Gull had said something about three weeks. But of course it might go a week more or less, depending on accidents. Anyone from Stavanger knew about stormy weather, not that any was in the immediate offing, for when Øistein climbed the ladder to the foredeck, the late afternoon sun peeped out to gild a lovely tree-hedgehog of coast, and off the stern lay a pastel island of high yellow and green shadows, the ocean almost reddish-grey against it. Ahead stretched a promontory of some sort. The *Hyndla* was sailing parallel to a cloud-pleat, aiming for a ridge of blue knuckles (the sea very calm, the glass falling slowly). Two sailors footed in another sail. Bendik Hermansson, who had also sought out good air just now, remarked that he had never seen such peculiar seamanship. Øistein declined to reply, for he had begun to wonder whether this fellow talked too much to no purpose. So they stood smoking their pipes while the glass fell a trifle further, and presently the waves roughened, so that the grey sea was sliming the scuttles belowdecks as the grey coast grew blurry. Preferring to delay his return into the odors of vomit, fish-oil and fouled diapers, Øistein remained on deck for another half-hour, until one of the Suldal men said he could make out some sort of high black shining, about two or three points on the starboard bow.

8

Now the sea began to foam in earnest, and waves rained down across the scuttles. The passengers were all good Norwegians, even the landsmen, so however they might have felt, they showed no fear of those glassy, icy sheets of spray in the milky sea. Presently the horizon disclosed mountains like the long black teeth of a wool comb. Øistein, who had never sailed far up the coast, but trusted in his calculations of how far the *Hyndla* had gone, supposed that this might be Ytre Sula or Sandøyna, not that either place boasted cliffs as grand or dark as this.

Passengers to their berths, said Captain Gull. The sailors were already unreefing the mainsail, an action which the former herring fishermen among the emigrants thought incomprehensible. Now the foresail had descended, and they were winching down the spar.

Belowdecks the four-tiered berths ran perpendicular to the ship's axis, interrupted by a narrow corridor. At the top of each bunk on its corridor-facing end was a knurled knob whose purpose Øistein had not perceived. Two tall sailors now came in and gave each knob seven turns. With each turn the berths contracted a little into the wall. Kristina inquired what they were doing. A sailor said: You'll see. It's a narrow passage.

And so they approached a cliff of hard grey rock, which suddenly gaped open for the *Hyndla* to enter, then closed behind her. All the passengers could tell was that the scuttles went dark—for the passage was as narrow as the Vågen itself, that long sea-mouth whose jaws are studded with hordes of white wooden house-teeth.

Following up his earlier supposition, Øistein decided that they must have turned in to the Sognefjorden, which is the widest introitus hereabouts, but not a single town appeared; moreover, two of the Suldal men had fished the fjord as far up as Balestrand on many an occasion, and they swore that this was no place they had ever seen. Bendik Hermansson, however, was certain of their proximity to Balestrand, for there was nowhere else that they could be. Now it is common knowledge that as it runs upstream at Balestrand, the Sognefjorden jogs sharply north by northeast and narrows into the Færlandsfjorden, presently passing Sogndalseggi to the east before reaching the many-armed spiderlake called Jostedalsbreen. Even if they could have somehow missed Sogndalseggi, which was practically impossible, the Suldal men said, the channel should have widened out. And why they should be carried deep inside Norway was beyond them. Bendik Hermansson persisted in his position that they had not yet reached Balestrand. Once Øistein, who was of a practical disposition, realized that they knew no better than he where the *Hyndla* had carried them, he returned to his berth to see how his wife was getting along. Reverend Johansen sat on a trunk, reading aloud from his Bible. An old man was groaning and vomiting. The women knitted. Kristina had grown quite fond of the minister, and in truth she might have wondered once or twice how it would have gone with her, had she married so distinguished a man. He had just come to the verse which runs: *Carry me, O LORD, that I may cross this circle of guttering fire; and against my enemies lend me Your sword that strikes on its own. Against the trolls deliver me; from the blue flames deliver me, that I may come safe into the Kingdom.*

There was a fisherman named Einar Sigvatsson, who had sailed widely in the days when people still hoped that the herring might be found. His brother had finally persuaded him to go out of the country. So both Sigvatssons were on board, with their wives and children, together with Einar's mother-in-law. Kristina and Øistein had struck up a liking for that family.

9

Coming back on deck once the whistle sounded the all-clear, Øistein discovered that the *Hyndla* appeared considerably smaller, for not only had all her sails disappeared but even the mast was broken down, its lowest stalk lashed tight against the deck and the remainder unscrewed into lengths of pole. Meanwhile the sailors were already turning certain knurled knobs upon the corners of the forecastle cabin, so that its roof crept down toward the deck. This accomplished, they unstepped the walls to fold them in. Now they turned other screws, and all along either side of the *Hyndla* uprose a low wall of oarlocks.

They had entered a very deep and narrow gorge, whose river, strange to say, flowed away from the sea. Overhead Øistein saw unfamiliar stars. This river was very dark, so that its ripples resembled silver inlay in a black iron axehead. Øistein stood watching for a long time, while the other passengers murmured around him. Presently there came a sort of dawn, and he began to perceive that the cliffs between which they sailed were white-patterned with petroglyphs of long ships which resembled worms rolling up their necks in agony because they had been pierced with upright rows of little sticks, which must have been either their masts or their passengers. Then the cliffs drew apart, so that he commenced to hope that the short passage might become more quotidian, but soon enough he saw that they had merely passed into a long ovoid lake, with a rocky islet in the middle; and evidently the cliffs closed in again not far ahead.

He wondered how Kristina might be faring belowdecks. At that moment she was quieting Einar Sigvatsson's daughter Ingigerd, who was a fine girl, well brought up, but passing fearful of the dark, as it now came out; so Kristina entertained her with tales of the cannery, where she used to stand with the other girls at the gutting tables, her toil lit by candles planted in heaps of herring. Ingigerd inquired whether she had been afraid.— Kristina laughed at her.— Afraid or not, child, we did the work. Now don't worry. Your father will come down for you soon.

For whatever reason, some voyagers had grown shy of the captain. Spying him behind the helmsman, Øistein went straight up and asked for an explanation.

Haven't you seen a neap tide before? laughed Captain Gull. The sailors were all grinning at Øistein, who knew well enough that this was no neap tide.

Men commenced to raise their voices. Bendik Hermansson and the reverend essayed to come forward, but the two tall sailors informed them that since it was dangerous to crowd around the helm, they must wait their turn.

Captain Gull was smiling a little, his strangely refined white fingers stroking his beard, and he said: Øistein, you and your wife are reasonable people. I'm trusting in you to make the other passengers see reason.

Then kindly do the same for me. Where have you brought us, captain?

I informed you at the outset that this route is my business. Other masters would love to learn it, not that there's much danger of that. Are you satisfied?

Why is your crew contracting the ship?

Well, well, it's a very narrow passage, you see. And several of you embarked with too much luggage, against my advice—

We got no such advice! shouted Bendik Hermansson.

That's as may be. We'll be stopping at that island, where we'll cache all unnecessary things. One valise per household can be kept, and no more.

But, captain, that's not right! You never told us before—

Øistein, most people aren't prepared to consider what a voyage of this sort entails. Had I warned you in advance of every conceivable difficulty, you might have backed out and gone to my competitors, who would have told you what you wished to hear. Then you would have been no better off, since everybody goes to the same place.

That's not so. Some ships sail to New York and some—

Believe me, you all would have come to this sooner or later.

But, captain, how will I manage in America without my tools and seeds? What about the people who laid out every kroner they had on food and extra clothes, or Reverend Johansen, with all his books?

Overgazing him with angelic eyes, that seraphic oldster replied: Øistein, we all hold onto what we think is precious. We even convince ourselves that we'll never manage without it. When your father-in-law died—see, I know about that!—your good wife could hardly endure to live, as you well remember, but then she persuaded herself to live, *for you*—

Who told you that?

And now our Kristina's living for herself again, as she ought to. An admirable woman you have there! And Reverend Johansen only needs one book to practice his calling. As for you, my friend, I don't mind letting you in on a secret: There's treasure ahead! In the place where I'm taking you, you'll find something that will set you up for life. This is for the best, you'll see. Tell everyone. Now leave me to my business, for the helmsman needs me.

Finding nothing more practical to do, Øistein did as the master had told him; and on account of his clear and simple manner, not to mention those intimations of treasure, the passengers stayed calm, their pallid faces flowing in the darkness like stained glass figures framed in lead, Reverend Johansen comforting them with the verse which goes: *For the gate is narrow and the way is hard, that leads to life, and those who find it are few.* Meanwhile Kristina proved yet again that no one on this earth is as hopeful as an emigrant bride.

10

But soon the passage became rather narrow even for its own passengers. The *Hyndla* was now not much more than a keel. Her freeboard had so far diminished that Øistein could have knelt on deck and touched the waterline. The thwarts had already been swung into place and the sailors were sitting down to row, while the purser sat on the harness cask, neatly crossing names out of the ship's register. Indeed, a number of emigrants had disappeared, Bendik Hermansson for one, and there seemed to be small use in searching for them. Several people had turned against Øistein, whom they considered to be, if not an accomplice, at least a pawn of the captain, but when he asked what else he should have done, they found nothing to say. The women kept weepingly outstretching their hands to the island where their possessions had been offloaded; its rock-darkness was nearly out of sight now. The Suldal men huddled together, evidently meditating the seizure of the ship, and although it pained Øistein that they distrusted him, he could not judge their notions; at any rate, they too soon vanished, together with all their families. Although the orange lanterns still shone on either side of the forecastle, as if the voyage were continuing well, as perhaps indeed it was, the shrinkage of the vessel, and the diminution of the people on it, soon became more rapid. The *Hyndla* appeared to be increasing speed; foam flashed against her sides. In a single long chest abovedecks remained all possessions that the passengers could not wear or carry; and their quarters had contracted to such an extent that sitting up was out of the question. Kristina thought that they might as well have been herring laid side by side into a rectangular tin.

Einar Sigvatsson's mother-in-law Holmfrid now fell sick, and although the other women did everything they could for her, it appeared that she might not recover. In the morning she too was gone, and nobody could say where she had taken herself; that was peculiar enough, and very upsetting to little Ingigerd, of whom Kristina had grown fonder than ever. She told the child all the other stories she knew, good tales like herring shining in the sun; but presently she ran out of anything to tell, and so lay in her bunk, staring up at the bottom of the next berth while the child wailed and fretted. Reverend Johansen continued reading aloud from the Scriptures, and wondrous pretty his verses sometimes proved, especially the verse *Glasir stands gold-leaved before Sigtyr's halls.* But where might Øistein be? He had always been known as someone who thought for himself. Couldn't he save them from any of this? After all, Captain Gull appeared to listen to him. So she tried to be calm and awaited better news.

Kristina had once imagined that she knew sorrow, when only now, on this narrow passage, had it truly begun. Whatever we are used to, however unpleasant it may be, is better than being deprived of everything. Well, God willing, we won't lose everything! By now all she wished for was to be restored to the miseries which had troubled her. Lying on her back side by side with the other passengers in the stinging acid stench of vomit, the vinegary smell of sweat and the sour-sweet reek of foul fish, with the ceiling pressing ever more closely in, again she made the time pass, if only to herself, by remembering her old home, since America was but a void to her, and this narrow passage did not seem like anything to be fancied. For a fact she should have comforted little Ingigerd, but instead she lay silent with her eyes shut, slowly chewing on a bit of flatbread. Yes, she felt homesick for the sweating, crowded blocks of wooden houses of Stavanger; even the slopridden mud-alleys between them were wider than her present situation. Once upon a time she had belonged to the triple line of pretty young women in their dark dresses and white aprons, their hair bobbed tight as they stood over the great salting-kettles, each nearly as large as the one which Thor won from the giant Hymir. Kristina's frying pan was as large across as three burly men. Although she used to dislike the smoky fishy smell, racked barrels and salt-burned wooden ladles, enduring those years only because she could get no other work, she missed the cannery now; she would have been grateful to wake up unemployed in Stavanger again, quarrelling with her jobless husband, looking forward to hungry years. The patient dread in Øistein's face, which he ingenuously supposed he concealed from her, sickened her with worry; and that was how she finally learned that her late mother had warned her well: Marry carefully, Kristina! Young people think they can put on a ring and get help and pleasure for nothing. Really the best you can expect is an exchange of burdens.— In any event, she could hardly blame her husband as some of the other women on the *Hyndla* were doing, since they both knew very well that it was she, Kristina, who had chosen this conveniently short passage.

She still kept a few kroner hoarded up, thinking to spend them in America; but all at once it came to her to approach Captain Gull, who had appeared so sprightly and kind back at home. Perhaps money would save the Pedersons. Instructing Ingigerd to guard what remained of her property, Kristina ascended to the deck. She found the master standing smilingly at the bow, while the helmsman dismantled the wheel. Before she could speak, he laid a hand upon her shoulder, and once again it came to her how fine he was.— Still you refuse to trust in me? was all he said. Have faith, Kristina; everything will come out for the best.

Too soon, they reached their next narrowing. Ice-walls rose ahead like terraces of frozen waves, riddled with electric-blue cracks.

It's my duty to go this time, said Reverend Johansen. And I'd like to leave three things behind for your help, but the captain informs me there's only room for one. So choose, dear friends!

But quickly, please, said the purser. We're coming to a particularly narrow part.

What are the three things, reverend?

Faith, hope and charity, of course. Now, I can't help but wish you'll choose faith—

Hope, said Kristina, and nobody contradicted her.

So be it, said the reverend, and withdrawing a sky-blue jewel from his waistcoat pocket, he slipped it into her hand, perhaps because he liked her best. It was a lovely stone which reminded her of the many-ledged glacier wall above the milk-blue sea.

He was smiling at her. Gazing into his face, she murmured: Did I choose wrongly?

Well, from my own selfish point of view, hope was the easiest to give up. I wouldn't be much good in my vocation without faith, and charity comes in handy just now—

All right, sir, come along! said the purser, and the two tall sailors grabbed the doomed man under his arms and heaved him over the side. He sank instantly. His killers sat down with their mates. Slipping their oars into the crutches, they began to pull, so that the blue terraces on the dull white glacier passed slowly by.

A broad low cave now opened in the wall of whitish-blue ice-teeth, and with uncouth gestures the nameless helmsman guided the rowers in. Down went the *Hyndla*, far beneath the bottom of the greeny-grey sea.

As you can well suppose, the emigrants' situation had become as narrow as the square entrance to a turf-roofed mound, all square inside. Remembering his old nightmare of suffocation, Øistein found himself in need of unceasing efforts (not unlike a rower determined to go forward) to keep his horror at bay. Sometimes the nausea in his throat or the cold wet constriction in his chest grew indistinguishable from panic, and when the last children still remaining began to scream, goggle-eyed like the old wooden-carved gods, he was tempted to violence, just to quiet them, because their cries bore the timbre of his own soul's desperate voice, the useless wailing of life itself when death's fingers close about our throats. Gasping in deep moldy draughts of darkness, he reminded himself that there was no hope in any event, so that to act ignobly could not purchase him a single extra breath. He had sought to persuade the other passengers to keep watch night and day upon the deck, so as not to be tricked anymore, but they were too terrified to creep abovedecks, even the Sigvatssons, from whom he would have expected better help. The last of the Suldal men concealed themselves beneath some planks, hoping to be forgotten, but they too disappeared. Well, after all, even the narrow passage must reach an end. Determined to retain his evenness, Øistein reminded himself that in every ancient barrow, so it was said, one must worm-crawl through the entrance tunnel, but once inside, it grew possible to stand, and perhaps even with outstretched arms remain unconfined by the dank dome of darkness overhead. Perhaps the passage would be like that. Chewing a plug of tobacco, he comforted himself with the parable of the thread within the needle's eye. He surrendered as well as he was able to the Lord's will. But what helped most of all was Kristina's strength for him, and her need. They had married until death. Well enough. He would not be so cowardly as to let the earth cave in on him first, so that his wife must die alone.

11

Now the sailors set to their oars, which were actually spades, of course; and the *Hyndla* proceeded like a millipede through the dark earth. Actually it was not as dark as one might have imagined, the ceiling being thick with glowworms, which gave the Stavanger people comfort, reminding them of when racks of head-skewered brislings and of herring like long silver jewels illuminated the old days of the canneries. Well, never again would they hear winches and chains bearing that treasure of silver tins. No, this narrow passage was not the pleasantest place, but it would surely end soon enough; and even now there was something merry in Captain Gull's flittering blue eyes. So they sailed blackly under the worm-stars, and the loudest thing they heard was the singing in their own skulls. Einar Sigvatsson whispered into Kristina's ear the rumor that trolls had been heard coming on board in great numbers, but she turned away, declining to listen. From time to time the cook opened the harness cask, from which he fed the crew a meat of salted dead men. The passengers for their part had almost nothing to eat; most of their food had been cached on that island in the dark lake. Beside his wife Øistein sat quiet, clenching his fists. His horror and terror of asphyxiation kept fingering him, in much the same way that in the sagas that blind and treacherous prisoner-king Rörek continually explored his cousin, King Olaf, to find out whether he were armored; for what he wished above all was to stab him. In this situation, Øistein, who yet half believed in the treasure beyond price which Captain Gull had promised him, sometimes found it helpful to row along with the sailors, not least because, good son to his father, he hated idleness. But presently anxiety for his wife arose in him, so, laying by his oar (at which the sailors shot him wolfish grimaces), he returned into the darkness where the passengers lay, and there was Kristina with her hands across her breast, silently praying, the drops of sweat on her face as richly silver as the hordes which once came to light in the dark water back in the days when the nets rose up full. Again her beautiful desperation strengthened him.

There were hardly any passengers left. Einar Sigvatsson remained, with his youngest son Arnvid, but his wife and daughter and all his brother's people had been taken, with ogres and trolls now snatching people right and left. Katrina felt very sad about little Ingigerd, but most likely the child was in heaven. Einar appeared half crazed. Øistein said to him: Now we know for certain that they mean us ill, so I propose that we attack them before they thin us out again.

Einar answered: That's all right for you to say, because you have no children, and your wife could get through life without you, but some people prefer not to leave their dependents alone in the world.

Then Kristina said: Let me go and speak again with Captain Gull, which everyone approved, even Øistein, because it postponed the moment when something must be risked.

So once more she crept forward, and there stood the captain, looking as ready and cheerful as ever, although most of the crew had disappeared, and just then the purser leaped headfirst over the side, burrowing greedily into the earth. As Kristina had borne him a grudge ever since the death of Reverend Johansen, this sight caused her less horror than one might have expected; and in any event she had come on business.

The master inquired how she was, and she could not but reply that she was well. Something about him put her at ease, as if even now matters must come out for the best. Aside from Øistein, he was the only one whom she now could see and hear without some sensation of distance. He smiled at her, and his blue eyes sparkled. Laying a hand on her shoulder, he remarked: Sooner or later, my good woman, emigrants discover that patience is better than hope. Because when hope is gone—

But I still have that, said Kristina, confidingly drawing out the blue jewel that Reverend Johansen had bequeathed her.

May I see it? he courteously inquired.

She placed it in his hand, and for a moment he closed his fingers around hers. Holding the lovely stone close to his eyes, he studied it for an instant. Then he blew on it, and at once it turned black.

Counterfeit, said Kristina dully. Who would have thought . . . ?

Not at all! laughed Captain Gull. But it was perishable. I've preserved it for you, in a less brittle form. Don't thank me. We're through the worst, my dear! Go encourage the others, for I've got much to do.

When he returned the stone into her hand, she discovered that it had grown heavy and cold. Nothing could be accomplished by complaining, so she slipped it into her pocket and crept back into that tight and chilly coffin where the last passengers lay, and all of them as utterly white as halibut-flesh. She had little to tell them; their voices came faint in her ears. The matter of the jewel confused and in some measure discredited her, so that it seemed just as well left locked up in her breast. Einar kept praying aloud with his son. When she offered to share the last piece of flatbread, they would not take it. She could barely hear her own husband, who whispered something about *this villainous Captain Gull, whom I hope to see hanged in chains.*

Now came footfalls, and to avoid turning into figures of bygone people scrimshawed on cracked ivory they fell silent and lay very still. As usual, it was no use. This time, instead of sailors it was trolls who threw back the lid and reached in. They bit people's heads off and ate them right there. Then they went away, and only Øistein, Kristina and Einar were left.

They lay in silence until they heard someone coming. Desperately Kristina seized her husband's hand. He could feel the blood pulsing in her fingers. For his part, dread tightened down upon him like his dead father's great vise, the diameter of whose screwthreaded cylinder exceeded a grown man's clasp; for a moment it comforted him to remember those hand-planes and pulleys, the staves steaming, his father smilingly tightening the iron hoop on a new barrel, then shaking hands with Mr. Kielland's father, with the wooden-wheeled cart of crates, baskets and sacks all lashed down tight. Øistein encouraged himself: My father was never afraid of anything.

He stared at Einar, who kept watching him as if he were the sort who steals Bibles from a church.

Again the lid creaked back, and they saw the last worm-constellations overhead in that moldy dirt. Captain Gull bent smilingly over them. Remembering that pale face which had watched their embarkation from between the pairs of triple panes of their old home, Øistein could not decide if there were one or two of those specters. What could he do but clench his fists?

From here on out, said their master, we'll only have room for two passengers. I'll return for your decision.

The instant he turned away, leaving their prison open, Einar rose up with an old-time ryting-knife* and attacked Øistein, who, expecting this, immediately struck him down with punches. Trolls gathered around, howling with laughter. Making use of their acquiescence, Øistein, who had not been wounded, began to drag Einar toward the railing.

Help me! he shouted at Kristina.

No, she said. I refuse to murder.

He shouted: Would you rather it was I?

Just then Einar got to his knees and stabbed Øistein in the thigh. The trolls applauded. Enraged, Kristina thrust her knitting needle under the man's ear. He fell more permanently, and the couple heaved him over, but not before they helped themselves to his ryting-knife. He had little time to rest, for the instant he landed, a greenish-grey hand burst out of the dirt and snatched him away.

The ship was neither more nor less than a large casket now, sliding down across the dark dirt by itself. The sailors were long gone, while the trolls leaped on and off the bowsprit as easily as walruses, and presently dove down into the ooze until not even their hairy feet could be seen. Øistein stood motionless. His good wife took his hand. She had come to resemble her mother, who in her last years grew stooped from carrying too many buckets, and grey-faced from malnutrition. Now for a long time the Pedersons stood clasping hands, and Øistein's heart grew hard and cold to anticipate the passage's next narrowing. He whispered: When he comes—

Turning toward them, Captain Gull gently said: If you, Kristina, and you, Øistein, do not yet hate each other and yourselves, then you cannot continue on with me.

Oh, yes, Kristina assured him, patting her husband's hand. We hate each other.

At this the master laughed, and then, one by one, removed his eyes,

---

* A sheath-knife or dagger.

which until now the Pedersons had never realized were made of glass. He flung them up into the air. Two ravens swooped to swallow them.

The captain's eyesockets were a trifle horrible, to be sure, but so many peculiar things had already happened that Øistein and Kristina made no remark. Besides, Stavanger people have no time to be squeamish.

Now he was removing his face like a hood. When they perceived his true appearance, it seemed to the Pedersons somehow right, which is to say in accordance with his true nature—but if so, why had they not much sooner perceived what he was? A case may be made that the *Hyndla*'s passengers should have seen through the captain at the outset, but I disagree, for the face of death, whenever it remains unveiled, is customarily concealed by the living. Six feet of earth, and then we turn away! Oh, but we know—or should know—but why bring little Ingigerd to nightmares and tears? True love defies "reality" for as long as it can—and besides, Captain Gull had always been such a pleasant old gentleman!

Until then, Øistein and Kristina had been prepared to give up everything simply to get through the narrow passage. But they declined to give up each other.

Well, said the skeleton, are you ready to decide? At this stage I like to invite the last pair to gamble—

The Pedersons knew what to do. Øistein gripped Einar's ryting-knife in his right hand, while in her left, Kristina held her cousin Eyvind's awl, whose end was as sharp as a marline spike. While the skeleton cocked its skull in a soothing grin, no doubt supposing itself still in command, they rushed over the railing and leaped straight down, Kristina comforting herself with the words of Christ, *Whoever seeks to gain his life will lose it, but whoever loses his life will preserve it.* This must be the end. Truth to tell, she felt much the same way that she used to on those black January mornings in Stavanger when she had finished making her husband's breakfast and must now go out into the miserably cold streets if she were to arrive at the cannery on time. As for Øistein, he likewise expected the trolls to tunnel up and devour them right away. They had not very far to fall. And so they struck the dark moss-riddled ooze.

Strange to say, perhaps because they had consigned themselves to the soil of their own volition, they did not sink; nor did any wound-eager entities wriggle evilly up. The coffin kept speeding away at a good pace, as if it were still somehow a ship under benefit of tailwind, and the skeleton stood motionless on it, watching them. Soon they could no longer distinguish its dark eye-holes.— What became of Captain Gull? I myself ask this after every funeral. Reader, you might suppose that he turned into a seagull and flew away, for his purpose was completed this time; he had brought the monsters their prey, and could now return to fetch more, such being the weird which had been cast upon him; how disappointed he felt at the Pedersons' escape is another matter of which I feel uncertain, being unadept at reading the facial expressions of skulls. But there is no purpose in my going on about him.

Well, said Øistein, what now?

It's too far to go back, replied his wife.

Yes—

Then we'd better dig.

And with Cousin Eyvind's awl she began to bore them a crawling-hole. Øistein did his best to help. Feeling hard up in the clinch, as the saying goes, he kept muttering: No hope for it, no hope . . .— You may be sure that by now they both were homesick enough for the fish-perfumed grey cobblestones of Stavanger, but emigrants cannot take great account of sorrows and difficulties; they must keep right on; and so Øistein cleared away the dirt that his wife so magically loosened, while she for her part kept digging straight down, almost cheerfully as when she used to help her mother carry the family's dirty clothes to the pond behind the Domkirke; sometimes the melodies of choir practice would reach them as faintly as if elves were singing from under a mountain, and then she and her mother would cinch up their skirts and wade into the cold water, soaping and scrubbing, chatting at first, until they grew too chilled to speak; and other women and children dirtied the water all around them, so that one could not expect to get one's underdrawers much whiter than grey, which success being accomplished, Kristina and her mother walked shivering beneath the yellow-leafed trees, through the mucky meadows, circling the long steep spine of the Domkirke's roof, fronted by its twin turrets, silent now, commanding the grove around it, beyond which the first hints of wooden-house multitudes peeked here and there, loud children weeping and fighting, outhouses stinking; although Stavanger hardly went much farther than Sølvberggata in those days, the walk home seemed to take forever, especially with the wet laundry so heavy, and they had to descend nearly all the stony narrow windings of Finklamauet Street to the house where they lived in those days, when her father was a herring fisherman and liked to be near the harbor; by then they would have warmed themselves into a sweat, and if her mother were cross she would stride on ahead as rapidly as the longhaired witch who bends her face toward the earth, while the girl struggled not to be left behind, but if her mother were in good temper she might tell the adoring child a story, for instance about the great fire, which broke out on Breigata Street and ruined more than two hundred homes; Kristina had been born before then, but of course she could not remember it; and by now they were nearly home, ahead of them the white sails shining in the silvery harbor, so her mother sent her with three copper coins to knock on the diagonal door cut under the corner of the neighbor's house, and buy eggs and perhaps milk or carrots, then rush straight back to help cook supper: herring, of course. What was there to do but work, and never complain? *The last shall be first and the first shall be last,* said her mother. Before she was forty-five, she profited the coffin-maker's shop.

Now they began to hear sounds below them, as if people were cutting up a stranded whale.

Kristina whispered: Dig more quietly, because if any of them hear us, we'll be hard pressed—

Wife, your advice is always good.

Holding her breath, she pricked their course downward with Eyvind's awl, which suddenly broke through into phosphorescence—at which point the dirt gave way, and the Pedersons tumbled down into a cavern where there were ever so many weird flames like the points of a skull's yellow smile. In the air, smooth old Saami ships kept swimming through the long diagonals like rain or sunrays which possibly had already existed in the rock; perhaps it was rock they were in, not earth; or might it be the case that when darkness gets dark enough, the atmosphere itself thickens into something approaching coal? Anyhow, it was certainly a wide open country they'd fallen into. As far as the Pedersons could see, tall grey she-trolls, naked but for necklaces of whorled silver beads, stood smoking corpses over bone-fires. Although she said nothing to her husband, Kristina thought she recognized Bendik Hermansson's carcass. In fact she was reminded of the cannery, with the lines of herring hanging down from skewers passed through their heads.

Howling like dogs and seals, the monsters now rushed toward them, ready to scream and harry, to burn and bite. Their lank grey hair was fishy-wet, and their teeth resembled the cracked dark rock between glaciers. Kristina overcame her horror by pretending they were women with bad skin from the burns of the herring-brine; she had known many like that back home in Stavanger.

Well, goodbye, wife, said Øistein.

Squeezing his hand, Kristina pityingly replied: It may be worse than that.

Indeed, Captain Gull's skeleton now arrived, enthroned on the rotten coffin-lid which was all that remained of the *Hyndla.* Rising, the thing raised its yellow hand, at which the she-trolls halted and gruntingly returned to their business.— Well, well, you certainly made a fool out of me! it chuckled. Got both yourselves here, yes indeed, the full pair. Made an even shorter passage, you did . . . Quite an occasion, it breezed on.— Welcome, welcome to America! Now stand up tall, both of you, because it's time to present you to the Great Troll. Kristina, my dear, have you saved the jewel that the reverend left you? You know, the one I helped you with—

Although she felt nothing for that monster but hatred and terror, the woman now found that she could not remove herself from its ascendancy. With a fixed smile she grabbled in her pockets, while Øistein quietly wiped the ooze out of her hair.

Perfect! the skeleton chortled, clapping its fingers together with a hateful hissing noise. Give it here.

The most unpleasant errand Kristina ever undertook was touching that bony hand, but she had to do it, so she did, and the skeleton received her talisman.

Thank you, my dear, it said. Now let me think . . . Oh, yes!— Capering and sniggering, it lobbed the dark stone into the nearest corpse-fire, while the troll-women ducked back, wiping their sweaty foreheads. For a moment nothing happened, and then the jewel exploded, giving off a sweet incense of blackberries, sunlight and church candles. The trolls wrinkled their noses. The vapor hung there for a moment, then darkened into dust.— One more illusion disposed of! explained Captain Gull.

It now began to lead them downward, into the same cold stillness which comes to Stavanger at the beginning of a rain, deeper and deeper, until the Pedersons had practically forgotten their names, and eternity glowed like blue cloud-light on the domes of their grey skulls.

Øistein said bitterly: A narrower passage than we expected, captain!

Well, man, you paid your money, so make the best of it, and after that no words were said.

Further they went, to Skullheim and below. Øistein felt ever more hopeless, although there was nothing to do but keep Kristina's spirits up, after the example of that rich man in Stavanger who bought his family a grave beneath the choir, just in case they could still hear the music. Troll-women, muck-furred corpse-gulpers, stretched out their hands to touch them, cold yet hideously active. Everyone was toiling—and on that ac-count, hope returned to the Pedersons like sunlight seen through many columns of drying sardines; they began to realize that they might do well enough for themselves, even here. For all they knew, there might be a passage back to Stavanger—a long one, to be sure, but given time enough they could dig their way with Cousin's Eyvind's awl. So, following their master, they entered the monsters' larder as inevitably as baskets of her-ring getting winched up the sides of those narrow sharp-roofed ware-houses; and there was even a simulacrum of the great wooden hand, ever so familiar, which pointed upward in the window of Mr. Kielland's shop, with a necklace of amber and carnelian looped about its wrist; at this sight the Pedersons' memories flew out of their hearts as bright as new wet clots of wool in a farmwife's dark doorway, and Kristina, feeling ever more at peace, recollected from her girlhood, although she could not have said why it now so consolingly haunted her, the great dew-studded spiderweb of a nettle colony, all plants growing outward from an empty ring, interlacing their bristly leaves. As for Øistein, he contented himself with the faith that at least he and his wife would remain like-minded forever.

The passage was as dark as the nets which hung in the fishermen's empty houses, but there began to be great phosphorescent side-chambers at left and right. All the people who had ever died lay smoked and gutted like Norwegian brisling, Mediterranean sardines; imagine the cans of sardines laid out in double rows of five in each pan, four pans per rack, on the bed of the lidding press and you can imagine how the human corpses looked, with she-trolls busily laying them in iron coffins and slathering them with oil.

This way, said the skeleton. Here's where you Pedersons will find yourselves most useful. Øistein, you can still make barrels, I hope?

It led them through the row of furnaces—crisscrossed logs in their dirt—then nine times nine racks of corpses getting smoked; the Pedersons had to admit that even this was better than sharing a house with twenty people forever. But for a moment Øistein impractically wished that he could have seen Kristina once more in some more pleasant place, even the most verminous street of Stavanger, and even with her back turned as she crept wearily away with a bucket of dirty clothes to wash; if he only could have known, he would have run after her, kissed the striped hem of her long grey skirt—

And they came into another cavern, nearly as large as the first, where to support any conceivable silver-weight in their winches' grasp, slant beams ran down much of the oozy fronts of the tall, narrow warehouses, most of which still sported pointed roofs as in Old Stavanger; within their lightless rooms, dead women, including Kristina's mother, toiled waist deep in a stream of silver treasure, and the kerchiefs were open like flowers on the women's heads . . . and so at last, their hearts like wet grass on an autumn's evening, Øistein and Kristina saw where all the herring of Rogaland had gone.

THE QUEEN'S GRAVE

But how is that future diminished or consumed, which as yet is not? or how that past increased, which is no longer, save . . . in the mind . . . ? For it expects, it considers, it remembers . . .

Saint Augustine, *Confessions*, bef. 430 A.D.

1

My mind bloomed white as yarrow on the queen's green grave. On the queen's green grave I lay all night, my face down in the cold wet grass, my purpose right-angled like a wool comb, because Ingrid, beautifully cruel, had promised to leave me unless I brought her a true swan-shirt. It was hardly the first thing she had asked of me, and I wondered how soon she would finish weaving the cloth of her discontent. So far I had wisely bowed my head to her demands. My obedience was resistance, because it delayed our separation. On this occasion her bright and narrow lips had smiled so freshly that I could not imagine refusing her—all the more since she so evidently hoped I would fail. When one is young, and sets his heart on another person, whatever unwillingness she raises may be interpreted optimistically, as mere admonition, rather than as the dreary verdict that it impels: convicted of unloveability; sentenced to loneliness! So I gave Ingrid's evasions and commandments their most splendid possible construction, hoping that we might yet get along; and because we are all of us passing changeable, at least until our bones get exposed, what could prevent her from possibly discovering more use for me? Three years she allowed me, most of which I spent wandering uselessly among the bird-lakes of Lapland, whose dark shore-rocks are scratched with fleets of swan-necked picture-ships. I importuned goosegirls and witchwives, haunted rookeries by moonlight and was gulled out of all my silver by knowing cormorant-trappers. Guarding my breath within me, I even sought beneath the water the horse, the fish and the iron snake. My perseverance lacking sorcerous qualities, I surfaced with nothing but muck and ice. When I look back on that time I can see that its sorrows and difficulties prepared me for my interview with the queen—but these had begun the instant I met Ingrid; and, for that matter, what would have caused me to love her, had my elders not raised me to love trials for their own sake? To submit, not to Ingrid but to suffering, in order to pay my weird fates their fair price, that was what I did, while the cold water ran out of my aching ears, and I coughed up mud. With what contempt Ingrid would have beheld me then, she who dressed herself so perfectly in black, silver and white, just like the autumn sea! Once more I dove, grappling myself down by the reed-roots, caressing the ooze in those same breaststroke-arcs by which a bellycrawling mason lays down tile, but the most promising thing I could grasp was a pebble. When I crawled out, goose-flocks overflew me, as white and perfect as the breasts of Ingrid.

To be honest, I cannot tell you why I should ever have appealed to her. Almost any other man would have paid three years for the privilege of hunting her a swan-shirt; at least, so the cormorant-trappers told me, grinning. As for me, I loved her, to be sure; I adored the sweet hands of my Ingrid, and the way she watched me with that soft smile of hers whose meaning I thought I knew, not to mention her dark eyebrow-arches. But what does a woman do with a swan-shirt but throw it over her shoulders early one morning and fly away? By now you can tell that my mind circled round and round Ingrid, with more longing than understanding. My dreams and desires concerning her, whatever else they might once have been, had long expressed themselves as mere directional pressure, much as the pallid grasses point downriver from beneath some black current where the salmon no longer spawn.

A certain cormorant-trapper's widowed daughter, pitying and desiring me, offered not only to weave me a swan-shirt but also to love me and care for me until death, in the fine turf house her dead husband had left her, on the top of a windy hill of reeds. She was a woman of such kind ways that when she came out her door in the morning, ducks, geese and even seagulls would alight in a circle around her, upstretching their necks and opening their beaks, as if for food; what they truly yearned for were caresses, which she gave them. In the side of the hill she had dug a secret cave, which could be reached only through a tunnel behind the kitchen stove; here she hid away cormorants from her angry troll of a father, and when she brought me into that place, simply trusting and loving me, I upraised my candle and saw that in that vast hall of dark dirt she had even made a black lake, glittering with fishes of copper and gold, so that her cormorants could feed and entertain themselves. She and I might well have found joy together. But since I had made up my mind to something else, there was no help for it.

In other words, this story does not exactly begin on the night when Ingrid first asked me for her heart's desire, nearly closing her heavy eyes as she lay there naked, slyly, sleepily watching me, with one hand on her knee and the other between her gaping thighs. Naturally I wanted to make love right then, but Ingrid refused. Sweetly faithless she had smoothly become, so soon as she felt herself sure of owning me. Whenever I for my part begged for some assurance to keep, my entreaty was as a stone dropped down a dark well; I never even heard the splash. But Ingrid did smile, calmly and beautifully; that was what she gave me just then; I longed to lick her white teeth. Or if she had only slapped me a few times, sharply, so that I could taste each sting, that would have nourished me equally well. I informed my Ingrid that what I wished was for her to trust and depend on me. I desired her to be my linen-goddess—the one I lived for. She replied that she had tried such an experiment once, with someone who brought her such jealous misery that she became abject.

What happened to him? I said.

Oh, one morning he turned into a white pig. Do you want to see him? He's in the swineyard. You two might find common topics to grunt about.

Well, I'm not him, I told her; you can depend on me.

Then do bring me that swan-shirt, said Ingrid. In not a day more than three years, and in the meantime I don't promise to be faithful.

I'll set out in the morning. Will you give me some bread and cheese to carry?

What you don't understand, said Ingrid, is that any help I gave you would only make it worse.

2

The cormorant-trapper's daughter warmed me in her bed, beat the dirt out of my clothes, fed me the best she had, saw me to the door, kissed me, and for a parting token gave me a twisting arm-snake of good red gold. I thanked her with all my heart.

I've spoken with the swans, she said, and it seems that swan-shirts are even rarer than they used to be. I wish you'd take mine; it would save so much effort! I've only worn it once, to make sure I wove the right magic. Surely Ingrid wouldn't mind that.

Well, I would, I said.

Have it your way, she answered. All the Valkyries who used to turn into swans have flown away. So you'd need to find a witch to make you one. From what the wind tells me, the greatest witch alive is this Ingrid of yours. Tell me, does she do anything in bed that I can't do?

Well, she has a certain way of smiling that's not a smile, and she knows how to leave me lonely when she opens her legs, so that no matter how deep inside her I go, I can never reach her, which makes her a goddess, or at least an infinite dream. And since she never gives me anything, nothing from her appears imperfect.

I wish you joy of her, said the cormorant-trapper's daughter. My advice is to inquire about swan-shirts at the queen's grave.

I asked her which queen—for there are as many queens as there are women—and the cormorant-trapper's daughter replied: Good Queen Hnoss was the wisest of all, or at least so the seagulls tell me, and they've flown even to the other side of the sea.

I thanked her again. She smiled at me, quite cheerfully, then went inside and shut the door.

As I set off into the wind, I had to wonder whether I were doing the right thing. The cormorant-trapper's daughter truly was so goodhearted. Besides, her bed was a veritable nest of eiderdown; no chill could ever get in there. And for some reason I could never even imagine dwelling forever with Ingrid, in her tall narrow house on her meadow of butter-rich grass. But I could see no help for it, so I kept walking, in search of the queen's grave. Soon the night was as dark as an iron axehead.

3

Yes, the queen's name was Hnoss, meaning *jewel,* which so many precious women have been called since the time of Freya's elder daughter. She lived in the time when the sea was higher than now, and keys' heads more complex than their stems. But in her day as in ours the highest human office was that of giver; and indeed this woman gained strange renown for her generosity, as you will hear; for when a friendless old thrall fell down sick before her hall, she had him carried to the hearth and nursed; once he strengthened sufficiently to go his own way, she gave him a gold ring for his family. And as I tell this over, it strikes me that this Hnoss was not so unalike to the cormorant-trapper's daughter—still another reason I might have done just as well remaining in her company. But how are we to know what others are? Ingrid's soul, for instance, was lightless, and of course that ancient thrall was not what he seemed. What woe he might already have worked upon our kind is unknown; for what malice he had come there is likewise concealed; but thanks to her kindness and healing leechcraft, the queen became the one and only member of humankind who receives praise in the *Jötunsbok,* the Book of Giants; and I have even heard that on her account the end of the world was put off by seven years. As for the king, his lendermen and thralls, and all the other hard people who grubbed over that turf until it devoured them, they doubtless took what they could of her. All the *Morkinskinna* says of her is that she was a good queen, who received everybody well, and furthermore brought good seasons, although ordinarily those are said to be brought about by kings. Never a wife gave birth but the queen sent something to her, be it a cooking-pot or a length of wadmal cloth. She was an unparalleled weaver, and introduced the lovely elf-stitch, which no one alive can duplicate—all the more reason to inquire at her grave about swan-shirts. Besides, when she died she must have gone to her friends, and one of them might know where I could get a swan-shirt for Ingrid.

4

So I walked all the way around the world, beginning to wonder whether my resolution might prove as fatal as King Swegde's vow to seek Odin's dwelling-place; a dwarf enticed him into a boulder, promising him his heart's desire, and he never came out. The longer I searched, the less I cared for gifting Ingrid and the more I desired the swan-shirt for myself, although perhaps I had no use for it, either. So I became old, hence unworthy of the loving gaze of Ingrid with her freckled young face. I had to remind myself of the fact that I loved Ingrid so very much, because she was beautiful and her vagina knew a special sucking trick. Counting red cows and black cows on the old green grave-mounds, I proceeded toward the queen's grave, which, as a kindly sexton told me, lay on the sea-meadow just over the hill from Ingrid's. That night I dreamed three times of Ingrid calmly refusing to make love to me, and each time I woke up in tears with an erection. Tomorrow would be the last day of my three years.

5

Ingrid lived where the sea resembled the interior of a mussel shell, and in her back meadow, just past the pigsty, rose Frey's mound, a fine old green hill where long ago, it is said, there was a door with three holes in it, one for gold, one for silver and one for copper; into these people paid their taxes to the god, in exchange for fat cows and good seasons. Since Ingrid had told me to keep away from there—and she never expressed her prohibitions but once—I avoided that place now, with its breath-sucking wind, all the more since I preferred for her not to catch sight of me until I had succeeded or failed. Besides, why should I mind detouring around a hill when I had already circumnavigated the world? Around the hill I went, and then down to the salmon-creeks and sheep-fields where all the lesser mounds were. One cold sunny morning long ago, before I ever met Ingrid, I came here to watch the salmonberries dance in the wind with the sea so bright behind them, while I wondered why I was squandering my life. Now that my life had been safely spent on Ingrid in any event, that flock of regrets had long since flown off to roost on some younger hero's shoulders. Rich in moss, grass and islands, such most happily remained my life; and even if my travels had not precisely accomplished my hopes, there is something to be said for not sitting at home, especially just now, when, feeling excited that I could soon present myself to Ingrid one way or the other, I enjoyed so sweetly striding along, with ahead of me the sea-ribbon wrapping grey and ultramarine around green grass. Past where I was going, the pale reddish dunes reminded me of Ingrid's pubic hair.

At first I could see that long green howe among the lesser gravel-scattered graves, but as I drew closer, the lowlier mounds puffed up their own claims, for, after all, every barrow-wight deserves to be noticed, even if he can only boast of dark iron tweezers and a green-rusted cloak-pin, while his gruesome neighbor might be squatting on an entire moldy sack of tarnished silver coins with holes in them. I suppose that the scald Einar Audunsson had their realm in mind when he sang:

A troll will scarcely sit at home
if he can dig a new kingdom

—a verse whose main virtue is to frighten children.

Out of a hole now rose an old woman in a moss-colored dress. Her hair was as the lank orange sea-grass between graves, and she said: Love me, and I'll weave you a mole-shirt, so you can creep among the roots with me forever.— I can't say this offer left me unmoved, but since I had come all this way (never mind that had I avoided tramping all the way around the world, this place wasn't but two hours from Ingrid's house), it seemed most befitting to persist in my purpose, so I gave her a kiss, although her frozen mouth tore the skin right off my lips, which she considerately salved with troll-fat, and then she pointed out my way across the green waves of howes over the fields, to where the queen's grave rose alone. Where King Yngvar was buried I wished to ask, but dreading either to pay the fee of another kiss or else to disappoint her by turning away from her hard and glistening blue-grey mouth, I thanked her with all my heart, sending my best wishes to her cousins the moles, at which, scratching my shoulder in what she meant to be a caress, she chuckled fondly and melted back under the earth. As for me, I made my way toward those white sheep-ovals in a line halfway up a rock-boned emerald hill all by itself, not as high as some, but all the same it must have cost her thralls and lendermen some pains to build. Between afternoon and evening I got there. Forgetting the old woman with the orange hair, I wondered what could be as chilly as the green-maned shoulder of the queen's grave, where I threw myself down, breathing in the scent of wet dirt; and now the autumn sun made landfall at the rocky river-mouth, rested upon the sea-horizon like a fabulous egg, then left me, just as Ingrid meant to do.

So darkness oozed up out of the sea, and presently a whole crew of grave-wights wailed and giggled all about me, longing to be givers or tak-ers, if I were only willing; and to me each proposition seemed as good as the next, except of course for Ingrid's, so I declined them all with thanks, at which some of them turned sour, and even snicked their teeth at me, while the rest either popped back down to their bones or else took on that lovely abstraction one sees on women's firelit faces when they are plaiting cord. I was introduced to a fetching goddess of an old headdress; I met many goddesses of the serpent's bed; their dead flesh was as white as the barnacles on black rocks. Without boasting I assure you that had I wished, I could have been suffocated in a troll-woman's bristly arms; she offered honest lust, and her breath was as cold as frozen meat. An elf-wife kissed her hand to me and gave me a silver coin. A troll-hag took a jab at me with a poisoned ice-needle; that was when I found out that my gold bracelet from the cormorant-trapper's daughter gave me magic protection, which I had to confess made me all the fonder of her. At any rate, I continued about my business of waiting for the queen. And soon enough, being no less weak and flighty than I, those ghosts and such moaned back down to their holes.

Now indeed came the time to lay down my gift from the cormorant-trapper's daughter, which I had faithfully kept upon my wrist all over the world, sometimes thinking, I admit, to offer it to my darling Ingrid, although she would have repaid me with anger—for Ingrid could be superstitious; I had found her unwilling to give her arm to be devoured in the gape of a gold bracelet of unknown provenance, in case it enslaved her by means of some spell. Kissing the arm-ring, I laid it down in the grass, and prayed the dead queen of her kindness.

First came a silver-blue shimmering of noble lady-sprites—evidently the mead-maidens and weaving-dames of Queen Hnoss's court. I bowed to each and all, wishing them joy of the cold air. And presently, when the night once again became as cold and black as an iron axehead, two skeleton-hands blossomed up through the turf, offering me a wide bronze bowl with snakeheaded handles. Even in death she remained a generous queen; her husband King Yngvar must have been very lucky, at least at one time. Had I accepted this gift from her, all might have gone differently, for me if not for Ingrid. Instead, I placed my silver coin in it, and greedily it rushed back under the earth.

Now the queen's old skull emerged from the turf, without hesitation, as if she did not know or did not care how hideous she might appear to me. In fact I have never met a woman entirely without charm, and this goes equally for dead ones, so the queen and I got on well enough. She wore a long-sleeved, wine-red dress with braids of gold and silver at the sleeve. Her hair, wet like fresh-cut grass, was combed down as carefully as the threads in her warp-weighted loom, and she wore snails for ear-rings.

She offered me a gold axehead which was shining with engraved serpent-men, but all I prayed of her was that snowy swan-shirt.

That's good, then, said the queen. You passed the test. You refrained from what you couldn't use.

I've heard of your openhandedness, said I. That's why I came to you.

I'll give you all a man desires, she replied. First, I'll give you a bride.

Ingrid?

Ingrid is not for such as you. It's wandering she'd rather be, and good riddance to her. Your destiny is the cormorant-trapper's daughter. Do you remember her name?

Turid, I said. The instant I said it, I fell in love. *Turid* means *beautiful.*

That's right. For the rest of your life, whenever you forget what you need to do, ask Turid. She'll take care of you. Do you promise me?

I swear by Freya.

You could have sworn by me. But here's how you get the shirt: Open my grave at sunrise, and dig down to me. Cut off the little finger of my left hand, and leave everything else alone. Cover me up again, or my hus-band will punish you. As soon as you see Ingrid, throw my finger in her face.

And when the shirt comes, shall I keep it for Turid?

No, man, you must give Ingrid the shirt, so that she has had her use of you. And take back the arm-ring that Turid gave you. It will defend you against Ingrid. Farewell.

On the queen's green grave I lay all night. A maiden in weeds of gold smiled sadly, reaching for my hair. Whenever trolls sought to choke me in their lichen-scabbed arms, I diverted myself by thinking about Turid. Was she lying awake? When I last left her house, a morning sun-ray had struck the crossbars of her leaning loom, and her bread was rising.

6

At dawn small dark birds exploded from a leafless tree, and the salmon stream began to glow. I peeled the turf off the summit of the queen's grave. Then I dug down with a sheep scapula until I found a bog-iron brooch, whose edge scraped the earth as nicely as could be. So I came to the rectangular stone-walled trench. Closest to the surface, but in a side-chamber, I uncovered the skeletons of all those court ladies I had glimpsed the night before, the cruel clay having long since tightened about them, drawing their skulls together like a woman's yarn bobbins. Begging their pardons and giving them each a kiss, I kept digging, a chore which although it was not easy proved less tiring than my walk around the world. Before noon I reached her. There she lay, rubble of bone in rags of linen, and no sadder thing have I ever seen than the dead queen's broken twill.

Once she had reigned here with her skeleton-hands outspread across her ribs like fans, but slowly the worms and roots dislodged her finger-rings; then they bent her ribs apart and groped up toward the sun. Then a farmer dug her up and robbed her of her spider-figured golden brooch. A subsequent crofter showed better heart, although his deed might have been misguided; thanks to him a rune-cut lead cross was buried with her in the grave. Gently setting this aside, I stroked away the dirt from the queen's hand, and found that the little finger was all the poor lady had left. There was no need to cut it off; it came up in my hand.

At her side the tines of her bone comb lay outspread like the fingers she no longer had. At her feet was a cracked bowl of dark clay, with my silver coin in it.

Behind her head a stone passage went down. With the sun now over-head, I could see some way in. There lay good Queen Hnoss, and far be-neath her was a boy's skeleton on its side, gaping like a panting dog.

Bowing to my hostess, I gave her back her lead cross. Then I covered everything up, and replaced the living turf.

7

It was night when I came home to Ingrid. I fear I was haggard and grubby after my travels. The door opened, and there stood Ingrid, who always made her dresses so elegant with the bright hooks and waves of tablet-woven braid. She was decked out as if for company, in double brooches, and a thrice-bright woven braid across her breast, a chain of silver dipping down. Perhaps it was I she had been waiting for. Her hair was brighter than morning sunlight on the sea, and she was smiling her old smile of mirth without cheer, brightness without friendliness, invitation without promise. Needless to say, I desired her as much as ever.

You didn't bring it, I see, was the first thing she said.

Straightaway, I threw the queen's finger-bone in her face, and my poor Ingrid went pale and rigid. Then she began marching into the darkness. Thinking it a pity for her clothes to get spoiled, I helped her out of them, not that she thanked me, and then allowed her to go nightwalking in her shift, as so she plainly desired, with her pretty bottom showing, and her not even knowing it. The last I saw of her, she was already in the sky, trudging obediently off across the moonbeams, her hands out before her as if she were a timid child on horseback who dared not let go the reins.

Thinking I might as well get something for myself out of all this while my darling was gone, I pushed her bedstead aside, which she had told me never to do, and behind it were three secret chambers connected to Frey's mound, one for the copper, one for the silver and one for the gold. Since there was so much more copper than anything else, I decided not to deprive Ingrid of what she evidently preferred to collect, and contented myself with taking all the gold and silver I could carry. Then I pushed back the bed and sat eating up Ingrid's bread and cheese, for walking all the way around the world is hungry work, never mind digging up graves, and Ingrid had neglected to offer me anything. After that I felt caught up on my obligations. The only other thing I might have done was to set free her enchanted pigs, but for all I knew they were happier as they were; I myself could have made the best of it as one of Ingrid's pigs, provided that she pulled my tail every now and then.

Here at dawn came my poor Ingrid, creeping down from the white sky's grey cloud-cobbles, sinking to the ankle in the wet green pasturage churned up by the cows, shivering and sweating without knowing that she did, with her blonde hair down, her night-shift sopping wet and that swan-shirt, courtesy of the cormorant-trapper's daughter, held tight against her bosom.

I threw the queen's finger-bone in her face again, and back to herself she came, my sweet old Ingrid, awarding me quite the hateful look.

Needless to say, I was wearing Turid's arm-ring, so Ingrid couldn't enchant me. She stood there dripping with dew and rain, and her mouth twitched while she decided how best to lay hands on me.

Good morning to you, I said.

In a rage, she bit her lower lip. Just then she noticed what she had in her arms, and her expression changed. Right away she commenced to coo and sigh over it, kissing the feathers one by one, until she remembered me again and sent her evil eye my way, in case I meant to rob her of her fine swan-shirt.

Where did I get this? she demanded.

You went barefoot to Lapland and back, I said. An easy walk, I should say, since you didn't get any blisters.

That was when she finally realized that my heart had changed. I should have felt sorry for her, but my indifference resembled the green grass that conquers a pillaged grave-hole.

Sulking, Ingrid rushed off to the duckpond to bathe. I made a point of not watching. When she returned, the morning was strengthening, and she was naked and white to tempt me.

Well, said Ingrid, don't you even feel like making love?

But your swan-shirt came a day late.

Oh, don't worry about that, said she, as sweet as I had ever heard. The main thing is that I have my heart's desire, no matter how. And so we'll live happily ever after, until I leave you.

When might that be?

That's no concern of yours. Now, do you want to make love or not?— And she swung her hips a trifle, so that I knew what she wished me to say.

Since doing the opposite of whatever she asked was bringing me such success, I said: Well, well, Ingrid, since that swan-shirt put us both to so much trouble, I'm curious to see how you look in it.

Of course Ingrid could not resist that; she longed more than anything to become a swan and fly away. So she pulled the beautiful thing over her head, slid her arms through the sleeves, and she was naked from her belly down, while from her belly up the perfect white swan-feathers sparkled like sea-waves, each one of them trapped so cunningly in the alternate-leaved V's of linen, the quills rustling so sweetly with her heartbeats, and her long blonde hair spilling loose and windblown across all that precious whiteness, although I must admit that this set me to thinking of the queen's hair ornaments scattered about her hairless skull. Turning her back to me, she began singing down to the grey ocean. Then she turned into a white swan and flew off.

As for me, I went home to my Turid, whose ways were as bright as lake-edge flowers. On the way I reburied the queen's finger-bone in her grave, and poured in a double handful of gold, because a generous queen can never have enough of that. I also gave a gold coin apiece to the elf-wife and the old woman with the orange hair. As for the silver, I scattered that from mound to mound, so that the other wights would have joy of me.

Turid was standing in the doorway smiling, with a serpent-pin at the throat of her soft grey shift. She had the white breast and proud neck of a Norwegian wooden church. We went straight to bed. Once I asked her what she saw in me, and she replied that she liked a man who was easily satisfied. I gave her the rest of Ingrid's gold, or Frey's as I should say, which she buried in her cave of cormorants, in case we might ever need it. From what the birds told us, Ingrid was very happy, and enjoyed taking her lovers in the air. (I fear her pigs all starved.) Whenever she flew to our house in hopes of bewitching me again, Turid went out to deal with her, and hid me in her eiderdown nest. In time she gave me a whole brood of bird-children, and our life together grew as moist as sea-wind over the sweet-grassed graves.

STAR OF NORWAY

To never again suffer the failing of the light I thought to give anything. We played on an old mound. The blue-grey light of spring clothed us all night. But to never again suffer the failing of the light, to have done with dancing strings of birch leaves, wasn't that to change fear for sorrow?

Between grey lakes and black rocks rose a hill:— There's my house.— Take me with you.— Too steep for you!

Behind the hill was her favorite river.— Then let me go there with you.— You'd never come back.

She undid her hair.— Let me touch it.— It will cut you.— Let me marry you.— Then we're married.

More lovely than white flowers in spring are the blue-black berries of the coffin-tree.— Come with me. Then you'll understand the old rock carvings.— But I refused to leave the wind-dance of birch leaves.— Come with me. Then I'll kiss you on the mouth.— Where will you take me?— We'll climb the coffin-tree into the sky.

Behind the wall of Christmas trees I ate berries from her hand until the cramps began. Then we laughed and went crazy. When I was light enough to stand upon the crest of a pine tree without bending it, I could climb the coffin-tree.

Because she would not hold my hand, I remembered someone else's arms like birch branches shaking against the grey sky. Had she or someone else been crying? But I'd lost the long stone tunnel into spring.

More lovely than white flowers in spring is the loveliness of a dead woman's white arms.— Why is it so cold?— It's not cold. Come to me.

VI

THE FORGETFUL GHOST

1

After my father died, I began to wonder whether my turn might come sooner rather than later. What a pity! Later would have been so much more convenient! And what if my time might be even sooner than soon? Before I knew it, I would recognize death by its cold shining as of brass. Hence in those days, I do confess, I felt sometimes angry that the treasures of sunlight escaped my hands no matter how tightly I clenched them. I loved life so perfectly, at least in my own estimation, that it seemed I deserved to live forever, or at least until later rather than sooner. But just in case death disregarded my all-important judgments, I decided to seek out a ghost, in order to gain expert advice about being dead. The living learn to weigh the merits of preparation against those of spontaneity, which is why they hire investment counselors and other fortune-tellers. And since I had been born an American, I naturally believed myself entitled to any destiny I could pay for. Why shouldn't my post-mortem years stretch on like a lovely procession of stone lamps?

If you believe, as H. P. Lovecraft asserted, that all cemeteries are sub-terraneously connected, then it scarcely matters which one you visit; so I put one foot before the other, and within a half-hour found myself al-lured by the bright green moss on the pointed tops of those ancient stone columns of the third Shogun's loyally suicided retainers. Next I found, glowing brighter than the daylight, more green moss upon the stone railings and torii enclosing these square plots whose tombstones strained upward like trees, each stone engraved with its under-tenant's postmor-tem Buddhist name.

The smell of moss consists of new and old together. Dead matter hav-ing decayed into clean dirt, the dirt now freshens into green. It is this becoming-alive which one smells. I remember how when my parents got old, they used to like to walk with me in a certain quiet marsh. The mud there smelled clean and chocolate-bitter. I now stood breathing this same mossy odor, and fallen cryptomeria-needles darkened their shades of green and orange while a cloud slid over the sun. Have you ever seen a lizard's eyelid close over his yellow orb? If so, then you have entered ghostly regions, which is where I found myself upon the sun's darkening. All the same, I had not gone perilously far: On the other side of the wall, tiny cars buzzed sweetly, bearing living skeletons to any number of premortem destinations. Reassured by the shallowness of my commitment, I approached the nearest grave.

The instant I touched the wet moss on the railing, I fell into communication with the stern occupant, upon whose wet dark hearthstone lay so many dead cryptomeria-tips. To say he declined to come out would be less than an understatement. It was enough to make a fellow spurn the afterlife! I experienced his anger as an electric shock. To him I was nothing, a rootless alien who lacked a lord to die for. Why should he teach me?

Humiliated, I turned away, and let myself into the lower courtyard behind the temple. Here grew the more diminutive ovoid and phallic tombs of priests. Some were incised with lotus wave-patterns. One resembled a mirror or hairbrush stood on end. I considered inviting myself in, but then I thought: If that lord up there was so cross, wouldn't a priest have even less use for me?

So I pulled myself up to the temple's narrow porch and sat there with my feet dangling over, watching cherry blossoms raining down on the tombs. The gnarled arms of that tree pointed toward every grave, and afternoon fell almost into dusk.

A single white blossom sped down like a spider parachuting down his newest thread. Then my ears began to ring—death's call.

So I ran away. I sat in my room and hid. Looking out my window, I spied death prising up boards and pouring vinegar on nails. Death killed a dog. What if I were next?

2

Not daring to lose time, I decided to seek a humbler grave. And right down the superhighway, past the darkly muddy rectangles of rice fields scratched with light, I discovered a wet grey necropolis upon a ridge crowded around with shabby houses. At first I wondered what it would be like to live in that neighborhood, with death right above everybody. And then I remembered that all of us do live there.

The sky had cleared well before twilight. I killed time, so to speak, in a narrow little eel restaurant. Within the lacquered box which the old man served to me, wormlike nut-brown segments lay side by side on their bed of snow-white rice. They were delicious. I felt as if I were getting advance revenge on the nightcrawlers which would eat me someday. And I cried out to the old man: Aren't you glad we're still alive?

Sometimes, he replied, I forget about everything but paying my taxes.

By now the moon had risen. Ascending the steep path, I arrived at the thicket of gravestones and found a meager one with just a few lichen-specks on it. The name on it was nearly effaced, and three neighboring steles shaded it so effectively that I had reason to hope that this soul might not be proud. Thank goodness!

I bowed twice from the bottom of my heart, clapped my hands, and knocked upon the tomb. Right away the ghost swam out. He had a wide, pallidly smiling face, and was serenely rigid, glowing like a spray of cherry blossoms in the sun. His eyes were mirrors in which I did not see myself.

Yes? he said. Who are you? Have we met before?

I don't think so, I replied.

Well, said he, in that case I'm at a loss. I wasn't sure if I remembered you.

At first I thought him sprightly as well as spritely; his movements were as crisp as the golden characters of the Lotus Sutra marching down blue-blackness, each column ruled off with gold, each letter even both horizontally and vertically with all the others.

I asked his name, and he said: Well, I used to be— Actually, what does that matter? By the way, this moonlight is almost too bright. Doesn't it hurt you?

Not really.

Oh. I wish I could be as strong as you.

He liked to interrupt me as eagerly as raindrops leap up from stones. In his words and flights he made flashy starts, but soon began to amble uncertainly. He was an entirely friendly ghost; I can't say I disliked him.

I inquired how to avoid suffering after my death, and he flittered about like an immense carp, smiling so widely that for an instant I took alarm and wondered if he meant to eat me. I asked if I were tiring him; I offered to run away, but he said it wouldn't do any good.

What's your aspiration? I wondered, and he told me it was to lick the sweat from a young girl's leg just one more time—he had grown too uncertain of himself to aspire higher than that.

I tried to learn whether life without consciousness might be preferable to consciousness without life; but to calculate the answers he needed to count several secret variables simultaneously upon his misty fingers, and soon lost track of where he had started. Of course he could not inscribe the sand with anyone's memorial stick, nor borrow pen and paper from me, being utterly permeable in relation to objects.

Well, then, you wouldn't be able to lick anyone's leg, I reminded him. My satisfaction, in which I could not help but bask, consisted of the fact that this ghost was dead and I alive. I was safer, more superior, less likely *ever* to be dead!

His eyes kept goggling. I asked if I would die soon.— Prune? the ghost echoed in bewilderment.

We continued to discuss the matter of suffering, and he suddenly cried out: But just now I can't quite remember what *suffering* means. So sorry! How do you spell it?

S, u . . .

Beg your pardon? *F?*

S.

Are you quite sure?

He had forgotten just enough to make a conversation exasperating, but not enough for him to give up hope of communicating his thoughts, such as they were, and of listening to me, in an effort to remind himself of what life was, and perhaps even to escape, however momentarily, into some pretense of life of his own. And how I longed to escape from *him*! I would have done nearly anything to avoid becoming his younger brother. Unfortunately, it wasn't up to me. As for him, was it his fault that he wasn't alive? Many times I have seen old men go through the motions of picking up the young girls who would joyfully have let themselves be carried away in ancient days; it's as if one needs to learn over and over the lesson of loss, and even then one hopes that since the rules altered before, they might change back again. But they never do, at least not for the better; and although I sought to be as patient as I could, I increasingly resembled the ignorant, bustling child who grows annoyed when its grandfather fails to accompany its lunges to and fro.

He wanted to know the current prices of everything.— How many golden ryo? he asked. How many silver kwan?— He imagined himself to be au courant, since he had not yet forgotten those two bygone coins.

Well, I finally said, I was thinking—

Are you always thinking? interrupted the ghost with extreme interest.

Yes.

Sometimes I don't think about anything, the ghost confided.

And is that relaxing? Would you rather not think than think?

Is *relaxing* a pattern or a sound?

A pattern.

And what was it you were trying to ask me?

Never mind.

Oh, you forgot? That makes me feel better. I sometimes forget things also. Do you know why?

No.

I was hoping you could tell me why.

I'd wanted to learn to die, but instead was condemned to try unavailingly to teach a ghost to live. Did it follow that perhaps I could help him forget that he was dead if he in turn taught me to forget that I lived? No matter; I found myself ever less ambitious to ride to death in a palanquin shrine. I'd rather keep hold of my flesh, at least until rain falls in Tokyo and people run away with newspapers over their heads.

The ghost would not stop asking me questions. I finally said: Ask the grass. Ask why it lives.

What an intelligent idea! he said. He bent shyly down over a tuft, and I sneaked away. Perhaps I'd return to the cemetery where the third Shogun's lieutenants dwelled. I'd dwell again in the shade of the tall cryptomerias. From the spreading cherry tree, there'd come a pale pink rain. Didn't I possess places to go? Wasn't I a fellow who once might have been slightly in the know?

But without the ghost I quickly remembered my helplessness in this alien environment and repented of my cruelty. I had lost myself among the crowds of tombstones. Bumping accidentally against them, I discovered myself hounded by marching ghosts in laced red corset-armor, their legs wound up in white like mummy-worms, their faces phosphorescent blotches of horror. They could not really strangle me, but their touches chilled me; my bones ached with cold. Ahead of me loomed an immense black whirling wheel—my death, no doubt. Well, well; it was going to be *sooner*! Somehow I reached the edge of the cemetery and leaped into the darkness. I fell and fell. When I came to earth, there was scarcely any pain, which made me wonder whether I had died.

Overhead hovered a familiar pallid, plump-cheeked shrine figure. The ghost had fluttered off to wait for me. He was very good at that.

What was I supposed to ask the grass? he inquired.

Ask which one of us is dead.

Dead? Is that spelled with an *x* or a *z*?

A *z*.

Just a moment. I'll go find out. Actually, I was wondering the same thing.

He flew slowly away, but when he returned his flight was as long and straight as one of the bolts on a sanctuary door. He reported: The grass said just forget you're dead and then you can go on. Let's both do it.

Well . . .

But last time didn't you say that it's spelled with an *x*?

I demanded to know what he meant. The ghost sighed: Don't you remember how often you've been here?

THE GHOST OF RAINY MOUNTAIN

1

To reach Rainy Mountain one must pass Dripping Pine, where after getting drenched with many silver drops one will hear a crow cry four times.

When Rainy Mountain is dry, even should the day be cloudy and windy, and the peak manage somehow to conceal itself within grey vapors, the mountain remains diminished by being seen, like our childhood homes which once sheltered and imprisoned us so grandly. At such hours paltriness afflicts its pines and cedars, and the spreads of blossoming cherry branches at its foot resemble nothing better than pallid scars in its dark jade flesh. Roofs, wires, aerials gash its lower reaches.

Above the gravel lot between two houses runs a mossy wall over the top of which flower mediocre shrubs beneath a yellow fence which halfway hides a wide pink cherry tree, and beyond that rise the foothills of Rainy Mountain. When the storm clouds begin to swarm, Rainy Mountain appears nearly sinister, while on sunny days the way from here to there is so ordinary that most people would rather entertain themselves at home. (To be sure, some wealthy, lonely man might extend himself so far as to to hire black-lacquered hair and a white-lacquered face in a cinnabar kimono whose metallic flowers shine like jewels; but that he can do in any teahouse by the river.) As for me, I preferred to go farther. Attached to the railroad station stands a small clean tourist office whose three-color map still delineates in a curving route of yellow dashes a self-guided promenade around the circumference of Rainy Mountain, but if you ask the stylish young woman about that, she will explain that two years ago a spring flood washed out the footbridge, which the prefectural authorities will have rebuilt by the beginning of next summer. She apologizes, then brightly recommends the geisha dances of the Three Fern School. There also happens to be a wonder-working Buddha (now retired), five minutes' walk past the hospital. If you inquire as to whether Rainy Mountain is haunted, she will clap her hand over her giggling mouth. This happened to me, and I for one was charmed.

Praying to Batoh Kannon, the horseheaded mercy goddess, I set out to

449

seek a ghost whom I could love; for I had recently met with disappointments, perhaps on account of my sunken eyes. It was a good day, a rainy
day. The mountain could have been a cloud. I hoped and hoped through
the green cloud-ribs of a pine tree in spring rain. Although she had never
explored in that direction (having been transferred from Niigata just last
winter), the girl from the tourist office had declined to accompany me.
Smiling and bowing, she said that she must work.

I arrived at the yellow fence by the cherry tree, and seemed to spy a
dashed yellow line upon the asphalt path. An old lady cycled past me,
sounding her bicycle bell as politely as a cough. I wondered where she had
come from, and where I was in life. Ahead, the sky was very dark. The
breeze expressed the sad rattlings of sticks. When I thought ahead I grew
almost afraid, and yet how I longed to do what I was doing! Whether or
not I ever returned from Rainy Mountain, I knew that I would be changed;
not changing would have been unendurable; even the yellow fence sickened me with sameness, never mind the world behind. All the misty
summer-leafed hills of my youth, and the thunderstorm days which magnified them, now invited me to take my adventure on Rainy Mountain,
however lush or eerie this might turn out; for I had been too timid or obedient to ascend them when it could have done me good. What had I grown
into? And where might Dripping Pine be? Descending a minuscule dip, I
reached the remnant of the footbridge. The creek being low, I easily
skipped across, not disturbing a certain muted orange carp.

Tall cryptomeria trees with slender chains around their waists now
outlined my way. Ahead of me, the mist held its breath. If I could see inside Rainy Mountain, would it be the same as seeing inside a cloud? This
question could only be answered through love, or something else of a
similar name.

At the summit of a low hill which had been invisible from the town,
the path turned under a many-branched pine whose needles urinated
upon me, although there was no longer any wind. Immediately afterward, a crow cawed four times. Before me rose a pyramid of greybearded
mist.

Bow two times, clap two times, then bow again, all from the bottom of
one's heart. This is how one is advised to behave at Rainy Mountain.

In Rainy Mountain there is a door whose dark jade shutters bear vermilion-sashed panes, and whose hinges are engraved in crowds of flower-crowned hexagons. I bowed two times; I clapped twice; I bowed. When this door opened, a certain crow cawed three times in the trees behind me.

Within was a wooden lattice-gate. Peering through its vertical bars which had once been green and were now white-streaked like moldy meat, I could see the vermilion steps to a black door with shiny brass hinges, a black door slammed exceedingly well shut! Bowing once and then once more, I clapped the first time and the second, at which the crow cawed twice, and as soon as I had bowed once more the wooden gate opened.

Bowing and clapping before the black door, I then bowed and clapped. The crow cawed. I made my final bow. When this door opened, the ghost of my dreams flittered out.

Her eyes resembled orange slits of light in a black lantern. From her skull sprouted double tassels, as if of horsehair, banded white, then red, then darkish brown with grey streaks showing miscellaneously. Her skirt might have been slats of bamboo chained into tight vertical parallels all around the widening trunk of a giant cypress. Between her breasts, an incense-hole was smoking.

Since she now grinned at me with all her sharp black teeth, I hoped that this particular specimen of ghostly nubility was interested in me, although with ghosts one can never be sure. For that matter, how could I even be sure of myself? Not long after a young girl left me, seven doctors had diagnosed my syndrome as anililagnia, which is to say, sexual interest in older women. Well, when does that become necrophilia? If the lady happens to be a ghost, should we select a different syndrome?

Here she came, her movements as complex and asymmetrical as a Japanese garden. Just as the sheen of rain on vermilion-lacquered shrines is counteracted by the dulling down or darkening of the cloudy atmosphere, so my ardor failed a smidgen, I do confess, the instant that she unfurled her iron claws; but I reminded myself not only of my prior intention to surrender to love, but also of the evident fact that now was no time to be undiplomatic—after all, what in the Devil's name had I expected her to look like?—so I strode forward to embrace her, hooking my thumbs most conveniently on her cold ribs while her talons settled upon my collarbones. She smelled of moss, not death. Narrowing her glowing eyes, she inclined her head to kiss me. Those teeth of hers could have nibbled my lips right off, but since she derived from a gentle species, kissing her proved no worse than pressing my mouth against a cold railing. To tell you the truth, I was reminded of the vulva of that young woman who had recently decided to leave me; visiting for old times' sake, she lay down on my bed, so I naturally slid my hand up her skirt, caressing for the sake of those same old times the perfect closed lips of the slit I used to know, at which she opened her eyes and murmured: Stop.— The ghost of Rainy Mountain uttered no such prohibition. Her claws rested ever so delicately around my throat.

She taught me how to beat the lacquered drum, and make the dead dance. When she opened her legs, I found myself looking up into the petals of a gilded lotus. She showed me what lies hid in vermilion darkness. With great kindness she presented to me the hidden opening of that crypt where the urns of our cremated hopes are buried. Entering my preordained place, I became as free as rain falling down a yellow moss-hole.

2

Oftentimes I fluttered out of her, after which we drifted hand in hand through the soft cool mists of Rainy Mountain where nobody else ever came. Educated into confidence, I now began to reach inside her to withdraw the urns of my hopes, one at time. The lids had been screwed down for eternity, but not far from the door to our vault, a rusty iron band ringed an immense cedar; this served for an urn-smasher. Just as most nongaseous chemical elements in our universe appear white or silvery-grey (not to mention the odd yellow, purple or gold exception), so my pulverized memory-ashes tended to resemble gunmetal, with more or less of a turquoise component; once an urn offered up a mound of granules as scarlet as ladybugs, and I wondered what that particular hope had consisted of; unfortunately, the undertaker had engraved his urns with nothing but my postmortem name, so that the only way to identify their contents would have been to taste them, a prospect of peculiar loathsomeness for me who still lived. Moreover, my sweet Rainy Mountain ghost used to hover behind my shoulder, watching these various residua depart. She might well have felt neglected had I displayed much curiosity about my own waste-years. Affectionately she traced her claws down my back, her rickety metacarpii reminding me of long sticks rattling in the wind. In the drizzles of Rainy Mountain those heaps of urn-matter quickly liquefied and flowed away; although drops of the scarlet element persisted among the moss like menstrual blood; I almost dabbled my finger in the stuff.

Around that cedar tree, urn-shards slowly assembled themselves into a ring-shaped midden of irrelevance.

3

Stroking her smooth hard breasts, I learned how to pleasure her, at which she would sigh like a child blowing through a bamboo pipe, the breath which issued between her cold black teeth then taking on the odor of pickled metal. Now that she permitted me to withdraw my urns of departed substance from between her thighs whenever I pleased, I felt quite satisfied, not having considered how any such procedure might have compromised me.

But one rainy night after nibbling sweetly on my lower lip in her accustomed manner, her gaze glowing right through my closed eyelids (it now seemed less orange than ocher—perhaps the hue of a tiger's-eye stone), she abruptly unflexed her claws to full length, which she had never yet done before; and then, as I ought to have expected (no wonder that the girl from the tourist office had declined to accompany me here!), rocketed into the mist like an owl-faced moon, plunged down, and in several slow and, I must confess, excruciating swipes, eviscerated me, so that I too became a ghost, with my intestines left to hang high up on that iron-banded cedar (a crow cawed four times).— More rapidly than the living might suppose, I came to resemble her, not only in my hollowness but also in my ability to fly. Thus I could be to her all that she had been to me; and on certain very humid nights, while the entire mountain wept most pleasantly, she liked to muse in the air beside me, her slit-eyes glowing with affection, her black mouth smiling; and then, in much the way that the giggly hot springs waitress pulls off each new guest's shoes, she would reach into my unsexed pelvic cradle, presently withdrawing some urn or other of her own cremated past, cradling it in her gristle-blue arms as she bore it above the treetops, in the fashion of the seagull which soars before dropping a closed clam onto sharp rocks. These pulverized hopes of hers, if such they were, appeared less bluish-grey than mine, more charcoal-like; for isn't each disappointment unique? I admit that I never could have foreseen discovering my dead past within her, much less hers within me—hadn't I come to her alive, and hadn't I treasured my ignorance of whoever she had been before our first meeting? Well, this must be what love is.

4

Surreptitiously I alighted on a single shard, touched my forefinger to a lingering rosy drop of my former substance, then sucked. At once I retasted the humiliation which had permeated my flesh when in my youth a woman I admired met my praises with wary condescension; and at the shining ball to which I brought her, nobody smiled at me all night; she went off and danced with anyone and everyone, while I sat among the old ladies on the long sofa against the wall. One of these kindly souls, laying her wrinkled hand upon my own, said: Dear, it happens to all of us.— That was when I first perceived the comforts of anililagnia. With the right sort of woman, I too could be free; I could be a grey ghost.

Since it was now her turn, my Rainy Mountain ghost swiggled her claws inside my pelvis, withdrew another leaden-colored urn, smashed it against the cedar, and gloated cat-eyed over the blackish powder spilling out. How could I know what she really felt about it? Flittering down to lick up a granule of her discarded old substance, I understood at once how it had been for her on her sixteenth birthday, when she was rejected at the first dance. Grimacing cheerfully and smacking his lips as he pulled, the dark boatman had ferried them all across that river of dirty jade. The farther they went, the cleaner the water became, until it was as crisp as the pleats in the schoolgirls' navy-blue knee-high skirts. Docking, they awaited the headmistress's signal. When she raised her arm, they filed by threes into the distant living world of summer: Die if you leap down there! And indeed they were all dead now; but she was the only one before me who had become a ghost upon Rainy Mountain. The girls formed ranks upon the edge of the outdoor stage, their shy hopes nearly as pale as the sun between the evening clouds. There came flutesongs and the crackle of those two flaming tripods, raining sparks some of which flew diagonally upward across the illuminated yellow-green tree-scape, vanishing into the rainclouds. The boys filed out in chorus, led by the child with the queue, her little brother, who had rotted for a hundred years now in a bomb crater, with mud in his mouth. In his white *tabi* socks he knelt, awaiting the next flute. It could never have been this way; certainly the face of the boy who eyed her across the polished boards could not have been a mask ivory-colored in the light; nor was his kimono greenish-grey, metallic and tarnished, the effect antique unlike the fresh green trees; but within the ancient soul of my Rainy Mountain ghost, semblances had decomposed and revivified in other images; rendering what had happened all the more true. That was why the ashes of her bygone disappointment tasted metallic to me, like the golden fan ahead and upward of that boy's forward-bowing face; he came slowly gliding out with unearthly music toward the girl, sad and demonic now, a golden skull with a golden queue, catching the red flickering light—then halted, and although every other pair in the facing lines had met, touching fan to fan, and begun to dance, the dead boy in the ivory mask now struck the fan out of her hand, wheeled and rose up into the air like an incomprehensible ghost! Now every mouth was laughing behind a fan—laughing at the girl, who in her humiliation sank slowly to the ground.

5

For love and pity I kissed her then, with the dark powder of her life still staining my vaporous lips. Nibbling me fondly with her sharp black teeth, she gestured as if to imply that she felt flattered by my interest. I supposed that she had lost the capacity to weep—although it might also have been that this youthful incident had grown trivial to her. For a fact, she appeared less affected by it than I.

Until now she had (for all her manifold ectoplasmic virtues) reminded me of the woman I once knew who eternally alluded to her secret gynecological difficulty but refused to explicate it. Now I was getting somewhere with her, thank goodness; my darling Rainy Mountain ghost might even love me! Or did she hate me, or did she consider me merely as a thing upon which to feed? She had killed me (I decline to accuse her of murder, since I had given myself to her of my own choice), in order to render my bony substance fit to entrust with the regermination of her own forgotten secrets.

Just as at dawn a sleeping lover's face so often appears young, open, yet far away, like a *zo-onna* mask, the countenance of my Rainy Mountain ghost opened unto me as if I were lying beside her on a tatami mat, marveling at her hair. Most days and nights we played with one another as luminously as green- or red-skinned demons on a golden screen. In her yellow-orange eyes a reddish tincture sometimes teased me; could it have been the reflection of my own new ghostly gaze; did I sport red eyes? I hoped not to be ugly, for then how could she love me?

6

It was not until she had begun to draw her dead emotions out of me that I suspected how dejected I must seem to her, or anyone—and might well always have been, not that it mattered. But how can a ghost be anything but sad? In the words of Lord Tokugawa Ieyasu: *If you consider suffering as an ordinary state, you will never feel discontent.*

They say that the first Shogun would kill the songbird that failed to sing, the second would teach it notes, and the third would wait until it sang beautifully. Lord Tokugawa Ieyasu was the third. Well, then, like him I would now await the silent singing of my Rainy Mountain ghost in the same spirit that the growing pine needles reach up. Side by side we would learn how to gaze at white rain-jewels and pink magnolia blossoms. The reason I had first approached her was to overcome the defining human error of despising death's carnality. I had sought to offer my love and desire to her; now I continued to present it to her, continuing the love after the grave, trusting that the breath of corruption would in time become the breath of a flower.

7

The hinges of our home were all engraved in crowds of flower-crowned hexagons. Moisture beaded in tiny white pimples upon our black door. On the infrequent occasions when the mist blew away from Rainy Mountain, we withdrew to our vault and concealed ourselves within the skull of a stone lamp. She kept me company as elegantly as if she were kneeling on a white tatami mat, gently pouring sake. Helpmeets to each other, we disposed of our miseries, wearing the red laughs of white-toothed dragons.

The longer we dwelled together, the less I could remember. After a season or a century, she ceased to grow gravid with my burial urns. I continued to incubate hers, which she withdrew ever less eagerly. I could not tell whether my tasting of her bygone failures made her bashful, grateful or something else, but I continued to sample their dust, because I wished to know her. These sorrows of hers were pools of silvery-pink water flooding my old life.

8

Come the middle of a certain rainy morning, when a cool yellow sky somehow found means to insinuate itself between the clouds and the lowlands from which I originated, I could see all the way past Dripping Pine, beyond those high-crowned cryptomerias and down to the city whose front row of houses loomed two-dimensionally like a multitowered battleship. Surely now the railroad tracks must be shining wet, the ballast-stones soft and mossy, the girl at the tourist office sweetly composing herself to perish, for it must have been nearly a lifetime already since my death. Her flesh might have been as sweet to me as all the drops of rain on a plum tree's galaxy of tiny white blossoms, but I felt no regret, so well suited had I become to my own Rainy Mountain ghost. All the same, that was when I began to study her for hints of change, not realizing that I myself continued to alter, in contradiction to every supposition which premortem entities make about ghosts. It might have been that she was discovering secrets from the urns she drew out of me, although so far as I could tell, the powders which swirled and tumbled from each terra-cotta vessel remained identically ebony—well, their separate blacknesses might vary by a hint of purple or green; or was that merely a trick of my glowing eyes, whose color I could never know? For my part, whenever I tasted the ashes of her life, my love for her softened further, like the mellowing rice brandy which learns to conceal its power within sweet water-blandness. Turning toward me like a slow whitish-beige fish, she taught me how to silhouette myself upon the moon. Her fixed face, the grey-and-black teeth in her dark mouth, her hand frozen on the bamboo staff she sometimes carried, and the fantastic smokelike hair around her skull, all seemed cheerful to me now. From the side, her mouth was a downcurving crescent of darkness. As a girl she had been taught to express not with the face but with the heart; and I would have said that she did so to perfection, although just what she expressed I cannot tell you. She had learned that when one wears one's death, it grows difficult to look down. When one emerges from a mist or a vault, one cannot feel one's feet, so it is best to hover. In company one wears, for instance, a memory of the V-necklined dark kimono with the white chrysanthemum pattern, the lavender obi embroidered with white plum blossoms— no matter that what's left of it is three fibers, four worms and a pinch of ashes.

For her fan I gave her a dewy fern, with which she danced for me on the rainiest nights. It soon decayed, but then we learned that she did not need it; for when she danced, our memory of her fan moved as inevitably as water.

9

When she withdrew her final urn from my bones and broke it, I greedily descended to nourish myself on its blackish cinders, and at once tasted the occasion when she had first masked herself in a mirror room, pleading with her Elder Sister: I just wish to be more and more feminine. That's my wish.— Never before had I heard her voice, nor would I again; and these words reached me by bone conduction, as if they derived from my own speech resonating within my skull. How often do we need to remember our own words? Most often it is the words and deeds of others which most eloquently relate our own chapters. Masked, the girl took her place among the kneeling geishas, who locked their hands in their laps. I awaited her error. How would it come? Just as lacquer wears off a shrine's door, revealing grey wood, so our expectations flake away, leaving dullness struggling to disguise itself in Rainy Mountain's grey clouds. When would Elder Sister slap her in the face? Bowing, the shamisen-player glided to the corner, then knelt and tuned her instrument. The girl arose. It was her turn to dance.

She disappointed no one, not even herself. Her excellence remained as pure as mountain rainwater. No one could strike her or do anything but bow in awe and gratitude. Here came the clatter of prayer-coins falling between wooden slats while people bowed—to *her*! To her they clapped two times. She was someone accomplished, even great, who founded the Three Fern School of Rainy Mountain. When she died, crowds burned incense for her.

To be sure, her most fearsome disappointments outlived her—the reason she was compelled to become a ghost—but thanks to these last ashes (which I assure you appeared no different, at least to me, from others), she now spied light instead of darkness through her own skeleton's latticework. Was she looking out through black-lacquered blinds at the pale branches of early spring?

Until now I had supposed her to be my counterpart. Well, perhaps she was. If only I had tasted that scarlet powder, I might have learned that I too contained more than disappointments.

So was she happy now? Her orange gaze found something in the distance. But then it seemed once again as if she were seeking something within me. Just as out of Keisai Eisen's woodblock prints an Edo beauty peers sidelong with her glossy black eyes, kissing the air with her tiny red mouth, just so my Rainy Mountain ghost studied me as if she were sorry for me. Her smile resembled one of those multiplying triple circles in a green pond when the rain begins, the ripples pulsing faster and faster, while beneath them, unaltered, comes a carp-flash in the greenish water, a pallid sparkle of shrine-gold. As slowly as a Noh actor, she rotated away from me, as if she were turning upon an invisible roasting-spit. More curious than alarmed, I flittered round to learn her smile's next chapter. Naturally she couldn't have forgotten me! Her twin orange eye-beams yellowed the grey-clouded summit of Rainy Mountain. Her gruesome arms sprang out of immobility, her claws parted, and then, head bowed, she flew away forever over Rainy Mountain, with her long hair dripping down her bowed back.

10

So now I was the ghost of Rainy Mountain, the only one. But I preferred not to be alone, since that made me so very, very disappointed! You might call me a hateful spirit, but nothing I was or felt could have been prevented. No doubt this latest bitterness of mine was already smoking down to nothing inside my soul's crematorium. But where were all the other urns, whose contents must have been as lovely as certain scrolls of the Lotus Sutra, each a particular hue and decorated with its own calligraphy and stamped crests? When my Rainy Mountain ghost remembered achieving her wish to be ever more feminine, she had improved her destiny; and I thought to do the same. So I set off in the direction that my mate had gone. But I was merely a ghost now—worse yet, an abandoned ghost, with less ichor inside me than any windblown dragonfly. So I fluttered along quite haltingly, much as an old woman clings to every wall, branch or railing that she can, since a fall will be disastrous. That was why it took me quite an eon to fly all the way to the peak of Rainy Mountain. By the time I got there, I would have been tired, if a ghost could ever get that way; perhaps when I am old enough I will indeed feel such a sensation; anyhow, I cannot say that I even remember what the summit looked like; but it must have been very, very grey. Behind a lichened torus, there might have been a vast stone ring filled with greenish water. Perhaps I cannot recollect it because I could not find my reflection in that pool. But I believe there was moss on a stone lamp; it must have been soft like pubic hair. Over this I drifted. Then I passed on through the clouds. No pine dripped on me; I heard no crow.

Emerging on the far side of Rainy Mountain, where it was windy, I heard before I saw it the rattling against the metal railing of those long narrow sticks with black characters on them. Cherry blossoms hung sickly in the streetlight behind a giant spreading tree. Here stood the narrow stele of a family tomb and there another, each stele upon its nested pedestals, each pedestal bearing a pair of silver cups for flowers and often an oval mouth for incense; sometimes a family crest had been etched into the stone. All this reminded me of something I could scarcely name. Between two silver cups lay a groove for incense, at which I finally remembered the breasts of my sweet Rainy Mountain ghost!

More clammy gusts played in this pallid forest of sticks which reached up toward the greyish night sky of Tokyo. Seeking to decode that long sad rattling, I reminded myself: Could they talk, this would be the only way they could do it, since nothing else moves.— Ever more desperately hopeful waxed my longing to see something, even something gruesome, for instance a ghoul or vampire shambling toward me up one of the long narrow alleys of gravestones. For to exist is to be alone.

Stopping at a very dark-shadowed tomb (streetlight glinting silver on its nearest flower-cup and on one granite corner-groove), I discovered the stone to be already engraved with nine names, in each case first the postmortem name and then the secular one. If only I knew what my Rainy Mountain ghost had been called! (I should have known; why didn't I?) Then I could have drifted from tomb to tomb with some pretense of purpose. But didn't I have all the time in the world?

Glumly I regarded the tomb, which seemed to stare back at me, for its two glowing cups resembled eyes in a black square stone face.

Falling back on hope, I bowed twice, clapped twice and bowed yet again. Here at once came my Rainy Mountain ghost with a horde of her bygone friends, some of them bearing twin lanterns and fresh white chrysanthemums, most of them skeletal, a few with the heads of foxes or horses, but all of them with their long black tresses perfectly combed. Spying me, they halted as if in confusion. Then, in that universally known gesture of threatening rejection which the dead make to scare away the living (but wasn't I one of them?), they signified in the air: What cures you harms us, and vice versa. So stay away; stay away!

Ignoring this—what harm could they do me?—I sped toward them almost as rapidly as a cherry petal whirls down an April brook. They wavered, but disdained to sink back underground. So I peered between my sweetheart's legs, but she was incubating nothing of mine. I won't pretend I was surprised.

But as I hovered disconcerted, she reached into my bone cradle, pulled out an urn and shattered it against the tomb while her companions tittered. I oozed down upon the blue-black ashes to taste them. Thus was I apprised of her final disappointment—her sojourn with me. After that, nothing remained to me but the words of Lord Tokugawa Ieyasu: *Blame yourself, not others.*

THE CAMERA GHOST

1

In Kabukicho a certain crow caws and memory sticks protrude from behind the concrete wall. Unless you know somebody here, you will not
think much of this spot—just another cemetery from the Meiji period!
White apartment towers stand behind it; plastic pallets sometimes lie
before it, mingled with cardboard boxes which once held frozen fish.
Seeking the past without expectations, I entered through the open gate.
A pine tree was slowly lifting the flagstones of the Naito family tomb. A
woman was walking, with her eyes nearly closed, and two incense sticks
smoking in her left hand; she was striding down the path of concrete
flagstones to her family's place. Whatever she would meet there would be
hers alone, no matter whether she thought of herself as belonging to others. Charmed by her beautiful accomplishment of grief, I dreamed of
photographing her. But she disappeared.

Approaching a vermilion-headed shrine high above whose bell was
painted a golden swastika, I bowed and clapped my hands twice, hoping
to see what was gone. The incense-bearing woman had expressed no
such prayer, I guessed; she would have felt she'd done enough. *Let the
dead bury the dead,* said Christ; while the cremated Buddha, smiling,
blew smoke-rings as he rose away from his pyre. I for my part thought:
Everything ought to be remembered forever.

Bending over a nearby tomb whose inscribed characters were moss-
greened, I now descried the representation of a camera, which in my
situation I considered lucky. Bowing, clapping and praying for old things,
I remained there for the duration of two joss-sticks, then departed the
cemetery.

An old man came walking slowly, dressed in tan, with a rust-pocked
little Leica dangling from his shoulder. To speak more correctly of his
outfit, it consisted of a tan-green coat, dark tan pants, pale beige hat and
white gloves. At his shoulder hung a cracked briefcase. He came to me,
leaning slowly on his black cane. I was prepared for him; I was the
watcher on the side.

I assured him that since he must be the lonelier of us two, I would help him however I could.

He replied: You didn't call me on my account, so no misstatements! What do you want? Speak quickly; my bones hurt!

Well, sensei, I remember film, paper, chemicals and cameras, real cameras—

I might know a little about those, he allowed, and we both grew happy.

And afterward, with your permission, I'll buy a bottle of snow-white sake and pour it over your grave.

At this he graciously bowed. Perhaps his other followers had died or forgotten him.

Walking side by side, we passed another young lady; soon she would be smoke and ashes. I said: How sad!— The girl did not hear; she was already gone.

He asked me: How long can you remember her?

Photography remembers, I insisted.

So does imagination.

It only thinks so. You're testing me, sensei.

Yes. Now answer at once: Would you rather have her before you all the days of her life, or make a picture of her which would be safe forever in some place you could never see?

The second, of course. It would be for her, not for me.

Good. Now tell me what she looked like. Be accurate.

I can't remember. How long has it been? She was beautiful. Did you see her face? She—

Coughing smoke and dust, my companion remarked: I've managed not to regret my death. Anyhow, it's time to make your wishes clear. My dead bones, you see . . .

Perceiving how frail he was, I bowed to him and clapped two times, at which he wearily nodded. A funeral shop stood in that block, with open double doors. I escorted him inside, and he inhaled three breaths of incense. That was all he needed. As soon as the clerk approached me, I apologized, and then the old man and I went out.

He said to me: Describe your own regrets. Please get to the point.

I told him that I reckoned my life from before and after the day when film went away. Of course I grieved for the sake of all cameras, but particularly for one of mine which was constructed entirely of metal, silk and glass; this machine had always been heavy around my neck, and even when it was new, other photographers had laughed at me, disdaining what they called its obsolescence. What knowledge it ever brought me I cannot say; whether it made me more or less fitted for life I can answer only too well (my dreams fading secretly in albums, so that I need not see); nonetheless, my camera was everything to me. Needing no battery, nearly impervious to humidity or shock, it could resist a century as easily as a speck of lint. Its round eye was brightly tireless. I told the old man that my camera saw ever so differently from me, and yet it never lied. If it never wept, sometimes what it saw touched the eyes of others. Well, now it had starved to death. Defying reality, I saved a few rolls of film in my freezer; the cosmic rays must have fogged them by now.

The old man nodded patiently, swaying.

Actually, I said, it may be a capability of the silver halides in the film to record mood itself.

You see, imagination does remember!

No, sensei. Only photography can be trusted.

Is that so? he inquired, patting my shoulder.

That was how we spoke, strolling together down Tokyo's narrow wobbly streets of cyclists. It was Golden Week, and so the vacationers streamed through Shinjuku, where photo store barkers and presenters of priceless facial tissues were chanting.

We recalled cameras and film, he and I, calling them up to praise them. We were proudly, loyally bound by former ties. Smiling and tapping his cane, he described to me a certain elegant wooden pinhole camera with brass fittings: a tiny, topheavy toy from 1899 it was, with nested tapering lens-snouts, the viewfinder like a clotted bubble on the side; not long ago I had seen one much like it for sale in an Argentinean fleamarket; when I raised it to my eye, it showed me nothing but cracks and glowing dust. Hearing this, the old man grew melancholy and shook his head. I told him that when I declined to buy that camera, the vendor had tried to sell me an old rotary telephone. Smiling, the old man said: How sad.

We stood there before the five-storey photo store which no longer sold film, while faces orbited closer and closer, passing on to be replaced by others. (As for the old man, perhaps he disliked noise and movement.) Lord Kiso and Kanehira, Komachi and Yokihi, I saw them all there. Across the street rose an immense department store whose façade had been silkscreened in the likeness of a young girl with emerald-green sunglasses and short brown hair. As I think about it, this must have occurred a long time ago; certainly it was before the great tsunami of 2012.

I confided to the old man that my camera used to see anything, be it wild grass or breezy leaf-shadows on a wall of galvanized zinc in an alley in the middle of a spring afternoon. It had saved from death the four schoolgirls of the black skirts and shiny black loafers and glossy black hair, not to mention the old bicycle with the sad handlebars.

I bought my camera in that shop over there, remarked the old man. In those days, cameras were all of metal.

There must have been some wooden ones, I said, and he laughed in delight, saying: Yes, yes, you remember; you too are old!

2

In the department store's seventeenth-floor restaurant I ordered two cups of steaming sake, the kind which was flavored with something like incense, and the old man bowed over his, smiling as if he could enjoy the fragrance.

From his briefcase he withdrew a tiny portrait, printed without error, of a geisha kneeling with her white hands folded. Strange to tell, I nearly seemed to remember her. Her skirts spread out wide around her in a pool of embroidered light. Fearing to touch, I bent over the picture as he held it in his hand. Rescued forever was the bright white parting of her ink-black hair and the long drop of her kimono sleeves. I seemed to hear the sound of snow. The neutral white of the photographic paper distinguished itself from the white, white, living white of her face powder. She was a shadow like a ghost on the paper wall, hair perfectly separating down each side of the head in a series of infinitely thin parallel ink-lines. In a moment, when she rose, her wide sleeves would cause her to resemble a flying bird.

I said: How beautiful!—to which my companion remarked: She has died.— Then he put the picture away.

Well, sensei, you saved her! What about the negative?

Don't worry. It's in a dark cool place.

The waitress brought two more cups of sake. She was old, plain and tired; I wished I could have photographed her. My companion inclined his head to her and she bowed.

Now I know you're worthy, he said. The others only cared about beautiful dead women.

Ordering more sake, which warmed me until I felt immortal, I proclaimed (the waitress clapping her hand over her giggling mouth) that anything dead is especially beautiful, because everything that is never stops deserving to be, and since the living can take care of itself, the bygone calls for chivalry. Meaning to compliment him, I said: Sensei, you and I are both tender toward those departed beings—

So. You know death, said the old man very pleasantly, and at the last moment I perceived his irony, which resembled the reflection of white thunderclouds in a wind-rippled pool of the darkest indigo. I managed not to fear him—after all, if he'd wished, he could have preyed on me in the cemetery—but perhaps I lost a certain confidence. His eyes were unwinkingly bright. Insisting that I presumed comprehension of no mystery, and that my intentions were but to honor, safeguard and facilitate, I drank my sake very quickly, in order to calm myself, while he for his part held his cup just below his nostrils. Before I could have clapped my hands once, the cup was empty, the liquor vapor, and the vapor gone within his skull.

3

From his briefcase he now took out (as we enthusiasts like to do) more photographs he had made. He even had a loupe with him, in case I wished to inspect the grain. So I ceased to doubt his friendship. And first he showed me a photograph of the place called Hanging Blossom: rocks as complex as vulvas, and curves of glossy-leaved shade on that one fantastical rock which was too complex to be retained in the mind. Yes, this was memory, the thing nearest of all to perfect love. How patiently I had reprinted this negative! But no matter how many hours the darkroom robbed me of, I (who have small aptitude for anything) had never been able to bring out every tone which dwelled in its grain. In our craft we remember a proverb: *In each picture, three thousand secrets revealed!*

Well, how many of us can elucidate them? Not I, not yet; I was sincere but lacked right understanding. But the old man had made so fine a print that I now remembered the shapes of summer water-lilies just beyond the viewing frame, and past them the reflection of Rainy Mountain; I even began to perceive the blurred brightnesses of large fishes, which reminded me of the shiny eyes of a woman who had been crying; her name was Dolores and she said she loved me; there might be other clues of her among the trees which resembled dreamy roots and vipers in that ginsenglike forest. She had died a year ago. The perfection of the old man's photograph made me feel as joyful as if a new bride had moved into my house.

Smiling, he now remarked (although I cannot claim we spoke in words): I was once your camera. How sad; how sad!

I remembered that I knew that, after which I remembered photographing the geisha kneeling with her white hands folded, who had afterwards sat on my left, with her young hands gently, relaxedly resting on the sake pitcher, ready to serve, and when I asked her to explain the dance she had just performed, the one about Rainy Mountain, she said: I think it implies a love affair, and some woman has come to see her lover. When I danced I was dancing for you, and so you were the lover I came for.— Now her dance was ended; it would never be danced that way again. When I photographed her bowing, that was already something different; my memories turned to dreams, darkening down, darkening down.

Slowly raising and lowering his hand, the old man said: I used to be your friend. I saw and remembered for you! Are you blind now, and have you forgotten all the beautiful things?

But, sensei, how can it matter what I forget? I never saw like you! Anyway, once the photograph is made, the subject will be safe!

He kept saying: So sad, so sad!— Then I remembered that his bones hurt.— Pressing more sake upon him until he grew drunk, I asked how he felt about that geisha portrait, and he said: Every picture tortures me.

I wished to photograph him, in order to hide and cherish him like the ashes of someone loved. Was he two or were we one?

4

Again he asked why I had disturbed him, and I answered: To save every-thing.— He said: That's why you're expected tonight.

5

It was the time when people begin to go away, and the cemetery crows stop cawing, the hour when the crickets sing: *How sad, how sad!* Think-ing that what had been might be again, and thirsting for those beautiful things—which is merely to say all the things I had seen, ever brighter by contrast with my greying life, not as if they were any better than what-ever the moon would reveal tonight, or the sun tomorrow, although it did appear (but why should this be so?) that these things were truest of all, truer still because once photographed, printed and toned they could be held in my hand, moved closer and farther from my gaze or studied at various angles, without changing—or if they did alter it would be slowly, over the progression of several lifetimes, so that their degradation could be ignored or denied—I opened the gate, which someone had closed at dusk, and strolled past the pine tree whose roots kept stealthily parting the flagstones of the Naito family tomb just as I once parted my bride's skirts. Whether something was spying on me I could not tell. The moon was as white as a geisha's neck. The memory sticks were black. In a newer briefcase than the old man's I carried a bottle of snow-white sake. I felt afraid, but hoped to cross the Bridge of Light. My heartbeats resembled the many holes within the dark skeleton of a dead lotus. Bending over my camera's tomb, I bowed and clapped my hands twice. Oh, I was no unin-vited guest! There came an odor of smoke and stale incense, a warm nau-seous dizziness as of fever, and so I felt allured.

Fulfilling my promise, I now poured out sake in my teacher's honor, and there at once he stood, taller than a cryptomeria tree. His forehead was too high to be visible, but when an oval of darkness grew more opaque I understood that he had opened his mouth.

Praying for everything I had seen and known to be saved, I flew up past the stone lamps, up the wet lichened wall of black stone cubes, to the ver-milion façade inset with brass-framed phoenixes and dragons. The old man's jaws closed around me with a click. Now I could be happy, in the place where pictures are made.

And so I had entered my old camera, or his, which was magnified—or, more likely, I myself had shrunk, after the fashion of old things. The vast metal plate had clicked shut behind me; I remembered that. My fears departed, my longings now shut out, I thought to guard my unfinished dreams. I found myself in the rubescent light of an antique darkroom, whose trays of hyposulphite and boiling selenium gave off those choking sulphurous and briny stenches I loved so well, here in the place where no voice is heard. Within the reel where the fresh film canister would have been seated, I presently discovered a spiral staircase which led me to a round chamber where some high-shouldered daguerreotypist with his back turned toward me was fuming mercury, the silvered plate already tilted to the proper angle. Since he had not observed me, I quietly re-descended. The stinging vapors of the selenium now attacked my eyes and nostrils. Passing them by as rapidly as possible, I met with a tray of running water, a still tray of hypo clearing agent in which several sheets of paper floated face down, two trays of fresh-smelling fixer, a vinegary tray of stop bath, which of all my chemicals I used to find most unpleasant to mix, then a tray of developer evidently of the warmtone type, for its exhalations made me nauseous and itchy at once; in the red light, the latter liquid appeared tarry, evidently from precipitated silver; it must have received several sheets of photographic paper already. At last I reached the takeup reel, and, instructed by symmetry, easily discovered the other staircase which took me, as of course it would, to my old enlarger, whose timer was singing away the seconds while the incandescent bulb glowed white, projecting upon the wall above and behind it crooked rays like the legs of a shining spider whose head was the bulb itself. Musing over the easel, where the light cast down the negative's image upon the paper, stood that same tall, high-shouldered gentleman who had been and perhaps still was fuming mercury in the other tower; he now turned toward me, with an agility I found unwholesome even before I saw his face, which was as featureless as the paper's latent image. So was he infinitude or utter negation? Just then the timer flicked off and the chamber went dark. Sensing, although I could hear nothing, that he must be bending toward me, as if to get his long pale hands about my neck, I rushed down the stairs, not knowing whether he were an inch behind or had returned to withdraw the exposed sheet of paper, which in any event he would momentarily be carrying down to the chemical baths, because this is how we photographers bear our messages from this world to the world which will come; and indeed, just as I reached the door at the base of the tower, although I had heard no footfall behind me, I felt breath on the back of my neck. The horror I experienced then, when I comprehended that his mouth could be no more than a handspan away, and that his arms perhaps already drew in about me, ought to have stupefied me, in which case I could have been developed and pickled just like the kneeling geisha, but somehow I was able to throw myself down the last step and roll into the sticky, poisonous concretions beneath the long shelf-sink of trays. Now in the rubescent darkroom atmosphere I could see his tall, slender legs, white as a crane's. His semiskeletonized majesty was as coherent and inevitable, if not as visible, as the sheen of brass chrysanthemum bolts marching in double rows up the black wood of a drum tower. He was as immense as a cedar. Although I supposed that he would promptly bend down and reach for me, he hesitated, perhaps for fear of exposing his fingers to chemical contamination, and therefore staining his prints. And very possibly he held that sheet of lightstruck paper in one hand. If he slipped it into the developer tray, I would gain five and a half to seven and a half minutes while it traveled from bath to bath, each station of which he must rock like a baby. If he set it down anywhere else, it might be ruined by some unseen chemical. While he pondered, I crawled as swiftly and silently as I could toward the other end of my camera, burning my palms and knees in puddles of ferricyanide bleach. My gorge rose and my eyes watered, but my heart pounded for fear of him who (or was it his twin?) now knelt down ahead of me, fishing for me with his long arms. Reversing course, I spied his double likewise hunting me—no shelter within this dark world! Nothing remained to me but to crawl out between those pallid twins, who straightened at once, as I could see all too well in the ruby light, and began to stride toward me with the delicate rapidity of spiders. Fortunately, I now reached what my hands remembered, for I had loved this camera so well that its workings nearly matched those of my own nerves and bones; here was the cam which used to come into play when I pressed the shutter release. Even as my two enemies commenced to strangle me, I rotated it ninety degrees, then pulled, so that the great spring-loaded mirror whirled beneath us as the lens opened and let in moonlight. I glimpsed my own desperate face, silvered down by the lunar rays. Clutching at their own eyeless, noseless faces, which were already blackening with the reliable rapidity of unfixed silver halides, the demons froze, and then, far too late, sought to preserve themselves by dunking their heads into the two hyposulphite baths. Re-opening the lens again, reassured by my orbiting flash of face, I this time employed the moonshine to discover the inner catch on the camera back, during which instant my enemies, all the more discommoded by this second exposure to light, trembled hopelessly, while fixer ran down their legs; and pitilessly I pressed the catch, which swung the camera back utterly open.

Although it was worse than foolish of me, for their hearing must have been unimpaired, and they could have trapped me between them in that corner, I skipped around them to peek at the photograph just ripening in the developer, and now, like those monsters, commencing to darken into ruin, and I saw a beautiful picture of mine which I had never printed— the face of the woman I loved. Too late!— As I remember this now, the taste of selenium rises in my gorge, and my eyes begin to sting.

Flying out of the old man's mouth, growing as I fell, I glimpsed the two demons, who were already smaller than a pair of chopsticks, staring blindly into each other's ruined faces, as if they recognized that they were or were not the same. I thought: Was it not lonely enough without this?

Grinning like the iron-crowned demon of Kibune Shrine, the old man now bent over me, and placed his Leica around my neck. No one visits him anymore, and so I say to myself: How sad!

6

The names of those two demons who hunted me I never learned, but upon opening the old man's camera I found in place of film a tiny scroll in characters of pure gold within sky-blue windows, like certain copies of the Lotus Sutra. I unrolled and viewed it frame by frame, weighting down each rectangle with my ten-power loupe. I seem to remember reading it long ago, in the Imperial Anthology of the Ten Excellent Silver Zones.

Now you have seen my true shape;
there is no difference between us, you and I;
for we both dwell in darkness, in order to devour the light.

My ashes abandoned by my smoke,
I am one and the other, the same,
two empty things which never will share a grave.

Down this road we go, we go;
delusion's road, where we go between death and life,
here where we pluck tender images out of light;
here we toil out our lives, gathering moonlight out of jade.

All is vain, even escaping from vanity.
My only hope, blind death, kills the eyes on my face;
but each eye remembers the other
and new pictures bloom up for the plucking,
so that I can never rest, never rest.

I have vanished into the dark, to gather light with you.
You are my brother; I am your smoke.
This is of all teachings the most excellent.
In every grain of silver is a palace of practice
where every being is enlightened for thirty-three million eons.

Here is the dwelling place where all is seen and nothing is known,
the place of those removed from this world,
who offer this world their love.

7

Sometimes I wish I might never desire the beautiful things which dead eyes can no longer see. But who would I be, if that were so? Sometimes I wish to be awakened from sad dreams, but not from this one. Until I have saved everything, I refuse to rest. Then I'll show you how a man should die! I'll vanish into the dark, and rise forever above the pines, nevermore to see! But not yet, not yet; nor will I pray to lose my delusion. When I finally leave this world in funeral-smoke, may all I have seen remain.

8

The waitress who had served us sake in that seventeenth-floor restaurant was there every day; she was wrinkled and yellow and her back ached. Was it she or I who had forgotten to be alive? Bowing, clapping my hands twice, I prayed: Please let me save you from death.— She nodded, smiling bravely. So I raised the old man's Leica, although there was no film in it. As soon as I gazed through the viewfinder, I found that she was a rain-jeweled branch of pear flowers, unchanged from long before. After this she bowed and said: We have met, so we must part.

How shall I bear this pain? Still I see her; now she has passed away.

THE CHERRY TREE GHOST

If cherry blossoms were never in this world, how serene our hearts come spring!

Ariwara no Narihira, *bef.* 880

1

Yukiko's dark little mouth was a plum in the newfallen snow of her face, and her eyelashes were as rich as caterpillars. Even her Elder Sisters, who were very strict, confessed that when this young woman opened a sliding door, following each of the prescribed motions, the effect became perfect. At the Kamo River Dance, even amidst an explosion of geishas in white flower parasols, all of them as stunning as cherry blossoms, it was she who stood out; and had I ever seen her myself, I would have painted her image upon my camera's polished mirror, making copies in paper and silver. When a man looked up her sleeve while she poured sake, and won a glimpse of her crimson undersleeve, he could not look away; and once two tipsy Kabuki actors fought over her sandal, while her scarlet-lipped white face watched from the doorway until the Elder Sisters summoned help. When a closed palanquin carried her from place to place, people would follow in hopes of glimpsing her perfect hand. Whatever Yukiko was, had or did, years after her disappearance Noh actors continued to discuss the way her white-powdered face used to become ivory when she leaned forward in torchlight, pouring sake for them, the golden maple leaves on her jet-black kimono flickering like stars, the rice spirit streaming in an arch of silver from the mouth of the wooden bottle. The Elder Sisters gave it out that she had made an advantageous marriage in a far-off country. Of course most of them were angry and hurt, while the rest feared that some demonhearted suitor had made away with her.

It happened when she turned twenty. There were pink cherry blooms and wet white tulip-cups of magnolia beneath the grey clouds. Ever nearer drew the night when she must *change her collar*,* as they say in the flower-and-willow world.

---

* A *maiko* is a young apprentice geisha. (This category exists in Kyoto only.) She dresses more vibrantly than her Elder Sisters. Her kimonos often sport accents of red, the color of sexuality and

The ancient poets teach that veiled beauty is the profoundest type. Much as autumn foliage barely seen through mist outranks the untrammelled scarlet of the leaves themselves, thus a geisha's beauty to a *maiko*'s. As for Yukiko, she preferred to continue as she was, so day and night she prayed to Kannon, goddess of mercy: Preserve me from the hollow chests, yellow teeth, bad breath and grey hair of my Elder Sisters! Don't turn me into smoke and dirt like them! Let me wear all the colors until I die—

It was February, so she wore a daffodil hairpin. Then it was March. Presently came April. Directed by her Elder Sisters, for the first time she did up her hair in the *sakko* style and blackened her teeth, because it was her final month as a *maiko*. Again and again she stopped by Yasaka Shrine, praying to Kannon. Her heart resembled a red tassel trembling against a round mirror. To shorten her obi, and hide her hair beneath the *katsura* wig, to put on lower clogs and a plain white collar, to know that the older she became, the plainer her kimono, this might be the fate of others; but she felt so sorry for herself that she wept in secret—not much, because that would have spoiled her lovely eyes. Her red collar was already almost obscured by swirls of silver thread when she prayed to Kannon, bowing and clapping two times.

Again she prayed, and in the darkness eight-armed Kannon appeared, stiff and tall, clasping two forearms at her heart, with her other wrists upraised, her other arms outstretched. It must have been because the girl paid threefold reverence to the Three Buddhist Treasures and twofold reverence to the Shinto gods that Kannon took pity on her. Sad and a little stern, darkskinned, in a robe of tarnished gold, the goddess bowed her wide-eyed face toward the girl, promising to preserve her beauty over a long span of years. Yukiko would become a cherry tree, and every spring she would come into flower. Only then would she become again a *maiko*. Thus for but a handful of each year's days would she incarnate the lovely being who she now was. Her month would last a decade; her year, a century and more. At other times she would be a cherry tree.

The goddess warned her: What you wish for may not be for the best.

---

youth. In her last year, her red collar is gradually altered, month by month, into a silver one, until she has entered into the more somber maturity of geishahood.

You will be trapped in many births and deaths. The sadness you experience will be your retribution.

The girl bowed meekly, her eyes closed as if she were remembering the first song of the cuckoo; and Kannon was touched.

Are you satisfied? asked the goddess.

Yukiko nodded. At once joy overcame her.

2

When she first reappeared to her Elder Sisters they screamed. It had been several springs; they all looked older, and two new *maiko*s had been taken on by the house. The Emperor had been exiled, they said. Bowing to each, clapping her hands (which made even less noise than before), she requested forgiveness, and promised to return each time the cherry blossoms opened, for so long as they should wish. And because she was rare in several qualities, and cost them nothing, they accepted her; she proved good for business. So the sake flowed sweetly out from her sleeves, and the highest-ranking musicians came to pluck the strings of the shamisen whenever she danced, and even jaded rich men could never drink enough of her. At first the other geishas hated this new Yukiko, for even the way she stamped her feet could not be imitated, no matter how brilliantly they danced, and never mind that their wardrobes entailed kimonos of lavender with golden cherry flowers, and pale pink cherry blossoms upon night-blue, and more others than I could ever tell, while she wore always the same yellow kimono with the pink and white blooms, wrapping herself in layers of farewell, smiling with her perfectly blackened teeth, bowing with perfect grace. When the two *maiko*s and Yukiko danced the Miyako Odori, Taeko wore pink and Sachiko wore blue, while Yukiko wore yellow, of course; cherry blossoms were on their kimonos and on their scarlet obis, and cherry-blossom hairpins adorned their hair. Taeko and Sachiko were beautiful, Yukiko was the one whom they all watched. Who can compete with the moon? The woman who tries is mad, and geishas need to be businesswomen. Therefore they made their peace with this willow-eyebrowed girl, who readily advanced their names to men who desired other company, as sooner or later most men did, since only for six days or seven could one see Yukiko, to whom her Elder Sisters now spitefully referred as the Cherry Tree Ghost, a name which hurt her because she believed herself to be alive.

On this subject something will now be said. No one in this floating world has more discerning eyes than an old geisha, and as the cherry-springs continued to spend themselves one upon the other, the Elder Sisters watched Yukiko with small alert smiles, inclining their heads whenever she bowed down before them.— Younger Sister, they'd say, there's a stray hair on your neck. Please let me fix it for you.— Or: Dear Younger Sister, isn't that a loose thread on your sleeve? Please hold still.— And with this or that pretense, they looked her over close up, while she softly thanked them, knowing quite well that all was in place. It lay in their interest as jealous human beings to see her age, so that they could comfort one another with smiling assurance that she too must die. Spring fluttered down upon spring, with winter in between, and while the wrinkles of the Elder Sisters lengthened, and their chins began to multiply, they discontentedly agreed that no flaw yet appeared on Yukiko's face. But there was one Elder Sister whose eyes were sharpest of all, and among the many fields in which she hunted was Yukiko's collar, once scarlet, now nearly silver; and after half a century she thought to spy another silver thread. After all, even Elder Sisters make mistakes. Some observant Noh actors agreed that her movements were becoming more fluid, her sleeves slowly clapping and parting like the pulsations of anemones; but this signified nothing more sinister than her increasing mastery. Even behind drawn shutters, in that upstairs room lit only with candle-flames, and the simplest painted screen behind her, she appeared to be dancing in a sky of blossoms.

So there were men who claimed to love her, and as her Elder Sisters aged and died, other geishas learned to dance at her side, and new young men grew up to admire her. She had scarcely known anyone else. Her parents, who had sold her to the teahouse on her third birthday, were since ascended in cremation-smoke; likewise her brother, who had never visited her; now her brother's children followed the same road; so that her antecedents might as well have been the faded square vermilion seal of Hojo Ujiyasu, whose lines resemble a labyrinth. Perhaps Kannon weighed this when she considered Yukiko's prayer. What had the girl ever received but loneliness, humiliation, merciless practice and principled punishment, all of which produced in her the determined longing to embody grace? Had she *changed her collar* and grown old with the rest of them, she might have won allies, dependents, starstruck clients and perhaps even friends of a sort, although the sorrow which I have sometimes seen in the eyes of older women in that world makes me suspect that a strictly governed childhood can never be remedied. So Yukiko had abandoned nobody! None knew who she was, for she was a tree on the other side of Jade River, on a hill nearly as far away as Rainy Mountain; there she stood dreaming while the earth froze around her skirts, and her arms were as wrinkled and withered as her unremembered grandmother's.

When whitish-pink cherry blossoms began to swell in the whitish-grey sky, then Yukiko remembered who she was, and drew in her arms. Next, her mind itself burst into flower. Finding herself once more in the back room of the teahouse, with the round mirror before her and her wig on its stand, she brushed the white *shironuri* on her face. They learned to set that room aside for her on the night after the first cherry flower fell at Kiyomizu Temple.

What she was sufficed her at first—all the more as others died. (This speaks more poorly of them than of her.) How many women would decline to be beautiful forever, or even nearly forever? Although they came precisely to forget the iron-and-autumn world, after too much sake her clients might mention famines, rebellions and executions, and she gave thanks to Kannon that such matters could no longer touch her. Rice was cheaper or dearer, *maikos'* costumes unfailingly splendid; that was all. The geishas called her Eldest Sister. Her wrists bloomed slowly up, and she crossed her brilliant sleeves, singing "Black Hair." She seemed beyond change. But she had been given only until the blossoms fell, so that still her hours resembled those swirls of silver thread advancing around her neck, soon to meet beneath her shoulders and drown the scarlet forever. Thus each spring she *changed her collar*, becoming again a cherry tree in the lonely hills.

3

Presently she commenced to wonder whether she had been created merely to make others happy, not to be complete in and of herself. She danced just as her bygone Elder Sisters had taught her, not altering a single motion, and the quietly carousing old Noh actors who came here each spring compared her to sunshine at midnight, to a bare peak looming high over a snowy range, to snow in a silver bowl. Sometimes she called for a closed palanquin, and was carried to Yasaka Shrine to pray alone. The house paid for this; that was all she cost; her younger sisters shared her fees among them, saving for old age. Where she hid herself from spring to spring she never said; and if, as some people believe, secrecy in and of itself becomes truth, then her vanishings were preciously inexplicable lessons. By now the Noh actors were certain of her ghosthood. A goddess appeared singularly, whereas these regular apparitions of hers implied some form of unfreedom. So they called her to dance for them in that upstairs room, behind closed shutters, while an old woman sang and plucked the shamisen, and sometimes a young *maiko* beat the drum. Drinking in sad joy, the actors admired and pitied her.

The Inoue School expresses nothing in the face, everything in the movement. This too is a Noh actor's way. Mr. Kanze and Mr. Umewaka, present incarnations of those two great acting families, discussed with nearly unheard of approval her fixed gaze's projection of thoughtful sadness, her slow turnings and the way her wide sleeves hung down like wings. She filled their sake cups, and they smiled—for they could be cheerful enough when their masks came off. Another incense stick burned to nothing. On the following night Mr. Kanze was performing "Yuya," incarnating the sweetly dancing young girl, and he raised his wrinkled hand in front of his masked face, then turned, the lovely mask smiling and smiling; he seemed to move faster than Yukiko, and presently his head tilted down lower and lower, so that Yuya's mouth smiled upward in increasing sadness; and her wig of horsehair glistened. The cherry blossoms had already fallen—a matter of greater interest than the recent hunger-riots. After he had withdrawn behind the rainbow curtain and the apprentices carried away his mask and costume, he went out to an eel restaurant with Mr. Umewaka; where, having discussed the carelessness of choruses, the ignorance of certain members of the public and other such eternal matters, they drank sake, then more sake, upon which Mr. Kanze said: Our Cherry Ghost nears the end of her spring at last.

Oh, do you think so?

Did your father ever speak about her?

Not in my hearing, unfortunately. He preferred me not to be instructed by any geisha, however talented.

Of course, of course. When she danced the Yuya Dance for us the other night, it struck me as less fresh than ten years ago. And once my father told me that while her motions were nearly perfect, she had not yet mastered it. You know the second lowering of the fan—

Yes. She has certainly mastered that. In fact, I saw no error in her dancing at all, and as you know, dear friend, I'm very critical.

As I know too well, dear friend! Well, next spring let's bring our sons, so that when they're old they may begin to notice something.

My son's unready, unfortunately. He's ungifted, quite a shame to me—

Not at all! I'll never forget the way he performed "Yokihi." He truly brought her alive, and that daring choice of mask—

He insisted. Perhaps I shouldn't have indulged him.

So they praised one another, and eventually agreed to bring their sons to see the Cherry Ghost. And when the blossoms came, and they withdrew into that upstairs room where she poured out sake for them and their sons, who were beginners, men in their thirties, still encumbered in their acting by remnants of the deceitful "first flower" which pertains to a young body, Mr. Umewaka requested the Yuya Dance.

The Cherry Ghost demurred, saying: But since I performed it just last year . . .

Exactly. You possess such grace . . .

Please excuse my extremely clumsy movements. I feel ashamed to dance before you. But since you insist, sensei, I'll try my best.

The shamisen player was already kneeling in the corner. The Cherry Ghost began to dance.

That night Mr. Kanze said to his son: Watch her again in thirty years. She too is losing her "first flower," but I'm sure she's unaware of it.

4

In her old teahouse they learned to expect her on that instant when clouds of cherry blossoms filled the sky in Kyoto. Men waited to give her gold hair ornaments, which she passed on to her Younger Sisters. When the last proprietress died, her sisters retired, and rain leached through the rotten roof, she removed to a quiet house employing only three gei-shas, whose owner was old and expected nothing; she made them all rich. She had heard that Yoshitomo was dead, and the Imagawas nearly exterminated; but when she inquired after these matters, in order to overcome the shyness of a certain drunken samurai, he laughed at her and said: That was long ago!— Perhaps she had already known that; she might have learned it in a song. She danced "Black Hair," and a tear trav-eled slowly down the man's face. His uncouthness annoyed her. But isn't the lot of the perfect to be surrounded by the imperfect?— When that house likewise went out of business, she gave herself to one in the Ponto-cho district, thereby freeing it from a parasitic loan; thus she did Kan-non's will. After praying at Yasaka Shrine, she recommenced to dance in Gion, saving the establishment of a retired geisha who had slanderously been called unlucky. By now people interpreted her apparition as a sign of great fortune, saying: *The Cherry Tree Lady has come to us!* She never ate or drank, but took in the fragrance from incense sticks. Most people still said her face expressed spring.

She carries her ageing beautifully, the current Mr. Kanze instructed his son. You should remember her next time you perform "Kinuta."

Thank you, father. Is she truly a ghost?

Of course. So never fail to show her respect and pity.

If I were performing *her*, I'd need our youngest mask—

Don't go falling in love with her. You know where the prostitutes are.

5

In Kamakura stands a shrine to Eleven-Headed Kannon wherein the goddess is all hues of gold, crowned with heads; she is vermilion-lipped, yes, very wide-lipped, and guarded behind by a cloud-shroud of swirling gilded metal. Some people say that prayers at this spot find special favor. And that spring when Yukiko flowered back into herself, there on her hill which lay so nearly in the shadow of Rainy Mountain, she wept snowy tears, and longed to go to Kamakura, to pray that this strange weight be lifted from her. But she was bound to appear in Kyoto, in another teahouse in Gion, and from there she could by no means reach Kama-kura before the blossoms fell. For that moment she would have liked to keep her budding blooms in her sleeves; but out they came; and thus, freed from her prison of wooden bones, she became a lovely *maiko* once again.

Then that spring fled, as did the next, and the young Mr. Kanze began to grow old. When he visited her she danced, singing for him the old tanka: *Even the dream-road is now erased.*

6

Up on her hill, not quite in the shadow of Rainy Mountain, she gazed across the forests and plains, and the jade-grey river made broad white waves across the rocks. Her flowers had gone; soon she must lose her leaves within the pearlescent colorlessness of the autumn sky.

To be beautiful without loving anyone is as sad as to be unbeautiful and remain unloved. How could Kannon's warning have been false? Disregarding Keisei's *Companion in Solitude,* which warns that a lover's longings, or even the wish of a faithful old couple to be buried in the same grave, are crimes, she reached for love as a reprieve from her sadness.

In the following spring, there came into that ancient teahouse a hardworking sake merchant's spendthrift son. His father had engaged him to a gentle girl who was adept at spinning hemp cloth. One night during the Chrysanthemum Festival a little streetwalker in a striped cotton shift led him past chanting and torchlights, around three shrines, and thus to her pillow-room behind the reed fence, where they spent a fine half-hour, after which, happily kissing her hand, he departed, and then, perceiving that only a few copper coins remained to him, he turned around and gave them to the prostitute, who stopped washing herself just long enough to take them, giggled at his silliness, then showed him out again. Not daring to face his father, who would likely beat him, this improvident fellow, whose name was Shozo, began searching for a place to sleep; and wandering past those same crackling torches, which cast ashes into his hair, he spied the youngish Mr. Kanze in a carplike costume—scaly flames and white shell-scales below his waist, white openwork lace above—gliding forward as if the stage were moving beneath him; I swear he was three-dimensional against the suddenly two-dimensional trees; and sparks rushed up into the summer darkness behind him, while the flame-light colored his white mask to ivory and yellow and back again. The windblown pinetops resembled the swaying and pulsing of Kannon's spider-arms. And when that ivory mask appeared to change expression, what could it mean? Shozo had never wondered this before.

The next time that he could steal money from his father, he attended "Yuya," which Mr. Umewaka the elder happened to be performing. So it was that Shozo presently won a side view of a lovely female Noh mask in play, so that he could swim into the black gash between its beauty and the flabby bulge of an old man's throat; and because Kannon had led him here, to him above other men was it now given to achieve true love of woman, which is to say that his heart's flower would never wither on mere account of a woman's ageing.

His weary father dispatched him with a fine two-handled keg of sake in order to seal a certain betrothal. Shozo misdirected the porter and sold the keg. With these proceeds he attended Kabuki plays all afternoon, then found one of those high-ranking courtesans for whom the weightiest silver coin is not enough.

The next time his father threw him out of the house, he departed well provided with coin, which he purposed to squander in a geisha house. Kannon appeared to him in the guise of an old friend who often borrowed from him and never repaid. Among Shozo's virtues was generosity, or at least a sort of consistency: Just as he expected forgiveness from his father no matter what he had done (an expectation ever more often disappointed), so he helped anyone unconditionally. When his friend now approached him, Shozo thought, without resentment or even regret: I won't be hiring a geisha after all.— And he smilingly greeted the man.

Shozo, said Kannon, I've come into some money, so I can finally pay back every *sen* I owe you. Here it is, with thanks.

And the astonished young man received a heavy purse. Being an experienced traveller in our floating world, he quickly recovered himself, laughed and said: Come help me spend it.

No, I don't deserve that. If I were you, I'd go to that teahouse in Gion where the Cherry Tree Ghost appears. The blossoms will soon be falling, you know! I'm off to pick one for myself, if you know what I mean.

And his friend hastened away.

So that is what Shozo did, and that is how he met the Cherry Tree Ghost. It was the first of her seven days. People were already streaming to the Eastern Hills to view the flowers.

When from the side he saw her snow-white cheek through the curtain of cherry-blossom strings which issued from her hairpin, he remembered Mr. Kanze's Noh mask, and loved her because she was more than he could understand. Or perhaps he loved her only for her willow eyebrows. In any event, he longed to disorder her hair on a pillow. How should he proceed? He could hardly hope to persuade her with the maxim that life is brief.

The Cherry Tree Ghost rotated slowly toward him, smiling. Never suspecting that each perfect movement now came as wearisomely to her as do all their drudgeries to those poor girls who burn seaweed for salt, he began to learn the way that the little downward point of hair at the forehead rendered her face heartshaped.

That year the cherry blossoms at Kiyomizu Temple were especially fine. But he did not go there. The Cherry Tree Ghost danced for two nights—and then Shozo's money was finished . . . and after the fifth night an early rainy wind came down from the mountains, so that the blossoms began to fall. Shozo's desire followed her, leaving him alone.

As for her, she scarcely thought to see him again. But as soon as April's cherry trees flowered in Kyoto, he was waiting for her at the teahouse, this time with money earned honestly. He had even begun to please his father. But his filial piety was not excessive. Longing to see that supermortal geisha's black hair spread out on his hemp pillow, he had broken off his engagement; to him the admonitions of his parents were as treecricket songs. He craved to marry the Cherry Tree Ghost. As soon as she read his face, she commenced to suffer.

Old Mr. Kanze had lately died. When she danced, his son watched knowingly. The house was satisfied; money came in, and all the geishas bowed one by one to their Eldest Sister. Meanwhile Kannon guaranteed that Shozo's purse was full. And so seven nights spent themselves. In the floating world one rarely gets a keepsake, a bone-hard residuum. Flowers fall. Desperate to comprehend what captivated him, the young man stared owl-eyed, dreading to cheat himself with a single blink.— A *maiko* explained: The first thing we learn is manners: how to enter a room, how to smile, how to talk.— Then Shozo understood that the Cherry Tree Ghost's perfection came from experience.— Having lately studied *The Tale of the Heike* and the Threefold Lotus Sutra, he now knew many allusions, and even the Noh actors who patronized Yukiko's teahouse had begun to find him less impossible. On the fourth night he had a *maiko* convey to her a poem he had calligraphed on blue paper, with a willow twig attached:

> What will become of me?
> Flitting dream who ever returns
> to this fading world of ours,
> when will you perfume my sleep?

The Cherry Tree Ghost smiled as if she were proud of him, although her smile might also have been sad or mocking. While the *maiko* knelt waiting, she painted this reply:

> Where you will be
> and what you might dream
> when next the cherry flowers
> the cherry does not know.

The *maiko* glided back to Shozo, bearing this verse on a tray. Shozo's eyes would not leave the Cherry Tree Ghost, who, well knowing that certain matters must not be discussed, and that in life as in breath the pause is important, vanished easily away in a shower of fragrant white tears, her tiny dark mouth verging on a smile, in order to go happily; before another incense stick could be lit she had become leaves, roots and wood again, on that high hill overlooking Jade River and the meadows.

That year flowered, then fluttered forever off the tree. Because Shozo rarely made mistakes in business, he made profit with small effort. He attended performances of the Kanze School, and when the actors glided before him upon the Noh stage, he seemed to be viewing summer from the edge of Kiyomizu Temple, gazing down into the green and yellow-green treetops, the emerald-lobed clouds of trees swimming above the curvily tapered gable roofs; within that darkness lived a treasury of ghosts, beauties and golden secrets. What world was this, and how could he increase his understanding? Slowly Mr. Kanze (who was already near as old as his father had been) turned back onto the rainbow bridge, gazed down, staggered, froze, then raised his staff. What did it mean? Shozo imagined that every motion of his Cherry Tree Ghost must hide a meaning. How could he approach her until he learned it? With all his heart he prayed in the wooden darknesses of shrines.

The spring buds returned to the capital's river-willows, and after that he returned to the teahouse, more prosperous than before, but wearing mourning, for his father had died. Since he now had means, and she inclination, for a private hour in that upper room, where her obedient Younger Sisters had closed the reed-blinds, she played the koto for him, with those pink-and-white flowers blooming on her eggyolk-yellow kimono. His prayers redounded upon his face like hailstones. He informed her of his feelings, but because she considered that to undo the destiny woven by Kannon must be as impossible as to find spring flowers in autumn, she calmly discouraged him, then faded softly away, while her flowers issued down like tears.

7

He continued to read ancient verse, in order to become a less uncultured person. By the time he was getting whitehaired he had made progress; and because he spent so much money at geisha houses, several teahouse proprietresses bowed to him like cormorants. On the twenty-third spring that the Cherry Tree Ghost appeared before him, he recited Teika's tanka about crossing a gorge in an autumn wind, the narrow bridge trembling like the traveller's own sleeves, the setting sun so lonely, at which she hid her face in her sleeve. Just as after a rain at Nikko's temples the dark water runs down the deep square grass-clotted grooves between wall and courtyard, so at each separation their regret for the time they had already wasted apart and their bitterness against the loneliness now to come bled between their bones. So he promised to seek her without fail.

8

It was still spring in the capital when he departed, informing no one. The moon was less white than her face. Kannon had made him a rich man, so that he possessed leisure to wander through this world; and of his own accord he might have grown a trifle wise. Soon he could no longer hear the village women beating cloth.

Passing the edge of the grass world, he rounded the curve of cool-breathing overhanging forest and forded the first bend of Jade River, crossing from stone to stone. On the far bank he halted to pray to Kannon. Then he knelt at the water's edge. Seeking intimations of his delightful Cherry Tree Ghost, he saw a band of live white light: indistinct reflection of the white reeds atop the green reflection of the grass.

Now he ascended terraces of trees. Each time he crossed another bend of Jade River, the season latened. At home the people would soon be cutting out cloth for their new garments. It was high summer when he reached the forest gorge of hanging blossoms. Once that lay behind him, the nights elongated and the days began to chill. His hat blew away; his straw cape grew stained and torn. Disdaining scarlet leaves, whose noise kept falling upon the silence of vanished cherry petals, he wandered through this floating world, sometimes losing his way in the similitude of silhouetted tree-mountains, then praying to Kannon and choosing whichever path appeared most difficult; until he came to that abyss over which the bamboo bridge, with a single reed guardrail, swayed with each step, vibrating meanwhile in that cold wind as he picked his way toward the round red sun. The rotten bamboo began to give way beneath him. There was nothing to do but stride carefully forward. Although he was afraid, never in his life had he felt so free as in this moment between life and death, deliberately chosen, the outcome not yet known. Looking down into the gorge, he seemed to glimpse a dragon's mouth and eyes. The sun was setting ever more rapidly, and for the first time his foot broke through the bridge. Calling loudly and repeatedly on Kannon, he continued through the windy dusk, and suddenly the moon rose, and he found that he was crossing a vermilion bridge, of the sort used only for generals and Imperial messengers. So he passed each glowing vermilion-lacquered lamppost, with darkness on either side of him and even the dragon's eyes as far below him as reflected stars; so he continued along the curving plank-deck which hugged the steep round fern-rock. When he reached the far side of the gorge, it was a winter's dawn, and on the hill before him stood his Cherry Tree Ghost, dark, wooden and naked, with her leafless arms over her head.

He fell to his knees, kissing her high and low, but she neither moved nor spoke. After awhile it began to snow, and he weepingly retraced his steps.

Although the journey had taken most of a year, his return took but a day, no doubt thanks to Kannon's help; and once he had regained his home in Kyoto, the Flower Capital, where the servants had nearly given him up, he rested—for he was not young anymore—then spent the winter whispering entreaties to Kannon in the dim light of brass fittings on black-lacquered appointments of red-lacquered shrines.

In Kyoto there is a temple dedicated to the Thirty-Three Thousand Three Hundred and Thirty-Three Kannons. Believers raised up this structure in the twelfth century. Having purified himself, Shozo approached this place. He bowed three times; he clapped his hands twice. Kannon appeared to him at once, and said: It is not right for you to wish anything for her. You may wish only for yourself.

Then what should I wish for, goddess? I ask your advice.

If you call on me to decide, then I will send you away with nothing changed. Accept what you have.

But will I ever be able to marry the Cherry Tree Ghost?

If I tell you, that will change you. Do you wish to be changed?

To be as I am is misery.

What would you be?

I would be capable of happiness.

Then I leave you as you are.

Bowing and thanking her, he departed. That spring the Cherry Tree Ghost appeared within his house, and became his wife. He was happy then; all he wished for was to die in flower-rain, buried in pink cherry blossoms on golden silk.

9

Raising the wig from her head with both hands—for it was very heavy—she set it down on the stand which he had procured for her, and for the first time he saw her sweaty hair. She flushed. When he presently perceived her unpowdered and undressed, it became clear that she was not quite as young as he had thought. She might have been twenty instead of seventeen. A Noh actor would have portrayed her not with the *ko-omote* mask of the radiant girl, but with the *waka-onna* of the beautiful woman, and beautiful she was, if not so much as art could make her; and because this floating world is shallow, he felt disappointed for an instant, but then his love, desire and gratitude returned, for constancy was the gift which Kannon had given him so long ago without his knowing.

In the morning he asked when the blossoms must fall, and she replied: Tomorrow.

He grew pale. Powdering her face back into a mask, she fell silent.

She implored him to seek out Kannon again, since he had not yet availed himself of anything; but neither one could imagine what he ought to ask her. Of course he had long since erected a shrine to the goddess in one room of his house; there it was, indeed, that they had said their wedding vows on the previous night. Purifying themselves, they prepared to bow, within that frame of wooden darkness. She knelt down first, with the strings of cherry blossoms hanging from her long black hair, and he knelt beside her. They clapped their hands twice.

Folding a wide yellow sleeve across her breast, she began to sing to the goddess, who never appeared. Her complexion resembled clouds over snow.

10

At least they were happy together for seven days and nights every year, as if they could take the one thing life declined to give. As the old poem runs: *Better never to awake from this night of dreams.* He asked how it was for her to be a tree, and she said: Sometimes I seem to hear you calling me.

They liked to sit out at night, listening to the bell-insects, and often she would dance for him, pleasing herself with his sad joy.

In the colorless months of her absence he sold sake and prayed to Kannon. Whenever he went out on business, he often paused by dark wooden caves with weathered wooden pillars, because he yearned for the glimmer of the metal votive things within. The wheat harvest passed; trees flowered and withered. Crickets died away. Fearing the future, he gazed ever less openly at this world. At each winter's departure he pressed his forehead to the floor by Kannon's statue, awaiting his wife's return. And when his wife again departed, his belly grew foully pregnant with fear and his chest clenched around his heart. Bowing, clapping, he prayed:

Great Kannon, we thirst for your mercy!— He found himself remembering his Cherry Tree Ghost by the way that the wood-carved goddess gazed so softly down past him.

11

Of course he could not live to see her mature into a more sober elegance. Had Kannon so permitted, he would have companioned her forever. In each other they drank the sweet sadness nourishing the branch which has lost its blossom. On the trees, yellow leaves went trembling like the waving, ever reopening fans of dancing girls. Each winter the snow weighed down her branches more heavily.

Kannon flexed her spider-wrists, and he lost his memory (although it might have been that there was nothing to forget); hence to her husband the Cherry Blossom Ghost came no more. In time he died, blind to the color of spring. Each year was yet another dance of upraised flowers, then more rice-stalks reaped up. Knowing their attachment to have been a useless delusion, she now danced without hope or desire, and the Noh actors said that she had attained the true flower. But even before the great eruption of Mount Asama her tree-bark had come to resemble the cracked wooden face of an ancient Kannon statue. Each spring she returned to Kyoto, slowly upraising her tear-moistened sleeve, drinking in from various teahouse mirrors the agony of beginning to lose her beauty. Had a wise Noh actor or priest encouraged her to keep dancing, her sufferings might have made her truly great. But the patrons merely drank her in. So presently she gave up human society, preferring to lurk in shrines, gardens and cemeteries, sometimes gazing upon her dissolution as reflected in ponds. Hating herself, and fearing to be seen, she became as unpleasant as a woman who forbears to wash herself—which we would call retribution for her egotism, were not Kannon, as we know, merciful. There came another great famine, followed by village riots, but those places were distant, and she never heard about such difficulties. A certain stormy winter on her high hill cost many of her branches, and on her return to human form that spring, she stood beneath the Shijō-dori Bridge, staring into the Kamo-gawa River, and discovered that she was well on her way toward being today's withered old Cherry Tree Ghost who appears in the mockingly inappropriate garments of a *maiko*. She rushed from shrine to shrine. The wall-stones were wet with green moss, and very ferny. She began to dance, singing: *Even the dream-road is now erased.* Poisoned with despair, she considered drowning herself, but then Thousand-Armed Kannon rose up before her, a calm Crab Queen. Embracing her, the goddess kindly relieved her of her reason. Ever after, she has seen herself as a lovely ghost-lady from the Old Capital. All this explains why last week a reeking old beggar-woman crossed my path, opening and closing a ginkgo leaf which she supposed to be a fan, gesturing hieratically with her hanging-rag sleeves of yellow, singing: *The day is come again,* and last night when I went to drink sake, I overheard an ancient geisha entertaining a sad salaryman with a story which began: Eight hundred years ago there was a teahouse in Gion . . .

PAPER GHOSTS

It seemed that the faded vermilion of the shrine fence now resumed its ancient brilliance.

The Tale of the Heike, ca. 1330

1

On the day after the last performance, life had already left the Kabuki-za, whose purple awning-bosom, nippled with two white crests, now hung over nothing but dull glass darkness between the white pillars; and I, who could have spent more afternoons in that ever-ancient melodrama of tricks and colors, drinking beer and spying effortlessly on pasteboard-armored warriors, never mind the shimmering dragon-gods and the white-faced *onnagata*s* more beautiful than moons, remained with nothing but my own life to look forward to. Although I had fallen in love with any number of horsehair-wigged princesses, to me there had never come a moment when, as there did for that man in the Chinese legend, I would have entered the painted world forever. Instead I liked to watch it pass before me, noisy and bright, self-mocking and au courant, inexhaustible, the way we all desire our futures to be. To sit and watch ladies cross the bridge over a river of colored paper, isn't this perhaps the best of life?

The final performance took place during a certain business appointment of mine. While I was still young, money had begun to come to me; I spent it easily and forgot it, and since it kept me company as faithfully as air inhaled, I stopped regarding it, for no mortal can plan very far ahead anyway. Then it left me, slowly and with backward looks, to be sure, but without remorse; and I to whom it had come without my doing knew not how to get it back. Perhaps I could have hunted more cunningly, but my ambition, never vibrant, had long since faded like the ocean in an ancient *ukiyo-e* print. I attended appointments obediently;

---

* Kabuki actors who specialize in female impersonation.

shouldn't that have been enough? But the client, who two weeks before had regarded me with due adoration, must have investigated me (in his souvenir album of business cards I once glimpsed the skull-crest of Yama Detective Services); for he drummed on the table, yawned in my face, and disdained even to thank me for paying the check. How could I have expected this? Hadn't I already prepared a most pleasurable disbursement? I felt as astonished as the woman whose purse has been stolen for the tenth time. The client hissed something out of one side of his mouth; his colleague, whom to my recollection I had never invited—another ten thousand yen—stared at me and laughed. Their behavior was so outrageous that I should have been alarmed, but in truth it felt good to get away from them!

Nakano sat waiting at a café in the Ginza. Had she dolled herself up and accompanied me to the meeting, the client, a fellow womanizer, might have been less bored. But she wasn't in the mood; her mind had always contained one layer of kimono within the other. More industrious than I and until lately less successful, she had taken my money as easily as I gave it away; once it began to leave me, she demanded to know why I would not work like other people. I explained that I had never known how, even when I was very young and toiled late; because in those days it had been nothing to me if the boss kept me until nine or ten at night; I always knew that the curtain would rise upon my freedom, and ladies would take me by the hand and lead me over the bridge of vermilion paper. Now the curtain was descending. In last night's dream I had seen Nakano peering out through lace draperies behind the show windows at the Mitsukoshi department store, as if she had joined someone else's act, and so I woke up anxious. Once upon a time she used to meet me at the Imperial Hotel, in the lobby vast and clean where all murmurs are low. Her daughter needed a new school uniform, and I was supposed to pay for it. That was when my heart swelled with resentment, I won't say dislike, for my ungrateful client and his colleague, who had violated my right to easy money.

Etsuko's uniform was ready. In a twinkling the clerk had unfolded it so I could verify that it was perfect. I inclined my head. Thanking me in a chirp of little-girl sweetness, she re-formed it into its original rectangular bundle, which would have done credit to the most fastidious demonstrator of Euclid, wrapped it in sky-blue paper decorated with opened white books and golden chrysanthemums, wove a pink ribbon around it, crowning and locking it with three beautiful knots, bowed her head and offered it to me with both hands. Bowing, I paid, and again she thanked me as if I had done her the greatest favor in the world. As I left the shop she was already cooing and bowing to the next customer.

The uniform had cost twice as much as Nakano said it would. I began to feel worried and sad. How could my ease have come to an end, for no reason? In my life I had never squandered a single yen; every expenditure had gone to satisfy my very reasonable desires. For example, when Nakano required a new kimono, simply because she was tired of the ones her mother had left her, it made me happy to please her, never mind that we might have bought a car for the same price. What would I do now? I could pay next month's rent, but the month after might be chilly. For a good three years that client had fed me with projects; I had not changed, so why had he? Was I now expected to touch death's flat golden leafwork on the lacquered doors of night? It was clear that when I told Nakano what had occurred, she would look me over with hatred and contempt. Then I would pay for her lettuce sandwich, and we would go home to Etsuko. Nakano's lined face was proof that life wears us out, either through worry about losing what no one can keep, or by disappointment about never having gotten it. Tonight would find me sleeping on the floor, no doubt, while Nakano lay rigid on our futon, sobbing silently. Why didn't the client accept responsibility for that also? Tomorrow morning I should have been going away on another business trip: rainy white skies and concrete lattices smearing themselves against the windows of an express train. Tomorrow evening would then have clothed me in a sweaty yellow evening light on the return train to Tokyo, the conveyance hissing and humming, my ears singing the song of death. Although I disliked going away from Nakano and Etsuko, now I finally perceived how much I enjoyed those moments like flashing windows when one long train speeds past another, both reflected in the watery windows of rice fields; and of course I never failed to feel important when speeding across the sunset bridge.

An old woman whose spine was so badly crooked that she did not even reach to my waist staggered slowly down the sidewalk, clutching a shopping bag in each hand. Diagnosis: calcium insufficiency. Nakano's mother might have ended up like that, had she lived longer. The old woman stooped so far forward that from the rear she appeared to be decapitated. How much longer could she creep on, and how much pain must she endure—and for what? I would have helped her, but Nakano was waiting.

So I turned away down Chuo-dori, into the promenading crowds, the huge advertising screen in the cylindrical brand-name tower of the many windows, with the café at the bottom named after a mediocre coffee chain. Nakano had left the café, it seemed. Bowing indifferently, the waitress presented me with a note from her; I was no longer to trouble myself with her affairs. I thanked the girl and walked away, not knowing where to take myself; and not even the sunshine on the creamy golden calves of little uniformed schoolgirls consoled me.

Our flat lay an hour and a half from the Ginza: three changes of subway, a bus so crowded that one could rarely sit down, another bus and then a fifteen minute walk. Nakano had found the place when my income became less regular. Perhaps I should have gone straight there. After all, I needed to pack my belongings. Etsuko, who adored me, would jump up and down when I opened the door. I would take snapshots of her in her uniform, and her mother might smile for an instant before she expelled me. But when I reached the subway station, my legs declined to stop. Before I knew it, I had rounded the corner, and reached the Kabuki-za.

Instead of the accustomed line of ticket-buyers and -holders there stood a vague horde, most of them on the sidewalk in front of the theater, and others, the ones with zoom lenses or a yearning for lost panoramas, across the street. They aimed their cameras upward at the row of white-and-black-crested red beehive lanterns above the awning; above these, that familiar wide white arch with the flattened ends roofed the portico; then rose the high façade which was now merely an outermost sarcophagus. The signboards no longer bore the likenesses of brilliant warrior-actors and *onnagata*s in many-hued kimonos. This saddened me more than my own failures. The authorities had already fenced off the theater with black-and-yellow-striped plastic bars connected by waist-high plastic cones. I could have stepped over them, but someone would have scolded me. Gazing in beneath the awning, I saw a certain door striped wood-brown and tan—closed now. How many times had I entered it?

The window of the semicylindrical box office had closed, and inside, a white sign with black characters marched down it. Behind the purple awning, the three pairs of brass-handled, red-lacquered doors were shut, and through their panes I could see nothing but the crowd's dark reflections.

Behind the plate-glass windows of the Miu Miu department store stood two mannequins whose well-shapen legs were crystalline plastic, whose arms and heads were brass armatures and whose white skirts were embroidered with red fish-scales around their narrow waists. As I contemplated the glittering silver geoglyphs where their breasts should have been, that same bent crone approached me, creeping and groaning. She had set down those two heavy shopping bags somewhere, but seemed no less weighed down. Bowing, she informed me: Your prayers will no longer be accepted.

2

By the time I finally returned to our apartment, nobody lived there, and even the number had been obliterated. As I watched, workmen began to carefully demolish the building. A bridge of silver paper was rolling itself up into the sky.

I set down Etsuko's parcel on the sidewalk, knelt, bowed and clapped my hands. Then I rose and walked away, wishing to spend the rest of my money at once.

Across the street stood a stationery shop where I used to buy Etsuko's school supplies. She used to cry out for joy and clap her hands when I brought her a new pink notebook whose cover depicted yellow butterflies, or a bookbag dedicated to the goddess Amaterasu, or a lacquered vermilion pencil. Entering this establishment, and exchanging bows with a pretty, chirpy clerk in a black-and-yellow uniform, I discovered just past the magnifiers and inkstones a new subdepartment devoted to folded-paper figurines. A certain warrior wore wide-legged pantalons with a gold-on-cream pattern of upside-down waves; he was as flat and broad as a Noh actor. A certain slender lady, as faceless as a Heian beauty, lived straight and stiff in her cellophane envelope. The hem of her vermilion gown had been neatly creased back to show naked white paper. Most of these origami personages, as I should really call them, were not previously known to me, although I thought to recognize the last Regent of Kamakura. Their beauty aroused my greed, so I bought more than twenty of them. They were all the same price. Counting sweetly in a low voice, the clerk showed me the total, and bowed once more when I paid. The light gleamed on her edible cheeks.

Then I went next door and bought a bottle of sake which was wrapped in a brown-spotted bamboo leaf tied with coarse black cord. Since I still possessed money, I proceeded to the next building, where, abutting the wooden façade of an old shop, there rose a curvy-cornered pillar with a sliding steel grating which must have once opened and closed from side to side, and above this, red and white in plastic relief announced **TOBACCO**; and from the next storey upward it was all hotel. I checked in. They made me pay in advance. Then I took the elevator to my room.

3

The snow-white shoji panels beside my bed could open, disclosing a narrow space where a refrigerator squatted unplugged from its outlet and two chairs faced each other across a stained veneer table. Here I sat drinking sake and watching the silver dusk tarnishing the fog upon the forest hills, the whitewashed concrete buildings going grey. I felt safe, and hidden. Sometimes I closed the screens so that there was nobody but the empty chair and me.

Now the world was silver-blue and bluish-grey. The tatami mat beneath my feet was so warm and tan.

4

In the flats across the street a single window was illuminated, and within I thought I saw Etsuko, sitting on her heels as she always used to do when she was waiting for me to come home.

5

When I lay down to sleep, I dreamed of a jointed black wall, very shiny, glowing dully with elongated brass hinges in the shapes of nutcrackers, doublecrosses, nippled lozenges, chrysanthemums, insect-eaten leaves;

and silently this wall opened. At once I awoke. First I felt refreshed, as if I had slept long and deeply, but the instant I sat up I found that it was not even midnight. So I returned behind the shoji panels and sat watching the darkness.

At dawn, pale blue turquoise light pasted itself within the window, and I lay watching the fading peach-colored shadows of canted latticework upon the far wall of my room, the shoji screens beginning to go faintly whitish-blue. I was febrile. When I listened to the clock, it seemed that each tick was a wave carrying me toward the grave. Presently the turquoise departed from my window, and the world became greyer and greyer, its tones and lines softened by fog. So I rose and dressed.

The instant I pressed the elevator call button, the door to that conveyance slid open, and I was in an ugly steel chamber of approximately the same dimensions as the shower. The elevator stopped at each floor and opened. My room was on the fourth floor. The lobby was on the second. The hotel seemed to be owned by a middle-aged man and an elderly lady; I supposed them to be mother and son. They were indifferent almost to unfriendliness. Evidently they ran the place themselves without any helpers, because the outer door was locked after eleven at night. What I did not know was when it opened, and whether I could go out and wait until it was unlocked. So the elevator stopped at the third floor, then at the second, which was dark and warm, with a thick sleepy atmosphere, then at the first; and when I saw that the front door was not only locked, but sealed off with a heavy curtain, I gave up and decided to return to my room. The elevator awaited me. It stopped at the first floor, then slowly closed its door and groaned upward. When it opened upon the second floor, I saw that a certain luminescence was now swelling from behind the reception desk; but in that instant there was a sinister click, and then the second floor went dark again. Next came the third floor, and then the fourth. It was about five-thirty in the morning. I sat in my niche and watched the fog-tones brighten into peach. Some of the corrugated roofs were striped white in their grooves; what looked like snow must have been fog.

By seven-thirty I found myself overlooking a lovely snowy-fog-world, which appeared as warm as my shoji panels, for the forest hills were smoke-green near the sky and various shades of dark jade below,

although it is true that the white walls and roofs of the city crowded together not unlike tombstones.

I wondered how I ought to live.

6

Now nearly all the roofs were grey, although there remained a few turquoise ones and a green one and even one red one; no, come to think of
it, they were all different colors; and beyond them there might have been
mountains. In the jade-grey wall of tree-cloud I could see a swirl of pale
cherry blossoms. The sky was occupied by a narrow column of mist
which rose up to touch a horizontal cloud.

7

Since my money was even now unexhausted, I descended to the lobby,
paid for a second night, went out, bought three more bottles of sake,
again selecting that special kind which offered such lovely speckles on its
bamboo leaf, and returned to my room, which had been perfectly cleaned
during the quarter-hour of my absence. Double-locking myself in, I slid
the shoji panels apart, seated myself in one of those two chairs by the
window, opened a bottle of sake and began to organize my paper figures.
This took me all day. By evening I felt ready to remove them from their
transparent envelopes.

8

Three of them were courtiers, with topknots of lacquered black paper.
Upraising their red streamers, they showed me how sad it was when the
Heike fled the capital, bearing off the Child Emperor (whom I had not
purchased from the stationery shop, so I helped them represent him by
means of a monogrammed envelope which I had taken from the reception desk). The tonsure of another far more aloof cutout identified him as
the Cloistered Emperor who had commanded their removal from the
scroll of visitors, and dispatched the Genji warriors to hunt them to
death—hungry spirits, all of them, and as real as I once was. Lowering
my ear, I learned that I could hear their murmurings. The Cloistered Emperor was whispering verses from the Golden Lotus Sutra. His bland
voice reminded me of a poem about autumn wind.

When the last Kamakura Regent was forced to commit suicide, his soul became as slender as a Japanese lady's leg. He too was now a paper ghost, flat and stiff, with scallop shells and stars upon the night-indigo of his battle robe. Truth to tell, his epoch was so much later that he should have been sold in a different subdepartment. His topknot was lacquered shiny like the black taxicab which sighs across the castle bridge. He was the most melancholy heir of Yoritomo, who had destroyed the Heike as if they were insects.

In matching transparent packets, four Genji warriors with eagle-feathered arrows in their quivers stood ready to whisper their names to the Heike, and behind them I laid out Shunkan the lonely Genji exile, whom the Heike refused to recall from his hunger-island; chief among their unforgivers I lined up the Priest-Premier Kiyomori, who in his narrow splendor was as foolish as a paper ghost who imagined that he had attained everything; while up against the paper screen I placed six Heike warriors mounted on their paper horses and dreaming aloud of the capital even as they cantered through the air; behind them I found a place for that longhaired Genji horsewoman named Tomoe, so fearsome with bow and sword; and beside her I stood Yukiko the Cherry Tree Ghost (another cutout from a later period), in care of Yoshitsune the Genji hero, who wore a battle robe of crimson brocade. On top of the unplugged refrigerator I positioned Yoritomo. Sometimes I was horrified by Yoritomo's square white faceless head, his hair tied back with braided silver wires, but then I reminded myself that at their height the Heike had also been cruel.

As feeble as cherry blossoms they all glided to and fro, so that my niche behind the shoji screen grew nearly as crowded as a modern Japanese graveyard. Of all of them the one I loved most was the Jade Lady Yokihi, that celestially beautiful inmate of the Island of Everlasting Pain. Her dance was a poem which achieved its effect by omitting the one line in which its context was stated.

Rolling up my last thousand-yen note, I made a cone of it and inserted the tip in my ear. Then I could hear the paper ghosts whispering: *Shigemori is dead. The Cloistered Emperor has passed away. Why cannot I succeed to the position of one of these?*

I heard the Cloistered Emperor chant: *When the wooden lattice is darkened.*

And wherever Yokihi danced her Dance of Rainbow Skirts, the air beneath her tiny feet became illuminated, a miniature path to dreams.

9

In bygone days, when money still came to me as easily as air and the capital shone at Shikishima, a certain Pale Lady desired me, although I cared for her not; she shared my best friend's pillow in order to gain my address, then appeared before me in tears and with disordered hair, begging to sleep in my arms. I consented out of pity. Even when I was penetrating her she kept enumerating other lovers; all she truly wished was to add my name to her scroll. Many seasons later, when the woman I loved had abandoned me (I remembered gathering all the cherry blossoms which had fallen into *her* disordered hair), and I grew so desperate to be held that anyone would have served, I went to my Pale Lady, entreating her to give me comfort in her arms, but she refused with smiling cruelty. Now here she was, crisply remade in a flash of crinkled gold paper. I could not help but recall how I had felt on that occasion, although fortunately my former grief reincarnated itself less viscerally than merely visually, as when a paper general cuts open his belly with his black paper sword, and scarlet paper shows behind the cut. Lowering my ear, I heard her imploring me to do something, in a voice as weak as an autumn cricket's.

At any rate, she put me in mind to wonder whether all these paper ladies represented old loves of mine, and, if so, whether the rest of them were likewise the paper ghosts of my past.

The Pale Lady said: *I dream of you as I once did.*

(In the past I had waited for dreams, while Nakano went treading her double path.)

As for Yokihi, whom she represented or recapitulated I could not have said—perhaps Reiko or Michiko, although she might have been Mitsue. Her knee-length golden tassels tickled her pink-and-carmine robe, and her double mass of hair was ribbed with segments of both red and gold paper. Wondering and dreaming, I listened through my homemade ear trumpet and caught her murmuring: *It is really impossible to compare my heart to anything.*

Yes, they all must have been foam from the past.

10

They began to dance and masquerade. That was when I realized that I had never known love or beauty before. The long red and gold stripes of Yokihi's hair ornaments mad me explode with happiness. The Pale Lady took up a poisoned dagger and serenely glided across the floor.

If you have ever seen the wine-tinged rainbows of autumn foliage reflected in a river at sunrise you may be able to imagine how lovely it became on the air-bridge they created. As I gazed up into the blossoming hills, my heart shouted with joy, and my memories passed across the window.

11

Now I was pretty much finished. Lacking the funds for drunkenness, I purchased a bag of squid-flavored potato chips and set out to join the headbanded, high-cheekboned beggarmen whose heavy sweater-sleeves came halfway down their hands and who warmed themselves with cigarettes and sake as they sat playing cards and guarding their cardboard flat of eggs from other eaters. At first they threatened and abused me, but I charmed them with my paper ghosts, who glided to and fro on eerie errands a hand's breadth above the dirty sidewalk. No one could harm or catch them; they came only to me. The autumn winds might flutter them about, but between gusts they re-formed into vibrant arrays. I made my living by sitting on a piece of cardboard while they played around me, and passersby dropped coins into my hat. And so the money fell down upon me as easily as ever.

All day I watched elegant women passing before me, silently admiring and critiquing their performances, for I had become not entirely inexperienced. One day I walked all the way to the new Kabuki-za, just to look upon the theatergoers as they waited in line. When they had all gone inside, so that I had the sidewalk to myself, I entertained myself inspecting the posters of the latest beautiful *onnagatas*. Then I window-shopped at the stationery establishment where I had bought Etsuko's school uniform. Wishing to make gifts for my paper ghosts, I considered buying a pair of scissors. But which size was best? Wrinkling her nose, the clerk rushed out to the doorway and shooed me off.

I never visited the place where I used to live, but once I took my paper ghosts into a cemetery, where Yokihi danced alone for herself and me and the twilight was shining on the white characters incised in the dark glossy crowd of graves.

I missed Nakano more than I would have expected, which made me smile a little. As for Etsuko, I remembered how when she used to run into my arms her heartbeats reminded me of a ghost's long and gentle fingers clasped together. Had some rich woman dropped a million yen in my cup, I would have wished to find the girl, and buy her more uniforms and notebooks; thankfully, this did not happen. By now those two had become a pair of painted cherry-ladies against a crimson ground, and my paper memories of them were softened by a cherry tree's pink storm clouds on the verge of showering down its melting treasures.

In time I grew known among all the edifices from VOICE BAR to **GIANT ARENA**, whose hopes, like everyone's, had been tainted by death. For a backdrop I had houses, grubby little apartment towers and glittering corporate castles, all of which looked their best in the dusk. What mortal could fail to be allured by the flower-sleeve of Lady Yokihi, especially when she let down her hair to mingle with her gold tassels? Who could remain indifferent to the sufferings and machinations of the Cloistered Emperor? When I watched the glidings of my paper warrior-ghosts with their lacquered black topknots, I pretended that I too was brave and important, and the man who each day read yesterday's newspaper all day, pretending not to be unemployed, told me that he had begun to dream of himself in jade armor laced with black silk string. Adoring the movements of the Cloistered Emperor, the former soapland employee imagined that someday he might be invited to pay a visit to the Paper Palace. And whenever Lady Yokihi danced, the homeless women who were my neighbors seemed to become court ladies weeping behind jade curtains.

Atsumori, the flute-playing boy warrior, turned his horse in the middle of the paper river because a Genji warrior had taunted him with cowardice. He rode back to be decapitated—a fact of desperate pathos to my friend and neighbor the terminated salaryman who, unable to inform his family that he was unemployed, had long since become an emperor thin as paper, staggering in the darkness. And on the far bank, a Heike retainer whose crimson stick-body was crisscrossed with long narrow isosceles triangles of pink paper, tips pointing upward, began to draw his sleeves across his eyeless face in token of weeping. If only he had dared to rescue Atsumori, or at least die with him! Having stood ready to reward his fidelity with silver coins, which I planned to make for him by cutting out circles from a soapland advertising flyer, I now enjoyed the pleasure of despising him, while he wept and wept until we could all begin to see straw-islets in the lavender mirror of marsh water behind him. Atsumori's head was an oval of crinkled silver paper, with a crisp black topknot. For a moment it lay in a polyhedron of pink blood. Then the Genji warrior picked it up, along with the turquoise sliver of his victim's flute. Thus he had won two trophies. The child's head would be displayed in the capital, against the will of the Cloistered Emperor. The flute would eventually lead the killer to the Pure Land of Enlightenment, for it uttered notes like night rain. Meanwhile the retainer, yearning and despairing, opened his belly, and the blood was as scarlet as the ribbon in a *maiko*'s hair. As for the killer, when he mounted his brown paper horse, his yellowish-green paper trimmings rose behind him into a ducktail.

Although robbing me would have been as easy as snipping off a paper ghost's topknot, no one ever did it, in part because I shared whatever food I had, and it may be that some people feared that I might be magically protected. Dreaming away my days, praising moon-minted autumns, while Yokihi's or Nakano's fragrant black hair bloomed in my heart, and the paper Heike ghosts sang of creeping their forlorn way through wet bracken, I enjoyed the world beyond the paper bridge. A branch of flowers waved in the wind beneath a single cloud. I finally bought scissors at a convenience store. Sometimes I cut out swords or horses for my paper ghosts. A policeman bowed to the Kamakura Regent. Once two uniformed schoolchildren took photographs.

By now I had learned to hear my ghosts without my thousand-yen note, which had long since gone for less noble purposes. The Cloistered Emperor was always whispering: Disregard these hateful commoners! They are not human beings.

Just after the first freeze, that bent old crone who had first addressed me in front of the Miu Miu department store became one of us. My tent was in the park, while she was one of those who slept in box houses beneath that long overpass there in Shinjuku. Come winter she thickened herself in so many cast-off jackets that her stoop nearly disappeared within her tear-drop waddle. Creeping toward the public toilet, she smiled at me.

The former soapland employee became my friend, because he adored beauty of all sorts, and had nothing to live for. He pretended that we were two Genji warriors striding shoulder to shoulder, with our swords raised as we prepared to engage the Heike. Once he had owned a magnifying glass solely in order to inspect the minute black strokes of an *ukiyo-e* print's willow-shaped eyebrows; and when a portrait of some bygone courtesan especially allured him, he employed it to count her pubic hairs. Like me, he had been idle and extravagant. We agreed on lacking regrets, although his eyes were sad and he ached in his bones. Soon he was sitting beside me for half the day on my scrap of cardboard, sharing cheap sake with me, watching my paper ghosts and describing all the women whom he had loved. In particular, he remembered two sisters named Yoko and Keiko—especially when two of my paper ladies in white-crested pink ki-monos began to stride past a lacquered drum which I had cut out for them from a rice cracker package; their mincing little feet barely cleared my shoulder, and the former soapland employee said: Yes, they looked just like that, so beautiful! and he clapped his hands.— Now, that girl in the red kimono's a paper ghost, he said to himself, or perhaps to me. No, her hand's warm from the sake we drank together, so I know she can't be a ghost . . .— He was far more lonely than I. The paper he had been cut from was as black as the opened mouth-square of the Noh knee-drummer who glares straight ahead. No one gave him money, so I took care of him. Once when I came back from buying sake at the convenience store, I found him bent over my paper ghosts (who without me lay dead together in a plastic bag), and he was imploring: If you are someone from the capital, please inform the Emperor that I continue to exist.— He tried to steal Yokihi, soiling her in his attempts to lick the triple tines of naked skin on the back of her white-stenciled neck, but since she was nothing without me, he returned her with apologies, after which we became still closer.— When pneumonia descended on him, as it had last winter and the winter before, the old woman and I cooked soup for him whenever we could afford to do so. Just as the sun of late afternoon pinkens the lobe of a *maiko*'s ear, so his face grew flushed with fever and drunkenness. If you remember that famous Kabuki scene when Kiyomori confines the Cloistered Emperor in the Prison Palace, you will visualize my friend's papery gestures of sadness on the night when he told me how sick and desperate he was. He had always been one of those successful prophets who foresaw the worst, did nothing to avoid it, and then exclaimed in agony. Do you remember the Dragon God's final torment, when a gold-winged bird swoops down to steal his retainers? My bravely defiant friend performed the dance of losing, so that he grew bereft of all his supports. Then he disappeared beneath a flat moon of yellow paper. I could have been a retainer in search of his master. He had always been as invisible as a ghost hidden in skyscraper-shade, so without hope I hunted him here and there, attended by my faithful paper ghosts, who made my living for me even when I felt too dispirited to watch; my life remained as charmed as before, except that I worried about him as I never had about myself, or even Etsuko, who was surely better off without me. I could feel the corners of my mouth pulling down. *Wait awhile; wait awhile,* sang my paper ghosts. I bit my lip, warming my nose in my mitten or counting cracks in the sidewalk while my paper ghosts performed; sometimes I heard a coin fall into my hat. Then I wandered beneath another overpass. If I could have found him, what a fine dance Yokihi would have accomplished for his rapture! Even the Pale Lady would have entertained him, for she was an accomplished tease. Then he would have laughed between his coughs, which resembled the crying of migrating cranes.— It was not I but the man who eternally read yesterday's newspaper who found him dead in a public toilet. For a week I felt heavyhearted. But it was cold, and I too felt unwell; I had no strength to grieve for what could not be helped.

One evening the ancient woman, creeping toward me, with a cane in each hand and a garbage bag tied to her back, lifted up her head with effort, composed herself and inquired: Excuse me, but what do you pray for nowadays?

Although her question surprised me, I lacked any reason not to answer it, so I said: I prefer not to give up my hopes and desires completely. I hope not to freeze to death before spring. I always desire a little more sake than I have, but perhaps such wishes are permissible in my situation.

Do you expect your wishes to be fulfilled?

Well, I've left my expectations. Anyhow, I have my paper ghosts.

That's right. You're getting famous in Shinjuku. Even the Yakuza* are talking about you!

We seated ourselves on a piece of cardboard. My paper ghosts began to play, and so the Genji lady Tomoe, blackhaired and lovely, decapitated Muroshige of Musashi at full gallop, and his corpse took on the many delicious blues and violets in the kimonos and sky of an old *ukiyo-e* print of Kabuki actors. Yoritomo hanged Yokihi from a flowering cherry whose silhouetted branches writhed into brushstroked Japanese characters. One and all, they watched me serenely, as glad as I that they were dead to me.

A rich lady approached, carrying a shopping bag in each hand. Her hair reminded me of the wet sparkle of Nakano's spangled handbag and silver raincoat, so I smiled at her. She glanced at us in horrified sorrow, then hurried on without giving anything.

The old woman sat smiling down into the earth. I asked her: You're a goddess, aren't you? Did you give life to my paper ghosts?

Never mind. Would you like to be with Etsuko and her mother again?

Thank you, but I would rather not be selfish.

Commendable! said the old woman. You may come to me.

When she removed her mask, she became a young girl. She had long black hair like the Pale Lady, and when she smiled at me, I seemed to re-member an ancient moon rising over reeds.— I bowed until my forehead touched the sidewalk.

Then she removed her young girl's mask, and showed herself as an an-cient skull. I was afraid for a moment, but I bowed again.

She said: Are you disappointed?

No, goddess—

Just as in a blast of sunlight cherry blossoms may grow so distinct as to resemble paper representations of themselves, so this divinity became

* Japanese "Mafia."

ever truer or more false with each unmasking of herself, but in any case no more known; therefore, I supposed that some further aspect of her, no matter whether I ever saw it, might lie beneath the skull, which anyhow grinned at me as easily as did every significant entity in my life—and, after all, who can hope to rob the grave of its mask?

Come to Mirror Mountain now, she said. I felt free because my heart did not follow after her. Her bent spine was as erotic as the back of a *maiko*'s neck. So I entered her house, where the summer gardens and winter gardens of richness walled themselves around us both—but only for a moment, to remind me of the paper world I forsook. Our paper ghosts danced for us one more time, although they had all become skeletons. They sang a song about returning to the capital. Yoritomo raised his ribbed paper lance, which was more narrow and three times longer than a chopstick, and then the Pale Lady chanted: Now I sink beneath this mound of grass; now I will fly for awhile.— Then the magic went out of them. I had no complaints; the old woman and I were fond of each other. We earned hundred-yen coins and entertained our friends by acting out the old Kyōgen skit about the man who sings best while drunk and in his wife's lap.

VII

WIDOW'S WEEDS

Mrs. Wenuke Lei McLeod was an elegant widow of about forty-five. I met her through her younger sister Rileene, a former lover of mine who happened to be one of my wife's best friends. While we were intimate, Rileene had led me to believe that she and Wenuke must be estranged, so it was half a surprise when she invited me to meet her at Wenuke's place; but only half, because when love ends, many impossible things become possible.

Rileene had been a dark brown slender girl with curly black hair; I especially used to prize the sparkle of ocean spray on her bare brown breasts. She had wanted to marry me; I never trusted the stability of her inclinations. Indeed, less than two weeks after my wife's death Rileene was unfaithful to me with a Cuban woman named Carmen, who knew how to cook so well that Rileene now went around in maternity dresses. Once her waist had begun to spread, I took equal delight in watching how her fat buttocks swung apart whenever she squatted down. As for the perilous transmutation of love into mere friendship, that Rileene and I had accomplished with small graceful sadnesses and scarcely any resentments. Over time we grew proud of one another. Strange to say, Carmen disliked me. I certainly bore her no grudge.

Apparently Carmen did not care for Wenuke, either. I was led to believe that Rileene found herself easily bored in her sister's company; so, since her best companion could not be bothered to join her, Rileene picked up her little mobile phone, which was studded with miniature cowrie shells, and dialled me up.

The McLeod property had been in the Captain's family since the very end of the nineteenth century; and at one time it must have resembled the residence of a Yankee sea-trader right down to the widow's walk on the roof, but since the death of Wenuke's husband, if not before, the jungle had nourished itself on the place. Creepers grew up the shuttered windows, and the front porch was rotten enough that Rileene, who knew it so well that she must bring guests here frequently, had to show me where not to walk. The roof was sagging with greenery. Orchids grew down from the knocker of the front door.

As for Wenuke, she wore green and seemed exceedingly quiet. Her youthfulness surprised me. The instant I saw her, I had to have her.

Watching me, she smiled, her slit skirts half revealing her thighs, in the fashion of banana leaves in the wind. Rileene soon departed. Wenuke awarded her a fluttery little wave.

As I sat with her beneath a grand old banana tree, whose broken dark leaf-sails shook in the wind, spewing lovely drops of rainwater into our faces, we rocked in a rickety lovers' swing. Other men might have wondered how many had sat there with her, and whatever became of them. As for me, I was content with adoring the crescent-shaped shadows beneath her eyes. The Captain drowned in a tidal wave, Rileene had said. Fortunately, I have never been attracted to lucky women. Whenever a raindrop fell on her cheek, Wenuke licked it up with her surprisingly long tongue. My heart pounded. Presently she took my hand and led me inside the mildewed old house. I glimpsed vines growing up from the kitchen sink, a bathroom which was now a black hole in the rotten floor, bookcases screened by descending stalks of greenery. Wenuke took me up the black, rotten stairs, pointing to the places that were unsafe. Her bedroom was gloriously overgrown with ferns whose sweet scent masked the putrescence in the walls. The Captain's photograph still hung from a rusty nail which I could have pulled out with two fingers. He wore a worried look, and mold freckled his bearded face. I cannot believe he would have liked me. But Wenuke, seeing me study the portrait, insinuated herself and turned it against the wall. When the nail slipped out, the picture shattered on the floor, releasing a fat old beetle, perhaps the Captain's incarnation, that twiddled its feelers indecisively for a moment, then marched into a hole in the wall. Wenuke shrugged. I have never been attracted to sentimental women.

The bed was a stout mahogany four-poster whose canopy had rotted into something like a spiderweb; impatiently, Wenuke pulled it away by the handful, and once I saw what she was doing I helped her. We ripped away the sodden sheets. The mattress had long since reverted to moss of an almost shockingly emerald brightness. Wenuke was already unbuttoning her dress, which fastened from the back; I undid the last button for her.

2

I had guessed what she was, but that only increased my relish; for I knew myself to be a man of experience. Before I was entirely naked, she was already swarming all over me. Even her hair seemed to be twining itself around my throat. Her breath and body were deliciously humid, so that when I lay in her arms I felt all at once refreshed, intoxicated and suffocated. In any event, I could not get enough of her. The coffee-like odor of her armpits, her breasts like a cluster of green papayas around a white trunk, the perfect softness of her legs, her cool ginger-ginseng scent, these were like various desserts set before me on a porcelain plate at a fancy restaurant.

When she climaxed, she gave off a sudden medicinal smell.

3

On closer inspection I learned that the hair in her armpits was actually delicate green vines with leaves like miniature pearls. Her pubic hair was coarse and reddish-brown, like coconut fibers. Her saliva tasted like rainwater. There was a faintly sour-salty smell about her crotch after she had urinated, which she did only rarely and then in transparent brownish-green gushes.

She had a way of wrapping herself around me and drinking my sweat with her entire body; I could feel the trillion little mouths of her skin.

Just as influenza sometimes announces herself with a sweetly feverish lassitude—one wants nothing more than to remain on one's back, enjoying the ceiling through drooping eyelids; and it's only upon attempting to sit up that the discomforts of sickness become apparent—so what Wenuke was doing to me seemed but part of the sexual act itself, when she let down her long hair-vines and wrapped us both in cool green leaves. Sometimes I would dig my face into the crook of her arm, just to catch my breath, and afterward I would never be sure whether I had slept. In those years I often experienced dizzy spells, as do many men my age; and this sweet greenskinned woman of mine made me a trifle dizzier, but only when I sat up. But there came the time when I finally rose to dress, and she pulled me back down on top of her. Letting her win that contest, I entered her in a frenzy while she twined her legs around me, pulsating, biting me and sucking me. We slept. Then I truly needed to go; I had an appointment. I tried to sit up, but she would not disengage her arms. When I said her name, she opened her evil eyes with the sudden threatening boom of a wave against a lava-cliff.

4

Having enjoyed several experiences with supernatural lovers in the past, I was not in the least alarmed. The beautiful Chinese fox-spirits who suck semen out of a man until he dies can be beaten at their own game: sustained, repeated, remorseless penetration will kill *them* first, so that suddenly, in the middle of the act, the lovely longhaired lady squirming on the bed becomes a sad little fox-corpse with its tongue hanging out. As for the elf-ladies of Central Europe, I've found them innocuous, since all they truly desire is a man's happy surrender for twenty or a hundred years, which in any case spend themselves ecstatically, like a single night. What he-man would pass that up? Everyone you used to know will be gone, of course, but one can't be miserly in the game of love.

That is how life is for those of us who can be caught by the sudden, astonishing dearness of a strange woman's back.

If you want to know, I was in love with femininity. That was why I hazarded myself with supernatural bedmates. In my quest for the most womanly woman of all, I sought out her who was not half derived from man, which is to say her who had never had a father.

5

Regarding the fox-women I do admit that in each case I felt bad for doing it, but then I thought: It was her, me or abstinence; and neither of us had wanted the last! She would have murdered me if she could.

6

I remember the first, who tried her feeble best to be good to me, but dared not cease even momentarily from being good to herself as she saw it, which meant protecting herself from what she was doing to me by draining my semen; once I began to show signs of anemia she cut herself off from my neediness. Unfortunately, it is impossible to divorce a fox and live; these beings do not accept abandonment, perhaps because once they have attached themselves to a given host, severance would cause them great suffering. At any rate, she had a lovely voice and long brown hair—but what is the use of remembering her? When she died, I remember how the white waterfall of urine gushing between her dark thighs turned into a snowy tail.

Departing the room forever, I emerged into the Chinese beauty parlor whose beautiful hairdresser, in a polka-dotted miniskirt, was rapping the shoulderblades of a happy man.— I think you have very good time? she demanded, continuing her business as rapidly as a chicken-and-rice vendeuse can slice with her cleaver.

And I remember the latest, who kept striding and kicking, prancing and flashing various shades of leg and breast while her lies alone smiled in the friendly darkness. She possessed the small unwinking eyes of a splay-legged turtle. Unlike the first, she not only preyed on men, but camouflaged herself as a prostitute. Light puckered up on the floor. My semen trickled down her black bikini, as slimy as a worm. Pretending to be happy and desirous, she dragged me into the back room.

At her funeral an old Chinese lady raised an incense stick above her head, clasped her hands at mouth level, silently praying before the shrine, her eyes tightly shut, her lips clenched; I suppose she must have been the procuress.

Below, in the creamy brown river, floating shacks on logs like old houseboats gone to decay reminded me of other lives that she and I could have lived; and I remember a hill of flower trees, coconut trees, papaya trees; a railing whose tiles were hot to the touch; and a street on which headscarfed women slowly strolled. The ones who were fox-spirits in that town frequented either the Tong Chong Chinese Club or the Lai Zhu Unisex Hair Salon.

7

And regarding the elf-ladies, I truly have no regrets at all. Thanks to them, I have already lived a thousand years.

8

Once an elf-lady married me, and then left me largely alone while she went out to enchant other flies into her spiderweb. I spent most of that century chopping wood for her. Grey hairs grew from my chin as slowly as the stained glass windows of ancient cathedrals ooze from rectangles into trapezoids. Brown creeks unhurriedly undercut the leaning trees of my solitude and occasionally some long narrow weasel-like animal clattered from stone to stone, chasing a fish. When she returned at last, with a hypnotized knight clinging to the tail of her white horse, she set the knight to breaking stones, dismounted and with a laughing kiss set me free. It had all been a game. I felt joyous and strong as I wandered back into the world, and found a fairy hoard of gold upon the way.

9

Ultimately, the play of light through banana leaves leads one to heaven, which I now inhabited with my naked Wenuke, who seated herself on a river rock, laving her drawn-up thighs, her desire to devour me as sweetly naked as a baby's toes wiggling in its mother's lap.

Whenever I left, even for a moment, I was attacked by her sadness at my back. Moreover, each time I tried to get up from beneath her, I felt weaker and she clung to me with greater determination. I had no illusions.

Once upon a time, a certain carnivorous woman sought to do to me as she had done to my nine hundred predecessors. Just as a smiling Thai mother dabbles her child's face with sacred water while he grimaces, so this fiendish lover of mine began to baptize me with a silver poison drawn from between her legs; fortunately, I confounded her with my bezoar stone, and she perished in a single shriek. How and when would Wenuke make her attempt to murder me?

We sat alone together in her rotting house, and in the rocking chair which would have caved in beneath a child's weight she knitted me a green pullover, the threads blossoming one by one as her needle drew them up toward the light, her face calmly poised over the growing garment that resembled a swatch of turf; sometimes she smiled, and sometimes peeped at me as if she might be plotting something; but what if it was only that she loved me? I had hollowed out the handle of my keychain and filled it with a military herbicide. Do you consider me a scheming betrayer? But I never killed any lady except in self-defense.

I was in love with every one of them, for they eschewed the tiresome unpredictability of human women, who might start an argument at any moment, or decide to leave me. At least the supernaturals always knew what they wanted.

10

The carnivorous woman I mentioned had murdered my best friend five hundred years before; and when I encountered her in that alien city I suddenly heard the ghost of my friend laughing his happy sniggering laugh, watching me from overhead in the night, knowing my misdeeds, and a pet phrase of his came into my head; he said it and laughed, said it and laughed, but in the laugh there was only bitterness; he was saying his pet name for the woman who had now become my lover. Well, who was he angry at? She had destroyed him, not I. Her kiss was as lovely as the sea's salty spittle squirting up against the walls of my heart.

And then I saved myself from her and she died in that long scream.

11

Wenuke was certainly as tender as sautéed snowpea shoots in a careful Chinese restaurant.

She sucked the semen out of me with her mouth, and kept sucking, until finally, when she raised her face and looked at me, I saw it trickling from the corner of her mouth, and there were threads of blood in it. I felt so dizzy that I could hardly think. If I didn't get away right now, I would die. I stood up, clung to the bedpost for a moment and staggered naked down those rotten stairs, expecting her to pursue me with her whipping tendrils, but she lay as if uprooted; and presently, just before I fled the house, I heard from upstairs the beginning of a keening like the sobbing of a child left alone at night with a cruel mother, a sobbing that continues hour after hour while the child tries to do what the mother demands, always failing to please her.

There was a blanket in my car. I threw it over me and drove away. Then I telephoned Rileene, who sounded strangely surprised and resentful to hear from me. She referred me to a discreet doctor who was very knowledgeable about such cases. He prescribed a diet of beef broth and blood pudding. Within two weeks I felt as right as rain.

Rileene telephoned me to say that her sister missed me very much. What could I do? I drove back to the house. Wenuke was waiting and watching for me up on the widow's walk.

12

That first dusk we scarcely touched one another, and the darkness came by staccato stages, each as irrevocable as another spurt of India from an inkwell. It became pleasantly cool, and my elbows and shoulders tingled with mosquito bites no matter how much citronella I put on.

Her gaze was like some strange green rainforest pool.

I already knew who I was and what I wanted. I had become nearly as supernatural as she.

When the moon rose, she wrapped her long green fingers around my wrist and led me back into our bedroom.

For a surprise she had dug up some foxed old mirror and propped it up against the wall so that we could watch ourselves make love; and I was interested to see how thin and pale I had become. She looked as perfect as ever, of course. With a single tendril she began to stimulate my prostate; and I looked at myself. My panting reminded me of the way a lungfish's inhalations puff out small sacs next to its anterior fins.

Gazing at me with desperate love, she brought her face close to mine and extended her tongue until it blossomed in my mouth, wrapping round and round my tongue a dozen times and piercing it with suckers until I was happily drinking my own blood.

Just as in Paris they open the long green coffins bolted to the wall of the quai, and the books and prints within get resurrected, so my capacity for affection—I nearly wrote *infection*—got once more disinterred from within my breastbone by Mrs. Wenuke Lei McLeod. I almost believed that she had no heart to hurt me.

13

But deep underwater in dreams, a nurse shark's belly rising overhead like the moon, I woke to find myself struggling somewhere within her crotch, which was a deep weedy hole with black water shining across it like morning light on the blue sea. Blood was trickling from my nose and my nipples. I pulled out of her and tried to sit up, but could not.

On the other side of the bed, she knelt and motionlessly watched me, half smiling, silently weeping jasmine-fragrant tears.

14

I knew even then that she was as rare as a banana-colored eel, which every now and then, on long voyages, I have been lucky to observe languidly flicking its tiny front fins.

I threw myself wildly into her cool green body, and in her magic mirror I saw myself purple-faced and bulging-eyed, with the stuporous gape of a puffer fish, and just then one of her fingers sprouted deep in my anus, at which point I experienced agonizing pleasure and everything went black. When I knew who I was again, I found her sitting on my lap with all her myriad arms wrapped around me; and in the mirror I saw the white cilia of mushroom-gilled anemones wriggling like maggots.

When I finally left her for good, she wrapped herself around the bed-post like a black-and-green spider whose legs swell at the joints into leaf-shapes, clinging to a silk-wrapped victim, hanging in the wind.

15

After my escape from Wenuke, I wanted somebody more substantial, so I travelled to Greece, a country renowned for vampirism. After a few peasant funerals I found the right situation and was there alone, having bribed the mourners, when the girl's cadaver rose up off the table, stark naked and ready. There may well be nothing on earth (or under it) as delectable as a fresh young corpse with a waxy yellow complexion, sunken eyes, conspicuous ribs and the sweet odor of decay. I was intoxicated by that odor! I fell in love with her.

I think I'm probably not as good a person as you make me out to be, the corpse whispered.

She left for a moment to recompose herself. Returning to the unmade bed, I sought her traces and found upon the pillow a long black hair. When I touched it, my heart raced and my penis stiffened.

I belong to you, I said. I'll love you forever. I'll be yours forever—well, at least for the rest of my life, which is the best I can do.

Oh, I hope not, she whispered in dismay.

I prized her. But whenever she thought that I was not watching, she commenced to make metallic grimaces and jaw-workings similar to those of a coal grouper fish; and I wondered whether she longed to gnaw me up or whether she were simply tormented at not being permitted to rot away in peace. Her kisses had begun to stink.

When I asked her how to make her happy, she replied that she had always wanted to visit other places. I took her to Paris. In memory of Wenuke I proposed to her in the Jardin de Plantes, where just behind our bench a sandyhaired young cop stood clasping his white-gloved hands just over his buttocks.

The last time I had confessed was at the funeral of my calm and faithful wife. The priest, who appeared to be quite certain of his knowledge, had assured me that in the afterlife I would be placed in a cell, bricked in up to my waist, so that I could see only the top half of my pure and faithful wife, who thanks to celestial virtue would be able to see all of me; she would pity me without missing or needing me. That had made me sad, but I soon consoled myself. Being a good Catholic, I now decided that I had better go to confession again. When I whispered into the little window that I intended to marry a ghoul or vampire, the father assured me that I would be doing no harm since such creatures lack souls. If anything, he said, I would bestow the blessings of God on her through the sacrament of marriage. That night I said a few Hail Marys just in case.

I'm afraid I'll disappoint you, the corpse whispered. I kissed her forehead, which was as waxy as a banana leaf.

The priest sold us holy water, and we both drank it. On our wedding night I stripped my bride, flung her down on the bed and buried my head between her breasts, ravished by the overripe smell of her cleavage. One of her nipples came off in my mouth, and I swallowed it desperately.— I think I have a loose tooth, she giggled in a little-girl voice.— Suddenly I was stung with longing for Wenuke's breasts, which had been like many immature bananas growing upward in their hard green cluster. But what could I do about that now? Here was my lawfully wedded vampire; I drove my stake between her legs.

Where must Wenuke be now? I had sent her to a grey clear sea, calmer than its mosquitoes and raindrops.

By the next morning, my wife's flesh had further discolored into a semblance of the soft yellows and greens of fluorescent corals. I possessed her in a fury, trying to persuade myself that the creaking of the bed might be her sighs.

Once upon a time, in the jungle on the way to Wenuke's house, there had been lemon-colored flowers that smelled like armpits. Wenuke's armpits had smelled like flowers. And now my wife, whom I had thought to be a vampire but who was only a harmless corpse, opened her black mouth to apologize for leaving me, then began choking and retching as ants streamed out of her. What sort of universe is this, that suffering continues even beyond death? Love and pity both demanded that I give her the only gift I could, oblivion. I went to the desk, found a letter opener, and with it sliced off her rotting head. Her yellow arms continued to reach for me, and her breasts wept ichorous tears.

Rushing out of there, I found myself on the Quai des Grands-Augustins, gazing into a bookstore window whose gold-stamped red and black leather merchandise gaped open to drypoints and aquatints. I remember a volume of Villon depicting an old man facing a noose, another *Oeuvres* of Villon open to a longhaired, gloomy medieval fellow gazing out of a dark casement, his hands on his knees; I also recall some NRF volumes of Malraux, whose spines bore luscious blue and orange inlays that reminded me of fungoid domes. Should I take up reading instead of love? But these printed adventures promised me no better happiness.

I walked for hours. Then like a grave there awaited me the empty bed, the rumpled bed, my loneliness a physical illness.

16

After that, my lovers got worse and worse. One night I found myself trying to pick up a sweetheart at Casa de las Mujeres, which was a closet in a hotel in a hot border town; but there was nothing inside except a yellow old skeleton with long black braids that the moths had been at.

Then there was a bronze woman who turned out to be malevolent; although I certainly have the fondest recollections of her cunt, which was dark, ornate and incense-fumed like the mouth of some Chinese temple encrusted with stone lions from which red balloons dangle like breasts. Slowly, slowly she lowered her head, grinning perpetually. Whenever she undid her chessboard skirt, it clanged on the floor. She liked to grip my upper lip between her rusty little serrated teeth. I suspected that it would end badly, so I started secreting a blowtorch in my pocket. One night, pale-mottled and -bellied but otherwise nearly stone-colored, she lay pretending to be sleeping, her snout upward as we lay together on our boulder. I knew that when the moment arrived, she would deny me any warning; so I felt almost sick with anxiety. Now my memories of Wenuke came back to me like the sky seen through insect-gnawings in a broad-leafed jungle plant. Of course I had then been trapped in the analogous situation of waiting for her to strangle me with her green tendrils; but my distrust of Wenuke no longer felt real to me, being the habits which no longer served, and whose comforting instinctual run suddenly faltered into astonished sorrow. As for my bronze woman, however, when she opened her golden-green eyes and snapped her teeth at me, did she mean to sever my throat or was it merely in her mind to nuzzle me affection-ately? I would not harm her on mere suspicion; after all, this was sup-posed to be a love match. And her cunt was so interesting; it was perfectly smooth and cold; she always oiled it for me.

She could not speak; she only roared. In the end I decided that she was harmless. But I never slept easily beside her. When I left her, tears hissed and squeaked down her mottled cheeks.

17

Back in the time when I used to pass my evenings in Wenuke's house it sometimes took quite awhile for the sky to actually get black. When it was still a pale blue color, Wenuke would show me the first star, which was big and round and bright, and then the next two stars winked on quite suddenly, and often a firefly traversed a tree-silhouette, sometimes grey and blurry, and perhaps a bat came almost to my nose.

I remember the indefatigable screeching of insects, the gravelly voices of rivers and sometimes, when we climaxed, the clattering wings of dis-turbed birds.

Occasionally I considered writing a letter to Rileene, but inevitably concluded that she would think badly of me, or, worse yet, that she had conspired with her sister to kill me. But what if Wenuke had never meant me any harm?

18

Word came that my Greek corpse-bride had been resurrected, her skeleton-hands thrusting out of the ground like some Parisienne's high-riding breasts. I received indisputable evidence that she was sucking children's blood. That was low of her, but don't we all decay? I remember for instance Wenuke, whose crotch became a deep weedy hole with black water shining across its depths.

Of all of them, that Greek corpse had loved me the most. But my grief at losing her had dissipated. It was gradually being revealed to me that Wenuke was the one I had been meant for. And we were parted.

If I could only avoid ever seeing Wenuke again, no matter how much I missed her, then I would not be forced to experience my new relationship to her, which must resemble the viewing of a lover's corpse; she would still be there, but she could never be to me what she once had been. Each love has its habits, as I've said; and when that love breaks, the memories of those habits, or the attempted practice of them, comprise a skeleton of pain.

Meanwhile, there came a night event, a funeral, in fact; as you remember, I had met my Greek corpse at one of those; she knew that I would be at this new convocation, so I sent word to her by vampire bat to keep away; scanning the faces with a dread which would have erupted into anger had she been present in that cemetery of verdegrised urns on plinths, wilting marble mushrooms, I quickly began to feel her absence although I inspected each skull and mourner with an ever firmer despair; and when I saw that my ex-wife wasn't there, I felt a patient ancient sadness.

The bronze woman was present, but I avoided her green frog's grimace; later I heard that she had ripped a man's heart out.

I went to California and stalked a high dark ocean-horizon from behind palms and bungalows; until one stormy night I spied a sea goddess whose garters were frilly white wave-tops and lacy sea-spittle. I especially remember a pointed brown-green breast gushing white froth. Swimming in her foamy white petticoats and her long green seaweed hair, she sang me the same melody she'd sung Ulysses, which made little impression on me; I'd heard it all before. Needless to say, I finally penetrated her, which was quite a trick, as you would know if you'd ever looked down through the foam, deep down into a green vulva. She had eyes like mirror-wet sand. Wringing out her dark sea-black skirt afterward, on her tiny lava-islet decorated with skulls, she offered me eternal life beneath the water; unfortunately, I was already diseased by that curse.

19

The elongated reflection of a seagull on wet sand kept me company once she swam away (she was hungry, she said). Then I was very much alone; and *then,* just as a dark wave rises suddenly out of the darkness, breaks open into spume and sprays you, longing for Mrs. Wenuke Lei McLeod came to me, and in my vision she was as humidly cool and perfect as jungleside sea air.

20

After that, there were slow late night sounds of heels on the just-shined tiles of hotel lobbies whose inset patterns now receded ever more vividly to ever greater distances. Beneath a potted plant, a longhaired slender-necked woman waited for midnight, her hands in her lap. I approached her, almost weeping. When she caressed my arm, her fingers reminded me of a crested iguana, slowly drawing itself along a branch.

And I thought, my God, my God, I am so weary of being a murderer; when can I find someone perfect enough to kill me? Who will she be? Will she first permit me to gorge my desires on her white-banded flesh and bluish face? And just before it happens, as her mouth suddenly tightens and for the very last time I stroke the preparatory pulsing of her tentacles, would it be hypocrisy or love if I asked her to remember me when it was over, and perhaps even put on widow's weeds?

THE BANQUET OF DEATH

You must share death amongst you in order to exhaust it and cause its dissolution, so that in you and through you death may die.

Valentinus

1

In keeping with this aphorism, we formed a society, Goldman, Mortensen, Sophie and I, and commenced to hold secret banquets at the graveyard. Mortensen could read the gashes and angles of any rune on a stone. It was he who had uncovered certain possibilities. Although I now suspect that he doubted Valentinus, for curiosity he went forward, which is to say downward. I no longer remember why Sophie and I committed ourselves. Being younger in those days, we owned more to lose, but our losses seemed proportionately less permanent. As for Goldman, whom we acknowledged as our cleverest executor, he managed by virtue of feeling needed. Before the moon had waned twice he achieved communication with the dead.

The first was a very tall yellow skeleton, who began shyly enough with three taps from behind the mausoleum wall; I hypothesized that its skull must be the percussive transmitter, at which Sophie put her finger to her lips. We must have been happy then. Goldman replied three times with the tip of his pickaxe, carefully or solemnly. Within the hour, he and the skeleton were conversing in Morse code. Mortensen, who possessed equal facility with that system, now took the pickaxe and excitedly tapped out: DEATH MAY DIE. After a long time the skeleton replied: DIE. Sophie gripped my hand.— YOU MUST SHARE DEATH, signaled Mortensen, and the skeleton tapped back: DIE. As soon as that fingernail moon had misted over, the tomb-door commenced to creak outward, and within the slowly widening column of blackness I saw my first animated death's-head, which reminded me of another moon rising sideways, or perhaps of the peculiar yellow-white glare, which pretends not to be luminous but nonetheless imprisons our gaze, of a locomotive approaching in fog, before that single light has drawn close enough to subdivide into three. Anyhow, out it shambled, its long toenails clicking like a dog's, and joined us at our abominable table.— But this is extraordinary! said Mortensen. May I remind you all to repress whatever horror you feel?— We know that, said Sophie, carving up the meat.

In the service of mutual understanding, Goldman had prepared a vocal apparatus out of silk, leather, catgut and rubber, the bellows being powered by a shielded air compressor placed within the patient's ribcage. It was almost comical to watch him hook it up to the skeleton, which might have been wary, wooden or irresolute (lacking facial muscles, it conveyed no such niceties). Sophie stared; Goldman turned on the device; the skeleton wheezed: *I am dead.*

But *death may die,* insisted Mortensen, leaning forward.

Die, agreed the skeleton. Accordingly, it began to grapple at its ribcage, breaking out bone-slats, pitifully striving to pull itself into yellow kindling, as if dissolution could be something to yearn for.— You're mistaken! cried Mortensen.— Fortunately, Goldman the practical knew what to whisper.— I wonder what he said? I also wonder which premortem occupation taught him his tricks: Was he once a motivational counselor, an unlicensed abortionist or a combat sergeant? Strange to say, he lacked an interest in people. The outcome was that Old Bones gave over trying to destroy itself, its skull swivelling heavily down against its sternum even while it spied on us through the tops of its eyesockets. (The mystery of consciousness is no greater for a death's-head than for, say, Mortsensen.) Sitting down in its own flinders, it chewed a cutlet, and its jaws squeaked like unoiled hinges.

Second was the sad brittle lady with the spiderwebs in her eyes. She persuaded Sophie to tickle her inside her ribs. I suppose she climaxed. Her friends had friends, and before we knew it we who still lived were outnumbered.

We always began with a toast: *To death.* But you already know that what our society intended was its extirpation. To what extent the dead lay ready to ratify that project remained debatable, no matter how interestingly they enunciated through Goldman's apparatus. They resembled children in a way, or perhaps we were children to them; but they were less alien than loathsomely familiar. With the exception of the warlock, I acquit them of making illicit advances or offering temptations of any sort. They never even intimated that through their example we could shake off the misery of being alive. All we could hope for was a temporary compromise, so I believed; while Mortensen for his part demanded that we set out with the utmost straightforwardness to understand and obey the rules of death no matter how long that took. My reading of Valentinus was that whatever we might learn would derive from the reaction-process of consumption, not from the dead themselves. I might have been wrong about this, for whenever a corpse stalks toward me in the darkness, unfurling its putrid fingers, grinning, snarling or doing whatever else its rotting substance accidentally impels it to, even now I can't help but imagine (I wouldn't say hope for) a significant experience. Mortensen and Goldman disagreed as to whether the dead were enchained in forgetfulness or merely existed in a state of being which we had not yet mapped out. In either case, once we four and our new friends had consumed enough death, what lay beneath it must begin to show, like the fossil of a great beast in the bed of a receding lake. I refrained from voicing my minuscule differences of opinion, even to Sophie, since I had nearly reached that age (oh, but never quite yet!) when whatever we do is worse than useless; besides, seven years before, when our leader first opened unto us his sweet treasury of aspirations, we had hoped and believed. As dark as the way might be, the end was undeniably glorious.

2

Certain know-it-alls insist: Death is nothingness.— Lucretius pointed out that if this be so, there is literally nothing to fear. (The pain and grief of dying shine no relevance on the state of being dead.) But people do fear cemeteries, and still more the dead themselves—for in their progression away from us, corpses wax not merely pitiable but (if I may employ an unscientific term) hateful. Might this reaction of ours, which among living humans approaches the universal, be explained simply as the assertion of the life instinct? Mortensen posited otherwise (and when he did, a knowing eye sometimes began shining out of a hole in a hunk of fossil driftwood). Thus the four of us founded our society on the principle that death is a positive state, which the living acknowledge, although they pretend not to. The seeming malignity of the dead may be reduced to a projection of our desire not to comprehend them. Mortensen's anti-dote: Partake of death generously, with opened eyes.

Because the benefit for which we banqueted was so material, none of us broached the matter of whether we had accepted sorrow into our partnership. Speaking only for myself, I now wonder if some prior melancholy could have in some way weakened my constitution, or perhaps even my judgment, in the years before I haunted cemeteries. Concerning Sophie and Goldman I cannot say, but in his youth Mortensen seems to have imbibed the horror of some dying person's ever more futile, wordless and mad beseechings. Perhaps he had attended the deathbed of a slowly asphyxiating parent or spouse (there was a pallid circle of naked flesh on his ring finger). Valentinus teaches that once one crosses that particular divide, his gaze comes to resemble a cat's—although as I recollect that passage I find myself at sea as to whether the crosser was supposed to be the watcher or the performer of death. On the subject of Mortensen, I sometimes thought to read desperation in his eyes. Wasn't it something of just that sort which he meant to stamp out?

3

Sophie had the dreamy lips of a Sphinx. The first time that the dead lady kissed her, she barely managed not to scream. When we left the cemetery, she rushed to the bathtub to scrub herself; it took an hour before she called herself clean. Goldman reminded her that to get to the meat of death one does unpleasant things. She knew that, she said. Now I suspect that the only reason she declined to quit our society was her loyalty to me—although her smile always used to be sad in any case; and well before she first kissed me she had already begun collecting dead butterflies. As for my motivations, I should have asked Goldman, who remembered everything, and did not even express perplexity as to the effects of the foul medicine we so busily imbibed. He and I had first met at Mortensen's famous speech, which asserted that we who live resign ourselves to death for no better reason than people were once resigned to slavery, operations without anesthetic, and any number of such evils. Mortensen, you see, was young once. He hated suffering of any sort. His blood circulated at a velocity sufficient for hope, or evil-fighting. Once the audience had departed the lecture hall—which process took less than two breaststrokes of my watch's spider-arms since there were so few cultivated people in Boston, even including the county medical examiner and his staff—then we three ascended the steps to Mortensen at the podium, and the dusty purple stage curtain behind him became the opaquest entity ever when we clinked our water-glasses against his and toasted: *To death!* While he scarcely looked at Sophie, I knew that of all of us she had made the most delightful impression on him, not that it mattered to me. All I yearned for then was to accomplish something marvelous. Goldman was already proposing to fit us out with silver-plated pickaxes.

Although her sincerity attracted me, I barely knew Sophie in those days. She too must have grieved for some stale corpse. Soon enough I got fond of her and wished to save her from death; and had I resigned from the society there would have been no hope of that. For my own part, the more I banqueted, the less I cared about dying. Thus I seemed to be freeing myself from error.

Unfailingly strict, Mortensen quizzed her on the snake, the ibis, the eye. Although, indeed *because* she breathed the living's natural resentment of the dead, she did not fail him. More than any of us, it seemed, she longed for our purpose to be achieved. So on the following night, when we strolled down to the domes among the cypress trees, all four of us ready if not exactly hungry for the Banquet of Death, she saw the snake before Mortensen did, and when the eye appeared (on the site of a Masonic burial), she chaffed him on not having spotted the ibis. By now the graves were already opening like the covers of drowned books in a tidal current, and that night we met the warlock, who could transform himself into a worm whenever he liked. From him we learned that the Black Depths, as his kind call this earth, extend down into bedrock, and through crooked channels to the Red Place. This news expanded Mortensen's ambitions, not that I cared. (I mostly tried to avoid talking with anyone.) Mortensen, however, proposed to refrain from harrowing hell, since that might be construed as aggression, not to mention that it would destroy a previously unstudied system. Therefore we ought to form an alliance with its inhabitants, based on common interest. And so we wined and dined the warlock, famishing for knowledge and greatness.

By now I more definitely inclined against the miasma of vileness which ever overhung our banquets, like a wall of withered ivy. Perhaps you too would consider them dislikeable occasions. In the style of lovers and of alchemists, we sought to recombine opposites into some divine substance; so our repasts were invariably a mix of succulence and filth, our salad greens being jeweled with maggots, our bread baked from powdered bones, our savory meats basted with cadaveric fluid, while we drank fine old wine mulled with cinnamon and humerus-sticks, slurped up blood puddings topped with spun sugar, and (for our digestions' sake) finished with prunes stewed in rancid ichor. Nibbling Mortensen's earlobe, the warlock said he hadn't eaten so well for a hundred years! He was glad to share with us both life and death; he quite admitted to liking our point of view. I wish you could have heard the sound his eyeballs made when he rolled them. The fact that he kept clear of Goldman, who was so superior in emergencies, stimulated my mistrust; for with his inventory of evil tricks he might prove yet more practical than our cleverest member. In short, what if he cultivated Mortensen in order to gull him? Valentinus implies that death extends up as well as down, so why did the warlock harp only on the Red Place? Forcing myself out of silence, I inquired what he knew about worlds above. The warlock replied with a truly unpleasant grin that he declined to traffick with Celestial Assassins. I most tactfully sank my canine teeth into my lower lip until dawn arrived, and the dead had clattered, sunk or oozed back into their graves, at which point I made known my concern that our research emphasis might be disproportionately negative.— First we must get to the heart of death and share it out, explained Mortensen. Think of rotten leaves in a drainpipe. Until they're cleared nothing goes deeper. Then, when we've descended to solid rock, we'll change course, and drink sky nectar!— Meanwhile our banquets wore on, and I had so far advanced as to gulp a bowlful of corpse-suet without even seasoning it with a sprig of the wild fennel that grew so rankly in the cemetery. Each night I saw new egg-white faces bending over their portions, slurping up marrow through artificial beaks fashioned of unicorn's horn, while beneath the table dead cat-children prowled as wide-eyed as owls, opening their mouths in quest of food. On a gaunt horse whose bones kept falling off, a one-eyed man came riding. He reached into his chest, withdrew his heart and tossed it into our stewpot with a fuming splash. We toasted: *To death!*— Nor did the warlock's blandishments raise my eyebrows anymore. That gentleman was nearly intact, although his face was moldy. He had even kept all his teeth. One night in late summer he invited us to tour the ocean floor, which even at this date lies mostly uninhabited by the dead, although certain drowned people have taken it upon themselves to represent the rest of us. He explained that the Mummy Lady on Sophie's right would drown us in the stewpot, or else we could ask ghastly Mr. Mooncrow to gnaw our throats.— Well, actually, said Mortensen, we mean to stay alive, you see, forever if possible—

Oho! cried the warlock. Then we'll be great friends. But see here: To live forever one must die.

I glanced at Sophie, who merely gazed around the company with charming openness, and presently returned the topic to the Upper Realm, where perfect truth is said to live. At this the warlock contradicted his own dig at Celestial Assassins by inviting her on a midnight promenade, commencing immediately. Destination: the Tree of Knowledge! That was how I first learned that the dead can be unfair. Frankly, I felt indignant; I thought I had gotten away from that. But I held my peace as usual, and so those two went their private way, while Mortensen shared tidbits with the Mummy Lady, whose little eyes were as lovely as gold coins. How far had we diminished death thus far? Goldman had already departed the table in order to measure the apparent speed of the moon between his thumb and forefinger. That left me friendless—for it had long since been clear that Mortensen and Goldman considered me a nothing. All I had ever offered them was Sophie.

4

By Mortensen's command we now had to give up daylight altogether. On the final occasion, holding hands, Sophie and I walked our long street of dark cobbles, which were half silvered with New Year's sunlight, and passed the old man squeezing oranges for juice in his hand-crank press, while the ladies smiled beneath the parasol of his wheeled stand, licking their painted lips. Once upon a time we too had been his customers. Even now Sophie declined to say what the warlock had showed her.— At least tell me if you ate anything, I said, but she answered: Don't put me to the test.— Goldman and Mortensen were waiting at the cemetery gates.

The former was calm, and the latter smiled with the same hopefulness as a child who expects something appetizing for dinner. Here came dusk. Reentering these shady, sky-roofed corridors whose domed, crossed, gabled porticoes and engraved stone-wreathed cells exhaled a half-imaginary odor of decomposition, we burgled a mausoleum and broke open four coffins whose contents would thicken tonight's banquet. Here we promised to dwell until our knowledge could bring back the light. I admit that I would have hesitated, but Sophie swore her oath unflinchingly, and Goldman was so understatedly cavalier about everything that, reminding myself how grateful I had been on the night when Mortensen taught us to fix our meditations on the Dark Door, I too bound myself, at which a comforting dullness descended upon me.

Behind the concave-winged marble angel who clasped the gilded shell for FATHERS and FAMILY began a deep hollow where the Great Flood had wrenched away a full acre of old graves; and down there we held our nightly banquet, dining on overturned slabs, with crowds of new-made ghouls around us. Two or three times I thought about the street where Sophie and I used to live. It was as if I were at the bottom of a well gazing up at a blue marble of sky.

5

At first the banquets took place at what adepts refer as *the time of the living midnight.*— What is the color of death? Mortensen kept asking the dead. Soon he would have mapped the infinite. The warlock was with us from moonrise to dawn. He was gloomy, perhaps, but never asked for our pity. I nearly began to consider him a member of our society once I overheard him teaching Mortensen about the Bitter Sea. Rolling his last cigarette, Goldman recleaned the putrid bellows of his speaking-apparatus; while I modeled myself after the tall bronze soldier leaning on his saber before the wide rectangle of Pablo Riccheri's tomb. Sophie was copulating with a swollen blue man—for isn't miscegenation a sharing and exhausting of our common feast? After that I no longer wanted her.

We now ate nothing but cadavers and bones, aside from the occasional dead birds Sophie gathered just before dawn. From each repast to the next, it seemed, at least to me, that the light in our neighbors' eyesockets was rekindled; and as centipedes and ashes commenced to fall from their ears they attended to Mortensen with diminished apathy. We four agreed that we were indeed in some measure depleting their deaths; so that what we had done for them, they could do for others; perhaps by midwinter we would be prepared even to meet the denizens of the Red Place. I asked the warlock which fruit he had fed Sophie, and he replied: That must be concealed from doubters such as you.— Enough now, said Mortensen, cracking open a skull for me.— Once I had eaten, nausea and misery kept me quiet. I reminded myself that the death of the One gives life to many.

There came the night when the dead began to look around them of their own volition, and so they perceived each other's hideousness. Mortensen lectured them that the most hateful thing is to be dead in secret, because that avoids the question of what one *is*.

Die, said our tall yellow skeleton, in what I thought to be insolent or threatening style.

6

As it happened, this skeleton possessed a more excellent memory than most of the other dead; it could even remember kissing someone. I asked how we could kill death, and it said: *Love.*

Sophie demanded: What do you mean? If I loved you, could I kill your death?

The warlock said: Even Christians say you must give up your life to save it.

That's not to the purpose, said Sophie, almost sharply. I was asking about you people who've already lost your lives.

We're not *people,* laughed the blue man, behind whom several pairs of living eyes glowed as glossily as berries in various dead skulls.

We're advising you to die, the warlock reminded us. Nothing but cowardice keeps you from taking that step.

Goldman was completing his explanation to Mortensen about the mathematical proportions of skulls in relation to their inner content, so it was to Sophie whom I whispered my question: Could the dead mean us evil?— She turned away, leaving me to my own miseries. Now Mr. Mooncrow was leading her inside a dome filled with murmuring ghouls. I knew what knowledge she would give and get of him. Truth to tell, each night the dead seemed more active. So did the many beautiful things which claimed the moistness beneath our banquet slab before dawn: the snails whose jet-black shells glistened like cloisonné, the clean-picked little skulls goggling up at us like bespectacled elementary-school students who hoped to be called upon by the teacher even as luna moths emerged from their nostrils; the hard seedpods filled with stars. Beneath the table, sweet small bats were parting purple-velvet leaves of funereal cabbage with their darling claws, so that they could watch our demonstrations. The bird-skulled woman bowed and pecked at her glass of urine-infused wine, as if she might soon pay attention to me. Perhaps if each one of us swallowed down more, we could reverse all imperfections, and achieve what Mortensen had begun to call *the dark comfort*. Watching me, or so I supposed, certain decayed banqueters worked their jaws, as if they were preparing to speak. Had Mr. Mooncrow uttered a syllable just now? Perhaps it was merely that my hearing was sharpened since I had so long avoided the hummings of the sun. (I should have asked Goldman about this.) Turning his back on the rest of us now that Sophie had gone, the warlock passed his hand over the ground, and blue hands began to claw themselves out of it. Meanwhile the Mummy Lady played with Mortensen—who, truth to tell, was undersexed; but he rose to the occasion, thereby fulfilling the interests of science. The warlock raised his glass to mine and toasted: *To death.*

Since my curiosity had not died yet entirely, I asked him whether there might be a Dead Book of the Dead with naked meanings in it, which would save its reader even at the cost of death to many others, but he replied: Has your name been spoken?

By whom? I said.

Then you're among the ignorant, said he, baring his teeth. I walked away, but the skeleton followed me, saying: *Die.*

Goldman was digging a rectangular hole. Even he had begun to shrivel a little bit—but then, don't we all? One of the articles of our society was that we must resist pitying one another, much less ourselves; anyhow, Goldman, surely the most sensible of any of them, was by that very token my most depressing companion, at least among the living, so his decay touched me less than Sophie's.— When I took him aside, he said: Analyze the problem. Do what you have to do.

Die, the skeleton advised me.

Accordingly, I took up Goldman's pickaxe. Mortensen would not approve, and indeed I rarely sanctioned my own deeds anymore; be that as it may, I smashed that skeleton, skull and spine, while other dead sat eating. Mr. Mooncrow and I collected the fragments and threw them into the stewpot, and Sophie, obediently opening her cunt, satisfied Goldman. I tried to remember the way her eyes used to be when she daydreamed. Saying nothing about my transgression, Mortensen ladled out the latest broth. The stench of his breath was worse than my coffin's. To tell you truth, I hated my existence. I poured out rainwater from an antique ewer, but no one wanted any. Goldman's corpse-women kept wandering to and fro among the tombs, gathering shrouds with which to feed the fire. Sophie scratched herself with her long black fingernails. Her hair was finer than spiderwebs. The warlock and Mortensen discussed the wisdom of worms, and the interesting operations of decomposing corpses. It was not unpleasant. In a very committed voice Mortensen asked Mr. Mooncrow what, if anything, the dead might feel for us, at which his interlocutor contented himself with so horrific a hoot that all the churchyard owls came wheeling round his grisly head; Mortensen muttered inexplicably: Give and take, that's all.— I sat remembering how outside the cemetery one often saw a mother lift up her child as it smiled into her face. How many times had that action been carried out in this world? There was certainly no more need for it. I was sick to death of it, and so for a moment I nearly became desperate.

Mortensen and the warlock now raised a new toast to necrophores, while a furry, moldy woman paired up with a beautiful dead Gypsy to carry to our larder a body which might still be breathing—an appetizing development which appeared to fascinate the shy, worried-looking woman-thing whose chalky face glowed as she squatted between two graves, lowering her slender arms, casting off her mushroom garments.— Who strikes down the wicked? groaned the blue man.

Why the scene should have wearied me I cannot tell; anyhow, I strolled up out of the hollow, and arrived at a glowing hole in the hillside I had never seen before, doubtless because Mortensen was right, and ever more of whatever contained death was revealing itself as death receded, leaving decorations behind. As I looked in I could see a fair sepulcher, and within it a lady's corpse, nude and greenish-yellow like some deliciously unripe fruit, and in a ring around her, five hundred worms were chasing each other in such perfect array that I marvelled. When I asked her name, she replied: I call myself alive, but am I rooted in anything?

Remembering the warlock's words, even if not understanding them, I asked: Has your name been spoken?

Do you have the knowledge to name me, or would you eat first?

Mortensen had rehearsed us on the three perturbations of life: fear, grief and desire. All are but vain reachings after life itself, whereas in death there is nothing but peace—if one sets aside the dead's angry hunger after the living.— So I said: Would you eat with me?

We'll eat knowledge down to nothing.

I said: My first duty is to eat death.

When I climaxed inside her, it felt more as if she had climaxed inside of me. I was filled with her death. She asked no question afterward; better yet, I felt even less for Sophie, as if I were lighter in my guts; my gross matter was becoming moss. Sobbing, Sophie stuffed herself with dead meat. As for me, I was eating less than I was supposed to.

And someday, said Mortensen, we'll make it so we won't die. Not ever. And all the dead who aren't *too* dead might even come back to life. And then cemeteries will never again be places of horror and sadness.

What will they be then? asked Sophie.

First they'll be museums. And then, when we don't even need to remember death anymore, they'll become fields, gardens and homes.

Sophie cracked a marrowbone between her teeth and said: But if no one dies, won't there be too many people?

That won't be our problem. We'll have solved the greatest problem of all time. Let someone else fix that one.

Mortensen sat smiling with love for the future. Goldman, whom I knew less than anyone, kept the fire going, and there were now three more shriveled corpse-women who always helped him, stirring the ladle round and round and moaning like the wind. So we made our toast: *To death!* Dead children took Sophie by the hand, and led her to places where corruption had advanced so far that there was nothing left to do with its traces but scrape them up and dump them into the cauldron.

Before dawn we invariably withdrew into our open coffins, and Mortensen would edify us with such old poems as:

Search while thou wilt, and let thy reason goe
To ransome truth even to the Abysse below.

We three lay staring straight up at the spiderwebs at such moments, and a black marble statue of a nude woman watched over us. Sophie was asleep, her face a purple jelly-jewel, more ovoid than it used to be, her blue hands slightly swollen. My growing indifference to everything deepened my trust in Mortensen, who had so consistently proclaimed that the living and the dead are one.

7

Yes, we were sharing in death, although (with the possible exception of Sophie) we had not yet learned any Names, much less been called by our own. We had achieved first emptiness, then delusion, then the contemplation of delusion, so that we could commence to understand that even emptiness is a delusion. And so we did not care when the warlock, who might have been testing us but more likely was merely lonely, informed us that he knew the whereabouts of hidden treasure. I can't say whether anything terrified him. Even had he offered to mix the most precious jewels with the most rotten carrion, it would not have fit our program, unless his stones were small enough to swallow whole. Likewise, Mortensen's reminders of our purpose might as well have been an accountant's sums. I felt certain that our project could never, no matter how brilliantly it might succeed, lead us into any freshness of being. That might have been another reason that all three of the other members of our society grew ever duller in my estimation.

But Sophie still sometimes reached out, however mechanically, for a dead child's hand. Twice she devoured banquet-meat as she was expected to, then rushed off to vomit between the tombs. Many a shy corpse shambled after her.

Mortensen enthusiastically informed me: This so-called hateful state she's in must be her dialectical maximum. It will intensify, and then she'll be free.

Sophie whispered: I'm not worth anything. I eat filth and death.

Mortensen confided: She's our treasure. She's deeper than any of us.

There came the happiness of another banquet, where we and our dead friends all felt like ourselves, throwing the pallid exoskeletons of crayfish out of our abundant boiling-pot, so that the armless, legless dead could graze them up; and Sophie withdrew into the tall chalky corpse-weeds whose leaves were many-fingered hands. Agreeing with Mortensen that the finest course is to face everything, I drank off another bowl of a highly disagreeable soup—although it had begun to strike me that the eating of death might signify far less than I had imagined, for in death even the sorrow dies, leaving mere innocuous moldiness. Was this the secret we had devoured so much to find? If not, how would we know when we attained it? The greenish-yellow lady with whom I had eaten knowledge reached for another tidbit, moaning: Why did no one save my life?—which I interpreted as evidence that she was closer to us than were we to her.

Now it was winter. The corpses had begun to pillage each other's coffins for firewood, and some of the bolder ones pulled the weaker apart, so there was always something to eat.

We're on the verge, said Mortensen.

The warlock confided: Soon I'll be Lord of the Ten Thousand Things.

Looking up from the fire, Goldman asked: What about us?

His three corpse-ladies sang: Die.

I thickened our broth with the contents of a much-cracked cremation urn, and Mortensen revealed more to us about the peculiar perfections and beauties of death, which do not lead to rest. For Goldman I cannot speak, but Sophie and I already knew everything.

8

One very cold night Mortensen, shivering, withdrew, and sat against a decrepit monument, saying: Too much unshared death! No matter what we choke down, we'll never reach the bottom of the bowl!— At this, his interlocutor, Mr. Mooncrow, hooted, leaping over a family tomb. The fellow had been literally skin and bones, and now look at him! As for Mortensen, he'd become a creature of angles, gaunt and wretched. Thus both approached their zenith, there in the place of marble tombs eroded into dead white woman-silhouettes. Through the dreamy dullness which defined us I felt grief's bite, but why? Wearying of my eavesdropping, I stole away to inform Goldman or Sophie of our leader's despair; for in our line of work one of the last enthusiasms to perish is the desire to tell tales. I encountered Sophie first. She was cutting up a dead child. Her hair had gone grey, and she wore dead beetles for earrings. Almost pityingly (although she never opened her eyes), she replied: Now you see the obvious.

Then why go on eating wormy meat?

We'll never get the taste out of our mouths now. And if we run away, we'll die eventually and come back to this.

But if we reach the Red Place—

The same. Even when I eat their hearts I've stopped believing in sweetness.

Mortensen said—

He's exhausting life and death. He's almost won.

What about you?

I wanted eternal life for you. Don't you remember what we promised each other?

No.

Instead I found myself remembering daylight, *the time of the dead noon;* I remembered standing where the terra-cotta sidewalk tiles are shadowed, and the old man pressing oranges into juice, the ladies smiling thirstily all around him as I stood ankle-deep in the paper ruins of the old year. My greenish-yellow lady was claiming prior acquaintance with me, while the blue man said: Whatever will become of us has already become of us.— Sophie was plucking somebody's long white hairs out of her mouth.

I asked her: Did you ever eat the fruit of the Tree?

Look into the warlock's face, she replied, and tell me what you think he's eaten.

When Mortensen returned to the banquet, Goldman's corpse-women were gnawing soup bones into pieces so that the marrow would come out. They sang: *Die!*

Mortensen instructed them: Get ready. Now. *Live!*

At once, Goldman sank the pickaxe into Mortensen's head. He fell without resistance. Happily clacking their teeth, all the dead crowded round to get at the blood.

Goldman and I looked at each other with relief. Now that Mortensen had crossed to the other side, he would know everything for us, and tell us what to do.

And so we waited. Sophie sat naked in the weeds, eating Mortensen's liver. I still halfway expected her to find a jewel inside. The warlock's eyes were as beautiful as butterflies. Mr. Mooncrow rose horribly tall, and a hundred dead children awaited carnal knowledge.

Unlike the rest of you, said Goldman presently, I never deceived myself.

THE GRAVE-HOUSE

Once upon a time I built myself a house beneath a delightful tree, but late on a certain afternoon I began to get old. The sounds of the evening unnerved me as they had never done before. I drew my curtains in order to feel more safe. Then it got very dark, and I slept a long time. When I opened the door in the morning, I discovered bulldozers digging everything up. A man in a hard hat told me to get out; this property had been condemned for nonpayment.— Why not? I thought. I'm too old for this.

I bought myself a well-made house in the city and furnished it as comfortably as I liked. This time I made certain that everything was paid for. No noises ever came through the windows. My soft bed whispered ever more sweetly to me at night, and warm air sang to me from the ceiling ducts. I went to the door, but the door said: Do you really want to go out? Stay awhile; you'll be so much happier here.— Warm sticky drops of something fell on my head. I looked up, and saw that the ceiling was salivating. This house of mine meant to eat me! So I rushed to the closet to get my coat, but the closet said: I wouldn't do that if I were you.— I pulled at the doorhandle, but the closet remained as tightly closed as the vagina of my first girlfriend, who had never been in the mood. I sat down on the bed to decide what to do. The mattress felt softer than ever, and I became a trifle sleepy.— Now wouldn't you like a little nap? my pillow whispered. I'll give it to you just the way you like it.— So I lay back on my soft, soft bed, and my pillow wrapped around my face to kiss me. In an instant I couldn't breathe.

After I ripped the pillow's flabby folds off my mouth, goosedown started whirling around me like malignant snowflakes, seeking to choke me. I leaped up, stepped into my shoes and kicked the closet door until it squealed. When I turned the knob, it opened with a sob and a shudder, wetting my hand with its tears.— I thought you loved me, it said.

I do love you, I said. Now where's my coat?

Wouldn't you rather play dress-up? The weather report predicts a cold front. If you stay indoors with me today, I'll show you costumes you've never seen. You can be either a king or a queen.

If I play with you today, will you try to stop me from going tomorrow?

I've always loved you, said the closet. It will never be easy to let you go.

Well, if I stay here forever, what do you have to offer me?

What do you mean? What way is that to talk to someone who would give you everything?

If you'll give me everything, start by giving me my coat.

Are you saying it's over?

Of course not, I said, stroking the shiny cool doorhandle in just the way it liked. I'm going shopping so I can bring you back some lovely, lovely clothes.

Do you promise? whispered the closet.

I promise.

I put on my coat, but just then the refrigerator spoke my name. It wished to offer me a really, really fancy piece of cheese. The instant I heard that, my mouth began to water, and once *that* happened, the ceiling dripped more saliva on me. That discouraged my appetite, so I went to the window to investigate the weather. But I lacked means to determine whether or not the closet had lied, because rain was running down the inside of the pane—the tears of my house, which feared that it might not be able to eat me.

Since the door refused to unlock, I broke the window with the base of a gooseneck lamp whose head kept hissing, swiveling round and attempting to bite me. By now the world had grown dark. I smashed out every last shard, threw that quacking, squawking lamp into the hole, and poised myself to escape from my grave-house. Perhaps I should have departed sooner. The bathroom door kept slamming to and fro, the lights glowed red, and the oven timer was screaming. To tell you the truth, I wished that I could have seen something more than blackness outside. How far down did the night go?— It's past your bedtime, the house threatened.— Leaping into space, I said to myself: This is the last time I'll ever allow myself to get old.

DEFIANCE

People also tried to defend themselves with hands and feet, and they twisted around and twitched like frogs. After that he had them also impaled and spoke often in this language: Oh, what great gracefulness they exhibit!

Manuscript no. 806, monastery of Saint Gall (*ca.* 1462)

So Abraham took Isaac up onto the mountain, a three days' journey, and tied him hand and foot upon the mound of firewood, so that he could be roasted after he was bled, but Isaac cried: *Why, father?*— It seems that Abraham could not answer. The slaughter-knife trembled in his hand. The boy shouted: Father, please, father, there's a ram in the thicket behind you, caught by both horns! That's what God intends!— The old man declined to look. Ruthlessly he raised the knife. Swallowing, the boy closed his eyes.— My son, said Abraham, you must look me in the face when I slit your throat. Then God will see that you give yourself willingly.— At this, the child commenced to scream, and so the two bondsmen came running. Until then Abraham had preserved hope that God's messenger would call down from the sky that he had acquitted his heart and could slay the ram instead. But when the terrified servants panted into sight, the ram tore himself loose, so that there remained only human victims to choose among. What should the father have done? The servants were of unknown blood; for in their infancy he had found them beneath a blasted tree, their mother dead beside an empty water-skin, and he drove off the jackals which were already grinning in their faces. They owed him life, so why not reimburse himself from the both of them, in order to ransom Isaac, whom he loved more than anything but God? Besides, they ought to pay the forfeit for driving the ram away. So he rounded on them with his upraised knife, while Isaac seized the opportunity to untie himself and flee, since after all no one had obtained his consent to this business. He ran eastward of Eden, this being the direction which Cain had chosen before him; and thence the Lord permitted both those outcasts to depart, for He punishes unto the seventh generation, and had He slain Isaac then, there would have been no children to slay. Knowing that he could never again enter his father's tent, nor lie in the lap of his mother while she groomed his hair, he aged a hundred years, travelling on into the fabulous lands, and God bore with him, for the sake of the seventh generation. And Isaac bowed low before God every day, offering Him the best of everything that he found, but he was not answered. And in the three-hundred-and-thirty-third year of his age he took to wife Dark-Eyes, a princess of the land whom he had allured in defiance of her father, for, being accursed, he owned neither sheep nor goats; no silver pieces lived in his belt; and his home was a certain cave whose entrance he sealed up from within every night, so that the jackals, men and angels who hunted him would wander away bewildered. Dark-Eyes's father promised him death should he ever visit again, but Dark-Eyes loved him, although why that was she could no longer have said after the first hour of their elopement, when she finally saw his unhooded face. Therefore, thanks to God, she repented that she had given herself to him, and during those morbid cave-nights when he would have slept in her arms, she sat against the wall, cursing him and herself. So she perished, without creating a new generation for God to punish. Then Isaac in his grief entreated forgiveness of her dead carcass, covered her face in an old goatskin, the finest he had, and upraised his slaying-knife to end himself, for he hated the days of his life, and resolved to recompense God for what he had stolen from Him. But had he died then, there would have been no seventh generation, and so the Lord made it fall out that a certain proud and beautiful woman now came riding up upon a camel, calling Isaac by his name. Just as his father had done, he fell into hesitation, and presently rolled aside the stones from his cave, at which she lowered her pitcher to him that he might drink the wine of peace, and carried him away to the mountains where a shady, rapid river flashed near as white as sunlight beneath cloudy green leaves whose like he had never known, and here the gates of a marble city opened unto him, for she was a great queen, whose name was Joy. When she had led him into her palace he knelt before her, touching his mouth to her right foot, and swore an oath to serve her forever as her loving consort, since she had returned his life to him, and together they dwelled in happiness for seven times seventy-seven years, making many children, so that someday there would be a seventh generation to torment to the utmost and finally blot out. In his great gratitude he drew water for her like a woman, while she protected him like a man, so that even the angels could not find him (God, of course, knew his whereabouts), and he tilled the soil like a man, and she wove their clothes like a woman, and when they were alone he played the harp for her while she sang in her soft small voice, upraised her little hands, and slowly danced, naked but for three silver necklaces. Then came an easy trifling hour of sleep, which resembled both of their conceptions of death. And every morning she said to him: Drink, and every evening he said the same to her. And he fashioned bracelets to gladden her wrists, and she washed his feet in flower-water. Then one night after her hair turned grey she dreamed of the sharp-toothed tomb which already opened its jaws to receive them, and in this dark mouth of death flickered seven red serpent-tongues of eternal fire fashioned and lit expressly to torture them forever, so that God could receive the payment of the first generation, but Isaac kissed her, saying: So wan a curse as death bestows upon our extreme old age need not be feared, for our very souls are worn out now, from too much living. Speaking for myself, eternal misery can be no worse than what I suffered before I met you.— But she replied: I have never been in anguish as you were, so I lack practice and experience. Husband, I'm afraid!— Then he said to her: I promise to lie beside you forever, and so long as God keeps me in consciousness to be tortured, I will say your name in my heart, and call upon you, and make my love for you a prayer for all the ages, and I swear to keep faith that you will do likewise for me.— So they comforted one another, and when their tomb roared out for them with the voice of seven lions, they entered it willingly, and their children, the second generation, walled them up, at which everyone's punishment began.

TOO LATE

It was getting late when I learned how much I liked the redbrick buildings; here's one with an octagonal tower! I cried to myself; and although it was cold, the round light-balls of a Christmas tree far within the dark reflections of towers in the panes of brass doors on Yonge Street made me feel vaguely expectant, as if somebody might want to give me a present. Well, the phony snow and plastic evergreens in the window which announced *RETAIL OPPORTUNITIES* got me over it. I felt colder than ever; in fact, it was so chilly that I could only be warmed by a woman with the sleek fat rounded thighs of a Maillol sculpture. None of the parka'd prostitutes on Wellesley Street were shaped like that, but I followed one for thirteen blocks, just to be certain, and her availability made me happy. What were my fantasies but fantasies? All the same, when she finally got into a man's car I felt sadder than ever.

In the door of a once ornate storefront now concealed behind brown papers, a puffyhaired Asian teenager smoked his cigarette. Nodding at him, I went to *ZANZIBAR—The Girls Never Stop—IS NUDE HOT EROTIC LADIES SMOKING ROOM INSIDE* and stood at the door waiting to see if the sign could be true, and before it got much later I had to admit that it was, for a woman in a camelhair coat clicked rapidly down the street, gripping both shiny black gloves in her naked right hand. The *NUDE HOT EROTIC LADIES SMOKING ROOM* tempted me, but, fearing the cover charge, I chose instead to stroll along University Avenue, adding my mite to the crowds with folded arms, Santa Claus caps, jackets and red balloons, awaiting the Santa Claus Parade! In their perambulators, babies outstretched their lobster-red mitts at the sun, and I thought: What if they're right?— So I returned to the octagonal tower, determined to go up in the world.

The lobby resembled the wide-waisted skirts of a fifteenth-century German cruet, brass or bronze, polished almost to gold, like a creek bottom when the sun strikes right; and the elevator arrived at once—and almost too late just the same, I had better add, for it would soon be closing time. But I pushed the button, and soared so rapidly that the instants nearly went backward! If only I could have gone a trifle faster and higher, I might have lived forever.

From the fifteenth floor I could see clear into Charlevoix County: wiggly-squiggly lines of delicious coldness, the road, hills and houses, frosted over with raspberry vanilla and blueberry ice cream.

From the twenty-ninth floor, Canada's trees rose snowily or not beneath my mountaintops, inviting me to admire the sea-view of Lake Superior. I could almost see a peaceful, stylized woman framed by pale green hills.

From the thirty-seventh floor I could see all the way to the beginning of the Great North, whose ruffled snow invited me like a loved woman's frilly underpants between the shadowed knee-hills of frozen sky-stone, and my soul rode away on spectacular waves of snow, ice and clouds like eagle-armies above.

From the eighty-eighth floor I discovered mountains like immense blue teeth; then a bird's wing of cloud above the fog.

The penthouse on the one-hundred-and-forty-seventh floor was windowed all around like a greenhouse. Up here I could easily make out the curvature of the earth. The first telescope angled due north, but maybe it was actually a kaleidoscope, because when I placed my eye against it, everything exploded into sunny blueprint abstractions of an astronomical character. Had I only spent my life learning and reasoning, I might have been able to interpret that message, but it was too late for that.

There was also a telescope pointed due west, and it showed me the brassy sun fleeing across the Pacific. This comprised futurity, and I longed to see my destiny here. After much labor I finally saw myself on one of the Queen Charlotte Islands, on my ninetieth birthday in a nursing home. I asked the lovely darkhaired nurse to kiss me, but she wouldn't because I was so old and gruesome. So I begged her to spit in my mouth—that way I wouldn't contaminate her—and she kindly did. I had to hurry now; this sunbeam was speeding on! For my birthday present I begged her for an injection of potassium to stop my heart; through the dusty window of the nursing home I could not quite read my lips when I made this plea, but because I knew myself, I knew what I was asking. The nurse smiled, stroked my hair and nodded. Just before her needle went in, I understood that after the carrion died, I would rise up from it, take her hand, and she and I would walk away together. She loved me! Wishing to gain some benefit from her love before it was too late, I raised the telescope up into the air, trying to spy on the two of us; but we were already gone, or else she had already buried me; either way, I had missed the train.

Hoping to do better, I pressed my face against the southern telescope. The instant my eye crossed the border, I was ambushed by grief; scanning streets where I had once been with a woman I had been far too late for, I felt the grief rise up in me like the numbness of an oncoming brain clot; I hoped to avoid focusing on where she lived; but the farther away I swiveled the telescope, the more anxious I became; why wasn't I going where I should be? Not caring to miss my opportunity, I finally aimed my gaze at her living room window; she was watching television and eating ice cream with a nice young man who kept kissing her hand; my God, she didn't even have hair under her arms; they were *both* too young for me; I'd been born too early, which is to say too late! Raising the telescope despairingly upward, I saw storybook airplanes ascending with live soldiers waving at me through the windows and descending laden with flag-wrapped coffins. Quickly I swiveled the telescope away, incredulous that I had failed to remain with the woman and the country that I still loved. And when I stood away from the telescope, it was as if I were departing from her city in the early morning dark, unable to accept that I had not made myself known to her. For some time, she had still loved me, and grieved in bewilderment that I would not be her friend. I had seen the same uncertain friendliness on the faces of the soldiers who had waved to me. They wanted me to accompany them on their mission; one corporal had even offered me his binoculars as he shot off to his death.

Needless to say, there remained the telescope oriented due east, where come spring the melting roads of Québec would be chocolate under the snow. I approached this eyepiece with a sense of excitement. And what would you know? I found myself peeping in on Lilian Terrace! That nice girl was in her high heels, and her nipples were very, very pointed. I spied a snowy landscape painting on an easel behind her, her garment draped over the chair. Well, after that, I wanted to be as Canadian as a beaver dam silhouetted beyond constellations of tree-forms rising up into the cirrus clouds and downward (reflectively) into splendid brass-dark pools. To hell with soldiers and ice cream eaters! Never mind that nurse! As for the sunny abstractions, I had time to figure those out whenever I wanted to. I felt so Canadian that I even wanted to take part in the Santa Claus Parade.

A gentle gong sounded four times: closing hour. So I rode the elevator back down to the lobby and went out into the snowdrifts in the ice-blued streets of Old Toronto, whose picket-fences were almost lost in winter; and the only ominous factor was the red maple-leaf flag at half-mast for me above Grosvenor Street. I felt hungry, but I gathered sunlight's warm patches between shadow and wind.

A little girl's hair blew straight back behind her as she rushed toward the parade, holding her father's hand. A woman's hair streamed behind her and her cheeks turned red and white with cold, just before the man she loved kissed her. A girl in a knit wool cap shivered and smiled. Among the parents and children holding hands on subways, bundled babies, couples holding hands nakedly in the cold, I searched for the Canadian girl for whom I had been meant, and the later it got the younger I became, until beneath the yellow-banded sky of late afternoon I found her, on a bicycle, her books in the basket behind her; and because she was meant for me, one of her books fell into the snow. I ran to pick it up. Smilingly, she asked me to walk her home. I was now so young that I had become too small for my wrinkled skin.

I accompanied her through tall narrow slices of shadow, sky on cloud between them, while she confessed that she had always been lonely. (A girl in a hooded white parka with rabbit fringes was shivering; I knew that I could make her warm, but I had to be faithful to the other one forever. Inspired by me, a man ducked down his head against the wind and hurried to the parade.) And now we had arrived at a bank of brick-celled house-flesh with tall windows bulging out, the roofs steep and peeling very sharply against the cold sky; they'd been maimed by a million frosts. I understood that even here life must sometimes be as dull as a sidewalk between office towers when the winter sun goes behind a cloud, but my face burned for that one girl in the lovely chill of Canada. I had become fourteen years old.

My girl went up the steps to a creamy door beneath a lavender snow-roof against a certain tall narrow yellow housefront. She went in, and it was too late for me to follow her, too late!

Grey hairs rushed out of my pores until I seemed to be covered in seal-skins. I sought other *RETAIL OPPORTUNITIES*, but all the women screamed.

In Canada my friend North, who had once been nervous to the point of making others sad and angry, was now at last happy, with a paunch; his wife was lovely; they had daughters and a nice old house; they fussed happily in the kitchen, cooking scallops from Novia Scotia, talking about the old characters on Digby Neck. I too could have been a Canadian. I could have married the right person. I could have been younger. But it was too late.

VIII

WHEN WE WERE SEVENTEEN

I pray you, my friend, look into thyself, and endeavor to find out in what part of thy composition is the *prima materia* of the *lapis philosophorum*, or out of what part of thy substance can the first matter of our stone be drawn. Thou sayest, it must either be in the *hair, sweat,* or *excrement.* I say in none of these thou shalt ever be able to find it, and yet thou shalt find it in thyself.

Francis Barrett, 1801

1

Less than a mile within the posted limits of our city, at the intersection where Mr. Murmuracki's establishment used to be, a left turn parallel to the cemetery will bring you past the old gas station to frost on the weed-islands between which white-beaked dark birds dip down at dawn, and sunrise arrives half-seen above a wind-riddled thunderhead, hurling down slantwise rays through every wound. Mist-fingers grope up out of steely pools. Suddenly color returns to the world, silvers going red, lovely russets and greens introducing themselves, the long rays of light now floating on the cress. Across the levee, a file of ducks swims in the ditch of ice-colored water which once morning reaches it will return to algae-green. Back at West Laurel Hill, whose original wall commences two and a half miles from here, sun-rectangles and polyhedral shadows decorate the frosted grass between the plinths, and the headstones remain partially silhouetted against the rising sun. An approximation of their projections could be made with the most elementary mechanical drafting instruments; while here at the marsh the shadow-patterns remain too grand to be understood, supernatural powers being in fact so feeble that darkness owns greater power around rivers than around graves. Now warmth touches the railroad embankment, unfurling downward, releasing the mud's smoky smell, until all the things of this world—those galls on that oak tree, the dead reeds, the hank of down from last year's cat-tails, the clot of spiderweb, that snorting otter rolling in a sunny patch of grass, the meadow's stripes of silver and russet—appear fixed in their

553

true natures, as if a flashlight-beam would prove them to retain their present forms no matter how powerful tonight's darkness.

A neighbor of mine once whiled away a summer here. I will not write his name.

2

His greyhaired ladyfriends still flattered him that his hair was not grey, merely grey*ing* a trifle at the temples. He avoided mirrors; and the neighbors with whom he was growing old treated him as if he were as young as they, so he returned the favor even though he knew that unlike them he truly *was*—or at least younger than he looked. One morning his stomach felt a trifle upset, but the next day found him as healthy as ever; and yet he seemed to be losing his appetite; he used to love bacon and eggs, and now the smell made him sick. The nausea descended like snow, almost imperceptibly coating the inside of his throat, piling up flake by flake in his chest and drifting down into his belly. For years he had been overweight, so this was actually fortuitous. He abstained from fatty foods more easily than ever before; and if his face began to draw in, well, didn't that mean he'd soon be lighter on his feet? The doctor gave him four months.

The instant he was alone again, he sat down at his desk.

His best friend Luke had been a practical soul who took pleasure in errands checked off, a bare desk and taxes paid early. He gave away most of what he owned, dispatching each thing to whoever he supposed would use it best. They scattered his ashes in the mountains.

Before Luke, and partially coterminously with him, there had once also been a certain tall, skinny friend called Isaac, whom he never would have known were it not for Clara, who had loved Isaac in high school and still alluded sadly to *the summer when Isaac went away*, which is to say from everyone, and of course from Clara in particular. She must have just turned nineteen, which would have made Isaac twenty-one, so this neighbor of mine who now had four months left had been twenty-two and already engaged to Clara when she asked him to meet Isaac. At that time he dreaded new people, not to mention any boy for whom Clara evidently still cared, but he obliged her, as a peculiar result of which he and Isaac became close. Nearly forty years ago now (it must have been the spring after Clara threw him out), he met Luke, and presently introduced him to Isaac, who among other virtues declined to possess more than he could carry on his back. Luke guardedly admired this. Wherever he went, Isaac journeyed deep, and kept on going. He was hardy, abstemious, longlegged, cheerful if fidgety, generous if spendthrift, capable of opening his heart and therefore of exciting affection in others, particularly women; and, above all, light in his travels. His bugbears were dishonesty and uncleanliness. Narcissists readily fail to notice that honesty can be unkind, while filthiness derives no more frequently from culpability or innate foulness than from helplessness or brokenness. Isaac's stellar fidelity to himself rendered him accordingly liable to fits of capricious extremism. Hence *the summer when he went away*, Clara's seventeenth. Luke used to observe that whatever meanness someone committed elsewhere would eventually repeat itself at close hand, and in due course Isaac *went away* again, into the desert, where he decided to live out his life. Luke, who kept up a love of hiking literally to the end, was impressed, indeed, almost haunted by his example, and used to praise him, but that methodical breaking of contact with his old friends partook of cruelty, at least from the standpoint of my neighbor with the upset stomach, who had never respected the decisions of Buddha and Jesus, let alone (for instance) Clara, to abandon those who loved them. Isaac did not mind breaking women's hearts; he felt what he felt, so why live a lie? When he *went away* from my neighbor, a woman told him to do it—for in between leaving women, Isaac made them his empresses. Perhaps what Luke admired the most about him was that he seemed never to regret himself. So Isaac *went away*, and my neighbor heard nothing of him for years. Presently, by some accident (Isaac needed help in obtaining antibiotics), they became friends again. But once my neighbor began to get fat, Isaac grew contemptuous. For his part, the fat one imagined that he had done a lot for Isaac, materially and otherwise; loyalty was his particular fetish, which must have been why he remained faithful to all his many girlfriends. One night after a certain favorite had jilted him, he sought to express his grief to Isaac, who knew her moderately. It was sad, no doubt; the fat man felt quite weak just then; he nearly wept while relating his pain to Isaac—who promptly *went away* from him for good. Somewhere on the other side is a gentler valley of milky-green rivers whose broad rapids enclose many-ledged islands upon each of which a skeleton may sun itself, but whether or not Isaac got there I cannot say. Were one to know a spiderweb only by glimpsing it edge-on, that would still be understanding of a sort; therefore, he and Isaac comprehended one another. To Isaac's way of thinking, he must have been as flabby and unclean as he looked; while to the fat one, this second betrayal was unforgivable, not that forgiveness was relevant. In point of fact, the fat one was goodhearted enough, like most people of his temperament; and had Isaac ever called upon him he would have been as agreeable as he supposed he had been to Clara (who, I must admit, had gone away not thinking highly of him). Who are we, then, the inhabitors of our courteous actions, or the happy perpetrators of our malignant fantasies?

Over the years the recollection of Isaac became apparently indifferent to him; he did not mind when Luke invoked him; and when Luke commenced giving away his possessions, it even comforted him to imagine his friend as entering into the situation of Isaac, who, having already disencumbered himself of his one piece of furniture, a mattress, slept for a final handful of nights on the carpet of his rented room, and was now, in the space of a quarter-hour, loading everything he owned into his backpack, preparatory to striding forever into the wind of the white canyon. If such could have been in even the most metaphorical sense Luke's destination, then his passing out of sight (let's say into the relative brightness of the lunar highlands) escaped being terrible. Of course my fat neighbor knew it to be terrible and worse; all the same, when his own turn came, he found himself preparing to unlock his desk, so as to make disposition of what was most precious of all his treasures—namely, the letters from all the women he'd loved.

3

In fact, two desks belonged to him. One was an antique rolltop formerly his father's. Prior to becoming old he'd wondered what to do with it. Never practical, he employed its pigeonholes for the adapters and plugs of lost electric-powered devices, which might yet reveal themselves (for in those days it was patent that he would live forever); not to mention the fat old analog microphone, the flash cards he had once made in order to dither with the Inuktitut language, broken pencil leads, pens which might or might not be out of ink, boxes of color slides whose subjects he had forgotten (but worth saving in case some of them might be naked pictures), spectacles which no longer befitted his eyes, keys to forgotten chests, padlocks, apartments and houses, and an empty pill bottle which remained eligible for one refill fourteen years ago. Luke gave him those pills when he developed a certain intimate complaint.

It makes me happy to think of you having this desk, his father had said. The son already owned the other desk. He liked his father's desk and vaguely hoped to someday work at it in a worthy manner. His father had been as uncluttered as Luke. Seeing what became of his desk, his father said nothing.

When he sat down to cross his arms on its bed of darkgrained red-stained maple, he knew that his father must have rested his elbows here in some analogous configuration, wide-eyed in his spectacles, sipping tea, steadily and probably contentedly preparing business drafts. His father had always been a light sleeper, and in early middle age sometimes worked through the night. Once the boy himself had insomnia, and came barefoot and quiet into the study at dawn, peeping at his father, whom he loved very much but of whom he was somewhat afraid. His father did not send him away. They sat together, his father working prodigiously over these papers which the child could not understand: the boy in the leather armchair, his bare feet cold, his father at this desk. It was one of the few objects he could imagine which appeared both precious and dependable. Even now he could barely grasp both of its curving wings when he outstretched his arms. Of course his father had been a bigger man in every way; once his mother had them stand back to back to be measured, and his father was a quarter-inch taller.— I want you to have this, his father said when his parents moved away. But while his father lived, the desk was not so much used as imposed upon. This box of rope, scissors and string, what would happen to it now? He opened the drawer which contained a wooden gouge, perhaps his father's, a box of Luke's travel slides, the hair ornament pertaining to a bygone girlfriend (the scent of her cheap pomade, somewhat simplified by the decades, nonetheless resisted them), a square of the red cloth in which his signal pistol used to be wrapped, and the red pinwheel which his daughter had awarded him when she was in elementary school (nowadays her children preoccupied her so happily that he preferred not to inform her of his condition); and then he closed that drawer again, gnawing on a pain pill. The next drawer down was so full of unlabeled color negatives that it barely closed. He pulled it out an inch, just to remind himself that someday—as if there were still a someday!—he would sort all those images, and even utilize them. Shutting that one as best he could, he drew out the drawer containing an obsolete "Guide for Expeditions to the Canadian Arctic Islands," a galvanized nail, a bottle of expired sulfa powder for frostbite, a photograph of a very young and handsome Luke (he ought to mail it to the widow, who continued unremarried), a pamphlet which discussed the breathing holes of ringed seals and the overwintering strategies of bearded seals, and a moon map, copyrighted thirty-five years ago. Half-smiling, he browsed for a moment over the craters of that bluish-grey disk. When he was a schoolboy, the teachers used to promise atomic-powered lunar travel "in our lifetime." He had always wished to visit the moon.

4

But it was not in his father's desk but in his own that he had to search. The stout square legs of this ugly if likewise capacious item, whose smooth top was wood-patterned laminate, doubled as filing cabinets. The left side being unlockable, he used that for his contracts and other such items which he never would miss if someone stole them. His father would have guarded them better. The righthand cabinet was for old love letters; those he had locked up years ago. Where was the key? Over the years he had dropped all keys extraneous, unknown or momentarily unnecessary into a ceramic dish on his father's desk. As it was, he still carried too many around—the price of owning properties, leasing mailboxes and hiding secrets.

And so in advance of dawn he was on his knees before the desk, wearily trying this key and that in the spiderwebbed lock on the inner side of the righthand leg. He seemed to remember a brass, short-necked entity with a trapezoidal head. But no object of any comparable description served. Could the lock require oiling? He would spray it as soon as he felt less ill—any day, no doubt. First he'd better open it. An impatient craving overtook him for this forgotten miniature country, whose people and landscapes he once knew so well. In his healthier years, boredom had impelled neglect; and so he had commenced the effort half expecting to be stupefied by futility and disgust the instant he gained admittance; but with every failure his longing waxed.— That's life, thought the dying man.— In his haste he made the mistake of trying only the most likely keys in each ring. Then he started all over again, more systematically. One brass key whose head happened to be ovoid penetrated to the hilt, but declined to turn. A loose silver key leaped from his fingers and disappeared into the dusty darkness. He reached for it, but his stomach checked him at once. Rising, he swallowed two codeine pills. It was sunrise. He lay down, his eyes slowly half-closing.

When he found the key three days later, he had given up looking for it. Most certainly he had tried every key in the ceramic dish. This one, the ugly-headed object, lay beside the dish as if it had always been there. He turned the lock and opened the drawer. So many women! Luke had met several of them.— Bella struck me as brilliant from the beginning, he said. But she never did her homework. I wonder if she's lost her mind?— Then for a moment the two friends would remember Bella together, and because Bella had been so long ago there was no pain, only the moderate pleasure which scientific colleagues might share when they identified another previously uncatalogued virus.— Beatrice was my favorite, Luke would say. I felt like she and I had a lot in common. What a goddamned nightmare she was. Have you heard from her?— And he would feel happy that Luke was remembering him by remembering his girlfriends.

He scooped up letters and let them fall. Now he was getting tired. At the very bottom (for she had been his first) lay the sack of letters from Victoria, in the fat envelope and the thin one.

He smiled; his heart beat fast. It was she whom he now most longed to know.

5

Had he first met her in later life he might have found her ordinary, although she probably wasn't, this slightly plump blue-eyed blonde who had once been most provisionally his; and if he could have come across her now as she was then, he would simply have turned away from seventeen-year-old jailbait. But since he had known her then as *he* was then, he was free to claim her.

People smilingly refer to "puppy love," for most of us do pass through it. Considered as a stage of character formation, it becomes innocuous, necessary. In its throes, of course, sufferers perceive it differently. His passion for Victoria had been absurdly noble. He accepted any negligence from her, even cruelty, without complaint; and while an onlooker might have been functionally correct to posit in this the desperate resignation of a lonely, unloved, self-despising adolescent, all the same, the boy *did* love her with all his best impulses. Yes, he lusted after her, as well he should have; certainly his infatuation remained nearly unencumbered by self-knowledge, let alone any comprehension of the girl herself; but it is touching and commendable as well as laughable that he would have done anything for her. And when she ended it, he imagined in his grief that he would never again be able to give himself to another as utterly as he had to her. In fact, as was proved by all those other letters in his desk drawer, he managed quite well—but had he done any better than manage? In the sensitivities of children—to raised voices, violence against animals, the softness of grass—there lies, if not wisdom, an empathy, which it is one of maturation's express purposes to blunt. So our smiles when puppy love gets mentioned are not entirely mocking; we remember when we were better. For a year or two, until he forgot her more thoroughly, he was pleased to blame Victoria for the ever increasing selfishness which he deployed in his romances. Irregularly bright glades of memories, hedged in as if by marshes or poison oak, comprised most of what he had left of her. In the arms of subsequent lovers he orbited over the Marsh of Mists, then the Marsh of Epidemics, the Marsh of Decay, round and round, and it seemed that the future would always be peach-colored like the June sky at sunset. By the time he was middle-aged, he and his male friends agreed that it was a fine thing to know exactly what one desires in life, and to demand it of each night-companion (ghosts rising up like angry bluejays at dawn). They convinced themselves that the young women who in truth had no more use for them than for their worn out grandfathers would have constituted annoyances, because, being young, the women must not have figured themselves out. Oh, how fine to have oneself figured out! To be an adventurer in a mystery, asking for nothing, speeding through space toward the silver-goldness of the Lunar Alps, and seeing for the very first time a round dark crater (Victoria's navel) aglow along part of its circumference, and otherwise shadowed—to bear happy hopes of knowing the Rhipaean Mountains, the Rheita Valley, the Sirsalis Rille, when knowing them would actually be above our capacity, or else be death—to experience each moment with Victoria as so perfect that its recollection fills up the darkest separations from her—to feel dizzy at the first sound of her voice—how preposterous! So he locked her letters away and mislaid the key.

6

Just then it was enough simply to lay out those two large envelopes on his desk. He sat there with his right hand on them until the doorbell rang. His next door neighbor had offered to drive him to the hospital.

At some point we ought to discuss palliative care, said the doctor.

Don't worry about it, he replied. I have guns.

For an instant the doctor appeared offended. Then he drummed his index finger rapidly on his knee and said: Have you ever tried antidepressants?

The neighbor drove him home, and he thanked her. Another neighbor whom he barely knew had sent him flowers. That must mean that he would die. He smiled, thinking of Victoria's letters. The evening sky glowed white, and the scent of jasmines descended upon him. All at once he grew rich in hopes and projects. But when he went upstairs, all he looked at was his moon map. Then he lay down.

That night he dreamed that in his father's desk were two drawers which somehow also existed as doorways. One of them had always given onto sunlight before; now its interior was nearly as dark as the lunar seas, which are really lava. The other, which had been dark, seemed to have taken on depth and luster, like an attic filled with someone else's dust-gilded toys.

7

From the fat envelope he first drew by chance that letter from thirty-five years ago when with her typical self-fullness she called herself *lonelier than an angel must feel. What am I doing? And I feel rebellious. I want to disagree with everything you said in your letter and I want to escape the caresses. I want to be left alone.* But he couldn't take that hint, not in those days when he had no one else. Thank goodness he'd since been given love by others! His memories of them resembled lichen on the shoulders of a semilegible gravestone.

Having forgotten her for so long, he had evidently attached to her a spurious sweetness; and as he continued to pick through those envelopes, each with its thirteen-cent stamp, he grew melancholy, although not overmuch, to see how greatly she had resented and sought to escape him, in part because he had not been a wholesome giving sort, but also because she had been, as she kept saying, restless, almost as if she sensed she would die young. If anything, it was to her credit that under the circumstances she sent him so many letters—although she might have done so simply because she had not known herself—or been instilled with a habit of polite kindness . . . How could he even remember her, especially when he had never known her? Calling her up now was equivalent to imagining how it would have been on the moon when the so-called planetesimals were striking, exploding and cratering.

Scratching his grey cheeks, he found himself even less convinced that he liked this dead young woman. Of course, he barely liked himself now (never mind that he'd indulged himself unfailingly); so what would he have felt for that skinny, acne'd teenager who offered Victoria so little beyond his need—and, of course, that most undervalued of treasures, unsullied adoration? Isn't that what we want others to feel for us, even while experience renders us incapable of giving it to them?

Well, even nowadays he considered himself less selfish than some. For instance, he had never loved any woman the less for being plain; that remained to his credit. All the same, how lovely Victoria had been!

8

In the drawer there were photographs and faintly scented hairclasps, withered flowers pressed within small folded squares of watercolor paper, photographs of women's faces and bodies, single earrings, half-rings and other such love tokens, postcards from unforgotten Asian prostitutes (he still imagined that he never forgot anybody), a tiny wax-sealed bottle which contained green liquid, happy letters, beseeching ones and ones which promised or sweetly commanded (he had already destroyed most of the angry ones), roots and nests of memory all in a mucky tangle, living in the decaying matrix of too many years—and, yes, back at the very bottom again, hence appropriate to Victoria, the fat envelope and the thin one. The fat one held the letters from when they were seventeen, each one in its original envelope, the righthand side of which had been carefully, reverently slit open by the idolatrous boy. Yes, thirteen-cent butterfly stamps! Had life truly been so inexpensive in 1977?

The thin envelope contained their early middle age, when she had decided to reestablish contact with him. He had opened these communications almost carelessly, discarding the envelopes. By then it had not been such a thrill to receive letters from a woman—particularly from one who had jilted him. As might be expected, the papers were in no kind of order. They now seemed as bright as sun-caught dust-grains on a spiderweb over dark ivy. He took up a pink sheet of paper and read: *I know I said I wouldn't write.* Evidently, like Isaac, she had broken off with him again; he couldn't remember. Well, she was married. He had been mildly surprised and pleased to hear from her at all. In those days they each sought to respect the lives they had made. *I lied,* said the letter. *I've just been told that I have invasive breast cancer and will have a mastectomy and removal of the lymph nodes within the week. I am scared to death. I have three small children, one almost five, a three-year-old and the baby is ten months. I cannot believe this is happening. I am not vain; I do not care about my chest, but I want to live. Do you believe in God? I'll have radiation and chemotherapy. So, tell me. This fear, I can smell it, is it like being in war? What do you read when you are afraid? You don't have to write; you don't even know me, nor I you, and as I said before, my husband would hate this. But I still need to write it. If I figure out why, I'll explain someday.*

In another yellowing envelope with a thirteen-cent Liberty Bell stamp and a 1977 postmark lay a cheap machine print whose color had shifted redwards. His smiling blonde Victoria, clasping her hands across the waistline of her leopard print skirt, holding a blue balloon (on the reverse she'd written *always the child*) was now almost a redhead. The shadows of the park had gone plum and winelike. Victoria stood flushing as if she were drunk, embarrassed or filled with desire for him to whom she had given this portrait. She was still a virgin then, at least so far as he knew. The blue sky had darkened; the balloon's shadows were purple. When he saw this photograph now, it meant more to him than before. She had sent it to him, so he had supposed, as a halfhearted appeasement; doubtless he had been hounding her for a picture, and on the back she had also penned *Well, I'll do better but please accept this anyway.* Doing better would have in his seventeen-year-old definition entailed writing: *I love you.* Well, why should she? Being young, she possessed the pleasure of declining to define herself. And she hadn't loved him, or if she had, it meant nothing in the end. Cocking her head, tossing her breast-length hair, Victoria smiled widely at him from the wine-rich past.

It was in fact a treasure that she had given him. No one else would ever get another from her. Unaware of her own death and his elderly ugliness, the girl offered him her bare knees, and the wind pulled her balloon eternally away. It looked to have been spring; the trees were barely in leaf. At whom was she smiling, and why? He had never thought to ask. With his now characteristic resentful suspicion he unfolded the accompanying letter, whose cheap white paper had shifted nearly orange, and read: *I think I'm going to miss you. Our relationship is different now, but I feel happier about it*—because I was gone, he thought. *My sister and I are expanding our minds by watching* Rebel Without a Cause *on television. I hope it ends soon. I hope you hold at least fond memories of this place and me and semi-dormant expectations. Needing you again does not totally please me—I think you realized that. Is there anything you don't realize about me? If there is, I fear distance can only make it easier to see. Please keep your promise. When you decide to break it, please give me a little time and notice. Will I suffer withdrawal symptoms? Love, Victoria.*

So she *had* loved him, at least on that day. What more could he have asked for?

9

And once upon a time a certain witch had loved him, too. As one might expect, she was passionate; there was no end to the things she could do in bed. In his memories she resembled the silvergold disk of the evening sun in a wall of wild grapes. Although he had enjoyed her body, she otherwise bored and occasionally frightened him, whereas he had been the love of her life. She had risen up as if out of the ground to seize hold of him, jealous of every instant that he failed to inhale her breath. He never comprehended why she loved him; nor could she understand why she remained unloved by him.— It's not simple chemistry, said the witch. If that's all it were, I could fix that with two potions. What's your astrological sign?

He told her.

Oh, said the witch. Well, no wonder.

Indeed, she could have made him love her, through much the same procedure as the one through which an impure tomb-spirit may be tricked into inhabiting another dead carcass. To her credit, she did not want that.

One morning she went away. Her parting gift was a tiny bottle of green liquid. She said to him: This can be used only once. If you pour it out on something belonging to a woman, the woman will appear before you.

He thanked her.

She gave him a locket whose window disclosed a many-fingered glob of mercury. For years she had worn it between her breasts. She said: Pour out the bottle on this, and I'll instantly return to you.

I understand, he said.

Don't call me back unless you want me. Otherwise it will hurt me too much. Do you promise?

I promise.

You'll use it for some other girl, I know. You don't care about me.

Of course I care about you. I love you—

Then marry me.

No.

Please, why can't you love me?

I don't know.

Is it because I'm old?

You're not old.

What is it about me? wept the witch. Nobody loves me.

I love you.

Goodbye, said the witch, and walked away without looking back.

10

He lay awake in the darkness thinking about Victoria until it began to seem as if she were thinking about him. His stomach hurt. He rose and visited the bathroom. In the mirror by the medicine cabinet, he saw the specter of himself, unshaven, pale, grimacing and bewildered, with dark hollows under his eyes. How could this be him? He tried to smooth down his sweaty grey hair, swallowed two antacids and three pain pills, and returned to the darkness. Now he could nearly see Victoria standing over him in midair. She too was thinner than formerly, but no less beautiful. Her long hair, which he had remembered as sunny yellow, now appeared silver-white like lunar beams—not grey like his, but as young as ever. He was neither ecstatic nor afraid. A slow joy settled upon him, as if she were bending over him, tossing her hair upon his chest.

11

He knew that a wall of agony awaited him; he was already in its shadow. Above swam the pitted moon; below hung a pale gall alone in an oak. Of course this had little to do with Victoria, who might indeed distract him from his impending appointment with the wall, which for some reason he began to imagine as pertaining to an old-fashioned New England churchyard. He had never visited her grave, and in fact had scarcely wondered where she was buried. A quarter-hour on the computer sufficed for that: West Laurel Hill, near the edge of town. A map appeared on his screen. He zoomed in and in, until the site had minutely located itself.

The grand trees behind the entrance arch recalled a trifle of the verdancy which framed our great nineteenth-century mausoleums, supposedly forever. The hill which once looked down on forest, church, field and brook, warning off colored people and Jews, was now an uninspired slope of homogeneous late-twentieth-century slabs. The great stele of every rich man was ringed round—at a distance, to be sure—by granite footnotes to the poor, many of which flew miniature American flags. It was late afternoon. His stomach ached. A bird-shadow sped over the breathless grass, whose scent resembled cured tobacco. Each tombstone's zone of shade had contracted, hiding all but snout or whiskers under the cracked plinth. Now he passed through another wealthy old section.

Bemused by those dishonest arched doorways which looked from hill-sides, as if the dead could see out and the living were invited within, he remembered his dream of his father's desk. Bypassing two marble cornu-copias which had been gnawed at by automobile exhaust, he arrived at the new section containing Victoria's hill—more precisely, a modest mound whose crest alone had been sold by the time the twentieth century began. He sorted through the lesser bric-a-brac of modern tombs. In a thicket of stair-plinthed granite crosses, square slabs, gravestones which epitomized the negative spaces cut out of archways, he presently found a monument to Mrs. Emilia Woodruff, who lay SAFE IN HER SAV-IOUR'S ARMS, and beside her rotted Victoria.

  She had sent him another photograph; the baby, who sat in her lap, wearing a plaid skirt, must have been about ten months. What if he and Victoria had had children? He remembered her eidetically from the time when she had been his sweetheart. In this family photograph (already time-stained on the back—a blotchy scarlet like some rare lichen), she failed to resemble the girl he had loved. Her blonde hair had thinned a trifle and taken on a reddish tint—the color of the three children's hair. Although she had lost her baby fat, her face remained unwrinkled. Had she owned so many freckles at seventeen? She was smiling, and he liked her cheekbones very much. He assumed the person at whom she was smiling to be her husband. She and the children were sitting on the steps of a suburban house, evidently gazing into the sun, because she was squinting, as was the middle child, who was grimacing, clutching his toy spaceship. The baby was clenching her fat white little fists, staring side-ways at the eldest boy, whose eyes were also narrowed against the light but was seeking in sweet submission to look into the photographer's eyes. Victoria's expression could have been read as happiness or compliance. She wore green. With the infant on her lap and the two others on either side of her, drawn in by her pleasantly pale hands, she concealed most of her body from him in this image, which no doubt she had chosen for just that reason; she had stepped out on her husband, but innocuously, care-ful to assert her familial self. Had the husband discovered who had re-ceived this photograph, he could at least have told himself that Victoria was not alone in it; moreover, her collar came up nearly to her chin. She wore white crescent earrings. No, she did look happy! She was the center of a young, healthy and prosperous family. Now she was a skeleton, or ashes. *You will not be aware of this,* said another letter, *but it is the anniversary of my mastectomy and I am supposed to be happy that I survived and all of that.*

Now with the mourners and other regular people gone, the front gate locked, the crows returned to the cemetery grass, watching him sidelong through their metallic ring-eyes. In case there might be a watchman, he hid inside the bell-cupola of the Bartlett mausoleum. The moon emerged suddenly, much as illnesses, realizations and heartbreaks so often do; so that it was now time to call up Victoria. How welcoming would she be? Sometimes in that last year he used to telephone Luke to see how well he was enduring, imagining that he was performing some virtuous duty, only to discover that Luke was bored with talking, or with him. Why shouldn't this be worse?

From his shirt pocket he withdrew the card through whose means she had first reestablished communication: distantly formal, and as haughty as ever—how he would have hated to be married to her! *You, for all I know, do not remember me. But, I think you remember at least a little.* That was Victoria for you—certain of her effect. *I've always felt bad for snubbing you so awfully. There were extenuating parenting and adolescent circumstances, but I was very horrible. I'm sure you would have been dumped (or vice versa) but later I learned to do it and accept it with some small degree of grace.* The next lay tidily folded in its envelope, with a cancelled twenty-nine-cent stamp of wild columbine: *Even though I have been thoroughly faithful in every possible way, Ryan, I think, lives in fear he'll lose me to something: a cause, a job, another man,* and I'll bet you liked it that way, didn't you, Victoria? The third was typed singlespaced and went on for several pages. She had confessed to calling him and then hanging up. *There are probably unresolved feelings for you that probably contributed to my feeling embarrassed. Please be flattered. I don't have feelings for many people—at least, not embarrassing feelings! I think it is ridiculous that there has to be closure for every relationship, friend, choice.* Yes, you would think that. No wonder you hated to die. *I can't tell if you mind questions. I think that in fact you do. I hope this reaches you before you are gone again to find your cigarette stand girl. How were the polar bears? The cold north, it sounds very appealing to an ice princess like me.*

*I dislike other people's children but they like me because I treat them
well and feed them and bring goldfish to class.*

The moon resembled a marble wreath when he poured the liquid onto
Victoria's grave.

12

Her smile was a flower without scent. He felt more saddened than be-
guiled.

13

When he came home, he took his pain pills and pored over the moon
map. Then he read two or three of her oldest letters. Playfully, the cancer
flexed its fingers within his entrails. Taking up a pen, he began to write a
reply, for practice, so that he would know what he ought to say to her.

14

The second time he visited, worn down by the sweaty brightness of his
summer evenings, Victoria was sitting on her tomb, in one of those mid-
length skirts which had been in fashion when she was seventeen, with
her white hands in her lap and her knees shining like moonlight. She had
combed her hair just so over her shoulders; he had never seen her so formal. She gazed straight ahead.

You must have suffered so much, he said.

Don't speak of it.

He thought her way of expressing herself old-fashioned.— Do you
mean it still hurts you? he said.

Actually, I guess it doesn't make any difference now.

The last time I called you, the nurse said you were too weak to talk.
And then I didn't know for a long time. I was afraid to disturb your family. But I could imagine your physical agony, and the emotional agony of
leaving your children behind—

She turned half away.

Has he remarried?

I think those questions are intrusive, said Victoria.

Which ones?

Any of them. I'm not asking you any.

I did notice that. Come to think of it, maybe you don't know if he—

You believe that I don't want to know anything about *you*.

Or maybe that you know everything you care to. Can the dead read minds or see the future?

I've learned not to force any issue, said Victoria.

Why should that be such a secret? he demanded, which he would never have done at seventeen.

Surprisingly, she smiled at him.

He said: Next time I'll bring you flowers.

You're having a bad year, aren't you? said Victoria.

You could say that.

You think you used to love your life, but you never did.

How do you know?

I'm not in a position to complain about anything.

Not with a marble slab on your chest! he replied, meaning to be wry but merely achieving bitterness.

Sometimes it hurts me. It's the heaviest thing I ever had to bear.

I'm sorry. You're having a bad time, too. Should I get you out of there?

It wouldn't do any good. But flowers, flowers would be nice—

What kind would you like? I never got you any before, so I don't know.

I love moonflowers. But you won't be able to get them. You don't even know what they are.

At seventeen he would have been crushed or at least disconcerted. Now he barely noticed humiliations of this sort. Rising, he said: I'll bring you six white roses.

To go with my complexion?

And with your pretty winding-sheet.

I'm not wearing one.

Then don't wear anything.

Victoria's ghost giggled. He blew her a kiss and went away.

15

The disk on the lunar map was more or less the same tarnished yellow-silver-green as the key which had finally unlocked his desk drawer. Through the loupe which formerly belonged to Luke's jeweler friend Raymond, he observed the Fra Mauro formation where Apollo 14 landed.

The enlarged dots taught him nothing, for even the acutest seeing, if it is of the wrong sort, can mislead more perplexingly than sincere blindness. Do you believe me? Sit down at the cemetery's edge; send your eyes into the ground. Behind the raspberry leaves lies a fern between whose green ribs ivy manifests itself like grey-green shadow; between the ivy leaves hang teeth and fangs of crisp darkness scattered in air as if new-smitten from a monster's jawbone; but now, just when you begin to wonder whether you might in time perceive moonflowers within those black places, the noon sun intrudes, perching like a hot puppy upon your shoulder, panting light into your sweating ear, slobbering rays of brightness into the sweet black places, chasing away their darkness more quickly than your vision can follow; so that all that remains behind the ivy leaves is tea-brown dirt partitioned by grey stalks. Now you must go away until late afternoon; not until then can you ever hope to find moonflowers. So flee the sun; lay down the loupe; and may the eyeballs of desire be your jewels.

Below the Mare Tranquillitatis, just east of where Apollo 11 touched down, the narrower, canyonlike windings of the Mare Nectaris went south, petering out in a confusion of craters of which Fracastorius (latitude 20° S) was the most impressive; and in the cratered badlands to the northwest was Catharina, which allured him because it was a woman's name. Rheita, Vega, Biela, Messala, Agrippa, Caroline Herschel, Gemma Frisius and Hypatia kept her company. He had a fancy that after he died, if he really wished to, he could take Victoria to that region. Well, wasn't it all fancy at this stage? There was no reason he should prefer her over others, since for so long she'd scarcely visited his thoughts. Come to think of it, that might be the very reason he dwelled on her—because he *hadn't;* in which case the excavation had to do with self-knowledge. But what the dirt that rooted her had to do with the moon, that he certainly could not say.

16

Not wishing to show himself up by asking for moonflowers, he wandered discreetly into a florist's shop, glancing into the dimmest refrigerator cases in case some bluish-white or greenish-yellow blossoms might whisper. Before he had completed his escape, the darkhaired young woman coaxed him back, promising that she could help him. Like many people who work with plants, she had unassuming ways, which must have reassured the shy and the sorrowful. He hesitated.

If you feel like describing the occasion, said the woman, carefully snipping off a rose stalk, I might be able to put something together for you.

Thank you, he said. But it's difficult to describe.

I understand, she said. Well, thank you for coming in.

Do you always have white roses in stock?

Almost always. Most of the time you don't need to call ahead.

Thank you, he said. The woman gazed after him in alarm; he must have looked unwell. When he got home, he vomited, then lay down for the rest of the morning. In the afternoon he telephoned the doctor.

Can you explain your problem? said the advice nurse. The doctor will call you back.

I'm dying.

Sir, if this is an emergency you'd better come straight in.

It's not an emergency.

Then what would you like the doctor to do for you? Do you need a refill on your pain medication?

I'd like something stronger.

Then you'll need to make an appointment. What's your date of birth?

I could give you my date of death.

That's not what we go by, sir.

What do *you* go by in your life?

Sir, the doctor can fit you in tomorrow at three-o'-clock. Make sure you bring your insurance card with you.

You, too, he said. He hung up, chewed up three antacids as delicately as if he were making love to them, waited a quarter-hour, then swallowed three pain pills.

Down on the far side of the cemetery lay Hal Murmuracki's Chapel of Flowers, an establishment whose black hearse never left the carport and whose lights whispered day and night through the closed blinds. It was early evening now, and the pills supported him. He turned the long door-latch. On the left an old man sat behind a half open door, verifying accounts by means of a silent adding machine.

Yes, said the man. Please sit down.

I'd like some flowers. To . . .

What kind of flowers?

Moonflowers, he replied.

I don't believe I've heard of those.

They're . . . Well, I've never seen them myself.

Just a moment, said the old man. He summed zero to zero, slowly, then shut off the adding machine.

For a remembrance, is it? the old man asked sadly.

Yes.

She must be very special to you. Well, let's see what we have in our floral section.

Across the hall was a door inset with a black window. The old man knocked three times, then unlocked it.— It's only me here today, he explained.

The darkened room, not much larger than a closet, smelled of jasmine and sweet pea. The old man turned on the light. There was nothing inside but a sink and a long steel table.

I'm expecting a delivery right about now, said the old man. Ah, here it comes.

Through the mail slot sped a cylindrical tube wrapped in black paper. The old man caught it as it came, then slowly rolled it round and round on the table.— Yes, he said, this must be your order. A hundred dollars, please. It's best to keep them in the package right up to the graveside, because this species is perishable, unfortunately. Quite light-sensitive, you see. They might last until sunrise tomorrow.

Thank you for helping me.

You won't suffer as much as she did, said the old man. Don't be afraid.

Are you Mr. Murmuracki?

No, I'm his father. Would you like a receipt?

Suspecting that this might be a test, he gazed into the old man's sorrowful eyes and said: I trust you.

17

Thank you for coming to see me, said Victoria. It makes me happy. There's not a lot to do down here.

Nor much for me up here. I'm glad it's getting dark—

I loved what you said to me last time. It had me laughing and laughing . . .

What did I say? Anyhow, were you truly laughing?

I was laughing down here but I didn't want you to know.

Why didn't you?

So you wouldn't have power over me. It's bad enough that you called me up. I had no choice but to come to you.

If you'd had a choice, would you have come?

I have a choice now. I don't have to be with you unless I want to.

Well, that's a compliment, he said wearily.

Don't get irritated. If you do, I'll hide. What did you bring me?

Moonflowers, I hope.

Did you really? It's been ages since anybody brought me a present! Please, please open them right now. Oh, they're pretty!

Where shall I put them?

Lay them down across my headstone, and then I'll sit here and hold them in my lap, like this. Do I look beautiful?

So beautiful—

I'll tell you a secret. I've never seen moonflowers before!

Where did you learn about them?

A long time ago I overheard the family in that mausoleum arguing. It was quite nasty, actually; I won't repeat what they said. And the wife said that she wouldn't forgive the husband for a hundred and one years, unless he gave her moonflowers.

And did he?

I don't know. How could he get them? I don't care about that couple really, although the elder daughter can be sweet. I don't care about very many people. Do you think I should keep flirting with you like this?

Well, why do you suppose I'm here?

For love or advice.

Or both, if you're interested. But I've spent so many years assuming that you weren't—

But here you are, she laughed. As if we might have a *future*.

Or a past.

It upsets me that everyone up here mentions the future so unemotion-
ally. Why don't they scream *death, death, death*?

Because we—

Because you don't care! It's too awful and far away.

You're not far away. Not from me.

No. But I'm awful. I was always awful to you.

You're being nice to me right now. What was in your mind when I
came to you?

Well, my first thought was, you still have the hormones of a seventeen-
year-old, and you'll never get beyond that with me. Then I thought: How
sweet, actually! You must have considered what would cheer up a rotting
skeleton with her eyesockets full of worms—

But that's not your form—

Look! See!

He nearly screamed. But he compelled himself to be brave, and advanced toward her with outstretched arms.

At once she became as pale as a spring sky at twilight, but she was wa-
veringly seventeen. The beauty of that he couldn't bear; he would rather
have her be a skeleton.

18

One of the reasons Victoria had left him was that at seventeen he was in-
tensely morbid, and when he sent her a notebook filled with poems about
skeleton women, she responded with angry disgust. This notebook and
her final letter to him lay within a large yellow envelope in that drawer of
his desk, buried, probably accidentally, beneath her other letters; whenever he saw that yellow envelope, which had turned orange with age, he
felt sickish, and so he had never looked inside it since that first time, when
they were seventeen. (Very slowly and cautiously, in tiny bites, he chewed
a wisp of bread, hoping to calm his stomach.) In point of fact, whatever
nausea the envelope recalled or engendered could not have afflicted him,
since he forgot it for so many years at a time, and never reopened it. Since
then he must have become, it seemed safe to say, a successful, alluring individual, for just look at all those letters from other women! When he
was seventeen, no girl but Victoria had been at all interested in him. The

reason that the envelope's contents might unsettle his belly was that (until we begin dying, of course) the future is a new blank notebook unmarred, in which all our wishes may perhaps be written, while whatever *has* been written, being utterly real, must be utterly imperfect. And thank goodness he had done better and better since then! Why on earth would he care to wallow in the grief and humiliation of that time before he had begun to do well? Hence opening the notebook would have been painful enough; as for rereading Victoria's stinging final letter, no, thank you.— So as he pulled fat or thin envelopes out of that pile, at first it was with a feeling of sweetness; and then, as the probability of drawing a letter similar to the one in that orange envelope increased (and probably he would open the orange envelope sometime, out of mere thoroughness), he found the nausea beginning to waft up out of his guts and into his throat.

19

And yet, strange to say, Victoria had herself been morbid. She had written him a romantic letter: *Jesus, I want to die of leukemia, too!*

Why on earth had the two of them wanted that? He had forgotten. And there were ever so many letters left to reread; perhaps he would never find the answer; very likely neither of them had known, being only seventeen.

(Seventeen is actually a perfectly aware and decisive age, he reminded himself. I am no wiser than I was then—merely farther away from being seventeen.)

It was certainly strange not to remember the circumstances of so peculiar a thing. Why had he written those poems? And what was he supposed to be learning now? But since his reacquaintance with Victoria had rendered the close of his life a sort of fairy tale, such incidental failures of recollection and understanding failed to trouble him. On certain hot afternoons when he felt so unwell that even a crumb of bread on his tongue made him retch, and Victoria's letters were too much for him, he lay down with a volume of someone else's fairy stories. One of Hermann Hesse's parables accompanied someone away from the blue iris flower of his childhood. *With growing sorrow and fear, the poor man painfully saw how empty and wasted the life behind him had become. It no longer belonged to him but was strange and disconnected, like something once memorized that could be recalled only with difficulty in the form of barren fragments. For* the man who loved Victoria, the past was not this way. To be sure, it no longer belonged to him, but he did not wish to be seventeen anymore; and however much he had forgotten scarcely mattered, since he would so soon lose the rest. Moreover, had his life been any more empty than Victoria's, or anyone's? Could he have done better? If not, regret would be misplaced. So the hot days embraced him as he lay sweating and queasy on his bed, and only occasionally did her old letters speak to him. Sometimes they charmed or embarrassed him, but did they hint at anything of which he had lost sight? Had Isaac been correct in his way of life, and Luke in his death, then the thing to do was to open his hands and let the letters fall away. Well, should he? The women whom he had clung to (and who had clung to him), the erotic gardens in which he had played, entering and leaving them through caverns of loneliness, these had offered him ever so many blue irises, including Victoria herself; and the flowers, now pressed and preserved in his desk drawer, retained as much fragrance as any dying man deserved. They proved that his life had not been wasted.

20

The night grew as dark as a mausoleum's doorway. Victoria had told him how to find the spot where the Spirit of Progress had updated the cemetery wall into a chainlink fence cut with a hole. Through this he now came and went as he pleased, counting off stone Sphinxes, eagles and doves to avoid getting lost. Sometimes he heard the muffled rhythmic clapping of unseen wings.

My first child was the politest, she said. He never comes here. Of course, if he did, he couldn't see me. There's no helpful witch in love with him. How she must hate you!

You haven't met her, evidently.

Why should I take the trouble? I'm not interested.

But you mentioned her.

Well, I admit to feeling flattered that you used her potion or whatever it was in order to see me! And since you chose me over her, I certainly don't need to be jealous, do I?

No.

But I think you should go home and live your life. You don't have much of it left.

Do you know when I'll die?

Yes, but cross my heart, I'll never, ever tell you! No one truly wants to know.

How much do you miss your life?

I miss my children. I certainly don't miss you. I miss my house. I miss—oh, we had an aquarium with a catfish in it that kept swimming madly around, trying to die; I used to go down there in the middle of the night to watch it . . .

And what did you feel?

Now I know I was watching myself, but at the time I just felt amused, the way I used to when I hurt you and you tried to hide it from me; I think I've always been a sadist, although I've never done anything terrible. Or have I? How terrible was I to you?

I don't remember.

You see? That's how it is!

21

He asked about the neighbors, and she said: I don't particularly like the family next door, because they don't engage in intellectual discussions; they'd rather give impressions and unanalyzed opinions. Of course, I'm not exactly brilliant myself, so that's ungracious of me . . .

And who's on the other side?

That woman is thoroughly unpleasant. All she likes to do is chew the dirt in her grave. Oh, dear, I shouldn't have told you that, because—

So that's what happens.

Not to all of us.

What happens to the rest?

Victoria smiled.— Someday I might tell you.

Annoyed and weary, he considered walking away. But then he remembered that his illness caused him to be irritable, just as Luke had been whenever the pain tired him without making him desperate or confused.

As if to further spite him, she added: Actually I like them all. I don't have anybody else who goes back so far. Certainly not you.

But we've known each other forty years.

I think we haven't. You'd forgotten my name until I wrote you.

No, I hadn't.

But what kind of memory do you actually have? You think that you remember things, but you're actually at the point where it all goes away.

Will it come back when I'm dead? Don't ghosts remember everything?

You're always fishing for answers. I think we should just agree that I don't have to tell you anything.

Spoken like a seventeen-year-old girl!

Well, I'm immature. I married at twenty-one so I would never have to have another affair to get what I wanted.

What exactly did you want?

I won't tell you.

Naturally. Well, did you get what you wanted?

She was silent. Then she said: I hope you've found your satisfaction somewhere. If my husband had ever cheated I'd have killed him.

If you mean sexual satisfaction, I don't aspire to that anymore. I'm dying.

I think you do still have desires.

Well, what a fruitless conversation this is.

Then go home.

So long.

Don't go. I'm bored here. I'll apologize if you ask me to. Will you ask me to?

He shook his head, smiling.

At least stay until the moon comes up.

All right.

He lay down in the cool grass, slowly curling in upon his side, weary almost to death, seasick at the dancings of the dandelions. Grass-shadows sawed across his face; he closed his eyes. Was that Victoria stroking his hair, or was it the wind? The spasm departed; he stood up. On the knoll where the nineteenth-century rich were buried, something tall turned away from him. The evening sky remained brightly pale. From the swamplands not far off came the humidity of grape-leaves and oaks.

Are you better? she inquired.

Sure.

Do you want to talk about you or me?

Let's talk about you.

But we always do. I think we should talk about you.

We'd both rather talk about you.

I can feel the moon coming now.

There it is.

You can only see it, but I can feel it.

Did I ever tell you about that moon map I have?

Which edition is it?

I don't remember.

I used to have the third edition; for awhile it was over my bed at college. I taped it up the day I left you. Do you mind my telling you that?

Not at all.

How old am I right now?

You know.

In a way I am still seventeen, said Victoria. If I weren't, you wouldn't be here. And at seventeen, please understand, I wanted someone to love my mind before my body. I held any boy who showed interest in my body in great disdain. Not that my body's in very good shape now, as you saw. But my *spirit*, that's not so bad, is it?

Your spirit, or ghost, or whatever it is, is very pretty. You look seventeen to me.

If my husband had called me up, I'd look twenty-one.

So he never did cheat? At least I never read his obituary!

I was all he could handle.

Does he have someone or not?

Don't ask about *now*.

Why won't you tell me what you know? The end will be easier for me if I could expect—

It won't, believe me.

Are you able to haunt your children? Because if you can't, I'll go and report what they look like—

No, said the woman in the ground.

Are you afraid?

I'm trying to protect you from understanding, and *you just won't let me*—

By the way, I'm not afraid of what anybody looks like. Be a skeleton again if you like; I don't care.

You'd probably like it. You see, I do remember your poems—

What do you want to be?

Right now? Well, beautiful, of course. And—

You are, Victoria, I promise.

Actually, until you started coming around, it never occurred to me that I could escape some of this horror by pretending. I do like to pretend, because it passes the time.

Then do you want to pretend that you're still my sweetheart?

Oh, grow up! laughed Victoria.

22

He never felt lonely anymore. Even when she was not thinking of him, she awaited him. Perhaps this should have frightened him, but, after all, he had initiated their reunion of his own desire, and nothing happened except when he wished it to; she could not come to him. He avoided visiting on holidays, lest he meet her family, although he inferred that they no longer paid their respects. When he and Victoria were seventeen, they had needed to get around their parents to arrange their retrospectively innocuous meetings, and this felt nearly the same.

I've thought of you all the time and kept quiet, she said. What would you like to hear about tonight? The couple next door, the woman who chews dirt, the sounds that the rats make? Sometimes I think if I can only strain my eyes hard enough I'll be able to see through the darkness; and then I start to see a star or maybe the moon, and then I remember that I don't have eyes and if I could see anything at all it would only be a maggot crawling across me. I can't see you and you can't see me—

Yes I can.

I remember my children over and over, of course. They must be quite different now.

Then you don't know anyone's lives. Now I finally know—

I like to tell myself the plots of books I've read—

Victoria, how much has dying damaged you? And is there anything good?

It was nauseating. It went on and on until I was semiconscious, and then the pain would wake me up, or I would start hemorrhaging or vomiting, and sometimes my children were standing there crying, not that they understood. I had wanted it to be over, but then when I saw them I panicked again; I was afraid of leaving them without a mother. By then I usually couldn't speak to them, or if I did it hardly made sense. And the morphine made the nausea worse, or maybe it caused it; I don't remember. And . . . Did you ever live in Baltimore? I managed a whole year there, across the street from a funeral parlor, before I got married. The man next door beat his wife every Friday night.

No, I never—

I want you to go there and see if that's still going on, said the ghost. I'll give you the address. Because it's getting to be an effort to hold onto everything. Does that answer your question?

I'm not sure.

Then I'll tell you a little more, since I'm the only one you've kept up with who's gone through it. At first you can't do anything but fight it; you keep trying to protect yourself against further injury and agony and degradation. The first day they gave me chemo, they put the needle in, and I started vomiting right there at the hospital. I vomited for four days straight; my husband almost went mad. I lived for almost two years after that, although for awhile I did get better, but that was just the beginning. You feel that it's unbearable, but you have to bear it. Then it gets worse, and then much worse. You go into shock, but somehow you still know that this truly *is* unbearable, and you're getting so hurt now that nothing can fix you. Then you start breaking into pieces. It's like that point in childbirth when you realize you have no control and you're irrelevant. Some people never come back together; they go straightaway into the same condition as that lady next to me who can't do anything except chew on dirt. But for me . . . well, after a long time my pieces flowed back together like mercury. I think that all of me is back, but I don't know. What do you think? Tell me! I can't ask anyone else. Do you think any part of me is missing?

No.

You're not just saying that? Promise—

I promise. To me you seem the same.

You know, dying hurt so much that for a long time I kept expecting to keep hurting. And at first I was changing so quickly, but now . . . How long have I been dead?

Thirteen years, I think. Well, let me read your—

You mean you don't know?

How would I? You didn't exactly tell me! And I didn't ask your husband. But I always read your headstone when I visit you. What does it say now? It's so dark. Anyway, when it comes to arithmetic—

That's right. I always got better grades than you.

That must have been one of the reasons you looked down on me.

Of course! But I don't now. You're so nice to come here, especially at night. I'm getting used to not having anything.

I can imagine.

But when I was getting chemotherapy, I learned to like having no hair.

Such beautiful hair . . .

Not having to toss it out of my face . . . My eyes seemed larger and more intense. That was nice. But it was humbling, of course, and being in the ground is so much worse. Did you know that lovers often come here at night?

I'm not surprised. After all, he remarked bitterly, here I am, with you.

Disregarding this, she said: When I see a very female female, with cleavage and long hair, flirting with somebody at the side of my grave, it makes me sad. Last summer, or maybe the summer before, a couple made love on top of me, and I was a little titillated, but mostly I was angry. At *them*. For being alive and showing me no consideration. But why should they?

You can flirt with me.

I did just now, a little. But I don't feel anything.

You never did, with me.

That's true. How stupid that you're the only one of us two who cares! Or do you? Aren't you just going through the motions?

Aren't we both?

Look, I'm not *with* anyone! Certainly not with you. The way you act toward me reminds me of how it was when the baby was crying or my husband wanted me back the way I used to be. Believe it or not, I have no desire to feel sexy. I'd rather feel alive. I'd like to heave this marble slab off my chest and *breathe*! I—

Victoria?

What is it? Oh, is it time for you to leave? Well, goodbye.

Victoria, do you want me to get you out of here?

You asked me that.

But if I—

And put me where?

Maybe in a fancy flowerpot. We can grow whatever you like on top of you, some black roses or—

Let me think about that. I like making you come to me. Maybe that's the best I can expect now.

I'm not feeling well. I'm going home.

Run along then, said Victoria, and he almost hated her. At least this was not the same misery she had caused him when he was seventeen.

23

Of course their doings had not brought him misery alone; that was why he remembered her so fondly, or gratefully, or something. They had kissed and caressed several times, and once it went farther. He remembered her in his bedroom on that summer afternoon—where had his parents been?—and they had drawn the curtains. She stood nude before him, the blonde locks licking down around her nipples as she smiled unreadably, doubtless prepared to withdraw herself at any juncture, as was her right; and he fell to his knees, burying his face in her bright blonde crotch. Then somehow she was in his bed with her legs open. It was his first time, although from what she later intimated, perhaps simply to push him away, it might not have been hers; he'd neglected or declined to ask, as was his policy on so many subjects. So he adored her, and it was all perfect. He would have given anything to keep it from ending. It did, and Victoria, triumphant, alarmed or simply cool, dressed and rapidly departed; he was not to call her without further instructions. That was the day of his great joy. Not until he was twenty-one did he penetrate a woman; but what Victoria had allowed him was no less intimate than that. That was his glory; she was forever his, at least in a certain seventeen-year-old kind of way. And in the painfully lovely brightness of his last summer, Victoria was whispering to him almost like the wind, or perhaps like a rotten tree rocking in the wind. She had opened her legs, and then . . . His belly ached. In the west, two silver dragon-continents faced off upon the moon's yellow disk, the sky's red gashes bleeding orange and a pair of raptors taking wing—dew on every railing and plaque, and outside the wall and across the street, doorknobs and porches wet in the country of the living.— Victoria said: When I was seventeen and I got a sunburn, I liked it because it made the *hidden me* look so white . . .— And his old penis nearly stirred, to remember her white parts. She had been like the moon, or like a concert singer's voice alone in the darkness, living and altering. He seemed to recall her sitting at the next table at the high school library, turned slightly away from him as she studied for her chemistry test, her handsome legs bare above the knee, the creases behind her knees calling upon him to lick them, her plump, pale buttocks, which he was to see and touch only that once, announcing themselves to him within the paisley dress, her arms alive with pinkness, her hair a brilliant straw-blonde: all these attributes were hers; this was *her*, but, being seventeen, he never thought to inquire what else might be her. And her breast, or some other woman's, green and hard in his mind as a half-made acorn, it dazzled him, as when one has sat in the sun too long and wishes to pass into the shade. Then came that maddening tenderness in his sides, nausea in his throat, and he forgot to breathe when he saw her.

24

In high school they took mostly different classes; she nearly might as well have been IN MANSIONS ABOVE. They used to pass in the hall, and exchanged notes. Who would have supposed that this beautiful girl named Victoria would actually write to him? He knew he would keep her letters forever.

25

What might he keep of her now? Had his life-horizon continued to roll indefinitely forward, like a planet's so called "terminator" where night gives way to dawn, then he might have wished, "forsaking all others" as the wedding vow put it, to lead her past the ruined angel whose marble hands would never come unclasped, then through the gate, for he most certainly lacked any wish to dwell here with her, eating dirt—but the rules have little to do with our wishes. Nor, it seemed, did Victoria yearn to abide with him. Wouldn't she rather flitter around her abandoned children? And why shouldn't she? Wouldn't that be the best, most loving thing, to reincorporate her with them? But if that wasn't practical, and if Victoria grew fonder of him, and therefore he of her, and could he but live aboveground awhile longer—or for that matter dwell in death with her—where should they abide? In the years when Luke and his wife used to quarrel, they had maintained separate residences, she not being above locking him out of the bedroom in the middle of the night, for which cause he discouraged her from selling her place and moving into the house whose mortgage he had finally almost paid off—what if she evicted him from his own bedroom? When his last illness softened their wills, they removed to a new home, where indeed they must have lived happily ever after, for the widow still remained there. At this stage what could one hope for but the mitigation of loneliness? He had to confess, it hurt his heart to think upon Victoria lying alone down there in the dirt, forever, no matter what she said about the neighbors. For all he knew, they might be one of her sad caprices, and whenever he quitted her she lay isolated and helpless, spinning out her skein of inventions just to kill more years and hours. The way she spoke mainly of herself, and then so inexactly (one shouldn't say evasively), conveyed nothing. He pitied her for being dead. Goodhearted, thinking merely to save her, in much the same way that Isaac ought to have rescued him from his needs and griefs, he sometimes, as you know, imagined carrying her far away from both their pasts—for example, to the moon, which might be the place to which her neighbor's tomb was referring when it asserted: IN MANSIONS ABOVE. In one of her letters from when they were seventeen, she had written: *I am what I pretend to be.* Do pretend, Victoria. Come to the moon with me; pretend away.

Bemused, Luke used to ask why the fat one needed so many women whispering in his ear, like a crush of cottonwoods around a sulphur spring; although Luke loved his moody but affectionate wife sincerely, he detested depending on her, or, worse yet, her expecting him to take care of her as if she were a child.— If I choose to be with her, he said in those last years, then I need to allow her to modify me.— Hence Luke sought to learn from his Stephanie how to be cheerful, at which she intermittently excelled, especially in the morning; and how to be effective with strangers by being social; that came easily to her. He admired her beauty even as she aged. Truth to tell, Stephanie was a fine-looking woman. In shape and deportment she partially exemplified a certain tall ex-ladyfriend of my neighbor's named Angeline, who had jilted him more cruelly, since with greater awareness, than Victoria; but Angeline's signature characteristic was treachery, while Stephanie adored her husband desperately even when she raged against him. They were both loyal. After he moved out, the marriage appeared to lack what a young person might call a "future"; then it got better year by year; and the month before his death Luke calmly reported (which seemed impossible) that it was improving day by day. Whenever his surgeries, chemotherapies and radiation treatments reduced him to that state of dependence which he so greatly feared, Stephanie ruled him with great love, showing his oldest friends the door when he tired, hounding the doctors to be less absent, sleeplessly spoonfeeding him her heart's best blood. Stephanie and the moon-gazer invariably got along well, because the latter respected her authority. She told Luke that she loved this fat friend of his; she was sweet that way.

Even while praising Stephanie, Luke occasionally used to invoke another woman. Long before Stephanie, he had loved an Eve with commendable seriousness, admiring without knowing her, barely revealing his interest, perhaps to prevent her from disdaining him. Before Eve lost her youth she moved away and married someone else. Her name came sweetly to Luke's lips. After uttering it he'd say: And then I realized that what I thought I remembered was just pieces of a dream.

What would have happened if you'd married her instead of Stephanie?

Oh, nothing. Stephanie's perfect for me.

For our dying moon-gazer, as for Luke, the Eves, the Angelines and their sisters were heavenly dreams; through them his life might be infinitely multiplied. Just as he grew better acquainted with his father after the latter's death, once he knowingly began to die he came to know his bygone women better; they could no longer save him, but their images comforted him; it might have been that way for Luke with his dream-Eve, who was one of his dearest secrets—not to be exposed to others.

Asked whether he might find Eve after death, Luke, as so often when she came up, changed the subject. Perhaps by then he had managed to lay aside his dream of her, for even before he met Isaac, Luke had always wished to depart an empty house, carrying the fewest necessities on his back. As for Isaac, he had certainly left nothing behind! He might still be alive in the stillness of rock-crowds in some dry wash, alone in the desert where it becomes practical to listen to life and death. As for Luke, where he had gone was unknown. He had always been stronger than this fat friend who survived him. To the southwest the gibbous moon remained high over the snow-corduroyed rock-hills, while the sky grew orange over the sharp blue ridge behind which the still unseen sun was approaching. Luke and Raymond planned out their climb, while the third one, the fat one, sat by himself. Raymond sought to persuade him along, kindly assuring him that it didn't matter if he couldn't make it, but he preferred not to be the cause of failure on what might and did prove to be Luke's sole chance to reach the summit; so he sat alone, his incapacity (which scarcely humiliated him at all) as glaring as the line of a salt lake on the horizon at noon. To be sure, he would have liked to keep them company—for much the same reason that he later wished that there might be a way to reach the cemetery through the drawer of his father's desk—or instantaneously to traverse the Straight Wall of the moon.

In the summer after Luke's death he had walked to the shore of a certain high lake and sat on the rocks for a long time, watching the cattails trembling and the clouds pressing as tightly upon the mountains as hands smothering someone's face; and the water altered from ultramarine to turquoise to milky grey as he sat there with the tears coming so easily and silently that he felt healthy while the wind carried off his tears as quickly as they appeared; and he sat in a kind of ease, listening to a bluejay, waiting for the tears to cease, so that he could return into the sight of others without embarrassment. On the far side of the lake rose a saddle between snowy mountains, too far and high for him to aspire to, although perhaps Luke could have reached it. At last a cold wind arose from the lake, and overcame his remaining tears; as he sat shivering, he couldn't help but wonder how the smallest birds stayed warm. Sometimes in his boyhood he used to see frozen sparrows in January; how did the others get through to summer? That might be one more thing which he used to know. His teeth chattered. A robin darted on the gravel beach, seeming to play with the waves, chasing them out and flying back when they came in. He felt chilled now, so chilled! Then he began to get dizzy. He sat for a long time, until the sun returned, and the wet rock took on color.

Stephanie, greyhaired and crushed, still worked (and kept an ageing quarter horse); once or twice a year he phoned her and they spoke of Luke, not for more than twenty minutes. What Luke had left in her heart was, of course, the couple's secret.

It was the anniversary of Luke's death. He telephoned her. She asked how he was.— No complaints, he said. What about you?

She was in debt. Luke's estate resisted liquidation; it tired her so; she didn't know how to go forward.— To this he didn't know what to say.

A cramp stuck him, so he said goodbye, perhaps too quickly; unaware of his condition, she might now suppose that he felt bored with her. But what was he supposed to do? Soon enough, like Victoria, he would lack the capacity even to roll that gravestone off his chest. The nausea was a longnecked bird within his chest; now it opened its wings. He could not imagine how this could be necessary. Why shouldn't he have lived forever, becoming ever happier and richer? (Not even his witch lover could have promised that; in fact, her love kept dragging him down beneath the ground.) Withdrawing the moon map from his father's desk, he searched for a likely growing-place for those chilly, waxy flower-buds which had so pleased Victoria; they were bluish, almost grey, yet also as brilliant as the white lip of a calla lily on a sun-field's edge. Perhaps they originated in the Marsh of Sleep. This was one of the questions which it was surely inappropriate to ask of Mr. Murmuracki.

There was a telephone message from the entity pretending to be his doctor: A new insurance form was required of him. The laboratory informed him that he was expected for more blood tests at six forty-five tomorrow morning, and he was supposed to have been fasting for twenty-four hours. Meanwhile into his mail slot came an invoice for forty-seven thousand dollars, which the insurance company declined to pay on his behalf, although the patient advocate in another city might or might not adjust the bill. He made two phone calls on this subject, listening to recorded music until pain and nausea released him. Wondering how much of his life he had dribbled away on such unworthy matters, he decided that he would lose no more time on doctors, except to get more pain pills. If they made it inconvenient to get those, he would go straight to the graveyard and dwell with Victoria.

He lay down. Closing his eyes, he seemed to perceive a moist, heterogeneous blackness crawling with stars. Somewhere within it, the tall blue people sat on high thrones, and the laughing green people rolled from side to side. Whom these might be he did not know. Seeking to dream of Victoria, he sank deeper into that blackness. The blue people were watching him, evidently from farther away. The green ones had gone. He heard something chewing, but it was his heartbeat. His ears were singing and roaring; he must have chewed too many pain pills.

26

Once he surprised a certain long green swamp-snake, and after smoothly backing away, her tiny head raised high to watch him, the creature suddenly flashed her long white belly sideways, whipping her head around to point into the highest darkest grass; then she was gone, presumably underground. His dream went away similarly. In its first recession he thought to keep all of it in his understanding, but then it somehow turned, and some essential yet already meaningless edge of its anatomy glittered like sunlit water on dark rock, after which he could remember only that he had dreamed of Victoria very beautifully and possibly happily.

It was dawn. Pain greeted him. Staggering to the toilet to vomit up blackness, he exhausted and disgusted himself. But the sun shone in on him through the bathroom window, so he chewed up five pills, swallowing them very slowly and carefully, with innumerable sips of water, so that he would not sick them up again, then rose to his knees. He asked of himself whether living remained worthwhile, and replied that it was. He then asked what he wished to do with his days. To be sure, the answer had something to do with Victoria, but just then he desired, he knew not why or how, to *express regret,* or undo or redo the past. Luke, who in that last year had sometimes been angry, often grieved and occasionally felt gratitude, used to remark that what he felt at any moment was less important than that he attend to those feelings and feel them to the full. One trait which he and Luke possessed in common was adeptness at drinking the bitter cup. So he sat on the toilet, with the sun on his face, feeling sorry for himself, then expressing regret indeed, earnestly, for all the women he had not loved better, and the many lessons he had never learned, including uncovering who Victoria had or might have been to him and why he had written her those poems. But above all he regretted his years of near indifference to the sun and the stars.

Now he felt better. Chewing two more pills just in case, he stood up. He went downstairs to the kitchen and made himself a banana milkshake. He drank it in careful little sips. He washed the blender. This took him half an hour.

He opened his front door, meaning to go out into the day, but the sunshine nauseated him instantaneously. Bitterly he crept upstairs to lie down like a corpse in a coffin, staring straight up at the ceiling until late afternoon.

27

Do you remember when you said you like to pretend?

So?

Well, you know, Victoria, I was just reading in one of your old letters about that Indian print bedspread you spread out in your window seat at college; and if it would please you—

I thought I'd already left you by then.

Not quite.

Yes, I do remember, and I hung some ferns from the ceiling—

And your moon map—

No, that was when I left you.

And on the walls you had prints that argued with each other—

Correct! Did I write you which ones?

No.

I must not have wanted you to know.

I didn't keep any secrets from *you.*

You can guess now, if you like.

Well, you were very intelligent and didn't want to be conventional—

Was I?

Were you conventional?

Yes.

I think you aspired to an upper middle class life, which was what you came from. When you were seventeen you tried to run away from it, but you wanted children and security, and—

Are you criticizing me?

No. I think you did well. I wish I'd had both of those together. When I was seventeen I—

Tell me.

Actually, I don't remember much about when I was seventeen. I'm sorry, Victoria.

Well, this is all very pleasant! she cried bitterly, and he realized that forgetfulness terrified her.

What did your Indian print bedspread look like? I can try to buy you one sort of like it, and I'll spread it over your grave when I come visiting, and we can sit on it.

That's sort of girly.

Well, isn't that the sort of thing you—

Actually, I don't feel like pretending at the moment.

And my stomach is hurting me, so I'll be going.

Did you know that I can see your tumor?

What does it look like?

It's like a blackish-purple jellyfish with a mushroom head. Very delicate, with translucent tendrils; there's one coiled most of the way around your backbone; when it reaches your throat you'll die. It's beautiful.

Thanks for that. I'll see you when I feel better.

Don't wait too long. And bring a nice bedspread or blanket for us to sit on. I want blue and—

I'll pick out the pattern.

I offended you, didn't I?

You did your best, he said, laughing a little. She laughed like water coming out of a narrownecked bottle, and he went away.

28

When he was seventeen he used to feel grief almost unto despair whenever his meetings with her had been concluded; he certainly felt nothing of the sort nowadays; of course, he had been granted quite a few years to get over the loss of her—and now she couldn't get away from him. Even if she declined to come out he would know that she was lying on her back six feet under him, with darkness in her eyesockets.

29

Tell me about all your women, she said. I vaguely envision your life as a very complicated orgy, with all sorts of women loving you and then hating you.

No, it hasn't been like that, although I've certainly loved a lot of them.

Actually, don't tell me. It's not that I'm not curious. I'd just rather not know.

You'd respect me more if I were a ladykiller.

I do prefer strong men. If you've let them all do to you what I did to you, that would disgust me, to tell the truth.

Do you remember the high school dance, when you invited me and then picked that boy who was—

Smarter and better put together? That wasn't me. That was Zoë Conway, who became a state prosecutor. Of course my news is out of date, but I think that if she had died I would have heard about it. You invited me to the dance, but I turned you down. We all gossiped about it.

And Zoë disinvited me at the last minute, so I never—

What changed you? Because, now that I think about it, you actually are a ladykiller, a very successful one. You know how to keep my interest. You don't need me the way you used to—

Because I'm dying.

No, that's not all of it.

Well, I've had a lot of pussy in my time. That gave me confidence. And I've been good at pleasuring women, which is the most important thing.

What would you like to do with me right now? Not that I'd let you.

First I'd strip off that winding-sheet of yours—

Why do you keep calling it that? It's my favorite leopard print dress—

And I'd very carefully brush the ants and dirt off your bones. I'd get in between your ribs and clean with a child's toothbrush. And while I did that, I'd be singing to you, songs from when we were seventeen. I'd clean out your eyesockets with cotton swabs, very very gently, in case there's anything left, and I'd comb your hair—you still have some. I'd comb it straight down your backbone. I'd brush your teeth for you, and I'd kiss you where you used to have a mouth. I'd scour out your pelvis with sweetgrass and lavender oil. Then I'd start kissing you there. I'd lick your bones right *there*. And afterward I'd go to a jeweler and buy a ring that would fit your pretty skeleton-hand, Victoria . . .

At least you can make me laugh. Honestly, I don't find much to laugh about when you're gone.

Do you wish I stayed longer?

Actually, your visits make me guilty. You don't have much time left, and I'm not giving you anything.

Yes you are.

Do you love me?

I'll take a leaf out of your book, and say: *I'm not going to tell you.*

I don't love you at all. But I'm undeniably attracted to you.

Because I'm alive, I guess.

That's much of it.

Would you ever choose to live with me? I mean, if you couldn't go home—

You do love to make up stories, don't you?

So do you, darling! This morning I was rereading one of your old letters—

I told you to destroy them!

Well, I didn't, because I was in love with you—

But I *told you*!

I never promised.

Yes you did.

Anyhow, you wrote it exactly a week before my seventeenth birthday (you were always conscientious about dating them, Victoria). You had dreamed you had sleepwalked to the shower, and later you wondered if you had really dreamed it or—

Did you ever show my letters to anybody?

No.

Swear it.

I swear. But what does it matter to you?

Well, it does. It may seem stupid to you—

What's the longest you've cried?

Here? Sometimes I've cried for a year or two straight. But I'm enjoying your visits now, even if I occasionally get irritated.

Thank you.

By the way, do you have a best friend?

He's dead.

Then I might have met him.

No, he's not at the cemetery.

What's his name?

Luke.

Of course I don't know him. Why is he your best friend?

For years he was almost like my older brother. He taught me how to organize weight in my backpack. Whenever anything went wrong in my house, he could usually fix it or tell me how to. There were certain things he didn't deal with, like leaky roofs or doors out of true. He did a lot for me. When my father was alive, he and my father used to do things for me . . .

It's good to be sad, said Victoria. That makes you more like me.

Gazing up at the constellated sky, he felt as if he were about to sink into black water which was snowed with cattail-down. It was getting dark earlier nowadays. Carefully he inquired: Can I love you except by being sad about you?

I'll consider that.

Luke was very wise. He said so many things that I always remember. For instance: *Don't keep making the same mistake. Make a different mistake.* And I could talk to him about my love life. When I was younger I used to ask him for advice, and then when he was suffering with Stephanie I wanted to give him advice, just because I loved him and that was something I could give, and sometimes it helped him, or her, but he was more his own man than I was. Now I think I'm becoming more my own man; I don't know why—

Because you're dying.

Into his mind came Luke's assertion that dying could become freedom. Even while he felt relatively well, Luke had begun giving up ever more experiences and aspirations as well as things, in order to die better. But he and Stephanie never had children. That must have made it easier. Victoria had fought death, for her children's sake.

Luke, to whom trust came hard, had gentled toward him over the years, but until the end, so it seemed, could not help but suspect even this close friend of selfish motives. If he made a date with Luke for lunch, Luke would pick him up at the station—then let fall some grim remark which implied that Luke knew very well that his friend was using him to get a ride. Or he might give Luke a book he had read and liked, in which case Luke might say that it must not have been a good book, or the moon-dreamer would have kept it. As for him to whom Luke had given so many rides over the years, he himself had surely been negligent or ungrateful on occasion; he and Luke had hurt each other every now and then, mostly by saying no. Of the two of them, Luke was more generous with his capabilities, having more; while the moon-dreamer more easily gave away money and possessions to others. What Luke did for his wife—the repaired washing machine and balanced checkbook—often went unnoticed by her; what he blamed her for were her temper and her flightiness. It must have been his cancer which inspired or compelled him into trusting Stephanie. About the cancer Luke once said: What I hate more than anything is throwing up. That must be the reason I got this disease, so that I have to throw up over and over again.— And so it might be argued that the illness refined or at least steeled him, or at least that he could have made a virtue out of his suffering. Not Victoria!

Why are you quiet? Do you need to go?

Victoria, tell me how long I have to live.

I already said I wouldn't.

But you know?

Of course I do.

If I had a month, I'd live differently than if I had three, or—

And then you'd want to know whether I love you, and what I will and won't do, and which sort of *future* we'd have, when I've already told you how I feel about futures. That was another reason I left you. You demanded certainty from me. What seventeen-year-old girl can give that?

But you married at twenty-one. Are you glad that you did?

I'm so grateful that I had children.

When we were seventeen, you told me that you might marry for money. You were laughing when you said it—

If I'd lived to be forty I might have had an affair. Maybe with you. But I never would have married you.

Why not?

Because nobody changes very much, so what I disliked in you would have remained. Besides, you wouldn't have loved me as much as you did before. It's refreshing to be adored. You'd stop doing that if you knew me—

I don't adore you now.

Well, that's not very nice! I'm going now.

Turning away from him, Victoria sank under the grass. The last he saw of her was her beautiful blonde hair.

30

He had forgotten that she had sent him more than one photograph. As he sat in his study that afternoon, too unwell to consider going to the cemetery, he withdrew a letter from his father's desk; on the back of the envelope she had written *amusing enclosures* and *Inside are pictures!!!!! Lions + tigers, monkeys, cats and zebras* and she had drawn a heart dripping two drops and then she had written: *If I wrote you in French could you understand it?*

For a time he held the letter in his hand, smiling. How many pictures had she sent him, after all? (The more he read, the more she was winning him over.)

She was at the zoo, and her lovely hair was blowing. Perhaps her sister, who might still be alive, and if so perhaps a grandmother, had clicked the shutter. She had lowered her head and closed her eyes when she smiled. In a high-necked white blouse and a paisley skirt, she stood before a giraffe, which cocked its head at her, its neck at a rigid near-horizontal, while she held a small blue balloon at her left breast, clasping her pretty long fingers together across her waist, the string wound around them. This photograph had not decayed so far into the red as the other; the sky was purple, the phony rocks reddish, the animal perhaps a bit more red than brown, but Victoria had barely begun to flush; her hands remained as fair as ever, and her blonde hair scarcely intimated red. He turned it over. On the back she had written that she loved him.

My mother is fine—no complications, no cancer. Help me. I know you are. Love me.

Victoria, he cried out, *help me; love me!*

No one answered.

31

There remained to him this sweet world of unread letters; perhaps it was better to guard them as if they were the future, rereading only a few; they were his treasures, or possibly the verdict against him. The true horror, much worse than that of the death which already drooled at his shoulder, was the fact of who he had been at seventeen. The reason he had clung like death to Victoria was that hardly anyone else would come near him! In high school he finally began to have friends, for the hormonal allurements at puberty can be so irresistible that we learn to disguise our faults in hopes of losing later rather than sooner; the shy girl parts her hair over what her mother helpfully assures her is the uglier side of her face; the farmboy takes more showers, and the boy who loved Victoria learned to hide his kinship to ghouls, skeletons and rotting corpses; in his summer nightmares the graves flipped round like lazy susans to fling death in his face! He always woke up smelling it. Years later, when he witnessed death without dreaming, he found that it smelled quite different—more vomity when fresh, more like garbage later on—but the death in his dreams intermittently continued to exude a sulphurous vileness, perhaps because he had once believed in hell, not to mention his own badness; certainly something about him was wrong, and when he was young his schoolmates would tear at him in a frenzy, children scratching at their common scab; he never should have existed at all! Later he disguised this fact; hence women loved him. Was it because he focused the lens of his own so-called love upon pleasuring them, so that, lost to his expert ministrations, they mistook procedure for soul? Give the devil credit; he'd had a knack; even Victoria, his first patient, appeared to enjoy the operation as far as it went. Better yet, he performed it sincerely. But certain natures are born in the shadow. In his first grade art class he was already drawing pictures of lightning-storms, carefully coloring the sky black and purple. Why are some people like that? I repeat: He should never have seen the sunlight. Nor did he mean to see it. When Luke and Raymond departed on that final hike, the reason that the moon-gazer stayed behind was that he'd spoil everything otherwise; he'd never been able to live among others; he slimed over everything he touched! No wonder Victoria fled him! What he should have done upon receipt of his fatal diagnosis was to remember all this, in order to begin to answer the question: Why am I this way? Some creatures are shadow-born, yes, but *why*? And who are they? Were death oblivion and could he rush into it, like a child darting under the bedclothes at night before the monsters come, then there might be scant interest in hunting this subject, but Victoria's postmortem consciousness unfortunately proved that avoiding or denying one's identity is not so easy. Once upon a time there had been that witch who loved him, the one who mixed green potions; why hadn't he loved *her*? She knew who he was (he supposed), and even liked it. But Victoria, who rather than being noble was possessed by a selfishness as ordinary, healthy and therefore as good as the movements of her bowels, intuited who he was and knew that she had to get away. He said to himself: To begin to see myself I must diagram the movements of the living ones whom I repel. Death had struck Victoria, shattering her skull and cramming fistfuls of worms inside her brainpan. She had sought to run from death, which had begun with a kiss, sucking those round pale breasts with which he had played in his seventeenth summer, then insinuated itself within the glands, clawing into her armpits, nibbling here and there until her strong young bones were breached—and she screamed, wept, vomited, perhaps prayed or pretended to for the sake of those children to whom she clung as he once had to her; she would have done anything to be selfish and move her bowels a little longer. Now her bowels pulsed with moonlight; to him she was more beautiful than ever. But she had gone over *there*, to this other man whom she had married. And when he was a child, the other boys, punching him a few times, had then kicked him into his place, which was westward of here, where the moon rose. Had he stayed hidden on the lunar surface (or at least concealed between broken marble urns), no one would have troubled about him—but perhaps the moon was another of those localities which were too good for him. Waiting for the school bus, in one of those winters before Victoria wrote her first note to him, he stood by himself, and then a girl in a ski parka grappled him, having fun, bullying him but also being sexual with him, and of course that excited him; he didn't know how boldly to grapple her back; it lasted but a moment, and then a strong, healthy boy, who hated cancer, came and punched him in the face. He had never told Victoria, who felt his unwholesomeness anyhow, sure enough. The fact that he later learned to love himself because women loved him is evidence that evil things need not find trouble in continuing to exist.— But *why* was he evil? It kept coming back to that. Had he asked the other children, and had they been able to articulate their loathing, they might have said: Because you're *different.*— And why was he different? Why does the rat seek out putrescent flesh? Rats aren't evil, are they?

He had just begun to nibble at a can of salmon when his cancer thrust a skeleton hand up his windpipe and his breastbone groaned with pain; no, that was him groaning. For a long while he bent over the sink, struggling to vomit. (If it were only true what the statues of angelic harpists promised: ASLEEP!) Finally the fish came up, streaked with black blood. Eased and exhausted, he lay down on the sofa.

32

In a rage he snatched up another of her unread letters: Now she was the one who demanded to know the future! *I always need to know everything for me to be comfortable.* She was just like him! Meanwhile he was everything he had disliked in her: suspicious, withholding, prissily critical, even nasty—while the poor girl timidly hoped for his approval, and even worried that she might be bothering him—how could he have not seen it? Again and again she worried that he would leave her; she reread his letters with foolish minuteness comparable to his—she was a darling, really; his *badness* must have driven her away.

He felt all the more ashamed, not only for having been harsh but also for prying into her heartpourings to her young boy—none of his business! He was an old man eavesdropping on children. So he turned to the letters from the year when she was dying, and read: *Are you really such a sweetheart? How could I have not known that about you? You know I don't want to ask you questions because I don't want to pry. Do you care if I do? Someday I'll write you about something—a really vivid memory I have of something we did in high school. You'll really laugh and kick yourself that you didn't know what I thought.* What right did he have to spy on this doomed married woman and the man with whom she platonically flirted? He was a grime-eaten angel whose stone trumpet was as cracked as his penis.

33

How have I forgotten so much? I was certain I'd never let go any of it. And it hasn't really been long! Why can't I remember more? It's as if my seventeen-year-old Victoria were but a blurry, roughed-out figurine of jeweler's wax—or a shapeless corpse. I'll go to her—tonight, and tomorrow night, if I'm well enough. No, I'll remember her tonight and study the moon map. Those photographs help me at least as much as does visiting her. And if I stay too long at the cemetery I'll get sicker; I can feel my tumor when I'm there, for some reason. So let me just read her letters once more—not the ones I don't remember but the ones I've come to know again.

Outside the window, his conception of Victoria hovered in the trees like a solitary gall.

34

So much of the loveliness of that summer had had to do with waiting for her; sometimes he met her once a week, occasionally more often. Until their next meeting he had her latest letter to read over and over with desperate happiness.

Shyly, desperately, happily the boy followed the blonde girl with his eyes. He slept with her letters under his pillow. Since she was more a part of her family than he of his, her letters sometimes described her brother and her sister, or her mother's health. He was never in her home; he never saw her bedroom.

Does old age invariably imagine youth to be a more innocent time? After all, babies keep getting made and grownups keep getting depraved. In any event, he almost never even held her hand. He never passed a night with her; nor was he with her at that moment past dawn when the cicadas begin to stridulate. He did remember meeting her in a park; he had walked and she had ridden her bicycle. The grass was so green around them that the greenness had stained the inside of his skull, although now it was verdigrised, a penny in a skeleton's hand. He remembered the summer humidity, and her lovely young face; but their time together never exceeded two or three hours, and sometimes she didn't come as she had promised.

35

Just as Victoria's not yet reread letters lay waiting for him nearly as invitingly as when they had been new—all the more now, perhaps, for the white envelopes had aged ever so delicately to cream, their thirteen-cent stamps were sweetly antique, the writing on them was precious since the hand was dead, never mind the modest yet significant alteration of the English language since then—and the unremembered contents could not affright him more than any page in some old love story (besides, it wouldn't end until that horrible orange envelope)—so this morning, and the summer world flowing from it, promised him an innocuous sweetness. The dawn was not far gone; the breeze was cool. Feeling less unwell than usual, he decided for that day to live his life instead of Victoria's.

Behind Hal Murmuracki's Chapel of Flowers was an abandoned gas station, after which the swamp began. Nobody he knew had gone there. In truth, he was less of an adventurer than Luke or Isaac; he entered the swamp almost as an exercise; had his tumor tortured him as much as usual, he would have been satisfied to be alone in repose, in his bed, his own place; he didn't need to set out anywhere; he was already suited to being dead. But (so Luke might have said) why not try what did not suit him?

As sky and meadows brightened behind the cool reeds, he felt grateful for the newness of life, and nearly believed himself to be healthy. Happy thoughts of previous women illuminated him in much the same way that morning light jitters back and forth on the spiderwebs between jade reeds; rather than perceiving complete strands, one sees continually altering segments of midair brightness.

When last night's darkness slinks back into reed-shade, one feels the opportunity to play an important part: Very soon I too will make something of myself; I long to; I expect to; for who could waste this morning light? Before the sun has drunk away everything, I will drink my share from the cool breath of reeds just as I have drunk and will drink again from Victoria's cool reed-breath . . .— But then, when the light exposes each reed in earnest, leaving only outlines shadowed, disappointment arrives.— Once he had seen the corpse of a young murdered woman who had been looking forward to a party. Not yet autopsied, she lay in her pink dress, with pink ribbons in her hair, her face bloody and yellow; and the stink of excrement from her abdominal wound was the smell of disappointment. Had her dress been alive, it would have wished to fly away from her; it could still be happy and dance. Here lay a woman who had very likely herself been happy sometimes, who had hurried in excitement to her death, and now there was nothing but disillusionment and failure.

In his memory that pink dress resembled a shady place not yet overrun by solar heat; still the night fragrance could hide here for another quarter-hour, defying the encircling day. But in full light, with the chance to make something of himself now once more safely past, the green reeds were going a lovely silver, their tips whitewashed so newly, the birds now awake (by now the cemetery grass would be a dreary orange-brown); and still he thought to improve his day just as morning gilds grassheads and wet grass. Morning presented him with the colors of berries and the songs of meadowlarks, the dark water beneath bright reeds, algae'd water like jellied jade, two rabbits chasing each other in a circle—and now in the widening of the morning, the smell of reeds and water began to be superseded by the delicious odors of trees.

36

The whipping of the trees made him queasy. It was the trees, nothing else. If only they would stop! Closing his eyes did not help, because he knew that the trees were still writhing. Making another effort, he stared them down. They swayed until he could no longer remember every place that they had been, which was when he vomited. So he got into his car and drove home. Needless to say, no time of day is as profitless to ghost-lovers as high noon, particularly in summer. Life sweats away our thanatotic idealizations, and then where are we? Toying with two of Victoria's unremembered letters, he smiled, but decided to treasure them as they were for a while longer. It was not right to decant her sayings when he felt less than his best.

It was a very hot day. He lay in misery, waiting for his prescription narcotics to rescue him. He would not reenter the hospital; those people would weigh down his misery with powerlessness, and he would still die. Cheered by his determination to be free (and forgetting that he had already made it), he opened a letter and read:

Dear Vickie:

You're tipsy. No, I'm sober. Then why are you writing this? Because I don't want to go too long without having him receive a letter even if it's not what he wants. Give him what he wants, Vickie. No, Victoria, I don't know what he wants from me. You do, mostly. What do you expect, a list of rules? Do this, don't do that? Pour your heart out to me, screw around all you want but leave me your soul. Write me intense romantic letters every Sunday over tea and biscuits. Scent your letters. Discuss your erotica. I'm tired. Who isn't?

In twenty years I bet I'll have breast cancer. I wonder what it feels like to lose a breast. If I'm going to be unhealthy I'm not going to live. Yes, you'll show them, won't you? Lung and breast cancer, kidney disease and maybe a goiter, and you'll just go and die. You're unstable, aren't you, Vickie? I admit it. Not everyone does. After I'm done with prettiness, I know what I am— silly as it is. Vickie, no one thinks I'm a rock of security, but do they know you're compulsive, self-destructive, paranoid? Probably.

Will this amuse him?

Are you amused?

I'll tell you, Vickie, when he answers.

Will he answer?

Sure, he's probably cross at me but he'll answer me.

       Love,

        Toria.

P.S. My mother has a tumor in her breast. I hope it isn't malignant. Selfishly, I'm worried not only for her but for me and the children I'll have.

P.P.S. I'm still getting the great American suntan in my wholesome sexy swimsuit and Riviera sunglasses. You in your hijacker sunglasses and me in mine, what a pair! I'm reading The Second Sex *by Simone de Beauvoir,* The Hite Report, *and* The Total Woman. *I've decided to become a man—grow hair on my chest and cultivate a tight ass.*

P.P.P.S. Purge the earth. Kill every third person. No, every fourth. No, just all those that protest.

37

Luke's friend Raymond had sometimes spoken quite calmly and freely of his first wife, the one who had left him and whom he still loved the most. And Luke used to take pleasure in speaking of Eve, whom, as he freely confessed, he loved because he never knew her; some years it had seemed as if he loved her more than Stephanie, out of self-spite or something more glorious. By the time he had thinned out, staggering dizzily and clutching at his greying head, he rarely mentioned Eve. As for Victoria, hopefully her husband had both known her and prized her over other women; whereas this formerly seventeen-year-old lover of hers was only now getting acquainted with her. What he had begun to learn from re-reading her old letters shamed him: even then she had offered him this knowledge of her, openly and honestly—perhaps because she did not love him, for if she did, would she have been so brave? Or did this conclusion simply indicate how debased his idea of love must be? But then who could be as cruel as Victoria, who when she went away to college liked to calmly, brightly write him about all the boys to whom she opened her legs? As to whether these revelations had hurt him at the time, he had no recollection. After her he had had, among others, a number of prostitute girlfriends, and even when his middleclass sweethearts cheated on him and lied about it, he never felt especially jealous—oh, a little, perhaps. Had Victoria broken him of that habit? He longed to rush off to the cemetery right then; he had many things to ask her. But some of love's most delicious business takes place behind the beloved's back—for instance, remembering her. There were times that long ago summer when he got to see Victoria for an hour—and then, while he was with her, he loved her so much that he wished they were already apart, so he could begin to remember her sayings and smiles; if he stayed with her too long, he might forget one or two of them. (Which ones *hadn't* he forgotten by now?) Smelling the insides of the envelopes, and sometimes peering inside them just in case there might be something still undiscovered which his dead girl had sent him, he chewed pain pills. He would have liked to ask Luke's advice: Next time he went to the cemetery, should he, so to speak, go deeper? At seventeen he had a male friend to whom he related every-thing, while Victoria must have had some other seventeen-year-old girl, or perhaps her younger sister, to whom she confided this or that about *him*—or had she truly been so strong, or isolated, that she kept him to herself? He wished to describe to Luke what it was like to see Victoria welling up out of her grave like a swarm of fireflies; sometimes her skull grinned at him like a stone lantern before the flesh seethed mistily and milkily over it. Knowing that the dead could come back was one of the great experiences of his life; he yearned to tell Luke all about it. But presumably Luke, being dead, already knew. Anyhow, shouldn't he have used the green potion to bring Luke back, instead of putting Victoria first? No; Luke would not have wanted to return; that would have been unkind. Then why wasn't it unkind to resurrect Victoria? Well, she was confined to her grave; it wasn't as if he had kidnapped her out of oblivion and imprisoned her like a pretty goldfish! Then where was Luke? What if he too were trapped? At least his ashes were scattered in the mountains. And Luke had assured him, he had insisted and promised (although how could he know?) that there was no postmortem consciousness; did that mean that Luke was safe from being one with the old man whose marble head gazed sternly out of the niche in his family skeletons' landmark?

Victoria, or at least her circumstances, might have intrigued Luke. If nothing else, Luke would have listened to him kindly and patiently. His grief for Luke was as deep as a bullfrog's voice in a sweltering swamp whose summer evening smell of sunburned live oaks now begins to ooze away at the edges, for fingers of coolness are oozing out of the muck; now the light softens from gold to white, and dusk dances on the triggerhairs of grasses.

(I try to keep my life at arm's length and just look at it, Luke once said. I haven't done a lot of things I wanted to do or should have done, but I don't pretend I have.)

Remembering when he and Luke were young and went hiking in the mountains together, he lay down, chewing more pain pills; the bottle was nearly empty. After that he might have been dreaming. Opening the middle drawer of his father's desk, he saw the dead moon in the black sky. He loved the sight. How often, if ever, did Luna duplicate herself? Wearily he crept to the window and found another moon there. Then he was sick to his stomach. Once that ended, he lay down on top of his unmade bed and closed his eyes. He saw the moon again. This time it appeared to be falling up toward the blue earth.

38

When he met Mr. Murmuracki again, he realized that he had lately been perceiving everyone else as if through glass, distant and muted. Only this old man did he see true.

He knew enough not to inquire about moonflowers. He said: I'd like to go to the moon.

Well, said Mr. Murmuracki, for that you don't need me. You need—

Excuse me, but I can't seem to find anyone else.

Ah. How much time did you say you had left?

I'd guess three months. But how can I know? My stomach hurts—

And why is it exactly that you thought I might be able to help you?

I bought my moonflowers from you.

Yes, I remember, but how does that signify?

I'd like to go to the moon because—

Yes. Why exactly would you wish to travel to the moon, especially in your condition?

If I could just see what's going on up there right now—

That's different. We do have a channel, to communicate with our suppliers. You'd be satisfied to observe it from the viewing room?

Have you been to the moon?

Oh, I've never missed a day of work. I'm much like your late father in that respect . . .

You knew him?

A fine man. One of the best.

Could I see him?

He's gone.

Where did he go?

Where you're going.

Will I see him then?

He's considerably farther away than the moon.

Oh.

Now, as I mentioned, we do have a viewing room. Whom would you like to see?

Victoria.

Of course. A pretty name, isn't it?

Yes—

You have very good taste, if I may say so, to feel as you do toward that lovely young woman. In her life she was, how shall I say, unappreciated—

But she—

Yes, yes, that's right. This way. Now, when you open the door, it will seem quite dark. Close the door behind you and wait for your eyes to adjust. Remember also that from here to the moon is a good light-second or two, as we both know from our college days. Just take your time. I'll be in my office up front.

Thank you, Mr. Murmuracki.

Within seconds he had become one of the elect who comprehend that the moonglare is caused by a certain pearlescent cloud-lid pressed tight over the Mountains of the Moon, whose fragile purple teeth and angles become black by contrast with this painful cloud and with the steep white bow of snow beneath; something about these entities makes for an awful and dangerous dazzlement.

Isaac was sitting alone and moody by the shore of a high cold lunar lake whose surface happened to be, in horrible contrast to Isaac himself, alive with earth-tides; he was picking moonflowers and dissecting them into nothing, ignoring Victoria, who hovered seductively at his shoulder, festively clad in her flesh; the breeze kept whipping her long blonde hair in Isaac's face; sometimes a strand of it flicked into his eyesocket, and then without looking up he brushed it away with his wristbone, meanwhile ruining more and more moonflowers, whose petals flew up like fireflies toward the lunar mountains. The roar of the lake-waves against the dun and cinder-dark moon rocks was so loud that whatever those two might have been saying to each other, if anything, could not be overheard; but presently Victoria began to ascend away, and as she cast one look over her shoulder, my neighbor who watched discovered her face sparkling with tears. Isaac never looked up. Pitying her, this sad watcher, whom both of them had rejected, leaped up to call to her; he thought merely to console her; *he* wasn't selfishly desirous! At this, Isaac gangled himself upright, a tall skeleton no longer in possession of all his metacarpii (no doubt he rambled hard here on the moon), turned round, waved and grinned at his former friend, who waved back neutrally, neither disliking nor blaming him but disinclined to be won over and re-abandoned (when he was young, he, like Isaac, had tried his best to make everyone love him, until failures taught him how to strengthen himself with the magic spell called *no*); whereas Victoria, flitting and hesitating, finally alit upon the water, at arm's length from the shore, wiped her eyes upon her fairskinned arm, and said: Hi.

Hello, he said. I was just—

I don't want to talk about it.

All right, he replied, mildly sorry that he could not help her. A moon-bird with a pearlescent beak rushed silently between them. He turned away as she began to strip, and Isaac swung the telescopic barrels of his eyesockets toward her. He left them then, approving of them both, wondering whether Victoria would succeed, in which case Isaac would certainly break her much-broken heart: all in a day's work.

Far away across the milky moon-lake, which widened and narrowed like a woman's body, there was a rolling rise of moon-alders and laval outcroppings, and beyond this grew many blackish-purple mountains of fantastic height, sharpness and fragility, like broken glass upended on narrow points, flaring out into double-bladed wings, and then terminating (where the clouds revealed it) in needles; and because he was on the moon, and therefore already partially of this place, he found himself able to speed as rapidly as a water-bird, if not as gracefully as his Victoria, over the waves and then up that lava-pored tree-swale and up a very steep yet rounded canyon to a glacier amphitheater amidst the highest peaks; and there, as he had suspected and hoped, walked Luke, quite steadily and still undecomposed; while at his shoulder now flew that naughty, never satisfied Victoria, so good at making herself and others unhappy, whispering, giggling, touching herself; just then she was a skeleton and did not seem to know it—or perhaps she had tried everything else and hoped to tempt Luke through this more advanced state of undress. Luke trudged on. Why didn't he fly like her? Well, he hated to cut corners. When she swirled down before him, seeking to clasp him in her bony arms, he pushed her away. She fell to the ground, perhaps on purpose, then leaped into the sky and streaked upward, leaving behind her a glowing trail of anger which condensed and fell to the snow as reddish-brown crystals which in turn sublimed into nothing.

Giving Luke awhile to recover from the irritation which Victoria must have caused, he presently overtook him, and called out. Luke uttered his name with cheerful surprise, and so he flew down to visit his friend.

How are you getting on?

Oh, not bad, said Luke. There's a million-year hike I plan to take, if I last that long, which I probably won't. What's going on?

Happily and excitedly he began to tell Luke all about himself. So often in their lives he had talked and talked, and Luke had patiently listened. At intervals Luke had called upon him in distress; but mostly it had gone the other way, and it was still like that. He requested advice, and Luke said: Well. I can tell you what I'd try not to do, not that I'm very good at doing what I'm supposed to. You've collected a lot of stuff in your life. Why not get rid of it?

I'm trying to phase it out in stages, he replied.

I'd say that's very sane.

How are you feeling? he asked again.

I have good days and bad days. Being dead isn't all that great, but it's not terrible. I try to appreciate what I can, like the earthlight on the snow over there. Where I'm heading there should be much more snow.

Then the wind began to hiss, whistle and shriek. Luke lowered his head, walking steadily into it.

The watcher hovered behind, as he had in life, perceiving now how steep and shadowed was that place between the rock-teeth. Here was he and there was Luke, with death snow-shadowed between them. There was Luke, going up into the blue sky of space. When the dying man departed the viewing room, he felt slightly ashamed that on his face Mr. Murmuracki could probably discern that loneliness, as if he had sat too long by the shore of that writhing lunar lake, while everyone else went about the business of living or being dead; he thought: Oh, no, to be lonely *forever*! and a high cold wind rushed down from the Mountains of the Moon.

39

When he found the little red book in which he had written his morbid poems, he felt revulsion and resistance. It was this object which caused Victoria to leave him. His final lover's letter to her was enclosed, carefully and viciously marked up by her. Setting it aside, he took the red book back into his hand. Pulling open the cover with his thumb was more unpleasant than it would have been to lever the slab off Victoria's grave. But he did it. The poems, of course, were very badly written, in an unhappy seventeen-year-old's unaware imitation of the Decadent manner. But it was worse than that—what had he been *thinking*? They described someone who looked like her, yet was dead and rotten. It was bad enough that he had written them; but why had he sent them to her? What had he supposed would happen? Now for a moment he excavated the grave of that pallid, skinny seventeen-year-old boy who had understood neither Victoria nor himself. The boy stared up at him. A beetle crawled across his spectacles. His desire to ask the boy anything fell away, for the boy knew nothing. He replaced the slab. Asking himself how he would feel if some woman wrote him poems like these, he answered: I would think her very sick. I would fear she meant me harm. I would get away from her—far away, forever.

> *There is a desert in your blonde-white hair*
>   *With lions sleeping in the sun.*
> *Your eyes are wide and deadly pools*
>   *That draw me under blue.*
> *Pretty bone-teeth glisten savagely*
>   *Veiled by the currents of salt-red blood, your lips.*
> *You watch me always, hungry;*
>   *Your smile is a tomb-sweet lure,*

and on and on, more gruesomely. He felt ashamed; he longed to destroy the book; it was horrible to him. But he had kept it so long, even if without looking at it.

It made him sick.

Now through the night-whipped trees I passed with silent tread, creeping through lakes of moldering leaves, filling myself with unspeakable etheric fires, whatever those might have been. *The grave awaited me,* just as it now truly did, when he went to visit the true Victoria, who was truly dead but not hungry for him and whose smile was no lure to anything horrid, or was it? *The grave awaited me. The sweet-smelling soil about it was repulsively soft, and I tunneled through it with loathsome ease,* no doubt because that summer he had been reading the stories of H. P. Lovecraft. *Through the soil, a green-white hand, blotched and cold, came groping in search of me.*

Now he remembered that for years he had suffered from nightmares of this sort, nearly every night. He must have been very ill.— Why hadn't he killed himself?— Women had saved him, one after the other.— Hadn't he hoped that Victoria would do the same?— She could have said: I'm waiting for you, and here's my hand; my hand's alive, and my smile's alive and I love you.— But who could have loved something like him? *Eagerly I scraped the earth aside . . .*

Flushing, he closed up the hateful book again and reinterred it in the envelope. He could bear no more of it today.

He chewed his pain pills. Then he lay down and waited for the syrupy narcosis to comfort him. He dreaded to meet Victoria's eyes.

He felt better. There was the envelope, lying on his father's desk. He longed to put it away in the drawer. Rising, he picked it up—and the red book broke through the brittle yellow edge.— Shame, shame, as pitiless as sunlit revelations of grime in spiderwebs!

40

Coasting over the lunar surface at a very low altitude seemed to improve his spirits, so he now did that nearly every afternoon, especially when it was too hot and bright to visit the cemetery: browsing across the moon map as if he were peering through leaf-holes into the light, loving the white shinings on the black and silver moon, searching for a certain un-known thing in craters on the night side of the terminator, while weary old Earth arose as jewel-green as a new oak gall. Whatever else was writ-ten in that red book of poems might if he were sufficiently fortunate be equally valuable. Consider the eighteen-year-old patient of Jung's who, having been preyed upon by her brother and a schoolmate, discovered that sorrow is a labyrinth of translucent glass, whose passageways gain in weariness and bewilderment by half-showing the adjacent ones, which may be their own turnings, and which continue even deeper into that green dimness of sea-glass; until she began to believe herself to live upon the moon, where all women and children had to be sequestered underground, in icy fissures in the grey moon-bone, in order to protect them from a certain vampire. Volunteering to kill this monster, she caused herself to be placed on a high tower in the middle of Lacus Mortis (45° N 27° E); and they gave her a knife before departing with protestations of admiring grief. Thus far in this tale, although it has been wisely called *the last receiver,* being the entity which communicates all rays and causes from the superiors to the inferiors, the moon seems no very pleasant place. But even before the dark predator came winging over the half-lit lunar canyons, she must have been lubricated by what prudes call curiosity; for she kept begging herself: Let me just find out what he looks like beneath his lush-feathered wings. *Afterward* I'll stab him.— Muffling his face in his black shoulders, contracting into his own long spine, like a folding umbrella, the vampire now settled silently onto the parapet, close enough for her to touch his elbow had she wished to. With extreme caution and delicacy, like a fisherman setting up his lures, he reopened his wings. His features attracted her far more than she could have imagined. Drinking in the sight of his beautiful eyes, she hesitated a trifle too long, so that he seized her and bore her off, through the dark grooves and into a pretense of brightness: green and orange swales, the roar of water dulling down the piping screams of death. What happened between them next Jung never reports, but I think it fair to suppose that there was kissing, sucking and tickling involved, for she soon considered the moon so lovely a place that she struggled against being cured and was thereby condemned to dwell on earth. What if the skinny, shy seventeen-year-old boy who loved Victoria had been of the moon-woman's type? In other words, what if he could have dug down through the cemetery loam and liked it? In his spirit he dreamed over his moon map. It also soothed him to sit at his father's desk and gaze at Victoria's letters, even without reading them; today he wasn't well enough for that. From the middle of the heap he withdrew a new one and placed it in an old pouch that he had, in the expectation of carrying it with him around his neck for several weeks, his joy in it slowly swelling—not at all the desperate joy which had inflamed him like longing when he was seventeen and she calmly slipped another note into his hand in the high school corridor, then rushed off to her chemistry class, or when a new letter lay in a slim white envelope in his family's mailbox, bearing a thirteen-cent Liberty Bell stamp or that butterfly or an American eagle gripping sheaves and arrows in its claws—and always her sweet name or initials greeted him on the return address, which she very occasionally typed but mostly wrote in her very slightly forward-slanting script: a new treasure to add to his hoard; ever so carefully he slit open the lefthand edge of the envelope. How his heart used to pound at seventeen! The pleasure he felt nowadays was a fiery, peaty spirit which had aged in an oak cask until its sting had grown capable of clothing itself with knowing discretion within sweet smoothness. Who could say which was better? Good boy, he drank whichever was available. Sometimes his loving pleasure in Victoria brought water to his tired old eyes.

It was a hot and utterly silent day. Smiling, he took the envelope in his fingers as gently as he could and kissed it. Just as some Saxons used to place a coin in a corpse's mouth, to keep it content with gnawing on that, so he clutched this letter of hers, and withheld other aspirations; but then the aspirations came anyway. Desire rose up gently within him, and he gave himself over, pulling the letter out of the envelope with much the same smoothness which had once informed his unhooking of women's brassieres (although in Victoria's case, his first, he had made several attempts, too flustered and ignorant to understand how the hooks went, until she finally undid them for him; and he kissed her delicious armpits). Now the letter lay undressed but still folded in his hands. He coaxed the folds apart. She loved him; she loved him; now she would say she loved him.

I can't really assure you that I didn't undergo some "psychic rape."

As usual, he didn't remember this at all.

I can assure you that I am doing much better. The first four days afterward were confusing. No desire to eat or sleep; everything about me deteriorated. I am now, in fact, a slim size 7, a considerable difference as you probably are aware. I was not affected for life. For me, at this time, I am just happy enough to go on living. No more emotional roulette. This will hurt you, because a part of our relationship was and is caught up in this spinning wheel. This is not saying we don't have a relationship, or that I'm negating what we previously established. Sometimes it seems that what we established isn't valid anymore. Maybe it still is but it will take time to know. I won't tell you what happened.

He had no idea how worried about her and selfishly anxious for himself this communication would have made him at seventeen. Now he felt sorry for her, of course. And as to whether or not they had engaged in a "relationship," how could that even be a question? This seventeen-year-old girl might assert herself all she chose, rejecting and raging, alluring and denying, but this old man, almost too old now to be her father, would not stop loving her; nor could she desist from loving him, for she was dead.

Of course she did right to leave me; all I cared about was keeping her; I couldn't have understood her, or been a patient, trustworthy pivot for her flitterings.

But I wonder how unhappy she was? I have been, I believe, very happy, although that may not have been apparent to others. (No, perhaps I have not been happy.)

At least she had her children. Very possibly she felt happy in those middle years when we didn't know each other.

And what happened to her, to make her write that letter? Should I ask next time I go to the cemetery? She might tell me now, but it must be a bad memory for her—best to leave it buried in the ground.

She did not love me. *She did not love me.*

But one thing I've definitely learned in life is recognizing when I'm not wanted. Victoria still wanted me then, even if only to gratify herself by keeping me dangling.— No, that's unfair; neither one of us knew ourselves, much less each other. And she wants me now—doesn't she?

Thus he overcame his disgust, grief and dread at his red book of poems, over and over again.

Whenever night came and he dressed to go to the cemetery, shaving himself carefully for Victoria, he felt anxious, excited, half-tempted to stay home, with an undercurrent of cocky desire just as when he used to set out to find prostitutes—but he was *old* now; all these feelings were weakened down a significant portion of the way to extinction; he didn't actually care so much; if he undressed again and lay down in bed it wouldn't be the end of the world—and something scary might happen at the cemetery; somebody or something might hurt him—but the prospect of sweetness awaited him, and he was so lonely; he yearned for an adventure; and even if something bad happened, how much could he lose? And if he stayed home, what did *that* make him? Once upon a time he used to go downtown to seek out women in the streets; and before that he used to get dressed for this date or that date; usually the girl ruled him strange long before the end of the movie; within ten minutes he knew she wished to escape him; it was to avoid that misery that he had hired or inveigled promiscuous women, who like him would settle for the satisfaction of the moment; so perhaps the same impulse now drove him to haunt a ghost-woman in the cemetery, who again would probably not be so choosy as to reject him. Something dark blue like an oil slick over black water slowly flashed between gravestones, hunching its dark shoulders; perhaps it was a lunar vampire, or one of Victoria's new friends (if she had any), or some animal. He decided not to mention it to her. He likewise declined to bring up the red notebook.

Victoria was waiting, sunning herself beneath the moon. He rolled out the blue-and-yellow blanket she had wished for, and she smiled. Her fingers were as white as her teeth.

He asked what it had been like for her on the first occasion when he called her out of her grave, and she hesitated, then said: I didn't know what to say; I was so excited about talking to you . . .

His heart began stupidly pounding; he grew nauseous. He said: Victoria, how do you feel about me now?

She quietly replied: I need to love someone, and so I've fixed on you.

Testily he cried out: Why didn't you love me when we were seventeen? You were my first; you know that. I still don't even know if I was yours; well, actually, of course that means I wasn't. I was so faithful and loyal to you; I worshipped everything you did—

Pityingly, the ghost stroked his hair. It felt like the slightest breeze; he could have been imagining it. She said: Well, I did love you sometimes.

I'm sorry; please forgive me; I . . . And it's just as you wrote me at the end: We would have left each other anyway.

But I do admit, he continued, laughing a little even as he rubbed his eyes, that even though I know that, I don't completely believe it. If you hadn't left me—

And if I hadn't died.

Yes.

And if you weren't going to die . . .

They both burst out laughing.

A moment later, he saw tears in her eyes. At once he took it upon himself to comfort her, soothing her, kissing the moonlight where her mouth should have been and promising to do whatever she might wish.

41

Later that night he was sitting beside Victoria on her grave when panting rapid footfalls came up the gravel walkway by the lake. Any instant, whoever it was would come into sight. Victoria vanished silently into the earth. Rising, he withdrew behind Mr. Arthur J. Bishop's tomb, leaning on the arms of the cross. The sounds got louder. He felt dread. Presently a chalky-featured man appeared, glaring straight ahead, running and gasping with his arms straight out. The man did not appear to see him. He kept still. The man ran out of sight. For a time he could hear him. Then, just as he had returned to Victoria's grave and was on the verge of trying to coax her out of the ground, he heard those evil, frantic footfalls coming back. This time, thanks to the configuration of the cemetery, he could see the man sooner and more clearly. His face was, in fact, horrible. As he approached, he seemed to scent something in the direction of Victoria's grave, for he glared up toward the two of them, showing his teeth. As yet he was some distance away, and not until he reached the stairs in the hill would he become a definite threat; all the same, it seemed best to retreat over the crest and down, which he did. Now he was temporarily out of both sight and hearing of that ghoul, who might, however, come loping around the hill in some unexpected direction, and so, hating to show his back to the darkness but not daring not to, he ran (in his own estimation) nearly as well as a young man, his heart tolling in his breastbone, and finally reached the hole in the fence and the single wan streetlight. He unlocked his car, entered it, started it, turned on the headlights and saw through that hole in the fence the hateful greenish-white face staring at him. Surely it would not come out here. There was a sharp cramp in his chest. He locked all four doors. Then he backed the car a good long block, until the hole could not be seen. He longed to live; he knew that now. So he had better organize himself. His way lay past the hole. He shifted the car into drive, then pressed the gas pedal halfway down, speeding back alongside the cemetery fence—and in the middle of the street stood that emissary from MANSIONS ABOVE, waiting for him with its mouth open and its arms stretched wide. He knew that if he slowed down in order to return to reverse, he would be in the thing's power. So he floored the gas, aimed right at the monster and ran it down. It panted and scrabbled even then; its long greenish hands broke off both windshield wipers, trying to pull itself up onto the hood. He kept driving, not knowing what else to do, whipping the steering wheel left and right until he had dislodged the thing. It was still squirming on the tarmac when he sped away, rounding three corners before he began to feel safe, slowing then to legal speed just before he passed the eternally shining sign, flickering with mosquitoes and midges, of Hal Murmuracki's Chapel of Flowers.

He got home, locked the door, and lay down gasping like his enemy, feeling nauseous in his belly and pained in his chest, with death's vomit choked through him like gravel, from deep in his guts right up to his tonsils.

He dreamed that the moon was a round bright pool in the sky which now rapidly increased in size until he fell into it, and he was swimming. Now he perceived that only part of it was bright. There he swam in mellow gold. But the instant he reached the shaded zone, the water or whatever it was became almost stingingly cold, and he seemed to see something like a low stone statue grinning at him.

Awakening into another stifling, nauseous dawn, he opened his eyes and saw the pale blue sky, which was in itself sufficient reason to have lived. He might have slept four hours. His mind was clear. It pleased him to be nearly alone in this new day. Perhaps death might be as fine as this, if he could only guard himself against the thing with the greenish-white face. He had not been afraid until now. Rising, he went out into the day.

42

Something was moving; something was watching him from behind his back yard hedge. It could have been a woman, or a man. Then he saw it no more. Why should it have been Victoria—and not something worse? Then he seemed to hear something creeping through the branches— well, actually, this is merely a metaphor for what he felt whenever he forced himself to withdraw another of her envelopes from the pile on his father's desk. Where was that greenish-white entity which seemed so desperately to desire him? What if it came inside the house?

After that, he began to dread reading her letters almost as much as he did returning to the cemetery at night knowing that that dead thing called Victoria awaited him; he had imagined that it was he who summoned her with the green liquid, but now he knew all too well that she whispered and murmured to him from under the ground and inside his desk until he grew helpless to employ the green liquid on anybody but her, or *it*, or whatever Victoria should rightfully be called. In truth there was probably no Victoria at all, but a nameless entity of unwholesome intentions.

Discovering the thirteen-cent checkerspot butterfly stamp and the thirteen-cent flower-and-mountain Colorado stamp, he felt fondness again and kissed the envelope. But he hesitated to learn whatever the thing in the cemetery might be whispering to him. No, she wasn't that, not then! Although this was a lengthy letter, she had denied herself the typewriter, in order to think before she said anything; this was sweet, not to mention reassuring. *Your longer, rational letter and the shorter, emotional one are in my mind. Your emotional one was what I thought I needed until my mother brought me down hard.* How could he imagine anything monstrous about his Victoria? *I'm tired of struggling between my guilt (and desire to be realistic) and my urgent inclinations toward fantasy and the unusual. I'm tired of thinking about our relationship. It is clear to me that it will have to be limited to paper for quite awhile; I don't even know about Christmas. If we survive all that I imagine we'll have our garden and breakfast in bed. That leaves us absolutely nowhere. Except that I'm rather emotionally involved and in love.*

That made him love her. In the dark, hoping that she was there and also that she was not, in which case he could run away with honor, he forced himself to enter the hole in the fence, then tiptoed through the forest of tombstones, sick with fear. All was silent.

Bending over her headstone, *Victoria, Victoria!* he called in a whisper.

Nobody answered.

Suddenly something pale rushed toward him from the black thicket of crosses farther up the hill. He leaped to his feet, deathly sick with terror. It was the ghoul; he would die now.

Boo! giggled Victoria. The pale blur had been her hair.

You scared me, he muttered.

Victoria laughed and danced. Her insides resembled black water silvered with thistledown.

What was that thing that chased me the other night?

It didn't chase you. You ran. That was how it noticed you.

Then it tried to attack me. I'm afraid I didn't kill it.

Of course you didn't. It's dead, just like me.

Whose side are you on?

Listen, she said suddenly in a low voice. I think it knows you're here. You'd better go now. I'll get in big trouble for telling you this.

I'll come back tomorrow.

Go now. I love you. *Run.*

He rushed away as quickly and quietly as he could, not knowing whether he was escaping the thing or approaching it, and fearing above all that it would be waiting for him at the hole in the fence—which of course it was. He saw it before it saw him. He burst out in a sweat. But he was relieved not to have it behind him. Very quietly he backed away, knowing enough not to return to Victoria's grave; sooner or later it would hunt for him there. First what he longed for was an open mausoleum to hide in. Then even a culvert would have done. Ducking down toward the lake, he soon spied the thing on the low hill he had vacated. Just as during an adagio movement a conductor's upside-down shadow clings to the podium's edge, its arms endlessly parting from and rejoining its sides with the same steady determination as a long-distance swimmer's, so this new graveyard thing stroked the belly of the night, glowing like a jellyfish. Fortunately it did not seem capable of scent-tracking like a hound. His heart pounding, he sidled behind a monument, then quickly ascended a narrow lane between tall dark tombs, realizing that he was nearly or already lost and therefore seeking the landmark of a tall narrow cross-crowned mausoleum which at a certain moment of each cloudless summer evening became as blonde as Victoria's hair; perhaps its cross would catch the moonlight a bit. But it didn't, and soon he was definitively lost among the graves. His belly ached. Around him the earth sweated out loathsomeness. He pressed himself in a shallow doorway and stood until the moon declined. It was the hour when frogs screech like birds.

In the almost-darkness, beneath the silhouetted trees, a glowing oval rose up, elongated and began to expand. He realized that it was coming toward him, and from its sureness it must see him. He had never before felt such terror. He tried to console himself by thinking: I ought to treasure this feeling. That means I still want to live, and therefore my life is valuable—in which case I should get away from *her*. Oh, please let me live, let me escape that thing—

Then Victoria's ghost rose up before him and said: You can go. It's all right now. Please; I'm tired—

Thank you, he said a little stiffly. How was he supposed to feel toward her? As he strode back to the hole in the fence, he realized that he didn't even care anymore whether the ghoul was there, perhaps merely because he believed that it would be gone, as indeed it was.

He slept until late in the morning. When he returned to the cemetery late in the afternoon, his belly sore from vomiting, a lawnmower was wandering through the hollow, which had formerly been a pleasant nineteenth-century pond where bereaved families picnicked. Here they were trimming the grass nearly to the roots, doubtless for the sake of hygiene. He saw the caretakers working around Victoria's grave. The grass had been torn up as if by some large animal.

He walked away, returning at night through the hole in the fence.

Don't ask me anything, she said.

Then he finally remembered that the caretakers must have removed the blanket he'd given her.

43

He did ask her, that time and the next; he pointed out, very reasonably in his own judgment, that since he came all this way to visit her, with his health not being of the best, it was only right that she inform him how much danger he might be in.

Well, I've already told you one secret thing, which isn't to say I gushed with confidentialities.

And you won't tell me anything more?

I don't want to be part of this.

Then I'd say you hold me pretty cheaply, he said, and maybe I won't come again. I have to say, Victoria, I feel disgusted . . .

Are the leaves back by now?

Can't you see them?

You know I can't! What is it you *want* of me? Why is everybody so demanding? All I want to do is be alone.

Then be alone; I'll go—

No. Listen. Promise to keep another secret.

I promise.

All right. I made him understand. Do you believe me?

Sure.

He stays under the lake. Go down there and—but he's not to know I told you.

Won't he figure it out?

He doesn't exactly think.

I'm afraid.

So am I, she said.— I'll hold your hand.

Will it hurt me?

I asked him not to.

What happens if we don't go?

He'll come here every night until he corners you. We'd better go now.

Why are *you* afraid, Victoria?

Please . . . I said I love you. Isn't that enough?

Elongating toward him in an ecstasy of avarice, the foul thing simpered expressionlessly. It sprang; he could hardly bear the horror. Sniffing him all over like a dog (its own odor almost unendurably foul), it drooled, dribbled and moaned. It afflicted him as relentlessly as a stench. When it got to his belly, it began to whine eagerly. Then it grunted. It sprang a few paces backward, then studied him, grinning. Its eyes reminded him of blue light-shards in black water. Victoria released his hand.

44

Shimmering like spiderwebs in a thick elderberry bush at dusk, the ghosts whined quarrelsome round and round their graves, much as Canada geese in autumn overcircle black swamp water, searching for what we do not know. No doubt he had imagined them. Victoria must know them all. He wished to ask what it was like underground, but this appeared to be another of her private secrets. Come to think of it, perhaps she didn't know anything. Why was she here and not on the moon? If he inquired as to the whereabouts and identity of the husband of this Mrs. Emilia Woodruff, on whose grave he and Victoria sometimes sat, would he be answered? If not, would Victoria's whims be to blame, or something else? During this last summer, wondering anything had become so considerable an effort that he felt guilty doing it and not doing it. There had been much sweetness in his relationship with Victoria; he had lived for her, and become better as a result, but now he could not tell whether the wrongness lay in her or him or both of them. When she had shut him out before, that felt different; he had been courting her. Perhaps even then he might have felt desperate and jealous when she kept something from him, but probably not; jealousy had never been his favorite vice. Nowadays what could be interpreted as a pattern of rejection still wounded him, coming from her; but being excluded from any particular thing left him indifferent. He was no crackshot astronomer, to map out her orbital period. Often he already seemed to be remembering both this summer and the other from some rainy, windy country. The whining of the ghosts, or insects, or whatever they were, made him look up from himself. Not seeing anybody else, not even Victoria, who had told him that tonight she wished to play by herself, he set out to find the green-faced thing again. After all, it was his dog.

Just as in the swamp he frequented he sometimes observed ripples starting and stopping in one place, then a darkness rising in the green water, a fin or narrow turtle-head showing itself before falling again, bubbling whitely as it vanished within its ripples, so it came from under the lake.

This time he felt more revulsion than fear. It somehow struck him that the thing was intelligent as well as sensitive, although he could not have defined its awareness or capacities. It grinned and grinned. He forced himself to stroke its head.

45

Victoria's blonde hair glared luridly against Mr. Arthur J. Bishop's black granite tombstone; she was sitting against it, running her left hand through her hair. She said: Tell me what it's like where you go, in the day.

Well, until I got sick I used to spend too much time at home. Now I can't even recall exactly what I did there. I lie down a lot now, of course, but when I'm not feeling too bad I try to go out. There are some reeds in the swamp down the road, and I love their jade-green color. Sometimes I think nothing's as beautiful as the silver-blue slime they grow from—

Except for me, of course.

That's right. Do you miss the sun?

The sun is horrible, she said quickly. Sometimes when I'm down in the ground, even as far as I can go, I feel it picking at me, rotting me and making everything worse. When my children and my husband all needed me at the same time, or— Anyhow, this is much more annoying than that. But there's not much I can do about it.

I love the sun.

Well, you're still alive. I suppose I did, too.

When I remember you, I think of summer. It seems as if it was always summer when we—

That's because we were only involved for one summer.

It was longer than that!

No it wasn't; my letters afterward didn't count. But what else do you do with your days? Why don't you have another womanfriend?

She died.

Did you love each other?

Very much.

Why did you call me up instead of her?

I don't know.

What was she like?

You know, Victoria, it would be one thing if you cared to tell me about your family, not that I'm even so interested except that I'd like to know everything about you, while you—

Let's not fight.

Speaking of daytime, is there somewhere you'd like me to go where you can't, so I could come and tell you about it? For instance, I—

No.

Whatever you say.

But do tell me more about your friend Luke. What did he look like?

You know what he—

Before he died, silly.

When he was young, he was an extremely handsome man. After his first tumor he aged quickly. Unlike me, he was never fat. He had brown hair and greenish-blue eyes with twenty-ten vision. He was very strong, with great endurance, and he used to be a mountain climber. He took care of himself in more ways than I did, so it's strange that he went first.

I wonder if he would have liked me?

I saw you with him.

What do you mean?

In the viewing room—

What do you mean?

Anyhow . . .

Maybe I would have made it worth his while.

No doubt. You have your charms.

Too bad you were never handsome. I might have stayed with you then, or at least stayed with you longer.

I hope you got what you wanted with your other men.

Did I hurt you just now?

Not at all. I've had harder lovers than you. But you haven't answered me. Did you get what you wanted?

Mostly. But it didn't mean as much to me as it should have. Maybe you were better off.

You think I got less?

You didn't get me!

Yes I did.

I'll bet you don't even remember me! I'll test you. What size was I?

Seven.

That was just for awhile, after a certain thing happened. I guess I have to give you half-marks. You did try, I admit. I don't know how I felt about that.

I loved you so much.

Why?

You were my first. Isn't that the best reason?

I demand that you destroy all my letters.

Why should I? What will you do in return?

I'll tell you bright new stories and sing you all the ghost songs I know. Ha, ha! I actually don't know any ghost songs.

Then tell me a story.

And you'll destroy my letters?

Not yet. But—

Here's your story: When I was seventeen, I used to wish for a big brass bed with someone in it to watch me combing my hair. And it had to be a brass bed that wouldn't squeak! I was always very particular.

This is your bed, Victoria. I'll sit here and watch you comb your hair whenever you like.

Well, I'm not seventeen now. Now I'd rather make friends with the sun again, which I actually can't. I like what you said about the reeds in the marsh. Are there many flowers?

It's too late in the season.

I wish I could stay up all day, see the sun and dance on my grave.

Will you dance with me now?

Did you ever learn how?

Not really, but I could try.

You were the worst dancer of any of them. Not only did you try to get too intimate, but you never learned my timing. That's why I only let you dance with me once.

I must be worse now. Old men with stomach cancer aren't known for their fancy moves.

Never mind. I wish my grave had a porch that we could eat dinner on.

You and me?

Yes.

It makes me happy that you would say that.

Well, don't get spoiled or I'll be bitchy again. I quite enjoy being bitchy.

And you're my favorite dead bitch both spoiled and decayed.

What do you like for dinner these days?

Nothing now. Before I had cancer, I used to sauté catfish with whatever green vegetables were in season. I had a girlfriend who taught me how to cook fish.

Was she good in bed?

Excellent.

As good as me?

I don't know.

It used to make me sad, the way I could wrap men around my little finger. I knew exactly what to do to drive them crazy. The only thing I didn't know was how to feel it.

Then I'm sorry for you, Victoria. I always felt it.

Well, we're both beyond that now, aren't we? It's nice to just be domestic.

Next time I'll bring two paper plates so we can eat together. I'll pretend to eat a little something to be companionable, and I'll set fire to your portion, so it can be a burnt offering, and you can hover over the smoke.

That sounds like fun! Will you burn incense to me? Then I'll perform a snake dance.

With or without clothes?

Whatever you like, darling.

You know what I like.

Of course I do. You're no different from the others.

46

Once upon a time in that swamp he liked to visit, a lost black crayfish on the path, seeing his approach, extended its pincers in what he presumed to be a terrified threat. The ghoul's attitude of menace now struck him as nearly as ludicrously innocuous as that. Nearly every night it rushed toward him, burying its snout in his belly. He thought: This is how it must have been for Victoria when I came to her, back when we were seventeen.

But when he was all alone at home, he frequently imagined that the thing would come bursting through the front door. Then he would hear it rushing up the stairs. He lay in bed watching the bedroom door and knowing that in an instant it would fly open and the ghoul would come leaping at him with its mouth already wide open to bite. Wishing to domesticate not only the thing itself but also his dread of it, he reminded himself that it was, so it seemed, his future. Perhaps he would learn to be fond of it, and then it would take him to laugh with the fat green people who lay on their backs beneath the ground, rolling from side to side and kicking like infants.

It was August. Behind the well-known headstones lurked other strange old beings which were actually familiar; by September, should he live that long, he might be able to make pets of them also. Each time he vomited, he felt freer. He no longer opened the hospital's invoices or returned the doctor's automated calls. He often lay on his back all day, imagining that he was thinking, and never lonely, thanks to the pain. He assured himself: Although I now belong to death, I can nonetheless own my death, just as I can own my memories of Victoria no matter who she was or is. And when I do take possession of and perhaps even love my death, then the other death which once corrupted me when I was seventeen, seeping out in my shyness and hideous poems, will be tamed, like this ghoul.— In point of fact, learning about himself had become ever more sinister; but since he was dying he lacked any obligation to continue this education.

In one of those lengthening nights when his belly was pregnant with foulness the ghost rose tall and narrow in the twilight, like an egret's neck, and said: When we were seventeen and my mother started reading your letters, I felt like a little girl who had her hands slapped. I knew that once I got away from her I would never want to come back.

Well, has she caught up with you yet?

She's looking for me, but I'm still hiding. We're both losing strength—

I can't understand the rules here.

You're making progress—

It's not very pleasant, is it?

I'm not brilliant, but I have so many friends even here. In the 1950s I could have been called the typical *golden girl.* Jane's temper, Mary's psychological problems, Cornelia's issues with her mother, they get to be too much sometimes, but they're all so self-centered that they don't listen to each other, and so I'd feel useless if I didn't listen. And there's someone else here who needs me. It embarrasses me to say so; he's passionate, and the things he says—

Who is it?

Your friend Isaac.

He smiled at that; he would have laughed but then his stomach would have hurt.

Does that offend you? she demanded. He said things to me that I wish you would have . . .

Which things? he asked, wearily pitying her.

If I told you, it wouldn't be the same.

Things I should have said when?

When you were seventeen, of course. You don't count now.

But I didn't count then, either.

Your interpretation disturbed me at the time.

My interpretation of what? I—

Listen: I had sex with you not for some quest or even curiosity but because I enjoyed it, I really did! It was just the right place and the right time. I didn't expect to find anything in what I did with you. I would have done it again if the opportunity arose. Actually I wouldn't have, you know—not with you. You were too . . . But I certainly did it with others.

I know, Victoria. And do you remember them all?

Actually I didn't sleep with as many people as you, so . . .

For an instant he could have been her age and coming closer, trembling with excitement, kissing her hard round breasts. Then he said: Victoria, I forget some things. It was awhile ago—

Of course you remember. Don't you love me? Aren't we seventeen?

Sure.

I'll skip over the first part. From there on, your analysis is fairly correct. It's a sad way to see me, though. I don't see myself that way. I see myself as one shallow but interesting person in a slump, rotting away until she gets up enough nerve or disgust to rouse herself.

And go where?

Smiling slowly at him, knowing that he would be captivated, she replied: To the moon, of course!

You're teasing me.

Maybe I am.

She parted her lips, and her pallid arms went up around his head like wind-whipped branches. When he sought to kiss her, he seemed to taste the cool breath of the ground.

47

So that was his last summer, summer vines growing as eagerly down into the sunlight as a certain seventeen-year-old poet had once imagined himself digging up his dead Victoria, while the lives of people he no longer knew streamed away through the evening, and his tumor blossomed with its own claim to life; he lacked the right to cut it short, lacking, indeed, much to live for, because Victoria had loved him only superficially and Luke was dead. Now he was entirely alone, in a world of water over muck and half-closed flowers, half-closed flowers of sorrow. Turning away from the evening sun to seek something for which he had no definition, some gleam in the blackish-green water between reeds, he cried out to himself: What did Luke teach me? Maybe he can save me. He . . .

But he used to tell Luke: You're my best friend.— And Luke did not answer.

That mattered, but not sufficiently to ruin anything. Once he accustomed himself to the fact that Luke was his best friend but he was not, or not necessarily, Luke's, he found the situation much easier than he had adoring the flittery Victoria when he was seventeen. For after all, Luke had steadily, loyally loved him. When his girlfriend Beatrice left him, Luke phoned every day, his love reaching like sunflowers. And perhaps Luke had known how to live, more than he had, or differently, or something.— Was Luke happy?— Not especially. So perhaps my life was not a failure, either. But what if it was? What would Luke say?

Luke was brave; he went away.

Isn't Victoria brave, then? Or *can't* she go away?

Returning to Mr. Murmuracki, he said: I'd like to visit Luke, if that's possible.

Of course. He's in the viewing room.

He asked himself: How could Luke have left me, when he was my best friend? But I wasn't his, or at least he would never say so, and therefore I . . .— Tears rushed down his cheeks, because when Luke was still alive he had not told him enough how much he loved him. More than Victoria, and . . . The touch of his fingers against each other astonished him; he wasn't yet dead! What should he be doing with the time? . . . Luke's greatest failure as a friend was that he had nearly always said no. And his greatest failure to Luke was . . . Well, who was *he*, but a wispy ghost like Victoria, good for nothing but mist?

Do you remember the way, sir?

I think so.

Then go the other way. It'll be your second left. By the way, Luke was a good man like your father. Take your time. I'll be in my office.

The door opened by itself. The viewing room was darker than any moon crater. How he loved the sweet loneliness of the moon! As soon as he had seated himself, the velvet curtain rose. Through the ground glass he saw a rock-maze on a steel-blue plain of moonsand—which of course was not to say that the cemetery's configuration could be overlaid upon some moon landscape. Now he seemed to be floating down a soft grey slope which shone with white boulders; he must be passing across the terminator. The moon was as rich as Victoria's shoulders when she was seventeen and eighteen and thirty-six and a rotting ghost. The moon was lovely-black like the shadow side of a boulder.

He saw snow along the razor-ridges of a desert range, all grey and ocher-grey down the canyon-outlined mountain-triangles in that mid-day glare, and then along the sandy basin rose a narrow snout of red earth-monster, still for so long that it might not have been alive, concealing everything above its neck in a sprawl of honeycolored sandstone mounds. Luke and Raymond had gone that way, over the monster's neck; and Raymond returned alone.

While he awaited them he felt that he could see time whole, as a rock with marvelous cracks. Every cleavage became a pattern or rune. It seemed to him that because the present travelled continually with him, it never ended, perhaps not even at death. This moment was ineradicable; therefore, so was he. It appeared that his present could never extinguish. Whether or not that was so, it scarcely mattered to him, although he did not know why it did not.

If anyone clambered up the moon-beast's snout, it disguised itself by means of simple immensity, so that its scaly wrinkles become ravines, its deep folds canyons, its bristly pores chalky-green squiggles of saltbush. The lid of its cunningly shut eye was nothing but sand. One tramped like a fly across its rocky brow.

Upon a rock, another fly, a black one, busily drummed with all six legs, then gripped with two and kicked with two, like an apprentice swimmer holding onto the side of the pool, and finally rushed loudly away.

By late afternoon, the long chocolate-red beast was purplish-black: nearly as dark as the crow which flew over, and the lake-line was now dull and inconspicuous; the western mountains were reddish-purple, their crests, snow and triangles alike all going shades of blue; and suddenly time began again.

Then it came twilight, the time of desert colors. Raymond, as calm as if he were in his apron, with his magnifying goggles pulled down into place as he bent over the grinding wheel (every woodenheaded gouge in its place, flat edge up, the many pliers claws-up against the window), arrived and said: He stepped off the path.

Well, he wanted to go.

Raymond nodded. He was half retired, slowing down; soon he too would die.

They told Stephanie that Luke fell.

Now the moon-beast was below him, the lunar surface sweeping eternally toward and behind him, and the complete blackness of a white-rimmed crater passed beneath him, while far off to his left he saw a spaceship like a golden firefly hovering on its tail not very high above the violet-grey plain. Here came another crater; he remembered the smooth dark dimple in the moon of Victoria's belly when she was seventeen. Thus all the moon lands, cold and white.

His father once bought him a set of compact binoculars, laughing with delight at the clarity of the lenses. The middle-aged son, who had never been able to see well or far, dully thanked him for the gift. He was grateful, but feared that his father had wasted money, for how could the son's useless eyes ever be worthy? He nearly felt as if he had cheated his father. From time to time, and more so after his father's death, he packed them along on his journeys, but frequently forgot to look through them. When he did remember to raise them to his tired eyes, he was not always certain what to zoom in on. It was always good to focus on a deer or a bear, of course; and at times they were capable of inciting in him the same pleasure he felt in handling a certain knurled chisel of Raymond's. When he left them at home, he felt regretful, even guilty; how could he be so inconsiderate of his father?

(The reason that he had declined to use the witch's green potion to bring back his father was this: He might bore his father. Surely his father was better off without him.)

There came a time when he returned the binoculars to one of the pigeonholes of his father's desk, and left them there. Perhaps he was already getting sick by then. One night he dreamed that he took up the binoculars again and looked through them, only to discover that they were two grave-wells, except that one lens showed nothing but dirt and darkness while the other revealed, far down the black shaft, a silver sprinkling of stars.

If there could be a place where one desired nothing, by virtue either of eternally shining joy or of nothingness itself, then it must be (so he supposed) a place where one would no longer learn anything, and therefore evidently a place choked with dirt and darkness if not with distracting light; anything without an end to it sounded nauseating. In which of the two wells would it lie? And where would Victoria be? Although she never seemed to blame him for calling her up, and nearly every night told him some new tale of the quotidian, prairie dog life of the cemetery's inhabitants, what if this spiderweb of other consciousnesses in which she seemed to exist were no more than the plausibly burrowing roots of one of those half-minute dreams which as we awake quickly grow down back into the past, so that for awhile we imagine that we dreamed for many hours? And why would she never tell him whether she had come from the dirt or the dark sky?

Now here in Mr. Murmuracki's viewing room he seemed to see farther and better than he ever had—perhaps nearly as well as Luke once did. But Luke did not come.

All the same, he knew that Luke had loved him and was loyal.

He remembered Luke saying: What I want is to be free. I don't want freedom from anything. I want freedom *for everything.*

At that time Luke was sitting in the kitchen, with a tear running down his face, because he was dying, and perhaps because he and Stephanie were not getting along.

48

When my neighbor awoke, he looked once more within the envelope which said *amusing enclosures* and *Inside are pictures!!!!!,* and there behind the picture of her at the zoo was a new photograph of her which he had never before seen; she was nude and smiling at him, and she was a beautiful old woman. Her wrinkled white breasts hung down uncut by any surgeon, and her blonde hair had gone greyer than his. She stood stretching her hands to him. Her body was the white trunk of a flowering tree, growing out over its reflection in the brown-green water stained by the rainbow of mud-spirits beneath.

49

It was so humid in the light that he could barely breathe. As soon as he strode into the shade, he realized without comprehending it that *the evening went on forever.*

However that might have been, no summer goes on forever; and only a very few more nights swam by, like water-birds uplifting their lovely heads, until two culminations arose—one in regard to Victoria, of course, and the other having reference to his sickness. He passed some days in bed, terrified of being alone with his death; he would rather have been attacked by the ghoul-thing than lie in his bed; but he would rather have died alone than to return to the corporation which called itself his hospital; very early one morning the disease momentarily opened its claws, permitting him to dress and drive out behind the cemetery. First the fear lifted, then the sadness; no matter that neither would keep away from him long. Two blocks past the stoplight he pulled over, got out and leaned across the hood, vomiting easily and almost pleasantly, freeing himself. Then he returned to the driver's seat, feeling not much weaker, and drove on, ignoring the cramp in his chest. There was a silver sheet of mist on the brown fields. Victoria must be sleeping by now. The upper edge of the mist kept rising up like spray, the mist itself creeping ever thicker and whiter beneath the orange sun, and now he passed Mr. Murmuracki's establishment, following the stripe of white mist beneath the grey trees, the rising widening silver mane of mist. When he reached the edge of the swamp and parked, the lower half of the sun's vermilion disk was darkened but not concealed by the mist. The air stung his nostrils. The reeds were silvered with dew, and a spiderweb cut with painful distinctness through the dawn fog. He strolled down into the murky dark, spiderwebs fingering his face, but already it was not dark anymore, the sun a ball of spiderwebs in the mist, the sparkling sunglow low through the dark trees. Here lay the long straight shadow of an oak tree across its own fallen leaves, which now glowed ever more red and coppery, as if they were metals heated from underground. The curlicues of oak leaves' edges grew more definitive as the light increased, and he thought about Victoria, not that his thoughts converged on any conclusion—rather the opposite; for just as when the sun makes ray-shadows in widening diagonals down through the mist, bluish-dark and whitish-grey, thus his so-called thoughts spread out across the world, doubtless accomplishing deeds of inestimable value. All the summer's cattail-down had now given way to spiderwebs. He began to feel unwell again. The line of shadow remained more than halfway up the reed-wall, but the sun was rising rapidly, so that tiny white droplets on the reeds suddenly came to life, as the sweat on Victoria's face once did when he was kissing her passionately; and the many little fingers of certain oak leaves were already bleeding; soon those leaves would fall. A thick plinth of gold-lit grass rose up around the base of an oak from a plain of flattened grass which was still silvered by shadow and dew, and on that tree was a single gall, rosy in the light. The day looked to be as lovely as the slough's scum, which was turquoise-green yet peculiarly reminded him of Victoria's moist young skin, because the way it bore those flame-tongues of brighter yellow-green light where the morning sun reached it created an impression of resilient firmness. Around him rose the water-metal songs of birds. He pressed on as if he were going somewhere, emerging into the wet warm golden grass which was horizoned by the shadow of the railroad embankment, two spiderweb-suns glowing in midair, pallid insects and thistle-motes flitting across them like microplanetoids, the geese calling overhead, the sun comforting his tired neck.

Now he could never get enough of gazing down into the dark water, with its greenbladed stalks paling as they went deeper. He peered and studied as earnestly as if one could truly understand the difference between water and air, which one needed to comprehend in order to determine where the downgrowing reflections of reeds might truly be, if they were anywhere. He thought to spend hours, perhaps the rest of his life, watching these water-pictures, which lived more active lives than their tangible upward-growing shadows, for as the water trembled, or a fish-moon arose in their mist, they altered as their doubles could not.

Perhaps it was in this place beneath the flocks of crying geese that he should have sought Victoria all along, rather than in her grave; for wasn't it merely the rotting part of her in the latter place, and isn't a ghost necessarily unclean by being chained to its carrion? A ghost, perhaps, might claim otherwise; but in any event, here amidst the paling reeds seemed as close as he could ever get to the lost bright part of her, which if it had been anything like his (not that he knew) must have died long before the rest.

He felt very ill now. When he breathed, the stinging air seemed to ripple around his nostrils, as if he were lying on the bottom of one of those sloughs where the sky puddled across the ground like mercury, and dark water were streaming across his face as he gazed upward, never to know who or what might be lying in any of those blackly bright pools around him.— He said to himself: I need to take stock here, and . . .

Unlike most of his other friends, Luke had always been able to understand the benefit of doing inventory; and when he told Luke that he had discovered this or that thing or act which he could sell, Luke approved, understanding the meaning of labor. If Luke were here now, and preferably still possessed of his superb vision, which had deserted him in his early fifties, then some of this might get categorized and even saved—for instance, these young cattails lying down together, their necks broken, their heads heavy with dew. Luke would have known what to do. In this Raymond had resembled him, for what could be more organized than the many shelves around Raymond's shop, and all his many cabinets, some with pull-out metal basins to catch shavings, wax dust and loose diamonds, and Raymond's various lamps, his footrest drill, the chisels all in place? Once he had been alone at Raymond's, the grinding wheel slowing down from a whir into a wheeze, and there had been silence, and before that, when he was seventeen, he was kissing Victoria, kissing her so greedily and gratefully; don't let the grinding wheel slow down. So what would Luke have said? He would have pretended to say something else, disguising his advice as valueless. Shivering, either with fever or with emotion, he thought about his best friend's death, and then Victoria's, although it was not as if he thought, much less had "learned," anything in particular about them, the dark little swallows rising on either side of him, the breeze refreshing yet somehow also hurting him, chilling his fevered face, his chest aching, a single monarch butterfly hanging on the tip of a reed, opening and closing its wings, jittering its antenna while the reed swayed in the breeze; and slowly, finally the insect expanded its wings. He thought about Victoria, his thoughts of her like dark swallows speeding away, the day resolving into reed-fingered sky-pools as his fever increased, and he glided over the grass. A fish snapped in the water. He sought to cool himself by touching a reed, whose chill stung his fingers and made him shiver without relieving him from burning. A half-torn formation of swallows swayed and twisted in the air until he grew nauseous. Wandering away from them, he forgot his own existence until the muck-perfume which he had been smelling since daybreak inexplicably called attention to itself, and he found the sun now high in a dark oak like a pure white gall. A dewdrop on a leaf twinkled whitely and vibrated. Sun-shards whitely cut the darknesses of various other leaves, while others were backlit entirely or in part, and many remained silhouetted. He could not understand any of this. Spills of sun-milk on the silver-red shadow-grass further baffled him. He vomited, although no blood came up. To pass here without even knowing why, in the tang of rot, the licorice of anise, as a meadowlark's notes bubbled up through water which was in fact air, this was his reward for having once been seventeen. Luke was right. It was better off to die alone, passing in and out of the sun, and perhaps when it happened he would even be grateful. All of his experiences had become lovely reeds around him. Craving the shock of coldness from them, he took up another of Victoria's long unread letters in his hands; he was standing over his father's desk, struggling against another cramp in his belly; now he was lying on the bed, chewing up a handful of pills. Silver lichens and withered berries hung inside his eyelids. Victoria's letter lay across his heart. After awhile the pills began to help him, and his sorrows sped away like morning swallows.

He lay on his back, his limbs as still as certain white bubbles on the black water; and now he allowed himself to remember his last meeting with Victoria.

50

Will you stay up all night talking with me? she had said. I feel so lonely.

I'll try, if my stomach doesn't bother me too much.

Don't bother if you don't want to; I don't care.

I hope you do.

Well, I like the feeling that there's someone here right next to me. That's what I always wanted. It didn't matter who it was. Don't get hurt; I'd rather have you with me right now than almost anyone—

Who would you prefer? Your children?

No, not them. They'd feel too sad here.

Victoria, what would it be like if I came down to you?

I'd hate it; I couldn't stretch out. That's how I always used to feel in college when some man spent too many nights in my bed.

Well, when I die—

I'd *hate* it, I said!

Then what did you get married for?

Oh, I wanted children. And he was right for me—very soulful, more intelligent than you, generous, a little detached—although he later did become jealous, especially when I took up writing you at the end.

He loved you?

They all did, or thought they did.

You must have been good in bed.

I wasn't totally sure about men at first. But after I realized I could fake anything, I did as I pleased. If they'd only known! But they gave me what I wanted and it was pretty easy to give them what they wanted, so I used them and never felt used.

Congratulations.

You never got to find out, but anyhow I was very good at it.

I'm glad, he said wearily. I did find out a little, since you and I—

Were *you* good at it?

Yes. Yes, I think so. I've gotten compliments—

Compliments don't mean anything, Victoria informed him with a smile. They're just something that women do.

Well, maybe some were more sincere than you.

Please, please don't get irritated! We're only chatting—

Were you ever my girlfriend?

Certainly not, the dead woman giggled.

I thought you were . . .

Listen. I keep telling you: Our physical encounters were very limited. I placed very little emphasis on them, but I came to see that you felt differently. You took them in their proper light, not as a game the way I did.

But since I took them in their proper light, then maybe—

I've never cared to feel obligated.

When you talk like that, I can't decide whether I'm alone with you or just alone.

When we were seventeen, I used to think you never got irritated.

Victoria, how old are you?

Seventeen.

51

I'm your past, she said after awhile, but you're almost nothing to me. Why am I saying this? What makes me so cruel? I don't understand myself anymore.

You didn't hurt me; I wish I could help you.

I believe in following my heart, even if it's dead and rotten. Even when I don't understand myself—

What do you mean?

I don't know. I see your tumor shining.

What color is it now?

Green. It's hurting you; you'd better go.

Will you allow me to visit you again?

Thank you for being a gentleman, said Victoria. Yes. I allow you.

Why can't I make you feel better?

Nothing can change me! laughed the lovely seventeen-year-old girl, her tears shining silver in the moonlight.

I don't believe that.

Do you want me to claim you?

Then what?

You just lost your chance. When you were seventeen you would have given yourself to me without any questions.

Victoria, you're such a tease! Do you want me to claim *you*? I offered to dig you up and keep you in a flowerpot. Didn't that happen to somebody's head in the *Decameron*? But he was murdered. Well, so were you—by cancer . . .

I want you to lie down with me.

52

She reached toward him, and he saw moonlight in her eyesockets. He knew that he truly was almost nothing to her, just as had been the case when they were seventeen. All she had ever desired, perhaps, was a partner with whom she could play again at the game of life. So he hesitated. When he began to turn away from her, he felt cold between his shoulderblades, as if something evil might reach for him. But what could harm him now? Moreover, why should her aspirations be judged unworthy merely because he signified little to her? And who had she ever been to him? The girl to whom he had written those morbid poems had certainly not been Victoria, but his own figment. He rose up from her grave. She said nothing, but a cold foul gust blew up around him from behind, stinging and numbing his lips. Now the back of his neck began to tingle as if spiders scurried on it. Perhaps she was angry. What did anything matter? All his memories—of her, Luke, his life and even the moon— resembled midges streaming up out of the sweating grass: at intervals the cloud of them took on certain provisional shapes which might have meant something, whereas the solitary insect which he squashed against his cheek had been so arbitrarily itself that his interpretative apparatus could not distort it into anything. Admitting that his life had been as meaninglessly active as bright green sedges writhing in the river wind impelled him into a consoling valuation of meaninglessness. The women who had passed over him like cool river waves over greenish sand, and certainly Victoria herself, what had they signified—for what did anything, when no life could be seen whole and coherently except by something which outlived it? This thought, self-serving as it might have been, he swallowed like one of his pain pills. Returning to her, he knelt down again, expecting to surrender himself to the mercy of some unclean thing, but there was nobody.

Victoria, Victoria! he whispered.

Slowly then she oozed back out of her grave, her face sparkling with silvery tears. He bent down low to kiss her, and as he approached her face he grew overwhelmed again, as he had at seventeen, by its loveliness, with the long blonde hair flowing over the blurred skull in semblance of a waterfall photographed in a lengthy exposure so that the impression of droplets and foam was retained in a statistical sort of form although there was only white haze; she smiled at him, and her bone-claws reached up through the dirt to rest lightly upon the back of his head as she drew him down to her, her wormy mouth widening until he drowned in her face.

53

Close upon dawn, exhausted, joyful, sad and nauseous, he seated himself on Mrs. Emilia Woodruff's headstone and said: Did you like it?

I found it very satisfying, thank you. But listening to the moon eats me up. Can you hear it?

No.

I shouldn't scorn you for that, but I can't help it. Does that hurt your feelings?

On the other side of Victoria's grave, the ghoul lay on its belly with its arms and legs splayed like a lizard's, and it watched him grinning and breathless. He felt something between pity and affection for the thing; doubtless they would soon become better acquainted. Perhaps it knew where treasure lay (another broken pot with tarnished ovoid coins).

Remembering Victoria's question, he replied: Not anymore.

Then I won't tell you what the moon says.

The ghoul fawned on him, grinning ever more widely until its rotting lips began to split. It smelled even worse than she. He said: Victoria, I'm not feeling good—

Well, you don't have much longer. I'm grateful that you choose to spend so many nights with me.

And after I—

Will you please stay until sunrise?

If you want me to. Do you see that thing over there?

Don't speak of it.

Maybe you don't care . . .

No, I enjoy these conversations, she whispered. But I feel at a loss.

Why?

What you said to me last time, I cherished that, I really did. But I don't know you!

What did I say?

Actually, right now I'm so bored and tired; I wish I could retreat farther down, deep down under the clay. I could . . .

You could what, Victoria? Victoria, is there something you'd like me to do?

Don't come anymore. Now that we've—

All right.

Why did you agree so easily? I wanted you to say—

I won't say it. As you reminded me, I don't have much time left. If you want me to go, I—

I'm sorry; I get cruel when I'm bored.

Then shall I go?

She did not answer.

Smiling wearily at her, as if he were the dead one and she a child exciting herself with grief and anger over an imaginary injury to her favorite doll, he asked: Victoria, why are you that way?

What do you expect? I'm thirty-six going on seventeen.

He began to shiver; he was only feverish. Dawn came.

I don't need anyone very much, she remarked. It's a cold feeling, a feeling where I know I should be crying and I can't.

Victoria, he said, I wish, I wish . . .

Well, goodbye, she said.

Bitterly he rose and turned his back on her. The sun was in his eyes.

54

In his last year, just before he declined to undergo surgery again, Luke had said: Sometimes I want something just because I used to want it. And if I think that through, then I don't have to want it anymore.

He had doubly cheated his witch lover, firstly by not using the green liquid to call her back, and secondly by saving a few drops of it, just in case. Now that he had no use for it, he poured it idly and thoughtlessly upon the earth-eater's grave. This is what he heard:

I can't forget Mama and Papa going away. Dear Jesus, help me forget! Papa had his new top hat on.

They prayed over me and he stood up, and he was leaning on his cane as if he'd turned much older; I was always his favorite. Every time he sobbed in his throat, I thought my heart was beating. What was that hymn they sang? It used to be my favorite. *Carry on the Calvary,* but I disremember the rest. He was holding Cornelia's hand; she was learning how to walk again, after her polio. And Mama had to keep telling Susie not to tease her. I don't know why she didn't just . . . Mama looked just like a black waterfall in her veil. And she turned her face away from me. Then they went walking together down that gravel path; I was hoping that Papa would look back at me, but he never did. He was too sad. The path's gone and so are the trees.

Not a word came from Victoria's grave. That was how it usually was when someone abandoned a lover. She had withdrawn from him absolutely. As for him, he was leaving her alone to be dead forever. When he died he would not see her. His stomach hurt. At the gate of the cemetery he wished to fall to his knees like a seventeen-year-old boy, but thought better of it—for now he felt angry with *her* for leaving him alone with the burden of life. Then he went home and unlocked his desk beneath the setting moon. All was silent. He took her letters in hand. They were very much out of order. The last one said: *So that's the bad news, but I won't die. I'm getting aggressive chemotherapy. I'll lose my hair. I just cut it really short. I'm still blonde. Something will grow back. I'll live because I want to live. I'm doing everything I can to live.*

IX

THE ANSWER

I asked the grave why I must die, and it did not answer.

I asked who or what death was, and it kept silent.

I asked where the dead I loved had gone, and its earthern lips did not open.

I begged for just one reply, to anything, and then its grassy lips began to smile. Moistening itself with its many-wormed tongue, it opened. Too late I realized the answer.

GOODBYE

With a heart full of hope, I look forward to the time when Jehovah God will deliver us from this painful system of things and lead us into an earthly paradise.

The Watchtower magazine, 2012

E*very man,* asserts a German psychotherapist, *passes through a critical age in which he bids farewell to youth and love.* This age begins at death. But I, arrested in my thanatosexual development, unceasingly relive my life, to which I do not care to bid farewell, not yet. I am a young ghost. Throughout this critical age (the deceased psychotherapist resumes), unsatisfied desires haunt us. What haunts me is my longing to breathe.

Because death is eternal, people suppose that it must partake of the infinite, in which case we could hope to enter ever wider if darker voids. In fact, each threshold is meaner than the last.

Throughout my life, but especially toward the end, when my heartbeats grew as slow as the drumbeats which announce a shrine dance, what I liked best of all was to sit behind the crowd of spectators, with my back against a tree as I inhaled the shade. If you have ever drunk in the humid sunshine of Kamakura in early spring, which is flavored, as is a fresh bun by its raisins, by pigtailed girls in white blouses and vermilion kimonos, you will understand me when I say that moments and instants can remain as distinct as the studs on a verdigrised bronze bell even in that languid ocean haze, when life and death resemble the square white sleeves of two shrine dancers slowly intersecting. Soon they would summon me to the dance, striking the gong which is shaped like a crocodile's mouth. Then, perhaps, I might no longer be able to enjoy the flutter of a young woman's eyelids, but I deluded myself that what I lost in colors and forms would be recompensed me in spacious ease, as if I would find myself lolling atop Kamakura's famous cliffs, which are grown with ferns and bamboo. Once upon a time before I died I sat beside a woman I loved, on a shady cliff-ledge marked with many stupas, gazing into the lapis lazuli fog of the sea. She took my hand, and we gazed down upon the waving tops of bamboo, which were russet green, and beyond them our vision flew over the steep low house-tops somewhere between pastel and metallic in their various shades, then lost itself in the pale bay. We slept in the darkness of her hair, and woke among Kamakura's blue hydrangeas, drinking up that summer, each humid green cliff-hill of which was so thick with growth as to resemble a single tree. Sometimes when she rolled her sticky body off of mine in order to drink green tea or make water, I even opened my eyes, faithfully hoping that somewhere within death I might pass into that blue-ceilinged room where seaside Kamakura pants with so many sharp green tongues. I have always wondered whether trees are speaking to me; and whenever they shaded me from the humid heat of Kamakura, nodding over me and glistening in ever so many coruscating greens like the foam from fresh-made powdered tea, I wished to thank them. Well, they shade me now. The huge-toed *nakai* trees bore into my bones. Whether she still lives I cannot say. Wherever she is, we cannot comfort each other.

I progress but slowly in learning how to be breathless underground, my mouth choked with earth, worms and rain-seepage passing through me, my rotting coffin collapsing on me, breaking my ribcage, showering me with earth.

It might be better could I forget our days in Kamakura, which were almost poisonously somnolent. After drinking in her love, each morning I was as a gasping, wilting leaf; a bamboo sapling exhausted by its own weight. Kites called above the treetops. Stroking my face, she wept for pleasure, and when I looked into her soul then I saw the yellow-green veins in a glossy blue-green leaf whose pigment is speckling off, leaving the yellow behind. Whether or not she loved me, she certainly lived me, and I her, I who can live no more. With her I anticipated life and death in Kamakura, both of them in the style of a japonica's roots tied down with moss so sweetly. We roamed the jungled cliffs whose names we did not learn. We lay kissing and gasping in the wet sunlight, hopeful of the time when the sea should darken and the breeze should dance in the cool evening waves.

I look back (or up); I imagine; I change flesh with the living, who through the law of compensation immediately find themselves in my shoes—which, to be sure, are of the finest patent leather, for *it is the custom for the barber to shave the deceased, to powder him, whiten his face and rouge his cheeks and lips, and dress him in a frock coat with patent leather shoes and black trousers, as if going to a ball, may God forbid— this shall not happen to Makso.* My shoes have swelled with moisture. They bulge with dirt and bone. Meanwhile I gallop around in clothes as yet unkissed by worms. Even when alive I showed little talent for living; now I show less, and when people see me they scream.

If only I could persuade the barber to rouge my cheeks! Then I might feel more handsome down here. I want to go to the ball; I'm ready to dance my rotten heart out. There's supposed to be a theater deeper down.

I'm trying to like it here. I know that I'm obliged to. Sometimes the vermin tunnelling through me give me pleasure of a sort, but it would be better if I could give up thinking. I can't breathe; therefore, I won't; I'm going to the ball; goodbye.

AND A POSTSCRIPT

There is a wall of ill, whose gate opens unto an archway formed of giant spiders squatting silently in a long row; and at this passage's far end there is a courtyard in whose center stands a woman barefoot, with dark red lips, who holds a bunch of flowers in her upraised hand. Tongues of white and yellow lace fall like fingers or pagoda-gables down to her ankles. Because she is alive, and I still have life in me, I pray to kiss the mud between her toes.

SOURCES AND NOTES

Since these stories are less ethnographically faithful than any of my *Seven Dreams,* I have not scrupled to operate an Anglo-Saxon charm in Bohemia, or even to alter magical names and terms to suit me. (May I be forgiven by all the demons and angels.) Notwithstanding, the basic laws of magic (sympathy, contagion, etcetera) strike me as psychologically true, so I have tried to respect them.

My Bohemia is an imagined construct. My Trieste and Veracruz both contain some deliberate anachronisms both architectural and otherwise. For instance, I wished to set "Two Kings in Ziñogava" sometime in the colonial period, when slavery was still common in Veracruz. But at this time San Juan de Ulúa was more of a fortress than a prison island. *Tant pis.*

EPIGRAPH

"It is the custom for the barber to shave the deceased . . ."— Pamphlet from the *Despića Kuća,* Muzej Sarajeva, collected in 2011.

TO THE READER

"Wherever there is a rose . . ."— Saadi [Sheikh Musli-Uddin Sa'di Shirazi], *The Rose Garden (Gulistan),* trans. Omar Ali-Shah (Reno, NV: Tractus, 1997; orig. Arabic [?] ed. *ca.* 1260), p. 186 (VII.19).

"There is no means through which those who have been born can escape dying . . ."— Paul Carus, comp. "from ancient records," *The Gospel of Buddha* (London: Studio Editions/Senate, 1995; orig. pub. 1915), p. 211 (slightly "retranslated" by WTV).

ESCAPE

As many of my readers know, the events related in "Escape" derive from a real incident (19 May 1993), whose protagonists were named Bosko Brkić and Admira Ismić. As in "Escape," he was Serb and she was Muslim. However, I have altered many other details. For instance, Bosko's family had long since departed Sarajevo; the couple were living together unmarried. They decided to leave not for the reason I have given but because Bosko had been summoned to report to the police, who of course were incensed against Serbs. I decided to alter their identities and their situation in order to respect the privacy of their surviving relatives. The family members in my account are composites of Sarajevans whom I interviewed, was told about, etcetera. Their relation to Admira and Bosko is entirely imagined.

In this story and in "Listening to the Shells," the various confused and contradictory later accounts by strangers of the couple and their deaths (including "No, no; he was the Muslim and she was the Serbkina," and "Actually, that's just an urban legend") are all verbatim as I heard them in 2007 and 2011. In 2011 a young Sarajevan woman summed up "that story on Vrbanja Most" for me: "He was Orthodox and she was Muslim. Today they are as famous as Romeo and Juliet. Just among the older generation they are popular, not the kids."

My one visit to Sarajevo during the siege (described in a chapter of my long essay *Rising Up and Rising Down*) took place in 1992, roughly half a year before the two young people were killed. Descriptions of the city in "Escape" and "Listening to the Shells" are based in part on my notes from that time and in part on my Sarajevo trip notes from 2007 and 2011.

Given names of characters in these three ex-Yugoslavian stories— People in this region would know which names are typically Serbian, Bosnian or Croatian. Some commonly occur in more than one group, such as Marija, which can be associated with both Serbian and Croatian women. I am informed (although I take it with a grain of salt) that a few names are still more specific; thus Indira might be a Bosnian girl from a mixed marriage or an atheist family.

Meaning of the name "Vrbanja Most"— My friend and translator Tatiana Jovanović writes, first noting that there is no considerable amount of information on this edifice, since "it is not beautiful or historically interesting compared to some other bridges in Sarajevo": "A name of the bridge 'Vrbanja' probably meant a willow grove . . . but some of researchers of the central medieval settlement (in Bosnia and Herzegovina) think that the name refers to [the] undiscovered key of 'Vrhbosne' (literally, the top of Bosnia). It was known also as 'Ćirišinska ćuprija' or 'Ćirišana'—i.e., 'Chirishan Bridge' [which] was a name of a small company that produced glue ("Ćiriša" . . . sounds [like] a Turkish word) . . . Probably, long time ago, in the ancient time, a wooden bridge was in this place, about which we can know because of discovery of some Roman bricks . . . in some fields in Kovačići, Velesići, etcetera. Bašeskija (an author, probably a historian) mentioned it [in] 1793 as a wooden bridge that was erected or renovated by a Jewish merchant. The previous one was destroyed by flood [in] 1791, and because it was needed to have a bridge in the same spot (especially for the Jewish people to go to their cemetery), the Jewish merchant paid for its renovation. It was restored again in [the] 19th c., but today, on the same spot, there is a new bridge made of reinforced concrete which was built after the Second World War."

The Serbian officers with stockings over their faces on the Vrbanja Most (just before the beginning of the siege)— Mentioned in Kerim Lučarević Doctor, *The Battle for Sarajevo: Sentenced to Victory*, trans. Saba Risaluddin and Hasan Rončević (Sarajevo: TCU, 2000), p. 35.

LISTENING TO THE SHELLS

Occurrence in the Orthodox graveyard overlooking Bucá-Potok— Related in Lučarević Doctor, pp. 29–31.

Comparison to my reporting from 1992 in *Rising Up and Rising Down* will show that my protagonist had it better than I did. Although my sojourn on the frontline was terrifyingly educational, if I had it all to do over again, perhaps I would rather spend my evenings at Vesna's, flirting with her and meeting her friends. Too bad there were no such people.

THE LEADER

Epigraph: "There is no life on the earth without the dead in the earth."— Branko Mikasinovich, Dragan Milivojević and Vasa D. Mihailovich, *Introduction to Yugoslav Literature: An Anthology of Fiction and Poetry* (New York: Twayne, 1973), p. 176 (Veljko Petrović, "The Earth," n.d.).

THE TREASURE OF JOVO CIRTOVICH

Epigraph: "I could have been unvanquished . . ."— Croatian Academy of Sciences and Arts, Ivan Supičić, chief ed., *Croatia in the Late Middle Ages and the Renaissance* (vol. 2 of *Croatia and Europe*) (London and Zagreb: Philip Wilson Publishers and Školska Knjiga, 2008), p. 122 (part of grave inscription).

Most descriptions of Trieste in this cluster of stories are based on visits in 1981, 2010 and 2012. Some descriptions of the old city are indebted to illustrations in *Trieste Dall'Emporio al Futuro/vom Emporium in die Zukunft, Dalla Collezione di Stelio e Tity Davia alle foto del nuovo millenio per la rappresentazione della città in un viaggio ideale* (Trieste: La Mongolfiera Libri, 2009).

Names of Serbian settlers in Trieste, events relating to the two Churches of San Spiridione, descriptions of those churches, the Triestine doings of Casanova (which actually occurred in 1772–74), the Triestine Serbs under the Napoleonic occupations, etcetera— After text and illustrations in Giorgio Milossevich, *Trieste: The Church of/ Die Kirche des San Spiridione* (Trieste: Bruno Fachin Editore, 1999). I have altered history rather freely. The real Jovo Cirtovich (or Curtovich) did not arrive in Trieste in 1718 but was born then, in Trebinje, Herzegovina. He first visited Trieste in 1737. According to Milossevich, p. 34, he "was certainly not a refined person. He was a practical man aiming at essential things and full of new ideas and initiatives." Apparently he began his career as a porter. This historical Curtovich would have lived in his warehouse (built in 1777), not on the hill. The Orthodox Church, or, more accurately, the first Church of San Spiridione, was built for both Greeks and Serbs in 1753 (thirty-five years after my Cirtovich's arrival), visited by the Tsar in 1772, left in 1781, by the Greeks, who wished to worship in their own language, decked out with a pair of Muscovite bell towers in 1782, demolished in 1861 to forestall a potential cave-in, and rebuilt somewhat later in the form which I describe here. My invented Cirtovich married in 1754. Tanya, whom like all his children I have invented, would have been born in about 1764, so her father's last voyage took place when she was fifteen. The names of Cirtovich's brothers are all genuine. About his father's death I know nothing. In 1806 Napoleon took ten rich traders hostage until Trieste paid him a vast tax; among them were the historical Jovo Cirtovich and Matteo Lazovich. Those two were incarcerated again in the third French occupation (1809). Cirtovich died that year, aged ninety-one, having outlived his children even though he had married three times. His brother Massimo closed down the family business in 1810.

Some details of Serbian dress and Orthodox tradition are indebted to Prince Lazarovich-Hrebelianovich, with the collaboration of Princess Lazarovich-Hrebelianovich (Eleanor Calhoun), *The Servian People: Their Past Glory and Their Destiny*,

2 vols., ill. (New York: Scribner's, 1910). A few incidents of life (for nineteenth- and early-twentieth-century Montenegrins) under the Turkish occupation (for instance, a man's execution by flogging in the market square) are indebted to Milovan Djilas, *Land Without Justice,* anon. trans. (New York: Harcourt, Brace, 1958).

Serbian attitudes toward the Ottomans, and toward the Battle of Kosovo— Here is a typical (pre-1991) assessment: "During the Turkish occupation, the Serbian Orthodox Church was the only force that kept alive the national spirit and the hope for a better future."— Mikasinovich, Milivojević and Mihailovich, p. 2. Djilas relates some horrible stories of opportunistic murders of their Muslim neighbors by Orthodox Montenegrins, while also relating a few Turkish atrocities. A dark view (and widely subscribed to nowadays) of Serbian historiography is summarized in Branimir Anzulovic, *Heavenly Serbia: From Myth to Genocide* (New York: New York University Press, 1999).

Several Serbo-Croatian (as the language was still called in 1980) folk proverbs are taken, more or less altered for style, from Vasko Popa, comp., *The Golden Apple: A Round of Stories, Songs, Spells, Proverbs and Riddles,* ed. and trans. Andrew Harvey and Anne Pennington (London: Anvil Press Poetry, 2010 repr. of 1980 ed.; orig. Serbo-Croatian ed. 1966), pp. 26, 32, 33, 41, 48, 65, 93.

Various obscure Roman coins, cities and provinces (Cyrrhus, Panemuteichus, Bithynia)— Some of my information comes from A.H.M. Jones, Fellow of All Souls College, *The Cities of the Eastern Roman Provinces* (Oxford: At the Clarendon Press, 1937).

"Take counsel in wine . . ."— Benjamin Franklin, *Writings* (New York: Library of America, 1987), p. 1187 ("Poor Richard's Almanack," 1733–58).

Captain Vasojević— The proud clan of this name was famous for its raids against the Turks.

Decline of Ragusan trade in the early eighteenth century, together with its causes and effects— Information from Francis W. Carter, *Dubrovnik (Ragusa): A Classic City-State* (London and New York: Seminar, 1972), pp. 407–14.

Some descriptions of Dalmatian medieval religious art and architecture and of Glagolitic derive from illustrations and text in that previously cited volume by the Croatian Academy of Sciences and Arts. Other descriptions are based on my notes from visits to Dalmatia in 1980, 1992, 1994, 2011 and 2012.

Archimedes's suppositions— *Great Books of the Western World,* Robert Maynard Hutchins, ed.-in-chief, vol. 11: *Euclid, Archimedes, Appolonius of Perga, Nicomachus,* var. trans. (University of Chicago, Encyclopaedia Britannica, 1975, 20th pr. of 1952 ed.), p. 525 (Archimedes, "The Sand-Reckoner," *bef.* 212 B.C.).

"The Sultan's rivals dragged him down from the sky" in 1730. This ruler, Ahmad III, had regained Morea from Venice in 1718, the year that Cirtovich arrived in Trieste.

Grisogono's Venetian circles for calculating the heights of tides— From 1528. Grisogono was born in Zadar.

Description of traditional Serbian marriage customs— Based on research and translation by Tatiana Jovanović. The source was Emma Stevanović, Faculty of Philosophy; Tatiana says "she was a student probably in a department of Ethnology." Much to my disappointment, Tatiana "omitted the most melodramatic and patriotic parts."

Descriptions of the squid-entity in the dark-glass, of cephalopods generally, and of nautiluses— After photographs, diagrams and textual information in: Richard Ellis, *The Search for the Giant Squid* (New York: Lyons Press, 1998); Jacques-Yves Cousteau and Philippe Diolé, *Octopus and Squid: The Soft Intelligence,* trans. J. F. Bernard (Garden City, NY: Doubleday & Co., 1973); and Peter Douglas Ward, *In Search of Nautilus: Three Centuries of Scientific Adventures in the Deep Pacific to Capture a Prehistoric— Living—Fossil* (New York: Simon and Schuster/A New York Academy of Sciences Book, 1988).

The fumigation of a coffin, and the rite with coins— Lazarovich-Hrebelianovich and Lazarovich-Hrebelianovich, vol. 1, p. 70.

Porphyry's claim about Plotinus— *Great Books of the Western World,* Robert Maynard Hutchins, ed.-in-chief, vol. 17: *Plotinus: The Six Enneads,* trans. Stephen MacKenna and B. S. Page (University of Chicago, Encyclopaedia Britannica, 1952), p. vi (introduction).

Various (but not all) descriptions of Marija Cirtovich and her attributes (affinity for doves, different-sized eyes, etc.)— After illustrations of Mother of God icons in Alfredo Tradigo, *Icons and Saints of the Eastern Orthodox Church,* trans. Stephen Satarelli (Los Angeles: J. Paul Getty Museum, Getty Publications, 2006; orig. Italian ed. 2004).

The papyrus from Heracleopolis, and other such (e.g., the wrapping of the crocodile mummy)— All these are, alas, invented, but some details relating to handwriting, sites of excavation and the like derive from information in E. G. Turner, *Greek Papyri: An Introduction* (London: Oxford at the Clarendon Press, 1968).

Description of the Sphere of Fixed Stars ("that great blue dome of ultramarine")— Based on the ceiling dome of San Spirodione Taumaturgo in Trieste.

Description of "the gloomy latitudes"— After a visit to Patagonia in December 2011.

The magical procedures followed on the island— Abbreviated from Sayed Idries Shah, *The Secret Lore of Magic: Books of the Sorcerers* (New York: Citadel Press, 1958), pp. 25–27 (The Key of Solomon, Son of David).

"The Patriarchs": "There is no resurrection without death."— Actually, Patriarch Gavrilo (1881–1950), as quoted in Anzulovic, p. 14.

The silver likeness of Saint Blasius— Seen by WTV in Ragusa (Dubrovnik).

Description of Mrs. Cirtovich— After a bust by Ruggero Rova (Trieste 1877–1965), *Il Sorriso,* 1910.

The Serbian crosses of black tar— Montague Summers, *The Vampire in Europe* (New Hyde Park, NY: University Books, 1968; orig. ed. 1929?), p. 159.

The lucky man who dies at Easter— Lazarovich-Hrebelianovich and Lazarovich-Hrebelianovich, vol. 1, p. 26.

"Society has no way out of disappointment . . ."— Djilas, p. 257.

THE MADONNA'S FOREHEAD

In some versions of the tale of why she bled, a frustrated player threw a *boca* ball at the Madonna's forehead. In the others, someone threw a stone, not a brick. She was the Madonna delle Grazie, or "Dei Fiori"—by one account the property of the family

Fiori, since she was found in the nineteenth century when someone was digging in the Fioris' garden.

"we may conceive of the masochism merely as a painting . . ."— Wilhelm Stekel, M.D., *Sadism and Masochism: The Psychology of Hatred and Cruelty,* trans. Louise Brink, Ph.D., vol. 1 (New York: Liveright, 1953 repr. of 1929 ed.), p. 210.

Varying opinions regarding the Madonna's forehead— In the end our disagreements solidified into two factions, which assembled themselves in the appropriate cafés. Speaking on behalf of the old men, I want to dig my finger's crook into your collarbone so that you'll believe me when I insist that life was much better when we possessed as many theories as Triestini, and discussion was as many-grooved as the costumes for "Aida" . . .—when we could mumble into our grappas about the Madonna, our mumblings even extending beyond the metaphysical to erotic considerations, so that the rancor with which we contested our interpretations of her spilled blood could, just like our city's yellow, soapy-feeling old marble, dissolve decade by decade in the acidic air. Oh, but human nature's not like that! At my stage of life, all I want is the lovely blue sky with grey cream in it; and however bad it was, the past stays safely past; *that* Trieste's always misty blue and white like a faded travel poster. Until the Romans roofed this territory with their authority, it was contested among Illyrians, Istrians, Celts and others; and after the Romans, first Venice, then Austria and finally Italy got their hands on it. Napoleon was here in 1797, just for the day. But I didn't live through most of that, so it's pleasant to talk about; I never oppose local color; in fact, I'm proud of that blue-and-red fragment of the old Teatro Verdi.— Nowadays it's less complicated. There are only two factions: the light and the darkness. Of course, I forget which is which.

CAT GODDESS

The bright yet pastel-like oil paintings of Leonor Fini celebrate femininity, androgyny, narcissism, surrealism and decadence. Often her women are Klimt-like in their pallid elongations. Aside from her cats, she loved nothing better than a good quarrel; best of all was when she orchestrated a falling-out between two of her friends. In 2009 I visited a postmortem retrospective of this great artist's work at the Museo Revoltella—the perfect venue, I decided, admiring some more Tominzes in gilded oval frames: near-naked young women fiddling with themselves. In the dead Baron's library, the backs of the chairs were carved with twin caryatid-like females who played quite busily with their own breasts. The red velvet cushions reminded me of Leonor Fini's lips. Mostly, of course, I studied Leonor's paintings. Entranced, I expressed my appreciation to the coat check girl. She smiled and said: Can you catch me?— Before I realized who she was, a strangely pallid corseted woman in a lace-sleeved red tunic was running through Trieste, daring me to kiss her. Lace around her throat, lace between her legs; oh, my! Finally she permitted me to grasp her from behind while she leaned against an antique column. As it happened, in those days I was still as handsome as Napoleon used to be back in 1805, so when I asked for a kiss, I hoped for assent, but she said: I'll only make love if you act like a woman.— When I finally agreed, that wary-eyed tease, as magnificently black-clad (in gloves, dress, the whole works) and as regally bored as the Duchess of Aosta, refused to take anything off. Maliciously giggling, she next proposed that I act like a cat. But I did not wish to. Fortunately for my aspirations, the previous night I had caught a ghost-fish, which I was wearing around my neck (for creatures of that sort never stink), so I held it out into the air behind Leonor's ankles, and then, just as I had hoped, three of her ghost-cats crept out of nowhere to bat that spirit-meat between them and finally share a few nibbles. This sight softened my friend, so she led me into an irregularly edged apartment tower whose windows, each of a different shape, were shuttered by concretions of unpainted planks; and in one room we lay down together to fill each other with Trieste, where the afternoon sky is bluer and the trembling bedroom curtains so much whiter that they might as well be silver and gold.

Several descriptions of Leonor Fini's paintings and of photographs of her derive from illustrations in: Museo Revoltella Trieste, *Leonor Fini: L'Italienne de Paris* [exhibition catalogue] (Trieste: 2009), and Peter Webb, *Sphinx: The Life and Art of Leonor Fini* (New York: Vendome Press, n.d.).

A few descriptions of elegant Triestinas are based on photographs in Elvio Guagnini and Italo Zannier, eds., *La Trieste dei Wulz: Volti di una Storia: Fotographie 1860–1980* (Trieste: Alinari, 1989).

The shy little marble girl— Sculpted by Donato Barcaglia, 1871. Now in the Museo Revoltella in Trieste.

The story (which Leonor especially loved) of Maximilian and "La Paloma"— From Webb, p. 10.

The "slim, lovely young wasp-waisted beauty in a black jacket-skirt and black tights who held a whip and sometimes permitted him to feed tidbits to her pet bulldog"— Based on a painting by Giuseppe de Nittis, 1878, *La Signora del Cane (Ritorno dalle Corse)*, which I saw at the Museo Revoltella.

Description of Rijeka— After a visit there in 2009.

The pale man in the photographer's doorway in Prague— After a photograph in Pavel Scheufler, *Fotografiké Album Čech 1839–1914* (Prague?: Odeon, 1989).

Leonor's inability to face the death of her own cats— Webb, p. 207.

Leonor's interest first in cadavers, then in mummies and skeletons— Somewhat after a direct quotation in Webb, p. 11.

"I dislike the deference with which your Rossetti's been treated."— Ibid., p. 71, somewhat altered.

The perfumed cat excrement at Leonor's— After Webb, p. 46, who implies that the story may be apocryphal.

The pale women wading naked in dark water— After Museo Revoltella Trieste, pp. 160–61 (*La Bagnanti*, 1959).

"The men around me are dead . . ."— Altered from Webb, p. 143.

"I prefer cats . . ."— Altered from Webb, p. 25.

"femininity triumphing over a city"— Webb, p. 11 (Leonor is describing her relief of Amazons trampling men).

The "woman not unlike Giovanna, but with still longer, richer hair"— After Museo Revoltella Trieste, p. 125 (*Streghe Amauri*, 1947).

Descriptions of mummies, Sekhmet, Hathor, etcetera— Based on visits to the Museo Egizio di Torino in 2009 and 2012.

THE TRENCH GHOST

Description of the trenches at Redipuglia— After a visit there in May 2012.

"I am not this."— This simple yet profound point is indebted to *I Am That: Talks with Sri Nisargadatta Maharaj,* trans. from the Marathi taperecordings [*sic*] by Maurice Frydman, rev. & ed. Sudhakar S. Dikshit (Durham, NC: Acorn Press, 1973), p. 59: "To know what you are you must first investigate and know what you are not."

Description of the pillboxes at Tungesnes (on the coast west of Stavanger)— After a visit there in September 2011.

"Find what is it that never sleeps and never wakes, and whose pale reflection is our sense of 'I.'"— Sri Nisargadatta Maharaj, p. 12.

"the pinnacle of military deployment approaches the formless."— Ralph D. Sawyer, with Mei-Chün Sawyer, comp. and trans., *The Seven Military Classics of Ancient China* (San Francisco: Westview, 1993), p. 335 ("Questions and Replies between T'ang T'ai-tsung and Li Wei-king" [written in Tang or Sung period], quoting Sun-tzu).

"It is the body that is in danger, not you."— Sri Nisargadatta Maharaj, p. 412.

THE FAITHFUL WIFE

A few details of daily life in preindustrial Bohemia are indebted to information in Sylvia Welner and Kevin Welner, eds., *Small Doses of Arsenic: A Bohemian Woman's Story of Survival* (New York: Hamilton Books / The Rowman & Littlefield Publishing Group, 2005), pp. 4–23, 33–35. [The letter-writer's surname is not given; she is simply introduced as Tonča, writing to her son Jaroslav. Her childhood recollections take place in the early twentieth century; I have assumed that the early-nineteenth-century existence of Michael and Milena's family was no richer than hers.]

Return of female Romanian vampires; tale of Alexander of Pyrgos— Summers, *The Vampire in Europe,* pp. 310, 232.

The Bohemian custom of masking oneself on the way home from a funeral— Ibid., p. 287.

The seventh Mansion of the Moon, called *Alarzach*— Francis Barrett, *A Magus, or Celestial Intelligencer: A Complete System of Occult Philosophy* (Secaucus, NJ: Citadel Press, 1975 pbk. repr. of 1975 ed.; orig. pub. 1801), Book I, p. 154.

The tale of Merit— Her grave-goods and her husband's are on display ("the tomb of Kha") at the Museo Egizio di Torino.

"I have found a woman more bitter than death . . ."— Heinrich Kramer and James Sprenger, *The Malleus Maleficarum,* trans. Rev. Montague R. Summers (New York: Dover, 1971 repr. of 1948 rev. ed; orig. Latin ed. *ca.* 1484), p. 47. (Sentence originally began with "And I have found . . .").

The vampire who first chuckles, then whinnies like a horse— Pëtr Bogatyrëv, *Vampires in the Carpathians: Magical Acts, Rites, and Beliefs in Subcarpathian Rus',* trans. Stephen Reynolds and Patricia A. Krafcik, w/ bio. intro. by Svetlana P. Sorokina (New York: East European Monographs, dist. Columbia University Press, 1998; orig. French ed. 1929), p. 132.

The Dark Man by the water ("he torments people when he finds them by the waterside")— Ibid., p. 133.

The eleventh Mansion of the Moon, called *Azobra*— Barrett, p. 155.

"Some say that vampires have two hearts."— Information from Radu Florescu and Raymond T. McNally, *The Complete Dracula: Two Books in One! Combining "Dracula, a Biography of Vlad the Impaler," and the bestseller "In Search of Dracula"* (Acton, MA: Copley, 1985), p. 95.

Some of the later descriptions of Milena floating in her bath are inspired by Bonnard paintings.

DOROTEJA

What is done with cristallium etcetera— Dr. G. Storms, *Anglo-Saxon Magic* (The Hague: Martinius Nijhoff, Centrale Drukkerij N.V., Nijimegen, 1948), p. 235 (The Holy Drink against elf-tricks). Since I have moved this spell to Bohemia, I changed elves to goblins.

"This is my help against the evil late birth . . ."— Ibid., pp. 196, 199 (Against Miscarriage; original reads "this *as* my help . . .").

Rite of washing in silver-water on New Year's Day— Bogatyrëv, p. 42.

Churchgoing of dead souls on Holy Saturday— Ibid., p. 68.

The dead woman who returned to bite her husband's finger— Ibid., p. 120.

THE JUDGE'S PROMISE

Epigraph: "And finally let the Judge come in . . ."— *The Malleus Maleficarum*, p. 231.

The incident in Neinstade (which supposedly took place in 1603)— Elaborated after Summers, *The Vampire in Europe*, p. 201.

"the ill-fated Bohemian rectangle"— Phrase quoted in Joseph Wechsberg, *Prague, the Mystical City* (New York: Macmillan, 1971), p. 1.

Police work of Frederick the Great and the Police President of Berlin (both actually in the early nineteenth century)— Clive Emsley, *Policing and Its Context 1750–1870* (New York: Schocken Books, 1983), pp. 99–100.

Location of the Golem's corpse and Dr. Faustus's residence— Wechsberg, pp. 5, 38.

Travails of Bohemian linen-weavers— Jaroslav Pánek, Oldřich Tůma et al., *A History of the Czech Lands* (Charles University in Prague: Karolinum Press, 2009), p. 292.

Description of the second medallion of the sun— Information from Shah, pp. 46–47.

"And though it was sore grief to us to hear such things of you, inspector . . ."— Tweaked a trifle from *The Malleus Maleficarum*, pp. 255–56 (formula uttered to a penitent relapsed heretic).

Characteristics of various demons— Shah, pp. 86–88.

Definition of *Abnahaya*— Barrett, p. 156.

The witch's purpose in digging up a dead man's head— Ibid., p. 108.

"The Romanians say that a vampire can go up into the sky . . ."— Information from Summers, *The Vampire in Europe*, p. 306.

The myth of a secret tunnel from Prague's Jewish Ghetto to Jerusalem— Wechsberg, p. 29.

The witch-events of Saint John's Day— Bogatyrëv, p. 76.

"this sort of creature does not give anything for nothing."— Shah, p. 80 (*Grimorium Verum*, oldest known version 1517).

JUNE EIGHTEENTH

Epigraph: "So long as there is an Emperor . . ."— Joan Haslip, *The Crown of Mexico: Maximilian and His Empress Carlota* (New York: Holt, Rhinehart & Winston, 1972 repr. of 1971 English ed.), p. 367.

Various information on Maximilian's life and career was obtained from Haslip, and Jasper Ridley, *Maximilian and Juárez* (New York: Ticknor & Fields, 1992).

Maximilian's aspirations: a castle and garden by the sea— Haslip, p. 113. Some of my descriptions of Miramar are a trifle anachronistic, since the place was merely a "bungalow" when he and Charlotte lived there (Ridley, p. 185).

"Owing to some radical defect in the Mexican character . . ."— R. Lockwood Tower, ed., *A Carolinian Goes to War: The Civil War Narrative of Arthur Middleton Manigault* (Columbia: University of South Carolina Press, 1992 pbk. repr. of 1983 ed.; orig. ms. prob. *bef.* 1868), p. 322 (Appendix II: The Mexican War Service of Arthur Middleton Manigault).

Maximilian's china blue eyes and beautiful teeth— Information from J. J. Kendall, Late Captain H.M. 44th and 6th Regiments, and subsequently in the Service of His late Majesty, the Emperor of Mexico, *Mexico Under Maximilian* (London: T. Cautley Newby, 1871), p. 157. According to a German observer, however, the Emperor's "chief defect is his ugly teeth, which he shows too much as he speaks" (Haslip, p. 235).

"Matters ran on pretty well for the first two years . . ."— Kendall, p. 185.

"No Mexican has such warm feelings for his country and its progress as I."— Charles Allen Smart, *Viva Juárez: A Biography* (New York: J. B. Lippincott, 1963), p. 357 (said in 1865).

Ten-year serfdom for negroes— Ridley calls this "particularly ironic" (p. 216) since Maximilian had just abolished peonage. The new decree was for the convenience of ex-Confederate colonists.

"We see nothing to respect in this country . . ."— Haslip, p. 268.

"If necessary, I can lead an army . . ."— Ibid., p. 302.

Details of Maximilian's last days and execution— Ridley, pp. 262–77, Haslip, pp. 484–98.

"I am here because I would not listen to this woman's advice" and Maximilian's reply— Slightly reworded from Haslip, p. 494.

Curtopassi scissoring away his signature— Thus Haslip. According to Ridley (p. 265), it was Lago.

Descriptions of retablos— After text and illustrations in Elizabeth Netto Calil Zarur and Charles Muir Lovell, eds., *Art and Faith in Mexico: The Nineteenth-Century Retablo Tradition* (Albuquerque: University of New Mexico Press, 2001). The votive caption in my text is invented.

Description of the Holy Child of Atocha— After two illustrations in Zarur and Lovell, pp. 108–9.

"in France it was no longer permissible to be mistaken."— Haslip, p. 196.

The reality of Princess Salm-Salm's seduction attempt, which is reported in several biographies of the Emperor, does not convince Ridley, who asserts (pp. 266–67) that it "sounds like the gossip of an officers' mess."

The various discontents of Charlotte— Haslip proposes (p. 127) that "Maximilian, who was neither very virile nor highly sexed and who was only attracted by the novel and exotic, found that with Charlotte he could no longer function as a man."

"You must stay here for the night . . ."— Haslip, p. 487.

The gardener's daughter in Cuernevaca— Ridley, p. 171. According to Haslip, she was the gardener's wife. Concepción Sedano is said to have given birth to Maximilian's son in August 1866 and died "of grief" the following year. The son might have been a man who was shot as a spy in France during World War I.

The slave-girls of Smyrna— Ridley, p. 50.

Reading material of Miramón and Maximilian— Ridley, pp. 270–71.

First dream: Description of Maximilian's embalmed corpse— After an illustration in Gilbert M. Joseph and Timothy J. Henderson, eds., The Mexico Reader: History, Culture, Politics (Durham, NC: Duke University Press, 2002), p. 268 (letter from Empress Carlota to Empress Eugénie, 1867).

Details of Maximilian's postmortem journey: The Novara, the hearse in Trieste; the marble tomb in Vienna— Gene Smith, Maximilian and Carlota: A Tale of Romance and Tragedy (New York: William Morrow, 1973), pp. 284–85.

"Anything is better than to sit contemplating the sea at Miramar . . ."— Haslip, p. 361.

"Just as when upon first penetrating the Brazilian jungle he nearly shouted for joy . . ."— This sentence is grounded in the following haunting words of Maximilian's, which do indeed refer to the Brazilian jungle (1860): "It was the moment when all we have read in books becomes imbued with life, when the rare insects and butterflies contained in our limited and laboriously formed collections suddenly take wing, when the pygmy growth of our confined glasshouses expand into giant plants and forests, . . . the moment in which the book gains life—the dream reality" (quoted in Haslip, p. 130).

Maximilian's order for two thousand nightingales— Haslip, p. 361.

Second dream (based on the sacrificial incarnation of Tezatlipoca, whose name is also transliterated Teczatlipoca)— J. Eric Thompson, in charge of Central and South American Archaeology, Field Museum, Chicago, Mexico Before Cortez: An Account of the Daily Life, Religion, and Ritual of the Aztecs and Kindred Peoples (New York: Scribner's, 1937), pp. 205–210. The victim was chosen from a pool of idle young men who were kept on reserve for the purpose. His enjoyments lasted for a year; he was not unlike one of our American range cattle, who wander freely under the sky, grazing and copulating until they pay our price (which at least spares them old age). Tezatlipoca's four wives were Flower Goddess, Maize Goddess, Water [Goddess?] and Salt Goddess. On p. 212 the author remarks: "This ceremony signified that those who had had riches and pleasures during their life would in the end come to poverty and pain."

Description of the quetzal-feather headdress— After an illustration in Brian M. Fagan, Kingdoms of Gold, Kingdoms of Jade: The Americas Before Columbus (New York: Thames and Hudson, 1991), p. 12.

"amidst cool night winds"— One meaning of "Tezatlipoca" was "night wind." Another was "youth." He was "associated with human rulership," all three of these details according to Joseph and Henderson, pp. 75–76 (Inga Clendinnen, "The Cost of Courage in Aztec Society").

The obsidian mirror— This was another reified meaning of the name Tezatlipoca, who represented war, darkness and masculinity. The surrogate's death facilitated the potency of other men. Zarur and Lovell, p. 104.

Description of the sacrificial stone basin— After an illustration in Fagan, p. 21.

"Never complain, for it is a sign of weakness."— Ridley, p. 48 (one of Maximilian's twenty-seven principles).

"God bless the Emperor!"— Haslip, p. 498.

Carlota: "One sees red . . ."— Smith, p. 291. [Ellipsis in original between "gay." and "The frontier."]

The incarnation of Teteoinan— Details from Thompson, p. 186.

The incarnation of Ilamatecuhtli— Ibid., p. 191.

"Well, you have your butterflies . . . the age of seventy."— Altered and expanded from Haslip, p. 160.

THE CEMETERY OF THE WORLD

Epigraph: "Woe is me, Llorona! . . ."— Margit Frenk et al., comp. & ed., El Colegio de México, Cancionero Folklórico de México, tomo 2: Coplas del Amor Desdichado y Otras Coplas de Amor, p. 122 (3646, "La Llorona," trans. by WTV).

The two possible origins of the plague— I have invented both of these. However, my description of the old volumes in the Archives of the Ayumiento de Veracruz (from which, thanks to translations by Teresa McFarland, I did garner a few rhetorical flourishes, together with the fact of the conversion of the municipal slaughterhouse into a barracks in 1648) is based on examination of them in January 2011, and in particular on the following: (1) Año 1608–1699, caja 01, vol. 1. (2) Caja 3, año de 1804; libro n 98 tomo 5. [As you can see, the cataloguing is inconsistent.]

Founding of Villarica, and the date of its removal to Veracruz; situation of the garrison, and a couple of other such details— Two Hearts, One Soul: The Correspondence of the Condesa de Galve, 1688–96, ed. & trans. Meredith D. Dodge and Rick Hendricks (Albuquerque: University of New Mexico Press, 1993), p. 159n. In this place we are told that "lack of city walls made the [new] settlement vulnerable to strong north winds," but in Veracruz I was informed that the city was "the cemetery of the world" for at least two centuries in part because of the fetor within its walls, so for this story I chose to follow local knowledge, or legend, and mention walls. Veracruz may or may not have been erected directly over an Indian town. A conquistador who was there locates it "a mile and a half from this fortress-like place called Quiahuitzlan" (Bernal Díaz [del Castillo], The Conquest of New Spain, trans. J. M. Cohen [New York: Penguin, 1963], p. 114).

Visual reckoning method when entering Veracruz Harbor— "In the old days navigators got into Vera Cruz by the picturesque means of steering so that the tower of the Church of San Francisco covered the tower of the cathedral . . . How the vast, shining wealth of Mexico poured into Europe through this port . . . [!]"— Edith O'Shaughnessy [Mrs. Nelson O'Shaughnessy], Diplomatic Days (New York: Harper & Brothers, 1917), p. 12.

The Marqueses del Valle were Cortés's descendants, and for some years they ran the port of Veracruz.

Miscellaneous descriptions of Cempoala, the Casa de Cortés and Veracruz generally, including of the "haunted" houses (which were in fact pointed out to me as such)— From notes taken during that same visit in 2011.

The life and goddess-avatars of Malinche— Information from Anna Lanyon, *Malinche's Conquest* (Crows Nest, Australia: Allen & Unwin, 1999).

Doña Marina's statement that *"she would rather serve her husband and Cortés than anything else in the world"*— Bernal Díaz del Castillo, *The Discovery and Conquest of Mexico 1517–1521,* ed. Genaro García, trans. A. P. Maudslay (New York: Farrar, Straus & Cudahy, 1956), p. 68. This is another translation of the Díaz text cited earlier.

Legends about La Llorona and other ghosts in Veracruz— From stories told to me by taxi drivers, etcetera, in 2011. Here is a fine one: A driver said that once he was driving to Cardel in his taxi and he saw a woman in a white dress standing at the edge of the road. She waved him down and asked him to give her a ride, all the while keeping her face hidden from him. La Llorona was frequently spoken of in these parts. She was said to wear a long white dress. She had long black hair down to her ankles and a horrible horse's head. So the driver drove past the strange woman, who was likewise dressed in white, then made a U-turn in hopes of seeing her from the front. At once she disappeared.— "What would she do if you'd said: *Oh, you're so beautiful!* and kissed her face?"— "The man would die at once," he said, bored. "Did you ever see the ghost of Malinche or Cortés?"— "Not around here."— "What about the old gods?"— "Not in this zone. But up at Cempoala, if you go into the ruins, there's a big circle of stones, and if you stand at the middle of the circle and stare into the sun, the sun god's energy will pour into you and cure all your problems."

The castle— I asked a man about ghosts, and he said: "Oh, yes, La Llorona can be heard in the castle. At three or four in the morning, you can see swings moving in this playground, if no one is there. You can feel them coming out to follow you. There are other presences in other buildings, but the castle is the worst."

Description of La Llorona after Ricardo feeds her the jade bead— After an illustration in Rubén Morante López, *A Guided Tour: Xalapa Museum of Anthropology,* trans. Irene Marquina (Xalapa: Gobierno del Estado de Veracuz de Ignacio de la Llave y Universidad Veracruzana, 2004), p. 147.

The golden parting gifts from La Llorona— Based on real Aztec goldwork on display in the Baluarte. Ordinarily they would have been melted down by the Spaniards, but the galleon sank. An octopus fisherman found them in a wreck, and went to jail for not disclosing them.

TWO KINGS IN ZIÑOGAVA

Epigraph: "But what does the social order do . . . ?"— Jan Potocki, *The Manuscript Found in Saragosa,* trans. Ian Maclean (New York: Penguin Classics, 1996 repr. of 1995 ed.; orig. French ms. *ca.* 1812), p. 517.

Common Spanish reference (*ca.* 1625) to an elegant, white-dressed black woman as a *mosca en leche*, a "fly in milk"— Herman L. Bennett, *Africans in Colonial Mexico: Absolutism, Christianity, and Afro-Creole Consciousness, 1570–1640* (Bloomington: Indiana University Press, 2003), p. 19.

A few details of religious coercion and sacramental fees are taken (perhaps not entirely accurately, since Veracruz is not in the valley of Mexico) from Charles Gibson, *The Aztecs Under Spanish Rule: A History of the Indians of the Valley of Mexico 1519–1810* (Stanford, CA: Stanford University Press, 1964). Some descriptions of masters' and mistresses' cruelty to slaves are derived from period woodcuts reproduced in Benjamin Nuñez, with the assistance of the African Bibliographic Center, *Dictionary of Afro-Latin American Civilization* (Westport, CT: Greenwood Press, 1980).

Description of the aventurine cask— From information in the Condesa de Galve, p. 143. Aventurine was a kind of glass containing scintillating particles.

Description and history of San Juan de Ulúa— After a visit there in 2011, and information from Teresa del Rosario Ceballos y Lizama, *Una visita al pasado de San Juan de Ulúa* [contains abbreviated English trans.] (Veracruz?: self-published?, 2010). For the legends of Chucho el Roto and the Mulata de Córdoba, see p. 69. In English the island's name is often spelled "Ulloa."

"*Mestiza*, goddess of the orient . . ."— Frenk, p. 376 (5182, *estrofa suelta*, trans. by Teresa McFarland and WTV).

Franciscan desire to create a Kingdom of the Gospels in Mexico— Alicia Hernández Chávez, *Mexico: A Brief History*, trans. Andy Klatt (Berkeley: University of California Press, 2006; orig. Spanish-lang. ed. 2000), p. 38.

"Stretch out your arms, *negrita* . . ."— Invented by WTV.

Benito Juárez: "*I know that the rich and the powerful . . .*"— Smart, p. 355 (said in 1865).

The Blue Range in Moquí Province (believed in from end of seventeenth century until the nineteenth)— Luis Weckmann, of the Mexican Academy of History, *The Medieval Heritage of Mexico*, trans. Frances M. López-Morillas (New York: Fordham University Press, 1992), p. 39.

The Amazon of Ziñogava; characteristics of Amazons; claim of the Tarascans— Ibid., pp. 51, 49.

The skeleton hand— A not entirely uncommon Gothic element. For instance, I once read an English tale about a woman who was murdered by a rejected suitor on her wedding night. No one could prove anything against the man; the body had disappeared, and so had he. Her skeleton was found years later; her sister asked that the hand be cut off, in case it could bring about justice. One day the murderer came into the bar where it was displayed (yes, in a velvet-lined glass box, although in this version the velvet was black, not red, which I thought better for a Mexican setting), stared at it in horror, approached the glass box, touched it, and blood appeared on his fingers.

The crocodile "bullfights" of Dorantes de Carranza (*ca.* 1593)— Weckmann, p. 122.

"Much do I care for my María . . ."— Frenk, p. 121 (3636, "*¡Ay!, qué diantre de María,*" trans. by WTV).

The head's magic power— This may not touch your belief, but in 2011 I saw for myself how some pyramidal little tugboat could pull a long, many-smokestacked

Rickmers freighter right past San Juan de Ulúa and out of Veracruz Harbor without seeming effort.

First arrival of Cortés at San Juan de Ulúa— Bernal Díaz, *The Conquest of New Spain*, p. 69. On the next page this conquistador describes the future site of Veracruz as "no level land, nothing but sand-dunes."

Colors and significances of ancient Mexica directions— Zarur and Lovell, pp. 98–99. *"they are dead; they will not live . . ."*— Isaiah 26:14.

Description of the Queen with "her eyes squinted shut like a corpse's"— After an illustration in López, p. 153. "The closed eyes and the open mouth of this female figure indicate that she is dead."

The two fountains of Huasteca and the magic mountain with the petrifying river— Weckmann, pp. 40, 39.

The shrub called *hueloxóchitl*—Lieut. R.W.H. Hardy, R.N., *Travels in the Interior of Mexico, in 1825, 1826, 1827, and 1828* (London: Henry Colburn and Richard Bentley, 1829), p. 533. I have Mexicanized the orthography of Hardy's *huelosóchil*.

"engordar el cochino"— Christoph Rosenmüller, *Patrons, Partisans and Palace Intrigues: The Court Society of Colonial Mexico, 1702–1710* (Calgary, Alberta: University of Calgary Press, 2008), p. 45. This may be an anachronism, since the phrase was current in 1710, but then again perhaps it was in use a half-century earlier; therefore, dear reader, please let me off the hook.

Punishment of concubinage— Weckmann, p. 455.

"Sad is my heart, *negrita . . ."*— Frenk et al, p. 5 (2773a, *"El Siquisirí,"* trans. by Teresa McFarland and WTV).

Former name for San Juan de Ulúa: *Chalchiuhcuecan*— Francisco López de Gómara, *Cortés: The Life of the Conqueror by His Secretary*, trans. and ed. Lesley Byrd Simpson from 1552 ed. (Berkeley: University of California, 1964), p. 54.

THE WHITE-ARMED LADY

Epigraph: "For the white-armed lady . . ."— Snorri Sturluson [attributed; but the true compiler's identity is uncertain], *The Poetic Edda*, trans. Lee M. Hollander, 2nd. ed., rev. (Austin: University of Texas Press, 1962; orig. texts 9th–14th cent.), p. 161 (stanza 7; slightly "retranslated" by WTV).

WHERE YOUR TREASURE IS

Kvitsøy is an island about twenty kilometers northwest of Stavanger.

"Better is the end of a thing than its beginning."— Ecclesiastes 7:8.

"To what shall I compare the kingdom of God? . . ."— Luke 13:20–21.

The flower called *guldå*— Galeopsis speciosa *Leppeblomstfam*.

"I never knew you . . ."—Matthew 7:23

A *valurt*-flower—Symphytum officinale *Rubladfam*.

Rogaland is the district containing Stavanger.

"Do not lay up for yourselves treasures . . ."— Matthew 6:19, 21.

"Somehow Astrid helped her make up the money—in secret of course."— The following verse might apply to Astrid's pre- and postmortem doings: "But when you give alms, do not let your left hand know what your right hand is doing, so that your alms may be in secret; and your Father who sees in secret will reward you."— Matthew 6:3–4.

Bishop Eriksøn— Jørgen Eriksøn, the Bishop of Stavanger in 1571–1604, proved that the Lutherans were as firm against witchcraft as the Catholics. In 1584 Stavanger was the proud originator of the witchcraft law whose provisions eventually put to death about three hundred people in Norway, and we can give the Bishop some of the credit. The victims got hanged, burned or decapitated. In a portrait, the Bishop's immense red moustache bends down over his mouth like the eaves of an old turf house, and his dark little eyes are sad and watchful in his pink moon-face.

"Blessed are those who are persecuted" and *"blessed are the meek"*— Matthew 5:10, 5:5.

THE MEMORY STONE

Epigraph: "Most people say that the bride was rather gloomy . . ."—Diana Whaley, ed., *Sagas of Warrior-Poets* (New York: Penguin Books, p. 136, "The Saga of Gunnlaug Serpent-tongue," trans. Katrina Atwood). In the epigraph I have emended "Serpent-tongue" to "Serpent-Tongue."

The rock with the footprints and ship-carvings actually does lie in the center of Stavanger, and anyone who wishes can stand on it.

The description of the landscape near Valhalla is derived from notes I took around Lillehammer in 2006. I am especially grateful to John Erik Riley for a beautiful driving trip toward Jötunheim.

THE NARROW PASSAGE

Epigraph: ". . . *if foul witch dwell* . . ."— Hollander, p. 239 (stanza 28; slightly "retranslated" by WTV).

As mentioned in the source-notes to "Where Your Treasure Is," Rogaland is the district containing Stavanger.

According to this city's Sjøfartsmuseum, Stavanger was one of the main embarkation ports for American-bound emigrants from 1825 to 1870. And here my celestial captain requires me to insert an endorsement for *Den Norske Amerikalinje, eneste norske passagerlinje til New-York.* This ship made seven hundred and seventy transoceanic voyages, the last one being in 1963.

The discussion of emigration in my story (including the tale of the *Amelia*) relies considerably on information in Egil Harald Grude's pamphlet *From Vågen to America: The Migrant Exodus 1825–1930,* trans. Susan Tyrrel (Stavanger: Dept. Maritime Museum in cooperation with Stavanger Vesta Insurance Co., printed by Rostrup Grafiske A.S., September 1986). According to Eli N. Aga and Hans Eyvind Næss, *From Runes to Rigs: Cultural History Treasures of the Stavanger Region,* trans. Rolf E. Gooderham (Stavanger?: Kulturkonsult, 2001), the herring arrived suddenly in 1808

(p. 88); then (p. 94) "the influx of herring became more and more unreliable after 1850, and the fishery came to an end in the 1870s."

Some of my descriptions of Stavanger and the herring factories at this period are derived from illustrations (and, occasionally, text) in Susan Tyrell, *Once Upon a Town* (Stavanger: Dreyer Bok, 1979), pp. 26, 32–37, 75. Nowadays Stavanger is blessed with night-water twitching with reflected window-lights, and rain clouds hang nearly blue over the great oil ships, whose bridges glow more brightly than anything, while far-away ivory-yellow windows call across the black water.

Saint Mary's and Haakon's church— These are at Asvaldsnes (a visit for which I thank Mr. Eirik Bø), and here I first heard of that Doomsday legend.

Hjelmeland and Suldal are two contiguous districts to the northeast of Stavanger, which, as I have said, lies in Rogaland. Hjelmeland is closer.

Reverend Johansen's Bible passage: *"Carry me, O LORD . . ."*— Of course this is not a Bible passage at all, but a stanza from the Eddic poem "Skírnismál," which I have clothed in a pseudo-Christian disguise. The original reads: "Thy steed then lend me to lift me o'er weird / ring of flickering flame, / the sword also that swings itself, / if wise he who wields it" (Hollander, p. 67).

Description of the "petroglyphs of long ships"— After a photograph in *Frá haug ok heithni: Tidsskrift for Rogalands Arkeologiske Forening* (Stavanger), nr. 1, 2007, p. 17.

"For the gate is narrow . . ."— Matthew 7:14.

"Glasir stands gold-leaved before Sigtyr's halls."— Snorri Sturluson, *Edda,* trans. Anthony Faulkes (London: J. M. Dent & Sons / Everyman, 1992 repr. of 1987 ed.), p. 96 (my "retranslation" of a line quoted in isolation from *Skaldskaparmal*). The title may be unclear, so let me note that this book is not in the Elder or Poetic Edda, which I cite as "Hollander," but the Younger or Prose Edda, written *ca.* 1220–30. "Sygtyr" is one of Odin's many names.

The maneuvers of King Rörek— Olaf Sagas, pp. 196–97.

"If you, Kristina, and you, Øistein, do not yet hate each other . . ."—Cf. Luke 14:26.

Description of the pond behind the Domkirke— *Frá haug ok heithni,* nr. 1, 2004, p. 7 (Bodil Wolf Johnsen, *Byparken—En Historisk Oversikt,* landscape painting from 1852).

THE QUEEN'S GRAVE

Epigraph: "But how is that future diminished . . ."— Saint Augustine, *Confessions,* trans. E. B. Pusey, D.D. (London: Dent/Everyman's Library, 1962; orig. Latin text *bef.* 430 A.D.), p. 274.

Description of the queen's grave and its environs— After a visit in 2011 (thanks to the lovely Marit Egaas) to Hå Old Rectory, Nærbo, a seaside cemetery of sixty-odd Bronze Age mounds; and to Tinghaud and Krosshaug (near Klepp) where there is in fact an ancient queen's grave.

The first Hnoss, Swegde, postmortem taxes to Frey, etcetera— Snorri Sturluson, *Heimskringla,* Part Two: *Sagas of the Norse Kings,* trans. Samuel Laing, rev. Peter Foote, M.A. (New York: Dutton: Everyman's Library, 1961 rev. of 1844 trans.; orig. text 1220–1235), pp. 7–17. My Queen Hnoss is invented, as is her husband, King Yngvar, not to mention the *Jötunsbok* (I do wish that Frost Giants could write).

Einar Audunsson— My invention.

THE GHOST OF RAINY MOUNTAIN

Rainy Mountain is an invented place, but some of the landscape is indebted to the shrine of Nikko.

THE CAMERA GHOST

The watcher on the side— For readers who might not be familiar with Japanese Noh plays, the "watcher on the side," the *waki,* is the one to whom the story (usually one of suffering as a result of an undying attachment) is narrated. Several other Noh references appear in "The Camera Ghost." These would require much explication here, none of which is needed (I hope) to parse the story. A résumé of Noh characters and situations may be found in my book *Kissing the Mask.*

My camera's eye— It was certainly strict in its fashion, neither blinking away an annoying telephone wire nor softening anything sad with a tactful tear. But because it was so uncompromising, it taught me how to see more carefully, so that unwanted telephone wires became fewer over the years.

"Was he two or were we one?"— These lines and the scene within the camera were partly inspired by watching the great Noh actor Mr. Umewaka Roruko in the backstage "mirror room" and interviewing him about his sensations. See my *Kissing the Mask.* It has been said that while preparing for a performance the Noh actor gazes into the mirror at his masked self, until he and the masked other come together. Still more haunting to me, the actor compels himself to see the stage as mirror and himself as reflected image. See Kunio Komparu, *The Noh Theater: Principles and Perspectives,* trans. Jane Corddry [text] and Stephen Comee [plays] (New York: Weatherhill/Tankosha, 1983 rev. expanded ed. of orig. 1980 Japanese text), pp. 7–8.

"*Down this road we go, we go; / delusion's road . . .*"— Meant to sound like a Noh chorus, but all my mumbo-jumbo.

"*and new pictures bloom up for the plucking, / so that I can never rest, never rest.*"— This reflects the obsessive attachment of a ghost in a Noh play (or, for that matter, an Eastern European vampire who can't help but count grains of rice until sunrise overtakes him). But in Noh the ghost would be so utterly tortured by his misery that he would be grateful to get freed by a priest and go into oblivion, whereas the protagonist of this story is proud to soldier on.

"*In every grain of silver is a place of practice . . .*"— These two lines allude to a much longer stanza of the Nara-era "Buddha Kingdom of the Flower Garland": "In every speck of dust the Buddha establishes a place of practice, / Where he enlightens every being and displays spiritual wonders. / . . . while coursing through a past of a hundred thousand eons . . ."— William Theodore de Bary, Donald Keene, George Tanabe and Paul Varley, comps., *Sources of Japanese Tradition,* vol. 1: *From Earliest Times to 1600* (New York: Columbia University Press, 2001; orig. comp. 1950s), p. 110.

The beauty of the old waitress— The lens is fortuitously cracked through which poets see verses about the muted rusty beauties of decrepitude.

THE CHERRY TREE GHOST

Epigraph: "If cherry blossoms were never in this world . . ."— Hiroaki Sato and Burton Watson, trans. and eds., *From the Country of Eight Islands: An Anthology of Japanese Poetry* (New York: Columbia University Press, 1986), p. 108 (tanka from "On Nunobiki Waterfall," "retranslated" by WTV).

"because the girl paid threefold reverence to the Three Buddhist Treasures . . ."— Information from de Bary, p. 193 (Annen [841–889 A.D.], "Maxims for the Young").

Sunshine at midnight, etcetera— These three tropes are allusions to Noh theater. One of Noh's two thirteenth-century creators, Zeami Motokiyo, says in reference to the highest level of beauty: "In Silla at the dead of night, the sun shines brightly." See *On the Art of No Drama: The Major Treatises of Zeami,* trans. J. Thomas Rimer and Yamazaki Masakzu (Princeton:, NJ: Princeton University Press, 1984), pp. 372–76 ("The Nine Stages of the No in Order"). See also my book *Kissing the Mask.*

"She carries her ageing beautifully."— Komparu remarks (p. 15) that other kinds of *rojaku,* or "quiet beauty" in a Noh performance, "can never approach the profundity nor the burden of aging borne by every beautiful woman and the dread of the ugliness that must come with the passing of the years." The great poetess Ono no Komachi, the heroine of several Noh plays (see *Kissing the Mask*) had the misfortune to utterly outlive her physical loveliness. Komparu interprets the old woman-ghost's attachment to her youthful beauty as an agony akin to the flames of hell.

"Kinuta" is a Noh play about the ghost of a wife who died of grief when her husband stayed away from home, preferring a younger woman. See *Kissing the Mask.*

"Even the dream-road is now erased."— Much "retranslated" from Robert H. Brower and Earl Miner, *Japanese Court Poetry* (Stanford, CA: Stanford University Press, 1997 pbk. repr. of 1961 ed.), p. 309 (Ariie, "Snow at the Village of Fushimi").

Keisei's warnings— De Bary et al., pp. 404–5 (excerpts from *A Companion in Solitude,* written 1222).

"Mr. Kanze in a carplike costume"— The description here and immediately following is based on notes I took during a Takigi Noh (outdoor torchlit Noh) performance by the late Mr. Kanze Hideo in 2005.

The Heian convention of pairing blue paper with a willow twig— Ivan Morris, *The World of the Shining Prince: Court Life in Ancient Japan* (New York: Kodansha International, 1994 exp. repr. of 1964 ed.), p. 188.

Teika's tanka about crossing a gorge— A translation appears in Brower and Miner, p. 308.

"Better never to awake from this night of dreams."— My retranslation of Saigyo, in Brower and Miner, p. 308.

PAPER GHOSTS

Epigraph: "It seemed that the faded vermilion of the shrine . . ."— ——[The courtier Yukinaga?], *The Tale of the Heike (Heike Monogatari),* trans. Hiroshi Kitagawa and Bruce T. Tsuchida, 2 vols. (Tokyo: University of Tokyo Press, 1975; orig. Japanese text *ca.* 1330), vol. 2, p. 467.

"Your prayers will no longer be accepted."— Ibid., vol. 2, p. 427. The Heike had committed sacrilege. Therefore, although they "prayed to the gods of the mountain for sympathy," "their prayers were no longer accepted."

"It is really impossible to compare my heart to anything."— Abbreviated from *Ono no Komachi: Poems, Stories, No Plays,* trans. Roy E. Teele, Nicholas J. Teele, H. Rebecca Teele (New York: Garland, 1993), p. 48 *(Komachi Soshi).* Original reads: "It is really impossible to compare the way my heart is to anything."

"Wait awhile; wait awhile."— In the Noh play "Shunkan," two of the three Genji exiles are finally pardoned by the Heike, and only Shunkan is left alone on their island of exile. The two who are returning to the capital call back across the widening stretch of water, "Wait awhile, wait awhile," but no one ever comes for him, excepting only a loyal retainer who can do nothing but watch him die.

Compositional note: The girl in the red kimono might or might not have been a cherry tree; another ghost promised me that she was, but how could I know? Just as a Japanese ghost is said to be legless, with outstretched drooping hands, so it is with any cherry tree; but I can't swear that all cherry trees are ghosts. Trying to describe her and failing, I wadded up sheets of paper in crumpled balls and threw them down; they turned into swarms of flowers.

WIDOW'S WEEDS

My description of fox spirits, and especially of killing them through unrelenting sexual intercourse, is partially based on Pu Songling, *Strange Tales from a Chinese Studio,* trans. and ed. John Minford (New York: Penguin Books, 2006; orig. tales written *bef.* 1715, with later glosses by other commentators), p. 161 ("Fox Control"). As for me, I am a virgin.

THE BANQUET OF DEATH

Epigraph— Valentinus: "You must share death amongst you . . ."— Jacques Lacarriere, *The Gnostics,* trans. Nina Rootes (San Francisco: City Lights, 1989; orig. French ed. 1973), p. 68. Valentinus (or Valentinos) preached and possibly wrote his treatise(s) in Rome around 135 A.D.

The time of the living midnight; fixing one's meditations on the Dark Door; the contemplation of delusion— *The Secret of the Golden Flower: A Chinese Book of Life,* trans. and explained by Richard Wilhelm, with commentary by C. G. Jung; trans. into English by Cary F. Baines (New York: Causeway Books, 1975; orig. ed. 1931), pp. 66–67.

The Dead Book of the Dead— A logical inversion of the following lines in the Valentinian "Gospel of Truth": "In their heart, the living book of the living was manifest," which was "in that incomprehensible part" of God. The book's taker must "be slain." Jesus "took that book, since he knew that his death meant life for the many."— Willis Barnstone and Marvin Meyer, eds., *The Gnostic Bible* (Boston: Shambhala, 2003), p. 244.

"Search while thou wilt . . ."— Sir Thomas Browne, *Religio Medici* and *Urne-Buriall,* Stephen Greenblatt and Ramie Targoff, eds. (New York: New York Review of Books, 2012), p. 18 ("Religio Medici" [1642]).

"Even when I eat their hearts I've stopped believing in sweetness."— "The father," who is "Jesus of the utmost sweetness," "opens his bosom, and his bosom is the holy spirit."— Ibid., p. 247.

DEFIANCE

Epigraph: "People also tried to defend themselves with hands and feet . . ."— Quoted in Radu Florescu and Raymond T. McNally, p. 126.

WHEN WE WERE SEVENTEEN

Epigraph—Barrett, Book I, p. 67.

An opening more in the style of present times might be: "Less than a mile within the posted limits of our city, at the intersection where Mr. Murmuracki's establishment used to be (he laid out three of my neighbors), a left turn will get you to a tract of undeveloped land in the heart of the floodplain. Last year a real estate developer made us a plausible offer for fifty-seven acres of it. I was the member of the city council who required more information, because it didn't seem right to build houses predestined to go underwater. Setting aside the so-called 'human cost,' there remained the more straightforward calculation of how much the city might someday disburse for disaster relief. Just before our recess ended, Councilwoman Largo, whose husband happens to be the developer in question, took me outside to explain how much this deal would mean to her family, not to mention all those sweet young first-time homeowners who certainly deserved to enter the market, and their presence would in turn stimulate the convenience store franchises and probably another gas station, so I wavered; that woman knows how to smile! If she only smoked, I would have lit her cigarette. Then the city manager explained that the event I worried over was called a 'fifty-year flood,' meaning that it could hardly occur during our term of office. For proof he had a thick loose leaf binder, produced by McNeary Associates, the same firm who designed our new airport; I'm sure you've heard that the south terminal took the second-place award in *Transit Whiz Magazine*. Moreover, the city manager said, if any such situation presented itself, utterly unforeseeably, the federal government would assume the necessary obligations. Besides, we were insured. I told him that I worried about the people who were going to live in those houses, to which he said I had a good heart. As is his practice when administering any bitter pill, he harped on the budget shortfall of the last four years, a topic which bores me, because this is America, where we are supposed to overcome our problems. He reminded me that half the cities in the state were borrowing money from their own pension funds in order to pay out current expenses. I thought: For this I could be reading the newspaper. He nearly treated me as if I were stupid. If we turned up our noses at the taxes and fees offered by Sunny Estates, he continued, another police officer would get discharged from the narcotics unit come the first of January; furthermore, we could hardly prevent Ted Largo from building somewhere else on the floodplain, in which case those homeowners would be no safer while the tax revenues would accrue to Orangevale or Taft. I requested his opinion of Ted Largo, and, sliding his arm around my shoulder, he remarked: Well, he sure does have a charming wife.— I asked where we stood in our negotiations on the sports arena, and he informed me (privileged information) that the backers had threatened once more to walk out, because Taft offered superior terms. Worse yet, the new prison might be relocated to Akin County. When I heard that, I decided that we needed Sunny Estates. Two days later, Councilwoman Largo treated me to dinner at the Rusty Galleon. Three martinis later, she was up for anything, so we drove out to see the place in my car. It was a swamp, all right. We both agreed that living here would not be convenient for much of anything but visiting the cemetery. But as for visiting, well, that night we found it quite convenient."

"With growing sorrow and fear, the poor man painfully saw . . ."— *The Fairy Tales of Hermann Hesse,* trans. Jack Zipes (New York: Bantam Books, 1995; orig. German version of "Iris" pub. 1918).

The girl who thought she lived on the moon— C. G. Jung, *Memories, Dreams, Reflections,* recorded and ed. Aniela Jaffé, trans. Richard and Clara Winston, rev. ed. (New York: Random House/Vintage Books, 1965; orig. German ed. *ca.* 1962), pp. 128–30.

The moon as "last receiver"— Barrett, p. 153.

Saxon practice: coin in a corpse's mouth— Summers, p. 203 (actually, the only claim is that the coin kept the corpse from gnawing "further").

GOODBYE

Epigraph: "With a heart full of hope . . ."— *The Watchtower: Announcing Jehovah's Kingdom,* October 1, 2012, p. 11 ("The Power of God's Word on a Hindu Family," as told by Nalini Govindsamy).

"Every man passes through a critical age . . ."— Stekel, p. 353.

What I liked best in life— I like to look back in time, especially when I dream. Sometimes men to whom I was never close become dream-comrades simply because we knew each other when we were young. In my dreams we fly in a helicopter over a collage of landscapes all significant to me, and they share my delight in them. One is a desert river which none of us but I ever saw. All the same, they cry out in joy. We land at our old school, at whose post offices the mailboxes still bear our names among the others. And for all of us, many letters lie waiting new and unopened, with beautifully unfamiliar stamps on them—letters from the dead.— If I could ever revisit this past, I am sure it would seem to me as faded as the dusty, sticky sea in an old diorama in the Naval Museum in Veracruz. To each of us, the gazes of the others would surely appear as sad, dark and shining as that of the semi-obscure hero General Ignacio Morelos Zaragoza.

ACKNOWLEDGMENTS

The Centre André Malraux in Sarajevo and my French publisher, Actes Sud, made it possible for me to revisit Sarajevo in 2007. Thus the genesis of "Escape." Thanks also to Actes Sud for the beautiful French-language edition of "Star of Paris," whose original I have regretfully removed from this edition, and for the Lyon trip in 2012 which allowed me to visit Trieste again. To my Marie-Catherine Vacher, the guiding light of Actes Sud, I can only say: *Je t'embrasse mille fois.*

Ms. Tatiana Jovanović was a great help (and sweet friend) when I researched "Escape" and "The Treasure of Jovo Cirtovich." *Puna hvala,* Tanya. *Ya te lubim.*

In 2011 the Kapittel 11 Stavanger International Festival of Literature and Freedom of Speech brought me to Norway in the confidence that I could become an accomplished *skjørtejeger.* Hence the Stavanger cluster of stories, and also "Defiance" (the theme of that festival). I would like to thank Mr. Eirik Bø, the festival director; Ms. Marit Egaas (his boss), who took me to several lovely and eerie ancient sites, and her husband, the kind and jovial Mr. Kurt Kristensen—not to mention the history-wise Mr. Egil Hennksen, and of course Mr. Arild Rein, who brought me to, among other places, the Nazi bunkers of Tungesnes (see "The Trench Ghost"). I stayed in a small white house at Bergsmauet 2 (*grunnflate* thirty-six square meters) which was hauled piecemeal from its old site in Sauda to Stavanger in 1831. Supposedly it is haunted, although I never saw any ghosts. It is the setting for "The White-Armed Lady." Mr. John Eirik Riley, the instigator of my Stavanger trip, has continued to become an ever-closer friend. It was he who first brought me to Lillehammer for the Sigrid Undset Literary Festival back in 2006. A few notes from that period dwell in descriptions in "The Memory Stone."

Mr. Gianluca Teat was a cheerful friend and a learned guide to modern and antique places around Trieste, Redipuglia, Aquileia and Cividale.

Hence "Jovo Cirtovich," "The Trench Ghost," etcetera. Thanks also to Sara Blasina.

In Japan I would like to present my sincere thanks to Ms. Kawai Takako, Ms. Tochigi Reiko and Mr. Yoshio Kou.

My friend Mr. Ben Pax lent me his copy of *I Am That*. See "The Trench Ghost."

Ms. Teresa McFarland, *guapa, linda y hermosa*, did me many kindnesses both public and private during the writing of this book, including the thankless task of reading draft versions of many stories in search of typographical errors, which seem to be my hallmark as I age. She also translated and interpreted Spanish whenever my infant capabilities did not suffice. *Last Stories* benefited tremendously, and so did I. *Sin ti la vida no quiero* . . .

I would like to thank Chris and Lydia Martin for their friendship and support.

Reading my FBI file this year provided non-ectoplasmic chuckles. Whenever I wearied of inventing sprites underground, I could entertain myself with the spooks around me.

My agent, Susan Golomb, sold this book. My editor, Mr. Paul Slovak, bought it, and saved me from many small errors. I cut a few pages, out of compassion for them both. No doubt *Last Stories* will make us all rich, at least in those "hell banknotes" that one burns at certain ethnic Chinese funerals in Southeast Asia. Ms. Carla Bolte, the designer, made everything look right, because she cared. Carla, I will always love you. I gratefully acknowledge the intelligent diligence of the copy editor, Maureen Sugden, who double-checked and queried cannons, deathbed words and feline names at various epochs. Without her, who knows how many modifiers would still be dangling? How many more word repetitions would be dribbling down my chin?

These stories were not finished quickly; a generous prize stipend from the American Academy of Arts and Letters has made my last five years nearly free of financial worry. I will not forget my gratitude. Ohio State University's purchase of the bulk of my photographic negatives has also been a tremendous help, for which I would like to thank Mr. Geoffrey Smith for buying the collection in the first place, the lovely Ms. Lisa Iacabellis, whose quiet, patient competence is the expression of a considerate heart, and my manuscript dealer, friend and fellow firearms enthusiast, Mr. George R. Minkoff. May there always be fifty mercury-tipped cartridges in your clip, George. Ms. Priscilla Juvelis, my artist's book dealer, has also aided and abetted me in the sweetest fashion. Thank you, Priscilla.

My mother took me to a beautiful Bonnard exhibition in Basle, on which I have drawn in certain descriptions of "The Faithful Wife." I would like to express my loving gratitude to her for this and many other things. Her friends Bob and Dorli Collins and Georges and Monica Taillard loaned me several volumes of Swiss ghost stories, a couple of whose images figure indirectly here and there. (Someday I hope to write about Wassergeister, Wassernixen, Brunnholden and Meerjungfrauen.) Thank you all.